The Sapphire Brooch

The Celtic Brooch Trilogy, Book 2

Katherine Lowry Logan

Edited by Faith Freewoman
Cover Art by Damonza
Interior Design by BBeBooks

Website: www.katherinellogan.com

DEDICATED TO

~

Charlotte and Lincoln

Table of Contents

Part One

"History, despite its wrenching pain cannot be unlived, but if faced with courage, need not be lived again."

—Maya Angelou

1

Chimborazo Hospital, Richmond, Virginia, October, 1864

DEATH WAITED ON the other side of the partially shuttered window, pointing its long, bony finger at Michael Abraham McCabe. He didn't fear death, never had. Dying slow from a gut-shot was preferable to dying at the end of a rope. Either way, the shutters would open fully and Death would sling Braham's body over its shoulder and haul him the short distance to Hell.

Braham crawled his hand along the curve of his swollen belly. The bullet had branded him with a sizzling, red-hot poker, burning flesh and sinew down to the bone, and his body contorted in brutal agony.

Through dry, cracked lips he exhaled one word, "Water." He didn't need much. Only a sip to quench his thirst would do. He tried licking his lips but his thick tongue wouldn't slide across the chapped skin.

Behind his half-opened eyelids, wavy figures shambled around him. He blinked and tried to focus on the rows of beds filled with moaning men, wounded Confederate soldiers, not Yankee spies like him.

Johnny Rebs had tossed him onto a bed. "Don't let the bastard die," they had told the surgeon. "We intend to hang him."

The nurses called him a dead man walking toward the gallows.

That's what he was, but would Death take him by the hand before the hangman could put a noose around his neck? The soldiers had tried to beat the names of Richmond's underground network out of him. They couldn't. So they intended to strip him of what he cherished most—his honor. He would die the dishonorable death of a spy. And who would care? He was alone. Not only on this ward but also in life. He had no family. No son to carry on his name. All a man had at the end of the day was his honor, and the Rebs intended to dump his into an unmarked grave.

The door at the end of the building opened and rattled shut. "Where's the prisoner?" the man asked in a distinctive Virginia drawl.

Feet shuffled. A chair scraped across the floor. "Down there. Number twelve. If'n you ask me, the man's gonna die right soon," a young lad said.

"Are you the night nurse?"

"Yes, sir."

Boot heels thudding purposefully against the floorboards grew louder, sharper. Brisk movements churned up the air throughout the ward. Men turned in their beds to see the newcomer. Braham turned, too, and rerouted his attention from the sharp stabs of pain in his belly to the man striding toward him wearing a gray officer's tunic. He hadn't seen this surgeon before. Would he do anything different from what the others had done? Five or six surgeons had already examined him. Afterwards, they had walked away shaking their heads, saying, "There's nothing we can do for that one."

"Sir, we ain't got no other Yanks. Why's he here?" the lad asked.

"What? Oh…well, he was caught down by the railroad tracks. Quicker to bring him here. President Davis believes he can identify spies living in Richmond. Has he said anything?"

"I been here all day. He's yelped some but ain't said nuthin'."

The surgeon reached Braham's metal-framed bed and read the paper ticket hanging on the end of the frame. He had wondered what was written on the paper other than his name, date of admission, and injury. Instead of entering information about his regiment, had they written *Yankee spy*? Would they tie the paper to his toe when they buried him?

The surgeon tugged on his hickory-colored beard and furrowed his brow. "Is there an exit wound?"

"Nope. Still got that Minié ball in his gut. If it don't kill him, the hangman will."

The surgeon pressed his fingers against the inside of Braham's wrist and held them there. His touch was gentle, with an almost silky feel to his skin, and there were no slight pricks from sharp or ragged nails. Hands told a lot about a person, especially when they fanned a deck of cards or tended a wound or touched him in tender places.

Braham clenched his teeth against the chill brought on by another bout of rigors. "Water."

The surgeon's forehead creased as he lifted the dressing, pulling scab and crusted dirt from Braham's wound. When he pressed his fingers into Braham's belly, pain lanced through him, and he cried out, "*Ahhhh.*"

"Sorry." The surgeon withdrew his fingers and straightened, mumbling under his breath. Then he looked at the wound again. "How long has he been shaking like this?"

"Awhile, I reckon. How long you 'spect he's gonna live?"

"At this rate, only a few hours." The surgeon's baffled look pinched his brow. Braham had seen similar expressions on other officers weighing difficult decisions. What concerned this surgeon that hadn't concerned the others? It didn't matter. Not really. His pain would end in a matter of hours—one way or another.

Flickering candles threw enough light for Braham to look into the doctor's almond-shaped, blue eyes, now studying him with penetrating scrutiny. He tugged on the man's sleeve. "Water."

The surgeon turned toward the nurse. "Bring me clean bandages."

"My orders are to leave him be."

"I'm not going to watch a man die without trying to make his last moments comfortable. Now go."

The nurse gave the doctor a brusque nod, then spun on his heel. His boots scuffed along the floor, growing fainter with each hurried step.

The surgeon sat on the edge of a spindle-back chair and scooted it closer, scraping wobbly legs against the floor. Dust fountained off him, as if he'd ridden for a month without care for himself or his mount. He took Braham's bruised hand between both of his.

A velvety whisper sounded in his ear. "I've been sent to rescue you, Major. I'm getting you out of here."

Was he already dead? Was the Angel of Mercy upon him? Forcing words through his cotton mouth he asked, "Am I dead?"

"No, and you won't die today if I can help it."

"My legs won't carry me very far." Braham's shallow breathing grew quiet for a moment, and he remained motionless, save for a twitch of a small muscle beneath his right eye.

The surgeon let go of his hand and leaned closer. "Hold on, we're going for a ride."

Braham didn't know how it was possible, but he believed the surgeon would rescue him, and his spirit ignited with hope. Maybe Fate wasn't leading him to a slow death or a noose around his neck, but to a life filled with love, and a soul healed in the fertile soil of his vineyards.

The surgeon opened a sapphire brooch, held Braham's hand again, and stumbled through barely recognizable Gaelic. *"Chan ann le tìm no àite a bhios sinn a' tomhais an gaol ach's ann le neart anama."*

Braham sniffed, turning his head to pull air deep into his lungs. The autumn scent of burnished gold leaves and fermenting grapes lingered gently on night's breath. Where the scent came from he didn't know, but as fog engulfed him, he closed his eyes and translated the Gaelic in his mind—*Love is not measured by time or space. Love is measured by the power of the soul.* Then he took in another deep breath and exhaled, long and slow.

2

Battle of Cedar Creek, Virginia, Present Day

CHARLOTTE LYNN MALLORY'S boot heels clicking against the hardwood floor echoed through the quiet house as she swaggered out of the kitchen, down the long hall, and into the mansion's foyer, carrying a travel cup of black coffee. When she caught sight of her reflection in the gilded-frame mirror hanging over the acorn-patterned mantel, gooseflesh rippled on her forearms. She stopped and cocked her head left, then right, and then left again, but nothing changed. The image reflecting back in the polished glass was still not her own, but that of her six-times-great-grandfather, Major Charles Jackson Mallory.

"Good morning, sir," she said in her deepest voice. "Looking good today."

She glanced over her shoulder, saluting sharply to his portrait, which hung at the bottom of the square-ridge staircase that rose three floors. Her leg muscles still burned from her half dozen trips to the top floor to gather her reenacting equipment.

The portrait artist had painted her grandsire in full Confederate uniform. His left hand, which bore the family acorn signet ring, was prominently displayed on the hilt of his saber, and his other hand rested affectionately on his wife's shoulder. Not only did Charlotte's uniform match his down to the Virginia seal buttons, but so did her Lincoln-style beard and brown wig.

She squinted into the mirror, grimacing at a stray blonde curl peeking out from beneath her shoulder-length wig. *Well, that won't do at all.* She tucked in the errant strands, then scrutinized her face and head. Was there anything else amiss? Earrings? *Nope.* Lipstick? *Ha. That's funny.* At the rate she used the Bobbi Brown pinky-brown lip color in her purse, the tube would last another five years.

Charlotte set the coffee cup on the mantel and patted her hands down the front and sides of her dark blue trousers, checking for lose threads. Her tailor had reinforced the stitches where the black velvet side stripes and gold cords attached to the pants. He had also added extra padding to the cadet gray officer's tunic to give her a bulkier shape. She had dropped a few pounds while training for last month's marathon in Charlottesville, so the tailor padded the jacket instead of taking in seams he might have to let out later.

Over the past fifteen years, with the help of her tailor, makeup artists, and drama instructors, she had created a character so authentic that other reenactors failed to see the woman camouflaged under layers of wool, Ace bandages binding her breasts, and theatrical makeup. When she was in costume she rarely broke character. Even under the heat of a summer sun—"hotter than a witch's tit in a brass bra," as her Grandmother Mallory used to say— the beard, wig, and makeup remained in place.

Satisfied there was nothing unauthentic about her uniform to cause another reenactor to accuse her of being a Farbie, she donned her medical service cap with the letters MS embroidered in silver, folded her gauntlets over her belt, and practiced her best Ashley Wilkes smile. Actually, she'd much rather play a character like the scalawag Rhett Butler, but it wasn't the personality of her six-times-great-grandfather. Was it hers? *Nope.* She was safe and boring. She didn't even own a cat.

After grabbing the coffee cup and car keys off the table, she turned on the security system, closed the door, and sauntered out onto the double portico. A beautiful, brisk fall morning welcomed her. She paused on the steps of her family's two-hundred-year-old Georgian manse, located a half hour outside of Richmond, and sipped the black brew. Although she no longer resided in the mansion full time, this house would always be her home.

She raised her hand to shade her eyes from the bright sun glinting off the gold-leafed oak tree which had flourished between the house and the James River for over three centuries. Wafting off the water this morning was the warm scent of smoky campfires. Was it her imagination, or did the river shed memories of its own?

She went down a couple of stairs, thinking of the other soldiers in the family who had marched down them. Her ancestor, Major Mallory, had been the second one. The major had mounted his horse and ridden off to fight in the War of Northern Aggression. He'd been one of the lucky ones, though, and had come home in the spring of 1865 in one piece. Afterwards, he had spent a decade as a U.S. Senator working on reconstruction. The same Senate seat had been held by members of Charlotte's family until her mother, who had picked up the mantle following her husband's death, had died in office during Charlotte's junior year in high school.

The day was starting out perfectly, blessed with mild temperatures, a cloudless sky, and fall colors abounding in brilliant leaf showers. The planners of the 150th Reenactment of the Civil War Battle of Cedar Creek couldn't have wished for a more beautiful day.

This was Jack's kind of morning, too. Her older brother, a New York Times and internationally bestselling mystery author and the full-time resident of Mallory Plantation, was in the mountains, out of cell phone range, finishing the edits on his Revolutionary War mystery. He was tossing around ideas with his agent for his next book, but hadn't come up with anything specific. Inspiration would come. It always did, and then he'd rush off in a reckless dash, chasing his muse.

Charlotte reached her car, paused at the driver's door of the SUV, and took another lingering look around the grounds of Virginia's first plantation, settled in 1613. The current mansion, built in the early eighteen hundreds, replaced the original homeplace. Although the land was no longer an operating estate, its renowned beauty and history kept it at the top of the Commonwealth's most touted historic sites. If her work didn't require her to be closer to the hospital, she would live here. Her medical practice, though, was worth the sacrifice.

She climbed into the driver's seat, buckled up, and went through her checklist one last time, nodding as she mentally checked off each item. Confident she had everything she needed for the two-day event, she headed down the plantation's long driveway.

The oversized rural mailbox at the end of the drive was stuffed with magazines, bills, invitations, and announcements. She thumbed through the stack quickly. Most of her mail went to her house in Richmond, but occasionally acquaintances who didn't have her city address sent letters to the plantation.

In the back of the mailbox was a package wrapped in brown paper and addressed to her. The return address label listed Digby McIntosh, Solicitor, of Edinburgh, Scotland as the sender. She shook the box. Nothing rattled, but the timer on her iPhone beeped. She had set it as a drop-dead reminder. If she wasn't turning out of the driveway onto the main road when it went off, she'd miss the start of the battle. She tossed the package onto the passenger seat and drove down the lane. Her curiosity would have to wait until she reached Middletown.

Before turning onto the highway, she shot a quick glance over her shoulder for a police car hiding in the shadows. No policemen with grumpy faces were waiting in their usual hiding place. *Good.* If she got another moving violation, she'd have to go to traffic school.

At least twice a week she stewed at intersections, tapping her fingers against the steering wheel, waiting on lights regulating traffic on empty streets in the middle of the night. Nine times out of ten, she ran the red, and frequently a policeman pulled her over. She would then explain to the officer the minutes she lost sitting at traffic lights—when there were no other cars on the road—put her patients' health in jeopardy. Unless she discovered a better alternative, she'd continue to violate traffic laws in those situations and pray a traffic court judge didn't yank her license permanently, as the last one had threatened to do.

Besides, every so often she needed a whiff of danger.

Although she was often late, this morning's delay was unavoidable. After rounds, the chief resident had called her in for a consult. The patient had been shot in the abdomen during a liquor store robbery and was about to go to surgery. Over the course of her residency and practice in general surgery, she had operated on hundreds of gunshot victims and had become the go-to person for difficult cases. Most of her department and the nursing staff had known she was in a hurry to get out of town for the weekend to attend the reenactment, but medicine still came first.

During the two-hour trip to Middletown, she rehearsed the Civil War medical spiel she would give at the living history demonstration later in the day. She had given it many times but always added a new twist, some tidbit to entertain anyone in her audience who had heard her speak in prior years.

For today's talk, she added information on Mary Edwards Walker, a surgeon in the Union Army and the only woman to receive the Medal of Honor. The doctor had also been a spy and was imprisoned in Castle Thunder in Richmond for four months until she was released in a prisoner exchange. Charlotte was inspired by Walker's bravery and humanitarianism, and she often wondered if she would have had the fortitude to risk her life as Mary had done.

With fifteen minutes remaining before the battle began, she pulled into the battlefield parking lot. Drumming her fingers on the steering wheel, she drove up and down rows until she found a spot between a tree and a camper where she could squeeze in her SUV.

Whether she would have enough room to open the door was debatable, but operating in tight spots was a regular occurrence in her life. She held her breath while she pulled in. When she didn't scrape off paint, she let her breath out. If she scooted flat against the side of the car, she'd be able to exit the vehicle. Years of running had kept her long and lean, not *skinny*, in spite of what her brother and colleagues were fond of saying.

So what? Skinny could be sexy, too, right? Although, judging by the dearth of men in her life, maybe not.

The car's cargo space was packed with all the supplies she would need for the weekend: coolers, change of clothes, makeup case, cot, blankets, and food.

Before locking the car, she grabbed the package from Scotland and opened it. Inside was a Japanese puzzle box about six inches long. "Cool." She loved puzzle boxes, and the challenge this box promised gave her a little surge of excitement. She flipped it around in her hands, twisting here and there like a Rubik's cube.

"Major Mallory."

She glanced up to see Ken, her medical school classmate and longtime friend, waving from the other side of the parking lot. It had been a couple of weeks since she had talked to him, and she was anxious to hear about the new woman in his life.

She waved back, calling out, "General Ramseur." She slipped the box into her haversack, slung the bag over her shoulder, and forged a path through the throng of reenactors and spectators.

"I was worried," he said. "You're late. You okay?"

"A consult slowed me down." She gave him a hug before stepping back and giving him a once-over. "I like the new uniform."

He slipped his right hand inside his tunic, resting it over his heart, and placed his left hand on the hilt of his sword as if posing for the camera. "Worth every penny, don't you think?"

She straightened his collar. "You didn't find this on eBay. It looks custom made."

"It is. Your tailor does good work."

Brushing crumbs from the power bar she'd eaten in the car off her own uniform, she mentally counted the handful of times she'd worn it, grimacing at the low number. "He keeps altering my uniform. As little action as these threads get, it'll last a century."

"Then use it more often. Go to Gettysburg or Perryville with me next year. Get out of the rut you're in."

"I'm not in a rut, and besides, I can't take the time off."

"The hospital will survive a few days without you," he said.

"Sure. The hospital would be fine, but what about my patients?"

He threw his hands up in mock surrender. "There're a dozen attending physicians in your department. You cover for them all the time."

"I can't ask them."

Ken frowned, and the deep vee between his eyebrows made his disapproval obvious and also darned annoying. "What you're really saying is you *won't*."

This was a sore spot, and they both treaded its boundaries carefully. Ken accused her colleagues in Richmond of taking advantage of her. She didn't think they did. The other surgeons had families and lived in the suburbs. She lived alone in a house a few blocks from the hospital. Plus she was happy to help her associates out.

She made a tee with her hands. "Time out. Let's change the subject."

"Okay. Who are you inviting to escort you to the reunion next month?"

She fidgeted with the standup collar, which seemed to squeeze tighter at the mention of the soiree. "I don't know."

"I have a lawyer friend in Winchester who would—"

She shook her head, anxiety scoring the back of her throat. "You know the rules. I don't try to fix you up and you don't try to fix me up."

"Come on, Charlotte. You haven't been on a date since medical school."

"I haven't had a date lately, but I did have one this year. I'm too busy. I run early in the morning, I operate and lecture during the day, and I'm on call twice a week."

"You're not any busier than I am, and I find time to socialize. So, what's the real problem?"

Her tension turned into exasperation. "Can you believe men find me intimidating? The few who don't are egotistical workaholics who only want to get laid. I want more. I want to wake up next to a loving partner, and have breakfast with him, too. There aren't any romantics left."

Ken gave an exaggerated sigh, rolled his eyes. "You've got to be kidding. *You* want to be romanced? What happened to friends with benefits? You said it fit your life style."

"It doesn't work for me anymore."

She looked away, through the trees and above the red-roofed barn, toward the northern end of the Massanutten Mountain range. Ridges etched by thousands of years of wind and rain snaked down its sides. In 1864, tears and bloodstains had soaked the ridges and gullies when so many died on a foggy October morning. Like the land, she too was etched with crevices, or at least it's what her therapist had told her before she gave up counseling in favor of long-distance running. A rush of endorphins gave her more peace and satisfaction, involved far less hassle, and except for running shoes, cost almost nothing.

"Now I want more," Charlotte repeated. "And there's no one around to make adjusting my schedule worthwhile."

"You aren't looking in the right places."

"Oh, yeah? Where should I be looking?" she asked in a voice heavy with sarcasm.

"There're thousands of men here today. There's got to be one you might find interesting."

"I don't need a real or pretend soldier in my life. They play with guns. Guns shoot people. And then I have more work to do."

"So why are you here?"

"Because modern medicine started during the Civil War, and I find that piece of history fascinating. *I* don't come for the women and guns."

He pressed his hands against his chest in fake humility. "I feel so shallow."

"You said it. I didn't." She fiddled with the twisted haversack's strap, which reminded her of the puzzle box packed inside and the mysterious sender. If she mentioned the gift to Ken, he would tease her about having a secret admirer, and she wasn't in the mood to be teased.

"What's wrong with you?" he demanded. "You need to get laid, don't you?"

"Nothing's wrong with me a ten-miler won't cure."

"God, Charlotte. Running is a solo sport. Do something which forces you to interact with people. With men. Hell, with anyone."

"What do you think I'm doing here today?"

"Lecturing. You talk *at* people. You don't talk *with* them. There's a difference. Borrow a horse. Ride with the cavalry."

"I have my own horse."

"But you didn't bring him. Why not?"

A trail of ants near her feet suddenly became more interesting than the conversation. "If you *must* know, I didn't have time to get a current Coggins certificate, and they wouldn't let my horse in without one."

He shook his head, giving her a sigh with more than a hint of frustration. This bantering happened every time they got together, which was why they'd never dated. He loved her and wanted her to be happy. She understood his concern, and no one else had the courage to get into her face the way he did. He knew he could tell her the truth. Whether she listened to him or not, well, it was up to her.

Occasionally, though, she did want to smack him. She yanked at his arm. "Come on. Let's stop arguing. Hang out at the medical tent today."

"And do what I do every day but without the medical advances of the past century? Would you really like to go back and practice medicine the way they did then?"

"We've had this debate before."

"And we'll continue to have it." He focused on something in the distance. Probably a beautiful woman in the crowd. "You're coming over to spend the night, aren't you?"

"I brought my cot, but I'd rather stay in your guest room."

He gave her a brief, distracted glance. "We'll talk tonight over a good steak and a bottle of wine. I've got some ideas."

"Now, Ken—"

"I'm not asking you to do anything you don't want to do. Just listen."

She compared two uncomfortable situations: listening to Ken pitch the virtues of a few single men, or sleeping on a hard cot in the chilly night air. If she went to Ken's, she'd get a nice dinner with wine and she'd sleep in a comfortable bed.

"What kind of steak?" she asked.

"Ribeye and wine."

"Since you went to all that trouble, I'll listen, but I won't commit to anything more. The last time you fixed me up, the evening was a disaster from the get-go. Then it took weeks to get rid of the guy."

"I'm not saying another word until you've had a couple of glasses of wine."

"So I'll be what? More amenable?"

He grinned as if he had her cornered already. She would never again go out with a guy he recommended, but she was willing to listen. Half-heartedly.

When they reached the field hospital, he ducked inside the tent and brought out a small valise. "I have a surprise for you." He opened the valise, lifted out an envelope, and handed it to her.

"Greenbacks?"

"Your tailor gave me a lead. Turned out to be a good one."

She leaned in and kissed his cheek. "Did I pay you enough?"

"To the dollar."

She opened the envelope and fanned the neat pile of bills with her thumb. "There's a lot of money here."

He rolled his eyes. "They're greenbacks, Charlotte. You can't spend them."

"Oh, shush. You know what I mean." She stuffed the envelope inside the haversack with the mysterious box. "This is Jack's birthday present. He'll be thrilled. Thank you."

Ken pulled up two folding chairs and straddled one with his arms crossed on the back. "And how *is* Castle?"

"Argh." She plopped down in the other chair and leaned forward with her forearms on her thighs, her hands clasped. "The more popular the TV show gets, the bigger his head gets. He thinks he's the real life Richard Castle."

"He looks and acts like the character."

"He thinks he's invincible like the character, too. One of these days his research is going to get him killed."

Ken smoothed his mustache with a fingertip. "Why isn't he here today?"

"He's in the mountains finishing up his edits. Then he'll probably go to Washington to meet with his agent. He spends more time with her than he does in Richmond. He should move there." Of course, if Jack ever moved, Charlotte would be devastated. He was the only family she had, and she depended on him. They talked or texted every day, and had dinner one night a week. Most weekends, unless she was on call or he was out of town, she hung out with him at the plantation.

"He won't give up living at Mallory Plantation," Ken said. "It's part of his author brand. When's the next book coming out?"

"Early summer, I think. Now he's looking for his next project." She got to her feet, gesturing toward a group of men approaching the battlefield. "There go the safety marshals."

"Good. Let's get this show on the road."

A conversation on her right caught her attention. Although the voice was familiar, the long-jawed private wasn't anyone she recognized. He was marching with a group of schoolchildren around the battlefield's perimeter, toward Belle Grove Plantation, as part of the day-long living history activities.

"This was the most dramatic battle reversal in the entire Civil War," the soldier said, "and ultimately ended the Confederate presence in the Shenandoah Valley."

"My dad's in the Second Corps, Army of Northern Virginia," a boy in the group said, standing taller as he spoke.

"Mine, too," another boy said.

"My dad's in the cavalry," a little girl added.

Charlotte whispered to Ken, "Those kids probably know more Civil War history than most adults."

Another little girl looked up at Ken. "Are you a general?"

He stood and doffed his hat. "Yes, ma'am. Major General Stephen Dodson Ramseur."

"He got killed," the first little boy said. "My dad said the General got two horses shot out from under him. Then he got killed riding the third. My dad said he was a sitting target."

The group moved on, leaving Charlotte laughing and shaking her head. "Precocious kids."

"Glad I don't have any," Ken said.

"Doesn't the new woman in your life have a child?"

His grin tilted to one side. "And that's why she's no longer the new woman in my life."

"If you rule out women with children, the dating field will get smaller and smaller, especially at *your* age." She slapped her forehead. "Oh, silly me. Your field is ten years younger than mine."

His grin was at odds with his hard, penetrating stare. "I haven't seen *you* go out with a man who had children."

She widened her eyes for emphasis. "Well, I might if I was asked. I like children. I want one of my own someday."

He rolled his eyes, sighing. "You're thirty-eight. Unless you've frozen eggs, it might not happen."

"Well, thanks." It wasn't a topic she had ignored. In fact, she'd recently spoken to the Chief of Fertility at VMC about freezing her eggs, which she should have done ten years ago. She had decided to wait until the first of the year before scheduling egg retrieval. Then if her soul mate didn't show up by the time she turned forty, she'd use donor sperm. She already had a list of physical, personality, and interest attributes, along with health and educational requirements.

"And don't forget, I'll be your 'Mr. Goodsperm' any day, merely say the word. After all, I'm your fallback guy."

"I changed my mind since we had that discussion. You don't fit my new requirements. You have red hair, you're not an athlete, and you can't sing a note."

"At least you didn't say little dick or some other derogatory identifier."

"You call me skinny and flat-chested. I don't fit on your list either."

His eyes brightened, and he rubbed his hands gleefully. "But I can fatten you up and a plastic surgeon can add some nice, big boobs."

She took a hefty swig from her canteen, then wiped drops of water from her lips with the back of her hand. "I don't want boobs the size of the women you date. They'd get in my way when I operate."

He straightened his double-breasted frock coat and reclaimed his valise. "They wouldn't get in mine."

She puffed out her cheeks then slowly expelled the air. "Go meet your troops. This conversation is degrading fast."

"It always does." He wiggled a pretend cigar while bobbing his eyebrows Groucho Marx-style. "I'll see you at dinner unless you find someone interesting on the battlefield."

She wiggled a pretend cigar in return and chuckled. "That's not going to happen either."

3

Battle of Cedar Creek, Virginia, Present Day

DURING A LULL in the afternoon battle, she grabbed her haversack and canteen and settled in the shade of a tree to study the puzzle box, determined to unlock its secrets. She discovered two sliding parts in one end. When she moved one end piece, the opposite end moved slightly, unlocking a side panel and allowing a new piece to be shifted. The top partially unlocked. She closed it and started over by reversing her moves. On the sixth try, the top panel slid open. After a moment to savor her victory over the box, she opened the lid completely. *"Wow."*

Inside was an antique brooch, which looked Celtic in design, with the bluest sapphire—as clear as ice—embedded in the center. She studied both sides of the brooch, awed by the intricate metalwork. It appeared older than jewelry designed in the eighteenth or nineteenth centuries. She wasn't an expert, but her great-grandmother had been, and had given Charlotte several exquisite pieces. Since then she had developed an appreciation for antique jewelry.

She teased and stroked the brooch, tracing the design with her fingertip. For someone accustomed to saving lives by paying attention to intricate details, the hairline seam around the circumference of the stone was easy to spot. She knew it opened. But how? There had to be a clasp. She retrieved her MacGyver knife from her haversack and picked at the brooch until she found the problem. A tiny piece of the clasp had broken off. She used tweezers to pinch the silver tracery, and a cleverly constructed spring popped the top half of the sapphire open. She ran the tip of her finger over an inscription etched into the center of the stone. Hmm. Gaelic?

"Chan ann le tìm no àite a bhios sinn a' tomhais an gaol ach's ann le neart anama."

As she stammered through the last word, a groundswell of heavy fog smelling oddly of peat gathered around her. She climbed to her feet and tried to jump out of the fog, but it followed her. A vortex formed and swirled up her legs, creating a funnel of dense air. She edged forward, then back, dodged left, then right, but she couldn't shake off the fog. The funnel reached her chest and pressure squeezed from all sides.

The fog completely engulfed her until she couldn't breathe. Nothing existed beyond the gray, cottony cloud surrounding her. The jackhammer beat of her heart was deafening, louder than the cannons, which had roared throughout the day. She had entered a maelstrom of chaos and its bitter taste of terror.

4

Battle of Cedar Creek, Virginia, October, 1864

UFFLED CANNON FIRE, high-pitched screams, and clanging swords penetrated the fog. As the peat-scented mist thinned, the sounds of battle resurged in a clap of thunder.

Her head swam, and her heart raced in panic. A battle waged around her. "What the f—"

"*Run,*" a soldier yelled, pushing her. "*Move or die.*"

A line of men, sweat beading their faces, hurled themselves forward aiming bayonets and muskets. The roar of a passing train couldn't have been any louder than the rumbling artillery caissons. She inhaled fetid air seething with Minié balls and screeching shells. Barefoot and blood-soaked soldiers fell thick and fast amid the reek of loose bowels and searing flesh.

This wasn't a reenactment. This was a damnable *real battle.* How had this happened? Paralyzing fear rose from her gut, burned her throat, and a vile taste exploded in her mouth. Her feet became leaden as if ancient roots had erupted from the ground and entangled her feet. She couldn't move, but she had to get to safety. How she came to be here wasn't as important as surviving it

She tucked the brooch into her pocket and snagged the arm of a soldier dressed in gray with blood dripping down the side of his face. "Where's the field hospital?"

He shook off her hand. "'Bout half mile ahead."

If the Confederate Army was running toward the field hospital, it meant they were retreating. Hundreds of soldiers ran past her, through the smoky blur of gunfire, bleeding from open wounds on their heads, arms, and legs, and leaving a trail of blood in their wake.

She edged her way over to the tree line, tasting the gun powder-laden smoke. Soldiers trying to dodge the main rush of men crashed through the bushes. Battle conditions altered how things looked, but how could this possibly be worse? Dead and dying were lying in the shifting shadows of the maple trees. She was a doctor, and the wounded needed attention. There was no one else around to do it. If she ran for safety, these men would die. They needed her. Now.

The first soldier she reached was dead. The next had been shot in the arm, which hung limply at his side. A look of desperation clouded his eyes. She ripped off the bottom part of his shirtsleeve and fashioned a pressure dressing to stanch the bleeding.

"Can you walk?" she asked.

He nodded.

"Make your way to the field hospital."

"Can they save my arm?"

"Maybe," she said, before triaging the next wounded man, doing what she could do without medical supplies. She moved quickly from one to the other.

A field dressing team finally arrived. "You're needed at the field hospital, sir."

"Where is it?" she asked.

A private pointed. "Through those trees."

A bullet whizzed over her head. She ducked, her legs nearly buckling. She wrapped her arm around the trunk of a small tree and dug her fingernails into the bark. The wind set the branches to chattering exactly as fear had done to her teeth.

She had to get out of there. But where was she, besides stuck in the middle of a battle? She glanced around, looking for a recognizable landmark, something identifiable. Then she gasped, hardly able to catch her breath, not believing her eyes. "On my God."

Belle Grove Plantation sat several hundred yards behind her. Not only had she suddenly appeared in a Civil War battle, but she had landed in the middle of the Battle of Cedar Creek.

She pulled the brooch from her inside jacket pocket. Minutes ago, when she had clenched it in her hand, she had inadvertently closed it. Now she tried to open it but couldn't. Not without tweezers. She patted down her body, hoping they had survived the fog. They hadn't, and without them, she couldn't pinch the clasp. Her heart sank with a hollow thud, and fear rose, hot and heavy.

She sat back on her heels and pinned the brooch inside her waistband. Until she found a tool to help her open it, she was stuck. She had to find a place to hide. But what good would hiding do? None. She would be much better off if she located the field hospital where she could borrow tweezers. But if the army was retreating, the field hospitals might already be relocating. If she knew what time it was, she'd know the locations of the armies.

She looked up to study the position of the sun. Using the plantation as a marker, she could gauge the time. She knew the house faced southwest. If she turned her back to the house, due west would be over her right shoulder. Assuming the sun would be straight up at noon, and would set at six o'clock, her best guess was it was now around five o'clock. She couldn't schedule surgeries telling time this way, but for what she needed at the moment, it would do.

According to the battle timeline, General Early had already overrun the nerve center of the Union Army. If the Confederates were now running in the opposite direction, it meant General Sherman had rallied his troops and launched the Union counterattack. About now Custer and Ramseur would be meeting at the final Confederate battle line on Miller's Lane. General Ramseur was probably already wounded. If she could get to him, she could help him, maybe.

If she was going to try, she had to head toward Strasburg. The retreating forces and his staff would take him south of the plantation at the North Fork of the Shenandoah River, about four miles away. All she had to do was follow the Valley Pike south.

She double-checked her bearings as she ran, while bullets whizzed overhead. She had no helmet, flak jacket, or steel-toed boots, none of the protective gear she'd worn in Afghanistan during a six-week medical mission. She might as well be running unprotected through a minefield. She hunched over and ran faster.

An explosion fifty yards to her right filled the air with debris, and the ground vibration knocked her off her feet. She rolled to her knees, shaking, and crawled until her jelly legs worked again. As more explosions lit up the sky and shook the earth she increased her stride and pumped her arms.

The sun was setting by the time she reached Strasburg, where ragged and exhausted retreating Confederate soldiers, along with wagons and cannon, jammed the streets. Their all-night march and six hour hand-to-hand battle had done the men in.

Charlotte stopped each horse-drawn ambulance and asked the drivers if they'd seen General Ramseur.

Blank, anguished stares met her inquiry. "Dear God, he can't be wounded. Are you sure?" they had asked.

The smell of bodily fluids and fear saturated the air. Dirt, grime, and blood covered the soldiers, crusting their hands, their faces, their shaggy beards, and unwashed hair. Ripped trousers and mismatched uniforms made it hard to tell which army they belonged to. Only their tight, pinched, demoralized faces revealed their loyalties. They were from the south and, on this day, the gains made earlier in battle had now been lost in utter defeat. This was no black and white moment captured by a still photographer, but a bold, red fragment of time indelibly etched in their weary hearts.

Custer's Cavalry would arrive any moment and capture more than a thousand men. If she were with the mortally wounded general, she might be allowed to stay with him. But where was he?

"Help," a soldier yelled. She turned to see a man leaning out of the back of yet another ambulance, waving. "Here. We need help."

She wove her way through the retreating forces toward the wagon. "I'm searching for General Ramseur. Have you seen him?"

"He's here," the soldier said. "He's been shot."

Charlotte climbed into the back of the ambulance and knelt beside him. "General, can you hear me?" She ripped open his jacket and blood-soaked shirt. "I need bandages."

One of the soldiers pulled a white cloth from his haversack. "Will this do? It's the general's clean shirt." It would have to. She used it to stanch the bleeding from the wound under his right ribs, hoping to reduce the hemorrhaging. She couldn't do much about the blood collecting inside his chest, though. She found the second wound near the left side of the general's neck. Blood and air leaking from his bullet punctures were slowly collapsing the remaining functional lung tissues.

"I need a syringe and needle. Find one, *now.*"

"Where?" the soldier who had given her the shirt asked.

"Check the medical supply wagon." Her tone of voice was so urgent the soldier immediately jumped from the rear of the ambulance and disappeared. He returned shortly with a metal syringe and bandages.

Using an unsanitized needle went against every standard of care she knew, but it wouldn't matter. The general had a mortal wound, and her intervention would not save him, but her care could lessen his discomfort during his final hours.

After verifying proper placement, she gently inserted the needle into Ramseur's chest until she heard a small *whoosh* of air. She attached the syringe and pulled back on the plunger, relieving some of the pressure as she sucked off a mixture of fluid and air. His breathing eased a bit.

A Union officer came to the rear of the wagon, gun pointed. "Everyone out."

Charlotte swallowed hard. She knew the cavalry would capture them all, but she'd been so engrossed with tending to the general she hadn't paid attention to what was happening outside the ambulance's canvas walls.

"I have a seriously injured patient. I can't leave him," she said.

He motioned with his revolver. "Get out."

Charlotte asserted herself as the surgeon in charge. "Where is General Custer?" She held the syringe firmly in her still hand. "Tell him his friend Dod is mortally wounded, and I refuse to leave his side."

Another cavalry officer joined the first. "What's the problem here, soldier?"

"The doctor said the wounded man is a friend of General Custer."

Charlotte spoke again in a controlled voice which still retained an urgent appeal. She had to be the general's advocate. "General Custer will want to know. They went to West Point together, and they're old friends. General Ramseur needs a bed, and I need supplies to treat him. He'll die in the next few minutes if you don't help us."

"Get everyone else out. Guard the wagon. I'll find the general."

Moments later, the driver was turning the ambulance around. *"Clear the way."*

The ambulance moved slowly, bumping and jostling the general as it threaded a course through the once-crowded street now lined with surrendered Confederate troops. She didn't have to ask where the wagon was going. She knew their destination and what awaited her patient.

A Union surgeon met the ambulance at Belle Grove Plantation and directed stretcher-bearers to carry the general inside the house. "General Custer wants to know his condition."

"He was shot in the chest. The bullet tore through his chest cavity, likely injuring the lungs. Short of clamping off the injured blood vessels and removing damaged lung parenchyma, there isn't much I can do here, except continue to relieve the pressure when his breathing becomes labored again, and make him as comfortable as possible."

"What do you need?" the surgeon asked.

"Clean bandages, soap, and water," Charlotte said.

The stretcher-bearers carried the general down the hall and entered a room on the right, where they placed him on the bed. With modern surgical techniques and chest tubes, she might have been able to save him, but not in 1864.

She was sitting at the bedside, holding the general's hand, when a cavalry officer wearing tight, olive-colored corduroy trousers appeared in the doorway. A wide-brimmed slouch hat covered his yellow hair. His long, tawny mustache needed a trim. She recognized the tall, broad-shouldered, imposing man immediately.

"Thank you for bringing him here, General," she said.

Custer crossed the room and sat in a chair on the opposite side of the bed, scrubbed his face with his hands, smearing smudges of dirt. A mixture of blood and mud covered his jacket. "Is there nothing you can do?"

"Not here. Not now," she said with a solemn mix of sadness and regret.

How many times had she read the account of Ramseur's death? Dozens. And it was happening exactly as it had been reported. She'd been doing living history demonstrations for years and now she was *living* history. *God, how was it possible?* Her fingers grazed the bump of the brooch pinned to the inside of her trousers. *How could a stone do this to me?* She shook her head. She'd deal with how it happened later. For now, General Ramseur was more important.

A steady stream of officers moved in and out of the room during Ramseur's final hours. Some offered prayers. Some sat silently. All came to honor a friend. General Custer kept a vigil throughout the night.

As dawn broke over the valley and the death rattle continued, Ramseur's attempts to keep moving air into his chest weakened. Charlotte rose to stretch her legs, setting aside the cold compress she had used to wipe Ramseur's forehead. Custer picked it up and dabbed at his friend's face.

The general opened his eyes and spoke in a weak voice. "I have a new baby and I don't even know whether I have a son or a daughter."

A moment of truth arrived for Charlotte. She had failed to save him, but she would not fail to give him the one piece of information she alone had the power to give.

She leaned in close and said in a low voice, "You have a daughter. Her name is Mary."

The general's mouth lifted slightly on the right side in an effort to smile. "Send a lock of my hair to my wife Ellen and bear this message: 'I die a Christian and hope to meet her in heaven.'"

And with those words, the general closed his eyes and quietly slipped away.

Charlotte met Custer's steel blue eyes, now battle-weary and red-rimmed from a night of sleepless grief. "Thank you, Doctor Mallory. I will mention the excellent care the general received in my letter to Ellen."

Charlotte's chest hitched as panic swept through it. Her ancestor's name could not appear in the historical record because of something she did. "Please don't single me out, sir." She struggled to think clearly. "The general received excellent care from your surgeon as well."

He stood with his hat in his hands, nodded, and quit the room.

Charlotte went over to the window for a gulp of fresh air, but was almost suffocated by the smell of decaying flesh. The dead and dying of the two armies were commingled. Many of the wounded had crawled to the stream for a drink of cool water. Horses dragged damaged wagons behind them. Abandoned ambulances were still full of wounded soldiers. Cries of agony could be heard from every direction. Over eight thousand men had been killed, wounded, or captured, and many of the dead were in the plantation's front yard, stacked in gruesome piles awaiting burial. They would all be buried in shallow graves until they could be moved to their final resting places.

She turned away from the window. All these years, she had been so naïve. She'd studied history and reenacted battles and believed she understood the war. But she hadn't, not really. War was gut-wrenching, heartrending, and, above all, deadly. And she had come close to being a casualty. Was this the point of this trip back in time? To see the war as it really was. If so, she'd seen enough, and she was ready to go home. Her fingers grazed the bump of the brooch again. As soon as she had privacy, she would use the tweezers she had pilfered from the medical supplies and find out if the brooch would take her back to her century.

Boots clomped on the floor behind her. She turned to see one of the junior officers who had been in and out of the room during the night.

"General Sheridan wants to see you. If you'll come with me."

She patted her beard and wig, hoping she continued to look the part of Major Charles Mallory. As tired as she was, appearances still meant everything. Even more important, in this case her appearance might mean the difference between survival and death.

She was escorted to the front room Sheridan was using as his office. "Come in, Major. Take a seat."

She sat across the desk from a dark-eyed man with closely cropped hair. A man she knew to be a ruthless and highly decorated warrior. He picked up a quill pen and dipped it into an inkwell. "Name and regiment?"

His steely tone triggered the bad kind of shivers along her spine. She twitched and straightened her back. She would not let him intimidate her. Who was she kidding? She was stuck in the Civil War, for Pete's sake, and not at all sure how, or if, she could return home. Was she intimidated? Yes, by God, she was.

"Major," she stopped to clear her throat and lower her voice. "Major Charles Jackson Mallory, Second Corps Army of Northern Virginia."

The pen squeaked across the paper. "Where'd you receive your medical training?"

"New York Medical College."

"Do you own any slaves?"

"Of course not." She gulped, knowing she needed to temper her responses. "Our slaves have been granted their freedom."

"Yet you fight for the rebel cause."

"I'm a doctor, not a soldier."

"The Federals need good doctors, too."

Her mouth had gone dry as paper. She gnawed the inside of her cheek and tried to summon a little saliva. "Virginia is my family home and has been for over two hundred years."

"Where in Virginia?"

Fortunately, she knew her ancestor served the Second Corps until the end of the war, which meant he had not been captured in Strasburg. She would be safe giving him the answer to his question.

"Mallory Plantation is about ten miles north of Richmond."

"What would you do to save your home from being burned to ground?" Sheridan glared intently.

For one shocking moment the steady hand of time stilled. Had her presence in the past suddenly put her ancestors at risk? She took a long, steadying breath, then another, suppressing a roar of fear.

"Whatever I had to do."

She knew in her gut she had committed herself to a task she wasn't going to like. There'd be no return trip home in the near future.

He put down his pen, leaned back in his chair, and pursed his lips thoughtfully. Charlotte squirmed under the intensity of his glare. Then he sat forward again. "I've been ordered to send you to Washington."

She blinked and swallowed hard. "Why? You didn't even know who I was until a minute ago."

"Three rebel surgeons are now my prisoners. They'll spend the remainder of this war in prison. Do you want to join them?"

"They all turned you down." There was no humor in her voice, no pride, only a statement of fact.

He crossed his arms and stared down his long, straight nose, past the scar where she knew a bullet had grazed him. "One of you *will* go." There was no gloating in his voice, either, only the steely command of a general. The threat no longer hung in the air. It smacked her in the gut.

She swallowed hard again before asking, "When do I leave?"

5

Washington City, 1864

IN THE AFTERNOON, Charlotte and a small company of Federals traveled east on the Ashby Gap Turnpike, leaving Winchester behind. She had no choice but to go with them. Her ancestral home was at stake. If it was destroyed, it might possibly wipe out her existence, and her brother's as well.

Jack had to be frantic with worry, and Ken, too. How long had she been gone? An hour? A week? A month? When she went into the fog, she had dropped her haversack. Would Ken find it? What would he think happened to her?

Fear struck yet again, bringing fresh waves, unending waves. This was not a game. Her life was in danger. What would happen to her when they reached Washington? The bigger question haunted her as well. How was it even possible to go back in time? But the *how* didn't matter right now. Neither did the *why*. Surviving took her total focus.

The Union Cavalry treated her well enough, considering she was the enemy. Soldiers guarded her, but she wasn't restrained. For safety reasons, they had also given her a Union jacket to wear. She had cringed when she put on the smelly, bloodstained coat. Being inconspicuous came with a price.

Riding a horse through the fall chill without any privacy wasn't easy, either. She had a miniature case in her pocket to freshen her stage makeup, but the wig and beard itched. Fortunately, early in her reenacting days she had perfected the art of taking care of personal needs without drawing attention. It was all part of the gig.

The Union forces had control of the area, so the threat of being shot out of her saddle was low. She took her cues from the battle-hardened soldiers who formed her escort. When they eased their shoulders and talked about their homes in Ohio, Indiana, and Illinois, she relaxed, too.

As Washington drew closer, a sick feeling settled in the pit of her stomach. Nothing good could come of this.

The small party rode down the Columbia Road toward Fort Runyon, one of many earthen forts surrounding Washington. Before they were allowed to pass, their traveling papers were thoroughly inspected.

Charlotte and her escort then crossed the Potomac River by way of the Long Bridge and entered the city. Mud covered the streets and clung to wagon wheels and horses' hooves. The animals slung the gloppy mess onto the sidewalks and her trouser legs. Open ditches were filed with carcasses and sewage, which poisoned the air, gagging her with the stench of death and decay.

Although she'd had little sleep in the past two days, she was awake enough to know the Washington she knew was barely recognizable beneath the dirt and grime. They trotted their horses down Maryland Avenue toward the Capitol Building with its partially constructed dome. In the distance the Washington Monument was an unfinished, truncated shaft.

The dull rumbling of heavy army wagons across cobblestone and the steady tramp of marching feet met them as they turned down Pennsylvania Avenue. The grand city of the future was nothing more than a grimy military fortress and an incubator for typhoid and other diseases.

Charlotte's stomach growled, but she was afraid to eat anything unless she personally witnessed the food cooked, boiled, baked, or burned. The coffee, however, was cooked so black and thick germs couldn't survive. She wasn't so sure her stomach could, either.

Her vaccinations wouldn't completely protect her from the onslaught of germs which she knew outnumbered and outgunned the enemy here. Under such unsanitary conditions, disease could wipe out the city's entire population. Wherever she was going, she prayed for a hot bath and thoroughly cooked, edible food. She was as grubby as she'd ever been in her life.

The patrol continued along the avenue toward the White House. She knew Lincoln walked over to the War Department several times a day, and she hoped she might see him going by. She studied the faces of the men on both sides of the street, searching for the tall, gaunt President.

Her escort stopped in front of the White House. Although the building didn't have the additions made in the 1900's, the mansion was clearly recognizable.

"Are we...going inside?" Charlotte asked in a halting voice. The last time she'd been in the White House was six months before her mother died. Charlotte never thought she'd return. Never wanted to, in fact.

"Those are my orders," the company captain said.

She dismounted and stretched. Although horseback riding had been part of her life growing up, her busy medical practice didn't leave much time for riding. As a result, she'd be saddle sore for the next few days.

Days? She didn't have days. Jack would be sick with worry, and her absence would create havoc at work. What about her own distress? She'd fallen through some kind of frigging time warp and her life and her family's property had been threatened. Whatever the Union Army wanted her to do, it had better be quick.

She marched after the captain in charge up the steps, through the front door, and into the entrance hall. They made their way through the crowd, into the cross hall, then turned and went up the stairs to the second floor. At the top, they entered a reception room where at least a dozen men waited.

A thin, dark-haired young man with a widow's peak and goatee approached the captain. "Can I help you?"

She recognized Lincoln's secretary, John Nicolay, from old photographs in Jack's Civil War collection.

The captain handed Nicolay an envelope. "From General Sheridan."

"I'll make sure the President receives this."

The captain cleared his throat and nodded toward Charlotte. "The letter refers to this surgeon." Then he lowered his voice. "We gave him a Union coat. Didn't think he should come in here dressed in Confederate gray."

"Oh, I see," Nicolay said. "Wait here."

A few minutes later, Nicolay returned. "Mr. Lincoln wishes to relay his thanks to General Sheridan," he said to the captain. Then to Charlotte he said, "If you'll follow me, the President will see you now."

She gulped and pushed aside all thoughts of why she was flung into another time or how she was going to get home. The Make-a-Wish Foundation, sponsored by the time travel gods, had granted her wish to meet Abraham Lincoln. She pressed down the sides of the borrowed, loose-fitting, and filthy jacket, wishing she could stop in the ladies' room to make herself presentable.

Nicolay led the way into Lincoln's office.

The President stood at the back of the room, holding a document and gazing forlornly out the window toward the Potomac and the encampments of Union soldiers, a shawl draped across his shoulders. Secretary of War Stanton, an identifiable, round-faced man with a graying beard, was absorbed in reading a document, standing next to an old mahogany writing desk with pigeonholes full of books and papers. This was a snapshot in time, a photo which would trend on every social media site, and she blinked rapidly as if taking multiple pictures, hoping her memory wouldn't run out.

While waiting for the President or Stanton to acknowledge her, she took a quick inventory of the room. *Blink. Blink. Blink.* Jack would ask her later to set the scene for him, and he would expect her to describe the room in detail. *Blink. Blink. Blink.*

From her previous visits to the White House, she was familiar with the public rooms and the main rooms in the private residence.

The room Lincoln used for his office, located in the southeast corner of the second floor, was referred to as the Lincoln Bedroom in the twenty-first century, and it was the same room in which she now awaited the President's acknowledgement.

The gas lamps' dim, golden light provided spotty illumination of the green and gold wallpaper and dark green striped carpet covering the floor. There were no recognizable pieces of furniture. The only painting she could identify was the portrait of Andrew Jackson hanging over the fireplace. In her time, the painting hung over a doorway behind her. Folios of maps leaned against the wall next to the sofa. *Blink. Blink. Blink.*

"How did you come to be captured, Major Mallory?"

Lincoln's question jolted her. She snapped to attention then took a deep breath and blew it out slowly. "I was tending General Ramseur when his ambulance was captured in Strasburg."

Lack of sleep showed in the President's dark-rimmed, bloodshot eyes. He shuffled away from the window and sank into a chair at the end of a long walnut table piled high with maps and books. Directly in front of him was an eight-inch high pile of documents written on heavy parchment.

"How's the general now?"

"He was mortally wounded, sir. There was little I could do. God was not on the Confederate side at Cedar Creek."

"My concern is not whether God is on our side; my greatest concern is to be on God's side—"

The Lincoln quote was one of many Charlotte had memorized. She finished it, saying, "For God is always right."

Lincoln nodded. "Indeed, He is."

"Please, Doctor Mallory, have a seat," Stanton said

She hovered over a chair before sitting, studying Lincoln closely, as if he were one of her patients during morning rounds. Although lanky and plain-looking, his face radiated intelligence and kindness. The mole on his right cheek, the asymmetry of his face, large jaw, and drooping eyelid were all consistent with photographs and historical observations. He also appeared to be several pounds lighter than his reported one hundred eighty pounds. His hair was disheveled, but his clothes were neatly pressed. *Blink. Blink. Blink.*

She eased into the proffered chair, sat near the edge, and leaned forward, never taking her eyes off of him.

"You're probably wondering why you're here, Doctor Mallory," Stanton said.

"It has crossed my mind several times since General Sheridan threatened me," she said with a thread of steel in her voice.

"We need medical assistance which only you can provide." Stanton impaled her with a fierce glare having nothing to do with her and everything to do with her allegiance. To have to ask the enemy for help must have riled him.

"The Union has very capable doctors, I'm sure," she said.

Lincoln clasped his hands and rested them on the table. "This is a delicate matter and requires more than simply a capable doctor."

Stanton sat heavily in an armchair next to the window overlooking the unfinished Washington Monument. "One of our best agents has been wounded and captured. He's currently being held in Chimborazo."

"Chimborazo isn't a prison hospital. Why is he there?"

"He was shot while escaping. Chimborazo was the closest hospital. They want him alive for questioning."

"He should receive excellent care. Why do you need me?"

"You don't need to treat him. You need to get him out." Stanton enunciated each word for effect, especially the *get him out* part.

Whatever she'd expected to hear, this wasn't it. Chimborazo sat on top of a hill in Richmond. She couldn't march up there and steal a patient. "Do you have a plan for how it might be accomplished?"

Stanton tapped his cigar against the edge of an overflowing ashtray. "No. You'll have to devise a plan once you've made an assessment of the major's condition. It's to your advantage, though, that he's not in a prison hospital."

Lincoln's keen eyes challenged her. "Once you get him out, other people will take him to safety."

She sat back in her chair, not at all sure if what they asked of her was even possible. "If I facilitate a Union spy's escape, what happens to me?"

"You'll be free to return to your unit."

"None of this makes sense." Frustration throbbed in her every word. "I'll be considered a traitor."

Stanton puffed, filling the room with a cloud of smoke. "We're confident you can find a way without compromising yourself."

"*You're confident.*" Maybe it was time to yank off her wig and beard, confess, and throw herself on the mercy of the President, but it might get her thrown into prison instead. She waved away the smoke blowing in her direction. "If I don't do this, Sheridan has threatened to burn my family home to the ground. If I'm found to be a traitor, my neighbors will do it for him." She made a low sound, like someone absorbing a body blow.

They sat in silence as the noise level in the hallway increased in sharp contrast to the present-day White House. How did the President work in this environment with dozens of people waiting outside the door to see him? No appointment needed. All you need do is show up and wait.

"How serious are your agent's wounds? Is he able to walk?" she asked.

"We don't know his condition, but we have to get him out. He has valuable information Jefferson Davis wants, which could compromise a dozen or more northern sympathizers," Stanton said.

Something in his expression told her he wasn't telling the truth…or he wasn't telling *all* of the truth. "Will his information shorten the war?" she asked.

Stanton tapped his cigar against the edge of an ashtray already filled with a day's worth of ashes. "The information we get from the sympathizers is invaluable. If we lose even one, we lose a link which took us months to establish."

"Do you want the war to end?" Lincoln asked.

"I never wanted the war to start," Charlotte said. "But what's to stop me from assisting Jefferson Davis?"

"I'm a firm believer in people. If given the truth, they can be depended upon to meet the crisis. You want the war to end. This will bring the end closer." He picked up a pen and placed a sheet of writing paper in front of him. The scratchy nib didn't glide effortlessly across the surface of the paper, but it didn't seem to bother the President, who scratched away with a flourish.

"A ship will take you to City Point, where you'll be met by an escort who will introduce you to General Grant. Then he'll see you through the lines," Stanton said.

"Will I be on my own in Richmond?"

Stanton puffed more smoke in her direction. "You'll be met by a member of the underground."

Lincoln put down his pen, folded the note, and handed it to her. Then he sat back and swung his legs over the chair arm.

As she held the paper, still warm from the President's touch, her fingers quivered. "I need food, sleep, and a bath." Her voice was hoarse with emotion.

"It can be arranged on board ship," Stanton said.

She cleared her throat. "I have one more question. If your Richmond contact can get me in, why can't he get your agent out?"

Stanton's face tightened. "He's a railroad President, not a doctor."

"And one of the northern sympathizers you can't afford to lose." She looked first to Stanton, then to the President.

Lincoln reached out with his long arms and drew his knees up almost to his face. "He's one of them, yes."

"Does your agent have a name?"

Lincoln and Stanton shared a quick glance then Stanton said, "Major McCabe."

Charlotte rolled the name around her tongue. "A Scotsman."

"A lawyer," Stanton said.

"And a damn good friend," Lincoln said. "Bring him home."

6

City Point, Headquarters of General Ulysses S. Grant, 1864

AFTER A LONG day, Charlotte trudged aboard the sidewheel steamer *River Queen*, Grant's private dispatch boat. She could barely stand, but her mind wouldn't shut down. If she did sleep, she'd probably have fitful dreams about wounded soldiers and a magical sapphire brooch.

Charlotte's Virginia Civil War knowledge was legendary among her peers. She could be a winner on Jeopardy if all the questions related to the Commonwealth's history between 1861 and 1865, or medical history during the same time period. When Stanton told her she would travel by riverboat to City Point, she knew exactly where she was going and why. Since June, the small port town at the confluence of the James and Appomattox Rivers had been Grant's headquarters and the base for the forces fighting in Petersburg. Her meeting with Grant would take place at his command tent on the east lawn of Dr. Richard Eppes's plantation known as Appomattox.

Once on board the steamer, while she took a sponge bath and ate, she analyzed her predicament. There had been no flashbulb moment of enlightenment in the past forty-eight hours. It would be nice to open the brooch and disappear, but if she did, Sheridan would act on his threat. She still didn't understand why the brooch had carried her to the nineteenth century. Until she could figure out an alternative, she had to continue to play the cards as dealt, because folding gave her no hope of winning a return trip to her time with the home place intact.

When she finally climbed into her berth, she dropped off imme-diately into a much-needed, surprisingly dreamless sleep.

Now, as a new day dawned, she prepared for what was to come in much the same way as she prepared for surgery. She sucked in long, lung-filling breaths while thinking ahead to her meeting with General Grant. Visualizing Chimborazo was easy. From previous visits to the historical site and visitors' center, she was familiar with the Confederate hospital's layout, but she had no workable plan. Her only advantage was knowing the hospital guards would be more concerned with keeping the enemy out than keeping patients in.

A successful rescue depended on the extent of Major McCabe's injuries. *If* he could hobble, and *if* she could get him out of the hospital, her next challenge would be handing him off to a member of the underground. If he couldn't walk, she had few options.

She leaned her elbows on the deck railing of the *River Queen*, sipping coffee while watching the sun rise over the James River. The sight was as breathtaking as always. Workers were already unloading supplies from the hundreds of steamboats, sailing vessels, and barges berthed along the mile-long wharf. Even with the bustle and clanging, the busy port seemed more like a quiet resort town to Charlotte's twenty-first century sensibilities.

While she was in City Point maybe Grant would let her tour the six separate hospitals of the Depot Field Hospital, which was only about a mile from the wharf. The facility reportedly treated as many as ten thousand patients on an average day, which seemed impossi-ble.

What was she thinking? A wounded, possibly dying man was waiting for her. She didn't have *any* extra time.

"*Doctor Mallory. Doctor Mallory.*"

She jerked her head in the direction of the voice, scanning the crowded wharf. A short, stocky, weatherworn man with shaggy black hair waved at her with one hand while holding the reins of a pair of bay Morgans with the other.

Since she was back in her Confederate gray uniform, dockworkers turned and glared at her, their scowls lining their faces in the morning sun. Waves crashing against the pilings seemed to echo the men's obvious dislike of the enemy in their midst. The air was damp, and the uniform in question stuck to her. She'd gladly remove the darn thing if she had anything else to wear. She closed her eyes for a moment, trying to ignore the thunder of her heart, and listened instead to the rustle and grunts of the men unloading the ship's cargo. She'd much rather listen to their swearing than to the clamor of her own fears.

After the gangplank was lowered, she tromped down the ramp to the wharf, trading in the shelter and safety of the ship for unknown dangers. The man approached her, leading the horses, his lips set in a thin, resolute line.

His eyes probed hers, black and hard and scalpel-sharp. "I'm Gaylord. General Grant's expecting you. Let's go." The thin lips became even thinner. "Best to take off the coat. No need to advertise you're the enemy. Makes my job harder and might get you killed."

She bristled, counted to a quick ten, and then snapped back in a sarcastic tone. "What about my trousers? They're gray, too."

He shrugged. "Don't matter. Soldiers wear what they can strip off dead Johnny Rebs."

She doubted he'd do much to protect her if those same Union soldiers decided they wanted her pants, too.

She removed her jacket, folded it carefully, and then packed it in the saddlebag. If the jacket had been made of linen it would be one big wrinkle by the time they reached Richmond. But as a true and proper daughter of the South, she wouldn't be caught dead, even in hot, muggy weather, in white linen or white shoes after Labor Day. *Why was she thinking of linen and shoes when she was living in some kind of alternate universe?* Because time travel was impossible, or should be, but the dangers she faced were both real and deadly.

They found General Grant sitting outside his command tent under the golden-bronze fall foliage of a beech tree. Several officers relaxed nearby, studying maps. The general was gazing out in

Charlotte's direction, cigar in hand, as if waiting expectantly. She dismounted and tied the reins to a high line strung between two trees.

Charlotte knew horses, and recognized Cincinnati, Grant's striking black thoroughbred and son of Lexington, the most successful sire in the second half of the nineteenth century. The general was probably the greatest equestrian in U.S. history.

The general approached, puffing on his cigar. For a split second, she considered advising him to stop smoking before it killed him, which it would in 1885.

"Doctor Mallory." The soft-spoken, rounded-shouldered general extended a delicate hand. They studied each other, blue eye to blue eye. His wavy brown hair, untrimmed beard, mustache, and ill-fitting uniform gave him a rather scruffy look.

"It's a pleasure to meet you," she responded.

"I don't want to keep you," he said. "You have a hard ride ahead. I only wanted to express my appreciation and wish you good luck. I'm rather fond of Major McCabe."

"I look forward to meeting him. He has an impressive fan club," she said.

Grant's brow crinkled in a puzzled frown.

"Lincoln and Stanton said the very same thing," she added.

"Gaylord will get you to Richmond. Once there, he'll hand you over to a member of the underground who will get you inside Chimborazo. The rest is up to you."

"What if McCabe is too injured to move?" she asked.

He pointed at her with his stogie. Pungent smoke spiraled up in her direction, but she didn't dare move or wave it away from her face.

"Unless he's dead, you must get him out. Do you understand?" He might be a soft-spoken man, but his tone made his point clear. Very clear.

"Yes, sir."

He tipped his hat and walked back toward his tent.

"Let's ride," Gaylord said.

For someone used to giving orders, taking them was a nasty-tasting pill.

She swung her leg over the saddle, wishing she had a twelve-hour Aleve to ease the stiffness in her joints. The well-trained mount took off at a trot, and as they neared a bend in the road, Charlotte glanced back for one last look at Grant. He was poised outside his tent, following their progress and puffing. She put her hand to her hat and tipped it ever so slightly.

7

Richmond, Virginia, 1864

AT DUSK, CHARLOTTE and Gaylord dismounted at a dilapidated farmhouse on the outskirts of Richmond. A swinging shutter groaned in the cool breeze that skidded through the nippy air. Broken windows, a splintered door creaking on its hinges, and a porch sagging on one side where its foundation had crumbled added to the homestead's ghostly appearance. The hair on her arms rose, gooseflesh stippling her skin. The haunted house didn't bode well for what was to come.

The physically demanding horseback trip from City Point had taken them across rivers, over rugged terrain, and through forested regions. Since both armies patrolled the area, they had maintained silence throughout the twenty-five mile trek. The possibility of ambush at every blind bend kept her braced for an attack. By the end of the journey her fear was locked in her shoulders and neck, and she winced when she twisted to stretch the tight band of knotted, strained muscles.

"Who lives here?" she asked.

Gaylord threw his saddlebags over his shoulder. "No one now." He uncinched the saddle. "We're leaving the horses here. They'll be confiscated if we ride them into the city."

"What's to stop someone from stealing them from an abandoned farm?"

"Soon as we leave, they'll be taken to a safe pasture."

Leaves crunched underfoot while they hiked in the shelter of the tree line. As hot as the wool uniform often was, tonight she was thankful for the warmth it provided and that Gaylord allowed her to wear it.

Gaylord followed an invisible path. More than once, when she was convinced they'd reached an impenetrable thicket, an opening appeared. Not even breadcrumbs would help her find her way back. The arduous trek ended at a dirt road on the north side of Richmond.

"What now?" she asked.

"We wait."

While they waited in the shadows, Charlotte leaned against a tree and closed her eyes. She had learned as a resident to grab sleep when she could, and she quickly dozed off.

Gaylord woke her, whispering her name. "Doctor Mallory. Wake up. Your contact is here."

"Oh." She got up, stretched, and yawned.

The carriage door swung open as if it had been kicked. If she had been nearby, it would have knocked her to the ground.

"Good luck," Gaylord said, before disappearing back into the trees.

The little man hadn't been good company, but he was an excellent guide, and she had become comfortable traveling with him. Now the fear she held at bay during their day-long ride to Richmond came back in a rush.

She peered inside the carriage's window. Moonlight barely illuminated the street, much less the inside of a carriage, but she was able to discern the shadowy outline of a man in there.

"Your patient doesn't have much time. Please get in," the man said.

Was she really expected to get into a dark carriage with a man she didn't know? Yes, and hadn't she spent the day traveling through Virginia with a man she didn't know? She took a shaky breath to silence the warning bells clanging in her head. How many more hurdles would she have to jump before she could go home?

Reluctantly, she climbed inside and sat opposite a man with dark, curly hair and muttonchops. He rapped the ceiling with a walking stick. The driver snapped the reins and drove down Broad Street.

"Have you met Doctor McCaw?" he asked.

"No. Although I'm familiar with the work he's done at Chimborazo." He and her six-times-great-grandfather were contemporaries but, thankfully, they had never met.

"We play chess regularly," the man said.

Charlotte calmly rested steady hands on her thighs, but inside she was one big monster knot. "Your friendly game could yield valuable information for the underground. I'm sure Doctor McCaw hears soldiers discuss tactical options. Information the Union would find useful."

The chess-playing spy leaned forward, lacing his fingers on the top of the cane. "I told my colleagues it was mistake to trust you, but no one would listen."

"You have nothing to fear from me. I'm on your side."

He frowned, his dark eyes narrowed. "Pshaw. I know your family, Doctor Mallory, and there isn't a Unionist among them. I pray for all our sakes you're telling the truth."

She hoped he didn't ask how she was related, because she hadn't had time to invent a satisfactory answer, and fumbling for one would only make him doubt her more.

"When we get to Chimborazo, I'll go in to see McCaw. Major McCabe is in the ward closest to his office. My informant told me earlier today he wouldn't survive the night. He might already be dead."

"Then why am I going in there?"

"If McCabe has talked, we're all in danger. I could be walking into a trap tonight. We need to know. Grant needs to know."

"Why is he in Chimborazo and not in a prison hospital?"

"He was shot while trying to escape custody. It was the closest hospital."

Which confirmed what Lincoln had told her.

The carriage drove along the road at the base of the camp, then crossed the bridge at the back of the compound. A sentry came to the carriage door.

"Evening, Mr. Parker. Is it chess night?"

"I've come to beat McCaw again. Is he in his office?"

The sentry opened the door and glanced inside. Charlotte nodded. "Who you got with you?"

Parker pointed with his walking stick. "A surgeon from General Lee's headquarters. Saved him a long walk from town."

"Your lucky night, hey?" the sentry said. He closed the door and rapped on the side of the carriage. The driver continued up the hill toward the compound.

Her companion fixed her with a piercing look, and a hot numbness swept over her face. "We're both playing a dangerous game. I pray you're not here to entrap us."

It was, indeed, the most dangerous game she'd ever played, and one not of her choosing. But even given the choice, she would never have taken such a risk.

The carriage stopped in front of Laughton House, now serving as headquarters, which included the offices of the surgeon-in-chief, the surgeons-in-charge, and other necessary offices of the post. Immediately to the south were the hospital wards.

Mr. Parker straightened a perfectly straight cravat. "Are you ready?"

She nodded. Her pulse, which had been beating quickly, had settled down to near normal. Under the circumstances, it was the best she could manage. Although she wore the right color uniform, had the necessary skills for the job, and she was, after all, from Richmond, she was still an imposter, and it made this situation dangerous.

"If you can get McCabe into the carriage, do it, and then get out of here. I'll claim you stole it. Good luck."

They climbed out and the major entered Laughton House, leaving her to find her way alone, one more turn in a never-ending labyrinth twisting through a bloody battle, meetings with President Lincoln, General Sheridan, and General Grant, and now a seemingly impossible rescue mission at Chimborazo. Her life and family's property were threatened. She'd had only bites of food and very little rest. She had walked, run, ridden on a horse, in a wagon, on a steamboat, and in a carriage. Damn, she was tired, and she wanted to go home.

Maybe the end of the maze was around the next corner. She could only hope.

Since there were only a handful of sentries patrolling the grounds, she assumed the hospital didn't have many escapees. She turned in a slow circle to orient herself. The guardhouse and five dead houses sat on the northern perimeter. If McCabe had died, she would find his body in one of those. The patient wards, a hundred one-story buildings, were directly in front of her.

She proceeded slowly toward the building closest to the office, hands behind her, with her head bent in what she hoped looked like deep thought. If this wasn't the right one, given the vast number of wards, the sun would be up before she had time to search the entire complex. Her plan was to assess the layout, identify exits, count the guards, locate McCabe, and get him out of there.

She could do this.

A small shiver passed over her as she opened the door and entered a candlelit ward. The ward held two compartments separated by a low partition running lengthwise. There were four rows of metal beds and two centrally located stoves. *Blink.* Sliding wood shutters covered square windows, and were partially open. *Blink.* The door at her back remained open. *Blink.* Leaving it ajar would catch the guards' attention when they passed by. She didn't want that, but closing it would block her escape. She didn't want that either. Undecided, she flipped an imaginary coin. Heads. She closed the door.

A chair scraped across the rough plank floor and a young soldier snapped to attention, acknowledging her. "Evenin', sir."

She took a calming breath, decided to forgo formalities, and asked with a sharp tone but low-voiced, "Where's the prisoner?" She'd be in trouble if there was more than one.

"Down there." The soldier pointed toward the end of the row on the far side of the room. "Number twelve. If'n you ask me, the man's gonna die right soon."

Charlotte headed toward the patient. "Are you the night nurse?"

"Yes, sir."

With only one night nurse and no guards next to McCabe's bed, it might actually be possible to sneak the major out. A thought niggled Charlotte. If the patient didn't need a guard, he probably wasn't in any condition to walk out with her.

"Sir, we ain't got no other Yanks, why's he here?"

"What? Oh...well." She bit her lower lip momentarily, thinking. "He was caught down by the railroad tracks." The lie rolled off her tongue, and kept rolling. "Quicker to bring him here. President Davis believes he can identify spies living in Richmond. Has he said anything?"

"I been here all day. He's yelped some but ain't said nuthin'."

Charlotte reached the foot of the bed, studying the patient. He was lying on his back, observing her with eyes half-closed. A filthy blanket was drawn up over the sharp angles of his body. She read the paper ticket tied to the end of the bed. Only his name and date of admission—Major Michael Abraham McCabe, October 17, 1864. There was no information about his condition. She moved to the side of the bed, leaned over, and took the major's pulse. Too fast. "Is there an exit wound?"

"Nope. Still got a Minié ball in his gut. If it don't kill him, the hangman will."

"Water," McCabe said.

She lifted the blanket and gasped at the dirty dressing. McCabe's distended belly was grossly inflamed around the area of the bullet entry. She pushed on it gently.

He grimaced and cried out in pain, "*Ahhh.*"

"Sorry." The patient had rebound tenderness, probably peritonitis. More than likely the bullet had nicked the bowel. Although he wasn't actively bleeding, the shallow breathing, fever, and shaking told her he was heading into shock. If she didn't get him into surgery he would die in the next few hours. She looked at the wound again. She'd seen worse, and those patients had all died on the operating table.

"How long has he been shaking like this?"

"Awhile, I reckon. How long you 'spect he's gonna live?"

Charlotte tapped her foot, rapidly sorting through options. If she operated on McCabe here and he survived, the Confederate Army would hang him. "At this rate only a few hours."

He opened his eyes very slightly, only a sliver, but she could somehow see the color—emerald. He was a handsome man, even with all the swelling and bruises on his square-jawed face. Long, dirty blond hair lay across his forehead, covering most of an open cut above his brow. Over six feet tall, broad-shouldered, probably weighed one-eighty or ninety. If he couldn't walk, she couldn't carry him. She checked that option off the list.

He tried to lick his lips, but his swollen tongue stuck in his mouth. His pitiable attempt at communication touched her doctor's heart. This soldier wasn't ready to give up. And if he wasn't, then she wouldn't give up on him, either.

McCabe reached for her hand. "Water."

She glanced at the nurse. "Bring me clean bandages."

The nurse stared at her and shook his head slowly, his mouth going tight beneath his moustache. "My orders are to leave him be."

"I'm not going to watch a man die without trying to make his last moments comfortable. Now, go."

The nurse nodded, then spun on his heel and hurried away.

She sat on the edge of the spindle-back side chair, scooted it closer, scraping wobbly legs against the floor, and took the major's cold, long-fingered hand between both of hers. He would die soon if she didn't help him. But to help him, she would have to take him to her time and operate on him. Did she really want to do this?

The major's eyes were not quite closed and a sliver of white showed among the bruises. Was he trying to open them for one last glimpse of the world? If she took him to the future, this could be his one last glimpse of *his* world.

President Lincoln called him a friend. General Grant thought highly of him, too. Members of the Richmond underground risked their lives for him. All excellent character references.

Suddenly, her brain slammed against the question of the day, and she swallowed hard. Would the brooch take *both of them* to her time? Would the brooch even take her? And if the magic worked as she hoped it would, how would the major handle living in her time? What if he freaked out and told people he was from the nineteenth century?

She fought back a growing quiver of panic.

What if the major was married and had children? He'd never see them again. What if...

Stop it. Now.

Going through a litany of what-ifs didn't help a damn bit. She was stalling while the life of the man whose hand she held slipped slowly away. This was a waiting-at-the-red-light moment. She could waste precious minutes, or she could do something. Why did surgical decisions come so easily and all others seemed to require in-depth analysis?

It was *now* decision time. Do it, or walk away.

She took a deep breath and saw her decision flow out in the spluttering flame of the candle. She glanced over her shoulder at the flickering shadows. No one was paying attention to them. If anyone was, the light was too low to see clearly.

She turned back to the patient, leaned in close, and whispered, "I've been sent to rescue you, Major. I'm getting you out of here."

"Am I dead?" he whispered.

"No, and you won't die today if I can help it."

"My legs won't carry me very far."

Sweating profusely, as if she'd just run a race, she let go of his hand, reached into her waistband, and unpinned the brooch. The stone was hot, and not from the heat of her skin. Using the tweezers she'd stolen, she squeezed the clasp and sprung the latch.

"Hang on, we're going for a ride." *I hope.*

His mouth turned up in the faintest of grins. She imagined in his delirious state he was telling the Devil to go screw himself because he didn't intend to die today.

Well, I don't either.

Praying she'd been given a round trip ticket which allowed two to fly for the price of one, she held his hand and haltingly sounded out the inscription on the stone, *"Chan ann le tìm no àite a bhios sinn a' tomhais an gaol ach's ann le neart anama."*

8

Winchester Medical Center, Winchester, Virginia, Present Day

WHEN THE FOG cleared, Charlotte was still sitting in the spindle-backed chair holding McCabe's hand. He lay on the bed, moaning.

Street lights indicated she was no longer in the nineteenth-century. But were they in Richmond? Washington? Cedar Creek? At least they weren't in a Civil War hospital any longer. Any other place would be an improvement.

She'd made it back with a nineteenth-century spy, a bed, and a chair. How was she going to explain this? At least they were period appropriate.

She checked her patient. No change. The clock was ticking faster now, and he didn't have much time. She had to figure out where she was, then get him to the closest medical center.

Once on her feet, she had a better view of her surroundings. Several hundred yards away sat Belle Grove Mansion. "Oh my god. I'm back." Her first impulse was to jump up and down with overwhelming relief, but she forced her feelings under control. If her car was still in the parking lot, then she would allow herself a small shriek of joy.

She squatted next to the major. "I'll be back in a couple of minutes. Don't go anywhere."

When he didn't answer or grin, she ran like she was approaching the finish line in a race, holding nothing back.

Her SUV was where she had left it, squashed next to a tree. She let out a loud sigh of relief, and said a quiet, "Thank you, God." Her keys were in her haversack, and she had no idea where that was now. Of course, thanks to Jack, she had a spare key hidden in the front passenger-side wheel well.

Once underway, she turned on the high beams and drove across the field, stopping a few feet from her patient with the headlights aimed right at him. There was no way she could move him. She had to call 911.

She rummaged through her purse she'd left in the car, and extracted her cell phone...which still held a charge. But what really surprised her was the date. It was Sunday night. Only thirty-six hours had lapsed since she went into the fog.

She dialed, unsure of what her story would be, but well aware of time running out.

"What's your emergency?" the 911 operator asked.

"I'm at Cedar Creek Battlefield. There's a man in the parking lot who's been shot. He needs an ambulance."

"What's your name, ma'am?"

"Charlotte Mallory. I just found him in the parking lot." She almost choked on the lie but composed herself quickly. How many more would she have to tell before this situation righted itself? She shuddered. She couldn't worry about that now, or she'd stay blanketed in a sheet of fear that had been suffocating her since she landed in the midst of the Battle of Cedar Creek.

"An ambulance has been dispatched. Is he breathing?"

Charlotte hurried back over to the bed, sat in the chair, and put her hand on McCabe's chest. "Shallow breathing. He said his name is Major McCabe, and now he seems to have lost consciousness." She pulled off her beard and wiped her face with a towel she'd brought from the car, then removed the wig and shook out her hair.

"Please remain on the line with me until help arrives," the operator said.

The shrill of an ambulance soon cut through the night. She

grabbed the ticket off the hook at the end of the bed and shoved it into her jacket. Very little personal information was written on the ticket, but it would only confuse the police, especially the 1864 date. It was illegal to tamper with evidence, but right now she didn't care. If she got arrested, she knew where she could find a good lawyer.

"I hear the ambulance," she told the emergency operator. "The driver should be able to see my headlights." The ambulance pulled into the parking lot and stopped a short distance from her vehicle. "They're here. I'm hanging up."

She disconnected the call as two EMTs rushed over. "Gunshot to the abdomen. Looks like the wound is a couple of days old."

One of the EMTs checked McCabe's vital signs, and then looked at his wound. "You're right. This isn't recent." He glanced up at Charlotte. "You found him here? Bed and all."

She nodded, slowly. "And the chair."

The EMT shook his head. "Never seen anything like this." He turned to his buddy. "Tachypneic, tachycardic, and hypotensive. Let's get this guy into the ambulance. He'll need a miracle to survive the night."

They wheeled a gurney next to McCabe, then lowered it to the height of the metal bed. As one EMT tossed off the blanket then lifted an edge of the sheet, another slid a trauma transfer board between the sheet and the bed. The first EMT said to the other. "Slide him over on three. One, two, three."

McCabe groaned but never opened his eyes. The EMTs rolled him to the ambulance and guided the gurney in. While they called into the hospital and started oxygen and an IV, Charlotte sat in her car and called Ken.

"Where have you been?" he asked.

"It's a long story. I'm in the battlefield parking lot right now. I found a gunshot victim and an ambulance is here now. We'll be leaving for the medical center as soon as they get him hooked up. Will you meet us there?"

"I'm not on call tonight," Ken said.

Charlotte used a face cleansing cloth and washed her face while they talked. "I need you to do this for me. If he's going to survive, you're his best hope."

"I'm just pulling into my garage. I'll turn around and meet you there. Where's he shot?"

"Abdomen."

"And he's still alive?"

She threw the cleansing cloth onto the floor and opened another one. "I wouldn't be calling you if he was dead."

"Are you going to tell me where you've been? You've been missing for over thirty-six hours. I found your haversack with a strange-looking box. You met someone, didn't you?"

"Sure did. A major in the Union Army with a bullet in his abdomen. See you at the hospital." She hung up in the middle of Ken's next question.

She hustled over to the ambulance. "How is he?"

One of the EMTs climbed out and closed the rear door. "Not good. We're taking him to Winchester Medical Center."

"I'll follow you," she said.

Twelve minutes later, she whipped her car into a reserved space in the parking lot at the Winchester Medical Center's ER entrance and tossed her doctor tag onto the dashboard. If a parking attendant looked close enough, he'd discover the tag was only valid at her hospital in Richmond and would have her car towed. But that was another thing she didn't care about right now.

Ken pulled into a spot next to her and jumped out. "What the h—?"

She pushed him toward the ER entrance. "Patient *now*. Explanations later."

He followed the EMTs into the ER, barking orders. "Get him to the trauma bay."

The EMTs rolled McCabe down the hall and into the first available cubicle. They transferred him quickly to the hospital bed, then the trauma nurses went to work cutting off his shirt and trousers.

One of the nurses held up the bloody shirt. "These look like old-timey clothes. He must have been at the reenactment."

The other nurse, hooking McCabe to the monitors, said, "I thought Safety Marshalls checked all the weapons. How'd he get shot?"

Ken snapped on a pair of gloves and inspected the wound. "Change his oxygen mask to a one hundred percent non-rebreather and start a second IV. Hang LR and run both wide open. What are his vitals?"

If this had been Charlotte's hospital, she would be working on McCabe, but it wasn't, and she had no privileges here. She resigned herself to standing in the back, against the wall. Ken didn't need her watching over his shoulder.

The adrenalin that had been her constant companion throughout her ordeal was dissipating, leaving her lightheaded and exhausted. Or, maybe it was the diet of coffee and hardtack combined with little sleep. She considered a shower, a decent meal, and down time, but as long as the major fought for his life, she would stay close by.

The ER doc stuck her head in. Ken told her he was attending, and he'd call her if he needed help. Nodding, she watched for a minute then left. Technicians hurried in to assist Ken, draw blood and cultures, and take x-rays.

Charlotte's eyes strayed from the monitors, to the shredded, bloody clothes someone was shoving into a bag, to the naked man, modestly draped. He had a v-shaped, ripped, lean torso from his broad shoulders down to a distended abdomen covered with dried blood and reddened with cellulitis. Perfect symmetry and proportion till you got to his belly. Nurse this guy back to health and he might be a classic hunk. Great physique, and, based on his friends, he had to be intelligent. For now, she wouldn't hold the fact that he was a lawyer against him.

If he survived, how was she going to explain what happened to him when she was completely mystified herself? Maybe none of the adventures of the last few days really happened. Maybe she'd never left the reenactment. Maybe she'd slept through the last few days dreaming of being captured and meeting Abraham Lincoln.

Really? Then how did she explain the man attached to oxygen,

IV's, and monitors with a Civil War-era Minié ball, of all things, in his gut?

There would be consequences for bringing him home with her. When Jack heard her story, he would jump into the middle of the mystery wearing combat boots.

"Are the antibiotics in yet? Call OR and see if they're ready for us," Ken told a nurse, before turning to Charlotte and extending a professional courtesy. "Do you want to observe?"

"Yes." She pushed off the wall. Until she scrubbed away the grime, she wasn't going anywhere, especially into the OR. "I'll join you in ten minutes. Where's the closest shower? I've spent two days in the field and I'm way too dirty for the OR."

"Second floor call room," a nurse said. "You'll find clean scrubs in the cabinet."

Stress, sweat, and dirt melted away under the hot spray. Although she was tempted to linger, she didn't. Returning to her patient preempted her physical needs, including food. Her empty stomach growled. She hoped Ken still had steak and wine left.

As soon as Ken finished surgery, she planned to invade his house, eat, drink, and soak in the hot tub. She also had to call Jack to fill him in. If McCabe survived, he would need someone with him who knew his identity and could answer his questions. She had a full day of surgeries and office appointments scheduled for the next day, which meant returning to Richmond in the morning by six. After all she had been though, she needed to return to her normal life, to structure and safety. Jack would be psyched to babysit a nineteenth-century Union cavalry officer who also happened to be a spy. Perfect story material.

She dressed in scrubs and hurried off to the OR.

Two hours later, Ken had removed the bullet, repaired the bowel, and copiously irrigated the major's abdominal cavity. The police would want the bullet for evidence once it was released by pathology. When they questioned McCabe, what would he tell them?

Two police officers were waiting when she and Ken exited the OR. One man was tall and lean with close-cropped brown hair, and the other was a broad-shouldered blond with a grouchy face. She disliked them both on sight.

"Doctor Mallory?" thin man asked, approaching Ken.

"*I'm* Doctor Mallory." Charlotte glared at the man with an exasperated shake of her head. She was exhausted and not in the mood to be interviewed, but she knew from personal experience that if she ignored the police, they could be more problematic than the press. She would stick to the truth as much as possible.

The grouchy looking officer said, "We'd like to ask you a few questions about the man you brought in earlier."

"Have you learned anything about him?" she asked, hoping to deflect some of the attention from her.

"We were hoping you could tell us," thin man said.

"When we finished late this afternoon, I got in my car to go back to Richmond but decided to close my eyes for a few minutes before making the drive. The next thing I knew it was three hours later. I didn't realize I was so tired. Glad I didn't try to drive."

Heat crept up her neck as a ripple of tension went through her. Lying made her uncomfortable. She would not pass a polygraph test today. "Anyway," she continued, "I pulled out of my parking space and spotted someone lying on a bed. I jumped out of the car, and approached cautiously. I asked his name. He was still alert enough to answer 'Major McCabe'. I saw his abdomen and realized he'd been shot. I called 911."

The tall officer made notes. Grouchy just glared. If they were trying to intimidate her, good luck. She had been trained by surgical professors who had perfected the art of intimidation.

Thin man flipped a page in his notebook. "Have you ever seen him before?"

She shook her head. "He's a pretty good-looking guy. I would have noticed him."

"He told you his name was Major McCabe," thin man said. "Is that his rank or first name?"

She shrugged. "I don't know."

Thin man wrote in his notebook. "Why'd you call Doctor

Thomas? The ER docs could have handled the case."

"No, the ER docs would have had to call a surgeon. Dr. Thomas is the best. He's my friend, and I thought he'd find it an interesting case. Besides, he would have been pissed if he had missed this one."

Thin man tapped his pen against the notebook. "Is that right, Doctor Thomas?"

Ken gave her a wry grin. "That I'm the best? Yes."

"Did you see anyone else? There was a chair next to the bed as if someone had been sitting with him," Grouchy said.

Charlotte shook her head. "No."

"The bed and chair looked old. Very old. Have you seen them before?"

Charlotte gave him a *what-the-fuck* look. "Are you saying I'm old like the furniture?"

He had the decency to blush. "No ma'am. I meant that the bed and chair looked similar to ones I've seen in Civil War books. You're a Civil War reenactor. I thought you might have seen the furniture in someone's tent during the weekend's events. That's all."

"What happened to the rest of his clothes?" thin man asked.

"You'll have to ask him."

Grouchy shifted his squeaky, leather duty belt. The clatter from his attached equipment sounded like a Roman Army on the march. "We'd like to talk to him as soon as he wakes up."

"Fine. Check back tomorrow," she said. She wanted to tell him to put a little saddle soap on his Sam Browne to keep it from squeaking, but decided it would be wise to keep her mouth shut.

Thin man put his notepad in his pocket. "If you think of anything that might give us a lead on him, please let us know. We'll give you a call if we have any more questions. Are you going to be working at your office in Richmond tomorrow?"

"Yes," she said, smiling. "Call me there if you have any questions."

The officers caught the next elevator off the surgical floor, and Charlotte let out a relieved breath when the door closed behind them.

Ken eyed her from under his thicket of eyebrows. "That went well."

She linked her arm with his. "Do you still have those steaks? I'm starving."

"It's after midnight."

"My stomach doesn't care what time it is."

"I'll cook for you but only if you promise to tell me the truth about where you've been."

"Deal."

Thirty minutes later she was soaking in the hot tub with a glass of wine in her hand, while Ken grilled the steaks on his he-man barbeque, several feet away.

"Okay, spill it. Who's the guy and how'd he get shot?"

"You're not going to believe this, so I'm only going to give you the synopsis. Are you ready?"

"Go for it."

"Someone from Edinburgh, presumably a lawyer, sent me a Japanese puzzle box. Inside the box was a sapphire brooch. Inside the brooch were words written in Gaelic. I spoke the words, traveled back in time, and landed in the middle of the actual Battle of Cedar Creek. I was captured with the wounded General Ramseur and tended him all night until he died. The next day Sheridan sent me to Washington to meet with President Lincoln, who personally asked me to go to Chimborazo Hospital in Richmond to rescue Major McCabe, a secret agent. When I found the major, I realized he would die without antibiotics and surgery. The President had gone to extraordinary lengths to save him, so I did the only thing I could think of to give him a chance. I brought him here."

Ken pointed at her with the grilling tongs. "That story is so far-fetched not even Jack could have made it up."

"It's true."

"Well, if it's true, I have one question for right now. Did you tell Ramseur he had a daughter named Mary?"

"Of course."

"Then it was damn well worth the trip."

Her eyes widened, her jaw dropped. "You believe me?"

"Hell no, I don't believe you. I think you hooked up with some guy and have been screwing in the woods for thirty-six hours."

She lightly thunked her head on the edge of the hot tub. "Why do you do this to me?"

"Look. It makes no difference to me. In fact, I'm glad you got laid. But you were less than forthcoming with the police. Tell me the truth. Is your new lover in some kind of trouble?"

"*Trouble?* If I hadn't brought him back with me, and he'd survived, the Confederate Army would have hanged him. Trouble? Yes, he's in trouble. He's a Union officer who was caught behind Confederate lines out of uniform."

"Calm down. I'm on your side, remember."

"I've never lied to you or given you any reason to doubt me."

Ken flipped the steaks and adjusted the cooking temperature. "Just for the sake of argument, if he's who you say he is, what are you going to do with him?"

She put the wine glass to her lips and mumbled, "Take him back," against the rim, grimacing and doubting she had the fortitude to make another trip to the past.

Ken jerked his head in her direction, dropping the tongs, which skidded toward the hot tub. "*What?* You can't be serious. You barely escaped unscathed. Why would you return?"

"He didn't ask to come to the twenty-first century. He deserves to live out his life in his own time."

"If soldier boy had survived the gunshot, he would have been executed. One way or the other, his time was up. What you did was give him a brand new life. He needs to live out the new life he's got, not the one he would have lost."

She took a long drink that emptied the goblet, then held out the glass to Ken.

"Are you asking for a refill?"

"Yes, please.

"The steaks are done." He turned off the grill and shut off the gas value. "You need a towel. Hold on." He opened the storage cabinet and grabbed a pair of clean scrubs and an extra-large, fluffy towel that smelled faintly of Downy Clean Breeze dryer sheets. She wrapped it around her bikini-clad body.

"You know any man, even your nineteenth-century major, would fall in love with you if you'd only give them a chance. Open up more than a corner of your heart, Charlotte, and let some deserving guy in. Let him win the whole kit and caboodle."

"I'm not a contest."

"That's not what—"

She pressed her finger against his lips. "Not tonight, please."

He kissed the fingertip. "Okay, let's talk about the patient. He might not survive, although he looked better than I expected when we left."

She slipped into scrubs that smelled like the towel, clean and fresh.

"He'll survive."

"What makes you so sure?"

"Any man who can call President Lincoln and General Grant his friends, *and* can linger for a couple of days with a gut shot, *and* can fly through a two-hour surgery, is going to be hard to kill. Plus the bacteria infecting him have absolutely no drug resistance. I predict not only will Major McCabe survive, he'll probably handle living in the twenty-first century with aplomb, and will still demand to be returned to his time."

"If we're making predictions, I'll predict that the green-eyed major will worm his way into your heart. I'll even wager another steak dinner it happens before Christmas."

She laughed. "You've got a bet, and when you lose, I want sautéed mushrooms and a loaded baked potato with my next steak."

He put the ribeyes on a platter and opened the door into the kitchen. "Don't hold out for the mushrooms unless you intend to cook them."

She collected the bottle of wine and the glasses. "You know, Ken, you're forgetting the most important element in this conversation."

He put the steaks on the table. "What?"

"That the doctor-patient relationship is sacrosanct. The major is *my* patient."

He pulled the chair out for her to sit. "No, my dear, he's mine.

9

Winchester Medical Center, Winchester, Virginia, Present Day

SHIVERING UNDER A light blanket, Braham opened his eyes a bit. A noise, not a chirp or a squeak—unlike anything he'd ever heard—had awakened him in a dim room. The sound came from a box mounted on the wall with green, blue, and red lines jumping in time with the odd noise. If he had died, he was pretty sure he hadn't gone straight to hell. It was too damn cold. Cords hooked to patches on his chest led to the box on the wall. A thicker cord was attached to his arm with a tube extending to a clear, fluid-filled bag which hung from a hook over his bed.

An old memory of a clear rubber bag with an expiration date came to mind, and the shock of the memory was tantamount to dumping icy water on his groggy brain. His eyes bounced from one side of the room to the other as he tried to make sense of his surroundings.

A dim light in the ceiling cast eerie shadows against smooth, whitewashed walls. The glass door was partially open, showing the hall outside was also dimly lit. There was no movement in his room or out there. His high bed had a metal railing on both sides. His head was slightly raised, although he had only one pillow. A tall armchair with an extended back sat in one corner, and another small box was mounted on the wall across from the bed with large red numbers in a row: five, five, six. Could it be the time? If so, the room was so dark he couldn't tell if it was early morning or night.

He peeked beneath the bedcovers. Someone had undressed him. He wore a long blue shirt and nothing else. His pants weren't hanging on the end of the bed. What would he wear when he got up? And where were his boots? He couldn't see the floor next to the bed, but if his pants were gone, his boots probably were, too.

A band encircled his wrist. There was a line for the patient's name. His band read: McCabe, Major. Had he given someone his rank? No. The surgeon had called him Major McCabe.

Braham had thought he would die, but he hadn't, yet. If he wasn't dead, it appeared he had been transported to the future, maybe to Kit's time in the twenty-first century. Was he stuck here for the rest of his life, or could he go back? Kit had been given a choice to either return home or live permanently in the nineteenth century. Would he have a choice, too?

He once again studied the room, this time more slowly. He didn't want to miss any of the strange objects. Kit had worked in a hospital. Was this the one where she had worked? Did the surgeon know her? Braham absolutely must not tell anyone about Kit. When she left the present to live the rest of her life—married to Braham's best friend Cullen—in the nineteenth century, she had told everyone she was retiring to the Scottish Highlands to live in seclusion at her family's estate. He couldn't destroy her cover the way someone in Richmond had destroyed his.

A woman entered the room. "Are you in pain? We can give you drugs to make you comfortable."

"Who are you?" His voice sounded scratchy, as if he hadn't spoken for several days.

A brighter light came on behind him. "Charlotte Mallory."

He blinked several times as his eyes adjusted to the bright glow. Now he knew he was truly dead because his Angel of Mercy stood at his bedside. Blonde curls framed an oval face with a gently rounded chin. A slim and delicate nose with high cheekbones gave her the timeless beauty of sculptured masterpieces. His eyes lingered on her kissable lips for a moment before moving up to her almond-shaped eyes, bluer than blue. They were like drops from an April sky. His heart skipped a beat and then another, and he shivered.

"You're cold? I'll get you another blanket." She left the room, and when she returned, she spread another thin blanket over him which embraced him with radiating heat from toes to neck. She tucked the blanket under his shoulders. "This should warm you up."

"You have eyes like the surgeon who rescued me."

She leaned in close and whispered, "I am the surgeon."

"Aye. An illusionist?" He gave a weak chuckle and waved his left hand slightly. "Then all this is an illusion, too. You've cast a spell to mask my reality. I'm still a prisoner, but have no chains."

She raked her fingers through the hair, hanging limp on his forehead, pushing the rough whorls of hair away from his face with startling tenderness.

"You're no longer a prisoner. When you're more awake, I'll explain what has happened. You're safe now. No one will recognize you. No one will hurt you. Rest and get your strength back."

"Answer a question, and I'll wait for the rest."

She held up her finger. "One."

"When can I go home?"

A smile flickered at the corners of her mouth. "You wouldn't believe how many times a day I get that question. No one wants to stick around here." She put the finger to her cheek in a thinking pose. "Must be the food."

"You didn't answer me."

"You'll be in the hospital for a few days. Afterward you'll need time to heal."

His eyes focused on a card attached to a cord strung around her neck with her picture and name. "How did I get here, Doctor Mallory?"

"That's two questions." She adjusted the cords on his arm. "Gaelic words and a sapphire brooch. And before you ask, I don't understand how it works or why. I only know it did."

He gave a small grunt of amusement but lay still. A magical brooch was one thing he did understand, but he didn't intend to tell the doctor about Kit's ruby brooch or where it had taken her.

Another woman wearing the same type of shirt and pants entered the room. "I have his six o'clock meds," she told Doctor Mallory.

His Angel moved aside, and the other woman wiped off the cord to his arm before sticking something into it. She wrote on her hand as she left the room.

Doctor Mallory leaned over him again, tucked his arm back under the blanket, and he breathed in the sweet fragrance of her skin.

"Your doctor's name is Ken Thomas."

"I thought you were my doctor." He reached out a finger and traced the curve of cheek and chin. A fetching pink bloomed in her cheeks.

"This isn't the hospital where I work. Ken knows you're from 1865, although I'm not sure he believes it. My brother, Jack, will be here soon. He'll believe it, although not right away. He won't leave you to fend for yourself. I've got to go back to my hospital in Richmond, but I'll return tonight to check on you."

"If we're not in Richmond, where are we?" Kit's brooch had taken her back and forth in time, and to different locations. Doctor Mallory's must work the same way.

"Winchester, Virginia."

She turned to leave but he caught her hand. "Thank you for saving my life."

She smiled. "You're special to some very important people. The nurse just gave you some pain medication so you can rest. When you wake, Jack will answer your questions."

Braham drifted off to sleep, dreaming of magical brooches and his Angel of Mercy.

10

Winchester Medical Center, Winchester, Virginia, Present Day

BRAHAM WAS AWAKENED sometime later by a plain-looking woman peeling the sticky patches off his chest, along with most of his chest hairs.

"Ouch. Do you have to take all the hair, too?"

She pushed her glasses up her nose, smiling. "I'll try to leave you some."

Another woman standing on the opposite side of the bed said, "We're moving you into a private room, Mr. McCabe. You're doing so well, Doctor Thomas thought you were ready to get out of ICU."

Both women wore identical green pants and shirts. They pushed the bed, with him still in it, out of the room, through a set of double doors, and down a long corridor lined with a dozen numbered doors. In a few of the rooms men and women wearing similar shirts to his shuffled in and out, pushing poles with hanging clear bags also connected to their arms. There were no guards or men in uniform, which eased his mind considerably.

The women guided the bed into room 214. "Here we are, your new room."

A large window was covered with vertical hanging slats which allowed streaks of sunlight to filter into the room. Outside, far off in the distance, gold and red-leafed trees clustered between buildings with oddly shaped roofs.

Sitting in a chair next to the window was a man with neatly trimmed golden hair. He was concentrating on a rectangular, thin black box in his hand. A purple chambray shirt stretched over muscular arms and shoulders, and the sleeves were rolled to the elbows. He wore odd-looking trousers, and his black boots looked supple from frequent use. And he hadn't shaved recently.

Braham stroked his chin, listening to the faint rasp of his whiskers. Neither had he.

The man climbed to his feet, setting the black box on the windowsill. "That was quick."

"We just had to unhook a few wires," the woman said, attaching Braham's remaining wires to another box. "The floor nurse will be in shortly," she told him. "Do you need anything before we go?"

"No. Thank you," Braham said.

After the women left, another odd, melodic noise had him searching the room to find the source. It wasn't coming from the box on the wall.

The man pulled a smaller thin black box from his shirt pocket and poked it with this finger. Then he put the black box to his ear and said, "Hey, sis... At the hospital...Yes, they just moved him...What's up?" He went to the door and looked out. "They're not here yet...Thanks for the warning."

The man poked at the box again and returned it to his pocket. From what Braham could see, it was similar in shape and size to Kit's iPod.

The man looked completely blank for an instant and then he grimaced. "The police will be coming to talk to you some time this morning."

The man's chest lifted as his breathing deepened, and his brows drew together in thought. He wasn't pleased with the news. But why? And why would the police be interested in Braham?

Braham kept a wary eye on the obviously distressed gentlemen. "Doctor Mallory said her brother would be here. Are you Jack?"

The man paused at the end of the bed, rubbing the back of his neck. "Yes, I am. My sister thinks you need watching. She told me a pretty wild story. If it's true, I'd advise you to tell the police, when they get here, that you have no memory of who you are or what happened to you."

Braham cocked his head with interest. "Are you telling me to lie?"

Jack dropped his chin slightly to hide a smile. "I would never advise a client to lie to the police. But in this case, they would believe the truth was a lie, so it's best not to say anything."

"Should I hire you to represent me?"

"You could," Jack said, shrugging. "I have a law degree from Yale, but I don't practice."

"I have one from Harvard College, but haven't practiced for a few years."

On the bed was a white box, attached to a cord connected to the wall. Jack pushed a button on the box. The head of the bed slowly lifted, making a low, grinding noise.

He adjusted Braham's pillow. "What year did you graduate?"

"1848."

From the dark look in Jack's eyes, he was working hard to keep his temper from rising to the surface. "You *know* it's impossible, don't you?"

Braham forced a grin. "I thought you would believe your sister."

Jack picked up a cup from the bedside table with a small, bent tube angled horizontally out of it. He put the tube to Braham's lips. "Here's some water. Take a few sips." Braham did and found the ice water refreshing. "I neither believe nor disbelieve, but I do know she's never lied to me before."

Braham pushed the cup away and Jack returned it to the table.

"What did she tell you about me?"

Jack rested his forearms on the bed's railing and clasped his hands. "That you're a major in the United States Cavalry. That you were caught spying in Richmond, and that if you didn't die from your wounds, the Confederate Army was planning to hang you."

"And you don't believe it?"

There was a knock and two men dressed in blue uniforms entered without waiting for a response.

"Mr. McCabe," one of the men dressed in blue said. "We're with the Winchester Police Department, and we have a few questions for you. Is this a good time?"

Jack moved away from the bed, standing behind the police but staying where Braham could see him.

"Let's begin with your full name," one of the policemen said.

Braham glanced at Jack. "I was telling Mr. Mallory I don't remember my name, or where I'm from. Or anything else."

"Doctor Mallory said you told her your name was Major McCabe," the other policeman said.

"I have no memory of the conversation."

"The beating you took to your face and head could have caused memory loss." Although the first policeman's voice was amiable, his gaze was unblinkingly chilly. "What were you doing before the fight started?"

Braham had never lied before he went to work for Lincoln and Stanton as a secret agent. He had withheld the truth, but he had never deliberately lied. During the past four years he had perfected the art of not answering questions, and it had saved his life more than once.

He gave a weighty sigh. "I don't remember."

"You have a Scottish accent. Have you recently moved here?" the second policeman asked.

Braham shrugged. "I wish I could help you."

The first policeman pulled a card from a pocket inside his notebook. "I can see we're not going to get anywhere today. Here's my phone number. If anything comes to mind, give me a call. We intend to catch the person who shot you."

The other policeman scratched his chin. "I'd like to try something which might trigger a memory." He left the room and returned a minute later carrying a mirror. He handed it to Braham. "Look in the mirror and tell me who you see."

Braham studied the image in the looking glass. He had a bandage on his forehead and bruises on his checks. He hadn't shaved in days, and the stubble finished off his well-crafted image of a fearless and daring spy.

"I see one sorry son of a bitch. But not someone I recognize."

The policeman placed the mirror on the bedside table. "Thank you for your time. If you do remember any details, we'd appreciate a call."

The policemen left the room. Jack watched the door for a minute and then let out a breath. "You played it brilliantly. Almost convinced me."

"If I had given them my name, they might have learned I died in 1864."

The box in Jack's shirt pocket made a noise, and he answered it. "Your time traveler told the police he didn't remember who shot him...No, I don't believe him..." He handed the box to Braham. "Charlotte wants to talk to you."

He put it against his ear as Jack had done. Silence.

"Hello. Is anyone there?"

Braham jerked the loud noise away from his ear.

"Hello, Major McCabe. Are you there?"

Braham kept the box several inches away from his ear and said, "Yes."

"I can't hear you."

Jack took Braham's hand and pushed the box closer to his ear. "Don't talk so loud, Charlotte."

"Oh, I'm sorry," she said quietly. "Is this better?"

Braham whispered, "Yes."

"Major, don't talk to anyone else. If you have to say anything, do what you just did and claim you don't remember. If anyone discovers the truth, it could be a problem. We're trying to work out a plan now. Will you hand the phone back to Jack?"

Jack put the phone up to his ear and listened. "I can stay until he's ready to leave the hospital, but it would be easier for both of us if you transferred him to Richmond....Yes....No.... I'll talk to Ken."

The blood drained from Braham's face at the mention of Richmond. He tossed back the covers. A fire burned in his belly, his head hurt, and when he moved, he got dizzy, but he was not going back to Richmond. All it held for him was a date with the hangman.

A look of alarm flashed across Jack's face. He pressed his free hand against Braham's shoulder. "Hold on, buddy. You're not getting out of bed yet."

"I'm not going back to Richmond and give those Johnny Rebs another shot at me."

"He doesn't want to go to Richmond. He thinks he'll be killed," Jack said into the black box. "How much of a history lesson do you want me to give him? If he's going home, he doesn't need to know the future."

Going home seemed like a fine idea to Braham. He pulled up the covers.

"I'll sleep here in the room....Yep, it's a private suite....Yep, I talked to the admission's office....Yep, I'll pick up the tab and recoup my losses when I publish this story...Are you freaking kidding? *Of course I am.*"

Jack put the little black box back in his shirt pocket. "Okay, nobody's listening but me, and I want the truth. If you're married and spent the night with my sister, and then your wife showed up and shot you, I want to know. So spill it."

Braham used the white box to raise the head of the bed higher.

"My name is Major Michael Abraham McCabe. I'm a special agent for Abraham Lincoln. The President sent me to Richmond to meet with a group of Northern sympathizers. I was followed when I left the meeting, and had almost reached my rendezvous point when I was attacked by five Rebel soldiers. I gave as good as I got, but in the end, I was gut shot.

"They carried me up the hill to Chimborazo Hospital. I lay there for two days, in agony and dying. Your sister said she was sent to rescue me."

Jack scrubbed his face with his hands. "How long have you been a major?"

"Six months."

"How long have you worked for the President?"

"Since Gettysburg."

"Why are you lying?"

"I'm not."

"You and Charlotte didn't have time to concoct a similar story. You weren't talking when you got here. I don't know how it's possible, but I'll give you the benefit of the doubt for now. After all, I write fiction, and this sounds like the beginning of an intriguing mystery novel. I'll play along and see where it goes."

"I hope you get good reviews." Braham said, smirking.

"I usually do," Jack said. "Now, crank the bed down. I can see you're hurting, so I'll let the nurse know. She'll give you something to reduce the pain and help you sleep. We'll talk more when you wake up."

Within minutes a nurse was at Braham's bedside injecting medicine into the tube connected to his arm. Sleep came quickly, and with it, dreams of a lass with golden hair and eyes bluer than the waters of Loch Lomond.

11

Winchester Medical Center, Winchester, Virginia,
Present Day

RAISED VOICES WOKE Braham from a restful sleep, but he remained still, eyes closed. He listened to the discussion taking place in his hospital room.

"I told her I didn't like the idea at all."

From the tone of Doctor Thomas' voice, he's not happy.

"She's being overly protective. You know how she can be."

Jack defending his sister.

"I'd have released him to go home in two days. I don't see the point in transferring him to another hospital."

"You'll have to have that argument with Charlotte," Jack said.

"I will, but it won't do any good." Doctor Thomas huffed. "I'll sign the release order."

"You two are made for each other. I don't know why you never hooked up."

Doctor Thomas gave a derisive laugh. "Because I'm not a suitable mate. I don't meet all ten requirements on her must-have list."

"I'd say you meet the most important one. You're as committed to the practice of medicine as she is."

"Are you kidding? It isn't even on the list."

Jack laughed. "I don't know what else to tell you, Doc."

"Take her patient to Richmond, and tell her to forget the rib eye and wine. All bets are off."

Leather shoes squeaked across the floor and the door closed.

"You can open your eyes now," Jack said. "I know you're awake."

Braham pushed the button on the little white box and raised the head of his bed, grinning. "You fight your sister's battles well."

"I've been doing it since she could walk. I'm not likely to quit."

"You're moving me to Richmond? Are you sure it's safe?"

Jack chuckled almost soundlessly, shaking his head. "You'd be safer with the hangman. You don't know my sister."

Braham put his hand to his throat and swallowed hard. He didn't find Jack's comment the least bit humorous.

Jack pulled the thin black device from his pocket again, and Braham pointed his finger at it. "I assume the thing in your hand is a communication device. What's it called?"

"Smartphone," Jack said as he punched at it, and raised it to his ear. "Ken's going to sign the release order, but he's not happy." Jack also poked at the device he called an iPad with his finger while he talked to his sister about logistics. "Sure, I'll put him on."

He handed the phone to Braham. "She wants to talk to you."

"Hello," Braham said, mimicking Jack's tone. Braham didn't understand how Charlotte could hear his voice through the device, especially speaking normally. He intuitively wanted to raise his voice, but Jack didn't. So Braham didn't.

"I've arranged for an ambulance to pick you up and bring you here. You'll stay in my hospital for a couple of days. Do you have any questions?"

"Only one. When can I go home?"

"Soon. I'll see you tonight."

There was no softness in her voice. Only a rush to finish the conversation. He handed the phone back to Jack. "She must be busy." Braham shifted his weight in the bed, pretending her hurried tone didn't matter, but it did. He wanted the intimacy they had shared when she ran her fingers through his hair.

"She's always busy, but sometimes I think she's busier than she needs to be."

Braham scratched his whiskers. If he continued to look the part of a rogue, he'd never get any of her time and attention. Jack hadn't shaved, though. Maybe men in the twenty-first century didn't scrape their faces every day.

"I need a shave. Do I have time before we leave? I also need pants and boots."

"Your face it too cut up to shave, and you'll go in an ambulance in what you're wearing now. Tomorrow or the next day I'll have my barber come in and give you a shave and trim."

An hour later, rattling wheels approached their door.

"Looks like your ride's here."

Two men rolled a gurney into the room. "Mr. McCabe, we have an order to transport you to Richmond."

Braham didn't look forward to the future's mode of travel. He'd seen a picture of Kit with a conveyance she'd called a car. He didn't understand how it moved without horses, but he'd soon find out.

The men rolled the gurney next to the bed and lowered the rails. "We don't want you to do anything. We're going to lift and move you." They rolled him and slid something beneath him. "On the count of three. One. Two. Three." As his body jerked sideways, Braham groaned. "Sorry, sir." They settled him onto the gurney, tucked in the sheet, and strapped him in.

Jack picked up his leather satchel, slung the strap over his shoulder, and walked over to the gurney. "You're in good hands. Don't worry. I'll see you in Richmond."

When Jack left, Braham shivered. He knew no one other than Jack and Charlotte, and Doctor Thomas, and this strange world stymied him. In a short time he had become dependent on Jack to shepherd him through the strange customs. Braham's weakness and fear shamed him. What would he say to Kit when he saw her again? Admit her world frightened him? No, he would tell her he acclimated quickly. With that, he relaxed, slowed his breathing, and let his shoulders go slack.

The men rolled him head first into what looked like a miniature hospital room. One of the men climbed in beside him and locked the rolling bed into place. He attached the clear bag to a hook hanging from the ceiling. The walls were lined with cubbyholes and equipment.

"Are you a paramedic?" Braham asked.

"Pretty close. An EMT. Been doing this work for ten years now." How many paramedics could there be? Maybe he knew Kit. Again, Braham bit his tongue. He mustn't mention her name to anyone. "How long will the trip take? All day?"

"We're only going to Richmond. About two hours. You relax, lie back, and enjoy the ride."

The vehicle's rolling, swaying motion made him queasy, and he gagged. The EMT cranked up the head of the gurney. "Ask the driver to slow down." Braham said.

The EMT chuckled. "I doubt he's going more than five miles an hour." He put a cold compress on Braham's forehead. "Riding backwards often makes people sick. This should help."

Braham didn't think so. Jerky stops and starts kept his belly churning. All he could see through the back window was scenery. After a while he closed his eyes. When he opened them again, the conveyance was backing up to a building.

"When are we leaving?" Braham asked.

"We're here," the EMT said. "You slept through the entire trip."

The two EMTs rolled him out of the ambulance and into the hospital. As the gurney rolled down halls and around corners, Braham's view of the ceiling didn't change much. The confined space in the elevator made him break out in a sweat. When the door opened, and he was rolled out, he let out a long-held breath. He never realized how small, enclosed spaces terrified him, or maybe it was small, enclosed spaces *in motion* which terrified him.

He entered a room much like the one in Winchester, except he couldn't see any trees from the window. He groaned as the jolt of transferring into the new bed sent flashes of fire through his insides. The EMTs straightened him up, then covered him with the blanket folded up at the end of the bed.

"It's been a pleasure meeting you, Mr. McCabe. Get well soon."

The two men left the room just as Charlotte entered, wearing a white coat with her name embroidered in blue above the breast pocket. On the other side of the coat, were the words *UVA Health Systems*, also embroidered in blue. Her hair was pulled back into a tail at the nape of her neck, but a riot of curls fell lose around her face, a lovely face which appeared tired and drawn.

"How are you feeling?" she asked, reading a stack of papers the EMTs had given her. "This report said you were queasy. Are you still?"

He shook his head. The only thing wrong at the moment was he had to piss. He would have used the urinal, as Jack called it, which he refused to do in Charlotte's presence. Jack had assured him it was acceptable in medical situations, but it would never be acceptable to him. He squirmed.

Charlotte looked up from her notes, pursing her lips into a tiny smile. "The bathroom is behind me. Have you been out of bed since surgery?"

He shook his head again.

She put the papers down, lowered his bed, and helped him sit up. "You'll be wobbly. Put your arm around me."

He was almost twice her size. If he lost his balance, they would both end up on the floor. When his hand slid across her upper back and around her shoulder, her muscles flexed beneath his fingers. He cocked his brow in surprise. Although small, she might be able to support him after all. How could a woman who appeared so delicate have such strength? Her hands were not callused from heavy work, though. Where did her muscles come from? Kit was muscular, too. It must be the way women were made in this century.

"Are you ready?" she asked, gazing up at him. "Go slow, now. It's going to hurt a bit when you stand."

If he hadn't had to piss, he would have been happy to sit on the edge of the bed, with her arm wrapped around him and his arm around her, while he sniffed the pleasing apple scent in her hair and enjoyed the warmth of her body pressed alongside his.

How long had it been since he'd been with a woman? Not long.

So needing a woman wasn't the problem, it was because the woman in his arms was highly desirable. In fact, her presence was having an effect on him which would soon become obvious to anyone who noticed the tent in the front of his long shirt.

When he stood, he gasped. "*Damn.*" His rising tent collapsed.

"You had a serious injury. It's going to hurt for a while."

He took a step, then stopped. Sweat beaded across his forehead.

"Let's take another step," she said.

He gritted his teeth.

Charlotte pulled the pole with the plastic bag along with them. Inside the bathroom was a white porcelain bowl.

"Pee in the bowl, then push the silver lever down when you're done." She closed the door behind her.

Braham peed in the bowl, pushed the lever, and watched water swirl around and disappear. Hanging over the washbasin was a reminder note to wash hands. He did, although he didn't find any soap. When he finished, he hobbled back to the bed, holding tight to the pole for support.

Charlotte helped him settle in. She held up the little white box used to manipulate the bed. "This is the nurse call button, the bed remote, and the controls for the television. Did Jack introduce you to the wonders of TV?" She pointed to the box on the wall.

He shook his head.

"You want to go home, right?"

He nodded.

"Then we're going to be vigilant about what you see, who you talk to, what you do. From that box you can learn everything there is to know about the past and the present. If you stumble across information which has the potential to change history, I won't take you back. It almost happened to me. Sheridan threatened to burn down my ancestor's home if I didn't do what he asked."

"What did he make you do? Rescue me?"

"He didn't know what Lincoln wanted with a Confederate doctor, only that he wanted one. My point here is, I had no idea I could impact history so easily. My advice to you is don't even turn on the television, don't read newspapers or magazines, and, for God's sake, stay off the web. If you'll make a list of books you enjoy reading, Jack will get them. He might have some recommendations for you, too. In the meantime, take short walks and sleep. You probably haven't had much sleep in the last few weeks."

"When can I eat?"

"I see the orders are still NPO—nothing by mouth. You'll get clear liquids later today. See how you do. You're recovering quickly, and Ken and I believe it's because you have no resistance built up to the medicines we use to treat infection. Since you're doing so well, we'll advance your diet as quickly as your body allows."

"If I'm going to walk, I need clothes."

"I'll text Jack to bring you a robe and slippers. He should be here shortly. I'll be back later, probably this evening. If you need me before then, ask the nurses to have me paged. Any more questions?"

He shook his head, wondering what had happened to the sweet woman with apple-scented hair who'd wrapped her arm around him.

12

Mallory Plantation, Richmond, Virginia, Present Day

TWO DAYS LATER Charlotte released Braham from the hospital. Although he had pleaded with her to send him back to his time, she had refused, and instead sent him home with Jack, along with a long list of restrictions. He rode in a wheelchair to the front door of the hospital, where he sat waiting until a big black conveyance drove up and parked in front of him. Jack got out and came around to help Braham into the front seat.

"What do you call this conveyance?"

"A Land Rover."

Kit had referred to her conveyance as a car. *This must be different.* "Are all conveyances called land rovers?"

"Vehicles come in different makes, models, and prices. Land Rover is the brand name. There're different models within the brand. This is the Range Rover Sport." Jack showed Braham how to buckle his seatbelt.

Braham immediately unbuckled it. "I don't want to be strapped in. If I hadn't been so sick when I rode in the ambulance I would have yanked off the restraints."

"If we crash, you'll go through the windshield. Put it back on," Jack said.

Braham shook his head. "I'll take the risk."

Jack turned in his seat, glaring. "It's not your life I'm worried about. I don't want two hundred pounds landing on me. Put the damn belt on. We're not going anywhere until you do." Jack pulled his phone out of his pocket and pecked on it, ignoring Braham as he wrestled with the idea of being restrained.

"Don't like it," Braham said, securing the belt around him.

Jack's lip twitched as he pocketed his phone and started the vehicle. "You'll get used to it."

"I don't plan to be here long enough." Braham stared out the window at the unrecognizable city: paved streets, no grass, few trees, and hundreds of conveyances. "Looks like there're enough for the entire city."

Jack pulled away from the hospital and merged into a long line of vehicles, all different shapes, sizes, and colors. "Certain times of the day you'd think everyone who had a car was out on the roads. Traffic's a nightmare."

Braham rubbed his hand across the leather seat, the sparkling glass, and odd textures that weren't metal or wood or stone. "Your Land Rover looks rich, expensive. How much did it cost?"

"About ninety-five thousand."

"Dollars?" Braham whistled. "I've seen the war through the lens of economy and I understand inflation. What's the difference in the value of the dollar between 1865 and now?"

"When I stop at the traffic light, I'll look it up."

Braham spotted a light strung on a wire stretching from one side of the street to the other. The light turned from green to yellow to red. The conveyances going in the same direction and in the opposite direction all stopped, while the vehicles on his left and right moved forward. "I crossed this street a few days ago, dodging wagons and marching soldiers. Risked life and limb to get to the other side. The…traffic light?" he glanced over to see Jack's nod. "It's very clever."

Jack punched the keys on his phone again. Then the light turned green, and he proceeded through the intersection. He handed over the phone. "Read this. Then you'll understand why we call our phones *smart* phones."

Braham read the words on the tiny, colored glass. "Compute the

Relative Value of a US Dollar Amount."

Jack reached over and pointed to the letters fixed to little squares underneath the colored glass. "Enter the year, 2014, and the amount, $95,000, in those boxes. Then click calculate."

"The relative value in 1865 is $6,530.00."

What other kinds of questions could he ask this smartphone? His fingers itched to punch the letters and ask the one question weighing on his heart every waking moment: *What year will the War of the Southern Rebellion end?* He curled his fingers into his palm. His nails bit into his skin. The urge grew stronger, searing him with the urgent need to know.

He punched the W, then the H, then the E. He bit down on his lip. Hard. He punched the N. "How do you start a new word?"

"Hit the space key."

He ignored his inner voice shrieking to stop. His conscience. His moral compass. He hit the space key. Then entered the words *when will the war of the Southern*—"What do you do if you make a mistake?"

"Hit the arrow with the x."

He erased all the words and started again. *When did the war*—his breathing became labored. He closed his eyes. Sucked in his lip. Deep inside his soul he found the strength to resist. He returned the smartphone, Satan's tool, to Jack.

Jack glanced at the phone then shot a stern glance at Braham.

"When you say US dollar, do you mean United States?"

"The United States is referred to as—"

"You mean the United States *are* referred to?"

"It was changed after the Civil—" Jack stopped mid-sentence, his jaw noticeably tightened. "It's your intention to return to your time, isn't it?"

"As soon as your sister will take me."

"Then there are topics we can't discuss. Not even something as simple as a verb."

"Your use of the verb told me the states will be united again. Stronger than before. It will be easier to wait for it to happen, knowing it will." Tension eased from his body. He settled back into

the plush seat and closed his eyes. The car swerved violently to the
right, to the left, and back to right. Braham's eyes popped open. The
seat restraint grabbed him. He slammed his feet against the floor.

"God damn it," Jack swore. "Get the son of a bitch off the
damn road."

Braham's heart cannon-fired inside his chest. "Are you trying to
kill us?"

"I'm not, but that son of a bitch is." Jack pointed to a red car
moving significantly more slowly than all the other vehicles on the
road. "You okay?"

Braham patted the restraint across his chest. "Thanks to this. I'm
sorry I was initially resistant. It saved me from landing on you. All
two hundred pounds. The stitches in my belly would have come
undone and you could have had my guts in your lap."

Jack resumed his casual one-handed driving, laughing. "I can do
without the imagery, thank you."

Now he had confidence in Jack's driving skills and the vehicle's
maneuverability, Braham took more interest in details of the interior.

The seat was ample for his large frame and the leather was supple, but the interior had an offensive smell unlike anything he'd run
across during his travels in Europe or across the western part of the
country. He had invested large sums of money in real estate in San
Francisco and his vineyards in the Napa Valley, all wise investments
made in consultation with his bankers. He wasn't at all sure Jack's
investment in this vehicle had been a wise one. The vehicle picked
up speed. Jack changed lanes and pulled up behind a car small
enough for the Land Rover to squash.

"Why would anyone drive a small vehicle?" Braham asked.

"Gas mileage, wear and tear."

"In other words, it costs less."

Jack changed lanes again and increased the speed. Braham
gripped the seat, needing a distraction. "What are the parts called?
The dials, the different colored lights, and the map."

"The map is a Global Positioning System. You can plug in any
address and the map will show you how to get there. There's an

owner's manual in the glove box in front of your knees. The manual will explain what's what. This car almost drives itself."

"A car won't get me home."

"No, but it sure will make life easier while you're here, especially at the plantation. You might like to get out and see the place. It's beautiful this time of year."

"Do you have horses?"

"Not as many as we used to have, but I doubt Charlotte will let you ride."

"I've ridden every day since I could walk. It won't hurt me."

"Butting heads with her might prove you're stronger, but she's smarter when it comes to healing and medicine. Had to go a few rounds with her myself before I learned my lesson."

Not since his mother died had Braham been forced to listen to a woman tell him what to do or when to do it. He doubted he'd change for Charlotte's benefit. Then he chuckled at his lapse of memory. Another blonde-haired lass had told him what to do, and he'd listened, but Kit was the exception.

Being in the future unsettled him. Kit had expressed constant fear over how her actions in the past might affect the future. He had believed she worried needlessly. How could the actions of one small woman change the future? Now he was living in her time, he had decided to put on blinders so he could return ignorant of what was to come, but his natural curiosity was making the decision difficult, if not impossible.

He didn't understand the customs of the day, which drove him to seek understanding. The more understanding he had, the more insight into the future he acquired. When he returned to his time, would he be able to put his knowledge aside, or would he use it for personal gain and disrupt the future?

He'd consider the problem in more depth later. For now, he had to convince Charlotte to take him back. His country was suffering from an intolerable war, and his President was waiting for vital information.

Time travel, as he'd learned from Kit, was a persnickety venture.

While days passed in one time period, months passed elsewhere. The war could have ended by the time he returned. Would Lincoln think Braham had been executed, or would he know Braham had disappeared? He realized, with a disturbing sensation in the pit of his stomach, that dying seemed preferable to living with failure.

"Are you hurting?" Jack asked. "Charlotte said the trip to the plantation would be uncomfortable." He pushed back his sleeve and looked at the timepiece he wore on his wrist. "You can have pain medication now."

"It puts me to sleep. I want to be awake in the event I'm crushed beneath a pile of metal and glass," Braham said without humor. The scenery flying by made him dizzy. He needed another distraction. He opened what Jack had referred to as the *glove box* and removed the manual he had mentioned earlier.

Twenty minutes later Braham closed the book and put it back.

"A bit overwhelming," Jack said.

Braham closed the compartment door. "I know all the parts now, but I'm not sure, if I disassembled the vehicle, whether I could put it back together again."

Jack drew in his eyebrows, looking skeptical. "Twenty minutes and you know all the parts?"

Braham shrugged at Jack's disbelief. "I have a good memory."

Jack pointed to the roof. "What's this called?"

"Full size panoramic roof."

He pointed to Braham's head restraint. "And this."

Braham fired right back with the correct answer.

Jack pointed to the multimedia instrument panel. "And this?"

"Hard disk navigation system, Bluetooth phone connection, eight inch touch-screen, MP3 compatible audio disk."

Jack was slack-jawed. "How—"

"I told you. I have a good memory." God forbid, if Charlotte's brooch didn't work the way Kit's did, and he was forced to remain in the future, all he had to do was observe, read, and listen. If he did, he'd quickly learn all he needed to know about life in the twenty-first century.

"That's not a good memory," Jack said. "That's an eidetic memory. Do you retain everything you read?"

"Shakespeare, Plato, legal treatises, I retain after one reading. A technical or ordinance manual, similar to the Land Rover's, I would read again to confirm my knowledge."

Jack gave him an incredulous glare. "Only one person has been tested and proven to have long-term eidetic memory. I have an excellent memory, but I can't do what you do. Scientists would have an orgasm studying a time traveler with an eidetic memory."

Braham turned to look out the window, managing a grim smile. "I won't be here long enough to be studied."

Jack turned onto an open stretch of country road. "We're about ten minutes from the plantation."

"Beautiful country," Braham said. "I see the telegraph is still widely used. There are poles on every road."

"The poles actually hold lines for power and communication, not telegraph. The telegraph is mainly used these days for text telephone machines operated by the deaf."

A list of questions concerning the use of the telegraph immediately came to mind, but when he smelled brackish water and fish, it reminded him he was hungry, and he shoved the questions out of the way. "We must be close to the river."

Jack pointed off into the distance. "The James River is about a half mile away. The house backs up to the river. Beautiful view. I think you'll appreciate it after a week in the hospital."

Jack turned off the road onto a tree-lined drive and drove past a handful of brick outbuildings leading to a three-story Georgian white-brick manse with double-sided porticos, looking like an elegant fortress.

"Welcome to Mallory Plantation," Jack said. "My ancestors founded the place a few years after the settlers arrived in Jamestown in 1607. Charlotte and I are the tenth generation to live here." He pulled to the front of the house, cut the engine, and pointed toward the residence. "Flemish bond brick, dormers, even a three-foot welcoming pineapple on the peak of the roof."

"How'd it survive the war?"

"The pineapple? I guess no one was hungry for fruit?"

Braham frowned, once again stymied by the man's unusual sense of humor.

Jack rested his arm on the back of his seat and turned to face Braham. "If you posed your question to a resident of New York, they'd assume you were asking about the Revolutionary War. But if you posed the question to a person from the south, like me, I'd say, 'You mean the War of Northern Aggression?'"

Braham tensed, preparing for the same arguments he'd listened to for the last three years. "New Yorkers are fighting in the rebellion, too."

"Granted. But the south never—" Jack stopped and took a deliberate breath. "Never mind. We don't need to have this discussion. The short answer to your question is, the house sits way back off the main road. Soldiers making the trek in here would have to have come specifically to burn it down. They never did."

"Charlotte said Sheridan threatened."

"Obviously he never carried out the threat. Come on. I have orders to feed you lunch, guide you on a short tour if you're up for one, then make sure you rest."

"Don't you have a mystery to write?"

"I've got some ideas I'm tossing around for a new novel, but nothing has grabbed me so far. Got any suggestions?"

Braham limped toward the house, grimacing from the pain in his abdomen. "How about a time-traveling doctor and a beat-up old soldier? An old, decrepit soldier." He gingerly climbed five stone steps, cursing under his breath. He reached the portico, latched onto one of the support columns, and assessed the property.

A light breeze ruffled his hair. He breathed deeply, inhaling the crisp scent of autumn. A large oak tree standing between the house and river had to be three hundred years old. Its yellow and orange leaves swayed in the wind and rained down in a sudden gust of cool air. Falling leaves cascaded into one another as they rustled against piles accumulating on the ground. Squirrels bounced and darted in all directions, searching for acorns.

Jack bounded up the stairs behind Braham.

Braham searched the gray-tinted sky. The clouds were moving from the west. "Charlotte said she was driving out here tonight? It's going to storm. She should stay in Richmond."

"Weather never stopped her from doing anything she had a mind to do."

"She shouldn't be out by herself. It's dangerous. What if her conveyance breaks down?"

"She'll call Triple A." Jack put his arm across Braham's shoulders and led him toward the front door. "Let's get you settled. If you're not tucked in when she arrives, I'll lose our bet, and she'll win a thousand shares of my Apple stock."

If Braham hadn't spent the last decade listening to Kit's unusual vernacular, he'd be at a complete loss, with no idea what Jack meant. Braham knew Apple was a company which had helped make Kit's wealthy family richer. Whatever the company made, it wasn't fruit.

When Braham entered the entryway, his eyes went immediately to the stunning carved walnut flying staircase, which rose three floors without any visible support structure. Jack closed the front door and joined Braham at the foot of the stairs.

"This staircase is the most outstanding architectural feature in this old house."

Braham studied the underneath side of the first landing, pinching his face in concentration. "What holds it up?"

"There're two flat iron straps running wall to wall which allow it to float in place. Quite an engineering feat for the eighteen hundreds. A building inspector wouldn't approve it today."

"If it's all the same to you, I'd prefer not to climb any more stairs today. I'll sleep here on the floor." His incision burned as if a doctor was pulling out the stitches using fingernails.

"We have a guest suite down this way. You'll be comfortable in there."

Jack led him into a large and well-apportioned bedroom. The fireplace's hand carved woodwork featured more pineapples. The tall four-poster bed was the biggest Braham had ever seen. After the skinny hospital bed, he looked forward to having room to roll over. Two of the room's walls had floor-to-ceiling windows, bringing light into the dark blue room. A set of French doors were open. When he lay in the bed he'd be able to see the river.

"I put jeans, sweaters, underwear, T-shirts, and socks in the dresser. Shirts are hanging in the closet. The bathroom is stocked with personal care items. If you have any questions, yell. My office is across the hall and my bedroom is directly above." He took a piece of paper from his jacket pocket. "Charlotte shoved this into my hand when we passed each other at the hospital. You need two o'clock meds, a light snack, and a nap. She also listed four prescriptions."

Braham set four medicine bottles on the table next to the bed. "It's time for the antibiotic and pain medication, right?"

"It's what the note says."

"I don't want the pain medicine. It makes me tired."

Jack sighed. "You don't want to get on her bad side. If she said to take the pills, *take the pills.*"

Braham opened two of the bottles and poured out the necessary pills. "I need to move and get my strength back. Not sleep the day away." He'd hold the pill under his tongue until Jack looked away.

Jack handed Braham a bottle of water from a silver tray on the dresser. "Drink this."

Braham studied the bottle and gave an impatient huff as he pulled on the top cap.

"Twist the cap. It breaks the seal." Jack opened a dresser drawer, pulled out some clothes and tossed them on the bed. "Pajamas and a T-shirt. You might want a shower to get rid of the hospital smell. I don't know how Charlotte can stand smelling like sanitizer all the time. It dries out her hands, too."

Braham didn't think so. He remembered them as quite soft. They had warmed him when he shivered, comforted him when he was dying, and held a cup when he needed a drink.

"I'll go fix lunch while you shower."

"You don't have to do anything else. You've done enough."

Jack folded his arms, leaned against the desk, and crossed one booted foot over the other. "I spent two years in a Tibetan monastery studying an esoteric meditative discipline. For the first six months I couldn't speak the language or do the meditations. I felt inadequate and doubted my purpose for being there. A monk took me aside and said in English. 'Follow me.' He never said another word, and for the next six months I never took my eyes off of him. Then one day he said, 'Follow your own path.' I never followed him again. You said I've done enough. How much is enough when a person is in need?"

"Give a man a fish and you feed him for a day—"

"Teach a man to fish you feed him for life?" Jack finished Lao Tzu's proverb.

"You don't have to teach me to fish, but you might need to show me around the bathroom."

"Good idea. This shower has all the bells and whistles. Come here."

After Jack showed Braham how to operate the controls, he gave a two-finger salute and left the room.

Finally alone for the first time in days, Braham stared out the French doors, which opened onto the riverside portico. *Teach a man to fish. Fine.* But he didn't intend to stay. He didn't belong here. It was different for Kit. She was out of place to begin with, but not him. He had a home, a winery, and a law practice to return to after the war. He had a life planned out in intricate detail—a plan he would not veer from; a plan which included a political career. The door to the office of the Governor of California would one day have his name engraved on a brass plate.

He appreciated the Mallorys' time and attention, but he had to return. The President depended on him. He had responsibilities and commitments. How could he make Charlotte understand? Abandoning his life would be tantamount to asking her to give up being a doctor, and he doubted she would ever consider doing it. Then how could she expect him to give up his dreams?

13

Mallory Plantation, Richmond, Virginia, Present Day

CHARLOTTE KNOCKED LIGHTLY on Braham's door before entering quietly. The French doors were open to an exquisite view of the moonlight undulating on the surface of the river. The windows were slightly cracked, and a cool breeze rippled through the sheer curtains. Braham had fallen asleep on top of the covers wearing Jack's black pajama bottoms with a lightweight blanket thrown haphazardly over his legs. A white T-shirt stretched tight across his expansive chest, and a dusting of hair peeked through the shirt's V-neck. He and Jack could be bookends on a shelf stacked with romance novels featuring kilt-clad heroes.

Charlotte squeezed her arms to her chest, surprised by a warm swelling low in her belly. What was different about Braham now to cause such a strong reaction? What did she see she hadn't seen before? Different clothes? Shaved? Hair washed? All those things and more. In a restful sleep, pain had released its grip, relaxing the tightened muscles around his eyes. No doubt about it. The man was gorgeous, and blessed with a constitution she rarely saw in patients.

He stirred, and his eyes opened. "I worried about you driving here in the rain," he said in a raspy voice.

She turned on a lamp and the soft yellow light curled around him. "It stopped before I left the city." She crossed to the other side of the bed and placed her hand on his forehead. "Jack said it only drizzled here."

Braham's eyes probed into hers, green and hard and full of questions. "Do I have a fever?"

"You feel slightly warm, but my hands maybe cold. She rubbed them, blew on them, and touched her own forehead for comparison. "It's me."

He pulled himself up, grimacing slightly, and his biceps bulged as he leaned against the headboard and laced his fingers across his chest.

She had an insane desire to wrap her hand around his arm to feel muscle flex. A small knot lodged in her throat. "I'm glad you rested. Looks like Jack followed instructions for a change."

"Doesn't he always?"

"No. Not often." It took an effort of will to look away from his sculpted arms and the physical strength they represented. But she did, her eyes moving slowly down to his belly. The pajamas drew her eyes to the area of his incision and down further, to other parts.

She carefully lowered the elastic waistband and peeked at the incision, then gently palpated his abdomen. His body reacted to her touch, and she gently let go of the fabric, steeling herself to not react to his growing erection.

"Looks good." She cleared her throat. "It's healing nicely." She placed her fingers on his wrist. His pulse was strong and fast, but not from illness. So was hers. "Dinner will be ready in about thirty minutes. I'll bring a tray in for you."

"Are you cooking?" He watched her. His eyes were liquid and sleepy and full of desire.

Needing a distraction, she reached for an unopened bottle of water on the bedside table, untwisted the cap, and took a long gulp. "If any cooking's done in this house, Jack does it. He's an accomplished chef, and has far more patience than I do with certain things."

"Like what?" Braham asked, his eyebrow arching.

"I don't do well with patients who ignore my instructions and compromise their healing."

"I do what I say. Never doubt it." His biceps twitched ever so slightly, as if to reinforce the statement. "You saved my life, and I'm grateful, but in a couple of days I *must* go home. I have timely information about Richmond's defenses, the condition of Lee's army, and, most important, the movement of troops and material between the Petersburg-Richmond corridor and the Shenandoah Valley. Lincoln is waiting for my report, which will directly impact Grant's major offensives around Petersburg. I *have* to go back. Even if I wanted to stay, Charlotte, it's impossible."

Her eyes locked with his now, and she saw the faint lines of tension at the corners. A sense of foreboding settled in her gut. "You almost died. You're not even close to healed. You need to give it a couple of weeks, not a few days."

He tapped his fingertips together rhythmically. "I can't wait. I'll take it slow for a few days after I see the President. But I can't delay here any longer."

She pulled a reading chair closer to the bed and sat, sighing. "What if the brooch takes us back to Richmond? You won't have the strength to fight your way out."

He stopped tapping, steepled his fingers, and pressed them against his lips. "Where did you leave from? Cedar Creek. Right? And you returned there. If we leave from Washington City, we should arrive there as well."

"You obviously have more faith in the sapphire than I do."

He dropped his hands, shrugging. "It's my Celtic heritage, I suppose. A friend once told me some see darkness where others see only the absence of light."

Charlotte scratched gently at the side of her face, letting the thought swirl around in her brain. "What does it mean?"

He glanced out toward the river, and his voice whispered over her skin like the cool breeze blowing in through the window. "There is more to the world than we can see. Always keep your mind open. Even without light, you can hear and feel and taste. But if you close yourself off to other possibilities, you'll wither in the darkness."

He took her hand in his, with all its cuts and bruises from the fight he had been in, and, using a warm fingertip, traced the lines etched into her palm. The corner of his lip turned up in a wry smile. "When I lay dying, a doctor who I thought was a man came to my bed and held my hand. When I looked into his eyes, I knew I had a life yet to live. It was the darkest place I'd ever been, but I could feel and taste and smell the light."

His vivid memories held hope. Hers, on the other hand, had turned into nightmares. She shook off the edgy sensation triggered by her traumatic experiences after being catapulted into another world. "Another couple of hours and you would have been dead."

"You arrived when you were meant to arrive. If I hadn't been dying, there would have been guards posted, and I probably would have been chained to the bed."

Heat rose to her face and her heart raced. "Let's not talk about it. Are you hungry?"

"Yes, but first I need a commitment from you to take me back to my time. If you won't, then let Jack. But in two days, I must leave."

"You're not—"

"I don't require coddling. You have to let me go."

Her phone beeped, and she silently thanked God for the interruption. She checked the message. "I have to return this call. We'll talk about it later. I'll bring you a dinner tray, or if you'd like, you can join us in the kitchen."

"I'll join you. I need to get up and move around."

"Okay. Dinner isn't fancy. Come as you are."

He glanced down at what he was wearing, smirking. "A gentleman would never present himself at the table dressed so informally."

She laughed as she headed for the door. "What do you think Jack's wearing? A suit? Not likely. He'll be dressed just as casually. If you'd feel more comfortable wearing a robe, there should be one hanging on the back of the bathroom door."

She closed the door and rested her head against it while her hand continued to grip the doorknob. She had to emotionally swim against the current to disengage from the intimacy they had shared, and from intruding memories. She had dipped into a swirling stream, and the surface was rippling from the force of the undercurrent.

Fear of the ambiguous gemstone, memories of being in danger, and an attraction to a man from the nineteenth century she couldn't possibly have a relationship with, propelled her away from the door and up the stairs. She ran into her old bedroom she still used on weekends, stripping off her clothes as she headed toward the shower, hoping to restore her equilibrium. Her call could wait another ten minutes.

Thirty minutes later, she entered the kitchen, composed.

Jack was standing on one side of the counter, Braham sat on a barstool on the other. They were clinking their glasses of red wine, participating in a toast.

"To a profitable venture," Jack said.

Charlotte grabbed a glass from a wall-mounted wine rack, picked up the bottle of an Australian Pinot Noir, and read the label before filling her glass. "What profitable venture are we celebrating with a four hundred and fifty dollar bottle of wine?"

"Since you have an overbooked schedule, I decided to take Braham home."

She covered her mouth so she wouldn't spew the sip she'd just taken. "*What? You* decided? Don't you think I have a say here?"

He gave a deliberately nonchalant shrug. "It's the only logical solution."

"There's nothing logical about your proposition. You're always chasing a story, Jack. If you go back in time, I can't even begin to imagine the damage you could do."

Jack gasped, slapping his chest. "Oh, ye of little faith."

"When it comes to you, there is no 'little faith.' Only a huge faith telling me you'll get so caught up in researching the war that trouble will find you a willing victim. So forget it."

"Then I'll go with you. Remember, I'm a better fighter."

Her nightmares kept her from wanting to go back, but if she had to go, having Jack along would certainly help her feel safer. "Okay, but we're not staying. We'll drop Braham off in Washington and come straight home."

"You make it sound like we'll do a drive-by. Isn't it more complicated?"

"I don't even know if it will work again. And if we get there, can we get back?"

Jack picked up a piece of cheese from a snack tray of crackers and Brie. "Nothing ventured, nothing gained."

Charlotte plopped on a stool next to Braham. "I don't want to venture anything or gain anything. I only want...I don't know what I want, but I know what I *don't* want. I don't want to land in the middle of a battle again. It scared the crap out of me. I shiver in the night remembering the screams and the cannon fire and the bleeding, dying men I couldn't help."

Braham's jaw was squarely set and his upper lip compressed. He listened intently, his eyes roving from her to Jack and back.

"Take all the time you need to decide, sis. I'll give you five minutes."

When she caught Braham's eye, he smiled, but the smile was seemingly in contradiction with the weariness in his eyes.

Jack gave her his book jacket smile, the irresistible one capable of triggering emotional highs in complete strangers and making fans see things in a more favorable light. Like forking over twenty-five bucks for one of his hardcover books. He squeezed her shoulder. "Come on, sis. You met Sheridan, Lincoln, and Grant, and toured Washington and Richmond. The least you can do is give me a few hours to explore."

This would be a perfect time for a snappy retort at the smiling co-conspirators who were so busy manipulating her, but nothing came to mind. She'd already been to the past, thank you very much, and had discovered time travel was fraught with danger and rife with long-term consequences. But Jack would never believe her until he experienced it for himself.

It wasn't a Japanese puzzle box she had opened. It was Pandora's, and it had arrived without a warning label telling her to keep it sealed or suffer the wrath of the time-travel god.

If it was possible, Jack's smile grew across his face, to his eyebrows, and even his body was smiling. She finally acquiesced. "We're not staying overnight. A couple of hours, max. That's it. It should give you time to see Washington and stop by the White House."

Laughing, Jack said, "Let's eat. The steaks are ready."

After a delicious dinner which left them all moaning from too-full stomachs, they took cups of coffee to the library and settled into the deep, tufted leather chairs. Braham told the story he had promised during dinner.

"Although I was born in America, I was raised in Scotland from a very early age. My friend Cullen and I finished our education at the University of Edinburgh, then studied law at Harvard. When we finished our studies, we joined a small firm in San Francisco. Cullen met his wife on a wagon train heading west in 1852." Braham paused and studied the mug in his hand. His face betrayed nothing other than a look of fond remembrance, but then his eyes darted as if trying to grasp an annoying thought.

"They settled in San Francisco," he continued, focusing his attention once again on his listeners. "The next year they bought land in the Napa Valley and started a winery. A year later I started one, too. I discovered I loved nurturing the vines, putting my hands in the rich soil—" He examined his fingers, and he seemed to be surprised to find there was no dirt under his nails, "—and spending time with my horses rejuvenates my soul." He gave a one-shoulder shrug and sipped his coffee. Then added, "I solve problems working outside, even in the rain."

"The only problem I try to solve in the rain is how to get out of it," Jack said, chuckling.

Charlotte set her cup on the table next to her, checked her phone for emails, scrolled through several, but none of them seemed as important as listening to Braham's story. She put the smartphone down. "What about your law practice?"

"I spend most of my time in San Francisco, but I get restless and go to the winery every month or two for several days. If I run for a senate seat, it'll be harder to get there as often."

"State Senate or U.S. Senate?" Charlotte asked.

"By the time this conflict is over, I'll have had enough of Washington."

Charlotte and Jack laughed. "A hundred and fifty years, and some things haven't changed," Jack said.

Charlotte yawned. "It's late. I need to get back to town."

"Why don't you stay?" Jack said.

"I've got an early-morning lecture. It'll be easier if I go home tonight."

Braham glanced around the room, then looked at Jack. "You've got a lot of books. I'd like to select one to read tonight, if you don't mind.

"You mentioned reading Plato. I've got *The Republic, The Symposium, Phaedo,* and *The Trial and Death of Socrates.*"

"I'll take *The Republic.*"

Jack put his coffee down, went to the floor-to-ceiling shelves, and scanned the collection. "It's here somewhere. It was my grandfather's favorite book, too."

Charlotte found her thoughts drifting back to her earlier examination of Braham's wound, the pajamas, and his muscular arms. Her face heating, she yanked her attention back to the conversation. "It was also his father's favorite and his father's and his father's and his father's ad infinitum."

Jack gave an amused snort. "As far back as I can remember the book sat on the bedside table. He read passages every evening. If he traveled, he packed it in his suitcase. I'm surprised my grandmother didn't put it in the casket with him."

Braham joined him, moving slowly from one bookcase to another. "I think this is it." He removed a book, opened it, and thumbed through several pages. "He made notations in the margins. I'll enjoy reading his thoughts." He then nodded to Charlotte and Jack. "Goodnight."

Before he reached the door, he stopped. "There's a newspaper clipping in here dated April, 1965. It's for a memorial service to pray over the hundredth anniversary of the death of Abraham Lin—" Braham stopped reading and glanced up, ashen-faced.

"If April, 1965 was the one hundredth year," he rasped, "it means Lincoln died in April of 1865." Braham's hands shook so hard the laminated clipping tapped against the book's cover. "What killed him? This doesn't say." His voice was an anguished whisper.

Charlotte's panic hoarsened her voice. "We can't tell you."

Braham pounded his fist on the edge of a table, rattling the lamp and glass candy dish. "What the hell do you mean, you can't tell me? Lincoln's dead, and you can't tell me what happened?" He scanned the titles in the bookcase. "You've got hundreds of books here. One of them will tell me what I want to know."

"Stop him," she said quietly to Jack. "The Sandburg titles are right in front of him."

Jack squeezed Braham's shoulder. "Come. Sit down. Let's discuss this."

Braham shrug off Jack's arm. "Are you going to tell me what happened?"

"No," Jack said.

Braham grabbed a book from the bookcase. "*Abraham Lincoln: The War Years Volume IV* by Carl Sandburg. This will tell me." He glared at Charlotte and continued in a steely voice, "You've known all along he might be dead by the time I got back. Yet you never said a word. Why?"

Charlotte had the sensation of losing a patient on the operating table, knowing there was nothing she could do to salvage the situation. "Life is full of uncertainties. None of us knows what the future holds. You can't come here, soak up what's happened in the past hundred and fifty years, then take the knowledge back to your time and manipulate history. I won't be responsible for it happening."

"*Damn it.* You should have let me die."

Something in his voice and the way he looked at her made her heart knock against her ribs. "I couldn't. Lincoln recruited me to save your life."

He slapped the book against the doorjamb. "You saved the wrong man, Doctor Mallory. I don't have to read this to know he was murdered. We begged him to be careful. But he refused to listen." Tears glittered in his eyes. "I have to go home and stop this madness before it happens." Braham turned and left the room with shoulders hunched in sorrow.

Charlotte moved to follow, but Jack held her back. "He doesn't need us right now." He poured brandy into two glasses. "When he reads what Booth did, he'll demand to go back and stop the assassination."

Charlotte gulped her drink. "We've got a problem, then. If that's his plan, we can't let him go."

"We can't keep him. He's not a stray. He has a life he's entitled to live."

"Braham lost the life he had. We can't give him another one, and then let him loose to shake the fabric of our lives. Can we?"

"No." Jack freshened his drink, then tipped the decanter to pour more into Charlotte's glass.

She placed her palm over the top. "No more for me. I have to drive."

Jack sat and crossed his legs, his slipper dangling from his toes. "Braham's never questioned the whole concept of time travel. It's as if he already knew it was possible."

Charlotte tilted her head, considering the possibility. "He's opened-minded and accepts situations that aren't easily explained."

"He won't accept being stuck here."

"He can't see it from our perspective, and we can't see it from his. To us, Lincoln has always been a man carved in white Georgia marble, larger than life, the nation's quintessential self-made man."

Jack finished off his drink. "You're waxing poetic, sis."

"What? Are you jealous? Afraid I'll write a book of my own and compete with you?"

"I'd love for you to write a book. You've got an entertaining writer's voice."

She kissed his cheek. "Thank you. But I'll stick to surgery. I've got to go. Take Braham's temperature in the morning."

"I assume you mean figuratively."

She rolled her eyes. "If he's still set on a plan likely to derail the country, we'll keep him here. Maybe you should take him to Washington and let him see the Lincoln Memorial."

Jack's face brightened. "That's worth a try."

She slipped on her jacket and grabbed her purse off the entryway table. "Check on him later. I'll text when I get home."

She opened the door and a black cat darted between her legs and into the house. She jumped and slapped her hand over her heart. "*Where'd he come from?*"

Jack crouched down and called to the cat. "*She* showed up a couple of nights ago. Come here, girl." The cat rubbed up against Jack's leg, meowing. "She's healthy and well fed. Her owner probably dumped her in the field, hoping she'd find a home here."

"Just because we have a farm, people think they can dump their animals here. Did I miss seeing a signpost saying *strays welcome?* What are you going to do with her? You can't keep her. You're hardly ever home."

Jack eyed Charlotte with a speculative gleam in his eyes. "Isn't that what I've been trying to tell you?"

She threw up her hands. "Apples and oranges." She left the house, letting the door slam behind her, feeling a hard, un-movable knot in her throat, and cursing brothers, cats, and green-eyed cavalrymen.

14

Mallory Plantation, Richmond, Virginia, Present Day

THE SUN WAS climbing above the horizon by the time Braham finished the last book in Carl Sandburg's *The War Years* four-volume set. He knew how the war ended and how profoundly affected the country was and continued to be.

According to John Wilkes Booth's notes quoted in Sandburg's book, Booth believed Lincoln was a tyrant who had caused all the South's troubles, and that he, Booth, was the instrument of punishment.

If Braham had anything to do with it, those words would never be written. Booth would die before he could end Lincoln's life on April 14, 1865.

Braham sat in an upholstered chair in his bedroom, feet propped on a stool, staring at the river, unsure of how to proceed. He felt certain Charlotte would never help him return to his time, now that he knew of Lincoln's assassination. That meant he had to find another way.

What that would be, he wasn't sure, but the answers would come. They always did.

15

Mallory Plantation, Richmond, Virginia, Present Day

THE SOUND OF shuffling feet told Jack his houseguest was up and about and on his way into the kitchen. Jack closed the *American History Magazine* he was reading and shoved it into a drawer. Then he turned his attention back to the newspaper spread open on the counter, and glanced up when Braham entered the kitchen. Tired, drawn, red eyes. Jack had seen the face of grief too many times, and his heart ached for his buddy. He reached for a mug in the overhead cabinet.

"Coffee?"

Braham slung a leg over the barstool. "As black as you can get it." He nodded toward the paper. "Anything noteworthy happening in Richmond? Are the Yanks ready to invade?"

Jack gave him a squirrely grin. "Does a Detroit automaker looking to relocate count?"

"Is it cheaper to make cars here?"

"Tax incentives," Jack said.

Braham gave Jack a curious squint.

"The government collects taxes from individuals and businesses. It then gives tax breaks to companies who relocate to depressed areas. Saves the company money, and it's good for the local economy."

"Your traffic will become more congested."

Jack placed a steaming cup of coffee on the counter. "There's the rub."

"For in that sleep of death what dreams may come," Braham continued.

"When we have shuffled off this mortal coil, must give us pause," Jack said.

"There's the respect that makes calamity of so long life."

Jack gave Braham a soft punch in the arm. "You're the first person to ever share lines with me. Thank you."

"I enjoy reading Hamlet."

"Tonight we can entertain Charlotte with a theatrical performance."

Braham scratched his chin. "Doesn't Richmond have men's clubs? I would think you'd be a regular, not home reciting Shakespeare to your sister."

"You'd be surprised at today's men's clubs. And, no, I don't belong to one." He refilled his mug and stirred in a teaspoon of sugar. "On second thought, you might not be surprised."

Braham glanced down at the T-shirt he was wearing. "I'd need appropriate clothes. A uniform, perhaps. Where does Charlotte get hers?"

"There's a Civil War clothing store in Richmond. The owner makes custom uniforms. Whatever you need, he can make it. Women's dresses, too."

"I don't think I'll dress up in women's clothing. I'll leave dressing as the opposite sex to your sister."

"Who, by the way, asked me to check your temperature this morning, but—"

Braham held out his finger.

Jack looked at the digit, then at Braham's smirking face.

"Don't you have one of those clothes pins they use in the hospital?"

"Clothes pins? Oh. You're talking about a Pulse Ox." Jack chuckled. "I don't have one of those, but she asked me to take your temperature figuratively. Not literally."

The wheels behind Braham's eyes were spinning. After a long moment, he said, "She was asking about my mood, not my health."

Jack held his fist out for a fist bump but Braham looked at him awkwardly. "Bump your fist against mine."

"Why?"

"Just do it."

Braham gave him a fist bump which ended up being more of a punch. Jack spread his fingers and shook his hand. "Not so hard. This is an important guy ritual. Let's try it again. It's more about touching your knuckles than an actual punch." Jack reached out his fist again and Braham applied the right amount of force this time.

Braham glanced down into his coffee. "I can do a fist bump, but it doesn't mean I belong here. I don't understand your jokes or your customs. Helplessness is emasculating, especially for a soldier. I've spent four years in a war. I've done things I'm not proud of. But I never doubted my manhood until now. I've failed my President. I've failed myself. I don't know why I'm here."

Jack sipped his coffee, tapping his foot softly.

"You understand those sentiments," Braham continued. "They're similar to what you experienced at the monastery. I don't have six months to follow you around, to find my own path. The path I'm on leads to a tragic end. If you won't take me back, I'll find another way."

"Let's eat breakfast," Jack said. "Then I thought we'd go to Washington."

Braham arched his brows.

"Sorry, buddy. Not your Washington, but mine. There's something I need to show you."

Jack had his own important reasons for helping Braham return to his time. He wanted to go, too. He had done extensive research on the sixteenth President. In one article, he had described Lincoln as the captain who had guided America's ship through stormy seas of secession and civil war and then led the people to a safe harbor called peace. Following the release of the article, a line of text had trended on Twitter, which resulted in a bump in sales for both his fiction and non-fiction books.

He had planned to write a follow-up article about how Lincoln's untimely death had caused the President to become a martyr to the cause of liberty, but Jack discovered he had nothing new to add to the discussion. An interview with Lincoln, Grant or even Booth could give him enough new material to even write a full-length book. He framed the premise in his mind: How did Lincoln's mythic stature grow over the century to the point where he was now considered America's greatest President?

So all he had to do, Jack thought as he sipped his coffee, was help Braham understand how saving the President's life would prevent Lincoln from becoming immortal. Once Jack accomplished that, he would have to then convince Charlotte she wouldn't land in another high-risk adventure with bullets flying over her head.

Convincing Braham might actually be easier than convincing his sister.

16

Washington, D.C., Present Day

AN HOUR LATER Jack and Braham climbed into the Range Rover for their day trip to Washington. Jack put on his seat belt and so did Braham, sliding it easily across his chest and clicking in the latch plate without glancing down.

"You sure you're feeling up to this?" Jack asked.

"I'm not accustomed to staying indoors." He knocked on the window glass. "I'm still closed in, but at least I can have the wind on my face. Is Charlotte coming with us?"

Jack started the car and put it into gear. "She said she would call if she could rearrange her schedule. I doubt she'll do it. Nothing comes between her and her precious hospital."

"You don't like her work taking up so much of her time, do you?"

"I don't have a problem with her job. I have a problem with her believing she doesn't need anything else in her life."

Braham pushed the window button and watched the glass disappear inside the door, then pulled the button in the other direction, raising the window. "What do you have besides your books?"

Jack chuckled. "More than she does. Charlotte calls me a serial monogamist."

"What's that?"

"A person who moves from the end of one relationship to the beginning of a new relationship as quickly as possible. I'm not quite that bad. But what about you? Are you married?"

"Never found a woman with the right mix of cleverness and sass."

"There probably aren't many eligible women in Washington…in your Washington, I mean."

Braham chuckled, remembering the stack of invitations to dinner parties and balls he'd declined prior to leaving for Richmond. He intended to thank the President for rescuing him from dozens of overbearing mothers eager to marry off their daughters. "You'd be surprised how many educated and wealthy women there are, but none of them interest me."

"What? Are you hard to please?"

"I'd prefer to be the pursuer, not the pursued."

"I know exactly what you mean."

They drove down the lane, a country road lined with vineyards. "I've seen several vineyards. How's the wine?" Braham asked.

"Pretty good. It took a few years to get the vines established, but in the last two years The Lane Winery has won several awards." Jack's phone rang, flashing Charlotte's name. He answered using the Bluetooth speaker phone connection. "Hey, sis. What's up?"

"I cleared my calendar. Where are you?"

"We're not on the highway yet."

"Oh, good. Come get me."

Jack tapped his fingers on the steering wheel. "I'm not sure we want you to go. You'll put a damper on our conversation."

Braham shook his head and mouthed, "No, she won't."

"It'll take you thirty minutes to get here," Charlotte said. "You can tell Braham everything you know about women in ten minutes, all your dirty jokes in five, and how to avoid an STD in thirty seconds. You'll be talking sports by the time you pick me up, and I know as much about that as you do."

"What about the subtle nuances of dating in the twenty-first century?"

"From what your ex-girlfriends say, you don't know any."

Jack slapped his chest. "Insulted by my own sister."

Charlotte laughed. "I'm getting off the phone before you start in on me. I'll be waiting on the corner. Ciao."

"Don't make us wait," Jack said, but Charlotte had already disconnected.

"What's an STD?" Braham asked.

Jack turned up the radio to hear the news on NPR. "Sexually Transmitted Disease."

"Like syphilis and gonorrhea?"

"There are even more diseases now to worry about."

Braham turned down the radio. "I'm listening."

Thirty minutes later, they stopped at the corner of 11th Street and Clay. Charlotte jumped into the back seat. "So, how far through his repertoire did Jack get? Can you repeat any of his jokes?"

Braham turned in his seat, trying to stifle a smile. "I'm going to drive once we hit the ...hmm... interstate."

Charlotte smacked the back of Jack's head. "Don't you *dare* let him drive. Can you imagine the nightmare we'd have defending a lawsuit if Braham had an accident while driving your vehicle?"

"Calm down. It was a joke. You're more afraid of being sued than you were of Sheridan's threats," Jack said.

She put her head in her hands for a moment, then straightened. "If Sheridan had acted on his threats, you wouldn't be living at the plantation now, and if Braham causes a serious accident, a judgment against us could do what Sheridan didn't. Please don't let him drive."

Jack eyed her in the rearview mirror. "By the time Braham drives on the highway, he'll know what's he's doing."

"Promise?" Charlotte asked.

"Promise," Jack said.

17

Washington, D.C., Present Day

WHEN THEY REACHED Washington, Jack drove directly to his agent's office on Connecticut Avenue and parked in front of the converted Victorian home. "I'll make lunch reservations and send you a text where to meet," he said to Charlotte.

"I don't know why you didn't tell her you had other plans. Just because she calls, you don't have to jump," Charlotte said.

Jack slid out of the car and grabbed his leather case from behind his seat. "She makes my life easier, sis. It's why I jump."

Charlotte climbed into the driver's seat and adjusted the seat and rearview mirror. "You'll start talking book deals and forget all about us."

"I'll make the reservation as soon as I get inside. Promise." Jack closed the door and waved goodbye.

"I'm not holding my breath," she yelled.

Braham studied their interaction with intense interest. Although they often snapped at each other, they obviously adored one another, teasing relentlessly. He couldn't help laughing at their shenanigans, and when he did, they would glower at him with identical blue eyes. Because he had been an only child, he had spent much of his time with his friend Cullen. Being around Charlotte and Jack reminded Braham of how much he missed his friend, and how empty his life was without him.

A car pulled up behind Charlotte, stopping traffic. Braham paid close attention to how other drivers maneuvered their vehicles. It took him a moment to realize the car was waiting for Charlotte to move out of the parking spot. There wasn't much difference between driving a car and driving a carriage. One went faster than the other, is all. His spirits were bolstered knowing he would be able to drive the Range Rover as soon as he learned the rules.

Charlotte pulled out in front of the waiting car, accelerating quickly. Braham tugged on his seatbelt strap, checking to be sure the latch was secure.

"Relax. I'm a good driver. I've never had an accident."

"The speed limit is twenty-five miles per hour. Jack never goes over the speed limit. Do you?"

"No, and he doesn't speed now, because a few years ago he had a rash of speeding tickets and got his license suspended. He'd be in a mess of trouble if he lost his driving privileges again. The plantation isn't accessible using public transportation."

"You wouldn't be in trouble, too?"

Charlotte put on her blinker and changed lanes. "I live a few blocks from the hospital. I could walk if I had to."

"Driving doesn't look difficult."

"If you want to learn, you can drive around the plantation. But if you get a scratch or dent on Jack's baby, he'll put a noticeable dent in you."

A smile brought Charlotte's dimples out of hiding.

He wanted to kiss both of them. The idea enticed him. After his physical reaction to her touch last night, he had remained aroused until he learned Lincoln had been murdered. Now his body was betraying him again.

"If someone put a scratch on Liberty, I'd feel the same way"

"Liberty? Your horse?"

"A black Morgan. My cousin gave him to me when I left California. She said he was my Liberty Bell, and not to get him scratched, cracked, or broken."

"She must have a real sense of humor. Great name."

"Great horse."

Charlotte stopped at a red light and checked her phone exactly as Braham had seen Jack do dozens of times. When the light turned green, she put the device down and drove through the intersection, paying close attention to the cars around her. She didn't drive as close to other cars as Jack did, she held the steering wheel with a tighter grip, and she never looked at her phone while driving. A very cautious driver. Did it spill over into other aspects of her life? If it did, he had a greater appreciation for the risks she had taken to rescue him.

"You must not have had Liberty with you in Richmond."

"I left him outside the city."

She shot a quick glance at him, eyes wide. "At an abandoned farm house?"

"Yes. I was assured he'd be safe."

"That's what Gaylord told me when we left our horses there." Her shoulders tightened up so subtly, if he'd been sitting an inch farther away, he wouldn't have noticed. The trip must have terrified her.

"Gaylord's a good man," Braham said.

She bit her lip and made it swell slightly, looking highly kissable and in need of serious attention from him. It would take her mind off her fearful recollections. It would briefly distract him, too.

"And very quiet," she said.

They rode in silence for a few blocks. He didn't recognize any of the buildings, or the street, for that matter. Washington had changed significantly in the last hundred and fifty years.

He had to return home without delay, but how was he going to convince Charlotte to take him when her memories still triggered such fear? Short of seducing her, how could he get her mind off of what had frightened her? What would she find interesting about his life in Washington? How could he help her understand he had a good life, and he wanted to return to it? He was wealthy and well connected. He had property and friends and houses. He was gathering his thoughts, sorting through them when he said, more to himself than to her, "I wonder if my house still stands?"

"What?" Her eyes moved along his face and it felt as if they were probing his skin. "Where? Maybe's it's still there. What's the address?"

"In Georgetown on 31st Street."

"We're not far from there now. Let's go see."

An anxious dread stirred through him. What if they found the house in shambles? It would be humiliating to find property he once owned in disrepair. Maybe it wasn't a good idea to check. He gripped the edge of his seat as Charlotte dodged in and out of traffic before turning up 31st Street.

"What's the address?"

An awkward silence developed before he answered. "Sixteen fifty-five. Right side. End of the block."

The car crawled down a quiet street. He tapped on the window, pointing, and he sloughed his anxiety like old skin. "There it is."

After pulling to the curb, she turned off the engine. "It's gorgeous, and look, it's for sale. I'll see what they're asking for it on Realtor.com." She swiped her finger across the screen on her smartphone several times. "I found the listing. It says the house was built in 1812. Second Empire mansion, mansard roof, brick, nine bedrooms, nine full baths, four half baths, four stories, almost three-quarters of an acre, seven fireplaces, swimming pool, and—"

"I'm getting out." He opened the car door and stood too quickly. He gasped, doubling over as pain ripped through his gut. Most of the time the incision was little more than a nuisance, but every once in a while, like now, he thought he was back on his deathbed.

Charlotte jumped out and raced around to his side, putting her arm across his shoulders "Sit back down. You don't need to get out."

"No, I've got to walk. It's the only way I'll regain my strength. Just give me a moment." He took a couple of minutes to breathe deeply, "It doesn't pain me much, so I forget about it until I move the wrong way."

When the pain subsided, he stepped onto the sidewalk and looked over his former property with an appreciative eye. There was an addition on the back, but the main residence looked exactly as it had when he purchased it in 1862. The dwelling had been well maintained, and a sense of pride bubbled up at owning, or having owned this exquisite house. The sycamore tree he had planted spread its branches wide at a corner of the manicured lawn.

This was a home meant for a family. Children should be playing in the yard. Disappointment over what he didn't have wiped away his joy. There was only one person stopping him from living in this residence again, and she stood next to him.

"You can buy it back for sixteen million, eight hundred thousand dollars."

He stared open-mouthed, temporarily speechless. Finally, he croaked, "Sixteen—"

"Million," she said with a little sparkle in her eyes.

"That much money would support the war for a week. What makes a house worth so much money?"

"Location, nine bathrooms, and a swimming pool."

"There's much about your century which doesn't make sense to me."

They took their time, strolling around the corner, viewing the property from all sides. Then they returned to the car in silence. Charlotte drove back down 31st Street, and through congested traffic toward Pennsylvania Avenue. As they sat through the same traffic light for the second time Braham said, "I have to go back."

"Okay. I'll turn around up here. It is a beautiful home. We can take some pictures."

Confused, and with his thoughts in a tumult, it took a moment to realize she had misunderstood him. "I don't want to return to the *house*, Charlotte. I want to return to my time. I have to go home. You can't keep me here."

They let the statement hang in the air, swinging from concessions she wanted which he couldn't give, and acquiescence he wanted which she wouldn't give. So they sat in traffic—stalled. Tension filled the car until it became thick as his Highlander's burr when he and Cullen drank too much whiskey. He opened his window and cool air rushed in.

The fussy clearing of her throat brought him back to the present. "If you want to learn to drive, you can practice using my car. I'm not as picky as Jack."

Was her offer an attempt to bridge the gap between his concessions and her acquiescence? "I might put a few bumps and scrapes on it, but I'll try to put them where they can't be seen."

She mustered a slow laugh, and he liked the way it relaxed her face. Her hair fell softly over her shoulders and when she flicked it behind her ears, the scent of almonds wafted his way. Apples? Almonds? What other scents did she have?

"You'll probably catch on to the driving part right away. It'll take longer to learn the rules of the road. I'll ask Jack to get a copy of the Virginia driving manual. He can probably find it on the web."

"He's mentioned the web. What is it?" Braham asked.

"The Internet. You can find anything or anybody. I'll show you how to use the iPad."

"The thin, book-size, black box Jack reads?" Braham said, forming the shape with his hands.

"I have one in my bag you can use."

He tugged on his chin with his forefinger and thumb, staring out the window. "An encyclopedia in a small box. The world's knowledge at your fingertips. Maps, too?"

"Everything," she said.

He spotted the finished dome on the Capitol Building and gasped. "*The dome.* It's finished."

"1866, I think. It's being renovated now to repair hundreds of cracks."

His eyes remained fixed on the building, slowly roving from one side to the other. "Could you trade vehicles with Jack tomorrow? I'd like to get started." If Charlotte wouldn't take him back, he had to find another way. A plan was forming, and learning to drive was an integral part of it.

"Sure, why not? But if you crash, the impact will set your recovery back."

He returned his attention to the Capitol. "I won't crash."

Charlotte made a sharp turn, pulling into the flow of traffic on Constitution. The buildings, streets, cars, people, colors, lights, movement, and loud noises bombarded his senses. His head pounded and his heart raced. He had to block out some of the stimulation or he'd lose his mind. He focused on the cars and studied the way the drivers maneuvered through traffic. By focusing only on cars, he was able to shut out other distractions.

"A car's pulling out of a parking spot up ahead. Can you park there?" he asked.

"Where? I don't see it," she said.

He pointed ahead. "Next block. A little red car."

"I see it now." She put on her blinker and stopped, giving the driver of the red car room to pull out. "We'll have to walk about a block. Can you manage it?"

"I can. It might take me longer to walk back, though." He had to keep pushing himself. He couldn't return to Washington an invalid. He eased out onto the sidewalk, careful of his incision this time. No longer focusing on the cars, he looked around at the buildings. "The Washington Monument is finished, too, and still there. I don't know why it surprises me. I grew up in Scotland. Castles and churches have been around for centuries."

She buttoned up her coat against the fall breeze. "The dedication was in 1885."

"It was the tallest building in America at the time. I doubt it's true now."

"Still the tallest building in Washington."

He tilted his head to one side, enjoying the way she gestured with her hands, the bright expression on her face, and a spark of something unidentifiable in her eyes, as if she was trying to hide something from him. He didn't think it was about his health, and he already knew about Lincoln, so what was it? Whatever it was, he'd find out. Discovering secrets people wanted to keep hidden was, after all, his job.

He switched his attention back to their surroundings. "You

know a lot about the city."

Charlotte put coins in a box on one of the poles lining the street. "Jack had an internship between his second and third year in law school. I spent most of the summer here with him and learned my way around."

Braham turned in a slow circle, taking a picture with his mind's eye. "It's hard to believe it's the same Washington."

"What do you notice most?"

He glanced up and down the street, shaking his head. "You have to pay to park your Range Rover."

She shrugged. "Yeah, well, it's the price you pay for a premium parking space."

"You don't have to give it water or hay, but I'm sure you feed it some type of fuel. What makes it run?"

"Gasoline."

He puzzled through the tidbit of information for a moment. "Do you buy gasoline at a livery stable?"

"Hmm. Not exactly. We call them gas stations. You can find them throughout the city and at all the exits along the highway. The next one I see, I'll point it out."

He nodded again, checking items off a mental list.

"What else is different about the city?"

He gently took her elbow and led her down the sidewalk. He wanted to control their pace, but mostly he wanted to touch her. "There's no space between buildings. The streets are paved. It doesn't smell bad, but there's a distinct odor I can't identify."

She sniffed. "Exhaust from the cars, probably. What else?"

He closed his eyes for a moment to conjure up a picture of Washington in his time. Then opened them, blinking. "Troops aren't marching up and down the streets. It's noisier now, but much cleaner."

She pointed to a sidewalk running perpendicular to the one they were on. "Let's go that way. I want you to see a monument. We can take the elevator. There're too many stairs for you to climb."

His heart gave a leap at the thought of getting into another moving box. "I didn't like the hospital elevator. Too confined, and it went too fast."

"This one is slower. I don't think you'll mind."

He shook his head. "Smaller would be even more confining. I'll take the stairs."

The trees along their route shivered in the wind. The red and gold leaves glistened in the late morning sun. He would never have described Washington as beautiful, but he saw beauty now. War made cities ugly. Made life ugly, too. For a few moments, he would breathe in peace and beauty and let it calm his restless soul.

Charlotte pointed ahead. "Here's what we brought you to Washington to see. It's called the Lincoln Memorial."

He stared at a Greek Doric temple and the door slammed on any chance of calming his restless soul. Grief welled. "Did you think seeing this would change my mind?"

"I don't know if anything will change your mind. But you need to see what Lincoln means to the American people today."

"Don't you understand? *I don't care how people feel today.*" His throat was thick, raspy with grief, and the words came out hoarse and unrecognizable. He closed his eyes, hands clenched hard into fists at his sides.

She shook his arm. "Braham, look at me." He opened his eyes but looked away. She moved to stand in his line of sight. "If Lincoln hadn't been assassinated, he never would have gained immortality. If you love him, how can you possibly take that from him?" She pressed her hand to her chest. "I've met him. I stood before him in awe. Do you think I would have grown to hold him in such high esteem if he had died an old Illinois country lawyer?"

"At least he would have lived *to be* an old country lawyer."

She gestured toward the memorial. "But he wouldn't have all *this*, and he wouldn't have six million visitors every year."

Tears welled up in his eyes, and he could feel the burn of them. His upper lip quivered as he fought for control over his emotions. "Do *you* believe marble is an adequate substitute for a person's life? Because I don't."

"I think leaving a lasting legacy that symbolizes the expansion of rights and equality to people across the spectrum of color and backgrounds is a good thing."

His eyes flashed briefly before going dark and intense. "What the hell are you talking about?"

"*Equality*—the President's legacy."

Her statement made the rising mix of anger and grief harden. He didn't want a legacy. He wanted the man—alive, well, and leading the country.

She studied him with her huge blue eyes, a touch of tears shimmering in them. "I don't know what else to say. Come on. Let's go back to Richmond."

Charlotte had saved his life. He didn't want to hurt her. She had rearranged her day to bring him here. The least he could do was visit the monument. He didn't have to like it, but he owed her that much. "If what I suspect is up there," he paused and glanced over his shoulder, "I'll show the President the honor he deserves."

She wiped away a tear with the heel of one palm. "The elevator is this way," she said, nodding toward the side of the memorial.

He steeled himself, breathing through his mouth, preparing for what he knew would be more painful than a punch at the site of his wound. The impact would rip him open. "I'll not take the easy way up."

She shuttered, aghast. "There're *fifty-seven* steps to the top."

"I don't care if there are a hundred and fifty." Logic and the law were things he understood, and there was nothing logical about climbing those stairs in his condition, but he would not be seen as a coward. He raked fingers through his hair until they stuck in windblown tangles. He gave up on the tangles but not on his decision.

He took the first five stairs easily enough. By twenty, sweat poured down his face. His heart bumped hard against his chest, but he kept climbing. He counted each and every step. By the forty-fifth, he was winded and had to stop for a rest.

Charlotte wiped his brow with a handkerchief. "Let's sit for a minute, please."

He shook his head. "No."

The exertion burned his legs and the seams of his jeans strained around his bulging thigh muscles. The last seven stairs took him the longest. When he reached the top and had a full view of Lincoln immortalized in marble, Braham's legs faltered. He would have crumbled to the ground if not for a fluted column next to him. He clung to it, digging his fingers into the grooves.

Charlotte rushed to his side and put her arm around him, her face tense with concern. "Please rest. You can barely stand."

"It's not the hike weakening my legs, it's the view at the top." Despair cut through his voice.

After a moment, he regained his legs and took one step, and then another. His hands knotted into fists, and his jaw clamped tight to the point of shattering. He would not approach as a grieving friend, but as a soldier reporting to his commander. He willed his jaw, and then his fists, to relax. In Braham's heart his President was not dead.

He reached the base of the statue, which was surrounded by a rope enclosure. He unconsciously reached out, but the marble was too far away to touch. Shivering, he stared, lost in thought, and then finally read the inscription above Lincoln's image:

> *In this temple, as in the hearts of the people for whom he saved the Union, the memory of Abraham Lincoln is enshrined forever.*

Tears etched tracks of anguish down his cheeks. If Lincoln had only died an old man instead of being assassinated, Braham would lift his hands with joy at the breathtaking monument. But he didn't die of old age. And if Lincoln had lived, nothing would have stopped him from receiving the accolades he so richly deserved. The heat of vengeance, unlike anything Braham had ever felt before, seared him, leaving him rough-edged and blackened. He *would return* to his time, and he *would find* a way to stop Booth, or he'd die trying.

Charlotte joined him at the base of the statue, slipping her cold hand into his.

"The sculptor depicted him as I know him," Braham said, his voice quavering. He breathed slowly, fighting for control, and he rubbed Charlotte's fingers against the side of his leg to warm them. "Worn, but strong. One hand is clenched, representing his determination, the other more open, showing his compassion. He was a humble man. He would never have agreed to a memorial of this magnitude."

"He deserved a memorial equal to what he did for the country," she said.

"He died too soon." Braham's pain echoed in his gravelly voice. "If the President had lived his full life, they couldn't have built a memorial big enough to equal his contribution. I *will* go back, find the people responsible, and stop the assassination from happening."

"The conspirators were tried, and convicted, and four," she said, holding up her fingers, "were hanged."

Braham dropped her hand he'd been holding, turned, and headed for the stairs. He wanted to run away and grieve for the man he loved, whose friendship he cherished and whose wisdom he sought. Who would advise him now?

Charlotte followed him. "Braham, wait."

When he reached the top of the stairs, he grabbed the column for support again and stared out over a pool of water and the Washington Monument. "The conspirators won't need to be punished, because the assassination will never happen."

She glanced around, then leaned in, and said in a low voice, "You can't stop it. You can't undo all this." She waved her hands to encompass the building and grounds.

He started down the stairs, ignoring her plea. Although she had met Lincoln, the President was still only a marble statue to her. She didn't love him. If she did, she would want to right this wrong, too.

"I. Won't. Take. You. Back."

The breath froze in his lungs. No one had ever told him they wouldn't do what he wanted done or used such a tone of voice—not a client, not an employee, not a soldier, and *certainly* not a woman.

He gritted his teeth and turned to look up at her, the sun shining in his eyes. A shadow passed over. Then, as if lightening had struck, the pieces of his plan fell into place. He knew how he was going to get back, and he didn't need Charlotte or her brooch to get there. When the sun shone again, he said calmly, "We'll work this out."

"Yes, I believe we will." Charlotte's flat tone and blank stare managed to convey the exact opposite.

He fell silent for several moments, then roused himself as though coming awake after a bad dream. "Where are we having lunch?"

She checked her phone for a message. "Jack made reservations at the Occidental Grill & Seafood at the Willard Hotel. They have the best seafood in Washington."

Braham raised one eyebrow and crooked up a corner of his mouth in a too-knowing grin. "The Willard is still in operation? If so, I wouldn't eat the seafood."

Smiling, she slipped her hand into the crook of his elbow. "The food has improved since you were there. I heard they hired a new chef."

18

Mallory Plantation, Richmond, Virginia, Present Day

AFTER DINNER CHARLOTTE and Braham took their coffee to the library so Charlotte could teach him how to use the iPad. "You can access the digital musical collection from here," she said, pointing to an icon. Braham selected an overture by Mozart. When the music streamed from the hi-fi wireless speaker, his feet hit the floor.

"Where's the music coming from?"

"The speaker over there, on the bookshelf next to the window."

He found the source nestled on a lower shelf in the bookcase and knelt to examine it. No matter how she tried, she couldn't take her eyes off him. The plaid sport shirt Jack had loaned him stretched tight across his back and shoulders, highlighting his muscles. His hair, still damp from a shower, hung loose over his collar in tousled waves. She had seen almost every inch of his body, and she marveled at how beautifully God had knitted him together. Perfect proportions. Eye-catching. And he'd certainly caught her eye. She snapped pictures of him using the iPad camera. Then chastised herself for drooling over her patient. There were lines doctors didn't cross, and she was tiptoeing along the edge.

She took a breath, desperately needing a distraction. She tapped her fingers on the iPad cover. "Now you know how to turn on the iPad and have listened to Jack's long explanation of the Internet, what other questions do you have? Or, would you prefer to give me something to research?"

He stood and searched the titles of the books on the shelf in front of him. He pulled one out and leafed through it. "See if Montgomery Winery is still in existence."

Charlotte typed in the name. "This isn't your winery, is it?"

"My friend Cullen Montgomery owns it, or did in 1864."

The website opened and she clicked on the *About* page. "Looks like his descendants own it now. Meredith Montgomery is the current President, and the winery has been in the family for more than a hundred and sixty years. She's married to renowned Thoroughbred breeder Elliott Fraser."

Braham grabbed the edge of the bookcase, rattling knick-knacks on the shelf.

She looked up, startled by the noise. Braham's face had lost all color. She leaned forward in her seat with a slight pang, knowing he didn't want to be coddled, but she was prepared to go to him if he needed help. "Are you okay?"

He waved away her concern, but his color didn't return. "Fine. Keep reading."

She did, but her eyes kept darting between the iPad and her patient. "The Frasers have one son. When not at the winery, they split their time between a farm in Kentucky and an estate in the Scottish Highlands."

Braham sat heavily in the nearest wing chair, rocking it slightly, and put his head in his hands.

Charlotte jumped up then, dropping the iPad on the table next to the sofa and rushing to his side. "You're not okay. What hurts?"

"Must have been all the stairs I climbed. My legs gave out."

She pushed a footstool over to his chair and lifted his legs. "Put your feet on the stool. I'll get you some water."

He shook his head. "No water. Whiskey."

She gave his arm a reassuring squeeze, and the rigid muscles beneath her hand eased a little.

The visiting cat jumped off the sofa and followed her across the room to the liquor cabinet, where she rubbed up against her legs.

Charlotte scratched her behind the ears. "Go find Jack. Go." The cat skedaddled. "Good luck," she said to the vanishing animal. When Jack was in writing mode, he was capable of ignoring fire alarms.

She scooped ice into two highball glasses, then splashed whiskey over the cubes. The Mozart overture ended and the room-temperature spirits cracked the ice, roaring like an avalanche in the silence.

She handed Braham a drink. "Do you feel dizzy?"

"I'm fine." He took a long sip and the color slowly returned to his face.

Satisfied he wasn't in any physical distress, she returned to her spot on the sofa and was rejoined by the cat. "Struck out, huh?" She curled up beside Charlotter, purring.

"What else is written about the Montgomerys and Frasers?" Braham asked.

A chunk of wood split in the fireplace with a loud *crack*, and sent a swirl of sparks up the chimney and the scent of hickory into the room.

Charlotte picked up the iPad, tucked her feet up under her, and read more from the website. "The winery had a successful launch of a new chardonnay a couple of years ago. The wine is called *Cailean*. I've seen the wine at the liquor store but haven't tasted it."

"*Cailean* means child in Gaelic."

She cocked her head in surprise. "Do you speak the language?"

"Gaelic, Latin, Italian, Spanish, and French."

She wanted to ask him to translate the inscription on the brooch, but she didn't dare. They'd start arguing again.

"Jack's also a polyglot. He can't speak Gaelic, but he can speak the other ones, plus Greek, Japanese, and German."

Jack entered the room, heading straight for the liquor cabinet. "And a little bit of Russian." He poured a drink. "I just got off the phone with my agent. She wants me in Atlanta tomorrow, for two days. I'll have a car pick me up in the morning. Which means you can drive mine home and leave your car for Braham to practice with."

She gave Jack a brief, shocked laugh. "You can't leave Braham here by himself. He can come to Richmond and stay with me."

Braham rattled the ice in his glass. "I've been taking care of myself for a number of years. I can manage. Besides, I want to learn to drive, which I can't do safely in the city."

She removed a blue-patterned scrunchie from her long ponytail, finger-combed her hair, pulled it together, and then looped the tie around her hair again. Fiddling with her hair gave her a minute to think instead of spitting out her first response—*I'm not leaving you by yourself.*

"You just got out of the hospital and should have a caregiver close by. I'd stay here, but I'm on call for the next two nights."

"If you're working during the day and on call at night, what's the difference? He'd still be alone."

"The difference is I'd only be five minutes away."

"It's only two days. He can manage."

"Oh bloody hell, Jack. Stop thinking about what's most conven-ient for you and think about your guest."

"I *am*, sis. Braham would much rather stay here where he's famil-iar with his surroundings than spend two days stuck in your house where he can't even see the river. Right?" Jack said, glancing at Braham."

Braham cocked his brow. "Right."

Jack winked at Charlotte. "See? Told you." He sipped his drink. "Now, what did I hear about a winery?"

She sighed, shaking her head. Sometimes it was pointless to argue with her brother. He could bulldoze his way up, down, and all around her. If she was going to be home, she'd have a better argument, but she had a full schedule, so she accepted defeat and moved on.

"Braham's friend started a winery in Napa," she said. "It's still in existence and is operated by his descendants. It boasts the longest continuous operation of any winery in the country."

Jack gave her a broad smile. "A long weekend in the wine coun-try would be nice. I can schedule a book signing to make the trip tax deductible." He tossed back his drink. "I'll check my calendar later, but right now I've got work to finish. I'll be in my office."

"Would you like to visit the winery?" Charlotte asked Braham.

He gave an agitated sigh, then took a long swallow of his drink. "Maybe. Is there any more information about the man she married or his farm?"

Charlotte Googled Elliott Fraser. "He breeds Thoroughbreds and owns MacKlenna Farm in Lexington, Kentucky. The farm is a three thousand acre Thoroughbred breeding and training facility established in 1790. Wow. Impressive. The farm has also had several Kentucky Derby and Triple Crown winners."

Jack returned to the library. "Did you say MacKlenna Farm?"

"If you're going to eavesdrop, why don't you stay in here?" Charlotte said.

"I can't, really. But did you say MacKlenna Farm?"

"Have you heard of it?"

"I met Elliott Fraser and Sean MacKlenna several years ago when I went to the Kentucky Derby. You had an emergency and couldn't get away. I'm glad you didn't go. Fraser would have hit on you. The guy is a drinker and a player."

"Not anymore," Charlotte said.

Jack scooted the cat out of the way and sat down next to Charlotte. "Guys like him don't change. Let me see his picture."

Charlotte clicked on several pictures of Elliott with his wife and child. "This isn't the face of a womanizer."

"Does it say anything about the farm's stallions?" Braham asked.

"The stallion with the smallest stud fee, five thousand dollars, is an eight-year-old named Stormy." Jack whistled. "What a horse. Look at this picture." He held up the iPad, showing off a magnificent stallion with three white stockings.

Braham took the iPad from Jack with a shaking hand. "I'd let this horse service my finest mare any day of the week. He's a winner." Braham handed back the iPad and poured another drink. "What time do you leave in the morning?"

"The car will be here at six," Jack said. "I've got an early flight."

"I'll be up before you leave," Braham said. "I don't want to miss a cup of your coffee."

"You can at least show him how to make it himself," Charlotte said.

"Oh, he knows. He prefers to have it ready when he comes into the kitchen in the morning. He can't stay at your house. You don't even have a coffee pot."

"I don't need one. There's a Starbucks at the corner."

Jack shook his head. "Sad."

"I'm turning in. It's been a long day. Goodnight," Braham said.

"Hey, if you need cash while I'm gone, there's a little bit in the top drawer of my desk."

Charlotte laughed. "It's his pizza delivery money."

"Glad to know. The pizza we had yesterday for lunch was good." He left the room, and a minute later they heard his bedroom door close.

"He had a rough day," Charlotte said. "You should have seen him at the Lincoln Memorial. It was heartbreaking."

"Then you were the best person to be with him."

"Not necessarily," Charlotte said. "I wish I knew what he was thinking. He's a very private person."

Jack enlarged the picture of Stormy. Then checked out the other stallions standing stud at MacKlenna Farm. "Braham's been a spy for four years. He's learned to play his cards close to his chest, for survival if for no other reason. I doubt you'll get much out of him." Jack handed the iPad back to her. "Beautiful stallions."

She set the iPad on the coffee table along with the charger and her car keys. "I wish I could do more to help him."

Jack gave her a hug. "You've done a lot for him already. Give him time. He'll find his way. If you'd let him back on a horse, he might feel like he had a bit more control of his life."

"I'd rather give him a watch. I learned the hard way that not knowing the time of day makes you feel even less in control over your circumstances. I didn't like it at all."

She rinsed out her glass at the bar and left it in the sink. "You know, two weeks ago, Braham was almost dead. He's making a remarkable recovery, but he's not healed yet. Let's see how he's doing next week. If he promises not to go galloping around the farm, he can probably ride. But not until then."

Jack grinned. "We don't have to gallop to go hunting."

Charlotte's mind spun with worst-case scenarios. "I only hope he doesn't go off hunting on his own."

19

Mallory Plantation, Richmond, Virginia – Present Day

AN HOUR AFTER Jack left with the car service, Braham carried a change of clothes and a sack of food out to Charlotte's Range Rover. If he was going to leave, it had to be now. Earlier he had read the driving manual on the iPad. He'd watched videos on YouTube, and he knew the rules of the road. The real question now was—could he drive a car Jack said could drive itself?

He started the engine and entered his destination in the GPS device. At seventy miles an hour it would take six hours to reach Lexington, Kentucky. He had calculated gas mileage, and driving at a constant rate of speed, he could make it on one tank of gasoline. If he had to buy more fuel he would use some of Jack's pizza money. He hated leaving without an explanation, but even if he had tried again to explain, he knew they wouldn't have understood.

He had called MacKlenna Farm and been told Elliott and his wife, Meredith, were at the farm until the end of next week. If Braham didn't leave now, he would miss the Frasers and the only means of returning to his time. The plan he had formulated might not work, but he had to try. Although he'd never been behind the wheel of an automobile, he dismissed it as insignificant. He would learn on the way and pray a traffic officer didn't stop him. He understood the traffic laws and how much trouble he could get into without a license. But he didn't think they would shoot him or hang him, and hopefully jails had improved a wee bit since the mid-eighteen hundreds.

He adjusted the seat and mirror as he had seen Charlotte do the day before. Then he put the car in gear. Before pressing the accelerator, he took a steadying breath. The moment he touched the accelerator, the car shot forward.

Braham slammed his foot on the brake and his chest hit the steering wheel. "Damn." He had forgotten to buckle up. He left his foot on the brake, put on the belt, put the car into park, and sat perfectly still.

While the car remained in park, he pressed the accelerator with a much lighter touch, listening to the roar of the engine. Obviously, he couldn't master driving techniques simply by reading instructions. He put the car in gear again and pressed on the accelerator. The car shot forward, but this time he didn't use the brake. Instead, he lifted the foot on the gas pedal a bit and the car slowed. He continued to practice both braking and accelerating until he felt familiar enough with how acceleration worked.

Feeling more confident, he followed the farm road and circled the plantation. Then he circled again. By the third time, his confidence had increased dramatically until he looked down at the speedometer. He was only traveling at five miles per hour. He stopped the car and pounded his palms against the steering wheel.

At this speed, he could get to Lexington faster riding a horse. He blew out a long breath and drove more circles around the farm, increasing his speed with each loop. When he felt comfortable at forty-five miles per hour, he ventured out onto the lane leading to the highway. As the first stop sign came into view, he stopped, and inched his way up to the sign. A car was coming from his right. He cringed, waiting for the impact he knew would come. The car zoomed by, and he relaxed. If he was going to panic every time a car came toward him, then he might as well turn around and go back to the plantation.

He pulled out faster than he intended and didn't turn the wheel as far as necessary, which put him close to the edge of the pavement. To avoid hurling off the road, he cut the wheel too sharply, causing the car to swing. He then yanked the wheel in the opposite direction. The rear end swerved from side to side, and he ran into the grass. He hit the brakes and threw the car into park.

"Damn." He slammed his palms against the wheel again, breathing heavily. This might be the hardest task he'd ever undertaken. He should practice more before he set out, but he had no time to lose. He took a moment to regain his composure then pulled out onto the highway. By the time he reached the I-64 West exit, his palms had stopped sweating.

He watched the gas gauge needle creep toward the halfway point with the same fear as going into enemy territory. What could he do if he ran out? Walk. But he wasn't going to run out. He had calculated carefully. He'd make it to the farm.

Toward ten o'clock he stopped, rummaged through his food bag, and gobbled a ham and cheese sandwich and an apple, getting back on the road quickly. At noon he passed the exit to Morehead, Kentucky, and pulled off to eat the other sandwich. He arrived in Lexington with little more than an eighth of a tank of gas left. Was it enough to get to the farm? If it wasn't, he'd get out and hike the rest of the way. He had the directions written on paper, just in case.

When he spotted a sign for a park, he pulled over, got out, and stretched his legs. Although he had spent the past seven hours rehearsing his speech to Elliott Frasier, he took the time to practice once more. His presentation was almost as important as delivering a closing argument in a murder trial.

After a quick walk through the park to loosen the tension in his shoulders, he got back in the car, followed the GPS directions, and thirty minutes later pulled up to the security gate at MacKlenna Farm.

A man stepped out the guardhouse. "Do you have an appointment?"

"No," Braham said. "My name is Abraham McCabe. I'd like to speak to Doctor Fraser about his goddaughter, Kit MacKlenna."

The guard went back into the guardhouse and picked up a phone like the one Jack had on his desk. Braham had decided using

Kit's name would be his best approach. It at least guaranteed he would get Elliott's attention.

The guard returned and the gate opened. "Follow the road to the house. Doctor Fraser will meet you there."

Braham nodded and proceeded down the road. The grounds had changed since his visit in 1852. There were more paddocks, more horses, and fewer trees.

The two-story red brick mansion finally came into view. The portico's four Doric columns guarded the residence as they had for more than two hundred years. He brought the car to a halt in front of the porch and after taking a moment to mentally prepare himself, he climbed out.

A tall, trim, distinguished-looking man with graying hair was waiting in the doorway. Braham could have recognized Elliott Fraser in a crowd. The doctor looked exactly like Kit's sketches of him. Braham took the stairs to the porch slowly, partly to avoid pulling his incision and partly to prepare for the conversation.

Elliott reached out his hand. "Mr. McCabe. Ye' certainly have a familiar name."

Braham shook the older man's hand. "After all Kit has said about you, I feel I already know you."

"Come in. We have much to discuss."

Braham followed Elliott through the door riddled with bullet holes. "Where'd the bullet holes come from? They weren't there when I was here with Kit in '52."

"The MacKlennas were attacked by renegade soldiers toward the end of the war. They saw the holes as a badge of honor and refused to replace the door." Elliott led the way into his office. If the leather chairs in front of the fireplace weren't the same ones, they damn well looked like it. The wet bar was a new addition though, and Braham was ready for a drink.

"What can I get ye'? Water? Soda?"

"Whiskey."

Elliott poured Braham's drink and got a bottle of water for himself.

"I thought you were a whiskey man, too."

"A few years ago I realized alcohol had more control of me than I had of it. Gave it up one day and haven't had a drop since. Don't miss it. I feel better, my leg healed, and I'm running longer distances now. Enough about me. Let's talk about ye'. My goddaughter mentioned a friend named Braham McCabe. But I don't see how it could be ye'."

"We're cousins," Braham corrected.

Elliott smiled. "Please, sit."

"My full name is Michael Abraham McCabe. I'm a major in the United States Cavalry." Braham settled into one of the leather chairs and Elliott sat in the other. "Cullen Montgomery is as close to a brother as I'll ever have. I've always trusted and believed him. When he told me Kit, your goddaughter, was from the twenty-first century, I was shocked, but I had no reason to doubt him. I know about Kit's ruby brooch. I also know there are three brooches. Kit traveled to the nineteenth century using the magic in the ruby. I was brought forward by the magic in a sapphire brooch. Now, I need to get back, as soon as possible."

Elliott remained stone-faced. "Go on."

"While reenacting the Battle of Cedar Creek, a surgeon from Richmond, Virginia was transported back in time to the actual battle—"

Elliott interrupted. "Have ye' seen the brooch?"

"Only a glimpse, but I heard the Gaelic incantation."

"Go on," Elliott said.

"During the battle, the surgeon was captured and subsequently accepted a mission at the request of President Lincoln. I was the mission." Braham stopped a moment and sipped his whisky, studying Elliott's face for a reaction. He saw none. Braham took it for a positive sign. At least Elliott wasn't dismissing him outright. Braham set his drink on the table and continued.

"I was shot and captured in Richmond while on a special as-signment for the President," Braham continued. "Lincoln needed the information I had obtained, and arranged for the surgeon to facilitate my rescue. When the doctor found me, though, I was dying. The only way to save my life was to bring me to the future. This all occurred two weeks ago."

"Then why are you here in Kentucky?" Elliott asked.

"She's afraid if she goes back again she might not be able to return, and the experience she had was quite frightening. As a doctor, she doesn't believe I've recovered enough to risk what could be waiting for me in my own time."

"Have ye' told her about Kit or the ruby brooch?"

Braham shook his head. "She only knows my friend Cullen Montgomery started Montgomery Winery, and Cullen is your wife's ancestor."

Elliott crossed one leg over the other, rested his ankle on his knee, and tugged on the hem of his trousers. "What do ye' want from me?"

Braham sat back and rested his hands casually on the arms on the chair. "To borrow the ruby brooch and return to my time."

"I can't help you."

"I think you can. The brooch seems to take people and return them to the same place, but in a different time. If I use the ruby brooch here, on MacKlenna Farm, then I should show up on the farm in 1864. If so, all I have to do is make sure Sean MacKlenna returns the brooch to its hiding place—" Braham pointed to the desk across the room "—inside your desk."

Elliott dropped his leg and leaned forward, pressing both hands on his knees as though to emphasize the importance of what he was about to say. "What ye're asking for is not the same as asking to borrow my car. There could be repercussions. I'll have to take those potential repercussions into consideration."

Braham willed himself to relax, to maintain his composure, but irritation slipped out. "*Doctor Fraser.* I'm Kit's first cousin. Which makes me your wife's cousin, too—"

"I'm well aware of the relationship."

Elliott's statement hung in the air.

Braham had practiced his speech for seven hours and it fell apart in less than five minutes. "This is a family matter," Braham said. "I need your help. President Lincoln is waiting for—and desperately needs—the information I have."

"It will take ye' weeks to get to Washington," Elliott said.

"Two and a half days by train. I should have been back two weeks ago. I can't afford any more delays."

"Give me a couple of hours. Let me talk to my wife—"

The woman Braham had seen on the winery's website when he had gone back and searched for Elliott's phone number entered the room holding hands with a wee lad dressed like his father in tan pants and a green shirt.

"About what?" she asked.

Both men stood. The toddler ran to Elliott. "Daddy, I took a long nap. I want to ride my pony now."

Elliott wrapped the boy in his arms with a hug. "Good laddie." He turned to Braham, smiling. "This is my son, James Cullen MacKlenna Fraser, and my wife, Meredith."

Smiling, Braham ruffled the wee lad's mop of brown hair. Then he shook hands with Meredith. She was a striking woman, with Cullen's black hair and blue eyes. Tall and lithe, she projected a gentle, trustworthy spirit, and he liked her instantly.

"Braham McCabe," he said.

Meredith eyed him quizzically. "Your name seems familiar."

A young man came to the door. "Is Cullen ready for his riding lesson?"

"*Kebin.*" The lad's big brown eyes opened wider with excitement. He wiggled to get down, then ran toward the man, who picked him up and twirled him around. "I ride Little Stormy."

"Okay, but tell Mommy and Daddy goodbye."

"Thanks, Kevin," Elliott said while the boy waved. "We'll be out in a few minutes to see you ride, Cullen."

Meredith sat on the footstool in front of Elliott's chair. "Sit down, please, Mr. McCabe, and tell me how you came to be here."

Elliott rubbed her shoulders. "By way of the sapphire brooch."

Meredith clapped. "*Really?* It brought you here? To MacKlenna

Farm?"

"No, to Richmond, Virginia."

"You're Kit's cousin, right?" She glanced around the room. "Where's the woman?"

"Who said anything about a woman?" Elliott asked.

"Of course there's a woman. The legacy of the three brooches says the magic in the stones unites soul mates. If Braham hasn't met her *yet*, he will."

"I can tell you emphatically the doctor who rescued me and brought me to this time is not my soul mate." Braham had intentionally ignored all thoughts concerning the brooches' legacy. It would cloud his judgment at a time when hard decisions needed to be made.

"He hasn't mentioned a woman, Mer," Elliott said.

Meredith smiled. "Only because you haven't asked. But I'm asking. There is a woman, isn't there? Who is she?"

Braham nodded, the muscle jumping in the side of his jaw. "There's no doubt in my mind you're Cullen Montgomery's great-great-something granddaughter."

"Six, I think." She merely smiled at him, showing dimples and a crease in her forehead which reminded Braham even more of his friend. "The surgeon who rescued you," Meredith continued, "must be *the woman*. What does she look like?"

"She has wild, curly blonde hair and deep blue eyes and she wears god-awful clothes she calls scrubs. She's small and *very* opinionated.

"Ah ha," Meredith said. "You're already in love with her?"

Braham's jaw dropped. "*No.* I barely know her. And unlike your sire, I didn't take advantage of Charlotte the way Cullen took advantage of Kit."

Meredith belted out a laugh. Then she grew solemn. "If you're Kit's cousin, it means you're mine, too."

Braham reached for her hand, took it between his own, and held it lightly. "Will you help me get home?"

She maintained eye contact while placing her other hand on top of his and patting it gently. Then she withdrew both of her hands. "I came late to this conversation. I don't know how you got here or how we can help you go back."

"He wants to borrow the ruby brooch," Elliott said.

"I vote you give it to him," she said. "He can leave it with Sean MacKlenna."

"Which is what I suggested, but Doctor Fraser wants to think about it."

Meredith got to her feet, leaned over Elliott's chair, and kissed him. "If Elliott wants to think about it, he has a good reason. I need to go watch Cullen's riding lesson. I'll let you men talk, and I'll catch up on the conversation during cocktails."

She left the room, closing the door behind her.

Braham finished his drink and took the empty glass to the bar. "Talking to her is like having a conversation with Cullen. They are very much alike."

Elliott stood. "Come on. Let me show you around the farm, and you can tell me about Kit. How many children does she have now?"

"She was carrying her fourth when I left for the war. Said it was her last."

"There's a portrait of her hanging at Meredith's winery. She was probably in her eighties when it was painted. Still beautiful."

"She's never stopped missing you. When I tell her about meeting you, she'll want to hear everything about you and the farm."

They went out into the corridor, and a golden retriever plowed into Braham, planting his paws on Braham's chest. Braham hissed, clutching the wound on his belly, but still managed to scratch the dog behind his ears. "Hello Tate. You remember me, don't you?" He had very fond memories of Kit's dog, cat, and stallion. They had gone back in time with her and traveled the Oregon Trail in 1852.

Tate barked.

Elliott patted the dog's head. "That's the most excitement we've seen from ye' in months. Now get down." Tate sat, his tongue lolling.

"Where's Tabor?" Braham asked. "As I remember, they were

never far apart."

A Maine Coon cat sauntered out of the front room. "There you are." Gingerly, Braham squatted and gave Tabor a rub, too. "It's been a long time, old girl. It was a hard trip we made." He glanced up at Elliott while continuing Tabor's rub. "My crossing wasn't so bad, but Kit, Cullen, and the critters had it much worse."

Elliott gave Braham's shoulder an affectionate squeeze. "Water under the bridge now. Kit and Cullen eventually got to where they needed to be."

Braham straightened, grimacing. "Now I'm in a similar situation."

Elliott grabbed a jacket and a green cap with a MacKlenna Farm symbol from a coat rack by the door. Jack had worn a similar cap with *New York Yankees* written on it. Braham hadn't wanted to offend Jack by asking why a good Southerner wore a Yankee cap.

"Cocktails are served at five in the library. Some of my staff joins us, including Kevin and David. They'll be glad to meet ye'. They're the only ones here besides Meredith who know the truth about Kit."

"If my memory serves, Kit called Kevin your aide and David your bodyguard."

"Among other things—"

"Doctor Fraser," an older woman called from the back of the house. "Kevin said you've got company. Is he staying for dinner? I need to know."

Elliott zipped up his jacket. "Yes, Mrs. Collins. He'll stay for dinner, and please have the guest room prepared."

Braham shoved his hands into his pockets. "I can't—"

Elliott held up his hand, interrupting Braham. "Trust me. It's simpler this way."

"But, I can't—"

Elliott gave him a direct look Braham found easy to interpret. He'd seen it on the faces of every general he'd ever met. "If I decide to loan ye' Kit's brooch, ye' won't need the room. If I decide not to, ye' will. In that case, I'll fly ye' back to Richmond in the morning and have someone drive the car. Unless yer Virginia host shows up on my doorstep, too."

"I don't know how she could."

"Don't ever doubt the power of a woman, the Internet, or a tracking device."

Dread hung in a tight knot in the back of Braham's throat. "What's a tracking device?"

Elliott pointed to a nearby table. "That." He picked up a small black box and tossed it to Braham. "The owner of the car ye' were driving knows exactly where ye' are now."

Braham's heart skipped several beats. "This wasn't in the car's manual. I would have read about it."

Elliott laughed. "There's no way ye' can learn all ye' need to know by reading a damn manual. If ye' and Kit aren't two birds in the same nest. I swear, she thought she could go back in time and cross the Oregon Trail because she had been in reenactments. She had a lot to learn when she got there, didn't she?"

He pursed his lips, thinking. If Charlotte and Jack knew where he was, they could show up at the door any minute. Or, would they? Charlotte wouldn't even know he was gone until after seven o'clock. Then she and Jack would have to talk, and then they would have to get to the farm. He had at least twelve hours to convince Elliott to loan him the ruby brooch.

"She did have a lot to learn," Braham said. "Mostly about herself."

"Changed history, too." He put his arm around Braham's shoulder. "Come on. Let's go see my son ride his pony."

Braham stopped when he spotted a portrait of a young, pregnant Kit hanging on the wall. "Sean painted this a few weeks before Thomas was born. He had an awful time getting her to sit still."

"No one recognizes her as the young girl who grew up here. I think it's the extra weight she's carrying in her face."

Braham gazed fondly at the portrait. Would he ever see her again? When they had said their goodbyes in California before he left for the war in 1861, they both knew it was a possibility, although they hadn't discussed it. Now he was in the house she grew up in, he ached to see her again.

"It would break her heart if I didn't come home," Braham said.

Elliott gave him a rigid smile. "Kit didn't fight fair either."

Braham mirrored Elliott's smile. "She said she learned it from you."

Elliott readjusted his already-straight ball cap. "I'll give you my decision after dinner."

Braham had the distinct feeling Elliott was stalling. But why? It wasn't like he could search the Internet for information about him. Braham didn't exist in the present century. And there was no way Elliott could find out about Charlotte and Jack. Braham had been careful not to mention any names.

Elliott's phone beeped. He checked the message. "Cullen's waiting. He's taking his first jump today."

Braham took a step backwards, slapping a hand over his chest as if that could contain his racing heart. "*A two-year-old?*"

"Don't look so shocked. How do you think Kit learned to ride?"

"But not at two."

"You're right. She was eighteen months when I put her on her first pony. Meredith wouldn't let Cullen on a horse before he turned two. We compromised at twenty months. Now he's almost three. Come on. If I miss this big event, I'm good as dead."

They hurried out of the house with Braham shaking his head. They reached the paddock just as the trainer lined Cullen up to jump a beam on the ground. Meredith sat on the top rung of the fence, softly hissing. Elliott put his arm around, patting her hip gently. "How's he doing?"

"He's fearless. But his mother is not."

"Did ye' double-check the harness?"

"And the helmet," she said, gripping the fence rail. "No cracks."

"Ye' should have bought a new one. The one he's wearing could have a hairline crack."

She looked down her nose at him. "I went over the dang thing with a magnifying glass. It's fine."

Braham rested his foot on the bottom fence rail, noticing Meredith's knuckles were white. He chuckled. Although projecting calm, she was still anxious. So much like Kit.

Elliott entered the paddock and leaned against the fence, arms folded, one leg crossed over the other at the ankles. His posture was relaxed, but his lips were pulled tight between his teeth.

"The first time I saw Kit ride, she was racing Stormy at Fort Laramie. She was riding up over his neck. I didn't think she could possibly keep her seat. Best damn race I've ever seen. Unconventional, but typical Kit," Braham said.

"Elliott raised her, you're her cousin, and I'm her six-times-great-granddaughter. When you see her again, will you tell her about Elliott and me and little Cullen?"

Braham gave her a lopsided smile, reflecting his anxiety. "Do you think I will?"

"What? See her again?" Meredith gave him a closed-lip smile which signaled to Braham she knew something but wasn't comfortable sharing it. "Elliott knows Kit loves you, and he would do anything for her. What do you think?"

Braham breathed a bit easier. It was what he'd been counting on.

Cullen's pony walked over the jump and everyone clapped. Kevin led the pony over to Elliott, who unbuckled his son. "Who's my winning jockey today?"

"I am, Daddy. Can I ride Stormy now?"

Elliott hugged him. "Not today, but soon."

Meredith jumped off the fence and took her son out of Elliott's arms, removing the helmet. "I'm so proud of you."

"Did I jump my horse like you do, Mommy?"

She kissed his cheek. "You sure did. Are you ready for a snack?"

He licked his lips. "I want a cupcake."

"Maybe after dinner."

"When we celebrate my 'complishment?" Elliott traded Cullen's helmet for a miniature MacKlenna Farm cap, and the lad straightened it on his head exactly as Braham had seen Elliott do earlier.

Elliott laughed and tugged on the cap's bill. "Sure, we'll celebrate yer accomplishment."

Although Braham was godfather to Kit's children and loved them dearly, he hadn't given much thought to having any of his own, but seeing Elliott with his son reminded Braham of his own father and the love they had shared. Maybe after the war, he'd look for a wife, have children, and teach his son to ride a pony.

"If Cullen is anything like Kit, you won't keep him on a pony for long. He'll be champing the bit for a bigger, faster horse."

"Which will be his mother's decision," Elliott said. "I won round one when he got to ride at twenty months. She gets to decide when the lad can graduate to a bigger mount."

"Kit and Cullen's biggest arguments have been over similar issues. They're learning the art of compromise."

Elliott threw back his head and laughed. "Cullen must be teaching her the art, because she certainly didn't learn it from her father or me." He picked up Cullen's helmet. "Let's go over to the stallion barn. Stormy's covering a mare at two o'clock."

They walked along an interior road lined with overlapping trees that formed a fall-colored canopy. Braham reflected on the quiet serenity around him. No guns. No cannon fire. No screaming soldiers. Yet in a matter of hours, if Elliott did what Meredith had predicted he would do, Braham would return to the war. It would only last a few more months, and then he could return to California, to his law practice, his vineyards, and his life.

Elliott interrupted Braham's thoughts saying, "Stormy's first yearlings will sell in February. Since he doesn't have any winnings or successful offspring, we're all but giving away breeding rights this season. Next year should be better. With his pedigree, he's bound to produce Grade One stakes winners."

"How many live covers will he do this year?" Braham asked.

"He has a book of two hundred," Elliott said.

"Kit has explained how things are done now in the breeding business. It's more complicated."

"A lot of money is at stake."

When Braham entered the dark, oak-paneled stallion complex, he gave a low whistle so as to not startle the horses. "These stallions live better than the majority of the people in the nineteenth century."

There were six stalls with brass nameplates hanging on each. A brick floor and a cupola gave the barn a fit-for-a-king appearance.

A handler dressed in heavy boots led Stormy into a larger room with a rubber floor.

"Stormy is a few pounds heavier than the last time I saw him."

"He lost a wee bit of weight during Kit's journey."

A mare restrained with a twitch waited for the stallion, the swathe of her tail held high, signaling her readiness. Stormy approached at an angle several feet from her nearside, instinctively avoiding startling her and causing her to kick out. He was fully erect. His handler allowed him to mount the mare. The mare lurched forward, but not far enough to put stress on the stallion's great muscles, already tense and straining in the act of mating. He signaled ejaculation by flagging his tail. A handler was ready with a bucket to catch the spillage as the stallion withdrew. From start to finish, it only took moments. Once the cover was complete, Elliott led Braham into a side room.

"They'll examine the semen under a microscope to confirm viable sperm," Elliott said. They stood out of the way, waiting patiently until the person looking through a microscope announced it had been a good cover. Elliott smiled, and he and Braham ambled back toward the house with Tate on their heels.

"Our stallions are too valuable to take any more risks than absolutely necessary. Everything is choreographed." Elliott opened the back door leading into the kitchen. "Are ye' hungry? Mrs. Collins can fix ye' a sandwich to hold ye' until dinner."

The aroma of roasting meat made Braham's mouth water, and his stomach rumble. "I can wait."

The woman working at the stove said, "You can't come into my kitchen hungry and not eat. I fed Doctor Fraser a couple of hours ago, so the complaining stomach I hear ain't his. You sit. I'll whip you up enough food to put hair on that big chest of yours."

Braham gave her a teasing smile. "Yes, ma'am."

"I'll leave ye' with Mrs. Collins," Elliott said. "I need to return a couple of calls."

Braham read the Lexington Herald-Leader newspaper while he waited. Every article he read generated a dozen questions, and he wished he had Charlotte's iPad. The idea of access to unlimited knowledge both baffled and intrigued him. There were several things about the twenty-first century he'd miss, especially Charlotte.

He hadn't even had a chance to kiss her.

20

MacKlenna Farm, Lexington, Kentucky – Present Day

ELLIOTT ENTERED HIS office already busy checking emails on his smartphone. He closed the door behind him. David was sitting at the conference table with two laptops, notes scribbled on a legal pad, and the tracking device from Braham's car.

Elliott sat next to David and picked up the device. "Thanks for leaving this on the hall table. The expression on Braham's face told me he had no idea what it was. So what'd ye' find out about him?"

David put down his pen and picked up the legal pad. "The vehicle is registered to Doctor Charlotte Mallory, the daughter of Jackson and Margaret Mallory. Both parents were U.S. Senators. Both died in office. Charlotte went to Duke Medical School, did her internship and residency at Cornell, then returned to Richmond to practice medicine and teach. She has an outstanding reputation. No malpractice claims. Is well thought of by her colleagues. She's a marathoner. Has qualified for Boston but cancelled. No reason given."

"Probably her schedule," Elliott said. "What else?"

"Her brother Jack Mallory is a New York Times bestselling author."

Elliott nodded his approval. "I've read his books. He writes mysteries and suspense. Good storyteller."

David continued. "Neither one is married. Jack resides at the family plantation, which has been owned by the Mallorys since

1613."

"One family?" Elliott was not only surprised but thunderstruck. "Since close to the founding of Jamestown, which was a long time ago."

David looked at him, his eyebrows raised in an unspoken question. "How do ye' know so much U. S. history?"

"After horses, history was Sean's favorite topic."

"Which Sean?"

"Kit's adoptive father, Sean the sixth." Elliott tugged on his chin. "Matter of fact, Sean the fifth was a bit of a history nut, too. They talked. I listened. They were proud of the farm's history. It was once part of Virginia, given by a land grant to James MacKlenna in 1790. But it isn't as old as the Mallorys'. Very impressive."

David sat back, shaking his head. "Do ye' want to hear this or not?"

"Not all at once. I probably paid a thousand bucks for the quick information. I'd like to savor it a bit at a time. Feels more like I'm getting my money's worth."

David stood, dropping the legal paid on top of the conference table. "Call me if ye' can't read my notes."

"I'm teasing ye', lad. Sit. Get on with it."

David shifted his solid frame in the conference table chair. He flipped a page and continued reading through his notes. "Charlotte took McCabe to the Winchester Medical Center on October 18 for treatment of a bullet wound in his abdomen. She claimed she found him in the parking lot following the reenactment of the Battle of Cedar Creek.

"McCabe told the police he didn't know who he was or who shot him. He stayed in the Winchester hospital for four days, then transferred to the Virginia Medical Center. He was released into the care of Jack Mallory, who also paid his medical bills. Mallory caught a flight to Atlanta this morning and has a two-night reservation at the Ritz-Carlton. Charlotte was on call this evening, but she's changed her schedule." David flipped a page on the notepad. "We ran the prints we got off the car. One set matches Charlotte's—"

"Why are her prints on file?"

"She volunteered for a six-week program to provide surgical assistance in Afghanistan."

"That took guts."

David grunted. "Another set matches Jack Mallory's. He was arrested in college for public intoxication. The case was dismissed. Arrested a few years ago on a murder charge—"

"*What?*"

"He was interviewing a biker gang and was arrested with them. Nothing came of it except an article he wrote afterwards trended on social media. I'm sure it sold more books."

"What about Braham's prints?"

David shook his head. "The man is a battle-hardened soldier. Ye' can tell in the way he walks and stands, and ye' can see it in his eyes. But there're no prints in any database. No credit cards. No employment history. No birth record. Michael Abraham McCabe didn't exist before October 18."

Elliott sat back in chair. "What do you think?"

"He's either in the federal witness protection program, or he's telling the truth when he says he's from the nineteenth century."

Elliott guzzled a bottle of water then squeezed and popped the plastic. "I believe him." He then threw the bottle toward the trashcan like a basketball. It missed and landed on the floor.

David howled. "Jim Manning can do it without missing. Ye' can't compete with yer lawyer."

"They didn't have basketball where I went to high school in Scotland, and I had no interest in learning when I was at Auburn vet school. Ye're right. I can't compete with a guy who played at the University of Kentucky. Call him and let him know about Braham. Something might come of this later, and I want him in the loop. Let him know about yer investigation, too. His legal skills will come in handy when yer cyber snooping and questionable contacts get ye' into trouble."

"What do ye' want to do now?" David asked.

"Get Braham geared up. He'll need a uniform, weapons, greenbacks, a wee bit of gold. I want him to go back with everything he needs. After three and a half years of war, I'm sure Sean the first is pressed for funds. How long will it take ye' to gather supplies?"

"Four or five hours, and I'll probably need the plane."

"Kevin can fly the prop plane or you can take the jet. The Mallorys won't notice Braham's absence before seven or eight o'clock. Unless Charlotte flies in a private plane, she won't get a flight out tonight. My bet is she and her brother will be here first thing in the morning. Braham needs to be gone by then."

"I'll be in my office at the stallion complex if you need me. If I have to go out, I'll let you know." David gathered up his laptops in one arm. With his free hand, he tossed his empty bottle of water into the trashcan, then turned and left the house through the French doors.

Elliott moved to the window behind his desk and stared out over the paddocks. The office door opened behind him. He glanced over his shoulder and smiled as his wife came up beside him. He pulled her into his arms.

"Have I told ye' today how much I love ye'?"

She shook her head. "Not since I woke up."

"He put his hands to her cheeks, eased her head back for the kiss he planned to give her, but paused to gaze into her eyes. "I love ye', and I'll always be grateful to Cullen Montgomery for saving yer life."

"Did you tell Braham about Cullen's ghost?"

"No, and I don't intend to. Some stories don't need to be re-told."

He gave her a tender, lingering kiss, caressing her lips lightly with his tongue. The pads of his fingertips glided down her neck. Her hands threaded through his hair, now longer just for her. For moments like this.

"Are you giving Braham the brooch?"

"Oh, aye. I only needed to verify a few things."

She pulled away slightly and looked up at him. "Did you find the answers you wanted?"

He gathered her close, holding her tightly to his chest, his cheek pressed against her hair, relishing the sweet scent of her shampoo. "Most of them, but something doesn't seem right. I can't put my finger on it."

"Trust your intuition. Are you going to talk to Charlotte?"

He pushed Meredith's hair behind her ear and nibbled on her lobe, murmuring, "If it weren't for Braham, Kit and Cullen never would have found each other again. She would want me to do whatever he asks of me." He blew lightly on Meredith's neck, knowing it would tickle.

She giggled softly, and her laughter enchanted him.

"Even if you have reservations?" she asked.

He blew again, and she pressed her body firmly against his growing erection. Every time Meredith was in his arms, desire burned through him, and he wanted her now as much as he had the first night he met her in Scotland.

"I understand Charlotte not wanting to return for fear of being stuck there, but why would she object if he found another way?"

"Maybe she's already in love with him and doesn't want him to leave."

Elliott skimmed his hands down Meredith's hips. "He's leaving his love behind to honor his commitment to Lincoln. Honor I understand. But there's more."

Meredith held his look with a faint, sultry smile. "If he sees her, maybe it will be harder for him to say goodbye again. David told me she's an excellent surgeon, beautiful, and wealthy. What's not to love?"

"Maybe her wealth is the problem, since he would have nothing to offer her. Not even a name or family," Elliott said.

"Well, Braham has us."

The last rays of the dying sun fell softly through the window, crisscrossing Meredith's face with light and shadow. Perfect light to paint her chin and cheek and lips with his finger. "Yes, he does."

"I look forward to meeting Charlotte. I'll know right away if she's in love with him."

"And if she's not?"

Meredith rubbed against him "It could get complicated."

Elliott chuckled against her lips. "From personal experience, I know ye' can't fight love." He kissed her again, even more thoroughly. "When did we become such romantics?"

Her eyes sparkled with laughter. "When you decided you couldn't live without me."

21

MacKlenna Farm, Lexington, Kentucky, Present Day

ELLIOTT'S VOICE BLARED from a box on the kitchen wall. "Braham."

Braham jumped to his feet, then groaned, grabbing his side. Glancing at Mrs. Collins, he said, "What the hell was that?"

"If ye're still in the kitchen," Elliott continued, "please return to the office. Mrs. Collins, if ye're there, buzz me back."

Mrs. Collins pressed a button on the box. "We're both here, Doctor Fraser. I 'spect he's tired of listening to me blather on. He'll be right there." She picked up a plate of cookies. "Take these with you, David loves 'em."

Braham hoped Elliott was going to help him go home, because Braham didn't think he could tolerate any more fancy cars or talking boxes. He took the cookies and walked down the stately mansion's long hall and stopped at the foot of the center sweep of stairs, remembering the day Kit went into labor. Her water broke almost exactly where he was standing. It had been a day mixed with joy, fear, and a very long wait.

Cullen had passed out cigars, his face bright with exhilaration. At the time Braham had been elated for them both. Now, though, as a flood of recollections burst through the dam constructed to keep them in a hidden corner of his brain, a jumble of sorrow and loneliness overwhelmed him. He shook off the feeling, or tried to. Shoved the memories back behind the dam, or tried to. Stepped over the spot on the floor, scrubbing it from his conscious thought, or tried to. All he succeeded in doing was chastising himself for being full of regrets instead of being grateful he was still alive.

The door to the office was open. He knocked on the doorjamb. A young, strapping man, broad-shouldered and narrow of waist and hip, peered over Elliott's shoulder at the stack of papers he was holding. The lad had close-cropped brown hair and, when he turned toward Braham, revealed large brown eyes. He flashed Braham an easy smile. Braham recognized him for what he was—a powerful warrior.

"Come in. Sit." Elliott pointed to the man standing behind him. "This is David McBain. He's been busy since ye' showed up at the security gate." Elliott held up the stack of papers. "We know everything that's happened to ye' since ye' were supposedly found in the parking lot at the Cedar Creek Battlefield."

Braham's heart rate increased, but he steeled himself against showing emotion. He casually set the cookies on Elliott's desk and prepared to hear the word *no*. If Elliott did, in fact, turn him down, Braham would take his case to Meredith. He would not leave MacKlenna Farm without the brooch, even if he had to steal it.

"I believe yer story," Elliott said, "And because ye're my god-daughter's cousin, I've decided to loan ye' her brooch."

The words *loan ye'* swept away the top layer of tension Braham carried in his tight muscles. But only the top. What conditions would Elliott impose?

David picked up a few sheets of paper from the desk, came around to Braham's chair, and handed the pages to him. "We found reenactors willing to sell uniforms, pants, shirts, jackets, belts, boots, hats. Everything ye' need."

Braham thumbed through the pages, arching an eyebrow at the detail on the uniforms. Whoever made them knew what they were doing.

"You'll have to try them on, and a tailor will have to make adjustments, but we've been assured a complete uniform will be ready tonight," David said.

"As for weapons, those were harder to come by," Elliott said.

David flipped to the last page of pictures. "We did find a saber and two Colt revolvers. They're all in excellent condition, but I decided to go with these," he said, pointing to the pictures. "The revolvers are reproductions of the 1862 Pocket Navy .38 caliber. If I had my druthers, I'd send ye' back with an assault rifle, a sig, and a laser-guided furball."

The only thing Braham had understood was the word rifle.

Elliott held out an envelope. "David, hand this to him."

"Here's five hundred dollars in greenbacks," David said. "It's all we could find on short notice. Again, they're antiques, but I don't think this late in the war anyone will notice they're old."

"You've gone to a great deal of trouble and expense on my be-half."

Elliott sat back in his chair and folded his hands across his flat belly. A sly grin appeared on his face. "I can afford it. Kit would expect it, and Meredith told me if I didn't help ye' I would sleep alone tonight."

"Ye' need to rest now," David said to Braham. "Ye' been out of the war zone for a few weeks. Ye' need to prepare for going back in. Ye're still recovering from major surgery, too, which likely will slow ye' down a wee bit, and ye'll be more afraid to take a punch that wouldn't have bothered ye' verra much before. The guest room is prepared. Take a shower. Rest. When ye' get up, it'll be time to go." David tapped his forehead. "Ye' need to be ready up here."

His speech confirmed David was also a soldier, as Braham had suspected. Braham shook his hand. "Thank you."

David clasped Braham's shoulder. "I'd go with ye', but this isn't my war."

"Mrs. Collins has prepared Kit's room. Top of the stairs. Go rest," Elliott said.

Braham nodded. "I do have one question. Are you going to call the Mallorys?"

Elliott scratched underneath his chin with his buffed thumbnail, thinking. "If I don't hear from them this evening, I'll call the doctor in the morning and make arrangements to return her vehicle."

Braham tapped the envelope against his fingers. "When you talk to her, tell her…tell her I'm sorry I didn't thank her for all she did for me. And tell Jack, too. They're good people."

Elliott picked up his bottle of water, unscrewed the lid, lifted the bottle to his mouth, then paused. "I'll tell ye' what Meredith said, and ye' can take it or leave it." Without taking a sip, he screwed the top back on and set the bottle down. "She said, 'This won't be the end—'"

Meredith entered the room saying, "—of the Charlotte and Braham story. I predict this is only a crossroads. What lies ahead will be full of potholes, but if you are meant to be together, which I believe you are, you'll find a way through them, around them, and over them. And I look forward to the day when we're *all* sitting in this room together, Charlotte and Jack included."

Braham hugged her. Meredith had inherited the best of Cullen and the best of Kit.

22

MacKlenna Farm, Lexington, Kentucky, Present Day

BRAHAM WAS JOLTED awake in a not-too-soft, not-too-hard bed. His feet didn't even hang off the end. The only other bed he'd ever slept in that fit him perfectly, other than his own, had been at the Mallory Plantation. He bolted upright, and groaned when his sudden move pulled on the healing incision. More carefully, he leaned over and switched on the bedside lamp. According to the clock, he had slept for almost five hours. Driving, he had discovered, was stressful. His arms were still sore from gripping the steering wheel.

He looked around the room, since he hadn't paid much attention to the furnishings earlier. He wasn't an art aficionado, but he could identify the work of a handful of artists. Kit MacKlenna Montgomery was one of them. On the wall opposite the bed were paintings of Chimney Rock, South Pass and the Blue Mountains. They were painted from sketches she had made during their trip west in 1852.

He eased to his feet and headed toward the bathroom. A Union Cavalry jacket hung on the back of the door. He ran his hand over the wool and checked the hand-stitched seams where the lining and wool met. Excellent quality and workmanship.

Stacked on a chair nearby were trousers, a cotton muslin shirt, and a slouch hat. A pair of spit-shined cavalry boots sat on the floor.

How could anyone have entered his room without making

noise? He'd already noticed the floorboards creaked, and he was a light sleeper with excellent hearing. Either he'd been knocked out or someone with unusual stealth had come in and left the clothes. He rubbed his head. There weren't any bumps.

David McBain.

Braham had a new appreciation of the soldier's abilities.

On the desk under the window, he found a belt and buckle and leather-end suspenders, every item made with the highest grade leather. An old, moth-eaten uniform would have been fine with him, but as he had discovered, Elliott Fraser expected the highest quality in his animals, the people who worked for him, and goods and services he purchased. He wouldn't have purchased a moth-eaten anything.

Braham remained in the hot shower for a long time, letting his mind drift to Charlotte. If she knew there was another brooch, she'd call Elliott immediately to explain the real reason she wouldn't take Braham back to his time. Would Elliott still loan him the brooch if he knew Braham intended to stop Lincoln's assassination? Probably not. But David would understand why Braham had to stop an assassin's bullet.

He took his time dressing. Each article of clothing added another tug on his heart and mind, pulling him back into his century. He stood in front of the mirror, gazing at his reflection. At some point in the past four years he had become a soldier in his appearance, thinking, and behavior. He was no longer a lawyer, friend, cousin, nephew, uncle. He was a major in the United States Cavalry, on assignment to the President. He picked up his hat and gauntlets and mentally saluted his commander-in-chief.

Braham found Meredith and Elliott in the office, sitting in front of a blazing fire, talking quietly. He cleared his throat to announce his presence. "Sorry. I didn't plan to sleep so long."

"Wow," Meredith said, looking him over. She came close, fiddled with the jacket, and patted the shoulder boards. "I don't think we need the tailor. Do you, Elliott?"

"It's a perfect fit. David has a good eye."

"Do you have your money?" Meredith asked.

Braham tapped his chest. "Yes."

David entered the room behind him. "Here's the rest of it. A saber and Colt revolvers."

Braham tested the weight of the revolvers. "Did you fire them?"

David laughed. "Aye. I found the sights on the revolvers a wee bit crude, at least compared to today's standards. Be careful." He slapped Braham on the shoulder. "If ye' come back, I'll take ye' out and let ye' shoot with some real weapons."

Braham threw him a crooked grin as he strapped on the holster and saber. "You make it tempting, but I won't be back."

Elliott picked up the rosewood box from the desk, opened it, and removed the ruby brooch.

"The first time I saw this, it was pinned to Kit's dress. She was only a baby. We had no idea where she came from. We thought someone had abandoned her. I hope it brings you the happiness it has brought her." He handed it over. "Good luck, Major."

Braham turned the brooch over and over in his shaking hand. "I don't know how it works. Kit never told me."

"I've never seen it open, but I know how it works." Elliott showed him the clasp. "Press right there, and the stone will pop open to reveal the Gaelic. Once you speak the words, ye'll go through a fog. When the fog lifts, ye'll be someplace else. Hopefully right here, but in another time. Don't touch anything here. Whatever you're touching when you go into the fog seems to make the trip, too. Good luck, lad."

Elliott, Meredith, and David moved to the other side of the room. Elliott wrapped his arms around his wife. David snapped to attention and saluted. Braham saluted him in return. Blowing out a breath, he opened the brooch, drew his revolver, then spoke the words engraved on the stone, *"Chan ann le tìm no àite a bhios sinn a' tomhais an gaol ach's ann le neart anama."*

23

Mallory Plantation, Richmond, Virginia, Present Day

CHARLOTTE HADN'T CALLED Braham all day, and neither had Jack. They had decided to give him time alone to think. In hindsight, it had been a mistake. She had worried all day. After seeing her last patient, she switched on-call schedules with a colleague and rushed out to the plantation. When she got there, the house was dark and her car was gone. Uneasiness spread over her and the hairs on her neck stood up.

Braham could be asleep, and the car could be in the garage…or it could be wrapped around a tree, floating in the river…

Stop it.

The police would have called if her car had been in an accident. He's not hurt, he's only…what? Sitting in the dark?

She grabbed the house remote from the glove box and pushed a button to turn on every light in the house. Braham might want to sit in the dark, but she wasn't going inside without the lights on. She wasn't afraid of the dark, but she was afraid of bumping into a burglar.

She entered, but left the front door open. "Braham. *Braham.*"

There wasn't a sound. No radio. No TV. No YouTube videos playing on the iPad. She knocked on his bedroom door. The bed was empty, made without a wrinkle or a ripple. It was so tightly made, in fact, a quarter would bounce off.

Check the kitchen.

She rushed to the kitchen, calling him. Still no answer. There were no dirty dishes in the sink. No crumbs on the counter. The newspaper was neatly folded, as if it had never been opened. The den was empty and so was the library. He wasn't napping on either of the sofas. She searched Jack's office for a note. Nothing. She stood at the desk rubbing her forehead, thinking. Where could he have gone? If he'd taken the car, he could have crashed it and be back in the hospital. But why would he have taken the car out onto the road?

She opened the middle desk drawer. The pizza money was gone. Her heart sank to her stomach, then to her knees, and then puddled on the floor.

Scenarios fueled her imagination. None of them good. Did he drive to get pizza? Surely not. Then where was her car? She hadn't checked the garage. She darted into the mud room and flung open the door, and for a moment was afraid to look. Her hand hovered over the light switch. Finally, she flipped it on and her heart sank.

Empty. No car. No Braham. Nothing. She slammed the door. A chill seeped into her bones. Where could he have gone? Her cell phone rang. She ran back through the house to get it. Jack's name flashed on the caller ID.

"Hey, have you heard from Braham?" she asked.

"No, which is why I was calling. To see how he's doing."

"I've searched the house, he's not here, and neither is the car. The pizza money is also gone." She tried to keep her rising anxiety under control. It wasn't working. "He could be in a ditch dying."

"Don't get your panties in a wad," Jack said. "It's easy enough to find him. Hold on and let me turn on my Mac. Both of our cars have tracking devices."

"*What?* Why?"

"Call me paranoid. But the thought of a stalker harassing either one of us was not a pleasant one. I decided to take precautions."

"Where could he have gone? If he went out driving, he would have left the lights on in the house. But it was dark when I came in." She closed the front door and paced. "What's taking you so long?"

"Relax. Go pour a drink. Just another minute or two."

Charlotte went back to the library, poured a whiskey, and sipped. She pulled the rubber band out of her hair and gave her scalp a brisk finger massage. "I don't even see the cat."

"The cat's probably in the barn, and Braham's in Lexington."

"*He's where?*"

Nothing but her own strong will was holding her together at the moment. "He's lost his frigging mind. He drove a hundred and thirty-something miles. Are you kidding?"

"Lexington, Kentucky, sis. Not Virginia. He drove *five hundred miles.*"

"He's never driven a car before and he drove to Kentucky? Who is this guy? Superman?"

Jack let out a rumble of a laugh. "He's got balls. I'll give him that."

She wasn't much of a judge when it came to male genitalia, but yep, the guy definitely had balls. "Why'd he go to Lexington?"

"Well…he's at MacKlenna Farm. I'll let you hazard a guess."

She shook her head, shoving her annoyingly curly, now-disheveled hair off her face. "If he wanted to go to the farm, why didn't he ask one of us to take him? We would have been happy to go ourselves. Are you going to call the Fraser guy?"

"No. I don't want to show our hand. Braham doesn't know we know where he is. I'd like to keep him in the dark until I show up at the farm tomorrow."

"Until *we* show up. I'm going, too. Do you think this is about returning to his time? If so, running away won't get him home."

"Only one way to find out. I'm going to book a flight out of Atlanta to Lexington, leaving first thing in the morning. Can you get away?"

"I'll have to make some phone calls, but I can probably work it out. I don't know how soon I can get a flight leaving Richmond, though."

"Call Richmond Private Jet Charter and schedule a flight. We'll need return transportation anyway. I'll text you the number."

"What about my car?"

"We'll pay someone to drive it back. See how quickly the charter company can get you out in the morning and then call me back."

She dialed the number in Jack's text and was told it would cost a premium for an early-morning flight. She decided to let Jack negotiate a reduced rate later and booked the flight.

He called her before she could call him back. "What'd you find out?"

She drew circles and squares around the notes she'd made on a yellow legal pad. "They can get me to Lexington by seven in the morning. What about you?"

"Seven-thirty. I'll reserve a rental car. Get some sleep and try not to worry. We know he's safe."

"You're kidding, right?"

"Yep. Night, sis, and remember—"

She drew a huge circle around Braham's name, which she'd written in big bubble letters. "I know. Worrying doesn't take away tomorrow's sorrows, it only steals today's strength. And at this point, I don't have much to spare. Goodnight."

24

MacKlenna Farm, Lexington, Kentucky, Present Day

CHARLOTTE ARRIVED AT Lexington Blue Grass Airport at seven sharp. She'd only had a couple of hours of sleep, and one of those hours had been on the flight. A whole range of emotions had plagued her during those sleepless hours.

Although she was angry and hurt, guilt topped the list. She never should have left Braham alone. She had time available to take off work, yet she had left him to his own devices because of her obsessive-compulsive need to be at the hospital. If Braham had tried to explain to the Frasers who he was, they probably had him arrested. She and Jack might be spending the day trying to get him out of either jail or a mental hospital.

At baggage claim, near the terminal's exit, she sat ramrod-straight in an uncomfortable molded plastic chair, fidgeting because Jack's flight had been delayed thirty minutes. She tapped her foot and cursed under her breath with her mobile phone in the left hand while typing one-handed on her iPad with the other. Communications from staff filled her inbox, but nothing from Braham. She laughed then. He couldn't send her an email. He didn't have a computer, and he didn't know her address. And what would he say?

Hi Charlotte, I stole your car and drove to Kentucky.

Someone tapped her on the shoulder. "You ready?"

She jerked her head up to see her brother. "I'm sorry. I didn't know your plane had landed."

His eyes widened in frank appreciation. He hadn't shaved yet, and the stubble rasped when he scratched his chin. "So what's up with the dress? I haven't seen you in anything other than jeans or scrubs in months."

She shrugged. "Thought if I was going to pay for a private plane, I should at least look like I could afford it."

He held out his hand. "You can afford it. You have millions and never spend a dime. But give me the bill. I'm working a story angle, so it's a business deduction for me."

She slapped the receipt into his hand. "Gladly. It's all yours. You make more money than I do." She snapped her iPad cover shut and shoved it into her bag, and they headed over to the car rental office. "Do you have a plan for today? Are we going to treat Braham like a recalcitrant child?"

"Wouldn't work," Jack said. "We'll have to play it by ear. It depends on what he's told them."

"I doubt he's told them the truth. He'll probably tell them his ancestor and Meredith's ancestor were business partners, and he was in town visiting and wanted to meet her. At least it's what I'd say."

As usual, every woman they passed gave Jack a once-over. He was movie-star handsome, but he could be a jerk. "Slow down before I twist my ankle."

He glanced down at her feet. "You're wearing four-inch heels. You're liable to not only twist your ankle but break your neck." Jack's phone beeped with a text message. He read the message and returned the device to his inside jacket pocket. "Have you thought about what you're going to say to Braham when you see him? Probably not. Which is why you're all dressed up." Jack eyed her closely. "You're even wearing mascara. *Charlotte has a boyfriend.*"

Her face heated. "Stop it. Why do you like to embarrass me?"

"Because it's fun."

"I think it's bullying. And I didn't dress up for *him*, but I do have a few well-chosen expletives written down."

Jack held the door to the car rental office open for her. "Your vocabulary doesn't extend beyond two four-letter words—damn and hell. Maybe you should practice them on me first. Let me hear them. Give me your best shot."

She gestured with her middle finger, hiding it behind her purse so only he could see.

Jack threw back his head laughing.

Fifteen minutes later they were pulling out of the airport in a rental car. "What's the address?" Charlotte asked.

He handed her a sheet a paper. "Enter this into your phone and tell me where to go."

They followed the directions to New Circle Road and exited on Old Frankfort Pike. "This road is beautiful. The rolling hills and white plank fences remind me of Virginia."

"Until 1792, it was Virginia." Jack drove slowly so he could enjoy the view along with her.

"How long has MacKlenna Farm been in the family?" she asked.

"It went bankrupt a few years ago and Fraser bought it out of bankruptcy."

"How sad it's not in the family now," she said.

"Well, it still is, sort of. Fraser's ten-times-great-grandfather was the illegitimate son of James MacKlenna, who founded the farm."

"You've got to be kidding," she said. "How'd they ever figure it out? They had to at least go back to the seventeen hundreds."

"The article I read last night said Meredith discovered the connection while she was doing genealogy research in Edinburgh. James MacKlenna immigrated to America and fought in the American Revolution. He was given the land as payment. He then returned to Scotland, where his brothers and sisters lived. He married and had a son, Thomas, who came to America and started MacKlenna Farm."

"I wonder if there're any records in Ireland about the parents of the Mallorys who started our plantation."

"If anyone ever traced the family, I never heard about it, or never heard anything other than the Mallorys were Ulster-Scots."

"What is Ulster-Scots?"

"Presbyterians from lowland Scotland who settled in Ulster and subsequently immigrated to America."

"Hmm. You know what we need? An Aunt Mimi."

"A what?"

"I have a friend who has an Aunt Mimi. She's the family geneal-ogist and has given all her siblings a binder with their entire family history. It's pretty cool."

"Maybe you can hire her to trace the Mallorys."

"I'll ask." Charlotte's phone beeped and she checked the mes-sage. The office was confirming she'd be back tomorrow for her appointments. She responded quickly and turned off her phone. She didn't want any interruptions when she met with the Frasers. She rolled down her window to breathe in the cool, crisp air. "If I can't hire Aunt Mimi, let's go to Ireland and trace the family."

"Sure. When are you going to take time off?" Jack pulled up to a security gate and leaned out to address the guard. "My name is Jack Mallory. I'd like see Elliott Fraser. I don't have an appointment."

The guard pushed a button and the gate opened. "Follow the road. You'll end up right in front of the mansion."

Charlotte frowned, gave her head a single shake. "This doesn't make sense. Why have a security guard if you're going to let everyone in?"

Jack looked at her and arched a brow slowly. "I was thinking the same thing."

"How would you explain it in a book?"

He gave her a brief snort. "I'd say the people in the car were expected."

Charlotte turned and glanced back at the guard. "He's on the phone now. So he's probably letting someone know we're on the way. But they can't know who we are or why we're here."

"Don't be so sure."

Charlotte looked out the window at the paddocks and barns. "This farm is incredible. They've spent millions on the grounds alone."

"According to the article I read, Fraser has millions to spend." Jack stopped the car in front of the mansion. "Let's go see Braham."

She followed Jack to the front door. "I hope he's not in jail."

A tall, lean, good-looking man with graying hair opened the door. "Jackson Mallory. Doctor Mallory. Please come in. I'm Elliott Fraser."

Jack and Elliott shook hands. "We met several years ago. The year Big Brown won the Derby. You were with Sean MacKlenna."

"2008." Elliott's dark eyes went curiously blank for a moment. Then they snapped back, and he said. "I'm sorry. I don't remember."

"I was with a large, rowdy group of investors and it was a quick introduction."

Elliott gave a relieved sigh. "Thank you. I'm usually good with names." He gestured toward a beautiful woman with short, dark brown hair who was coming down the stairs. "My wife, Meredith."

Charlotte extended her hand to Elliott and then to Meredith. "It's nice to meet you both."

"Welcome to MacKlenna Farm," Meredith said.

A line of concern drew Meredith's brows together as her eyes searched Charlotte's face. She smiled at Meredith but quickly broke eye contact. What did Meredith see in her face to cause such concern? Charlotte didn't know, but couldn't worry about it right now. She glanced around, for once ignoring exquisite antiques and paintings, searching for Braham, surprised he hadn't made an appearance already.

"Shall we go into my office?" Elliott said. "I know you must have questions."

A man with a military demeanor entered the room through French doors opening onto a back portico. Elliott didn't introduce him. The man didn't sit, but remained standing, close to the doors.

"Where's Braham?" Jack asked.

"Please sit down," Elliott indicated the sofa. He and Meredith sat in matching chairs facing them.

"Where's—" Jack said.

Elliott held up his hand. "Before I explain, let me tell ye' a story. A few years ago, the owners of this farm, Sean, we called him the sixth, and Mary MacKlenna, were killed in a car accident. Their adopted daughter and only child, Kit, survived the crash. While going through her father's papers, she discovered a letter, a journal, and a Celtic brooch with a large ruby at its center."

Charlotte gasped.

Elliott continued, "Kit used the brooch to go back in time, where she met Cullen Montgomery. She and Cullen married—"

Jack interrupted, "And started a winery which is going strong today." He glanced at Meredith. "Your winery."

Elliott sat back, wearing a wry grin, and watched the exchange.

"You're correct," Meredith said. "When Kit crossed the Oregon Trail in 1852, she met her cousin."

"Ohmygosh," Charlotte said. "Braham's her cousin?"

Meredith nodded.

Goosebumps peppered Charlotte's arms. "He knew Kit was from the future. Which is why—"

"He never seemed as shocked as he should have been," Jack said. "Then he also knew Kit had a brooch. But why did he come here? Her brooch would be in the past with her."

"It must not be," Charlotte said. "That's why Braham's here. To use her brooch instead of mine."

"He was here," Meredith said.

Charlotte leaped to her feet. "*Was? No. He has to be here.*"

The man by the door took a step forward. Elliott held up his hand and the man moved back.

"We did an investigation, beginning with when he was discovered in the parking lot at the Cedar Creek Battlefield, through when he left Mallory Plantation yesterday morning. We decided he was who he said he was. Once that decision was made, there was no reason not to loan him the brooch."

"Did he tell you why he was so determined to return to his time?" Charlotte asked.

Elliott crossed his legs and pinched the crease in his kakis. "He said Lincoln was waiting for the information he collected while in Richmond."

Charlotte buried her face in her hands, shaking her head. "He's

going back to stop the assassination by killing Booth." She looked
up into Elliott's stark white face. He'll change history in a major way,
one sure to impact all of us."

Elliott and Meredith shared a grim glance. "Which I assume is
the reason you wouldn't take him back?"

Charlotte nodded. "That and other reasons."

"He said you were too afraid to go," Meredith said.

"It's true. I've never been so scared in my life. I spent six weeks
in Afghanistan and was frightened a few times, but I didn't live in
terror the way I did going back in time, especially when I landed in
the middle of the real Battle of Cedar Creek. I had hoped Braham
would want to stay here. Plus, I have a horrible fear of getting stuck
there if I go back again."

"Kit went twice," Elliott said.

"But she must have stayed the second time. Was it her choice, or
was she stuck?"

"Braham confirmed what we read in her journal," Elliott said.
"It was entirely her choice."

"Then how did you end up with the brooch?" Jack asked.

Elliott pointed to the large mahogany desk. "She left it in a se-
cret compartment of this desk. If Braham didn't arrive at
MacKlenna Farm, he promised to go there and put the brooch back.
If he did put it back, it would be there now."

"But you haven't looked," Jack said.

"I will, right now." Elliott opened the drawer in the center of the
desk, reached in, and a secret compartment opened in the top. He
pulled out a small rosewood box, opened it, and turned it for all to
see. A ruby brooch, identical to Charlotte's except for the stone, sat
nestled in satin.

Charlotte gasped again. "Oh, my God. He made it. When did he
leave?"

"Late last night," Meredith said.

"Time doesn't necessarily move at the same rate here and there.
Braham could already be in Washington. He could already have
killed Booth." She dug through her purse for her smartphone. "I've

got to check."

"There's no need to check," Elliott said. "If he had changed history, our frame of reference would not be to Booth and the assassination. Matter of fact, we wouldn't care whether he went back in time at all."

"Booth traveled around. Braham will have a hard time finding him, especially if Lincoln sends him out on another mission."

"We have a small window of time to stop him," Jack said.

"*We?* I'm not going back. I don't understand how the magic works, and I might not be able to return."

"Char, you don't have to go," Jack said. "I will."

Charlotte jumped up. "No you won't. I'll never see you again. You're too impulsive, Jack. You do things without considering the repercussions. History will change because you're there snooping around. I won't let you go." She paced the room. "What I don't understand is why we have identical brooches. Are there others?"

"There's one more," Elliott said. "An emerald."

Jack's face tensed with excitement. "How do you know?"

"When Meredith and I met, we discovered my great-great-great-great-great—"

"I read your story in a magazine article last night," Jack said.

"So it makes you the last MacKlenna, even though you carry another name," Charlotte added.

Elliott smiled. "Not anymore. Our son Cullen is the last."

"To answer your question, the MacKlenna family has one of the brooches. The Mallorys have another. Do we have a family connection?" Jack asked.

"I don't know," Elliott said. "Mallory is Irish, not Scottish."

"We're Ulster Scots," Jack said.

"From the lowlands. The MacKlennas are from the Highlands. Meredith is the genealogist in the family, and her cursory research last night didn't unearth a connection. If there is one, she'll find it, though. Where did your brooch come from?"

"It was mailed from a law firm in Edinburgh," Charlotte said. "I haven't contacted them."

"If you'll give me the address, we'll check it out when we go to Scotland for the holidays. I have a feeling our lines will connect at some point."

"Find the other one and destroy them all," Charlotte demanded. "They're dangerous. I wish I'd never opened my mail."

Jack put his arm around her shoulders. "It's okay, sis. We'll find a solution."

"Let's go home." Her voice sounded thick to her own ears.

Elliott handed Jack a business card. "Send me the address and any other questions you have."

"I'm not sure I trust the topic to email."

"You have a secure system and so do we," Elliott said. "David made sure of it."

Jack's face pinched with clear irritation. "How do you know?"

"As I explained earlier. We investigated Braham's story. You were part of the investigation."

Jack's face relaxed. "I would have done the same. Is there anything else we need to know?" Meredith and Elliott exchanged significant glances. He squeezed her arm affectionately. "No. Nothing else."

They escorted Jack and Charlotte to the front door. "Your vehicle should be parked in front of your house by the time you get home. When we learned you had chartered a jet, we took the liberty of having it delivered. If you decide to go after Braham, please let us know."

"We're not going," Charlotte repeated, shaking her head.

Jack shook Elliott's hand. "We'll keep in touch."

Charlotte and Jack drove away, both lost in their own thoughts. Not a word was uttered between them during the drive back to the airport. Jack returned the rental car, and they walked over to the private plane terminal and boarded their plane, which was already standing by.

About a half hour into the flight, Jack said, "We have to go, Charlotte."

"No, we don't," she said. "The stone is dangerous, and so many things could go wrong. We don't know how it works, or why, or where it could take us next. I don't trust it, and you shouldn't either."

"I do trust it, and I'll go by myself."

"That. Will. Never. Happen."

Something flickered deep in Jack's eyes, and he shook his head slowly. "Then you're responsible for whatever happens to Lincoln and the history of disenfranchised people in the United States."

She glared at him, struggling to find words necessary for a coherent rebuttal, but none came, and she gave up. "You can't blame that all on me." She punched down on the arm of the seat. "You're brilliant, successful, drop-dead gorgeous, but you're impulsive and spontaneous. You act on whims, and, while it makes for great fiction, in real life, actions can have unintended and disastrous consequences."

She tapped her chest with her fingertip repeatedly, and swallowed against tears. "You're unaware of the stress and consequences you cause me, or the impact your thoughtless choices have on my life. On me."

Charlotte turned to stare out the window at the beauty and calm of the blue sky while she tried to breathe through her urge to either sob or scream.

When her breathing returned to normal, she continued, "I thought the monastery would help you learn to see more than one step ahead. Instead, all it did was provide coping skills to deal with regret and remorse when you finally realize you messed up. Again.

"Like two days ago," she turned in her seat and faced him squarely. "Braham needed a buddy. I'm not his buddy. I'm his doctor. You two were getting on famously. But you were focused on your new book proposal. I ended up with him in Washington when you bailed, and it was an upsetting day for him. You let him down, Jack. You let me down.

"I have a very inflexible schedule. I couldn't be there twenty-four/seven, because I work at a job where I have no control over when I'm needed. I was counting on you to help acclimate Braham to this time, to technology. I wanted you to make him want to stay. And what did you do? You left him by himself and now he's gone."

Jack's face was a billboard of remorse. "I'm sorry. I didn't—"

"You're full of regret now. But if you had taken the time to think about the impact of your actions on anyone else…" She threw up her hands and swallowed, hard, again. "Forget it. Some day you might learn to base your decisions on logical thought, not emotion."

Jack slammed the cover to his iPad and tossed the device on the seat in front of him. "You're not without blame, Charlotte. I screwed up. I accept it, but can you? You never should have brought him here."

Her chest tightened and anxiety ambushed her. "I couldn't let him—"

The astonished look on his face instantly changed to total disbelief. "Did someone name you God, and then fail to send the message to the rest of the world telling us you were in charge?"

"We're not talking about me."

"Then maybe we should. You didn't think about the consequences of your actions either, so don't give me grief about my inadequacies."

She adjusted her seat, leaned back, and closed her eyes. "We're done talking."

"We have to go after him. You have a responsibility to clean up this mess."

"A mess I didn't make," Charlotte said in a dismissive voice, refusing to acknowledge there was any truth in what Jack had said.

He sat rigid in his seat. "Listen to yourself. Sometimes you're off-the-wall crazy."

She had learned long ago to be careful, to edit what she said to him. After all, he was a lawyer and a wordsmith. When it came to their *discussions*, she couldn't compete with him. He always spotted holes in her arguments and threw them back at her with a blazing, fastball pitch.

But he was right. She had messed up. Braham should have died in Chimborazo, and now she had a responsibility to clean up her mistakes. But she adamantly refused to go back in time to make it happen. There had to be another way. She was an intelligent person and could solve this dilemma without putting her life in danger again.

25

Mallory Plantation, Richmond, Virginia, Present Day

CHARLOTTE HAD ALWAYS seen herself as a pragmatist, quick to make surgical decisions and expedient by nature, but personal decisions required time, thought, analysis, and more thought.

At the hospital, she remained a hundred percent focused, but she struggled with the dilemma of what to do about Braham and the assassination. She had gotten home after a thirteen-mile run, yet her head was as jumbled as it had been when she set out two hours earlier.

The situation had to be resolved somehow before she went nuts. Going nuts, though, was preferable to going back in time and dodging bullets and threats.

If she was ever going to find a solution, she first had to patch things up with Jack. She hadn't spoken to him since the flight home from Kentucky days earlier, and she missed him terribly.

Since she had the night off, it was time to have a chat with her brother. Should she apologize? For what? Jack was the one who skipped out and left Braham to his own devices.

If she didn't intend to apologize, then she needed to forgive him and move on. But move on to what? Braham was still an issue. The problem wasn't only about forgiving Jack. It was about going back in time and keeping Braham from changing history.

This was another red-light moment in her life. She had taken a chance, ripped through the last one, and look what happened. She had created a mess. She might as well run another one. It couldn't get any worse.

Wait a minute. The consequences could be a lot worse. She could get shot. She could be thrown into prison. She could...

Yes, she could even die, but she could also die in the next five minutes sitting in her living room. Her mother had suffered a fatal attack and died in her chair at work. A tight tug in Charlotte's gut caused a constriction around her heart. The loss of their mother had been traumatic, which was probably why she and Jack clung so tightly to each other.

Whew. Forty degrees outside and she was burning up. She grabbed a bottle of cold water, went out onto her screened-in porch, and looked out over her garden. Everything had been cut back to enhance next season's growth. She loved the beauty of Richmond in the spring. If she and Jack went back in time now, they might be spending next spring in Washington in the year 1865, long before the cherry blossom trees had arrived from Japan.

She rolled her cold water bottle along her forehead, from one side to the other. Was she really considering going back? Yep, she was. There was no other way. Braham had to be stopped.

Okay, then. Let's do it.

Two hours later, she marched into Jack's office at the mansion. He didn't bother to stop typing or turn away from his dual monitors. "Hey, sis. What's up?"

She plopped down in a chair on the other side of the desk. "I've made a decision."

"About what?" To be annoying, he continued typing. "A date Friday night? What you're going to do this afternoon? How many miles you're going to run this weekend?" He sat back in his chair and swiveled around to face her. He let the silence lengthen before asking, "Tell me your decision. I'm all ears."

She drummed her fingers on the edge of the desk. "You're also a butthead. But you know it already, don't you? And you also know *exactly* what I'm talking about."

He was pissed and hurt, and she was confused and scared. They would dance around each other until they found their way again.

He came around to the front of the desk, leaned against it, and crossed both his ankles and his arms. There was a glint in his eye and a half-smile he couldn't contain. He knew damn good and well what she was going to say, but he wasn't going to let her do it easily.

There was an uneasy rumble in her stomach. "Stop smirking. This isn't funny."

He held up his hands in a mock dramatic gesture. "I don't know what you're talking about."

Sometimes she wanted to haul off and smack him. It was a darn shame they had outgrown wrestling matches. "You were wrong to go off and leave Braham alone, but I forgive you. I want you to go with me to…" The next part snagged on a logjam in her throat. She grabbed a bottle of water off the desk, took several sips, and then tried again. "I want you to go with me to…to stop Braham."

He bit his lip, seeming to concentrate, then nodded as if he'd come to a decision. It was all for show, and she wanted to smack him, but it *was* part of the game.

"When do you want to leave?" he said finally, with a twinkle.

"As soon as I can arrange time off. I don't know how much I'll need. Maybe the rest of the year. Maybe more. It will be a setback for my career, but right now my sanity is a bigger concern."

He hauled her into a bear hug. "You're making the right decision."

She hugged him back. "Then why don't I feel better?" She pulled out of the embrace. "I'm going to the hospital tomorrow to talk to my colleagues. See if I can work out a schedule."

"I'll do the same. My agent will need to reschedule a few book signings. She's expecting an outline for my next book, so I'll have to promise to have one ready as soon as I get back." He picked up a legal pad and pen and jotted down a few notes. "No big deal, though."

"What about the plantation and your cat?" she asked, petting the animal curled up on top of the desk.

He continued writing. "We do have a farm manager, even

though he doesn't have much to manage right now."

Her phone beeped, and she checked the message. Ken was coming to Richmond and wanted to meet for dinner. She texted back a simple *yes*. "I'm on call tomorrow night, but on Sunday, let's have dinner and talk about what we need to do."

He tossed the notepad on the desk. "I'll add it to my calendar, but do you mind if we eat early? I might have something going on later."

She rolled her eyes. Her brother had more ex-girlfriends in Richmond then all of his single buddies combined. "Who is it this week? Susan? Laurie? Jennifer?"

He smirked. "Susan was last year. Laurie went back to her ex-boyfriend, and Jennifer was hinting about a ring for Christmas, and that was the end of that. This is someone new. I met her at Starbucks yesterday."

She stared at him for a long three-count. "Whatever." She shook her head, puzzled, but he was as puzzled by her opposite position on dating. "Okay, we have a date Sunday night, six-thirty. Text me where to meet, and I'll be sure we get through early enough so you can hook up with—" Charlotte threw up her hands, "—whoever."

When Jack couldn't contain his excitement any longer and started slapping high-fives with a poster of himself, she escaped the house, wondering if she was about to make another big mistake in her life.

Underestimating Braham was the first, trusting Jack was the second.

26

MacKlenna Farm, Lexington, Kentucky, December, 1864

W HEN THE FOG lifted, Braham found himself on MacKlenna Mansion's front portico. He leaned against the porch railing, waiting for a wave of nausea and dizziness to pass. He had no memory of his first passage through time, but this trip had been exactly as Kit had described—twisting and tumbling inside an enveloping, peat-scented fog.

He stared into the glow from the sidelights bracketing the door, much as he had years earlier when he had journeyed to the farm. Last time he'd been anxious in anticipation of a reunion of sorts. This time all he felt was a prevailing sense of dread—not about seeing Sean MacKlenna again, but about being pulled back in an atmosphere of uncertainty and violence—and the dread kept him nailed in place.

He glanced out over the surrounding fields. The colors of late fall were gone, and naked branches swayed and rustled in the breeze. Although the grounds were pristine, Braham's appreciation had been diminished by the beauty and refinement of the twenty-first century farm's manicured lawn, concrete driveway, and freshly-painted white plank fences.

He had also been tainted by being behind the wheel of a car, and how the slightest pressure of his foot against the pedal increased the vehicle's speed to a heart-stopping fifty miles an hour. For the rest of his life he would covet the sensation of high speeds and the accompanying rush.

Would he now view his proper world through soured lenses? Would his short time in the twenty-first century affect his life in the present? Of course it would. He intended to use what he had learned to change the future.

Still stiff from days of inactivity, he moved slowly toward the door, where he paused, his fist inches from the sturdy oak door. It's wasn't too late. He could still go back, but once he passed through the door…

No, he wasn't going back. He intended to save the President and would allow nothing to stop him.

The MacKlennas' longtime servant, Joe, answered the door. "Mistah McCabe, been a long time since you be here last." Joe ducked his head and opened the door wider. "Come in."

Braham handed over his slouch hat. "Afternoon, Joe. Is Mister MacKlenna in today?"

"Yes, suh. 'Spec he be happy to see you. You'n wait in a parlor."

The foyer spilled into the parlor, where the walls were painted a dark blue and matched the loch in the painting of Eilean Donan over the fireplace.

Braham glanced around the room to see what new pieces Sean had acquired since his last visit. Braham had used his memories of Sean's home for inspiration while furnishing his Washington townhouse. The house in Georgetown had been fully furnished, but the townhouse, across the street from the White House, hadn't included so much as a stick of kindling for the front room fireplace.

Braham turned toward the clomping of boot heels.

"Abraham McCabe." A grin split Sean MacKlenna's face, and he pulled Braham into a backslapping hug. "What are ye' doing here? Why aren't ye' in Washington?"

Braham opened his hand to reveal the ruby brooch.

Sean's jaw dropped. "Kit's brooch? How'd ye' get it?"

"It's a long story," Braham said.

"Then we need whiskey." He threw his arm across Braham's shoulders and directed him out of the room. "I heard birthing the last bairn was difficult for Kit. Heard she told Cullen to stay away from her or she was going home."

Braham laughed. "I doubt she held to the threat for very long."

As the two men walked down the hall, Braham glanced up the stairs, remembering the glorious weeks he spent here in 1852, and then again in 1858. "Where's Lyle Anne?"

"Resting. She'll be happy to see ye' again." He turned toward Joe. "Tell Sukey we've company for dinner."

"Yes, suh, Mistah Sean." Joe shuffled toward the back of the house, mumbling, "Yankee Major. Trouble comin'. Sur' nuff."

The masculine leather furniture in Sean's office hadn't been changed since Braham's previous visit. The surface of the large, burnished mahogany desk was unsullied by papers or knick-knacks. The shelved books in the cases were lined up flush with the edges. The trees outside the windows were kept clipped back to avoid interfering with the expansive view of the paddocks. So different, yet so similar to the look of Elliott's office.

Braham placed the brooch on the top of the desk. As he took away his hand, a chill hit him. He quickly clasped his hands behind his back. "I told Elliott I'd make sure the brooch was placed back inside the desk. I don't want my actions to interfere with Kit's future."

Sean reached into the center drawer, pushed the hidden lever, and the compartment popped open, revealing the rosewood box. He placed the brooch inside and closed the desk's secret pocket. "When you see him, you can let him know you fulfilled your obligation."

Braham gave Sean a direct look, while his gut tightened involuntarily. "I won't ever see him again."

"I canna believe it," Sean said. "Let's sit, and ye' can tell me how ye' got to the future to begin with, and what brought ye' here."

Once the men were settled in chairs by the fire with drinks in hand, Braham began his recitation, leaving nothing out except the primary reason Charlotte had refused to bring him back. Sean had made it clear years earlier, he didn't want to hear anything about the future.

Sean listened attentively, his chin resting pensively on his hand. "Both ye' and Cullen turned down the chance to live in the twenty-first century. Was there nothing to hold ye' there? Not even the love of a bonny lass?"

Braham sipped his drink, preparing to deny having any feelings for Charlotte. He cleared his throat. "Charlotte Mallory is a beautiful, intelligent woman."

Sean cocked an eyebrow. "And…"

Braham breathed in and out slowly to loosen the tightening knot in his throat. He propped his elbows on his knees, and after some more throat-clearings and hemmings and hawings, said, "I know the stone's legacy, but this situation is not the same as Cullen and Kit's."

"Once the stone's power touches ye', fighting the magic is useless. My great-great grandmother shared the mystery with my father. Auld granny said, 'The stone will take ye' to a world unknown, through amber light to a time not yer own, to the one of yer heart, and the truth ye'll be shown.'"

Braham dropped his head, shaking it and feeling his thoughts slosh around truths he preferred to ignore. Charlotte might come after him. If she did, the magic would weave its spell, and they might actually surrender to its sweet promise. But the promise could never be fulfilled in their case.

"There has to be a way to resist the magic before hearts are broken. I have no passion for living in the future, and Charlotte's passion is for twenty-first-century medicine. She would never give it up. It was different with Kit. She knew she belonged in this time."

Sean refilled both their glasses. "Being born in a time doesn't mean ye' belong there. Remember, when the stone weaves its magic, it reveals the truth."

"Nonsense." Braham heard the gravel in his voice. He took a big gulp of whiskey. "I need to get back to Washington."

"I'll take ye' to the Lexington railroad terminal in the morning. From there ye' can catch the Baltimore & Ohio Railroad to Washington City, assuming the Federals have control of the lines along the way. Several weeks back, Mosby derailed a Union train on the Baltimore & Ohio at Harpers Ferry and made off with a large payroll. They're calling it the Greenback Raid."

Braham flinched. "What's today's date?"

"23 November, 1864. How long have ye' been gone?"

"Five weeks. The President will believe I'm dead."

Sean steepled his fingers and tapped them at the tips. "Then he'll rejoice to learn yer' not. Do ye' want to send him a telegram?"

Braham shook his head. "I can't explain how I disappeared from the hospital in Richmond and then ended up in Kentucky. I'll wait until I return to Washington and tell him I've been holed up in Virginia until I was well enough to travel."

"Under the circumstances, I believe it's a wise decision."

A gunshot shattered a window in the office and crashed into a tea set on the table, scattering sharp fragments onto the Oriental rug. Stacked books toppled over, and Braham and Sean dropped to the floor.

Braham drew his revolvers. "What the hell's going on?"

Sean peeked over the edge of the sofa, his face white, eyes wide. "Deserters been causing trouble lately. I thought they were farther north."

A barrage of gunfire splintered the front door and pinged against the brick. The glass in two windows in the office exploded. Sean ducked.

Braham's heart pounded against his ribs so hard he thought they'd crack. He was battle-hardened. Why was he reacting like a raw recruit?

Gut-shot once, battle leery forever.

This wouldn't do at all. He wiped away the sweat streaming down his forehead and into his eyes, clouding his vision. He was a trained soldier. This was like getting back on a horse after a fall. He had to push on without being impeded by fear. He swallowed hard. It was true one of those bullets could rip another hole in him. And if it did, he'd either die or recover, but he wouldn't cower in a corner. He stiffened his spine.

He belly-crawled to the window to the sharp crack of bullets which flew over his head and ricocheted off the walls. "Keep yer head down," he yelled to Sean. Bullets smashed the wooden muntins separating the windowpanes, turning them into the sharp-edged projectiles which flew across the room and wedged into the furniture.

"Do you have guns in here?" Braham asked.

"Desk drawer."

"I'll cover you. Get 'em." He fired several rounds. "There're three in the tree line, two more by the paddock." He craned his neck to see the far side of the house. "Are you sure your family's inside?"

"Aye."

"Where're the slaves?"

"Don't have any. My father freed them years ago. Treating men like animals didn't sit well with a Scot's love of freedom. Most are still with us, working for wages. My men carry guns, but they're all in the fields. The women are in the cookhouse, and they have guards."

Braham raised his head far enough to see over the windowsill. The deserters were maintaining their positions. He kept them in his sights, but he couldn't afford to shoot and waste ammunition. He had to wait until they were closer.

"Will the men guarding the women come to the house?" he asked.

Sean shook his head as he cocked his rifle. "They have orders to lock the doors and protect the women and children."

Memories of being close to death warred once more with his soldier's battle instincts. "What about the men in the fields?"

"They won't hear the shots."

"Where's your warning system?"

"The bell is between us and them," Sean nodded his head toward the attackers while swinging his rifle toward the front of the house.

Braham swept his tongue across dry lips. "What's your plan for protecting the house?"

"Delay long enough to allow Lyle Anne and the children to get to the safe room and through the escape tunnel."

"If they haven't been watching the front door, they probably believe you're alone. It's a definite advantage for us."

Movement to the right caught Braham's attention. "They're about to make a move. How's your ammunition?"

"Got enough. And ye'?"

Braham steadied himself. "Elliott sent me back battle-ready. Thank God." As Braham spoke, he couldn't deny the raw sound of mingled worry and fear in his voice. The odds of repelling the attack weren't worth betting on. He sighed, hoping the carnage wouldn't extend to the family.

Firing in a single deadly salvo, five men rushed the porch. Braham got off several shots before taking cover behind the solid brick wall bordering the window.

"Did ye' hit any?" Sean asked.

"Maybe one."

"I got one rolling on the ground. Another one's limping."

Braham peered above the windowsill. "Three of 'em are hiding behind the columns. Is the front door bolted?"

"No," Sean said.

Braham ducked, giving vent to a loud expletive. "All hell's about to break lose. I'm going to the hall." He staggered to his feet. "If they burst through before I get into position, cover me."

He sprinted across the office to the door, then glanced quickly around the door fame toward the main entrance. Two men were peering through the sidelights, and the others were a shadowy presence behind them. Braham took aim and waited for the Rebels to crash through the front door. He held his arm steady and swallowed hard.

The Rebs fired indiscriminately into the front door, peppering it top to bottom. The gunfire shattered the glass panes in the sidelights, sending shards across the floor. There was a loud bang, and the door burst open, followed by three men barging in with guns blasting in both hands. Plaster on the ceiling crashed down and glass crunched beneath the scallywags' boots. The chandelier tinkled and paintings smashed to the floor, shattering the frames. Gunfire smoked up the foyer and bullets whistled around like hailstones in the gunpowder-scented air.

Braham fired through the smoke. One man dropped to his knees then fell face forward—dead or alive, hard to tell. Two others ducked into the parlor. He signaled to Sean his plan to go through the dining room and sneak up behind the intruders.

As they prepared to move out, Braham whispered, "If I get hit—"

"I'll send you back to Charlotte."

Sean dashed across the hall to take cover behind a cabinet. The Rebels pushed the parlor sofa to the doorway, creating a shield, then fired at them from behind it. While Sean returned fire, Braham ducked, rolled across the hall, jumped up, and ran for the dining room. He drew both Colts, then waited behind the wall separating the two rooms until he heard the floorboards squeak. Immediately he turned into the open doorway and fired, hitting both intruders.

"Got 'em." Braham kept his guns pointed at the two men as he cautiously approached the bodies. He kicked weapons out of their reach and checked for pulses. "Both dead."

"This one's dead, too," Sean said from the hall.

Braham holstered one revolver and reloaded the other as he approached the front door, heart pounding. He hugged the wall and peered out onto the porch. "One dead outside. Three inside. Don't see the fifth one." Braham inched out onto the portico, sweat pouring down the sides of his face, guns cocked.

Sean joined him at the doorway. "I think he's on the ground toward the side of the house."

"Cover me." Braham darted from one column to the other until he reached the end of the portico. "Looks dead from here." He kept his gun trained on the deserter while he jumped off the porch and checked the man's pulse. "He's not going anywhere. Believe we got all of 'em." Braham picked up the dead man's weapon and holstered his revolver. When he climbed back up onto the porch, he stopped at the bullet-riddled door.

"I asked Elliott the other day where the holes came from. Now I know."

Sean looked stunned. "As splintered as the door is, I'm not sure we can save it, but I'll ask the carpenter to do what he can."

They entered the house, crushing broken glass.

"It's over. Come on out," Sean said.

Joe was the first one to reach the foyer, shuffling and shaking his head. "Sur' nuff trouble came a home today."

Other house servants followed, carrying brooms and baskets, and talking low-voiced among themselves.

"Let's get these bodies out of here. Joe, send a message to the barn to bring a wagon, canvas, and a burial detail."

"Yes, suh, Mistah Sean."

Joe left the house, and the other servants went to work sweeping up glass and pieces of frames and plaster.

"I need a drink." Braham went into the office, dropped the dead man's gun on top of Sean's desk, and headed straight for the whiskey. His hand shook as he poured.

Sean joined him. "If ye' hadn't been here, I'd have died." He picked up the whiskey bottle, but set it down with a thud. His hand shook too much to pour.

Braham filled a crystal glass and handed it to Sean. "We should have jumped out of the window and run for help."

"Being a Scotsman is a blessing and a curse."

Braham took a long swallow, then refilled his glass. "Damn stubborn pride kept me in a fight with terrible odds."

Sean laughed. "Ye' didn't see me heading for the window, did ye'?"

"I'm glad to see you're both laughing."

Sean and Braham jerked around to find Lyle Ann, Sean's wife of ten years, standing in the doorway, hands on hips, dressed regally in a forest green silk gown, her hair still perfectly coiffed.

"Did you have to shoot up the house?"

Sean opened his arms and pulled her into an embrace, holding her close. Her knuckles turned white as she gripped his shoulders. "I had to give ye' and the bairns time to escape."

Lyle Ann gazed into her husband's eyes while she stroked his face tenderly. "You weren't supposed to put your life in danger. From the looks of the foyer, you should be on the floor bleeding, or worse."

Sean kissed her soundly before burying his face in her honey-colored hair. "Aye, if Abraham hadn't been here, I would be."

She glanced at Braham as if seeing him for the first time. The corners of her full lips turned up slightly in a constrained smile, but the tightness around her eyes remained, and her porcelain skin still lacked color. While the servants swept and picked up broken pottery and portrait frames, they kept glancing at her, as if their own composure depended on hers. If she broke down, they, too, would shatter into millions of pieces like the glass on the floor.

A tear slipped from the corner of her eye, but she didn't draw attention by wiping it away. Instead, she lifted her chin and kissed her husband's cheek. "I'll go settle the children. Their naps were interrupted." Her dress swished as she left the room, and her shoes made soft clicks against the floor.

"Sukey, Mr. McCabe will be staying for dinner, and please have a guest room prepared," Lyle Ann said.

Her exit was as smooth as her entrance.

Braham had never seen a woman so composed. Five minutes earlier her world had hung by a weak thread. Her home, her husband, her children, her life could have ended if he and Sean had failed. Kit, Charlotte, Lyle Ann…three Southern women with amazing strength and beauty.

For the first time he had a visceral sense of what it must have cost Charlotte to be caught up in a battle, dragged to Washington, and have her family and property threatened if she didn't do what the President required of her. She did what she had to do without complaint, but the experience had terrified her. After seeing the look on Lyle Ann's face, he realized Charlotte's fear had been the same or worse. Had anyone noticed her silent tears? Because he was sure she had to have shed at least one.

Braham finished his drink. "I'll help you haul off the bodies."

"Nay. Ye're bleeding."

Braham patted down the front of his jacket. "Can't be bad, I'm still standing." Then he noticed blood on his hand. "Must have gotten cut on the glass when I rolled across the floor. I'm very glad I didn't get shot again."

"I'll take care of the bodies," Sean insisted. "Ye' go find Sukey. Let her dress the wound, or I'll have to send ye' back to Charlotte for sure.

"I wouldn't be happy if you did."

"I hope I'm around when ye' finally admit ye're in love with her."

"It won't happen, and for God's sake, don't tell Kit I used her brooch. She'll send Cullen to find out what happened."

"Maybe he can convince ye' to go back," Sean said.

Braham shoved the guns into the smooth-grain leather holster. "There's no reason. I'm not in love with her, and she's not in love with me. She was my doctor. That's all."

Sean harrumphed.

Braham threw up his hands. "I'm going to find Sukey." He dragged himself along, trying to ignore a splitting headache, a burning incision, a fresh wound, and shaky legs. He'd thought driving fifty miles an hour had been scary. The prospect of getting shot again was a hell of lot worse.

27

En Route to Washington City, December, 1864

ON MONDAY FOLLOWING the MacKlennas' Thanksgiving Day celebration, officially set by President Lincoln as the fourth Thursday in November, Braham departed the farm, leaving behind a swarm of workmen repairing plaster and cutting new glass for the windows. Bloodstains had been meticulously scoured. Broken tables and chairs had been replaced with furniture brought down from the attic.

Though their faces were stoic, the MacKlennas couldn't mask their lingering fear. The war had hung around near their door, poking and prodding, for almost four long years. Finally, it had barged in with guns blazing, but thankfully he and Sean had emerged with only a handful of cuts and bruises, but the bloody skirmish still left people and property indelibly stained.

Braham and Sean drank and talked late into the night and, in a moment of weakness, Sean asked when it would all end. Braham gave him a peek into the future. Knowing the date seemed to lessen Sean's fears for his family and property. Although Braham didn't tell Sean about Lincoln's assassination, he did imply the outcome of the war, for many people in the South at least, would take decades, if not centuries, to accept. Now, as Braham prepared to leave Lexington, he wrestled again with the decisions he had made.

"All aboard," the station manager announced.

Braham lingered on the platform, statue-still, part of him pulled in a westerly direction, and the other determined to go east.

"All *abooaaard.*"

The train began to chug slowly out of the station. If he didn't go now, he wouldn't go at all. *Why am I hesitating?* Half the train passed the platform and still he didn't budge.

Charlotte's face flashed before his eyes. So did Lincoln's. Without honor, Braham had nothing. He had no choice. He snatched up the food basket Sukey had prepared for him and chased after the train. As the caboose neared the end of the platform, Braham grabbed the car's iron railing and hoisted himself aboard. He claimed a cracked leather seat in the back of the musty-smelling car, where he sat very still, staring off at nothing for a long time, with a gunmetal taste in his mouth.

The wheels clacked as they rolled off one rail onto the next. The snow flurries had stopped, leaving behind a brilliantly clear sky. The rolling hills of Kentucky's Bluegrass Region passed by quickly, one conical hill after the other. Dormant tobacco fields dominated the landscape while the weeks he'd spent in the twenty-first century dominated his thoughts—Charlotte's almond-shaped blue eyes and full, kissable lips, Jack's friendship, the Internet, driving a car with wind blowing in his face from the open windows. The lure of these memories had to be sealed away, hidden in his heart—forever.

In hindsight, the skirmish at MacKlenna Farm had been a blessing. The next time he encountered men with guns, he would be protected by his battle-hardened determination, now fully prepared to engage the enemy.

28

Washington City, December, 1864

THE TRAIN ARRIVED in Washington two days later, during a cold December rain. At a station prior to his final destination, he'd gotten off and sent a telegram to his Lafayette Square townhouse butler, advising the staff of his arrival. He often stayed in the city instead of taking the long ride out to Georgetown, and meeting with Lincoln and Stanton should keep him in Washington for at least a day or two. After a bath and change of clothes, he would present himself to the President and Secretary of War.

Though he knew they would press him for an explanation, he also knew he could never tell them the truth unless he wanted to be committed to the Government Hospital for the Insane. He would have to use the same answer he gave the police officers: *I don't have any memory of what happened.*

As to where he had been for the last few weeks, he would have to tell them Doctor Mallory had kept him at an undisclosed location until he was fit to travel. Would they believe him? He shrugged. They were more likely to believe a lie than the truth. At this point, all they cared about was when he'd be ready to return to work.

Two hours later he strode, outwardly confident at least, into the White House. When he reached the second floor, he ran into the President's short-tempered, dyspeptic private secretary, John Nicolay. Braham got along well enough with Nicolay, but he preferred to deal with Lincoln's other private secretary, the witty

John Hay.

"Major McCabe, you're alive. Mr. Lincoln will be pleased. Come quickly. He's descending the private stairs to visit the War Department. We'll catch up to him in the basement."

The gaslights threw a warm, mellow glow along a stuffy hallway lined with unwashed patrons. "We've had no news of you since Doctor Mallory was sent to arrange your escape. We assumed you were dead."

Braham followed the secretary through the colonnade. "I should be, but I'm not, yet."

"We're greatly relieved," Nicolay said. "There he is." A dozen yards ahead, the President lumbered across the lawn. "Mr. Lincoln. Mr. Lincoln. *Wait*, Mr. Lincoln." Nicolay waved his arms.

The President stopped and turned. When he saw Braham he opened his long arms. "The Prodigal has returned."

Braham jogged toward Lincoln, arriving breathless, his hand braced on his belly. Lincoln embraced him. "We heard you were fatally shot, and we feared you were dead. We've had no word, but here you stand. Doctor Mallory performed an astounding feat of magic."

Braham lowered his eyes, shaking his head. "I can't explain it any other way."

"Nicolay, find the doctor. I want him to work his magic and end this terrible war."

The President took Braham's hand and clasped it between his own. "I prayed for your return. My prayers have been answered."

"Congratulations on your reelection," Braham said. "I'm sorry I wasn't here to vote."

"It was a hard-fought campaign. The victory at Cedar Creek was instrumental."

"You need to be careful now. It's even more dangerous for you. I even dreamed you would be attacked," Braham said.

"Mrs. Lincoln has one every night. I'll tell you what I tell her. 'I confess, the first two or three threats made me uncomfortable, but having become familiar, I pay them little attention.' Besides, I have always thought *there's a divinity that shapes our ends...*"

Braham finished the quote from *Hamlet*, "...*Rough-hew them how we will*—. Maybe so, Mr. President, but—"

The President waved away Braham's worry with a flip of his hand. "Tell me, Major, what's the news from Richmond?"

If he couldn't convince the President to take the threats seriously, Braham would implement his own plan, even though he didn't, as of yet, have one completely formed.

"There's increasing desolation and rampant inflation. The election and fall of Atlanta has demoralized the citizenry. Deserters are pressed into service at the Tredegar Iron Works to free up factory workers for military duty. The functioning intelligence network is hearing rumors of the prospective evacuation of Richmond.

"What of Miss Van Lew?" the President asked.

"The Provost Marshal Thomas Doswell initiated an investigation of her." Braham laughed. "You should have seen her. With head held high, she insisted she was a victim of the espionage and treachery prevailing in Richmond. In essence, she threw the accusations against her right back in his face. Her cover of respectability remains intact because of her mother. Fine women, both of them," Braham said.

"The Union is deeply indebted to them. Miss Van Lew has aided the escape of Union prisoners, retrieved and buried dead soldiers honorably, and sends reliable information to Grant through her pipeline. I am still astonished she was able to place a spy in the Confederate White House."

Braham and the President walked in silence to the War Department building's entrance. Before opening the door, Lincoln said, "I want you to go back. The Union loyalists need a strong leader to ratchet up their activities. They remain firm in their resolve, but this war has to end soon. I need you inside."

"I'll be arrested as soon as I enter the city."

"Not if they don't know who you are. We'll cobble together a satisfactory disguise." Lincoln slapped Braham on the back. "Hell, we'll make you thin as a beanpole and ugly as a scarecrow."

The door opened and a solider held it while they entered. Lincoln removed his hat and unfurled his scarf. "A man approached me one day not long ago and said, 'If I ever came across an uglier man than myself, I'd shoot him on the spot.' I told him, 'Shoot me, for if I am an uglier man than you, I don't want to live.'" Lincoln burst into a hearty laugh and exclaimed, "Looks aren't so important. I got elected President, and I was the homeliest man in the State of Illinois."

The last place Braham wanted to go was back to Richmond. God help him. Even thin as a beanpole and ugly as a scarecrow, his very survival would be at risk.

29

Richmond, Virginia, Present Day

T WO DAYS AFTER Charlotte decided to return to the past she officially went on sabbatical. Surprisingly, her cover story—a six-month retreat in the Himalayas with her brother—was well received. Over the years she had sacrificed nights and weekends to help every member of the department. Charlotte could take the time off, the Chairman told her, but she needed to return by summer or the department would be short-handed.

With work issues resolved, Charlotte met with her CPA and established a bill-paying account. Until she returned, a bookkeeper would pay all her expenses from those funds. It was a setup similar to one Jack had established when he became a bestselling author and decided he was too busy to mess with little details like paying the plantation's electric bill.

Sweating from a long run, she now sat in her home office drinking a protein shake and reviewing her list again. Since her life revolved around work, she had few close friends who needed explanations. No pets. No vacations to cancel. No extracurricular commitments needing to be rescheduled. She didn't have much of a life outside of the hospital. Her lifestyle would change, though, when she turned forty and entered her Procreation Year.

After a shower, she headed downtown to the Southern Lady Suttlery, a supplier of Civil War reenacting supplies, dresses, and uniforms, where she spent the afternoon selecting fabrics and designs for a half dozen dresses with all the underpinnings, plus shoes, hats and accessories. Then she paid a small fortune for a one-week turnaround.

When she told Jack her dresses wouldn't be ready for a week, he immediately booked a flight to Los Angeles to pitch his story concept to a producer friend. She was glad to see him leave. He had been driving her nuts with his impatient excitement. She instructed him not to return home before she was packed and ready.

30

Mallory Plantation, Richmond, Virginia, Present Day

"YOU TOLD ME you were ready to go," Jack said, breathing heavily from dragging Saratoga trunks and portmanteaus down from the attic.

"Everything I'm taking is laid out on the bed in the guest room, waiting for the trunks. And you're not packed, so don't give me a hard time."

"There's an old valise in the attic I can use."

"Bring your clothes in here and I'll pack everything."

He left to get his clothes and Charlotte went to work, folding her dresses carefully to prevent as many wrinkles as possible. An hour later she closed the trunks and dragged them to the entryway. While she waited for Jack to return, she sat down with her laptop to answer last minute emails.

Jack entered the foyer jingling his car keys. "Are you ready?"

"Almost." She finished an email and clicked send. "Everything is packed. You have greenbacks to pay our expenses. What else?"

"The post office is forwarding the mail to our CPA. I'll set the alarm when we leave. The farm manager will take care of everything on the plantation, including the cat."

She opened the next email and quickly scanned it. "What'd your agent say in the call you just finished?"

"She was relieved I wouldn't be pestering her, but made me promise I'd have a draft to her as soon as I returned."

Charlotte fired off a quick answer to the email and sent a copy to her Chairman. Why were her colleagues asking her about the surgical residents' evaluations? She wouldn't be teaching for a while, all her required evaluations were in, and they all knew it. What part of the word sabbatical did they not understand? She turned her attention back to Jack. "How are you going to write a draft without a laptop?"

"In case you haven't heard, pen and paper were invented a few years ago."

"Ha. Ha. Well…speaking of writing, I have something for you." She dug into her computer case and pulled out a dark walnut leather journal. "Here. This is for your notes. You've never kept up with one before, but this one was especially made for you. So don't lose it."

He rubbed the distressed, smooth leather she'd had engraved with his initials, CJM, and then he fanned the textured artist pages, sniffing the mild, easy-on-the-nose leather smell. "It's beautiful. Thank you. I'll try to keep up with it." He slipped the book into his inside jacket pocket and picked up one of the trunks. "Good God. What do you have in here, lead?"

"Shoes." She opened the next email and read it quickly. This morning she was unusually testy. She had planned to fit in a long run to work off some of her mounting anxiety, but she hadn't gotten the chance.

"Shoes don't weight this much. I think you packed Thor's hammer." He set the trunk in the back of the SUV and came back for another one.

"You made our reservation at the Willard, didn't you?"

"Two adjoining rooms for one night."

"Where're your guns?"

"In the valise." He picked up another trunk. "You do realize this is the same list we went over last night."

"And discovered you hadn't made the hotel reservations. Today we might remember something else."

He carried the second trunk to the car. "You're sure the luggage will go with us? I hate to go to all this work then have them left behind."

"I don't know for sure, but Braham's bed and my chair both went into the fog and came out on the other side. As long as we're attached to them in some way, they should make the trip."

"I hope you're right. Oh, by the way, did you tell Ken we were leaving?"

She sent another email to cancel a speaking engagement at the Rotary Club. "I talked to him about ten minutes ago. He's insanely jealous." She glanced at Jack as he emerged from the porch with his long coat flapping in the wind and moving with his characteristic loping gait.

Jack snagged the last trunk and headed back out. "Did he say anything else?"

One more email. Then she'd be done, and she wouldn't have to put up with this political crap—budget cuts, medical records, Medicare changes—for several weeks. Taking care of patients was only a small part of her job and the one part she truly enjoyed.

"Yes, he hoped I wouldn't bring home another dying patient. Why?"

"Just curious about what he thought about you chasing after Braham."

"You make it sound like I'm chasing after *him* instead of...you know...chasing after him to keep him from changing history."

Jack came back inside, picked up his valise, and tucked it under his arm. "All I know is it was hard to sit in the same room with you two without getting electrocuted."

"What are you talking about? Are you writing romance novels now?"

He stopped, tossed back his head, and laughed. "Why do you think I always left the two of you alone? I was trying to help you out, sis. I figured if he fell in love with you, he'd stay and I'd get a huntin' and fishin' brother-in-law."

"You've actually gotten subtle in your matchmaking attempts. I didn't even notice."

There was an ironic twist to his lips and sparkle in his blue eyes.

"If you had, we wouldn't be hauling ass back to the Civil War."

"And you wouldn't be getting a bird's-eye view into your new story."

"We're both getting something out of this."

"You're wrong." There was the sharpest of prickles in her voice. "I'm doing this because what I've already done could possibly screw up history for everyone else. I don't want the responsibility. I'm not getting anything out of this except risking my life again."

"History is not going to get screwed up. I promise."

"Are you serious? You can't make that promise."

He smiled. "Maybe not, but it won't be from a lack of trying." He turned off the lights and picked up her black medical bag. "Cars loaded. Shut down your laptop and let's get out of here."

"I want to send Elliot and Meredith an email to let them know we're leaving. Then I'll be done." Charlotte had already shared her plans with the Frasers. At least someone would know where she and Jack had gone and why. Now she signed off, wondering if she would ever sign back on again.

She didn't want to go back in time, but she had to clean up her mess. If she had only thought through the possible consequences of her actions, she would have let Major McCabe die.

Ha. Who was she kidding?

The moment she saw Braham in that filthy ward, she'd known exactly what she would do, and consequences be damned.

She slipped the laptop into her leather computer bag and left it sitting by the entryway table. She managed one last glance around the foyer, imprinting the room on her brain, praying she would come home again. She sniffed. The scent of bacon Jack had cooked for breakfast lingered in the air. Braham had loved Jack's bacon and coffee in the morning. She shook away the memory and closed the door. There was no room for sentimentality. She had to stop Braham and make it home alive. She had six months.

God help them all.

Part Two

"I will do my part as if the issue of the whole struggle depends on me alone."

—Abraham Lincoln

31

Washington, D.C.—Present Day

A BRILLIANT SUN poked bold fingers through the empty branches of the willow oak trees planted along Pennsylvania Avenue near the Willard Hotel. The Christmas rush was at its peak, the city was festooned with wreaths and garlands with bright red bows, and hundreds of shoppers jammed the sidewalks. The Ellipse, with the National Christmas Tree glimmering in the center, was full of sightseers both young and old, milling around and posing for pictures. When Charlotte and Jack were kids, they never missed witnessing the National Christmas Tree Lighting Ceremony from President's Park. Now, since their parents' deaths, the event only triggered bittersweet memories. The holidays were tough for her, which was why she was always on call Christmas Day.

A doorman at the Willard opened Charlotte's door. "Happy Holiday, Doctor Mallory. Are you checking in or going to lunch?"

"We're checking in today, Gregory." She wouldn't have been able to call him by name if he hadn't been wearing a nametag, although she and Jack stayed at the hotel so often the staff remembered them. "I'll need the trunks brought to our suite."

The doorman smiled and signaled for a bellhop.

"Leave the car here," Jack told him. "I'll check in and then come back for it."

He tipped the doorman, then escorted Charlotte toward the entrance. As soon as they entered the lobby, Charlotte stopped short, taking in the breathtaking beauty of the antiques, marble columns, frescoes, chandeliers, poinsettias, and a floor-to-ceiling Christmas tree. Jack placed his hand in the center of her back and pressed her forward.

"Stop gawking. This isn't your first visit."

She sighed. "I know, but it still takes my breath away."

"So does the Grand Canyon."

"You're so unromantic. No wonder your little black book has only a few entries."

He cocked one brow in disbelief. "I love violins and candlelit dinners, and for your information, I have a full book."

"Ha. According to MacKlenna Farm's website, Stormy has a full book. You have Cliff Notes. And those candlelit dinners are followed by football or basketball games on TV."

"You don't know what you're talking about. Ginny loved to watch football and basketball games with me."

Charlotte dismissed his ploy with a wave of her hand. "She worked for CNN Sports, and you only dated her for a couple of months. Her travel schedule was worse than yours."

"Your love life is worse than mine, so stop picking on me."

They reached the registration desk and checked into their suite.

"Here's your key. I'm going to go put the car in the parking space I rented. When I get back, we'll have lunch and go over our list one more time."

"Do you want me to make dinner reservations?"

"I'm having dinner with my agent. You're welcome to go, though."

"Thanks, but no thanks. I'm going to enjoy room service and a long, luxurious bath, since it's likely to be a while before I enjoy either one again."

Charlotte watched her brother saunter away, wondering for the hundredth time, or more, why he sabotaged relationships. He refused to go to counseling, and every time she brought up the subject of their parents' deaths, he shut down. She wasn't forthcoming either, but at least she had given counseling a try. What the heck. They were probably stuck, going through life together forever, two people riding a tandem bicycle, trying to go in different directions, and too damn stubborn to let anyone else take the lead.

32

Washington, D.C.—Present Day

At SEVEN O'CLOCK the next morning, Charlotte swished through the hotel lobby in a deeply pleated, silk-satin Civil War-era walking dress in a blue and black checkered pattern, and carrying a long blue winter cloak over her arm. Jack had told her to meet him at the Christmas tree, but he wasn't there, so she tapped her foot, turned up her nose, and channeled Scarlett O'Hara. *"Fiddle-dee-dee. War, war, war; this war talk's spoiling all the fun at every party this spring. I get so bored I could scream."*

Several early-morning risers had snapped her picture using their smartphones. She smiled sweetly and threw in more fiddle-dee-dees as she turned this way and that for them. Wearing such an elaborate costume freed the little girl inside her to enjoy a flight of fantasy. She went a bit overboard with her channeling, but what the heck. The fun would end when she left the building.

"There you are," Jack said.

She blinked, and her mouth dropped open. The shock wore off and she shut her mouth, shaking her head. "Damn. You look *good.*" She straightened his cravat and hand pressed the shoulders of his frock coat. "The silk striped vest is a nice touch. I like it. Very handsome."

He stood tall and easy and smiled down at her. He did indeed look every bit the gentlemen he purported to be. The young women in Washington were in for a treat.

"Are you ready?" he asked.

"I should ask you the same thing. I already know how dangerous it is."

His face telegraphed his brotherly concern. "Do you want to change your mind?"

She shook her head and took a calming breath. "I don't want to go. Other than witnessing history, there is nothing enticing, entertaining, or healthy about what we're about to do. But's it's necessary. Regardless of how I feel about it, I have to go."

"The bellhop is taking our trunks to the corner."

She scrunched her face. "Is it a good idea to disappear in plain sight?"

"Do you want to duck into a phone booth instead?"

She smirked. "You're the writer."

"I know, which is why I picked seven o'clock to disappear. The street is empty. And it's cold outside and barely daylight. If you'll stop lollygagging, we'll get out of here."

She swooshed around his legs and stomped toward the door.

Jack chuckled close behind her.

A moment of levity before they spiraled into danger.

She stopped and dug in her heels. "But I don't want to go."

He put his hands on her shoulders. "You'll be safe. I promise. Now, let's get the flock out of here."

She supposed he meant to comfort her, but his words were like Band-Aids on an open-heart incision, and did nothing to assuage the fear churning in her belly. A strange breeze slithered by her, sounding like whispers of secrets. She shook it off, or tried to.

Their bellhop hovered at the corner of 15th and E Street guarding their trunks. Jack tipped the young man, but he didn't want to leave them until their transportation arrived. Jack assured him a bus would be by to pick them up in a matter of minutes, and they wouldn't need his assistance to get the trunks on board. The bellhop left, but kept looking back. Finally, Jack scooted them next to the side of the hotel and out of the bellhop's line of sight.

Charlotte sat on top of one of the trunks and spread out her skirt.

"It's time, sis. No one's around. Say the words and let's be gone."

"You're sure this is what you want to do?"

"Damn it. You're becoming obnoxious. Get the brooch and let's go."

The brooch and a pair of tweezers were packed in her reticule. Using the tweezers, she caught the edge of the broken clasp and pinched the pieces together until the stone opened. Then she patted the trunk beside her. "Sit, and let's hold hands."

They squeezed each other's fingers. Then after a silent prayer, she spoke the ancient incantation. *"Chan ann le tìm no àite a bhios sinn a' tomhais an gaol ach's ann le neart anama."*

As the peat-smelling fog engulfed them, Jack let out one of his boisterous laughs.

33

Washington City—December, 1864

A S THE FRIGID fog dissipated, Charlotte shivered, even in her long cloak. The mist's embrace had been suffocating as it twisted and tumbled her through a void black as coal and cold as ice. The vertical loops and inversions were made worse on this trip by an unnerving effect that shot her back and forth, scaring her even more than the previous trips.

Relieved it was over, she took several deep breaths. Big mistake. The smell of unwashed bodies and open sewers triggered bile up into the back of her throat. She gagged.

Jack put his arm around her shoulders. "Are you going to be sick?"

She fanned her face with her hand. "Give me a minute." A combination of smells and riding on a speed-demon roller coaster would upset even the most stalwart of stomachs. She closed her eyes and breathed in and out through her mouth until the nausea passed.

Finally, she said, "I'm okay now." She opened her eyes to see Jack standing with his hands on his hips, gawking.

He glanced down at her. "*We're...here.*" His voice was choppy with excitement, reminding her of a hound dog sniffing the scent in a relentless drive to follow a trail.

Gingerly, she stood. "You have a cast-iron stomach. The trip didn't bother you at all, did it?"

"Nah." He pointed over her shoulder. "Look. We're still at the

Willard."

She turned to look at the old building. She hadn't paid any attention to it during her prior visit, and now she saw there wasn't much of a resemblance to the twenty-first century hotel, other than being on the same corner.

"Let's hope we arrived in the right year, too." She pulled her cloak around her, trapping warmth between the heavy wool and her dress. "What time do you think it is?" Not that she had any place to be, but her entire adult life had been driven by the time. She glanced up, shading her eyes with her hand, and studied the position of the sun in a slightly overcast sky.

Jack stretched, cocking his head. "I'm facing north. The sun is to my left. It's after twelve o'clock, but not by much."

"A line from one your books, I bet."

"It is, and a bad one, too. Honestly, I have no idea."

"I'm glad your sense of humor arrived intact."

"Why wouldn't it? This is a game-changer for me. I have a good shot at getting another movie deal from this book. Don't mess it up."

"This trip is *not* about you." Her voice was sharp with agitation.

His nostrils flared, but he didn't snap back at her. "Maybe not, but I'm going to take full advantage of it. Now, I'm going inside the hotel to hire a carriage to take us to Georgetown. Will you be all right staying with the luggage?"

"I'm within spitting distance of the White House. What could happen to me here?"

"Yeah, right. Look what happened to you at the Cedar Creek reenactment."

"Good point. Go. Hurry. The sooner we get to Georgetown, the sooner we can find Braham."

He pulled down on his right cuff, then his left, straightened his jacket, and finally adjusted his hat, fidgeting. She'd seen him do much the same before an interview. "Stay put," he said, "and don't talk to strangers."

"Ha. Ha."

Jack strode toward the Willard's main entrance with shoulders squared, as confident as someone who belonged in this era. Nothing about his general appearance, hair or clothing, looked out of place…except he was clean and didn't stink.

Did she look out of place? She might be dressed authentically, but she saw herself as a plastic checker piece on an ivory chessboard. Wearing a costume and playing a role at reenactments was fun, but in the nineteenth century it rattled her. Her layer of disguise could be easily dismantled with a yank here or there. Although she had held it together under extreme conditions last time, could she maintain her disguise over the course of several weeks?

This trip she didn't intend to let herself be dragged off and dumped into another life-threatening situation. If she could find a small hospital willing to allow her to work, she'd be able to help with the war effort.

Her abilities had already won acceptance in the surgical world heavily dominated by male doctors, although it had been a long, hard-fought battle. And it was a battle she would have to fight again if she intended to practice medicine now. The hospitals needed doctors, but they would refuse to believe she had the necessary skills. Being a woman, she would need references, and she doubted the President would give her one. She doubted Braham, if and when they found him, would help her, either. He would want her gone, not entrenched in one of Washington's hospitals.

Glancing up and down the street, she saw hundreds of soldiers within a few blocks of where she sat. If he were among them, wearing a uniform, would she recognize him? How would he react to her presence? Would he be glad to see her? Probably not. Had he even thought she would come after him? She didn't know him well, but she knew him well enough, and he would be expecting her.

Three soldiers on horseback rode closer and reined in right in front of her. The man in the center wore an officer's double-breasted coat with one gold eagle on his shoulder boards. He dismounted, grimacing, then with a stiff leg stepped up on the sidewalk and out of a street which was little more than a channel of liquid mud.

"What sort of rogue would abandon a beautiful woman on the sidewalk?" Although his voice was amiable, his cognac-colored eyes were fixed on her with an unblinking chill.

She took a step backwards and glanced around, searching for Jack.

The man politely doffed his slouch hat, which bore the cavalry's crossed-sabers insignia. Wavy brown hair fell across his forehead. "Colonel Henly. At your service, ma'am. Where may I escort you?" He shoved fingers through his hair before resetting his hat.

"My brother has gone to rent a carriage and will be right back. But I appreciate your offer." She shivered slightly from the cold and from his chilling visual appraisal.

The colonel set his lips in a grim line and glanced up and down the street. "It's too cold for you to wait here. While my aides guard your luggage, I'll escort you inside the Willard where it's warm. You will wait for your brother there. Come along." He took her hand and threaded it around his proffered elbow.

"I'm sorry, but I can't leave without him." Being less than subtle, she reclaimed her arm, yanking it from the colonel's clutches. She quickly scanned the crowd. Jack was a good head taller than most men, including the obnoxious colonel, and she would spot him immediately. But he wasn't around to be spotted.

The colonel turned to his aides. "Guard these trunks, When the lady's brother returns, send him inside the hotel."

The aides dismounted and took up positions on either side of her luggage.

Unease gave her another reason to shiver. She rooted her feet to the planked sidewalk. What if they searched her luggage? Twenty-first century antibiotics and pain medications, as well as her Confederate uniform, were packed in the bottom.

"Come, before you freeze." The colonel had her hand tucked in the crook of his arm and was towing her off in the direction of the hotel, despite her protests.

"I'm sure you have other matters more important than seeing to my comfort." She could continue to resist him, stall to give Jack more time, but was it wise? He was a colonel, and she needed friends with connections.

"Protecting you from freezing is the most important task of my day. My men will notify your brother the moment he returns."

Her feet tingled from the cold. She truly did not want to stand outside much longer. The two men guarding her luggage stood at attention, appearing to take their task seriously. She didn't think they would have time to pick the locks and dig through her belongings before Jack returned. The colonel was pushy, but there wasn't a logical reason for her to remain out in the cold while soldiers guarded her bags. She took another look around for Jack. Then, reluctantly, she accepted the colonel assistance.

"What is your brother's name?" he asked.

"Jack Mallory," she said.

After giving his aides instructions, the colonel led her toward the corner. "How did you come to be stranded, Miss Mallory?" He glanced at her, waiting expectantly.

Cold prickled at the back of her neck. What in the world was she going to say?

Think quickly. Think smart.

"The carriage…we were in had a lame horse… and the driver put us out." She had been in the nineteenth century only five minutes and had already told her first lie. How many more would she tell? Jack's advice was to keep it simple and as close to the truth as possible. Hers didn't have any semblance of truth, but it was simple enough.

A look of astonishment on his face quickly changed to disbelief then displeasure. "The driver should be whipped."

"It's wartime. We have learned to adjust to unusual situations." She kept her voice light, not wanting to be overly dramatic.

They headed toward the hotel's entrance at an unhurried pace. She had the impression Henly wasn't walking slowly for her comfort. He had probably been recently wounded.

"It's almost eleven o'clock," he said. "The politicians should have finished their breakfast and hastened to the public rooms to mingle. It will be quite crowded."

They reached the main entrance and proceeded through a spacious corridor toward the hotel rotunda. Before reaching the rotunda, though, the colonel stopped at a news, books, and cigar stand. The banner over the merchandise proclaimed the cigars were *the best the market affords.*

"Would you mind waiting a moment?" he asked.

She shook her head, eyeing the books and folded newspapers. Above the headline was the date—December 8, 1864. Perfect. Booth should be in Washington, living at the National Hotel and romancing Lucy Lambert Hale. If Jack visited the hotel, he could find Booth, and possibly Braham as well.

A lanky, immaculately dressed man joined Henly at the counter. "Morning Colonel."

"Morning, Senator Sherman. I just read a report indicating your brother is halfway to Savannah. Does he plan to make the city a Christmas gift to the President?"

The Senator gave a nasal laugh. "A gift Mr. Lincoln would gladly accept."

Henly paid the clerk for a handful of cigars and tucked them into his coat pocket. "Pray Hardee realizes the futility of defending the city and surrenders before thousands more die and the city is burned to the ground."

Another man approached and asked to have a moment with the Senator. Henly excused himself and escorted Charlotte back out into the corridor.

"It's a bold move for General Sherman to operate so far within enemy territory without supply lines," she said. "It hasn't been tried before in the annals of war, has it?"

He arched his brow and frowned back at her in puzzlement.

"I heard someone refer to his march," she continued, "as a scorched earth campaign, designed to bring a quicker resolution to the war."

"You're not only beautiful but quite knowledgeable."

She shrugged, deliberately nonchalant. "Washington has dozens of daily newspapers. Many of them find their way out beyond the city limits. I read everything I can find."

The rotunda looked different from the one in the twenty-first century hotel. Instead of comparing the two, she blocked the hotel of the future out of her mind, and turned her entire attention to the features in the current one.

The vaulted ceiling was elaborately frescoed and supported by pillars. At the base of each pillar was a circular walnut-seating bench with cabriole legs and velvet cushions. Most were filled with overweight men smoking cigars. Other men clustered in small groups, buzzing with animated conversation. Certain words rose above the din: Lincoln, Sherman, Richmond, Lee, Grant, and the recent election. She craned her neck, searching for both Jack and Braham.

She assumed Jack was in the building somewhere. Was Braham? And, if he was, would he be in uniform? There were a few uniformed men, but most were dressed in business attire, including a top hat, fedora, or bowler. Jack and Braham were both tall enough to be seen above the heads of even those wearing stovepipe hats.

A majority of the men in the room carried canes or umbrellas they used for emphasis by either pounding on the floor or poking the air. Nine out of ten had facial hair—short beards, long beards, mustaches, goatees. None were particularly attractive, the beards or the men. And the smell of unwashed bodies saturated the air.

Henly waved one hand toward a vacant bench. "Shall we sit over there?" He ushered her around a group of men who were debating mercy for the vanquished and sectional reconciliation for the nation. The muscles in her stomach gripped. Mercy would fly out the window following the assassination.

Before she sat, she lifted her foot behind her, catching the bottom hoop on her heel, and placed the hoops on the back of the seat. She perched on the edge of the chair, making sure she wasn't rumpling or sitting on any of the hoops. The little trick saved her from the embarrassment of flying skirts.

"By the way," he said, crossing his legs, "where were you going when you were unceremoniously booted from your carriage?"

Oh, God. What am I going to say?

She and Jack had decided to show up on Braham's doorstep, hoping they would be welcomed, but they hadn't discussed how they would explain their relationship. Whatever their story was going to be, it had to be believable. She blew out a breath before answering.

"To my…cousin's house in Georgetown."

He pursed his lips a little, and thoughts flickered across his face. "I have several acquaintances living there. What's your cousin's name? I might know her."

She couldn't mask the associated guilt from telling another lie so she turned her head, coughing. Lying was certainly not her forte. "Major Abraham McCabe," she said between coughs. "Excuse me. I have a tickle in my throat."

Henly's turned the full force of his brown eyes on her and his eyebrows rose. "He's your cousin?"

She cleared her throat. To keep from telling a third lie she asked, "Do you know him?"

Henly sat back against the column and pulled his bottom lip out into a pucker, obviously thinking. "When was the last time you heard from him?"

She searched the colonel's face for clues as to the cause of his concern. Had he heard Braham had been captured in Richmond and was believed dead? Or had something more happened to him? A sharp pain grew inside her chest. "It's been a while, but if you have news, please tell me."

Henly's eyes darkened and were edged with concern and something else. "I heard he was captured and died from the wounds he sustained. I'm sorry to be the one to tell you."

"If he'd been killed, we would have heard."

"If you're on his notification list, a telegram would have been sent to your home. Where do you live?"

She stared ahead, wrinkling her brow in concentration, and told the truth. "My home is in Richmond."

Henly sat ramrod straight, and a muscle twitched along his jaw.

"We left some time ago, though," she added quickly, hoping he wouldn't ask how long ago. "We're Unionists and it was no longer safe to stay there." Her voice held a distinct quaver.

He leaned in confidentially. "I'm attached to the War Department. I'll see if I can uncover any information."

If the colonel worked at the War Department and hadn't heard Braham had survived Richmond, then either Braham hadn't yet arrived back in Washington, or the President had sent him out immediately on another mission.

A hand tapped Charlotte's shoulder, and she jumped.

"What are you doing here?" Jack's lips were set in a grim line. "Did you leave the trunks on the street?"

She came to her feet quickly. "Colonel Henly absolutely insisted I come inside with him. His aides are guarding them. He took pity on me when I told him about the carriage's horse going lame and how we were ejected at the corner."

Jack extended his hand to Henly. "I'm Jack Mallory. Thank you for taking care of my sister."

"It was an honor, but I'm afraid I shared bad news."

"It's about Braham," Charlotte said. "The colonel heard he was captured and died of his wounds."

Jack's jaw went slack and he put his hands to his hips. "We would have received a telegram or letter."

She cupped her elbows and shuddered. "Not if we aren't on his notification list." She felt certain the colonel was referring to Braham's October injury and capture, and not to a new one, but there was no way to know for sure without talking to him.

"I told Miss Mallory I'm attached to the War Department. If there is any information available concerning his whereabouts, I'll find out. Have you thought of staying at the townhouse he owns on Lafayette Square instead of Georgetown?"

"I didn't know he owned a townhouse," she said, feeling betrayed by another one of Braham's lies.

Henly glanced from her to Jack. "It would be more convenient to stay there than to travel out to Georgetown, at least until I can investigate his whereabouts."

"Do you know the address?" Jack asked.

"It's across from Lafayette Square."

Jack gave Charlotte a what-do-you-want-to-do look. "I have a carriage waiting outside."

Charlotte fidgeted with her cloak's top button. She didn't know what kind of reception they would receive from Braham's servants. It would be embarrassing and unexplainable if they weren't permitted to stay at the townhouse. They needed to sever ties with the nosy colonel immediately.

"Let's go to the townhouse, at least for tonight," she said.

Henly snatched his hat off the bench. "I'll escort you."

"It's—" she said with a snap.

"—not necessary," Jack finished her sentence, smiling. "We wouldn't wish to impose."

"You're new to town, and I insist." The ruthless edge in his low-pitched voice sent a shiver up her spine. Then he gave her a slow smile that revealed deep grooves on either side of his mouth. The smile did not appease her shivers.

They left by way of the ladies' entrance on Fourteenth Street, exiting the hotel a short distance from their waiting carriage, trunks, and the colonel's aides. Henly assisted Charlotte into the conveyance before mounting his horse for the short ride over to the townhouse. A few minutes later, the carriage stopped in front of an Italianate-style residence.

Would the servants allow two people they had never met to stay in Braham's home? She tried to focus on a cover story to tell the servants instead of the unnerving thump of her heart.

"Colonel, thank you for your assistance. We don't want to hold you up any longer," Jack said.

She didn't dare look at Jack. He would give her the same questioning look she wanted to give him.

"Nonsense," Henly said. "I'd prefer to see you settled before I leave. And maybe the servants have news of the major's whereabouts." He pointed toward the front door. "Shall we go?" Henly's eyes held the same unblinking chill as when she first met him.

Charlotte gathered her courage. Jack appeared to be his usual suave self, sauntering up the stairs to the sandstone door surround, where he clasped the doorknocker and tapped it several times, giving Henly his book jacket smile.

A butler smartly dressed in day livery opened the door. "May I help you?"

"I'm Jack Mallory and this is my sister Charlotte. We're Major McCabe's cousins and have come for a visit. Is he here?"

The man opened the door wider. "Come in, please." They did, including Henly, and the butler closed the door behind them. "The major said when you arrive, Miss Mallory, you're to have the house and staff at your disposal."

On a scale measuring from pissed off to grateful, she found herself somewhere along the center point, and could easily swing in either direction depending on what happened in the next few minutes. "Is the Major in Washington now?"

"He spent several nights here, but he hasn't returned recently."

Charlotte untied her bonnet and unbuttoned her jacket. "Would you have someone help with our trunks?"

"Yes, ma'am." He pointed toward a parlor to the right of the entry. "You'll be comfortable waiting in there while I see to your baggage and your rooms. I'll have refreshments brought in."

Charlotte handed the butler her bonnet and coat and entered the parlor with Henly and Jack.

"If McCabe was here, it means he survived Richmond. When I leave, I'll go over to the War Department. As soon as I have information on his whereabouts, I'll let you know."

The words *consult the President* were on Charlotte's tongue but she reeled them in before she actually said them. She had no doubt at all Lincoln knew exactly where Braham was and probably received daily briefings from him.

"Thank you, Colonel. You saved us a trip to Georgetown," Jack said. "We don't want to keep you from your business any longer."

"It's been my pleasure, Mr. Mallory, Miss Mallory."

Jack escorted the colonel to the door. "If I hear anything tonight," Henly said, "I'll send word."

"I'd appreciate it," Jack said. He opened the door and the colonel stepped out, and then turned back.

"With your permission, I'd like to call on your sister."

Jack glanced back at Charlotte, who was standing in the hall talking with the butler, but looking in their direction. "You'll have to take it up with her. She's never needed my permission before. I doubt she wants it now."

Henly set his hat on his head, glanced at Charlotte, and with a wry smile said, "I'll discuss it with her then. Good day, Mr. Mallory."

Jack watched Henly mount his horse, then closed the door. Turning toward, Charlotte he said, "What do you think of the illustrious colonel?"

She wrinkled her nose.

"That bad?"

She nodded toward the parlor. They entered the room and Jack closed the tall sliding doors.

"We should get in the habit of only talking privately," she said.

"I agree. There's too much at stake."

They sat on the sofa, close, so they could speak in low tones.

"I thought Henly was overly aggressive, and he refused to listen to me, but in the end, he was helpful. I'm not sure what to make of him." Charlotte picked up a small pillow and hugged it to her chest. "If the butler had said he couldn't allow guests to stay in the house without Braham's permission, or even that he'd never heard of us, Henly might have thought we were spies. I hate to think of what could have happened."

"Why would he have believed such a thing?"

"He asked where we were from. I told him we were Unionists from Richmond. I wasn't prepared to answer his questions and didn't want to tell more lies. His eyes told me he was analyzing every word I said. I don't trust him."

They sat in tense silence staring at each other for a minute, lost in their own thoughts. Finally Jack said, "Your story should work. But what I want to know is, why was Braham so damn sure you'd come after him when you insisted you didn't want to come back?"

She threw up her hands. "You probably understand him better than I do. You tell me. You did notice, though, he didn't make it easy for us. If we hadn't met the colonel, we would have traveled out to Georgetown and might not have learned Braham had been in town."

"He probably reported to the President and immediately received a new assignment. At least if he's out of the city, he can't shoot Booth," Jack said.

"Maybe Henly will learn something at the War Department."

"Henly will be back whether he hears news of Braham or not. He couldn't take his eyes off of you."

"I couldn't take my eyes off of him, either, but it wasn't because I was interested. He reminded me of the cops who hide close to the lane in front of the mansion waiting for me to break the law so they can pull me over and slap a citation in my hand."

"Then stay away from him. Since he intends to call on you tomorrow, should I tell him to leave you alone?"

"No, don't do it yet. I'll see him tomorrow. His connections might open a door to one of the hospitals so I can work while I'm here. I'll put up with him, at least for now."

"You might enjoy having male attention. Someone to take you to parties and the theatre."

"I don't want male attention, and *you* can take me to the theatre."

He tapped her cheek. "You don't? Then how do you explain the pinkish tinge on your face?"

She slapped his hand away. "If you think I could be interested in a controlling jerk like the colonel, you don't know me at all."

"Tsk, tsk. I know you better than you know yourself. Thoughts of the colonel didn't make you blush. Nope, you blushed because you pictured a soldier with steady green eyes and a knee-melting smile."

She threw a small decorative sofa pillow at him. "You *are* working on a romance novel, aren't you? Trying your lines out on me. What's your pseudonym? I know you have one. You are *such* a jerk."

Jack laughed and tossed the pillow back at her. "And you're such a liar. You've all but drooled over Braham since he came out of surgery and you saw the man beneath the blood and grime."

"And how do you know?"

Jack's eyes twinkled. "I have my sources, and a good reporter never reveals his sources."

She looked at her brother, those deep blue of his eyes, the straight line of his nose, the mouth so quick to curve up in amusement. He was a combination of both of their parents, and she loved him, but he sure did piss her off sometimes. It wasn't because Jack went looking for trouble; it was because trouble had a way of finding him. He'd never done anything illegal, but he had been beaten up a couple of times, which had scared the crap out of her. He never appreciated the true danger in his situations because he was always thinking about the story.

"Sources? I wouldn't call former bedmates reliable sources. Thanks to Ken's introductions, you've dated most of the nurses from Richmond to Winchester, so any one of them would have told you whatever you wanted to hear. They would even violate HIPAA to get back into your bed."

He pressed his hands against his chest, and managed to look crestfallen. "I can't believe how mean you are to me."

There was a knock on the door. "Come in," she said.

The butler entered. "Your trunks have been taken upstairs and luncheon is served in the dining room."

"What's your name, please?" Charlotte asked. "You've been most helpful."

"Edward, ma'am. Major McCabe was very specific. This is your home, and we are to serve your needs as long as you wish to stay."

"Would you mind serving us at the round table in front of the window?" she said pointing behind her. "I'd like to enjoy the view while I eat."

"Certainly." Edward left the room, closing the door behind him.

"I guess Braham wants to make up for stealing my car," Charlotte said, finally taking a minute to study the ornate room, which was painted and papered in vivid greens and reds. He had exquisite and expensive taste.

"He didn't steal it, he borrowed it," Jack said.

She ran her hand along the top of a walnut table next to the sofa from the Rococo Revival period. "What?"

"Your car. He didn't steal it."

She went over to the front window, pushed aside a swathe of lace curtain with the back of her hand, and looked out at the White House. "He didn't even have a driver's license. What would have happened if he'd been stopped? We'd have been in a world of hurt. I wish he'd been honest with us."

"He didn't intentionally deceive us."

She let the curtain drop back into place, still clutching a corner of the lace. "He deceived me from the very beginning. It never occurred to me he would find time travel acceptable. If I had known, I could have saved myself a lot of anguish. Now he's run off and we don't know where."

"If we find Booth, we'll find Braham. And I'll get a helluva of a story along the way."

34

Washington—December, 1864

CHARLOTTE JOINED JACK for breakfast in the dining room shortly before seven the next morning. They had eaten lunch and dinner in the parlor and retired early, so she had yet to tour the house. Her bedroom, complete with a feather bed, was elegantly furnished. She had slept well and woke up refreshed.

She found Jack sitting at the end of a long carved mahogany table with his journal and a sharpened pencil at his side. She paused in the doorway, taking in the complete dining room, not wanting to miss any of the sophisticated details. She imagined Braham selecting every piece of furniture for both style and function. He was a man of many talents—educated and wealthy—and she'd only gotten a glimpse of his multi-layered personality.

The ten chairs surrounding the long table had scroll arms, lion paw feet, and blue silk dragonfly upholstery. She ran her hand across the smooth fabric. "Sweet."

A clear crystal chandelier with silver finish accents hung above the table. Below it, Jack lounged at one of two place settings. Growing up she had been well schooled in china and silver patterns, but the azure china with its embossed bead edge was not a pattern she recognized. The Grecian pattern flatware by Gorham, she did. "Impressive."

"I hope you remember the finer details of this room. I'm only writing down what I see as important, like how many guests can fit at this table," Jack said, chuckling.

"Without looking down, tell me the color of your china plate," she said.

His eyebrows scrunched as he thought. "Green?"

She shook her head. "You're right. You won't remember. How about the paintings?"

He gave her an I-gotcha-there smile. "I may not notice china patterns and seat cushions, but I do notice paintings. The one behind me with the four boats is a Birch. My agent has a copy hanging over the receptionist's desk. The other three," he said, waving his finger around, "show the same technique in the clearly-painted waves, so I assume they're also by Birch."

She poured a cup of coffee from a silver pot on the sideboard. "A townhouse in Lafayette Park—across from the White House—and Birch originals. I'm—"

"Impressed?"

"And surprised. Aren't you?"

"Not really. He's well-traveled, educated, and wealthy."

"Where'd his money come from? Do you know?"

"He inherited money from his father, but a controlling interest in a California gold mine substantially increased his net worth." Jack folded the newspaper and pushed away from the table. "Will you be all right while I go out?"

"Depends on how long you'll be gone."

"Most of the day. I want to get a lay of the land. Our man's not in town yet, so I'll use this week to acquaint myself with the landmarks."

Charlotte winced, knowing Jack was referring to Booth. They had agreed not to use his name.

"According to my notes, he'll be here on the seventeenth."

Charlotte took her coffee cup to the table, and sat next to her brother, whispering, "Do you think Braham knows?"

"Sandburg's books are very detailed. We have to assume he's fully aware of the man's comings and goings over the next four months. Today I'm also going to visit the epicenter for journalists, talk to a few reporters."

"You mean there's a general location where they all hang out?" Her voice rose in disbelief. "They're not roaming the streets harassing people like they do in Richmond?"

"It's between 14ᵗʰ Street NW near the Willard and the Ebbitt Boarding House, and you need to get over your press phobia. So stay away from there. I don't want you arrested for attacking the press."

"Me? Attack them? Maybe I can convince the Confederate Army to target the area and blow them all to smithereens. I'll even send them the coordinates."

"I don't think a bomb would take out the entire newspaper row."

"Dang," she said, snapping her fingers. "What's at the location now? I mean in our time? Has to be better than a swarm of reporters."

Jack laughed. "The National Press Building."

She rolled her eyes. "I hate the press."

"You *do?*" Jack grinned and changed the subject. "It might be decent enough this afternoon for you to take a stroll through the park."

"I don't know all the social etiquette, but I don't think it's proper for a lady to go out alone."

"No, but the colonel said he would call on you. Maybe—"

She plopped her elbow on the table, chin in her hand. "I'll see him today and ask him if he knows anyone who can help me get approved to work in one of the hospitals. I'll feel better if I can work while I'm here, even if it's only for a short time. Apparently he knows a lot about Washington and the people who live here, but if I have to be on guard, it's not worth socializing with him."

"It's either make the effort or be bored. At least today he can take you to the park."

"Oh," she said, tilting her head slightly. "Should I give him a leash to put around my neck?" She grabbed her throat with both hands and made exaggerated gagging noises.

Jack took a large bite, murdering a plate of scrambled eggs. "The colonel might have news of Braham today."

"He might, but I doubt it. The odds of finding him, especially if he doesn't want to be found, aren't good. The odds of stopping him are even slimmer. I'm resigned to being here for at least four months." Except for the mission to Afghanistan, she'd never been away from her patients for more than a week, two at the most. And although she had planned for an extended leave, the knowledge that she could be gone for months created an odd emptiness beneath her breastbone.

"Then, you have to find a project. Don't you have two journal articles to write? Work on them."

She snarled, putting the full force of her frustration—at the restrictive status of nineteenth-century women and her pique at her *errant cousin*—into the long growl. "Longhand? You're suggesting I write and edit a detailed medical article by hand? I need my data, a computer, and the internet to get past the outline."

He wiped his mouth with a cloth napkin, grinning. "A surgeon needs to keep her fingers nimble."

She swatted her napkin at him. "There's a difference between keeping them nimble and writing with a quill pen until they cramp."

Giving her a broad wink he said, "They use dip pens now."

"Great. Just what I want. Ink all over my fingers."

35

Washington City—1864

Aᶠᵗᵉʳ Jᴀᴄᴋ ʟᴇꜰᴛ to go wandering about the city, Charlotte asked Edward for pen and paper. He brought her a metal nib pen, inkwell, and a sheaf of Braham's letterhead. She set up shop at the table in front of the window and outlined a promised article on the improvements in computer simulation as teaching adjunct for robotic surgery. Because she didn't want to waste paper, she took her time, composing sentences clearly in her mind before she wrote them. Her drawings would never be accepted by a publication, but they did have an artistic flair which made her chuckle.

At noon Edward brought in lunch, and at two o'clock, he announced Colonel Henly.

Ringlets had fallen across her forehead during her long hours bent over the table writing. She tucked them out of the way behind her ears, but the stubborn locks were too short and too curly to stay put without hair clips.

"Good afternoon, Miss Mallory." Henly strode toward her with a slight hitch in his stride, his steel scabbard clinking with each step. His jaw didn't have the tension of the previous day, and his eyes seemed clearer. She tried once again to tuck the springy wisps out of the way before giving up.

"Good afternoon, Colonel."

His glance drifted from her face to the drawings of abdominal organs spread out on the table. He frowned, his mouth twitching in disbelief.

"I'm writing an article I hope to see published in the Lancet, and I've written enough for today. Will you take me for a walk? I need exercise and fresh air."

With his eyes still on the papers he said, "It's chilly. Colder than yesterday."

"I know, but I need fresh air, if only for a brief stroll." She gathered the papers, tapped the edges on the table, and then stacked them neatly.

A few minutes later they waited on the corner of H Street and Jackson Place. A wind blew through the bare trees, making them whisper and creak. *What were they saying? Were they warning her? If so, they didn't need to go to all that trouble.* Fiddling with history could cause all sorts of complications, none of them pleasant. She looped her hand around the colonel's elbow as she stepped off the curb, and they crossed the street heading toward the General Andrew Jackson equestrian statue.

When they reached the opposite corner she asked, "Where's the closest hospital?"

He glanced around for a moment, as if getting his bearings. "The K Street Barracks Post Hospital, on K and 17th Streets. Why?"

"Because I need to do something useful. I want to work in a hospital." They began walking again. "The K Street hospital is only two blocks away? If I could volunteer there it would be easy for me to walk to and from work."

Emotions swept across his face, which made her wonder if he was remembering his painful hospital experience. He shifted his weight, grimacing slightly. "If I hadn't seen your drawings, I would have said you were too genteel to work in a hospital. Did you do the same work in Richmond?"

"I'm a trained surgeon, like Mary Edwards Walker, and I need to work. I have skills that can save lives. If I dressed in a surgeon's uniform, I'd be admitted to the surgical theatre, but because I'm a woman—"

"Other doctors would be reluctant to let you."

"Exactly."

They circled the statue of Jackson in silence. When they returned to their starting point, he directed her toward the street crossing.

"Might we stay out a few more minutes? I'm not ready to go back."

He slowed his pace. She stopped and took a long, hard look at him. There was an unnatural color to his skin, and the tightness around his jaw had returned. "You're in pain. Aren't you? Why didn't you tell me before you agreed to escort me?"

"You don't impress a lady by telling her you're injured."

She searched his face. "What happened to you?"

"I was shot several weeks ago."

"Where?"

"The Battle of Cedar Creek."

She shook her head. "No, I mean where on your body, if you don't mind me asking."

"I was shot off my horse. The bullet entered my back, and now it's lodged close to my spine. The surgeon said if he tried to remove it he could paralyze me, or worse, kill me. I'm able to walk now, though it is uncomfortable at best. They left me the choice. I could put up with the pain, or—"

"Possibly never walk again."

He smiled, but it didn't reach his eyes.

"Let's go back and have tea, then," she said.

As soon as they entered the front door, Edward said, "Tea is served in the parlor."

"How delightful. Thank you, Edward." She sat down on the bench in the foyer and unlaced her shoes, but before she took them off she noticed the colonel staring at her. "What's the matter?"

Shock jumped into his eyes. "You're taking your shoes off?"

Her head came up. "Of course. I don't want to track mud on the floor."

He glanced down at his muddy feet.

Edward pulled a white cloth from his back pocket, bent over, and cleaned the mud from the colonel's boots.

Charlotte removed both shoes and put on a pair of black kid leather dance slippers. She handed Edward her muddy shoes. "Would you ask someone to clean these for me?"

He tried not to smile, but his eyes twinkled. "I'll clean them myself, ma'am." He carried them by the laces to somewhere in the back of the house she had yet to explore.

"You're a most unusual woman, Miss Mallory," Henly mused.

She sat and poured cups of tea. "Please call me Charlotte, or if you need to be formal, then Doctor Mallory will do."

His full, symmetrical lips pinched in disapproval. "You *are* a most unusual woman."

She was not seeking his approval, and she intended to make it clear to him she was an intelligent and well-educated woman with strong opinions. "There has to be more to your name than Colonel Henly."

He nodded quickly, as if shocked by her question. He cleared his throat. "Gordon Frederick. If you're so inclined, please call me Gordon."

She sipped her tea. "Tell me about your injury. Did the surgeon see you at the field hospital?"

"Yes, and then I was examined by several more surgeons once I arrived back in Washington. I've been reassigned to the War Department, and Colonel Taylor now leads my regiment." Bitterness lingered in his voice. "I don't want to talk about me. I'd much rather hear about you. Where did you study medicine?"

"There's not much to tell." God, she hated lying; and yet here she was, at it again. "My father trained at a medical college in New York, and I assisted him for a number of years, learning as much from him as possible."

"Where is he now?"

She held Gordon's gaze a moment. Then her eyes dropped before saying, "He's attached to the Second Corps Army of Northern Virginia."

Gordon's upper body stiffened.

"I told you I'm a Unionist," she added quickly. "The split with my father has been difficult."

He set his teacup on the serving tray. "Your story is not unique. The war has torn apart families in the North and South—brothers, fathers, and sons fighting on opposite sides."

"At least Jack didn't join the cause."

Gordon's head tilted curiously. A faint gleam of something indefinable appeared in his eyes. "How has he stayed out of the conflict?"

A liar's edge of discomfort crawled up her back to the base of her neck, tingling and twitching. She glanced down at her hands, avoiding Gordon's eyes. "Jack is a journalist. He's been at most major battles." Once she regained a grip on her composure, she looked up at the colonel again. "He's a brilliant writer. He's visiting newspapers today, as a matter of fact. Maybe one of them will be interested in buying his dispatches. One day, I believe he'll write a novel of lasting importance."

"You have confidence in him."

"As he does in me," she said.

Gordon tapped his finger against his chin. "Jack Mallory. I don't think I've read anything he's written."

"Bylines aren't published so you wouldn't recognize his name."

"I'd like to read one of his dispatches. Maybe I can introduce him to a few editors. I know several. A recommendation might help him sell a piece."

She gave him a sweet smile. "I'm sure Jack would appreciate your help, if it's not too much trouble."

Gordon took her hand. His palms were sweaty and callused. "If you're serious about working in a hospital, I'll see what arrangements I can make."

"You're more than generous, and I am very appreciative." She withdrew her hand to pick up her teacup.

"I can get you in to see the right people, but you would have to prove you have the skills you claim to have. I can't speak to that."

"You came to my rescue yesterday, and today have made offers to assist both Jack and me. Our abandonment on the street was very fortuitous."

He gave a light laugh of false modesty. "I do what I can."

They both sipped their tea. She felt a question or statement hovering in the air between them. Could it be about Braham? She set her cup in its saucer. Not one to shy away from controversy, she asked, "What about my cousin?"

"Oh, well, yes, I asked Secretary of War Stanton about him."

"And?" Her voice climbed a notch in anticipation."

"He wanted to know why I asking. I told him Braham's cousin from Richmond was in town looking for him. He said he found it very curious and didn't have any information he could pass along. However, as I was leaving, Secretary of State Seward stopped me and extended an invitation to a small dinner party at his home this Friday. Would you like to accompany me?"

"He lives on the other side of the park, does he not?" she asked.

"Near the corner of Pennsylvania and Madison Place."

"May I send you my reply tomorrow?"

He gave her a half grin. "If the answer is yes, tomorrow will be fine."

For a moment she didn't reply. Then she said, "I'd like to mention it to Jack first, to be sure he hasn't committed us to another engagement."

The case clock in the corner struck four.

"I must be going," Gordon said, standing. "I have a five o'clock appointment. Tomorrow I'll call on Doctor Letterman at the Medical Department and inquire as to a position which might be appropriate for a woman with your qualifications."

"I'll look forward to hearing from you."

He lifted her hand and kissed her fingers. "And I look forward to hearing from you."

Charlotte stood at the window scrubbing her hand to get rid of the sensation of his lips. She had painted herself into a corner. Lincoln and Stanton had sent her *father* to rescue Braham. Now she showed up claiming to be his cousin and wanting to know his whereabouts.

Good God, what was she doing? Playing with history. Playing with people's lives.

Life was much simpler when all she had to worry about besides her patients, teaching, and piles of medical records, and whether or not she was going to get another speeding ticket.

36

Washington City—February, 1865

J ACK STOOD IN the doorway to Charlotte's bedroom, twirling his pocket watch by its long silver chain. "Big date?"

"I'm going with Gordon to Ford's Theatre to see the comedian J. S. Clarks. He wouldn't take no for an answer, and I do want to see the production."

Jack leaned against the doorframe and pocketed his watch. "I would have taken you."

"I know." She removed her grandmother's cameo from its secret hiding place in her knitting basket and pinned it at the center of the low, square bodice of her blue silk dinner dress. "I don't want to complain, though. Getting me a job at the hospital racked up lots of points for him. And he can be quite charming when he's not in pain or doped up on medication. Then he's unpredictable."

"Do you think he's dangerous?"

She swirled from side to side, checking her reflection in the long mirror. "He can be aggressive, but when I'm firm, he backs off. The trouble is, I never know which personality is going to show up."

"A real Jekyll and Hyde. Now you've told me, I'm not sure I like the idea of you going out with him."

"He's got connections and knows all the movers and shakers in Washington. I don't think we'd get invitations to important dinner parties and balls without him. Although none of them have led to a smidgeon of information about Braham."

"Stop seeing him, then. You don't care about the parties, and if they're not fruitful, there's no reason for you to go."

"You enjoy them, though," she said.

"I do. But I don't need Gordon to get an invitation." Jack sat in the chair next to the door and stretched out his long legs. "Do you think it's serious with Gordon? An unrequited love affair could get messy."

She stopped primping and studied Jack's face. On the surface he appeared relatively calm, but she sensed an undercurrent of concern. His tense neck and chin contradicted his relaxed posture.

"God, I hope not. I have no interest in him at all," she said.

"Because you're just not *into him*," Jack said, using air quotes, "or because of the difference in time zones? You can't have missed the way he looks at you."

"I've noticed the lustful looks, but I ignore them."

Jack smiled charmingly. The sort of smile that caused women to add their phone numbers and addresses to his contact list, then sneak a peek at his cell number in case he didn't call them for a date within the next forty-eight hours.

"Would he fit the bill as a sperm donor?" he asked.

"Hmm." She pulled her lower lip through her teeth. "He has the physique, intelligence, and voice. But there's something missing. Chemistry, I guess."

"What's chemistry got to do with choosing a sperm donor?"

She scrunched her face, thinking. "It does seem odd, doesn't it? I think I want my donor to be anonymous. Just a picture and facts on a piece of paper." She patted the sides of her hair to herd stray wisps back into place. The current style of parting a woman's hair in the middle, smoothing the sides over her ears, and then pinning a roll at the back of her neck, didn't work for her natural curls.

"Whatever you decide to do about Gordon, please do be careful. I don't want to have to beat him up because he misbehaves. Or, you could fix him. Then he might give up painkillers... unless he's already addicted."

"The bullet presses on a nerve in his back. Riding horseback aggravates the injury, and he can't get any relief from the pain. I wish I could help him, but I wouldn't attempt the surgery even in our time. Neurosurgery isn't my specialty."

"Don't worry about Gordon. Forget him. Braham's my ideal brother-in-law. He's a lawyer, he likes to hunt and fish, and he quotes Shakespeare, too."

"Pshaw. Braham? Our elusive *cousin?*" She collected her white leather gloves and slapped them against her palm. "I wouldn't be surprised to discover he's back in town and trying to avoid us."

Every moment her mind wasn't otherwise occupied, it drifted toward him like smoke from a tipi-shaped fire, spiraling in one direction—his. Even in the midst of minor surgeries the hospital had, out of necessity, allowed her to perform, her thoughts were of him—yearning to see him and wondering if he was well. The image she carried in her mind was of him sitting on a bar stool in the kitchen at the mansion, drinking Jack's coffee and laughing. His bright green eyes held a magical twinkle. The twinkle was what kept the pain of his betrayal manageable.

"By the way," she said, dragging her attention back to the conversation. "Did you finish your article on the inauguration? Gordon said he'd like to read it before it goes to print."

Jack crossed his ankles and folded his arms across his belly. "It's on my desk. I'm submitting it to the *Daily National Intelligencer* tomorrow. It was one of the hardest articles I've written."

"You're writing in the present tense. You have to back away from the historical Lincoln and write about him from today's perspective. It has to be difficult. What's the opening line?"

"Lincoln's second inauguration isn't taking place in a small country town startled by the arrival of a handful of soldiers, but in a city approaching triumph."

"I like it," she said. "You'd think with the scent of victory in the air, the sources you've cultivated would be freer with information. Someone has to know where Braham is. Have you tried John Nicolay or John Hay? They're the President's gatekeepers."

"And they keep his secrets well. Believe me, I've tried both of them. So has everyone else. They don't leak anything."

"And one day *the boys* will be responsible for writing the President's history and creating his legacy."

"And they're so young," Jack said. "I wish I had information to trade. They know where Braham is. I'd bet on it."

"Write a few good articles about the President and gain their trust. Might help."

Jack rose and went toward the door. "The article I'm submitting tomorrow will be a good start. Certainly won't hurt."

She returned the knitting basket to its place on the table and turned down the gas lamps in the bedroom. "Do you have plans tonight?"

"I'm dining at the National Hotel. Why don't you and Gordon join me for a late dinner?"

"I'm not up for your rowdy crowd, but thanks."

She sashayed out of the bedroom, her skirt swishing in the quiet hall. "Come downstairs with me."

"Why? Do you need protection from lover boy?"

"If I needed protection, you'd be going with us. I don't yet trust myself on the stairs in a long dress with all these petticoats."

"Ah, you do need my protection."

She gave Jack a knuckle punch to his bicep. His arms were so muscular, her light punch bounced off like a penny on a desktop. "You're arms feel like punching bags filled with cement. No wonder you don't have a girlfriend. Who'd want to snuggle up to those rocks?"

"You'd be surprised," he said, waggling his eyebrows.

"Egads. Get me out of here." Jack had been her protector since childhood, and she depended on him far more than she'd admit. Although she gave him grief over having no soft edges, she appreciated how hard he worked to stay fit, saying nothing of how her pride was tickled when he dressed in a tux.

"You didn't tell me about your meetings today. Did they go well?"

Jack looped her hand around his bent elbow and they started

down the stairs. "Yes, they did. My contacts now extend to the very bowels of the White House. Someone will talk. Someone always does. We'll find Braham. It's just a matter of time."

"Yes, but time is one of many things not on our side."

37

Washington City—February, 1865

M OMENTS BEFORE GORDON arrived, there was a crash in the kitchen followed by a glass-shattering scream. Charlotte and Jack ran to the back of the house to find one of the women servants holding up her scalded hand, crying hysterically.

Charlotte gave Jack's arm an urgent squeeze. "Get my medical box." Then she turned to Edward saying, "Get a bottle of whiskey."

Gordon arrived in the midst of the confusion, and demanded that Charlotte abandon the servant to her own devices. Incensed by his attitude, she wanted to tell him to screw himself, but instead she told him to go sit in the parlor with Jack, have a drink, and wait for her, or go to the theatre by himself.

"I'll wait. You have ten minutes."

It took fifteen minutes to settle the woman, treat the injury, and send her off to bed. Dealing with Gordon's passive-aggressiveness wouldn't be so easy. He barely spoke during the carriage ride.

At Ford's Theatre, the usher escorted Charlotte and Gordon down the aisle to their seats in the front row of a packed house. The production was minutes from starting. Gordon was fuming, and on their way down the aisle, he made a production out of speaking to everyone he knew except her.

She scooted into her seat and arranged her dress. "How did you manage to get such excellent seats?"

"I imposed on a personal connection and told him I needed to impress a beautiful woman."

She smiled, and tried to make her appreciation sound as sincere as possible. "Thank you. I am impressed, and I'm also sorry we're late."

"I should be used to it," he said with a slight snarl in his voice. "You make us late to almost every function."

She concealed an exasperated sigh behind her hand. Nothing she could say would appease him. If she was lucky, the show's humor would defuse the tension. If it didn't, and he was still as unpleasant after the show, she would insist he take her home and not out to dinner. Walking on eggshells around him made for very tender feet.

Since Gordon wasn't speaking to her, she surveyed the theatre and compared the architecture with the present-day theatre. The Presidential box, built into the proscenium arch, was draped with American flags and a portrait of George Washington. Charlotte's mother had held several Senate campaign fundraisers in the twenty-first century Ford's Theatre. Looking at the interior now, Charlotte was amazed at how accurately the building had been restored.

Gordon tapped her arm. "The show's starting."

The gaslights were turned down, the orchestra began to play, and Charlotte settled in for the performance. Then, moments after the music began, the conductor abruptly stopped. The crowd seemed to be poised, electric, waiting.

Charlotte leaned over to Gordon. "What's happening?"

He turned in his seat, craning his neck to see over the crowd behind him. "A special guest is about to enter, but I don't know from where."

The orchestra played the distinctive four ruffles and flourishes of *Hail to the Chief.*

"Lincoln's coming," she said to Gordon.

Heart pounding, she could scarcely contain herself as she watched the entrance to the Presidential box with shivers of excitement. She dug into her drawstring-beaded handbag for her camera, and then stopped herself. This wasn't the twenty-first century, where every moment must be captured on someone's cell phone, sent to Twitter or Instagram, and then out into the world.

Lincoln, followed by General Grant, entered the Presidential box.

She came to her feet, joining the audience in a rousing standing ovation. In her lifetime she had met the Carters, Bushes, Clintons, Obamas, and Lincoln. Now, the sight of him in the Presidential box, where in two months he'd be murdered saddened her. How could she live with herself if she did nothing, and allowed Booth to succeed with his diabolical plan? Wouldn't she be as guilty as the conspirators if she didn't try to prevent the assassination?

"You're shaking. Are you ill?" Gordon asked, with noticeable irritation.

She gave him a tight smile. "No." But she was ill. She was sick at heart.

Was Braham's plan to stop the assassination the best course? Would the country ultimately be better off if Lincoln survived? How could she do nothing and allow such a noble man to die long before his time? She studied the shadowy hollows and deep lines etched in angles across his cheekbones—so care-worn and weary. The job and the constant demands on his time were literally killing him.

He waved to the audience and Grant nodded. Then Lincoln took his seat in a comfortable parlor rocker and turned toward the stage. His hearty laugh could be heard throughout the performance. When the curtain fell, she didn't remember much of the play, but the President's laughter would echo in her heart for the rest of her life.

Following the performance, Gordon begged off a dinner invitation with fellow officers and spouses also in attendance. As they left the theatre, Charlotte said, "I would have enjoyed dinner with your colleagues."

"I'm not in the mood to share you with anyone tonight."

"Jack invited us to join him."

"I'm not sharing you with your brother, either. We'll dine alone."

Any other night, his possessiveness would have irritated her, and she might have insisted on going home, but tonight she couldn't see beyond her worry over Braham's plans. So she said nothing. She merely lifted one shoulder in a half shrug of acknowledgement and climbed into the carriage.

He grimaced when he climbed in, and she realized part of his problem was he was in more pain than usual. Maybe he would want an early evening, too. The rest of the night didn't bode well for either of them.

38

Washington City—February, 1865

CHARLOTTE AND GORDON were seated in a quiet, candlelit corner of the Willard dining room drinking champagne. The bubbly settled the tension between them, and it seemed to calm Gordon, too. Although there was still a noticeable tremor in his hand as he fiddled with the plain stem of his glass.

"You're in pain, aren't you?" she said. "We don't need to stay for dinner."

He gave her a warning eye. "My back is *not* the issue. There's a delicate matter I wish to discuss." His voice was sharp with agitation. He stopped fiddling with the stem and held up his hand to quiet her. "I saw the list of sick and wounded brought into the city today. I know the K Street Barracks Post Hospital received a fair number. The work is taking its toll on you. You're always late for engagements, and when you are present, you're distracted. I want you to quit working immediately."

She stared in open-mouth shock, temporarily unable to speak.

"Hear me out, please."

He took a sip of champagne, and so did she, but it did nothing to lessen her outrage. She inhaled through her nose, exhaled through her mouth. If she wasn't so conscious of needing to protect her hands, she would have reached out and slapped him silly.

"The war won't last much longer." His eyes were fixed on hers, but the only spark of life was a small glint which then disappeared into darkness under the low light of a gas lamp overhead. He continued, "When it ends, I'm going back to Ohio to take over the family store."

Her vision narrowed, as if she had entered a long, winding tunnel with only a small beam of fading light.

"I should discuss this proposal with your brother first, but he told me the day I met you he didn't make decisions for you. In light of that, I'm broaching this subject with you instead."

"Gordon—"

"Please, let me finish."

Their eyes locked and held. Her foot shook. If the conversation went in the direction she suspected, then a disaster was looming.

"We've only known each other for a few weeks, but we've grown compatible, nonetheless. You are as knowledgeable about poetry as you are about the army and politics. You have practicable opinions on every conceivable topic. You're well-read, and you have a unique sense of humor I find refreshing…most of the time." He placed his hand on top of hers. "I'm a man of means and can provide a comfortable lifestyle. I hope you will consider—"

Braham's doppelganger appeared in Charlotte's periphery. She did an instant double take. After tossing down a whiskey, the man opened a cigar case, extracted a black cigar, and held it to his nose for a moment. A match flared, then he leaned against the bar, one foot hiked on the lower rail of a stool, smoking.

Gordon looked to see what had caught her attention. "What the hell is he doing here? I heard the President sent him out on assignment."

She snatched away her hand, damp from his sweaty palm. "You heard what?" Ripples of shock pulsed through her. She put her fingers flat on the table and pushed her chair away.

Gordon grabbed the back of her chair, holding it in place. "*Sit.* You're not going anywhere."

"You've been lying to me. I've been asking you for two months—" She flashed her fingers in front of his face. "—if you knew Braham's whereabouts, and not once, not twice, but dozens of times, you've said *no*. Now you tell me you've known all along Lincoln sent him out on a mission."

Anger flashed up like heat rising from a boiling pot. She glanced over at the bar, and her eyes locked and held with Braham's. He saluted her with the two fingers gripping his cigar. Then, he turned, opened a door behind him, and quit the room. She peeled Gordon's hand off her chair.

"Now he's gone. I've got to go find him before he leaves again. Let go of my chair."

Gordon glanced over his shoulder. "If he went through that door, he's in the billiard room, and women aren't allowed in there."

In the brief time she'd been in the nineteenth century, when faced with blatant sexual discrimination she had remained calm, which had surprised her and given Jack a good laugh. But this time, cultural practices were putting a trivial and unnecessary obstacle in her path. She didn't intend to stand idly by and accept the dogma. She slipped out the other side of her chair and stood.

"Watch me."

"*Sit down,*" Gordon growled between clenched teeth, clasping her wrist with a yank, "before you cause a scene." His dark eyes narrowed and the vein at his right temple pulsed. "There are actions you can take in your own home you're not permitted to take in public. One of those is entering the billiard room."

Blood pounded in her ears. "If I can't go in there, would you please go ask him to come out? I'd like to speak with him."

Gordon shoved his fingers through his hair, leaving uneven ridges. "He'll be at the townhouse later. You can talk to him then."

"You don't know that." She set her feet squarely. "I have been waiting months to talk to him. If you don't go in there right now, I will, and rules be damned." Gordon made an exasperated noise deep in his throat, but it was his scorching glare which fueled her determination.

"I didn't know this side of you existed, but I shouldn't be surprised. Your father and brother have coddled you and allowed you to have your way. Your husband will correct this behavior with a lash, if necessary. Now *sit* down." His voice was as inflexible as a stone.

A lump of fear hardened in her chest, so she sat. She'd had professors in classroom situations and doctors in the hospital use a similar condescending tone with her, but no one had ever threatened her. Forget slapping him. Breaking a chair over his head would be far more satisfying.

Gordon got to his feet and threw his napkin on his chair. "I'll be *back*." The sharp-edged emphasis he placed on the word *back* was as relentlessly pointed as the final gesture of a conductor's baton.

Silently, she seethed, refusing to let her composure completely crumble.

39

Washington City, February, 1865

B RAHAM HAD GONE to the dining room at the Willard intending to have a decent meal. His stomach rumbled for expertly prepared food rather than something shot, skinned, and burned over an open campfire. He ordered a whiskey at the bar and drank the amber liquor in one long burning swallow.

"Keep 'em coming," he told the barkeep.

Damn Stanton. Braham had wanted to strangle the Secretary of War. Still did. He squeezed his fingers around the refilled whiskey glass, but it wasn't Stanton's imaginary neck in his stranglehold. It was Charlotte Mallory's. What was she doing in Washington? Yes, he had imagined her coming after him, even made plans for the eventuality, but he hadn't really believed she'd have the fortitude to make another trip to the past. Obviously, he was wrong.

If Braham hadn't been sitting at the large walnut table in Lincoln's office when the Secretary of War asked him to explain his relationship to Charlotte Mallory, his legs would have given out and he'd have hit the floor. Shocked? Hell, yes, he'd been shocked. His nemesis, Gordon Henly, had told the secretary Braham's cousin was in town searching for him. Braham had been forced to lie to Stanton and Lincoln. Did a damn good job of it, too. The lie had rolled off his tongue slicker than water off an oilskin duster.

"She's the daughter of the doctor who saved my life," he had told Lincoln and Stanton. And then, in answer to Stanton's question about why she was in Washington, he had said smoothly and wishfully, "She fell in love with me."

He squeezed harder on the glass—a substitute for *her*. His thumb glided up and down the soft, white skin of her long, elegant neck. He gulped the rest of his drink and slammed the crystal on the bar for a refill, not hard enough to break it, but hard enough to crack it.

The barkeep's brows furrowed, disapprovingly. "You cracked the glass."

Braham impaled him with a ferocious glare. "Add it to my bill."

He would crack a dozen glasses if it would ease the pain gnawing at his gut. The pain was not from the old gunshot wound, but from missed opportunity. He gave a derisive chuckle. Missed opportunity? Is that what he was going to call it? He had walked away from the only woman who had ever challenged his mind while she also stimulated his senses. His insatiable lust for her had given him a perpetual cockstand no other woman would ever satisfy. Stanton had asked if Braham loved her, and another lie had rolled easily off his tongue. No.

Did he want to see her? Yes. Would he see her? He shook his head, glaring at his fingers, now turning white from his grip on the tumbler. Again he shook his head. If he did, he might as well put a pair of ominous scissors in Delilah's hands.

He pried his fingers from the glass and reached for the cigar case in his pocket. He extracted one and gently pinched the cigar between thumb and index finger, working the entire length inch by inch, searching for hard or soft spots. Satisfied there would be no draw problems, he passed the cigar beneath his nose, taking in the sweet aroma. The full-bodied cigar and the libations were diversions. The smoky cloud masked the feelings of his heart.

A match flared. The barkeep held the light while Braham rotated the foot of the cigar above the flame, drawing smoke into his mouth. Pleased with the even burn, he leaned casually against the bar, one foot hiked on the lower rail of a stool, and puffed. His fingers found the glass again and squeezed.

Diners filled the room with their discussions of politics and the war. A man and woman sat nestled in the corner drinking champagne. The curve of her breast spilled from a dark green silk gown. His eyes followed the line of her long, elegant neck to a stubborn chin, full lips, a small, tipped-up nose, almond-shaped eyes, a face fringed with golden curls.

A beautiful woman.

His heart stopped…and then leapt to his throat, cutting off his air. He couldn't think. He couldn't move. He just stared. Then Charlotte's eyes found his. In that one moment he thought he would shatter into a thousand pieces. It was not only Charlotte, but Charlotte with Gordon Henly.

The man might be a highly decorated officer with a fine military reputation, but Braham had heard rumors at the gaming halls about Henly abusing the women at Mary Ann Hall's brothel so badly the madam had forbidden him to ever return to her establishment. Surely Jack could see the man beneath the uniform and warn his sister to stay away from the cad.

Braham's breath returned in an angry rush. He straightened, pivoted on his heel, and fled the room. An unaccustomed, twisted weed of jealousy sprang up in his heart, towering over all other emotions, stinging like nettles. He pressed his palm against his chest to smother the feeling, but it left blisters on his heart which burned when he breathed. He needed to get out of town. Now. Go where she couldn't find him. He hurried toward the hotel's rear door, barely acknowledging his acquaintances at the gaming tables.

"Major McCabe," Henly's voice rang out.

He couldn't ignore a senior officer. Braham whipped around to find the colonel weaving his way briskly around the billiard tables, his face a mask of granite.

Braham lifted his hand, held it in a salute. "Colonel." It took the strength of will to keep from ramming his fist in Henly's face.

They stared at each other in tense silence. Finally Henly said, "Your cousin wants a word with you." He smirked. "If she really is your cousin."

Braham's hand clenched at his side. To hit a senior officer would land him in the Old Capitol Prison. He relaxed his hand and shook out cramped fingers. "I'll meet her in the corridor."

Two days of hard travel, shock, and anger coalesced within him, making any plan more complicated than telling the simple truth impossible. The immutable truth bloomed in his chest. He would tell her what she wanted to hear, and then she'd go home—out of his sight, but not out of his head or his heart. He was doomed to die with her occupying most, if not all, of both.

Preparing to lose her once again, he marched out into the hallway, leaned against the wall, and waited with his arms folded tightly at his chest.

40

Washington City, February, 1865

CHARLOTTE TAPPED HER short fingernails on the lip of the table. A minute stretched into two or five or twenty. She had no way of knowing. What were Gordon and Braham saying to each other? Gordon was angry, but he'd been angry all evening, and since Braham hadn't sought her out, she assumed he was angry, too. But why would he be? He had assumed she would follow him back to his century, and she had. Since he didn't have any romantic interest in her, he couldn't be upset because she was having dinner with Gordon.

After an interminable time, Gordon strode back into the room. His face was shiny with nervous perspiration and there was no spark of victory in his eyes. Her mind was racing, and time had slowed to a stall. Why was Gordon walking so slowly? Was it to give Braham time to get out of the building? If Braham refused to speak to her, she wasn't sure what she intended to do, but whatever it was, it wouldn't be pleasant. For him. She swallowed hard to keep any possible nervous flutter from creeping in her voice. She put her hands in her lap, and crossed them wrist over wrist.

Gordon grasped the back of her chair. "He's waiting in the corridor."

She swallowed, dry-mouthed with excitement and apprehension.

Gordon's eyes locked on hers for a moment, the corners now deeply lined with tension. "He's leaving town again tonight, but he agreed to speak with you."

"He agreed? How lovely."

Gordon cringed at her acerbic tone.

She swished her way out of the dining room and into the corridor. Since the night she had driven up to the mansion and discovered Braham gone, she had wanted to take her anger and frustration out on him. But how? A sudden thought lay heavy in her chest, like a swallowed stone. Since he wouldn't listen to her logical arguments—and she wasn't one to cry or get violent—and, as far as he was concerned, Lincoln's welfare trumped her own, then what was left? Begging.

Braham waited at the end of the long hallway, one shoulder propped against the wall, arms folded. Tonight he was dressed, handsomely, in a Cavalry uniform, saber hanging at his side.

"Will you please give us a minute?" she said to Gordon.

"Make it quick. Dinner will be served shortly." He pointed to a bench next to the door. "I'll wait here."

She took a calming breath, and glided toward Braham. He gazed into her eyes for a long moment, a look to remind her he was everything she imagined, and much, much more. He levered himself away from the wall, fists on his hips—a ferocious warrior. He had added a few pounds. His uniform jacket was snug across his chest. But uniform or additional weight didn't halt her breath, or the long, blond hair brushing his collar, or even the grin tilting one side of his mouth. It was the hunger and longing swimming in the depths of his brilliant green eyes. If eyes were windows to one's soul, then he was gazing into hers as she was gazing into his.

Small lines were visible around his eyes as they widened in frank appreciation. "Charlotte." His voice was resonant, husky. Was he trying to ignore a swelling tightness in his body as she was with hers? "Why did you come, *cousin?*"

"You were expecting me," she said.

"I thought you'd come. Though I wish you hadn't."

"You lied to me and stole my car."

He rolled his shoulders in a defensive gesture. "I never lied to you. If you've talked to Elliott, you know why I didn't tell you about my cousin…my real one, I mean."

Being in his proximity after months of worrying about him knotted her insides. She clenched her hands beneath the folds of her skirt. "Lies of omission are still lies."

His green-eyed look was as shattering as a physical touch. "I learned that lesson years ago."

A protracted and awkward silence fell between them. "Come to the townhouse tonight. Let's talk over a glass of wine instead of whispering in a hallway."

Braham rubbed his chin, and his whiskers rasped under his fingers. "Are you afraid your suitor will get jealous?"

"*He's not…*" She took a breath and tried again in a calmer voice. "Gordon's been very helpful."

"I'm sure he has. It looked scandalous from where I was standing." His voice held a ruthless edge. "Of all the men in Washington, why him?"

"I secured a position at a hospital through his contacts, and he introduced Jack to several editors who want to read his articles." She crossed her arms and planted her feet, refusing to let Braham intimidate her. "Why do you care?"

He didn't answer. He let the words drift to the floor between them.

She tried a different approach. "Gordon said you were leaving again tonight. When will you be back?"

"I serve at the pleasure of the President."

She took another breath, searching desperately for something to say to make him understand why she was there and what she wanted from him. "Surely, the President will let you —"

He cut her off with an abrupt blast of fury, saying, "Mr. Lincoln expects me to do my job." His tempestuous tone died suddenly, and when she looked back up into his eyes, her throat was sticky as paste, and she turned away, willing the tears not to come.

Although the corner of the corridor they occupied was chilly, it was his impenetrable wall of indifference freezing her out. One last try; then she was done. "I beg of you, please don't change the future because of what you learned while you were with us."

There was silence, short enough to fill a heartbeat, long enough to pave the distance growing between them. She swallowed with difficulty and a tear slid down her cheek. Using his thumb, Braham wiped it away.

"I couldn't live with myself if I didn't try to change what's to come."

"But—"

He pressed his finger on her lips. Then said in words so thick with emotion he seemed barely able to squeeze them out, "Go home, Charlotte."

41

Washington City, February, 1865

GORDON SLAMMED THE carriage door, sat on the opposite bench from Charlotte, and said with a sarcastic bite, "A joyful reunion of *cousins*, followed by a lousy dinner with a less than charming dinner companion."

"I'm sorry I was distracted." Familiar anxiety clutched at her stomach, triggering a bitter churn. She'd had more than enough male attitude hurled at her for one evening. All she wanted to do now was go home, get in her jammies, and drown her sorrows in a glass, no, a bottle of wine.

"Distracted?" he said, sneering. "I'd call that a polite term for speaking only monosyllables during a five-course dinner?"

"I asked you to take me home before we ate, but you refused."

"Of course I refused." His absolute matter-of-factness sent a shiver running down her spine. He removed a tin snuffbox from his jacket pocket, tapped on the lid a few times, and then slowly opened it. "I wasn't going to let the son of a bitch ruin the rest of my evening."

"You obviously dislike the major. Why?"

He took a pinch of snuff between his thumb and forefinger and sniffed it sharply into one nostril, and then the other. "We had a difference of opinion a couple of years back. Nothing more, and nothing to concern you." He closed the tin and returned it to his pocket. Making no effort to hide his contempt he asked, "Are you in love with him?"

"No." There would always be loyalties, fears, and lies separating her and Braham. She wasn't in love with him, but even if she were she'd never admit it to Gordon. But if she wasn't in love with Braham, why did her heart ache?

The conversation died, and they rode in an exceedingly awkward silence until they were only a couple of blocks from the townhouse.

"Braham's appearance interrupted you earlier. I'm sorry it happened. You were talking about what you intended to do after the war. Would you like to finish now?"

The frown, which had lurked during the discussion of Braham, cleared at the mention of their earlier conversation. "No. It's late." He shrugged uncomfortably while tugging at his cravat.

If he didn't want to talk, it suited her fine.

The carriage stopped, and Charlotte couldn't get out fast enough. As they proceeded toward the front door, Gordon said, "We have a dinner invitation Friday evening—"

The timing was perfect. Gordon wouldn't verbally attack her in front of another person. Just as Edward opened the front door she said, "I don't know if I'm available. I'll give you my answer tomorrow."

"Good evening Colonel Henly, Miss Mallory."

She handed the butler her cape. "Is Jack home?"

"A man is with him in the study."

She glanced in the direction of the room Jack had co-opted as his office, located across from dining room and the ever-present coffee pot. "Do you know the man he's with?"

"Mr. Mallory didn't mention a name."

The door to the study creaked opened and Jack and his guest came out into the shadowy entryway. When she saw the visitor sauntering toward them, her heart lodged in her throat. Dear God, surely not *him*.

"Charlotte, my dear, and Colonel Henly, I'd like to introduce Mr. John Wilkes Booth."

She opened and closed her mouth in a futile search for something—something calm and rational—to say. Nothing.

Gordon shook Booth's hand with star-struck enthusiasm. "I saw several of your performances last year at Ford's: *Richard III, Romeo and Juliet, The Merchant of Venice*. I believe the Star hailed your engagement as brilliant and lucrative."

Gordon continued to gush on, further disorienting Charlotte. "You've had much success as a tragedian. Your swordplay and bounding leaps are spectacular. When will you return to the stage?"

Booth resembled a preening peacock, with his greatcoat collared in fur and a stick pin thrust in the center of his elaborate cravat. "I have no professional engagements scheduled. I'm more interested in investing in oil lands than acting."

The actor's sweet voice grated on her nerves. His risky speculations were the stock jokes of the day. A shiver rolled up the length of her body from her shoes to the top of her head. If she had not been well schooled in social graces from the time she learned to walk and talk, they would have failed her now, and she would have refused to touch the assassin's hand. Instead, she demurely lifted her fingers to greet him in a performance worthy of the stage he had recently vacated.

"Mr. Booth, what brings you to Jackson Place this evening?" she asked as civilly as possible.

His big, powerful hand contrasted oddly with his fine-drawn features. He was impeccably dressed. Even his hair was perfectly waved, as through he'd used a curling iron. She was not remotely impressed, and, in fact, thought he appeared vain and insufferable. He kissed the back of her fingers, gazing at her from beneath his long lashes. She quickly reclaimed her hand, wishing she could sterilize it. How could Jack bring this monster inside their doors? Inside Braham's home? Jack had some explaining to do.

"Mr. Booth agreed to sit for an interview," Jack said. "I'm afraid I've used much more of his time than he originally offered."

Edward handed Booth his hat. "I have a late appointment. Please excuse me." Booth bowed to Charlotte, then said to Jack, "I look forward to reading the interview." Booth left the house, his cape flowing behind his long strides.

Charlotte threw a cool, rigid look at her brother.

Jack clapped his hands together, rubbed them vigorously, smiled, and said, "Well, how was the theatre?"

Her performance would have earned an Oscar, and as long as Gordon remained at her side, she would continue to act the epitome of Southern graciousness, elegance, and hospitality. She had temporarily lost her composure at the hotel, but every daughter of the South had an occasional bad moment. The assertive side of her personality, which Gordon had seen earlier, needed to be curbed for only a few minutes more. Clearly, it wasn't worth the effort to rein in her assertiveness in her own time, but here expectations were different.

Gordon cleared his throat. "The show was entertaining and dinner was exceptional. However, both lost their flavor by the appearance—"

"Braham was at the Willard." Charlotte cut Gordon off abruptly, cringing as she did so, but it didn't keep her from continuing. "He came to town for a meeting with Stanton, but he's leaving now to go back to who-knows-where to do who-knows-what."

The expression on Jack's face was indecipherable. "Where's he been?"

"He didn't say."

"Where's he going?"

"He didn't say. All he said was he served at the pleasure of the President."

Another question hovered in the air between Jack and Charlotte. They eyed each other, but left the thought unspoken.

"Was he surprised to see you?" Jack asked.

Charlotte answered in a clear but soft voice belying her true feelings. "He knew we were here."

Jack snatched his hat and coat from the coat tree. "I'm going over to the Willard."

Gordon lips twitched in what might have been a faint smile. "Would you care to ride with me?"

She watched the two men leave, hoping Jack didn't haul off and punch either Gordon or Braham. On second thought, she still believed both men might benefit from having some sense knocked into their rocklike skulls. He had her blessing.

42

Washington City, February, 1865

B EYOND THE WINDOW of Charlotte's bedroom, moonlight painted a glittering trail across snow left over from a late winter storm. The only sounds were crackling fire and the wind groaning outside. The dark, velvety cloak of night would lift in a few hours and a new day would begin. Perhaps the dawn would illuminate solutions to this abominable situation.

She sat curled on the loveseat in front of the fire, massaging her forehead, nauseous with the onslaught of a massive headache. The book on her lap forgotten, she stared blindly into the flames, still shivering—a disastrous date, a confrontation with Braham, an unexpected and unwelcome meeting with Booth. One of the three would have been enough to send her into a tailspin. All three within hours of each other was sufficient excuse to pop open a bottle of valium. She had never taken the stuff, didn't have any pills with her, but had heard plenty of people rave about its calming effect. If she expected to ever be calm tonight, she'd need another glass of wine, or two.

What had Jack been thinking to invite Booth to Braham's house? If Braham had come home and found Booth there, one of them would be lying on the floor bleeding out right now.

Shivers rattled her teeth, exacerbating the headache.

The front door opened and closed and voices floated up the stairs. Golden light from the lamp in her room spilled out into the second floor's wide hall. Jack would, out of habit, stop by to talk before bed. A few minutes later, he sauntered in, carrying two glasses and a bottle of wine.

"Saw your light on when I came in. Thought you'd like a glass of wine after your exciting evening."

She held up her empty glass, smiling. "Perfect timing. Thank you."

He refilled her glass and poured some for himself, then squeezed and squirmed until he finally settled into the walnut lady's chair next to her.

She lifted the glass to smell the bouquet before taking a sip. "Did you find Braham?"

An impertinent grin livened his face. "I found him. He was working his way through a bottle of whiskey. You must have done a number on him."

She snorted and rolled her eyes "Who, me? I hardly said anything. He was as shut down as a condemned building waiting for the wrecking ball."

"Yeah, but I think he was the wrecking ball searching for a condemned building to plow into. He definitely wanted to pick a fight, but I wasn't about to give him an excuse."

"I begged him not to do anything based on what he learned in the twenty-first century, and he told me to go home."

"He didn't like seeing you with Gordon."

She jerked back with a start, the book in her lap landing on to the floor with a hollow thud. "Did he say so?"

"More or less."

She leaned over, grabbed the wine bottle off the floor, and read the label. "This is good." She took another sip. "Now don't be so cryptic. If he said something, tell me."

"He asked how you met Gordon, how often you spend time with him, and if he had seen you in scrubs with your hair down."

"Where does he come up with these things?" She pulled her feet up under her hip and snuggled once again into the sofa's soft, plushy cushion.

"Conversation with him tonight was like patting a porcupine," Jack said.

"Why was he so testy? Did he know Booth was in town?"

"Nah. His mood was directly related to you, and I enjoyed his suffering. Payback for lying to me." Jack gave her an unrepentant grin. "I made it worse by talking about how beautiful you looked tonight."

"Must be a guy thing."

"Right, like girls don't do it, too."

"Girls might play games, but they don't bring the enemy into the house." Her voice was hemmed with jagged edges of fear and fury. "What were you *thinking* when you invited Booth here? He's dangerous, and associating with him could be deadly."

A worry crease appeared over Jack's nose. He propped one booted foot on his opposite knee and picked at the threads of his wool sock, thinking. Finally, he broke his silence. "You're right. I shouldn't have brought him to Jackson Place. But I wanted to tape the conversation, and the noise at the National Hotel made it impossible to get a good recording."

"What'd he talk about… other than his gorgeous and talented self?"

Jack dropped his foot to the floor and leaned forward, holding his glass with both hands. "He asked what I thought of Lincoln. I said I admired him. He wondered how a good Southern gentleman could support a despot. I told him the focus of the interview was his career as a thespian, not his politics. He switched tactics and talked about the theatre and oil and land investments."

"Did you mention your meeting with Booth to Braham?"

Jack shook his head. "Braham's not an assassin. He might threaten, but he's got too strong a moral code. I predict when the date gets closer, he'll make comments to Lincoln about additional security, and on the fourteenth, he'll try to keep the President from going to the theatre."

"Since we don't know where he is," she said, "we can't keep him from interfering. He was in town tonight to meet with Lincoln and

Stanton. He could slip back into the city at any time and we wouldn't know."

"He ducked out on me tonight. He left to use the necessary room, and when he didn't come back, I went looking for him, but by then it was too late. He was gone. Which won't happen a second time." Jack sat back in the chair, stretched out his legs, and gave her his endearing raised-eyebrow look. "Now, I want to hear what happened with Gordon."

She looked down at her fingers, fussing with a hangnail.

After an awkward silence, Jack said, "You done stalling? Fess up. What happened?"

"I hate it when you're right. You had Gordon pegged. He was about to propose when Braham showed up. Boy, did that piss him off."

"Gordon told me I had done you a disservice by allowing you far too much freedom."

"What did you say?"

"I told him the same thing I told him the day we met in December. You make your own decisions."

She couldn't help smiling with relief. "I don't want to see him again. Not after the way he acted tonight. He might not even come back."

"Oh, he will."

"What makes you so sure?"

A dimple identical to the one she saw in the mirror every day appeared in Jack's right cheek. "Gordon sees it as a competition now, and doesn't intend to lose to Braham."

"*Men.* I don't intend to be a pawn in a chess game, and I certainly have no intention of being any Neanderthal's prize."

43

Washington City, February, 1865

A KNOCK ON Charlotte's bedroom door startled her awake. Her eyes popped open to see Braham standing in the doorway. "You left the door ajar. It's allowed all the heat to escape the room. And you look uncomfortable on the loveseat. Why don't you sleep in your bed?"

She yawned, shivering. "Jack stopped by to talk. I must have dozed off after he left." Although smoldering ash of a dying fire scented the air, he was right, there was no heat coming from the red, yellow, and orange embers. "I'm surprised you're here. I didn't expect to see you again."

"And I thought you'd be gone, too." His voice was low and husky.

"I don't make it a habit of disappearing into the night like some people I know."

He leaned back against the doorframe, wearing only a pair of trousers with suspenders dangling down his legs. Damp hair reaching his shoulders dribbled glistening drops of water onto his bare chest. The whiskers she'd seen earlier had given way to a smooth-shaven, expressionless face, but she sensed the roiling going on inside of him. He closed the door and sidled over to the fireplace where he added wood and poked the dying embers, coaxing it to reluctant life. He then turned to face her, the furrows in his forehead deepening.

"I had to leave Jack at the hotel tonight. I didn't want him to follow me."

She reached for a shawl tossed over the back of the loveseat and draped the warm velvet around her shoulders, snugging the ends close to her body. "Am I going to read about Booth's murder in the morning paper?"

He set the poker aside and picked up the bellows. A *whoosh* of air stirred the embers even more, until red-gold sparks burst into brilliant flames. "If you do, it won't be my doing."

He turned, and those kindling eyes of his pierced her soul, deeper than they had any right to penetrate. She squeezed hers shut, pushing away his intrusion. Could he see her defenses crumbling? Because they were. Like sand castles when the tide comes in. She couldn't speak; tears were too near the surface.

She took a breath and looked at him once more, saying softly, "Why are you here?"

Although the burning logs sizzled and popped, he poked at them again somewhat absentmindedly. "I didn't want our earlier meeting to be my last memory of you."

Unsure of him, and definitely unsure of herself, she asked, "What kind of memory would you prefer?" Heat radiating off of him, imagined or real, nonetheless warmed her. She loosed the ends of the shawl.

He set down the poker. "That's not a smart question to ask a man going off to war."

"Are you..." Her voice cracked, and she tried again. "Are you going off to war?"

"Yes."

He crossed the flat woven carpet defining the edges of the small sitting area in her bedroom. She patted the sofa cushion, inviting him to sit. His shoulder brushed her arm, and his face was but inches from hers. The expression he wore was soft, eyes unguarded. With surprising tenderness, he stroked her cheek with his fingertips, up and down like a narrow brush, painting the essence of her.

"Don't go."

He laughed softly. "It's my job."

She leaned toward him with her arm along the back of the love seat. "You scared me when you left the plantation. I imagined all sorts of things had happened to you, and almost all of them would have been better than what actually happened."

His large hand traced the muscles of her arm with unsuspected gentleness. He brushed the shawl off of her shoulder and pinched a bit of her gown between his thumb and forefinger, toying with it softly. His eyes roved over her hungrily.

"I'm sorry." There was a still, smooth tone to his voice, lulling.

The stew of her emotions came to a boil. "Now I understand how you can go into enemy territory and do what you do. It was no small feat to drive a car almost five hundred miles when you'd never driven before. You have nerves of steel."

"Sometimes." He let go of her gown and picked up one of her ringlets, carefully. "You looked beautiful tonight, elegant. I'd never seen you in anything other than scrubs and jeans." The fingers of his other hand swept seductively across her chest below her collarbone, above her breasts. "Your décolletage—" he raised an eyebrow, "—is not for cads to view. Next time, I suggest you wear scrubs. If there is a next time."

Heat rushed to her cheeks. There was nothing particularly revealing about the dress she'd worn tonight, at least by twenty-first century standards. Was it her imagination, or was he truly attracted to her? Did he find her desirable? Was his heart beating to the double-time cadence of a drummer like hers? "And now?" she asked, her voice soft, and she anchored her attention on him, careful not to move or blink or think beyond this moment. "How do you see me?"

"Very desirable." His mouth twitched with the tiniest and briefest of smiles. He dropped the curl and picked up another one close to her ear, bushing her neck with the back of his hand. "I like your hair falling down around your face and shoulders." He pulled the curl to his nose and sniffed, smiling.

She was silent for a long time, and so was he, seemingly content to listen to the wind. Embers fell apart and sparks floated like fireflies in the dimness of the room. She returned his gaze, waiting to hear the unspoken whispers hovering in the air. To say them would strip away all vestige of hope. He let the curl fall back into place, and, instead of picking up another one, he touched her cheek again. His scent was fresh and clean from the Proctor & Gamble white soap he had used, but there was an underlying scent—his own male musk—the kind of scent that pulled on a woman at a primal level. His thumb slid over the curve of her cheek, the line of her jaw, stopping at her mouth, gazing at her with a visual caress.

"I came for one last memory of you."

"So you said," she realized she sounded a bit breathless. "What you didn't say was what kind of memory you would prefer."

He nudged her chin up with his thumb. "I didn't, did I?"

She touched his arm, which was warm beneath his shirt, and a shudder went through him. It went through her, too, pulsing and vibrating, and she moaned with a rush of desire. It seemed so natural to slip into his arms and share a kiss. His mouth came down slowly, tentative at first, then he kissed her full on the mouth, pulling on her bottom lip with his teeth, lightly and erotically. His large, gentle hands stroked her face. When their tongues touched, she tasted sweet whiskey on his warm breath. His tongue moved against hers, tantalizing her mouth with thorough, languid movements. She kissed him back, astonishing herself with a depth of passion she had not believed possible.

He leaned back with a groan, pulling her with him until she lay on top of his sprawled body. Only the thin silk of her gown and the wool of his trousers separated their tightly strung bodies, each molding against the other. Braham gripped the curves of her buttocks and nudged her ever closer. The hard outline of his pulsing erection pressed against her almost bare thigh.

And she desired him as feverishly as he wanted her. She skimmed her hand down the side of his face, tracing the lines of his chin, his neck, to the hollow of his throat, and kissed him there. He shifted his fingers through her curls from her nape to her crown. He nudged her chin up and coaxed her mouth to stay open.

He tasted wild and fresh, and the touch of lips seemed like something other than kissing—more urgent, more relentless, eroding her balance. She clutched his shoulders, curving her fingers over the long plane of bone and muscle to the hard nape of his neck. If she could crawl inside his skin and know him, know the flesh and blood of him, know his thoughts, she would go now, this very instant, and never look back. She threaded her fingers through damp, satiny hair, cradled his head, and kissed him intensely. A desperate ache burst low in her belly. Responding on her need alone, she pressed his hand against her breast.

"Do you feel the beat of my heart, the hum of my soul?" she whispered.

His fingers drifted over the round shape, cupping the top of the slope until her nipple ached sweetly.

"Yes." There was a slight quiver in his voice.

"You've crumbled the defenses I created so long ago to keep from loving and wanting this much," she said.

As their looks entwined, her hands moved to his buttons, longing to feel skin against skin, and aching to show him, silently, the depth of her desire for him.

He held her tightly against him, slowing her hands, and whispered in her ear words she did not understand—Gaelic words, she suspected—words making the candle he had lit in her heart flicker with hope.

With a soft breath she asked, "What'd you say?"

"I'll live with your absence every day." He eased curly wisps of hair behind her ear. "You've bewitched me with your eyes, your touch, and yes," he squeezed her breast tenderly, "your heart. I thought you might have feelings for me though not so much as this. I care about you so much I canna take you now, knowing I must leave. And Jack would be a wee bit angry with me, too."

"My life is my own. He won't be angry. Come back with us."

He shook his head. "You know I can't."

She laid her head on his chest, relishing the warmth of his hand still cupping her breast. His heart thumped against her cheek, solid and steady, relaxing some of the frozen bands of fear plaguing her since he'd left.

She had saved his life, unaware this moment would come. But even if she had known he might break her heart, she would have handed it to him gladly, wrapped in a package tied with hope and longing. Strands of dread coalesced into the cold shudder snaking down her backbone and coiling in her belly, twisting and knotting her insides. Would the knots ever untangle? She doubted it. Desire for him would hold her captive, and she would continue to dream there would one day be a time and place for them.

44

Washington City, February, 1865

B Y THE TIME Charlotte went downstairs for breakfast, she'd only climbed halfway out of her pity party. Jack would want to know what was wrong, and she couldn't lie to him. He could be counted on to notice her hurt and disappointment. What was she going to tell him? Whatever she decided to say, it would have to be the truth. He had an uncanny ability to read body language and discern thoughts—not just hers, but everyone he met.

She whipped into the parlor and stubbed her big toe on the brick doorstop. "Ouch. Damn it, Braham McCabe. Why'd you put this frigging brick where I would be sure to stub my toe?" She hobbled over to the closest chair, sat, and rubbed her foot. "This is the third time I've run into it."

Edward picked up the brick. One corner of his mouth curled wryly. "I'll find another place for this nuisance."

"How about next to the major's bed? Let him find out what it's like to stub *his* toe."

After a minute or two, when the throbbing dissipated, she opened the sliding doors leading into the dining room, and let out a soft gasp. She clutched the doorframe as the blood rose warm in her cheeks at the memory of last night's kisses, and the sight of this morning's smile. Breathlessly she said, "You're still here."

Braham stood and pulled out the chair next to him. "Good morning. I hope you slept well."

Jack got to his feet, too, frowning. "How'd you know he was here?" His glance moved from Charlotte to Braham, then back to his sister. As he studied her face, it felt like he was prodding beneath her skin. "You have pouches under your eyes you didn't have late last night, and your hair is—" he waved his hands around his head, "—unruly this morning. Why?"

"Good morning to you, too, Jack."

"I didn't mean to insult you. You just look..." He cocked his head. "Tired and unhappy."

"I am tired." She sat and smiled at Braham. "Braham and I talked late last night."

"Talked, huh?" Jack settled back into his chair and picked up his coffee cup, but continued to glare. "Rather late, then. I went to bed after two o'clock and Braham hadn't come home by then. Staying up all night doesn't usually make your eyes red. You've been crying, I bet. What happened?"

She would have kicked her brother under the table, but she was sitting too far away. Instead, she glowered. "Don't let me interrupt your conversation. I'm sure you have more interesting topics to discuss than the redness of my eyes."

A servant came in and poured her a cup of coffee. "Thank you. I'll serve myself from the buffet when I'm ready to eat."

Jack set down his coffee cup, crossed his arms, and wiggled his index finger from side to side. "You stayed up late talking, and this morning your eyes are red from crying. What's going on between you?"

She rubbed her fingers slowly with her other hand, lips pursed in thought. "If you must know..."

Jack leaned forward eagerly. "Yes?"

"Braham asked me to marry him, give up medicine, and have a dozen children. I laughed so hard I cried and couldn't stop. I'm surprised you didn't hear me."

Braham pressed a crooked finger against his lips and coughed, his eyes twinkling. "You misheard, lass. Considering your age, I only asked for a half dozen."

She quirked her eyebrows at him. "Well, if I got lucky, I could have sextuplets, which would require only one pregnancy. Might be doable at my advanced age." She barely got a swallow of coffee down before she really did laugh till she cried, and then dabbed at her eyes with the cloth napkin. She lay her hand on Braham's arm. "I'm glad to see you, but I expected you to be gone by now."

"I was on my way out when I ran into Jack. He persuaded me to stay until this evening. If you're up for a ride, I thought we'd go to Georgetown for luncheon."

"And see your house?" She glanced from Braham to Jack. "I'd love to go."

Jack stood. "Good. It's settled. But first Braham's going to sit for an interview to discuss espionage during the war, so give us a couple of hours." He poured another cup of coffee and left the room.

Before Braham followed Jack to the office, he squeezed her shoulder and kissed the back of neck, blowing a tickle of warm air down the length of her spine. "I've thought of nothing but you in the last few hours. When we get to Georgetown, we'll find a few moments of privacy to talk."

She sat in much-needed solitude, smiling, thrilled at the unexpected gift of a day with Braham, but dreading another final goodbye. Her body warmed, remembering the feel of his lips on her neck.

Edward entered the room. "Colonel Henly is here to see you"

She smiled at Edward until his statement made a connection in her brain. A surge of anxiety settled in her empty stomach. "Tell him I'm not up yet."

Edward turned to leave.

No, she better not put Gordon off. He'd either wait for her to come down or he'd come back later. At least both Braham and Jack were in the house in the event he caused trouble. Best to deal with him now and get it over with.

"Never mind, Edward," she said, rising from her chair. "I'll see him in the parlor."

Gordon was standing in front of the hearth when she entered the room.

"Good morning, Gordon. Isn't it rather early for a social call?"

"I thought I'd save you the necessity of sending a note with your answer about our dinner engagement tomorrow night."

"I appreciate all you've done for both Jack and me, but after last night I think it's best if we don't see each other socially again."

A ghostly smile flickered over his lips. "I'd hoped your brother had impressed upon you—"

"Jack does not make decisions for me," she shot back. "He's told you so twice now, possibly three times."

The soft tick of the clock in the corner and the rising wind brushing against the windowpane were the only nods to time passing. The throb of her pulse beat inside her brain. She felt light-headed, dizzy, like she might faint from an empty stomach and the damned instrument of torture she wore over her chemise—a corset.

Gordon stared at her, his eyes traveling down her with unnerving thoroughness. His face darkened. He crossed the distance between them in two long strides, his fists clenched, his expression furious. She took a step backwards. He caught her face between his hands and turned her chin to the side.

"I heard McCabe's voice as I entered the house. And your lip is swollen, my dear. Did he fuck you last night? Never mind. Don't answer. Save me your sanctimony."

She gasped in horror.

"You're nothing but a goddamn whore."

She recoiled, jerking her head out of his grasp, irate over his jealous tirade. Goosebumps prickled across her arms and shoulders. Her throat tightened painfully, but she forced out strangled words, "Get out. *Now.*"

"Not until I get what I came for." He jerked her to him and grabbed hold of the hair, flinging the sterling hair comb across the room and unraveling the braided chignon at her nape. She cried out when he twisted her hair around his fingers to hold her still, and then he slapped her. Before she could knee him in the groin, he pressed his lips against hers in a bruising kiss, his lips hard and unyielding.

She pushed him off, and he grabbed her roughly by the bodice. The force knocked her off balance, ripping her dress. She scrambled for purchase, but fell sideways onto a table, knocking a stack of books onto the floor.

He raised his arm to strike her, but she dodged, turning her head to lessen the impact. His hand barely grazed the side of her face. "Braham and Jack are here. If I call them, they'll kill you. Go away." She swallowed hard, fighting back a spasm of shock in the pit of her stomach. Her mind was working furiously, but going nowhere. "If you're spoiling for a fight, they'll gladly give you one."

Gordon's brows slanted down like an angry hawk and his checks quivered with rage. He threw open the doors, and they rattled when they hit the wall. "You haven't seen the last of me."

"Oh, yes, I have," she said. "Don't call on me again. You won't be welcomed." Gripping the back of a chair for support, she called to Edward, standing at his post by the door. "The colonel is leaving and will not be back."

Gordon snatched his hat out of Edward's hands and stormed out of the house.

Her insides trembled violently. Clutching her arms, Charlotte went to the window, proceeding with her grandmother's fluid grace, the kind Granny was born with and never failed to exhibit in times of stress and violence.

"By doing it, you believe it," Granny had said.

And so Charlotte did it now. But she didn't have her grandmother's gumption, and she never would. From the window, she could see Gordon stomping down the street, through the snow, with anger radiating off him so forcefully ice probably melted beneath his feet.

"Is there anything I can do to help you?" Edward asked.

She pointed over her shoulder. "The books fell off the table. If you would put the room to rights, I would appreciate it. I'm going upstairs now. I'd like a bath, too, if you would send up hot water.

And, Edward, please don't tell Braham or Jack. There's no need for more violence."

"Certainly, Miss Charlotte."

As soon as she reached her bedroom, she dropped onto the chair in front of her dressing table and stared at her reflection in the mirror. Her head hurt where Gordon pulled her hair, and the curls were now a frizzy mess. She had a bruise developing on the side of her face near her hairline and another bruise beneath her jaw. She also had fingernail scratches on her chest where he had grabbed and ripped her bodice. Intellectually she had always understood drug addicts could be emotionally volatile, and had seen addicts out of control before, but their anger had never been directed at her until now. And she never wanted to repeat the experience.

She opened the window, scooped up a handful of snow from the ledge, and held it against the side of her head. When the first handful melted, she grabbed another. By the time the second compress melted, her bath was ready. A long soak would rejuvenate her. Before the trip to Georgetown, she would apply a bit of makeup over the bruises. If Jack or Braham discovered the colonel had carried his delusional jealousy to such an abusive extreme, someone might get shot.

45

Washington City, February, 1865

WEARING AN EMERALD riding habit along with a matching hat decorated with feathers, plump roses, and an illusion veil, Charlotte made her way to the study to find her afternoon escorts. Entering the room, she gave a fake cough and fanned her way through the cigar smoke to join them. Braham sat back, feet resting on the edge of the desk, puffing. Jack's cigar lay in an ashtray with streaming wisps of smoke following his pen as he drew the trench lines between Petersburg and Richmond.

Braham got up and offered his chair, giving her an appraising glance.

"What? Is something wrong?" she asked.

He shook his head, smiling with a glint of deviltry. "You surprise me, that's all."

Jack's eyes narrowed to crinkled slits. "You *both* surprise *me*."

Charlotte picked up Jack's cigar and tamped it out in the ashtray. "Just because you're living in the midst of smokers doesn't mean you have to smoke." She pointed at the cigar clamped at a jaunty angle between Braham's teeth. "You shouldn't be smoking either."

He gave her a subtle wink. "I haven't heard anyone complain about smoking since the last time I saw Kit. She's on a one-woman crusade to outlaw one of man's most profound pleasures."

Charlotte slapped her riding crop lightly against her leather-gloved palm. "Hundreds of thousands of lives would be saved if she's successful."

"Stop preaching, sis. Nobody likes to listen to a harpy."

"Smoke the damn things, then." She picked up a small tin, removed a lucifer match and tossed the unlit stick onto the map in front of Jack. "Here's a match. Fire it up."

He flicked the tiny piece of wood out of the way and the match rolled among the books and random pieces of paper cluttering the top of the desk.

"How much longer are you two going to be?" she asked. "I'm hungry. Should I have a snack?"

Huffing, Jack rolled up the map and stacked his notes, tapping the papers' edges against the tabletop until the pages were aligned perfectly. She chuckled at the habit they had both acquired from their fastidious mother.

"Let's roll," he said. "I wouldn't want you to faint from hunger." He glanced at Charlotte, his brows knitted in a frown. "Where'd the bruise come from? You didn't have it earlier." He leveled a glowering look at Braham, who returned the glare.

"Excuse me, sir," Edward said, standing in the doorway. "Colonel Henly left his gauntlets. Should I arrange to have them delivered?"

"Yes," Braham said. "I certainly don't intend to deliver them."

Jack came around to the front of the desk and looked closer at Charlotte's face. "Wait. When did Henly leave his gloves? He had them when he left last night."

Edward stared fixedly at Jack. "Earlier this morning. If you'll excuse me, I'll see to their delivery."

Braham's look could have peeled the hide off a snake. He turned on Charlotte. "Henly was here? And you saw him? Why in God's name did you allow the man back inside this house?"

"He was already inside when Edward announced him. I wasn't going to see him, but I knew he'd only come back."

Jack gave her an incredulous glare. "*And he hit you?*"

She cringed from the force of Jack's sizzling incredulity and the memory of the encounter. "He pulled, I pushed. I'm not hurt. He'll never be back."

Braham turned to leave. "The bastard won't get away with it this time."

Charlotte grabbed his arm. "He's a senior officer, Braham. Let it go."

"He sure as hell isn't mine," Jack said. "And I'm not going to let him get away with man-handling *my sister.*"

Charlotte rushed to the door ahead of them and stretched out her arms, grabbing the doorjamb on both sides. "Okay, guys. *Stop.* I'm not hurt, and I don't need the two of you to track him down so you can beat him up to satisfy your personal sense of honor. He's not worth it. Besides, if I had felt threatened, I could have hurt him. One punch to the area where the bullet is lodged in his back, and he'd been on the floor blubbering."

"You should have hit him," Jack said. "Next time I see him, I will."

Braham brushed the side of her face, close to the bruise. Then he cocked his head and touched her chin tenderly. His eyes blazed hot enough to scorch her. She moved back, not out of fear of Braham, but because she didn't want to be in the path of his righteous indignation when he exploded.

"You have *two bruises* and you expect me to do *nothing?*"

Jack and Braham stood shoulder to shoulder, cornering Charlotte and giving her no room to escape their glowering faces. "If you have two visible bruises, I'd bet my next book's royalties we'll find more, under the get-up you're wearing."

If they saw the scratch marks on her chest they would tackle each other to be the first in line to plow a fist into Gordon. She gulped and held up her foot. "My toe hurts."

Braham squatted and removed her riding boot and stocking and untied her garter. Her big toe had a nasty bruise. "How'd you get this, lass?"

She cleared her throat and told the truth while intending the statement to be misconstrued. She couldn't keep her eyes from blinking rapidly, though. "I kicked."

The corner of Jack's mouth ticked in visibly repressed anger. "Hope you gave the bastard a karate kick to the balls or the back. Either one would do satisfying damage."

Braham replaced her stocking, retied the garter, and slipped on her boot with sufficient skill to imply he dressed women regularly. She blinked as images of Braham with other women wrenched her ego into a state of raging jealously. Before her ego could grab her around the neck and make her believe Braham had hundreds of women ready to succumb at the merest twitch of his finger, she turned and marched toward the door. He caught her arm and turned her to face him again. The blaze in his eyes had cooled, although it was still there, humming beneath the surface, dangerous and deadly.

"Stay away from the bastard. If he hits you again, he'll inflict serious damage. Don't give him an opportunity."

She pulled her arm from Braham's grasp. "I'll make the promise to you if you'll make the same one to me. Stay away from the bastard."

46

Georgetown, February, 1865

AMBER SUNLIGHT POKED through a scrim of dirty clouds while the temperature hovered in the mid-forties, a beautiful day for a ride. The Georgetown house, located at the edge of the city limits, was only a mile and half away. It wasn't unusual for those who resided in the city to summer in a house a mile or two away to get away from the city's breezeless heat.

Charlotte had learned to ride sidesaddle during her early reenactment days. Her confidence had grown over the years, and now she rode comfortably both sidesaddle and astride. Today, since she was wearing a riding habit instead of her Confederate uniform, she rode sidesaddle on Scarlett Belle, Braham's chestnut Morgan. The hardest part of riding in a Victorian-era costume, she had discovered, was getting enough air while cinched into a tight corset. She had once come close to fainting, so now she carefully monitored her breathing. Shortness of breath was inconvenient, but her real fear was falling off with her dress tangled in the saddle. Breaking her neck or being dragged to her death seemed equally gruesome.

Braham led the way, weaving around wagons, marching troops, and walking wounded who trudged along muddy Pennsylvania Avenue. Charlotte had difficulty not stopping. She was torn between being at the hospital to receive them and spending the day with Braham and Jack. Twice, she reined in her horse so she could talk to glassy-eyed soldiers. The odor of their sweat and blood saturated her nostrils, but she ignored the smell, more concerned with their welfare than her own selfish comfort.

"It's not so bad, ma'am. I can still walk," said a young man wearing a bloody sling.

Another soldier said, "We got food, we got medicine. We don't need much more 'cept for the war to end."

A man on crutches shouldered his way into the small group gathered around her. "If you get a chance, tell Mr. Lincoln we'll fight as long as it takes, but we sure do want to go home."

The flood of wounded pouring into the city continued even as Braham led her and Jack across Rock Creek and onto Bridge Street. Had the gates of hell opened and spit out all the ragged and war-weary men in the Union Army? She would not be back at the hospital until morning, so until then she had only a smile or kind word to offer those who looked her way.

Braham turned up 30th Street and left the war traffic behind as they entered Georgetown's more dignified streets. While they rode past the red-brick houses, he and Jack discussed the city's defenses, and the animated conversation between the two devilishly handsome men attracted stares from well-dressed ladies wearing fancy hats and riding by in open carriages.

Charlotte paid attention to details, often picking up on inconsistencies between a patient's reported history and symptoms attributable to specific diseases. She was kicking herself now for ignoring Gordon's obvious symptoms. She had dismissed behaviors which normally would have triggered concerns about drug addiction, post-traumatic stress disorder, and abusive personality. She now was convinced Gordon suffered from all three.

She glanced over at Braham. He was quite a sight in his Cavalry uniform, sitting tall in his saddle, his chiseled features shadowed beneath a dark slouch hat, his well-trained mount responsive to the slightest shift of his weight. Her thoughts spiraled back to the moment he cupped her head in his large, gentle hands and kissed her.

She moaned.

He turned in her direction. "Did you say something?"

She shook her head trying to shake off last night's sensual memories. He reached for her gloved hand and fondled her fingers.

"Does your wee toe hurt?"

She couldn't help but chuckle. If she had stuck her toe in his face, he would have lavished the foot with affection. Someday she'd have to tell him she kicked the damn door stopper, not Gordon's ass, but for right now he needed to believe she could defend herself.

He straightened in the saddle, winking roguishly. "After luncheon, you can rest. You didn't sleep much last night."

She replied with a simple eyebrow arch before saying, "You didn't either. Maybe you need to rest, too."

He smiled. "I've arranged for Jack to meet the daughter of my neighbor. I think he'll find her enchanting."

"Did you know this, Jack?"

Her brother turned in his saddle, free and easy. "Know what?"

"Braham has a woman for you to meet."

Jack gave an easy lift to his eyebrows, widening his eyes. "Why do you think I'm out in front trying to hurry this party along?"

"Is Braham trying to pass off a homely young lady to occupy your afternoon?"

Jack turned his stallion to align his mount with hers so their horses were trotting side by side. "I asked him, and he assured me she's the most popular young lady this season, and I'd find her charming."

She gave her brother a frank, assessing look. "And Braham doesn't find her charming? Is that why he's introducing her to you?"

"He assured me he's not interested."

She thought a minute, then said to Braham. "Are you sure introducing the famously rascally Jack Mallory to your neighbor's innocent young daughter is wise?"

Braham shifted in his saddle. "The lassie's parents will be close by. But I'm mindful of Jack's reputation. I was in town for only an hour last night when I heard the first of several rumors concerning your brother. He's an object of much discussion and speculation. At least a dozen fathers asked me if I would vouch for his character since their daughters wouldn't stop giggling about him."

She gave Braham a fixed stare. "And did you?"

Braham's look jumped from Jack to Charlotte. "Without the slightest hesitation, I said I knew him well, he came from a wealthy, highly respected family, he was a writer with immense talent, and a man I was glad to call friend."

She glanced sideways at Jack, narrowing her eyes. "Sounds like excellent book jacket copy to me. I'd get it in writing while you can. And be sure to get a picture of Braham in uniform to go with the comment." Then she nabbed Jack's arm and squeezed. "And please don't seduce a virgin."

47

Georgetown, February, 1865

AFTER A DELIGHTFUL luncheon, Braham's neighbors the Murrays, along with Jack and Mary Ann, the Murrays' daughter, left for a stroll in the garden, with her parents following at a discreet distance. Charlotte watched the couple saunter along the snow-cleared pathway from the window at the back of the house. The wind had stopped blowing, and a brief glimpse of dark blue sky showed through the clouds, giving her hope it might clear the way for an early spring.

"I see why you thought Jack might find her charming. She's educated, well read, and has traveled abroad. She also fresh, innocent, and different from any woman he's ever spent time with. For her protection, though, I'm glad we're staying in Washington instead of next door. I'm not sure Jack could resist the temptation of a beguiling young woman."

Braham came up behind Charlotte and rested his chin on the top of her head, his hands caressing her shoulders. "He's given me his word he'll not deflower her."

She laughed softly. "I hope he didn't ask the same of you. Although deflowering me isn't an issue. It happened several—"

Braham pressed his fingers lightly against her lips. She turned in his arms to face him. His eyes were darker than their usual glacial green, and they were fixed on her, or at least pointed at her. "I don't want to hear about the man who took ye'."

She kissed the tips of his fingers and his mouth quirked wryly. "Why does your accent come and go?"

His brows knitted together briefly before he laughed, his body vibrating against hers. "I fall back into it when I'm with other Highlanders like the Murrays. Do ye' not like the sound of it, lass?"

"Ooooooh," she sighed, "I love it. It's musical and very romantic."

He took her hand. "Come, I'll show ye' the library. It's my favorite room."

When they reached a closed door, he said, "Close yer eyes." The doorknob clicked slightly before the door hushed open. The warmth of sunlight bathed her face. "Open your eyes now."

She did. She pressed her hand to her open mouth. "Oh my, what a beautiful room." She meandered across the parquet floor, glancing up, down, and around. "Are those all Birch paintings?"

"Not all of them."

A dozen paintings hung side by side between the top of the head-high, wall to wall bookcases and the ornate crown molding. The bookcases were filled to overflowing, a large library globe mounted on a three-legged mahogany stand sat in the corner next to a window, and a circular table covered with opened books and maps occupied the center of the room. Brown and gold curtains framed windows overlooking a private garden. A gold-upholstered settee and two chairs covered in coordinating green brocade clustered in front of the fireplace. A chandelier throwing off rainbows from the abundance of sunlight hung over the table. At one end of the room, a grandfather clock was nestled in an alcove between two bookcases. At the other end, an open three-panel door led into a room with a massive four-poster bed.

"You designed this suite of rooms, didn't you?" she asked, looking at him intently, seeing the side of him devoted to order and symmetry and simplicity. "You belong here."

He smiled slightly, and his face seemed perfectly at peace in sunlight which somehow washed away the worry lines normally etched in the corners of his mouth and eyes. Then in an instant his mood changed, and he wore an odd expression—tender, yet somewhat rueful. "The war—violence, death, destruction—stays outside this door." One of his powerful shoulders moved in a partial shrug. "I don't allow it in here, but it sneaks in when the door's left ajar."

"What will you do after the war? Will you live here?"

His lips stretched into a grimace which might have been intended as a smile, but fell far short. "I'll have had enough of Washington by then. I'll sell the house."

The heat of his energy was palpable, especially against the chill in the air. Perspiration gathered between her breasts. Feeling overly warm, she removed her wool jacket and opened the top button of her blouse.

"It's so beautiful here, especially this room." She relaxed onto the oak settee, casually rubbing her hands over its ornate carvings and silk upholstery.

"Aye, but I have a similar room in my house on Rincon Hill in San Francisco."

She removed her shoes and tucked her chilly feet up under her. "Three houses. Are you starting a collection?"

"There's one at the winery, too."

"Hmm. Four. You definitely have a collection. Will you move back into the Rincon Hill house and practice law again?" She picked up a Highland piper figurine off the table next to the sofa and examined it. The vivid detail and intricate workmanship were extraordinary. She set it down carefully, patting the piper's head, as if giving him permission to blow his bagpipes.

"Cullen is keeping the law practice going with only one other lawyer. There's too much work for them. They need me back."

"Is it what you want to do?"

He joined her on the sofa, stretching out his long legs, his arms draped casually along the back and arm of the settee. "I'm tired. I want to work at the vineyard for a while. Put the war behind me. Settle down."

Her mouth quirked as she met his eyes. "Get married?"

Shying away from the question, he half-closed his eyes, his long lashes shadowing his gaze. His strong, lithe form remained motionless for a moment. Then he gave her a serious look. "When I thought I would die at Chimborazo, I believed no one would care," he paused a moment, shrugging, "...except perhaps Kit and her father. Even their lives wouldn't be troubled much by my death. I don't particularly want people to mourn for me, it's well...I want to know someone will pray for my soul."

"A wife and children would pray for you."

"Aye. I hope it's not too selfish a reason to wed."

She sighed with exasperation. "You desire a family so when you die, you'll be missed? You're missing the point." She snatched up another figurine, one resembling a Scottish terrier and passed it back and forth between her hands, mentally weighing the small piece of pottery, wondering how much sense it would knock into Braham's impenetrable skull if she threw it at him. "What's wrong with having a family so you'll have a richer life, filled with love and purpose?"

He scrubbed his face, sighing heavily. Then he shook his head, his hair coming loose of the thong binding it at his nape. If he'd been a wet dog, water would have scattered across the width of the room. He turned his body to face her. "I have my law practice and vineyards. You have your hospital and patients. We both have lives with purpose. From what Jack says, your patients and students love you. If you can have a life with love and purpose through your work, it stands to reason the same is available to me."

She gently replaced the dog figure next to the piper and arranged them exactly as they had been before she fussed with them. "It's not enough for me—"

There was a knock on the door.

"Come in." Braham's voice sharpened with an annoyed edge.

The butler entered and handed Braham a note with a red wax seal. "This was just delivered, sir. The sergeant said he'd wait for your reply."

Braham put his thumb beneath the flap and withdrew a sheet a paper. His eyes were fixed, as though he were seeing something else, something far beyond the missive he held in his hand. Casually, he refolded the letter and slipped it inside his vest pocket.

Addressing the butler he said, "Tell the sergeant I'll join the general on board the *River Queen* at the requested hour."

The butler left, closing the door with a soft click of the latch.

Jolts of desire to make love to Braham shot through her and mingled with spurts of fear, bottling up in her throat. The decision to have sex, though, would have to be his, and damn him for being so stubborn.

"Will you tell me where you're going?"

"If I'm to travel on the *River Queen,* my orders must have changed. I don't know where Lincoln is sending me this time. Even if I knew I couldn't tell you."

She chewed her bottom lip in moody concentration, fighting a semi-hopeless battle to keep tears at bay. "I wish I could whisper the magic words and take you home with me again. If something happens to you, I'll never hear about it."

As he stroked the side of her face, tugging once again on her curls, a hidden smile popped out, dimpling one cheek. "Jack told me you won't leave until Lee surrenders. I catalogued all the reasons you should go, but he scratched off each one. I know now he won't alter his plans, and neither will you. It's reckless for you to stay, but you're both too damn headstrong to listen to reason."

"There's a triangle here," she said forming the shape with thumbs and forefingers, "and Jack and I are only two of the points." She wagged her thumbs. "You fit the definition of headstrong, too, and I'll add stubborn, bullheaded, mulish, obstinate, and pigheaded to the list."

"You've made your point, lass, and mayhap I am stubborn, bullheaded, mulish, obstinate, and pigheaded, but I'm nay reckless."

Reconsidering, she picked up the dog figurine again and fingered the fine whiskers carved along its muzzle and above its eyebrows.

"Before I leave tonight, I'll make arrangements for your safety. Gaylord has worked for me for a number of years in a variety of positions. He'll act as your bodyguard while I'm away."

Braham rose and crossed the room to a table holding a crystal decanter and glasses. He poured amber liquid into two whiskey glasses and handed one to Charlotte. "If you need him, whistle this tune." He puckered his lips and whistled.

"It's very familiar. What's the name?"

"Bach's *Minuet in G.* Try it."

"I'm a terrible whistler. Don't laugh." She wet her lips, puckered, then whistled. At first nothing but air came out. She tried again, blowing a steady stream of air, but managed only a single note.

"Curl your tongue, lass."

She wet her lips once more, curled her tongue and tried again and again. Finally, more than one note replaced the hissing, and she actually whistled a tune. "Okay, I've got it now." She took a mouthful of whiskey and let it trickle down the back of her throat, a warm and pleasing sensation.

"If you need anything, anything at all, Gaylord will come to you. You can trust him implicitly. He'll even deal with Gordon if he causes you more trouble."

"What created the bad blood between you?"

Braham sipped his whiskey, making no comment. Finally he said, "He wanted the position with Lincoln, but Sherman recommended me over him. Henly has a fine military record, and no one would suspect a violent streak twisted his character."

"He lives with constant pain. It can change people." She thought a minute. "He must blame you for his injury. If he'd had the job working for Lincoln, he wouldn't have been wounded at Cedar Creek."

One of Braham's eyebrows rose in an ironic arch. "But he might have been hanged in Richmond."

"Could Gordon cause a problem for you since he works at the War Department?"

"I'm assigned to the President. He's the only one who dictates where I go and what I do."

They sat in silence, save for the annoying tick-tock of the grandfather clock. To her ear it sounded out of balance, and ticked every half-second instead of every second. Or, perhaps it was because time moved faster when she and Braham were together.

In the room's semi-silence her stomach fluttered like lightning bugs caught in a jar. Funny she should think of lightning bugs now. Didn't fireflies blink their taillights off and on to lure a mate? Maybe the old cliché was more accurate for the moment—she had butterflies in her stomach.

She had a question for Braham, and it hung on the tip of her tongue, daring her to set it free—so she did.

"What are you going to do about Booth?"

"Gaylord's keeping an eye on him." Braham's voice was heavily laden with emotion and guilt, as if he had assigned his retainer a despicable task. "I won't kill Booth, but on the fourteenth, I *will* keep the President away from the theatre. Marshall Lamon warns him daily. He's even threatened to resign as his bodyguard unless Lincoln takes his concerns more seriously."

"Why does Lamon believe there's a threat?"

"He received a secret service report filled with warnings."

"Did you write the report?"

Braham didn't answer her question. He also had a way of hiding his expressions when he wanted to. She couldn't read a thing from his face, nor could she read the gold specks in his eyes like tea leaves. But she knew his heart when it came to Abraham Lincoln, or at least she thought she did. Even knowing, she had to try once more to get him to do something he absolutely would not allow himself to do.

"Come home with me." Her request ricocheted wildly around the room, as if looking for a place to land where it wouldn't cause an explosion. The place didn't exist.

With a sudden intake of breath, he came to his feet and strode across the room, where he paused spinning the globe, watching it twirl. It made several revolutions before coming to a stop. Then, as if his thoughts had settled, he pulled roughly at his collar and appraised her critically. "Abandon your machinations, lass. My life is *here.*"

Her heart closed in on itself. His statement stung like alcohol on an open wound, but she wasn't willing to let go of the conversation. "You could start a winery in Virginia, or write, breed horses, solve world hunger. I don't know. You're brilliant. You'd find something to give you purpose."

"Solve world hunger?" He laughed, but there was no humor in it, merely a low, mirthless noise. "Why do twenty-first century women think a man engaged in serious thought must be trying to find an answer to feeding the world's population?"

She smiled. Kit must have said the same thing to him.

She went over to the table holding the whiskey, set down her glass, then joined Braham next to the globe. "The problem is not whether we can solve world hunger, it's that we don't. But it's not what we're talking about right now. We're talking about—"

He wrapped her in his arms. "What *are* we talking about?" Their lips were mere inches apart. Their whiskey-scented breath mingled in the space between yearning and wanting. "Or, should I say, what are we *not* talking about?"

She reached her arms up around his neck, stroking the skin beneath his hair. He slid one hand into her curly hair, sending hairpins flying in all directions, pinging on the floor. Then, without smiling, without saying a word, without doing anything other than gazing into each other's eyes, Braham lowered his head to capture her mouth.

"The butler said they might still be in the library." Jack's voice preceded the opening of the door.

Jack, Mary Ann, and her parents staggered back, aghast, at the sight of Braham and Charlotte entwined in each other's arms.

"Oh, ah...Well, we'll be waiting in the parlor." Jack closed the door, leaving Charlotte and Braham in momentarily stunned silence. Then they laughed, and when their laughter died down, he cupped her face, softly tracing the bones of her cheek with his thumb.

"I do want you so."

If last night's kiss had been a lesson in restraint, then this almost-kiss had been a blatant invitation to misbehave. She glanced longingly beyond his shoulder toward his tall four-poster bed.

A devilish spark rallied in his eyes. "I know where your mind is roving. Mine's been there and come back again, but I won't sully your reputation nor dishonor Jack's trust in me. Come along now. Let's join the others."

He opened the door, but she backed against it and pushed it closed with her foot. Then she placed her palms on his chest. "Promise me you'll come back from wherever you're going."

"I promise."

"When you do, know this. I won't let you use concerns about my reputation or your relationship with Jack as excuses for not doing what we both want, and damn the consequences."

He put his hands to her cheeks and she placed hers on his. She painted the outline of his face with the pads of her thumbs, memorizing the look of him, the bones of his cheeks, the set of his eyes, the small scar on his forehead, capturing his image in case it should be her last glimpse of him.

"If you still want me when I come back, lass, I'll bed you," he said in a voice rich and smoky.

His arms tightened and brought her closer. She knew he wanted her, and she arched her body into his. He smelled of winter and whiskey, fresh air and soap, and wood and leather. A moan slipped past her lips, husky with need. She was hot and wet and forged with liquid fire. Her fingers spread across his wide shoulders and pressed into the muscles beneath his jacket. He was deliciously made, and she longed to taste him.

His lips found hers, with a touch at first, molding shape against shape, and then with a burst of hunger his tongue plunged far into her mouth, amazingly intimate. She returned his passion in equal measure. Even as she yearned for greater intimacy, she feared it. What if he transported her to another dimension with sensations so strong and rich and vital she wasn't able to let him go?

His mouth slid warmly down the side of her neck toward the slope where the muscle of her shoulder joined it, nuzzling her cool skin. "Undo the rest of your buttons."

Her fingers fumbled with the small buttons, but finally her blouse opened to him, the tops of her breasts spilling from her corset, full and inviting. He kissed the fullness of her and then he stopped abruptly and stiffened.

She opened her eyes and was no longer met by his bold, appraising look, but by blistering eyes blazing with fury. He dragged her across the room until the waning light from the window fell on her. With a frown, he pushed her blouse off of her shoulders. His hand shook as his fingers swept down the lines of each one of the marks Gordon's nails had raked when he grabbed her bodice and scratched her.

With a face twisted in agony and malevolence in his voice Braham said, "The son of a bitch did this to you?"

She jerked back, as if stung, as much from the memory of the initial trauma as from the vengeance ignited in Braham's voice. He stomped over to the table and strapped on his revolvers.

Charlotte dashed for the door and plastered herself against it. "You're not going after him. You promised me."

"It was before I knew the extent of your injuries."

"They're scratches, for God's sake."

He buckled the belt and adjusted the weight on his hips. "He'll not get away with this."

Charlotte buttoned her blouse and tucked the tail into her skirt. "What are you going to do? Challenge him to a duel? You can't. He's a senior officer. And you gave me your word. Are you going to break it after only a few hours?"

"It's your honor I intend to protect."

"The *hell* it is." She didn't know if it was what he said or the emotion behind it, but something reached into her heart and squeezed hard. "We were so caught up in the moment you were ready to yank up my skirt and take me against the wall after twice—" She paused and held up two fingers for added emphasis, "*Twice* telling me it wasn't honorable." Her face flushed hot and blood throbbed dully in her ears. She barreled up to him and jabbed her finger into his chest. "Running off with your blasted guns cocked is about *your* frigging honor, not *mine*."

She stumbled over to the settee, collapsed onto the cushions, and dropped her head in her hands. Something cold slid down her back, leaving icy uneasiness.

"I've never felt such desire," she said sadly. "If you hadn't stopped when you did, I would have ripped your clothes off, and after we'd screwed each other's brains out, we both would have been furious with ourselves. Me, because I don't want sex without love, and you because making love to me would have violated your blasted code of honor. Instead of running off to shoot Gordon Henly, we should pen a joint thank-you note to him."

Tears weren't flowing from her eyes because she had a well-honed ability to grasp temporary composure on demand. "I'm done here. I'm ready to go home. Do whatever you have to do." She knelt and scooped her hairpins off the floor and then, with a steady gait and her chin held high, she glided past him, slamming the door behind her.

After all, composure only lasted so long.

48

Washington City, March, 1865

T HERE HAD BEEN no word from Braham in more than a month. She shivered every time she thought about the day in Georgetown. They should have found time later to talk about their differences, but he had disappeared, again, making it impossible. How could two people be so attracted to each other when they had opposing views on almost everything else? Maybe the brooches had bewitched them both. Great. She hoped it didn't mess Jack up, too.

Since arriving in Washington several months earlier, Jack had attracted the fervent attention of a handful of young women Charlotte referred to as his groupies. Women flocked to him, falling easily into his bed, but rarely into his heart. Charlotte secretly blamed their mother for his behavior. If she hadn't withdrawn emotionally after their father's death, and left her children to sprout in an unattended garden, Jack might be able to form attachments that lasted longer than a few months. Charlotte's own issues were probably similar, but it was easier to be critical of him and ignore her own inadequacies. She would never admit it to him, though.

Jack had been inundated with invitations to balls and dinner parties, and for the last two weeks, events celebrating Lincoln's second inauguration had crammed his calendar. He often invited her to accompany him, but to Washington society, she was an eccentric old maid who preferred the company of wounded soldiers to participating in the glitter of the city's elite.

She had tried to beg off this particular evening's fete, which was being held two days after the inauguration, but Jack had insisted she attend and had promised to remain by her side to thwart unwanted attention. She believed it was the other way around and he was using her, but she agreed to go, hoping to speak to the President.

Four thousand revelers, drinking and dancing quadrilles and waltzes, had squeezed into the room on the top floor of the Patent Office Building. By the time the buffet—with its advertised bill of fare of oysters, roast beef, turkey, ham, venison, lobster salad, and an endless display of cakes and tarts—was served at midnight, the party-goers would be well into the cups.

Charlotte was people-watching when Jack nudged her. One corner of his mouth curled up in a cynical smile. "Don't look now, but guess who's sauntering across the room in our direction?"

"Please don't tell me it's Gordon."

While there was a short list of people in Washington she and Jack tried to avoid, there was only one person who rankled them enough to get her panties and his boxer briefs in a wad.

She turned, snapping open her fan, closing it, and snapping it open again, covering the lower half of her face. She could continue to let her fan speak its own language, but Gordon was perversely persistent and obviously didn't care if she wanted nothing to do with him. His absence in her life had been a huge relief. It had taken days for the scratches to heal and disappear, and she would never forget Braham's flaring nostrils and balled fists when he saw the marks on her chest.

A young woman with delicate features and gossamer-soft blonde hair glided across the floor beside him. Her left hand lay limply on his raised right palm. Because Gordon didn't consider Charlotte or Jack part of Washington's prominent and "must know" officials or entrepreneurs, his approach struck her as unusual. If he was seeking them out in public, it had to mean there was an ulterior motive hidden beneath his faux friendly exterior.

"Good evening, Mr. Mallory, Doctor Mallory."

"Good evening, Colonel." She gave a small shudder, moving a

barely discernable step closer to Jack, a step farther from Gordon.

"May I present Miss Cochran, daughter of Walter Cochran, the president of Washington Bank? I believe you met the Cochrans earlier this year."

Yes, she had met them at a dinner party she had attended with Gordon in late January. If he thought she cared about what he did or whom he did it with, he must be having delusions.

Miss Cochran curtsied, bobbing the flowers in her headband. She couldn't keep her eyes off of Jack, who looked very much like his book jacket photograph tonight—two-day stubble, manscaped to look un-manscaped, white shirt, and black suit.

Never one to pass up an opportunity to engage an admirer, he took her extended gloved hand, bent in a courtly manner, and brushed an air kiss over the backs of her fingers.

"Delighted to meet you, Miss Cochran." A smile stole across Jack's face and settled in. If Gordon had thought he would score points with Miss Cochran by introducing them, Jack's magnetic, no-holds-barred, and undeniably sexy smile had flipped the game to his advantage—game, set, and match.

Charlotte covered the lower half of her face, hiding her smile, and glared over its cream-colored lacework.

"I hope you'll allow me to add my name to your dance card." Jack's voice curled around the young lady, soft and warm as the dozens of wall candle sconces complementing the gas light chandeliers.

Miss Cochran giggled and, smiling sweetly, extended an elegant sterling silver fan card with attached pencil. "You may have a waltz, Mr. Mallory."

"You have no waltzes left to promise, my dear." Gordon's cold eyes flung shards of animosity in Jack's direction. The tone of his voice made it perfectly clear he would delight in cramming Jack's teeth down his throat. Charlotte missed neither the look nor the tone, and neither did Miss Cochran, who pursed pouty lips. Her long lashes dropped over amber eyes.

Gordon pulled her hand through the crook of his elbow and set it solidly against him. She couldn't escape his grip without jerking her hand free and causing a scene. "Come. I see Congressman Vallandigham." As he led her away, Gordon sneered over his shoulder at Charlotte, then leveled Jack with a malevolent glare.

Charlotte snapped open her fan and began waving it rapidly in front of her heated face. "Whew. If you weren't already on Gordon's undesirable list, you are now. Watch out." She snapped the fan closed and left it to dangle by the ribbon attached to her wrist.

"He resents me for not exerting control over you. If I had pressed his case, his name would be on your dance card tonight, not Miss Cochran's."

"He's delusional and dangerous," Charlotte said.

Jack dropped back into a boxing stance and tucked in his elbows. "He can bring it on…" He then placed his left hand at his check, his right hand under his chin, and shadow boxed, throwing a quick jab. "Float like a butterfly, sting like a bee." Then he did a shuffle on the balls of his feet.

Charlotte rolled her eyes, groaning. "Please don't antagonize him more than you have already. With no more than a smile and a few words you made him appear sexually inferior. He won't forget the insult."

"I hope he doesn't. But enough of him. The President and first lady have arrived. Let's go say hello." Jack threw a final double jab combination before taking her arm and escorting her to the receiving line. "Float like a butterfly…"

As they were standing in line to greet the Lincolns, the hairs on the back of her neck prickled. She turned slowly, casually glancing through the crowd until she saw Gordon standing on the edge of the dance floor, alone, staring at her like a predator salivating over a toothsome morsel. Small beads of sweat popped out on her brow. She shook her head, taking a long breath and settling her shoulders. She wasn't going to let him intimidate her.

"What's wrong, sis?"

"Gordon is standing by the dance floor alone. Looks like he's been dumped."

"Good. Maybe we saved the girl a few bruises, or worse."

Charlotte would have said more, but they had reached the front of the line. Lincoln looked dapper in his black suit and white gloves, and Mrs. Lincoln was quite elegant with jasmine and violets woven in her hair and a white satin off-the-shoulder gown.

"Good evening." The President's hand trembled slightly when it clasped hers. His soft brown eyes, full of speculation, remained on her face. "Doctor Mallory. I've heard stories about you lately."

"All good, I hope."

He gave a small grunt, and then his brow crinkled in amused approval. "You've developed a fine reputation since you've been in Washington." Then, in a voice so soft she had to lean forward to hear him, he said, "I hope you'll call on me soon. I'd like to hear how your *father* removed a dying man from Chimborazo."

An icy finger touched her spine at the emphasis he placed on *father*. She wasn't sure if he knew she had impersonated her ancestor or not, but it could get very complicated if he did. "I understand the miracle was accomplished with smoke and mirrors, Mr. President."

His laughter echoed throughout the room.

49

Washington City, March 28, 1865

C HARLOTTE FINISHED CHANGING the dressing for the final soldier in her thirty-two patient ward, put her supplies in the cupboard, and checked her inventory. The steward who performed the tasks of pharmacist, clerk, and general manager of the ward had already restocked the cabinet with medicines and dressings. Unless the hospital had an influx of wounded overnight, her ward was adequately prepared for the next day's needs.

The very day the surgeon-in-charge had given her responsibility for the ward, she had initiated the cleanliness standard now copied throughout the hospital. Patients were given wound care and baths daily, clean dressings were always used, sheets were changed when soiled, and floors were cleaned every shift if possible. Sick patients were no longer housed with the wounded, and caregivers washed their hands between patients. As a result, the hospital's infection rate had dropped significantly. She was still considered an oddity, but her skills had won over the majority of her critics.

A nurse entered the ward carrying an armload of clean linens. "Is your brother late tonight, Doctor Mallory?"

Charlotte tossed her apron into the dirty linens basket and rolled down her sleeves. "If Jack's busy writing a post, he often forgets the time. When his stomach starts growling, he'll remember it's time to pick me up." She considered walking home, but she had promised him she would never travel on foot without an escort. Society expected such a concession of a single woman. Jack, however, demanded it because of the implied threats from Gordon. Although if he hadn't recited a litany of horrific crimes against women, she probably wouldn't have bought into his demands.

The hospital's front door burst open, startling her. She drew herself up and squared her shoulders before cautiously peeking around the ward door to see who had barged in so energetically. It was Jack.

The chilly wind had turned his cheeks ruddy and his hair appealingly windblown. When he spotted her, his eyes remained unblinking on her face. "I'm late. Sorry."

She reached for his arm. "Something's wrong. What is it?"

He leaned closer and murmured. "Wait until we get outside."

Several convalescing soldiers had been playing chess or cards at tables set against the wall. They had all stopped playing to concentrate on Jack. Many held game pieces in their hands, as if their pause buttons had been clicked.

"It's time for supper. I'm hungry," Jack explained to the men with a shrug. They turned back to their games, clucking with disappointment like a yard full of nosy old hens.

She swung a cape around her shoulders and fastened the clasp. "Hope you're not expecting me to cook."

Jack waited until they were far enough down to the street, past the hospital grounds, before saying, "I heard a group of sympathizers has been arrested in Richmond and incarcerated in Castle Thunder."

"The invasion of Richmond is only a few days away. I'm sure they'll be all right," she said.

"Braham was arrested with them."

She dug her fingers into Jack's wrist. The stiff white edge of his shirt cuff crackled beneath her fingers. "*Not again.*"

He put his hand over hers, loosened her grip, and held her hand, squeezing gently. "I'm going to Richmond tonight to see what I can do."

"*No.* It's too dangerous," she said, her voice trembling.

"They evacuate—" Jack paused while a group of soldiers marched briskly around them and crossed the street, dodging several wagons. He waited until the street was clear before escorting Charlotte to the opposite corner. "As I was about to say, the prisoners will be evacuated before the Union troops arrive. If Braham is to be rescued, it has to happen before the prisoners are removed from Richmond."

She hurried out of earshot of other pedestrians crossing the street. "There's a network in place with people who can help. They've helped him before. Surely they don't need you."

"They needed you to get him out last time." The line between Jack's brows deepened again. "I thought you cared about him."

She snorted, and the white mist of her breath purled around her head like cigar smoke. "I do care about him, but he needs a new occupation. He's a lousy spy."

"Come on, let's get inside."

They continued to the townhouse in silence. When they reached it Jack said, "If prison officials discover who they have in custody, they'll hang him. Braham's already been convicted and sentenced. If I can get to Richmond, I'll find a way to get him out, or I'll bribe people to stall the execution long enough for the war to end."

She stomped up the steps to the front door. "You think you've got it all figured out, but you have no idea what it's like to have bullets flying over your head."

He put his arm around her and snugged her to his side. "I'm not going into battle."

She pushed away from him. "Lee's last offensive will be in two days, at Fort Stedman."

"Which is at Petersburg, south of Richmond. I won't be near the fighting."

She reached for the door. "You're absolutely right. Because you'll be here in Washington. You're not at home where you can jump in a car and drive down the highway."

"You traveled to Richmond a few months ago without a car. If you can do it…"

She shot him an irritated glance. "Let's get some things straight. I had a pass from the President, and he arranged transport for me on Grant's steamer. Those aren't available to you."

"I found the pass from the President." His voice held a little bit of steel.

She was stunned, and her mind refused to accept what he was saying.

"And before you say anything else, it hasn't expired."

After a long silence, she stormed into the house, slammed the door in Jack's face, and hurried to his office, where she ransacked his papers, determined to find the pass and tear it to shreds.

"*What are you doing?*" Jack asked.

"I'm going to tear it up."

Jack threw himself down into the chair, and it creak under his weight. "*Sit down* and get a grip. You're being irrational. I haven't seen you like this since…I've never seen you like this. What's going on with you? This isn't about going to Richmond, is it?"

She dropped into the chair across the desk from him. "You live in a pretend world where heroes always win and lovers find their happily-ever-after, but it's not the real world, Jack. Heroes die and people live sad, incomplete lives."

"What does this have to do with rescuing Braham?"

She glanced down at her hands, biting her lower lip, sorting through her jumbled thoughts. Then she glanced up to find him looking at her, a slight smile hidden in the corner of his mouth. "We're not heroes, Jack, and we don't have to pretend we are."

"Is that what happened at Cedar Creek? Were you trying to be a hero?"

She wasn't sure what to say, so she said nothing.

"You play it safe every day, sis. Yet all your patients and their families see you as their hero. The one time you do something *you* believe is truly heroic, not only did you almost die, but the plantation was threatened and you were forced into an even more dangerous situation.

"You saved Braham once and, as a result, you're here now trying to keep him from changing history. We can leave him in Richmond and let him die, and then go home confident in the conviction we've made history safe again. Is that what you want?"

"Damn you." She swiped her hand across the desk, sending a stack of books to the floor. "No. I don't want him to die."

"I don't, either. Somehow, I'm going to rescue him."

"Even knowing what's about to happen in Richmond, the fire, the devastation, the danger?" She was scared, but not for herself alone. The two men she loved could be taken from her in an instant. Her mother had lost the man she loved and had grieved for him for the rest of her short life.

Jack drilled her with a look of mild exasperation. "I don't know why the brooch was sent to you, but it was, and subsequently Braham's life was saved. Call it Fate, call it the work of the Cosmos, call it God working in mysterious ways. Something bigger than both of us is happening here. You once described me as a hound dog on the scent of a story…" His voice trailed away and worry clouded his eyes. Then he continued, "You probably got it right, sis. But there's one thing I know for sure, I will see this though, with or without you."

Her heart accelerated, thudding in her chest. "Where I go, you go. Where you go, I go. We're in this together. If trouble comes, we can leave on a whisper, but we can't if we're separated." The crutch supporting the weight of her resolve to be brave splintered into pieces, and tears hovered very near the surface.

Edward came to the library door dressed in his evening livery, smelling of sandalwood and wax, and calmly announced, "Mr. Gaylord is here."

Braham's retainer. Charlotte raised her eyebrows at Jack.

"Give us five minutes, then send him in," Jack said. The fire had burned down and the room held a chill. He tossed in more kindling and poked at the dying embers.

For a moment Charlotte thought she had stopped breathing, though her chest continued to rise and fall. She dabbed at the corners of her eyes, wiping away any telltale gleam of moisture, composing herself quickly.

Jack set down the poker, squared his shoulders, and conjured a smile.

The short, stocky man with a weatherworn face who had escorted Charlotte to Richmond months earlier entered the room. "Mr. Mallory, Doctor Mallory. I'll get right to the point. Major McCabe has been working undercover in Richmond. Last night, he was rounded up with other sympathizers and incarcerated in Castle Thunder. The major's instructions were to notify you immediately if anything happened to him while you were still in the city."

Jack sat on the edge of the desk, twisting the family signet ring around and around the knuckle on the third finger of his left hand. "I heard the news a couple of hours ago. Charlotte and I have been discussing what to do."

Gaylord's dark brows went up. "If you intend to attempt a rescue, I'll see you through the lines and provide an introduction to Miss Van Lew. She's quite resourceful."

"A Southern lady or Yankee spy?" Charlotte quoted the opposing labels from a book she'd read about the lady patriot. "How soon can you be ready to leave, Gaylord?"

He lifted a watch fob from his waistcoat, pursing his lips and frowning in thought. The fingers of his right hand twitched as if he were mentally counting. Finally he cleared his throat and said, "It'll take three hours to gather supplies and make necessary arrangements."

"Will we travel by horseback or boat?" Charlotte asked, doing her own calculations as to how long it would take her to pack.

"Time is of the essence. I'll arrange passage on the fastest ship available."

"How much money will you need?" Jack asked.

Gaylord waved his hand in a shooing motion. "I have access to sufficient funds." He then addressed Charlotte. "Since you have the propensity for dressing in men's clothing, I suggest you travel in disguise, at least until we reach Richmond. There, you'll be safer dressed as yourself. I'll arrange for the necessary work papers for you, Mr. Mallory, or else you'll be conscripted and sent to the front lines to guard the city."

Charlotte exhaled a thin stream of air. "Did you know I was a woman when you guided me to Richmond last October?"

One corner of Gaylord's mouth curled wryly. "Not at first, but within a few hours of City Point, because of your repeated scurries into the bushes, I suspected. By the time we reached Richmond, I was sure."

She had the grace to blush slightly. "You should have told me."

"It would have eroded your confidence."

She attempted a smile of acknowledgement. "You're probably right."

Gaylord then made a slight bow. "If you'll excuse me, I'll see to the preparations." He departed at once, leaving Charlotte staring out into space, her face scrunched in concentration.

Jack poured two glasses of whiskey and handed one to his sister.

"Thanks." She pointed her glass in the direction of Gaylord's withdrawal. "I'd call that a dump truck full of malleable concrete quickly set into a plan. No heroics needed. Just go here. Do that."

Jack raised his drink and gave a chortle. "Nope. It's the Cosmos working overtime." He emptied the glass and set the crystal on the table. "I'm going to pack."

After Jack left the room, Charlotte leaned back in the chair and twirled a pencil between her fingers. It popped out of her hand and hit the floor. When she reached for it, she spotted the corner of a familiar-looking piece of paper peeking out from under one of the books she had swatted off the desk. She picked up the paper embossed with the *Executive Mansion*. She placed the President's pass dated October 22, 1864 on top of the desk.

No heroics needed. Just go here. Do that.

Things were rarely so simple, though, and she seriously doubted this would be an exception.

50

Richmond, Virginia, March 31, 1865

C HARLOTTE, JACK, AND Gaylord dismounted at the same tumbledown farmhouse on the outskirts of Richmond where they'd paused months earlier. A warm breath of wind carried the sweet scent of flowering dogwoods, and their fragrance and the peace of the new-growth forest soothed her. Of course, the calm was only temporary, but she welcomed the short-term respite with relief.

During most of the trip Jack had jotted notes in his journal. "The novel is taking shape," was all he would say when questioned, with the added caveat that if anything happened to him, she had to save the journal. If anyone from the nineteenth century read his notes, more than Lincoln's legacy could be at stake. He didn't elaborate further, which was typical for him when developing a new story. Later, if she plied him with enough whiskey he might reveal a hint of the plot, but it would require her to drink as much as he did. For the foreseeable future, inebriation wasn't on her to-do list.

Gaylord gathered the horses in a cozy knot, and left them hobbled and snorting. Vapor from their mingled breaths formed clouds of white in the predawn light. With the horses settled, he pried up a porch floorboard and removed a metal box. Inside were several neatly folded sheets of paper. He gave them a quick perusal, then handed them to Jack.

"Those are special passes to get us through to Richmond. The other papers identify us as essential government employees. Without the documents we could be conscripted and sent to the front lines."

"We're bypassing the checkpoints, though, right?" Jack asked.

Gaylord nodded. "If you're stopped by the Rebs, you'll need a pass, or they'll toss you in Castle Thunder."

Jack stuffed the papers inside his jacket. "If I enter the prison, I'd rather it be on my terms, not theirs."

While Gaylord returned the box to its hole, Jack sat on the stoop and spread out a map drawn on tracing linen. Charlotte hunched beside him, studying the vicinity of Richmond and the positions of the battery defenses. He pointed to a spot on the northeast side of Richmond. "By my calculation, we're here."

Gaylord bent over Jack's shoulder, hands on his knees, viewing the map. "We're within the three-mile radius of the city on the northwest side. Both armies have holes in their defenses." He drew a line with his finger. "We'll sneak through this way."

"Is it the way we went last time?" Charlotte asked.

"The Rebs closed the hole we used, but they opened another one."

"And if the new one is closed?" Jack asked.

Gaylord raised his shoulders in the faintest of shrugs. "We'll find a way through the woods. Might take longer, but we'll get there."

As if acknowledging the truth of Gaylord's statement, the wind sighed softly through the budding foliage, ruffling the edges of the map.

"Give me the canteens and I'll refill them," she said.

Jack's eyes narrowed to crinkled slits as he scanned the encroaching woods. "Where?"

She jerked her thumb over her shoulder toward the spring Gaylord had shown her the last time. "Your preternatural hearing must need a tune-up."

Jack's eyes flicked up, assessing the surroundings, as he smiled enigmatically. "Are you talking about the spring hidden behind the scrubby growth of evergreens to the right of us, or the trickle of water over stone and pebbles to the left of us?"

She gave a snort. "Ha. Ha."

Jack refolded the map and returned it to his saddlebags. "Don't be gone long."

She gathered up the canteens and a small hygiene kit before trudging, mud-splattered and achy, off to the creek for her morning ablutions. Imagining a hot shower and breakfast, she momentarily considered zapping herself back to the twenty-first century, but the idea drifted away on the breeze like dandelion fluff. If she quit and went home, she'd have to give up on the task she'd begun, and quitting wasn't in her genes.

Braham's incarceration in Castle Thunder, a rat-infested hellhole with sadistic guards, no sanitation, and barely enough food to survive, weighed heavily on her mind. Gaylord told her he'd heard Braham had been dumped into the dungeon, which guaranteed he'd be among the prisoners who were tortured.

She pressed her hands against her chest, feeling hollowness there, an emptiness carved into her heart the night at Chimborazo when she'd looked into Braham's eyes and known she couldn't let him die. Putting him back together again after a second rescue wouldn't be easy. Not that it had been last time, but then she had the advantages of twenty-first century medicine. Until she knew the extent of his injuries, there was nothing she could do except worry, which she chose not to do. As a little girl she had memorized a worry verse from the Book of Matthew:

Therefore, do not worry about tomorrow, for tomorrow will worry about itself. Each day has enough trouble of its own.

Her anxieties firmly squelched, she returned to the farmhouse with refilled canteens and feeling somewhat refreshed.

"If you'll carry your haversack and water, I'll carry your carpet bag," Jack said.

She slung the haversack strap over her shoulder. "Sure. Thanks."

The weight of the tight strap pressing around her chest triggered a memory of archery class at youth camp. Instead of a quiver of arrows, she now carried a quiver of memories—the musky scent of Braham and the curve of his mouth as it fit perfectly against hers. In a recent disturbing dream, she had looked over the shoulder of a master painter and watched intently while he painted the curve of Braham's mouth, then painted the curve of hers, making one mouth. When the artist completed the painting, he sliced the canvas in half, leaving two unfinished works of art. She had awakened in a cold sweat and ended up spending the hours until sunrise sitting in a rocking chair, thinking.

Dawn was coming now, casting a bluish-yellow glow above a landscape dotted with wildflowers. When the sun came up, so would a profusion of brilliant colors, the work of a true master painter.

Gaylord made a round up motion with his finger. "Let's go."

She stopped ruminating and hefted the bag again, hoping the physical weight would distract her from the increasing weight of her worry. Pressing her right boot into the damp soil, next her left, then her right and left again, she eased into a comfortable stride which would keep her from lagging too far behind the men.

Allowing herself a small smile, she couldn't help thinking if Braham knew she and Jack were risking their lives to rescue him, the force of his explosive reaction would register on the Richter scale. But Braham's opinion in this case was irrelevant.

Jack had promised he would devise a plan by the time they reached Richmond. As far as she knew, he had yet to make it to the first rung on his plotting ladder. She was in favor of carrying Braham off to the future again, but it would only solve the immediate problem. He would merely turn around and come back to the nineteenth century, and there was no way she was going to live in a *Groundhog Day* time loop.

"Jack." She hurried up next to him, ducking under a low-hanging willow branch. "Do you have a plan yet?"

He slowed, pushing aside the hanging veil of branches to make room for her on the path, letting Gaylord gain a few yards on them. When they were safely out of earshot, Jack said, "The prisoners will be evacuated Sunday night for a forced march south."

She repositioned her haversack to ease the load on her shoulders, thinking about what dangers the evacuation would mean for

Braham. "Hmm. Then we have to get him out before then."

"I don't think so. We can use the evacuation to our advantage."

"What are you going to do? Pull him out of line while they're marching out of town? What if he's disoriented and resists?"

Jack put his finger to his lips, glancing ahead. "Shhh. The softest cry carries out here."

Charlotte covered her mouth, realizing her voice could have carried across the field in the morning stillness. She whispered between her fingers. "We don't know what condition he's in. He could cause a disturbance by not realizing we are there to help him. He has to know what to expect."

Gaylord stopped and signaled for them to catch up and follow the tree line to the right. In a low voice, he said, "Heard part of what you said. I agree. We need to get a message to the major."

She moved to stand beside Gaylord, keeping her voice low, too. "A Confederate doctor could get inside easily."

Jack came to a halt, pointing a finger at her. "You can get your crazy idea out of your head right now. You're not going in there."

She swatted at his finger. "Put your dictatorial brother finger away. I'm no longer your baby sister. I'm almost forty years old and can make my own decisions. If it's a possibility, we can't rule it out. I got into a Confederate hospital. I can find a way to get into a prison, too."

Gaylord came up between the siblings, giving a small, amused sort of snort. "Miss Van Lew will have suggestions. We'll sort out how to make it happen together."

For the next hour Gaylord skirted around rebel forces, taking roads and paths through the countryside and bypassing the home guards manning checkpoints. As they neared the city, Gaylord followed the James River to the southeast. Slowly, in the chill of the morning, they made their way through to the woods lining the rushing river, swollen from early spring rain.

Charlotte ducked into a dense stand of trees and changed out of men's clothing and into a traveling dress. Her preference was not to change, but they didn't have work papers for another man, and women didn't need them.

The trio arrived in Richmond, passing by the Tredegar Iron Works. At Cary Street, Gaylord left them with instructions to make their way to Miss Van Lew's Grace Street residence.

"She might have news of the major," he said in parting.

"If you hear anything, please send word." Her fear for Braham was almost strangling. Since he had already been tried, convicted, and sentenced, he could have been hanged by now.

No, impossible. She would know. There would be barbed wire tightening around her heart, a sharp tug in her gut, the intensity would create a cosmic disturbance. Maybe she'd be the only one to feel it, but it wouldn't diminish the intensity of the disturbance.

He was alive, and she knew it.

He was above all an honorable man, exuberant about living. A man so naturally sexual he intensified her own sexuality. A man both tender and intensely male who made her feel intensely female.

Yes, she would know.

She allowed none of these turbulent thoughts to cause even a ripple in her expression, though. Jack needed to believe she had her usual calm confidence, especially if Doctor Carlton Mallory intended to visit Castle Thunder.

Jack had a keen look on his face as he scanned the cobblestone streets. "We've spent most of our lives in this city. It's as familiar as Mallory Plantation, but this," he encompassed the scene with a wave of his arm, "is an alien place."

Charlotte hugged her cape tight around her shoulders and breathed out hard, followed by a long breath in, hoping the chill would calm her.

"There's an ominous stillness. Do you feel it?"

"Yes." Jack lifted his chin and sniffed. The expression in his intelligent eyes changed ever so slightly. "I smell it, too." He sniffed again. "It's the lingering smell of sulfur from cannon and artillery fire."

She twitched her nose. "You're more sensitive to smells than I am, but even I can smell it, hear it, feel the vibrations."

"Do you want to go by the prison on the way to the Van Lew's house?"

She nodded.

He pointed with a slight lift of his chin. "Let's head up Cary Street then, but don't make it look like we're casing the joint. If we get locked up, we won't be any help to your boyfriend."

She gave Jack a smile as thin as a razor. "He's *not* my boyfriend."

"The lady doth protest too much, methinks."

She'd never been able to put anything over on her brother. He knew her too well. But Braham wasn't her boyfriend. Wannabe lover maybe, but not a boyfriend. No matter how much she might wish for a future with him, they were both in the wrong place and the wrong time.

The tune to a Stevie Wonder's song surfaced in her mind, and she hummed a few bars while she and Jack walked down Cary Street to 18th. *Undercover passion on the run…For me and you my part-time lover.*

"There it is—Castle Thunder," Jack said, pointing to three old red brick tobacco warehouses. The buildings faced the James River, each one with dozens of barred windows open to the elements. A wooden fence encircled a small prison yard, and guards lined the tops of the walls.

A cool breeze had sprung up and was blowing the folds of her skirts around her legs. Dread of what they might find raised the hackles on the back of her neck. "I wish I knew which building he was in."

"Probably the one with deserters and political prisoners."

"Not much help unless there's a sign over the door. Whichever one it is, we've got to get him out."

He nodded cautiously. "Come on. Let's keep going."

They moved quickly though the shadowy street, peering in all directions and listening to groans coming from the prison's open windows. The rancid smell, a sickening combination of disease, sweat, and other bodily fluids coated her nostrils and clung there, magnified by her own fear. She chewed her lower lip as she tried to think of ways to get him out quickly and safely. They didn't have many. In fact, they only had one.

"Major Carlton Mallory is going to visit the prison tomorrow."

Jack's face assumed the Mallory look; a characteristic calm masking the rapid and furious thinking going on behind it. After a moment, his eyes bored into hers, dark and penetrating. "The prisoners incarcerated there are some of the most desperate men in the Confederacy. There's not a chance in hell I'm going to let you go inside that suffering, stinking pit."

Jack placed his hand on her back, heavy even through her riding cape. He guided her forward with a bit of pressure to keep moving. "The guards at the door are watching. Keep going." He guided her up 23rd Street toward Main.

"There won't be any wagons or ambulances available to evacuate the non-ambulatory prisoners. It would make sense for a doctor to go in there to evaluate the prisoners and get an accurate count of how many would need to be left behind. That wouldn't be dangerous."

He glanced sideways, tongue probing a back tooth as he thought. "I might have a plan, but it requires someone to get inside—someone other than you."

"I wouldn't want you in there either, Jack, but disguised as a Confederate doctor—"

He shook his head. "We'll work something else out. The place is a vast sinkhole of inhumanity."

"I wonder if any of those men will ever find their way back from the abyss of brutality."

Jack shot a glance over his shoulder toward the prison. "Abyss of brutality? Hmm. Nice word choices."

She thought about it, rubbing absently at her cheek. "It's not original. I read it somewhere. Epitome of inhumanity is a good line, too." They continued to the corner in silence and headed down another block toward Franklin Street. "I've been reenacting Civil War battles for the last twenty years, but walking past those warehouses, smelling the blistering stench, and hearing those anguished moans makes me realize what I've been doing is—"

Jack finished her sentence saying, "Honoring those who fought."

She glanced up at him with a lifted brow. "Those words aren't exactly the ones I would use."

"Don't belittle what you've been doing." He lowered his voice to a familiar pitch, trying to appear unruffled, but he marked every word with subtle inflection, a vocal cue to those who knew him well. "Every survivor will suffer for the rest of his life. Thank God it's almost over."

They reached Grace Street and climbed the short distance up Church Hill to the Van Lew mansion. The horizon to the east appeared gold-plated as a brilliant sun inched its way up through the orange hues of dawn. The sumptuous fragrance of showy pink Magnolia blossoms floated on the breeze. Grand homes lined both sides of this street. Charlotte stopped and stared, appreciating their beauty all the more after the degradation they'd witnessed. In the twenty-first century, half-million dollar row homes were crammed together in their places. Though still a beautiful street, it didn't have the charm and elegance the street possessed in the nineteenth century.

"One of my reference books mentioned that during the evacuation—" Jack said, but Charlotte interrupted him.

"What? I'm sorry," she said. "I was distracted. What were you saying?"

He frowned back with a look of puzzlement. "Pay attention. Stop woolgathering. I thought you wanted to hear my plan."

She might have laughed if she'd been in the mood for irony. After waiting with bated breath for two days to hear his plan, her mind took a break for a very few seconds to appreciate the scenery, so naturally he chose this particular time for his big reveal. She lifted one eyebrow at him. "Go ahead. I'm listening."

He glanced at her with a wry half-smile. "Are you sure?"

She replied with a small grunt of amusement.

"Okay, here's the gist of it. During the evacuation there was a confrontation with the crowd, and three of Miss Van Lew's cohorts slipped away undetected."

"Then Braham needs to be with them. Wait a second" She snapped her fingers repeatedly as she attempted to draw something from memory. "There are no horses, wagons, or trains in Richmond, at the present, right? So there's no way to carry wounded prisoners. If a prisoner can't walk, he won't be evacuated. Doctor Mallory has to get inside the prison to get a message to Braham to get in line with the Van Lew people and slip away with them."

"Are you out of your mind?"

She snorted.

Jack dug a knuckle hard between his brows, as if he was trying to press a headache into submission. "We'll find another way."

She was fired up, suddenly feeling quite herself, although there was a faint echo of constant, underlying fear. "I want to do this."

"What we want," he began in a voice inflexible as a stone, "isn't always good for us."

"Good God, Jack, stop acting like a parent and be my partner in this."

"When you were in high school and college, I was your only parent. It's hard to break old habits, especially when it concerns your well-being." He put his arm around her shoulders and pulled her close. "Let's wait and see if Miss Van Lew has any better suggestions."

Their walk up the street took them alongside the Van Lew's three-story white residence. The house took up an entire city block and sat at the top of the elegant Church Hill neighborhood. From the side street they could see the rear of the house, an imposing two-story Doric piazza overlooking elaborate gardens. Magnolia trees, hedges of privet, and box bushes wreathed the house and fell gently in a series of terraces down the hill toward the river.

"It's gorgeous," Charlotte said. "Old black and white pictures don't do it justice. Why in the world did they have to tear it down?"

A wistful, reflective smile crossed his face. "The city condemned the building in 1911. Folks thought it was haunted."

"Now I've seen all this," she said with a sweep of her arm, "I realize how much of historical Richmond will be lost to the future."

Jack pointed to St. John's Episcopal Church on the corner across the street from the mansion. "The church hasn't changed much."

"It's such a waste the Van Lew mansion didn't survive as well. Maybe we can find a way to save it."

He gave her a narrowed-eyed disapproving glance. "Are *you* suggesting we change history?"

She gave him the faintest of shrugs. "What harm would it do?"

"What harm? *Seriously?* If you make a small change for Van Lew—"

"I know," she said, flapping her hand. "If we do it once, we'll do it again for the next person who needs a different outcome."

"Exactly." Jack opened the whitewashed wrought iron gate leading to the mansion's front door. They ascended the left curve of the double staircase, up to the dwarf portico facing Grace Street. "Are you ready?"

She patted down and smoothed the front of her riding dress, then tucked loose curls back under her hat, wanting to be presentable when she met one of Richmond's most famous nineteenth-century personalities. "Historical people are challenging, because you might slip up and tell them something they shouldn't know."

Jack lifted the doorknocker and struck the ornate plate fitted to the door twice. "I have the same problem with the Booth article. I keep interjecting the future."

Charlotte glanced into the side windows. "Someone's coming." She patted her buttons to be sure all were tightly secured, then tugged on the hem of her jacket. "When will you finish it?"

"Be still. You're a fidgety butt."

A servant dressed in splendid livery answered the door.

Jack leaned slightly toward Charlotte and whispered, "To answer your question, I don't know if I will."

The servant inquired politely, "How may I help you?"

"We'd like to see Miss Van Lew on a business matter," Jack said.

They were invited into a massive entryway furnished as elegantly as any grand home in twenty-first century Richmond. A massive cut-glass chandelier hovered over the marble floor. Set in motion by the breeze coming through the door, the crystal teardrops tinkled faintly. Oil paintings lined the walls, stretching back into the heart of the house.

They were shown into a spacious front drawing room. Large open windows were covered with lace curtains blowing gently in a breeze carrying the fragrances of roses and jasmine. Charlotte paced along the room's perimeter, taking in every detail of the furniture, porcelain vases, and an exquisite classical sofa upholstered in a burgundy... something... with matching silk tufts. She ran her hand over the fabric. *Harrateen, probably.*

Several comfortable wing chairs were scatted about, some with books lying open on their seats. She flipped one of the books over to read the title. *Jane Eyre.* Amused, she returned the book to its original position on the chair. This room was comfortable, luxurious, and well used by the family.

Jack gave her a slightly reproachful look. "You're bugging me. Sit down and relax."

Before she could retort, a small, birdlike woman entered the room in a rustle of silk. Charlotte recognized Elizabeth Van Lew from the history books. Dark ringlets dangled around her face and softened her sharp nose, thin lips, and aquiline jaw.

"I'm Miss Van Lew. How may I help you?"

"I'm Charlotte Mallory, and this is my brother, Jack. We have a confidential matter to discuss with you."

Miss Van Lew waved her hand in a graceful, genteel gesture. "And it shall remain confidential. Please, have a seat."

Charlotte settled onto a settee. Jack remained standing, slouching elegantly, broad shoulders wedged against the mantle. Miss Van Lew took a seat next to Charlotte, arranging her skirts.

"Our friend Major McCabe," Charlotte began, "was rounded up a few days ago and incarcerated in Castle Thunder. I'm sure you've heard the news by now, although you may know him by a different name. We left Washington immediately to help facilitate his escape."

Miss Van Lew smiled faintly and shrugged. "An acquaintance

sent word I might hear from you, but I'm not sure why you've come to me," she said with a hint of concern.

Jack stroked the bronze statue of a lion perched on top of one of the columns lining the sides of the hearth. Their hostess's eyes followed his fingers while they familiarized themselves with the figure.

"We know the role you play in the Richmond underground and that you send coded messages to Grant," Charlotte said. "We also know you keep the cipher in the back of your watch."

Miss Van Lew's eyes widened and her hand shook noticeably.

"We don't have time to prove our allegiance to the Union or to earn your confidence," Jack said. "We're on your side. You have nothing to fear from us. We are most assuredly not here to betray you. A lengthy investigation would prove our loyalty, but we need your help immediately. Major McCabe's associate Mr. Gaylord assured us you would do what you could."

"The confederacy is doomed," Charlotte said. "They'll evacuate the city tomorrow, and Union troops will arrive on Monday."

Miss Van Lew's eyes were open and alert. She searched Charlotte's face, then Jack's. "How do you know this?"

"The same way we know about the crack in this creature's head," Jack said, patting the lion's head. "We also know it's been used as a depository for messages, and it regularly gobbles up Confederate secrets."

Their hostess's face lost all color.

More gently, Charlotte tried to reassure her by saying, "Your secrets are safe whether you help us or not."

"The longer the major remains in prison," Jack said, "the more likely his captors will discover who he is and hang him. He's an agent for President Lincoln. He was captured last fall, and Charlotte rescued him from Chimborazo."

"Why was he in Chimborazo?" Miss Van Lew asked.

"He was captured close to the hospital and shot during a scuffle. He was sent there because the Rebels needed him to survive so they could interrogate him. Thanks to my sister, they never got the chance."

"From what Gaylord told us, Miss Van Lew," Charlotte added, "Braham's been back in Richmond for the last few months posing as a professor of philosophy wearing a disguise. I'm not sure I'd even recognize him," Charlotte said.

"Please, since we are destined to become much better acquaint- ed, call me Elizabeth. And I would recognize the major," she said on a hastily exhaled breath. "I've been to several of his lectures and hosted a dinner on his behalf. He's brilliant, and very entertaining. He's using the name Charles Jackson."

Charlotte smiled discreetly at Braham's combined use of her name and Jack's. "He *is* brilliant, but spying is apparently not his forte."

"Avoiding capture is not his forte," Jack said. "We haven't had any news of him in three days. Have you heard about any trials or executions?"

Elizabeth clasped her hands so tightly in her lap her knuckles turned white. "No, and I would have heard."

Jack moved away from the mantle and parted the lace curtains to study the street. "I know you were under surveillance at one point. Are you still?"

"I don't think so."

He dropped the curtain and sat in a chair across from the sofa. "The prisoners will be rounded up tomorrow night and transferred to points south, out of the reach of the oncoming Federal Army. The evacuation of Richmond will provide us with an opportunity to rescue him."

Elizabeth's eyes darted from Jack to Charlotte and back again. "Is the government evacuating, too?"

Jack nodded. "Jefferson Davis will catch a late train out of the city."

Elizabeth clapped her hands. "I've waited four years to hear this news. But you said you've been traveling for three days. How do you know your information is current?"

Charlotte took a composing breath. "We can't explain how we

know. We can only tell you what will happen during the next forty-eight hours."

Jack leaned forward in his seat, rested his forearms on his thighs, and clasped his hands. "Three of your associates, Hancock, White and Lohmann, are with Major McCabe in Castle Thunder. Is it possible to get a message to one of them?"

"It will be difficult. They're in solitary confinement, often referred to as the dungeon."

"Do you believe the major has been tortured?"

Elizabeth reached out and squeezed Charlotte's hand. "The prison guards are known for their brutality. Major McCabe was captured at James Duke's tavern. He was there to assist refugees escaping to Union lines through Fredericksburg. He was tortured to reveal the identities of other members of the underground network. He never broke, although I hear he has suffered."

Jack's brow furrowed with worry. "Braham knows he only has to hold on until tomorrow. He's strong enough to manage it, I believe."

"He's not Superman, Jack. And I'm not sure he's fully recovered from the gunshot." If Braham needed extensive medical treatment when they found him, her small medical kit wouldn't be enough. Would he go home with her? Yes. She wouldn't give him a choice. Then she'd give her brooch to Elliott and ask him to lock both brooches up in a secure location—like Fort Knox, or the basement of the New York Federal Reserve Bank.

"What about the clergy? Can Reverend Moore get into the prison now?" Jack asked.

"Or a doctor?" Charlotte asked.

"A doctor would have the most success, but we don't have a doctor we can trust."

Jack skewered Charlotte with a long, cool glare, twitched his shoulders irritably, and then quickly hid his emotions behind a mask of pleasant blandness.

She kept her features composed, choosing not to have a body language battle with her brother, but then reconsidered, turned in her seat and gave Jack a good view of her back. "I rescued Braham from Chimborazo in October by impersonating a Confederate surgeon. This time I don't need to get him out. I only need to get a message to him. Do you think you could get me inside? I could tell them I'm there to evaluate the injured, or…something."

Elizabeth tapped the chair arms with white, elegant fingers tipped with neatly trimmed nails. "If the prisoners are going to be evacuated tomorrow then your idea might work. Will they travel by train?"

"There won't be any available. They'll have to walk," Jack said.

Van Lew shook her head, sighing. "With Lohmann, Hancock, and White locked up, all other operatives have had to shoulder extra burdens. It's why the major was at the tavern. The Confederates believe if they punish every Unionist, we'll scale down activities out of fear. What they don't understand is, their activities spur us to take greater risks."

"Someone betrayed the major last fall," Charlotte said.

"We believe someone in Washington or Maryland tipped off the authorities about our activities." Elizabeth went to the doorway and pulled the sliding doors together. "I'm a pragmatic person. And while I've patiently listened to your stories and predictions, I don't know how it's possible for you to have the information you have unless you're using a scrying bowl. In which case, I have absolutely no confidence in what you're telling me."

Charlotte's emotions were a turbulent cocktail of worry and fear, and she was having trouble accessing her well-practiced professional calm. If Elizabeth wouldn't help them, the rescue would be twice as difficult. "What we're—"

Elizabeth held up her hand. "Please let me finish. I have known Carlton Jackson Mallory my entire life. I've attended parties at Mallory Plantation and the Mallorys have attended dinners here. I've never heard your names mentioned. I don't know who you are, but you look enough like Carlton's wife Kathleen to be her twin sister," she said to Charlotte. "You could be a distant relative. I don't believe you'll betray me. I'm very fond of Major McCabe, and I can see in your eyes, Miss Mallory, you are, too."

Elizabeth yanked on a tasseled bell pull. "I have an appointment in the city center and may be able to have a plan in place by the time I return. In the meantime, I'll have rooms prepared for you. I'm sure after your long journey you'd like a bath and breakfast."

Jack reached into his jacket pocket, withdrew a roll of bills, and handed the roll to their hostess. "Thank you for trusting us. This money is for you, and for those people who'd be more receptive to turning a blind eye if they had cash in their hands. If food is available for purchase, you'll need to stock up on food and supplies. You might soon have a house full of visitors."

Elizabeth clasped the money to her chest and relief relaxed some of the tightness from her face. "If placed in the proper hands, these funds will help immensely. While you freshen up and rest, I'll call on a few people who might be able to help."

"Any news of Braham's condition would be welcome," Charlotte said.

Elizabeth wrapped her arm around Charlotte's shoulders. "With this money, I'll get more information than I could have without it. Rest now. I'll be back soon."

As Charlotte climbed the sweeping staircase of the Van Lew mansion, a premonition told her the next forty-eight hours would be worse than she could possibly imagine. Even with all she and Jack knew about the future, they knew nothing of Major Michael Abraham McCabe's future. Would he survive? Had he been living on borrowed time since his October rescue? Was she on a fool's mission? She couldn't answer her questions, but her heart urged her forward.

When she reached the top landing, Charlotte turned to watch Elizabeth swing a cape around her shoulders, pick up a fruit basket, and quietly leave the house. Charlotte prayed silently, hoping when she returned, she'd bring news…good news…because at the moment, hope was all they had.

51

Richmond, Virginia, March 31, 1865

L ATE IN THE evening, the atmosphere was damp and heavy, which seemed to match her emotional state. Charlotte, Jack, and Elizabeth had sneaked out of the mansion for a clandestine meeting. Elizabeth carried a basket of cakes on her arm to share with those less fortunate. The threesome hurried quietly through the darkened streets toward a farmhouse on the outskirts of the city, slipping from shadow to shadow under low, dark clouds. Grant's guns muttering in the background made the late-night conclave even more ominous.

They reached a white clapboard farmhouse with its curtains tightly drawn. A thin woman who appeared to be in very poor health, pale with dark hollows under her eyes, opened the door and led them across the yellow pine floors to the back of the small, cramped house. Two men, a father and son, sat on a long bench drinking tea.

"Did anyone follow you?" The woman looked like she had been pushed to the brink of her endurance. Her hands shook noticeably.

"Jack came along a short distance behind us, keeping watch," Charlotte said.

He gave the woman a tight smile. "No one followed us except an old hoot owl."

The woman's shoulders noticeably relaxed. "Sit. I'll pour tea."

Steam from the kettle on an old wood stove took the edge off the chill in the room, and the tension in the air dissipated along with the cold.

"If the rumors are true, the Union Army will be in Richmond in a matter of hours. Until they arrive, our lives hang precariously," Elizabeth said. "Neighbors who have accused us of siding with the enemy may take this opportunity to burn us out. Thank you for taking the risk tonight."

The woman touched Elizabeth's arm affectionately. "Thank you for the money, but we would follow your orders without question or payment. We haven't come this far to abandon the cause now."

Elizabeth covered the woman's hand with her own. "I haven't suffered nearly what your family has, yet y'all soldier bravely on."

The older man allowed a tinge of wryness to creep into his voice as he said, "Don't despair, Elizabeth. You might still see the inside of Castle Thunder."

Elizabeth chuckled, but it was a raw, nervous sound, without gaiety. "Then we must redouble our efforts. Over the next few days, Grant will need every tidbit of information we can gather. I've written to him letting him know a barrel of flour is now selling for over a thousand dollars, there is little food to be had, and our situation is deteriorating. But I also emphasized that we remain steadfast in our resolve to support the Union. We need to continue doing what we've been doing, but with greater caution than ever."

The woman and two men sat back heavily in their seats. Fear tightened the wrinkles in their leathery faces. The threadbare cottage and empty pantry shelves spoke of how destitute this family had become. Charlotte was uneasy drinking their tea, knowing they were sacrificing what little bit they had to honor Elizabeth and their guests. At least now they had money for food, if there was any left to buy.

Charlotte turned to look at the younger of the two men. He had a rattling, persistent cough and had been lethargic all during their conversation. "How long have you had a cough?" she asked.

"A couple months, I reckon."

"Can't get him to wake up long enough to eat nothin', neither," the woman said.

Charlotte would have had to examine him to be certain, but she was confident he had either TB or bacterial pneumonia. Either disease would kill him soon. She choked the thought off abruptly, before frustration set in. She had no magic pills available to prolong his life.

Elizabeth explained to the young man. "I already told Doctor Mallory you were recently released from Castle Thunder after four months in solitary confinement."

The man coughed again when he tried to speak. "I thought I'd die in their rat-infested hole."

"We need to get a message to a prisoner. Is it possible?" Charlotte had a rush of guilt over reminding the man of a harrowing experience he'd rather forget.

"Depends," he said. "The third story houses soldiers and partitioned cells for prisoners tried by court-martial. Dangerous and disruptive prisoners are on the same floor. The second story has the disloyal citizens and deserters. If you can get word to one of them, they'll get the message to those in solitary confinement."

The band of throbbing pain from the tension headache threatening Charlotte for several hours was getting worse. She pressed her fingers, warm from the teacup, between her brows. The heat soothed her chilled skin, but did little to relieve the pressure migrating toward the back of her head. She could recite the medical literature by rote: Episodic tension headaches are triggered by stressful situations. Thinking of Tylenol for her headache, she thought to ask, "Is there medical care in prison?"

"The warden sends prisoners to sick bay, where they're examined by the surgeon. There's no medicine for prisoners. If they're bad off, the doctor removes them to the hospital. They did nothing for my fever and cough. Just left me layin' on the straw."

"How often does the doctor visit?" Charlotte asked.

"He comes and goes. Has his own schedule."

"Does the warden visit the dungeon?"

"Ma'am, there ain't no real dungeon." His statement triggered another coughing fit, and he couldn't catch his breath. His mother tried to get him to drink hot tea, but he pushed the cup away. When he could speak again he said, "Cells used for solitary are small, no windows. Warden does the interrogation. Favors a whip mostly. Prisoners in solitary for misbehavin' won't see the warden. Won't see nobody."

"I've only seen the interior of the side building housing the women," Elizabeth added. "The prisoner we need to contact is probably in the front building."

"Confederate Army deserters and political prisoners are in the front building," the older man said. "It's where my son was held."

"I've seen the three buildings from the street," Jack said. "But how are they connected? What's the layout?"

"The front is fenced," the father said. "A long brick wall connects the two smaller buildings to the center building, making an enclosed yard for exercise and latrines. Guard boxes line the top of the walls looking into the yard. If you get into the yard, there's nowhere to run."

"If I impersonate a doctor, can I get to the cells used for solitary confinement?" Charlotte asked.

"Them guards would be suspicious if a different doc showed up," the coughing man said. "Doc never goes to the dungeon. If your man's there, he'll be staying put 'less he dies or the war ends."

Elizabeth set her teacup on the china saucer she held delicately in her palm with her thumb resting on the rim. "The war is going to end within days, and my sources tell me the prisoners will be evacuated tomorrow night."

"If it's true, the guards will be distracted and might not question a different surgeon."

The coughing man wrapped his fingers around a coffee cup and tapped the china. His eyes seemed to turn inward to a scene playing out in his tormented mind. "Prisoners have ways to talk to each other. You get a message to a prisoner, it'll find its way through the prison."

"Even to the prisoners in solitary confinement?" Charlotte

asked.

"When all you got to do is plan an escape, you become resourceful," he said.

The father refilled his cup at the stove, then went over to the window and pushed aside the homespun cotton curtain. After a moment, he dropped the fabric but continued to stare while holding the cup in his unmoving hand. Finally he said, "If you showed a signed order requiring you to check on sick prisoners and decide if they're fit enough to be evacuated, the guards wouldn't bother you."

Charlotte's fragile bubble of hope expanded with the heat from Jack's scowl. "How do I get an order?" she asked.

The father rubbed his stubbled chin. "I can have a forged order ready tomorrow afternoon. But if you get yourself into the dungeon, be prepared to see things you'll wish you hadn't."

Her mind quickly flashed to the inhuman conditions and atrocities she'd witnessed in Afghanistan, and the horrific displays of inhumanity on display at the Holocaust Memorial Museum in Washington. Nothing shocked her anymore, but it always saddened her. Knowing Braham was incarcerated under similar conditions chipped away at her heart. He was strong and healthy and could withstand deprivation and pain for awhile.

"What name should I use on the order?" the older man asked.

"Major Carlton Mallory, Surgeon, Second Corps Army of Northern Virginia."

The older man responded with a grunt, staring bleak-eyed into some invisible distance for a long time, saying nothing more. Then, coming out of his trance or bleary consideration he said, "A basket of flowers will be delivered to Elizabeth's house tomorrow afternoon. The order will be inside the false bottom."

Jack had been following the discussion, elbows propped on his knees, chin resting in his hands. He straightened up, saying, "Sis, I don't know if I can stand by doing nothing while you do this."

She chewed her lip, thinking. "You're the mystery writer. Come up with a better plan fast, because right now this is the only one with any chance of succeeding."

"I don't have one." Jack's voice was distant and distorted. Charlotte was often the brunt of his frustration when his muse misbehaved. She didn't like it any more than he did.

She gave him a cool look, folding her arms across her chest. "Okay. Let's play what-if. What could happen if I use old Mallory's identity to get inside the prison?"

The wavering candlelight caught his profile and threw the stubborn set of his facial bones into sharp relief, the reflection of the flame visible in his dark pupil. "Well…if someone recognizes you, they'd wonder why you're in Richmond and not with the Second Corps."

She threw up her hands. "Okay, then what? Help me out here." An invisible cord seemed to stretch between them, drawing taut and then snapping back on her, bringing along the rejection she had experienced when he wouldn't help her write term papers. There was no life lesson for her to learn now, as he had claimed when she was a teenager. So why was he was being so obstinate? "I need your help, Jackson Mallory. Braham needs your help."

Jack slapped the tops of his thighs, stood, and did a tight-formation pace, while his fingers plucked at his chin. Five sets of eyes observed pensively. Finally he stopped and lifted one eyebrow, glancing at the people sitting around the table.

"Can you limp?" he asked Charlotte.

"*What?* Replace my perfected swagger with a limp? Are you kidding? It's part of my persona."

He made a derisive noise in the back of his throat. "Don't reject it out of hand. If you can limp, it will give you a plausible backstory."

"Sure I can limp, but I'd probably forget which leg was the *bad* one."

"Put pebbles in your boot," the father said. "You'll have a fine limp, and you won't forget."

Elizabeth set her cup of tea on the table. "If anyone asks why you're not with your unit, tell them you were recently wounded and sent to a Richmond hospital to recover."

There seemed to be a consensus among the two men and two women, as they chatted and nodded, pleased they had solved the dilemma, and thus the argument between the siblings. Elizabeth pushed away from the table and wrapped her cloak around her.

"Thank you for meeting with us under such short notice. It's late, and we must return home now."

Charlotte allowed Elizabeth to leave the room first before she turned back to the family, and looked at the younger man. "I believe you were infected with consumption while in prison. Cover your mouth with your arm when you cough," she told him. "You need to isolate your son," she said to the mother, "or both you and your husband will catch the disease from him. Wash your hands and the dishes in very hot water. When food becomes available, be sure he gets a wholesome diet and fresh air."

Their eyebrows furrowed with obvious doubt.

"Are you a real doctor?" the young man demanded.

Charlotte nodded. "I'm a surgeon. Unfortunately, there is no medicine for your disease." Not yet, anyway.

She glanced around the small room, where germs would probably pass from one family member to the other until the disease killed them all. "Rest as much as you can, and everybody wash your hands." Charlotte left the house, doubting they would listen to her advice, and wishing she could do more.

Charlotte and Elizabeth locked arms and moved quickly through Richmond's dark streets, with Jack trailing a short distance behind, watching them with a protective eye. Once back at the mansion, the threesome relaxed in the library, drinking whiskey and reviewing their impressions of the meeting in the farmhouse.

A frown rippled over Jack's face, like a stone thrown into a puddle of muddy water. "You understand what could happen to you if the guards suspect you aren't who you claim to be." His sober voice matched the seriousness of his concern.

Charlotte wasn't sure what to say to relieve his worry, so she remained silent. If she did speak, her voice would betray her, exposing the fear clogging her throat. If Jack knew how afraid she was, he'd write himself into her role. While it would certainly create tension in the story he was writing, it wouldn't do much for the one they were living. He had limited tolerance for sickness and injuries.

"They arrest women for posing as men," Elizabeth said.

Charlotte glanced down at her tightly laced fingers and deliberately untangled them. Placing her hands on her thighs, she straightened her spine and got to her feet. She had no desire to be incarcerated, but she couldn't stand by and do nothing.

"If I'm discovered, you'll have two to rescue tomorrow night."

Jack set his glass on the table with enough force to put a fine-line crack in the crystal. "Don't be flippant."

Charlotte got in his face. "Then support me."

He picked up another glass from the serving tray and splashed whiskey into it. His eyes narrowed dangerously. "I can't."

She snagged fists full of his jacket and held on tight. The keening of the wind outside the windows whooshed into her heart, illuminating the one thing in the world she was most afraid of—losing Jack. If that was her biggest fear, then she now understood the monster crushing him. She relaxed her hands and smoothed the creases she had caused with her tenacious grip.

"I'll go to the prison late tomorrow afternoon, and if I'm discovered, which is highly unlikely, the longest I could be incarcerated is a couple of hours. But," she said with her mouth twitching in an attempted smile, "if doing this will cause you to stroke out from worry, I won't."

He hugged her, resting his chin on top of her head, his galloping heart thumping against her cheek. Her body tensed, except for her quivering chin, as she waited interminable seconds for the answer she expected him to give.

"I won't stroke out, but I can't promise I won't go barging in after you if you're not back in a reasonable amount of time." He held her at arm's length. His eyes bored into her with the precision of a diamond bit. "And my definition of *reasonable* is within the hour. Understood?"

Superficially, peace between the Mallory siblings was restored, but for the next forty-eight hours, the embers of uneasiness would continue to flare.

52

Richmond, Virginia, April 1, 1865

CHARLOTTE THREW BACK the covers and got up slowly. After a night of fitful sleep, she was stiff and achy. She needed an easy walk and a long stretch. Dressing quickly, she slipped out onto the back portico where a mélange of heady scents, flower fragrances, and freshly-turned earth wafted around her.

Hoping to enjoy a few minutes of peace before the household began to stir, she strolled barefoot around the terraces and breathed in the delicious scents of spring. Wisteria was blooming in big blue and lavender clumps on the side of the house, and beyond the garden full of dogwood blooms and fruit blossoms, a soft mist lifted over the James River. A brilliant sun inched its way up through the golden hues of a still and lovely dawn. The same smells, the same flowers, the same exquisite sunrise had not changed in a hundred and fifty years.

The first Sunday in April was Communion Sunday in Richmond. That hadn't changed, either. Charlotte, Jack and Elizabeth planned to attend worship service at St. Paul's Episcopal Church. The siblings, unashamedly, had an ulterior motive. They wanted premium seating to observe one of the last memorable days of the Confederacy unfold.

When Charlotte reentered the house, with her bare feet making soft pats on the hardwood floor, she found Elizabeth preparing to go out. "Do you still plan to attend church services? If you'll give me a minute to find my shoes, I'll go with you."

Elizabeth tied her bonnet strings. "I'm going to Capitol Square for news first."

Charlotte laced up her shoes and jotted a note for Jack to meet them in front of the church at eleven. A few minutes later the women headed down the sidewalk to find out what was happening in the city.

Warm breezes and the morning's exquisite beauty belied the anxiety rippling through the crowd milling around the War Department and post office. Everyone in Richmond was desperate for news from Petersburg. Charlotte knew the Union Army had breached the Confederate trenches in front of the city and the end of the war was at hand, but she couldn't tell the crowd what they desperately wanted to know. Instead, she scanned the panicked faces and for some odd reason remembered a line from *The Tempest. Hell is empty. And all the Devils are here.*

At eleven o'clock the peal of church bells signaled the start of services. Charlotte and Elizabeth met Jack at the corner of Grace and Ninth Streets.

"Did you hear any news?" Elizabeth asked.

Jack edged the women away from a group of men who had gathered in front of a park bench to discuss what would happen to Richmond if Petersburg fell.

"The Union breached the line in front of Petersburg. It's only a matter of time now," he said.

Elizabeth's pensive smile was shadowed at the corners. "If Petersburg is lost, Richmond will be evacuated, exactly as you predicted yesterday."

Charlotte took Elizabeth's arm. "Come on, let's go inside. More news should be available by the time the service is over." Together they climbed the stone steps, past the columns, and strolled into the building. Charlotte had attended services here as a child, but on this Sunday she wasn't remembering her past. She was reflecting on what would happen by the end of the day, and how it would impact the citizens of Richmond.

Jack escorted them to a seat on the back row of the elegantly simple church, where they could observe everyone entering and leaving. Charlotte was only interested in the comings and goings of one person—President Jefferson Davis. Within minutes of taking her seat, she saw him, dressed in an immaculate gray uniform and carrying his hat. His pale face showed no sign of emotion, leaving her to wonder what he must be thinking. He stopped at pew number sixty-three, halfway down on the right, and took a seat.

Charlotte couldn't take her eyes off of him. She'd had a bad case of idol worship in the presence of Abraham Lincoln, a man who would obtain mythic status. Jeff Davis, however, was an enigma, a man few in the future would want to acknowledge, much less celebrate.

Jack whispered into her ear. "Do you notice anything peculiar about the gathering?"

Charlotte perused the congregation, mentally making bullet points. "Most are women dressed in mourning clothes. Gaunt faces full of grief. A few men hobbling on crutches. The rest of the men look ill."

"Anything else?"

"Inside this building there's a pretense of peace and calm. Outside there's chaos and death. Why?"

Jack wiped the corner of his eye with a knuckle. "They're all Christians who went to war for the cause of slavery."

She would always be a daughter of the South, a Virginian, but she would never have fought for the South's cause. Why, then, had participating in reenactments been so important to her? Jack had asked her dozens of times, and she'd always shrugged and replied it was fun.

She had never opened up about the real reason: her grandfather. Reenacting had been his passion, and when she had been with him, she was embraced by his extended family of reenactors. It was all about belonging, about not being alone. Maybe it was why she had gravitated toward medicine—she was embraced and respected as part of the healing community.

The church sexton, a tall, portly man wearing a faded blue suit, marched down the center aisle. He stopped next to President Davis's pew, tapped him on the shoulder, handed him a piece of paper, and left.

Davis glanced at the note, folded it, and tucked it into his pocket. A few seconds later, while everyone watched, he rose from his seat and, with his posture straight and stiff, his demeanor calm, Davis walked down the aisle and left the building.

Elizabeth cupped her mouth and whispered, "What do you suppose the note said?"

"Evacuate tonight," Charlotte said.

"He's known for months this day would come. He'll probably send a message to Lee begging for more time," Elizabeth said behind her open fan.

Charlotte's mouth curled wryly. "You know him well."

Elizabeth sat back and folded her fan. A small, wistful smile drifted across her face.

In the middle of the sermon, the sexton once again strutted down the aisle and whispered, this time to General Joseph Anderson, who immediately rose and strode out.

Elizabeth opened her fan and whispered again, "I suppose the general has been tasked with carrying Davis's message to Lee."

After the service they found Capitol Square swarming with people. In front of the government buildings civil servants were throwing mounds of paper on a bonfire.

"They're burning all the incriminating papers," Elizabeth said.

Charlotte considered how she could douse the flames. Some of the papers might incriminate Davis in Booth's plot to kidnap Lincoln. What a coup it would be to save those messages for posterity. She hunched her shoulders and pulled her shawl tighter to ward off the sudden chill in the air and her even colder thoughts. History would have changed drastically if Lincoln had been kidnapped instead of murdered. If he had been kidnapped, she and Jack never would have followed Braham back in time.

She could make excuses, of course, but she had not asked for what had happened to her since she came into contact with the brooch. Nor had she fought against it. She had searched for Ramseur, convinced her twenty-first century medical knowledge could save him. It didn't. The repercussions of her single, selfish choice were spreading like a giant tsunami. How many lives would be swallowed? If she had returned home immediately, the story would have ended, but the story would continue now until she could convince Braham to leave history alone.

She might as well try to part the James River.

For now, she would stick to an achievable goal: by midnight she intended to have a recalcitrant patient firmly under her medical supervision.

She'd deal with tomorrow's problems tomorrow.

53

Richmond, Virginia, April 1, 1865

A FEW HOURS later, Charlotte was in the guest room at the Van Lew mansion, dressing in her Confederate surgeon's disguise. She hadn't worn the gray wool garment since rescuing Braham last October, and now here she was, planning to rescue him once more.

She'd never be able to wear it again without thinking of him. What would she recall when she reminisced? The first time she saw him at Chimborazo? No. How about the bulge of his muscles in a tight-fitting T-shirt? That was a good one. But a better sensory jolt was the morning she caught him fresh out of the shower with drops from his shoulder-length hair glistening on his chest, and his long legs sheathed in a pair of faded denims. And she couldn't forget the bare feet. She didn't know what made naked toes sexy, but he had beautiful feet. She should know; she'd seen more than her share, checking for weak or absent ankle pulses in her patients. She had first noticed his feet in the emergency room. Matter of fact, she had noticed everything about him then. Every naked inch. Even with flaccid man-parts, it was obvious he was…

A knock snapped her out of her reverie. "Come in."

Elizabeth swept in carrying a small basket. "I brought you some pebbles." She gasped and came to a sudden halt, almost tipping over. "Doctor Mallory? Gracious goodness. I never would have recognized you." She slowly walked a full circle around Charlotte, assessing the view from all angles. "What have you done with your breasts? And what happened to your slim waist? The coat makes you look thick in the middle."

"My breasts are bound, and the jacket is padded to give me extra bulk." Charlotte twirled the beard's long hairs at her chin. "The disguise fooled both Sheridan and Lincoln a few months ago, too, or at least I thought it did. I'm not so sure now."

With lips pursed, Elizabeth gently stroked strands of hair from the light brown wig Charlotte wore, finger-combing some of the hair back off Charlotte's face. "Is this real hair? Feels real."

"Yes, I wanted the disguise to be as realistic as possible."

Elizabeth heaved a sigh and folded her arms across her middle, the basket dangling from her elbow. "Your eyes are the only thing giving you away. Keep them averted, but in a distracted sort of way."

Charlotte averted her eyes, practicing, and spotted the four pills, two antibiotics and two painkillers, she had left sitting on the corner of the dresser. If Elizabeth spotted them, it could lead to awkward questions. Charlotte surreptitiously scooped them up and slipped them inside her jacket. The guards were unlikely to allow her to visit the prisoners in the solitary confinement cells, but in the event she could cajole her way in there, she'd find a way to press the pills into Braham's hand. Having relief from pain might enable him to walk out of the prison on his own. If he couldn't walk, she wasn't sure what might happen to him.

Her hands were steady as usual, but they were also stark white and cold, her tell in times of stress, and they were about as icy as they had ever been, even during cold January training runs. "Any other advice?" she asked Elizabeth.

"Be careful." Elizabeth reached into her pocket and handed Charlotte a piece of paper. "Here are your orders. I've reviewed the document carefully, and it specifically says you are to inspect all the sick, injured, and wounded to determine how many prisoners are unable to walk. I'm sure the Confederacy would prefer to leave all the prisoners behind. The army doesn't have food to feed them or medicine to treat them. However, they can't afford to abandon healthy prisoners who could then rejoin their units and swell the ranks of the Union Army in the field."

Charlotte studied the order, reading each line carefully and analyzing every word to be certain the document couldn't be misinterpreted. She didn't doubt Elizabeth, but thoroughly checking patient records and orders was a career habit she didn't intend to break. Satisfied, she slipped the document inside her jacket, alongside the pills. She then gently touched Elizabeth's forearm. "One day your contribution to the war effort will be fully understood and appreciated."

Elizabeth raised a dark, wing-shaped eyebrow. "I'd prefer to remain anonymous, if it's all the same to you. If the extent of my involvement were known, living here would be impossible. And this *is* my home."

History would show Elizabeth had been despised, seen as a lonely spinster, and called Crazy Bet. Yet she had the most giving heart of any woman Charlotte had ever met, and she was saner, not less sane, than her accusers. If Charlotte could do anything for Elizabeth when she returned to the future, it would be to put the myth of Crazy Bet in proper perspective. She may have acted crazy at times to throw off suspicion, but she was a pillar of reason in a world gone mad. Jack could write her story—the real story. Maybe they couldn't save her house, but they could resurrect her good name.

Elizabeth seemed lost in her own troubled thoughts now, if her furrowed brow was any indication. Charlotte tugged lightly on a fold of Elizabeth's sleeve, pulling her toward the settee, where they both sat, with Elizabeth fidgeting and glancing around.

"It's going to be an endlessly long night, Elizabeth, but tomorrow the Union forces will be here. All you've worked for is about to come to fruition."

Elizabeth lifted her eyes upward, as if looking toward heaven to pour out her thanks. "I can survive one more bad night, because I know when the sun rises, Yankees will be marching up Main Street."

Charlotte picked a handful of pebbles from the basket and sorted through them in her palm before dropping several of the small stones into her boot. "They'll march straight for the Capitol building, where they will unfurl the flag and raise the Stars and Stripes."

Elizabeth clasped her hands together and pressed them under her chin, as if in prayer. "The Union has always seen Richmond as the holy grail of the war effort, believing when they captured the city the horror would end."

"Seven hundred fifty thousand dead," Charlotte told her. "This war will always be a central, tragic chapter in American history."

Elizabeth clutched her chest as she gasped for a breath, shock on her flushed face. "Seven hundred fifty thousand? My heart breaks for all the wives and mothers and sisters."

Charlotte got up and tested the feel of the stones, which she'd placed evenly across the bottom of the boot for maximum discomfort, against the sole of her foot. She took a few steps, hissing between her teeth. The sensation was similar to walking barefoot across broken shells on the beach. There was absolutely no chance she'd forget which leg was supposedly injured.

Elizabeth remained sitting, distracted and muttering, her face now pale as she fingered the brooch pinned to her neckline.

Charlotte returned to the settee, relieved to take the pressure off her already-tender foot. She shucked her boot, removed half of the stones, and tried again. She only needed a reminder, not excruciating pain.

"I know you're curious about the information Jack and I share with you."

Elizabeth waved her hand in a shooing motion. "No, no. I have no reason to doubt you. Although I do pray the number of war dead is exaggerated." She fell into a troubled silence for several moments, then roused herself. "How can the country recover from a loss of such magnitude? An entire generation of men—husbands, sons, fathers, brothers, friends—gone."

Elizabeth reached for the decanter of sherry and crystal glasses on a small table next to the settee. Distractedly, she lifted the narrow-necked bottle while gazing out the window. "You seem to know the future, Charlotte. Tell me this. Will the South ever recover?"

Charlotte took the decanter from Elizabeth and poured two glasses. Then she sipped slowly, considering her answer. Finally, she decided to tell Elizabeth the truth. "The war has decimated the South, as you know. It's lost its manpower, roads, bridges, railroads, and will soon lose most of the labor force upon which it depends. A cycle of poverty is beginning. Income and wealth have already plummeted and will continue to do so. The Old South will take almost a century to recover before it emerges as the New South."

Elizabeth tipped up her glass and emptied the contents in one long swallow, her eyes tear-glazed. Her shoulders lifted and dropped on a shuddering breath. "I wasn't prepared to learn we have such a dire future."

Letting both warmth and apology show in her voice, Charlotte said, "I could have been less direct. Would you have preferred I coated the South's future in sugar to make it easier to digest? This devastates me, too. Richmond is my family's home."

"We've done what we had to do to get through the war. We'll do what we have to do to recover." Then the steel in Elizabeth's voice seemed to melt, though the gritty determination in her eyes did not. "I'll leave you now to finish your preparations." Elizabeth left the room, sniffling, and quietly closed the bedroom door behind her.

Charlotte went over to the window and gazed out over the lush gardens toward the James River, listening to the cannon and musket fire in the distance. She didn't have a view of the river from her house near the hospital, but she enjoyed the view from Mallory Plantation, where she spent most weekends.

She and Braham had ambled along the banks during his recovery. Their animated conversations had skittered across the river's surface like skipping stones. Had there been any other time in her life when she experienced such contentment? Why was he able to feed her soul in ways no other man ever had? Why couldn't she have found him in her own time?

She blinked and shook her head, making no sense of it.

Once the brooch had plucked her off the reenactment field, her life was no longer her own. Some puppeteer had a tight hold on her marionette strings, letting her periodically believe she was in charge of her life, but she had actually lost a great deal of control. Someone, or some *thing*, was pulling her strings, directing her movements. It was time to dance to her own music again.

She set her mouth in a hard, thin, resolute line. After today, there'd be no more adventures, no more danger and uncertainty. The twenty-first century was waiting for her return, and she was ready to go.

But wait a minute. There might still be a chapter to write. If Braham remained in prison, he would be marched south and would be out of Washington on April 14—the date of the assassination. He wouldn't have a chance to change history…but would he be able to survive until Lee surrendered?

She had returned to the past to stop Braham from changing history. But if she allowed him to die in captivity, she'd never recover from the guilt. She was damned if she did, and damned if she didn't. She snatched her slouch hat off the bed, forced self-flagellating thoughts from her mind, and limped from the room.

54

Richmond, Virginia, April 1, 1865

D R. CARLTON MALLORY hobbled down 18th Street toward Castle Thunder, humming low in her throat to warm her vocal cords for her male speaking voice. The distant din of cannons thundered over the city. Army supply wagons rumbled through streets clogged with bewildered people who roamed aimlessly. They were all waiting to see what would happen next. If she told the citizens the Yankees wouldn't hurt them, they wouldn't believe her anyway.

Over the trees, osprey soared through the warm air, patrolling the shoreline, their sharp, hooked black bills and white heads gleaming in the tranquil blue sky, while the sun dropped slowly in the west. The dang birds were probably more vigilant than the Confederate Army. Too bad they couldn't swoop down and carry Jack off and drop him in the river. Her brother's brilliant idea had lost its appeal a couple of blocks back, when jabs of pain from the stones in her boot began to ricochet up her leg. From past experience with running injuries, she knew pain reflected in tightness around her eyes. Ah, well. It would enhance her cover story, although at the expense of her foot and leg.

She patted her breast pocket. The crackling of paper reassured her the signed order was still there. She hoped the sweat trickling down from her armpits and between her bound breasts didn't soak the order, making it unreadable before she could produce the document for the prison guards. Although it gave her the authority to evaluate all sick and wounded prisoners held in all the Richmond prisons, she certainly didn't plan to visit all the facilities, but it was imperative the guards believe her assignment wasn't exclusive to Castle Thunder.

Jack was positioned on the corner across the street from the prison, exactly where he had planned, and was already shouting news of the evacuation to passersby. "It's time to say your mournful goodbyes," he yelled from the corner like a man on a soapbox. "The city will soon fall to the hated Yankees." His shouts provided a beacon for people who were swarming the streets searching for safety. Prison guards remained at their stations, although their glances and mutterings suggested even they were distracted by Jack's proclamations.

The dark wood of Castle Thunder's Cary Street entrance loomed closer with each hobbled step. How many soldiers and civilians had been dragged through the passage, wondering if they would ever emerge alive? She imagined men and women clinging to the door frame to keep from being thrown into a forgotten pit. Charlotte didn't plan to be another quill mark in the prison's ledger.

Her uniform was fittingly stained and worn and created the perfect costume for the role she was playing in the afternoon tableau Jack had scripted. She was used to telling patients what to do, and expected them to follow her orders. Jack, on the other hand, studied people and had a far better understanding of human motivational and situational behavior. He believed if he added to the guards' stress, their anxiety would reduce the attention they paid to their jobs and to Charlotte. She wasn't fully convinced, but she hoped he was right.

She was only a few yards away from her destination when a red-haired soldier skedaddled from Jack's corner, ran across the street, and dashed toward the door of the prison, where a gaggle of soldiers had gathered on the doorstep.

"*What?* The army's evacuating?" The reek of the soldiers' fear surged through the crowd like the leading edge of an incoming tide.

"Yep. Tonight." The red-haired soldier's voice wobbled slightly. "Depot's already pressed with civilians trying to get out of town 'fore the army leaves."

Another soldier raked fingers through his disheveled hair. "I need to get my family on a train right quick."

The red-haired soldier shook his head. "Only a few left going to Danville. No room on 'em. Folks are bein' told to go home or try the packet boats on the canal."

"Boats? Ain't no boats to carry nobody anywheres unless you can pay with gold."

A guard who had been listening from the door came out onto the stoop. "Won't do no good to go home. Damn Yankees will bust down the door and shoot 'em dead."

Another soldier rocked back on his heels, leaned against the wall, and shoved his hands under his armpits. "What about President Davis and the rest of the government?"

The red-haired soldier stretched his neck, looking up and down the street like he expected to see the Union Army marching toward him with guns cocked and loaded. "Heard they're packing up to leave tonight, too."

The rocking soldier stopped rocking. "Jesus."

The redhead punched him in the arm, flashing a nervous grin. "Didn't hear no news about him. Reckon he'll stay or go, depending on who needs him more."

There was a smattering of nervous chuckles.

Charlotte hobbled up to the group. "We're evacuating," she said. "President Davis is moving the government south. I'm here to count the number of prisoners who can't walk without support. Step aside. Let me through."

The soldiers came to attention, saluting. "Yes, sir. We heard. What happens to us if Richmond falls?"

Charlotte leaned on the silver-handled Malacca walking stick on loan from Elizabeth. "You'll keep fighting. If General Lee believes the Confederate cause is best served by abandoning the capital, you'll follow him."

"Can I help you, sir?" the red-haired soldier asked, holding the door for Charlotte to enter. "I'm on guard duty."

"Good. You can escort me to the sick bay."

As soon as she stepped past the prison door the smell of rot and decay assaulted her. The building had no ventilation, and the stifling air was like an impenetrable thicket of poison ivy. She angled her body back toward the exit and, without thinking, pressed her foot down hard on the stones, knocking herself off balance in an effort to avoid the pain. She toppled sideways, slamming her shoulder into the wall.

The soldier grabbed her arm. "You okay, sir?"

"Damn leg," she said. The stones were stark reminders of what she was doing and why.

The red-haired soldier, a private, told a guard stationed at a desk inside the door, "We're evacuating Richmond. The doctor's got to count the prisoners who cain't walk."

A coarse man, roughhewn, reeking of well-aged perspiration, and built like a bull, saluted her. Then he lowered his head, studying her. "Never seen you 'afore, Major. You got an order?" he asked in a deep, staccato voice. He set his jaw and slapped the desktop with stubby fingers tipped with dirty, bitten nails.

She pulled the order out and handed it over. "Can't have just anybody walk in off the street and demand to see your prisoners, can you?"

He read the document, or appeared to, before handing it back. "Like I said. Never seen you 'afore."

"You heard of Mallory Plantation? We've lived there for over a hundred years. I was with the Second Corps of Northern Virginia until I was wounded last month. Just now getting out, starting to walk a bit." She was jabbering and needed to shut up. "Can't stand for long. Haven't been able to operate, but I can do this job while others treat the wounded and prepare to evacuate."

The private, beanpole thin and jittery, moved closer to the desk. "We don't have much time. Yankees is comin'."

The sergeant's brow creased as he eyed the private. A moment of intimidating silence saturated the air around the desk. Then the sergeant hawked and spat a blob of tobacco juice, which landed on the floor with a splat, missing the spittoon by mere inches. Charlotte tamed her rolling eyes and moved her foot away from the dark brown spot, one of many wet patches on the wood plank. A trickle of sweat ran down the side of her face, but she ignored it, letting it plop to her collar. He waved Charlotte away as if she were an annoying fly. His lips compressed, showing only the edges of decaying teeth. "Private Franklin will show you to sick bay."

"And if I need anything else—" The front door blew open.

A half dozen guards rushed in, crowding the entry. She inched back out of the way, before they could crush her with grossly sweating bodies reeking of unwashed male, fear, and onions. The distraction was a welcome relief, and untied one of the many knots in her stomach. The men and their concerns should keep the sergeant occupied while she searched for Braham.

"Richmond's being evacuated—"

"They're opening the banks—"

"On a Sunday afternoon—"

"So customers can get their money to leave town—"

The sergeant worried the flesh of his lower lip with one of his crooked yellow teeth as he followed the conversations. "I ain't got no money to get out."

"The mayor announced to the City Council—"

"The government's leavin'—"

"Two militia companies are staying to protect the city—"

The sergeant spit again. This time he hit the spittoon. "Doubt they'll be able to protect the city from looters. Nobody wants to stay. Don't blame 'em none."

The buzz of activity surrounding the sergeant's desk continued. He gave the red-haired private a dismissing wave. "Whatever the Major needs, see he gets it."

The private pointed down a hallway. "This way, sir."

When they reached the end, he pushed opened a door. A guard, leaning haphazardly on the back legs of a chair, dropped his feet and jumped to attention, saluting. Charlotte gagged at the filth and fetid smell in the room.

"We're evacuating," the private said.

The guard's eyes widened. *"When?"*

"Tonight." The private swung his head, doing a sweep of the room, his eyes darting quickly from one row of prisoners to another. "The doctor's here to count the patients who can't walk."

"Got several. Where we takin' 'em?" the guard asked.

Charlotte continued breathing through her mouth, avoiding the man's sweet-sour odor. "South."

"By train?" the private asked.

She shook her head. "No trains. No wagons. No ambulances. Those who can't walk get left behind."

The bare rafters supporting the floor above creaked as soldiers moved around upstairs. Sturdy bars covered open windows, leaving the prisoners exposed to weather and temperature extremes. Dark splotches covered the dank prison walls. She hated to guess what caused them. Even the naked posts and beams were splattered with stains. Although she couldn't see the ticks, fleas, and rats, she knew they skirted the room, spreading disease. Even thinking about the vermin made her scalp itch.

The floor was slick with slime, and wet as well. Patients lay moaning on straw mats on the floor. Several patients, lying in their own filth, had pustulant sores. Others had wounds wrapped in old, bloody bandages. All the semi-naked men appeared emaciated. Those who were aware enough to notice her arrival, tracked her movements with vacant eyes.

Man's inhumanity to man. Robbie Burns got it right. But her favorite verse on inhumanity was from Alan Paton: *There is only one way in which one can endure man's inhumanity to man and that is to try, in one's own life, to exemplify man's humanity to man.* Her grandfather had taught her the verse, and it had probably been largely responsible for her decision to go to medical school instead of law school.

But right now she had to endure man's inhumanity. "I'll start at the far end and work my way back here." She needed a minute or two to compose herself, to shut down feelings, and turn off her emotions. Her cane thudded rhythmically against the floor as she shuffled down the long line of straw mats.

Her mind flashed to Lincoln's most prominent feature—the perpetual look of sadness. He'd been to the battle fields, he'd read the prison reports. No wonder he was so burdened with sorrow. She doubted she'd ever make it through a day in the future without having flashes of these men who'd been treated like rubbish.

When she reached the end of the row, she knelt beside the first patient. If he had been dead for a week, he couldn't have smelled worse. No bath in months, a bloody bandage around his leg. She didn't need to remove it to know the tissue beneath was gangrenous. He was a shell of a man with sunken eyes and a cachectic body.

"What's your name, soldier?" she asked.

His eyelashes fluttered and, after some effort, he opened his eyes, and said in a weak voice, "Private Jeff Dougherty."

"What hurts?"

"Not much don't hurt, sir. I want to go home."

She clasped a very dirty hand, but he barely had the strength to squeeze her fingers. "Just a few more hours," she said. "Can you hang on?"

"I'll do my best, sir."

"How old are you, soldier?"

He didn't change his pained expression, but something nameless passed between them. "Sixteen on my last birthday."

He was merely a boy who would never grow to manhood.

As she moved to the next soldier and the next, finding cases of dysentery, pneumonia, malnutrition, and infection, she no longer saw the filth or smelled the vile air, or cringed at the despair and inhumanity. Good God, their clothes were holding their bones together. She only saw dying men who wanted and needed comfort in their final hours. Saving them was impossible. No medicine. No decent food. No clean clothes or bandages. No one to provide care, fresh straw or untainted water. None of these prisoners could walk on his own. Most would be dead in twenty-four hours. Even if there was a way to take them all home with her, it was too late. The regret would linger in her heart for a long time.

A lost generation.

Getting a message to Braham seemed hopeless now. With a deep breath of the fetid air, she made a decision. She'd have to find the dungeon and do it quickly. Jack had threatened to come after her if she didn't return within the hour. He might have already dipped into the flask he'd filled before he left the Van Lew's. The liquor was not for him, he had assured Charlotte, but for nervous guards. He'd better have some left. By the time she got out of Castle Thunder, she'd need a stiff drink.

When she was in high school, if she didn't call him exactly when she was supposed to, Jack would come looking for her, and embarrass her so badly she wouldn't speak to him for days. If he came barging into the prison, embarrassment would be the least of their problems.

"Are these prisoners going or staying, sir?" the private asked.

"Not one of these men can walk, and I doubt many will survive the night. Are there any other sick or wounded?"

"All the sick ones are down here. The prisoners upstairs can walk."

"What about the prisoners in the dungeon or solitary confinement cells? What shape are they in?" she asked.

He shook his head. "Don't know."

"My orders are clear. Count the prisoners who can't walk. If there are any in those cells, I have to count them, too."

"Let me ask the sergeant."

She couldn't allow that. She looked down at the sterling silver-tipped cane, thinking fast, knuckles turning white. "Go ahead, but he said to help with whatever I needed. I'll wait here for you." She was taking a gamble which might backfire. "I can't stand much longer. Let's get this done, soldier." She put her full weight on the stones, grimacing from pain she didn't have to feign. Jack's brilliant idea was comparable to wearing an insole made of porcupine quills.

The private licked his bottom lip. After a moment he said,

"Never mind. Let's go." He pointed to a doorway. "The cells are on ground level, facing Dock Street."

Charlotte glanced toward the sergeant's desk. The group of guards, full of brag and bluster, was still standing at the entrance berating the Union Cavalry.

The private lit a lantern, and led the way down the stairs. With each step, the smell of decomposition grew stronger. She breathed slowly in and out through her mouth. Using the railing on one side and cane on the other, she was able to hobble down without putting pressure on her aching foot. As she came off the last step, her foot landed squarely on the stones and she let out a sharp gasp.

The private turned, jerked the lantern up high, alarm written across his face. The pulse at his temples beat rapidly. "We shouldn't have come down here. Going up will be worse for your leg."

Charlotte swiped sweat from her face with her jacket-covered arm, not wanting to put her hands anywhere near her nose, mouth, and eyes. "We're here now. Keep going."

Four massive oak doors lined the hall. Scurrying rats made rustling noises as they darted in and out. One ran over the top of her foot. She swallowed a scream. She hated rats. The overpowering stench of excrement, vomit, and blood curled around her stomach and squeezed.

"How many prisoners are down here?" She breathed through her mouth and hoped her breakfast would stay in her stomach.

"Four." He grabbed a ring of giant iron keys off a wall hook. Each key was about ten inches long, four inches wide. They clanked together as the private approached the last cell holding the lantern in one hand, key ring in the other.

Charlotte began to whistle.

The private handed her the lantern. "Will you hold this while I unlock the door?" With practiced ease, he inserted a key and a loud click reverberated through the clammy dungeon. More rats skittered by. Whatever her anxiety level had been prior to coming down the stairs, it had now doubled.

The door opened. He took the lantern and entered the cell. A

barefoot man in tattered clothes huddled in the corner. Hopelessness dulled his pale eyes. A chain attached to a heavy iron ball was
wrapped around his ankle, and had rubbed the skin raw. Where did
the guards think he would go?

"What's your name?" she asked.

"John Hancock."

Charlotte moved into the room and squatted close to him. "Can
you walk?"

He shook his leg and the chain rattled. "Not with this goddamn
ball and chain."

"How about without it?" she asked.

"Guess so."

"Good. You're being evacuated tonight. Be ready." Elizabeth
had told her if she saw Hancock, White, or Lohmann, to say the
words *be ready.* They would understand the message.

Before the soldier opened the next door, her whistle had been
cut short by another rat running over her foot. Her heightened fear
was taking its toll on the muscles in her neck, tensing them to the
point of rigidity, but she wouldn't leave until she found Braham.

"Don't think them rats like your whistling."

The second man was on his feet when the private held up the
lantern. "I can walk," the prisoner said in a coarse whisper like a
heavy smoker's. The blood splatters on his body and clothes told her
his voice had been strained by screaming, not smoking. His ankle,
too, was raw from the attached manacle.

"What's your name?" she asked.

"Bill Lohmann."

She gazed into his sunken eyes, trying to soften hers and convey
a sense of hope, much as she had done to scores of patients through
the years. "Be ready."

In the next cell the prisoner was also standing, eager to be told
he, too, would be evacuated. By the time they reached the last cell,
she was flushed with a rage so intense it seemed to scorch the very
marrow of her bones. How could people do this to each other?

The door squeaked open, and the private held up the lantern, as he'd done in the three previous cells. The prisoner was on all fours, trying to stand. He rolled back onto the floor, groaning. "I can stand."

Charlotte barely stifled a gasp at Braham's condition. She tried to calm her racing heart. She pressed her foot harder on the stones. The pain was a necessary reminder of the role she played. To rescue him, she had to allow him to suffer now.

"Don't think you can make it," the soldier said. He turned to leave, taking the light with him.

"No, wait." Charlotte went inside the cell. The miasma of death filled her lungs. In a pile of musty, foul-smelling straw, she spied a dead rat. She looked directly at Braham then. His eyes flicked to her, huge with shock. Sweat poured from his face, and the rags of his filthy shirt hung bloodied and sodden against his chest. Blood seeped from open wounds. A gash on his forehead was crusted with dirt, and one side of his face was swollen. Both his hair and beard were streaked with blood, but the corners of his mouth trembled in an attempt to smile.

She couldn't speak past the lump in her throat, past her scorching fury.

"What's your name?" the young soldier asked.

He didn't answer right away, and she wasn't sure he had any voice left after everything his interrogators had done to him. She held her breath, waiting. Then, his jaw clenched, he said through his teeth, "Charles Jackson."

The amount of suffering he had endured was unimaginable. Not being able to treat his wounds filled her with cold rage. To leave him behind, even for a short while, would be the hardest thing she'd ever done in her life. She struggled, but found her voice again and asked, "Can you stand, Mr. Jackson? If you want to leave here tonight, you have to walk." She slipped her hand into her pocket and palmed the four pills she'd placed there earlier. Then she stepped over to him and took his arm. "Let me help you."

The tobacco-spitting sergeant who had been stationed at the desk the floor above, entered the cell, shoving the door open so hard it bounced against the outside wall. He fisted his hands at his hips, and his bulk filled the doorway, muscles bulging, jowls quivering with fury. "These prisoners aren't allowed visitors."

She stomped down on her good foot, putting herself mere inches from the foul-breathed sergeant's face. "I am *not* a visitor. I'm a *Major* in the Army of Northern Virginia on assignment to evaluate prisoners for ambulation, which includes—" she jabbed her finger in Braham's direction, "—this man."

Braham staggered to his feet and managed a step toward the sergeant, his nostrils flaring. His eyes shone almost black.

She moved between the two men and pointed her cane at the sergeant. "This prisoner can obviously walk. I'm done here."

"All prisoners down here will be evacuated on the order of the warden. If they can't keep up, they'll be shot." The sergeant left the cell and shoved the door back against the wall again, metal bolt clanging against the wood.

Charlotte leaned closed to Braham and slipped pills into his hand, giving it a squeeze. "Rest up. You'll need to be strong for tonight." She intentionally did not look into his eyes. If she did, she would betray them both.

When she hobbled out, she asked, "Is he the final prisoner?"

"Yes." The private slammed the oak door and turned the heavy key in the lock.

The finality of the sliding bolt shattered her brief bravado. The hall, the door, the cell, quickly dissolved behind a layer of watery film. She stood cemented to the dirt floor. The rats could eat her shoes for all she cared. She leaned heavily against the door. As sweat poured down her face, tears poured through her soul.

"You coming?" the sergeant asked.

She cleared away the knot in her throat. "Yes."

"How many did you count?" he asked.

"Fifty-two," she said. "Some in the sick bay won't last the night. Everyone down here is on their feet and should be evacuated, even the last one."

"He," he said, thrusting out his thumb, "will be leaving, even if we have to skewer him with a tobacco stick." The sergeant spit more juice, hitting a rat. Then he yanked the keys from the red-headed private, gripping them tightly in his meaty paw. "The warden wants his neck in a noose as soon as he gives up the names of the Richmond underground leaders."

"Not sure it matters much now."

"Does to the captain." The sergeant nodded toward the stairs. "Let's get out of here."

His hand squeezed the keys, his knuckles scabbed and still bloody, and she knew his fist had been the instrument of damage to Braham's face. What a son of a bitch. If she ever saw him lying on the floor bleeding, she'd forsake her Hippocratic Oath and leave the room.

There is only one way in which one can endure man's inhumanity to man and that is to try, in one's own life to exemplify man's humanity to man.

"Aren't there exceptions?" she remembered asking her grandfather.

"No," he'd said.

Well, Grandfather, you were wrong.

She gripped the rough wood railing to steady herself. She needed the support, but she also was afraid she might run back to Braham's cell and put both their lives at risk. "Go ahead. It'll take me longer to climb."

The men climbed the rickety staircase, their boots scuffing against the wood. The sergeant spit as he climbed. She balanced her weight between the railing and the cane, protecting her bad foot, and hobbled up the stairs, slowly and carefully, whistling as she climbed. It was all she could do to leave Braham with a bit of hope.

55

Richmond, Virginia, April 1, 1865

B RAHAM AWOKE, AND immediate pain reminded him of his present condition. Instead of opening his eyes, he squeezed them tighter, as if not looking would change his situation. He had lost track of the days, but he thought the invasion was close. Maybe today. Maybe tomorrow. Could he take another day of the warden's tenacious interrogation? At the thought, his mouth moved soundlessly, his face contorting in a rictus of agony.

One more day. He could survive one more day, unless they resorted to bucking again. He had heard of the torture device, and knew it left no tell-tale marks, but had never seen it used until they did it to him. They forced him into a sitting position on the ground with bended knees. His wrists were then bound together and tied to his ankles, his arms cradling his legs. When the guard picked up a tobacco stick, Braham doubted his constitution would withstand another beating. The sergeant had laughed with calm callousness as he passed the stick over Braham's elbows and under his knees. He had then been forced to remain in the position for hours. When they finally removed the stick, his joints and back were frozen in the unnatural position, and were screaming in agony.

The door to the stairs leading to solitary confinement cells squeaked open. Fear crawled coldly through his empty stomach. Boot heels scraped across weathered floorboards. They were coming to interrogate him again. The warden always dragged out his approach to the cells, playing on the prisoners' fear until they sometimes pissed themselves. At first Braham had tried to hide his dread behind a mask of indifference, but soon enough it had been pitilessly stripped away. Now he only tried to survive.

Someone whistling outside his door brought him fully alert. It wasn't a sharp whistle to get someone's attention. It was a recognizable tune. He puckered his parched lips, but his swollen face made it impossible for him to whistle in response. He blew out a steady stream of air, but no sound. Then he heard the whistle again, and in his haze, he thought he knew the whistler.

Not Charlotte. Dear God, not in this demonic hold. It must be his imagination.

Thoughts of her had kept him sane during these long, cold nights, as did one of his favorite Robbie Burns songs which described her to perfection. *She's sweeter than the morning dawn...Her hair is like the curling mist...Her cheeks are like yon crimson gem...Her lips are like yon cherries ripe...*

God, he wished he could see her one more time. But what could he tell her that he hadn't already said?

A rat crawled over his shoulder and nudged its mouth into the open wounds on his back. He swatted at the creature until it scurried away. Braham rolled over onto his wounds to keep the rat from burrowing back in. The straw pricked at the cuts made by the dozen lashes he'd received within hours of being arrested. He sucked air through his teeth and rolled onto his belly, sucked air again, and switched to his side. He couldn't find a position to relieve the pains around his ribs. One of the many punches or kicks to his gut might have bruised a couple. They weren't sticking out, and he could breathe, so at least his lungs weren't punctured.

He rolled his tongue around his mouth. All of his teeth were still in place. The cuts on his head had stopped bleeding, but he'd had headaches for hours, maybe days. The growl in his stomach was louder now, too.

The first day, he'd removed worms from the bread he'd been given. Afterward, he ate whatever they gave him, which wasn't much. He was still alive, and although he'd come close to revealing everything they wanted to know, he'd managed to keep his secrets. The guards set out to unman him, steal his courage and self-control. They had laughed when he pissed himself and vomited, and then they had left him to lie in his own filth and blood. Knowing the Union Cavalry would soon ride down Main Street was the only thing keeping hope alive.

When he heard boots stomp down the wobbly stairs, he sat up, heart racing. If they were coming for him, could he endure another pummeling or the lash? They had started on his back, then his buttocks, and finally his legs. They had left him threatening to move on to his front next time. Give them what they wanted, or suffer the whip and worse.

"You'll never get a child on your whore when we're done with you," the guard had said.

The ring of keys clinked, and he shivered violently. His shaking leg rattled the chain attached to the iron ball, which he'd learned was too heavy to lift. A kettle drum pounded in his chest when footsteps reached his door. He let out a stifled groan as the men moved past his cell. The whistle again. The tune he had taught Charlotte. But she had gone home. His mind was playing tricks to torment him.

The bolt to one of the doors screeched opened and he heard voices, but couldn't distinguish what they were saying. The door closed. Another door opened. More discussion. That door closed. He attempted to stand but fell back on his bloodied ass. The door to the adjoining cell opened.

"What's your name?"

Braham heard only garbled words.

"Can you walk?"

He stilled to hear what was being said. Muffled sounds were muted by the roar of his heart pounding in his ears.

"Be ready." The words were spoken in a deepened, familiar voice. Terror seized his gut.

A key grated in the lock and a wave of torchlight fell into the cell, temporarily blinding him. He rolled onto all fours and tried to stand. If evil was coming through the door, he would meet it face to face, not as a coward groveling on the dirt floor. If it was Charlotte, he wanted to be on his feet to meet her.

The chain rattled and rubbed against his raw ankle, but he kept trying to stand, twisting and pushing. During the whippings, he had been handcuffed to the wall and the prolonged, awkward stretch had strained the muscles in his arms and shoulders.

Two men entered. The red-haired lad he had seen before.

"Give me a minute," Braham said. "I can stand."

The lad turned to leave, mumbling, taking the light with him.

"No, wait," the bearded officer said. "What's your name?"

He shaded his rapidly blinking eyes from the light. "Charles Jackson." Who was the bearded man? Why did he look familiar?

"Can you stand, Mr. Jackson? If you want to leave here tonight, you have to walk."

The voice sounded so awkward, so out of place, it made him cringe.

The bearded officer came closer to him and took his arm. "Let me help you."

Braham looked into the man's eyes. Memories returned in searing flashes. *The man had rescued him once before. He wasn't a man. He was Charlotte.* The shock was a bloody bayonet to the belly, ripping him open. Braham willed himself not to breathe, not to respond in any way. If he could react, though, what would he do, wring her neck or kiss her? He'd kiss her, and then he'd wring her neck—and Jack's, too.

The asshole sergeant who had paid frequent visits to his cell entered, yelling, "These prisoners aren't allowed visitors. Get out."

Charlotte whipped around and got up into his face, slamming her cane against the dirt floor in punctuation. "I am *not* a visitor. I'm a *Major* in the Army of Northern Virginia on assignment to evaluate prisoners for ambulation, which includes—" she pointed to Braham, "—this man."

The sergeant growled, raised a fist, and made a threatening gesture toward Braham. He willed himself to his feet and lunged forward. The chain, anchored to the wall by unbendable pins, groaned under the force of his weight, but held tight. A volcanic burn of fear scorched through him, and he pulled on the chain again, ignoring the raw pain in his ankle. Chained to the wall, he couldn't protect her. He couldn't do a damn thing.

The sergeant growled again before stomping from the cell.

Charlotte took Braham's hand and slipped something into his palm. "Rest up. You'll need to be strong for tonight."

God, he wanted to pull her into his arms, but he had to let her go without acknowledging her. She had entered his world of darkness and brought slivers of light.

She hobbled out, putting little weight on her right foot. She was hurt. He made a sudden move to follow, but the damn chain held his leg in place. Concern, not pain, had shown in her eyes. Was the limp a ruse? Maybe so. Maybe no.

The cell door slammed shut and the lonely darkness enveloped him once again, but he remained standing, listening. Boot heels scraping against the floor faded, but still he listened until the door at the top of the stairs closed and locked, and Charlotte's whistle became little more than a memory.

Pain flooded in again. Now it rated a nine, maybe ten. The gain of one or two points on the pain scale were the result of his carefully sealed heart cracking open. If Charlotte could find the courage to risk her life for him again, could he find the courage to love her?

Loving her was the easy part. Living without her would keep his heart chained to the iron ball for the rest of his life.

Slowly, he gathered his thoughts, sorted through them, and then set aside the ones he could deal with later. He opened his fist, and his fingers explored the items she'd placed in his palm. Pills? She had given him pills? As Jack would say, "What the fuck?" Jack would have slipped him a gun or knife. Damn women. They were naturally inclined to comfort a man, not protect him. If Charlotte was going to dress like a man, she should damn well think like one.

He dipped the ladle into the pail of stagnant water and swallowed the tablets, which he hoped were pain pills. If they were, the pain would start to slip away within minutes, and he'd have a few moments of peace, the first he'd had since he'd been thrown into the cell.

Braham managed his first smile in days. Cracks rutted into his dry lips. Freedom was hours away. Jack would be waiting to rescue him. But another problem hovered in the distance. Charlotte would want him to return to her time so she could put him back together again. The thought created one of those odd moments when his brain seemed to stop working. He forgot about loving her and living without her, and for the briefest of seconds he wished she had only been a dream.

56

Richmond, Virginia, April 1, 1865

CHARLOTTE LIMPED OUT of Castle Thunder. Her grunts of pain harmonized with the guns stuttering in the background. Sweat soaked her shirt, her scalp itched under her wig, her foot hurt, her heart weighed a ton inside her chest, and she'd bet her brass buttons there were tooth marks on her boots. "Damn rats." Her curse included not only the vermin, but the warden and guards, who were inhuman assholes.

She was spitting anger and frustration, and even shame for being part of a race which could birth such evil, vile people. Her lungs begged for a breath of unadulterated air. But the outside air was tainted, too. Not ripe with the stink of the prison, but with smoke from cannons and the sulfur byproduct of gunpowder. Bile churned in her stomach, inching up her esophagus. She couldn't remember the last time she threw up, but it was about to happen. Fortunately, when she reached the street corner, a cool breeze coming off the river brought a reprieve. She gulped in fresh air, forcing her lungs to expel the prison poisons.

Braham was alive. Injured, yes, but from what she'd seen, his injuries, while not minor, weren't as bad as she had feared. Concern for his emotional state, though, had her mind buzzing with speculations of all sorts. How much damage had the trauma of being locked in a claustrophobic, windowless hole and tortured for days done to his already troubled soul?

A hand tapped her on the back. Startled, a new surge of adrenaline pumped into her bloodstream. Grimacing, she jerked her head to look over her shoulder.

The red-headed soldier jumped back, saluting.

Her nostrils flared with disdain for the prison and everyone associated with it, even the one person who had seemed almost humane. "*What do you want?*"

"Sorry, sir, but Libby Prison is the other way." He pointed in the opposite direction. "I can get a wagon to carry you there. If'n your leg's bothering you."

Charlotte whirled around to face him, putting more of her weight on her bruised foot. The pain rocketed through her, and she wanted it to be visible in her face as a living, breathing thing. "It'll have…to wait." The words came out in a gasp. "Shouldn't have…climbed the stairs. I have to rest."

A closed carriage stopped on the street only a few feet away, and Jack leaned his head out. His face was white with worry and fatigue, and his features were drawn. While he didn't have the carved-in-marble appearance, he was close. Both his hair and beard stubble appeared darker in the shadow of the carriage.

"I noticed you limping, Major. Can I give you a ride?" he asked.

Her lips tightened into a thin line, and she clasped the guard on the shoulder. "Thanks for your help, Private, but I'll ride in this carriage."

"If'n you need assistance later, I'll be here to escort you."

Charlotte gave him a tight smile. Since he had helped her already, he needed to continue believing he had a vested interest in her assignment. "I'll find you. In the meantime, keep an eye on the prisoners in solitary. They need to walk out of here tonight. They don't need to be interrogated again beforehand."

The private saluted. "I'll do what I can, sir."

"I'm sure I can count on you, son," she said.

Jack opened the carriage door and scooted over to make room. "I've been waiting for over an hour." The edge to his voice had been honed and stropped to a fine point.

She stretched out her leg, resting it on the opposite bench seat. "I can't tell from your tone if you're relieved or angry."

"Both." His eyes remained on her, steady and unblinking. "You look horrible."

"Gee, thanks." Her voice wobbled a bit, but the tone echoed the intensity of his emotion.

He stretched out his arms and cracked all his knuckles simultaneously, something she'd only seen him do a couple of times, when his anger got out of control. The months he spent at the monastery had taught him how to manage his emotions.

"What happened? You're not hurt, are you?"

She shook head and steeled herself against the riptide of god-awful memories. "They didn't hurt me."

A hot blast of relief gusted out of Jack's pinched mouth, and he relaxed his arms. "Did you find someone to get a message to Braham?"

Recalling the face of Private Jeff Dougherty, she moaned softly then said, "No."

In the split second it took Jack to close his eyes and shudder, the red color of anger faded from his cheeks.

"I saw him."

"Sweet Jesus. He's in solitary. Don't tell me you went there."

"I had no choice," she said quickly, before he started popping knuckles again. "The men in sick bay are dying from untreated illnesses, in atrocious conditions. They couldn't get a message out of their mouths, much less out of the room."

A drop of sweat ran down the side of Jack's face. He didn't wipe it away. His hands lay folded in his lap. His breathing was easy and deep as he moved into the special trance state where he could find mental and physical calm. She'd let him remain there a few minutes.

As the carriage drove off, Charlotte glared at the prison until it was out of sight. The air was filled with a cloying mixture of Magnolias, gunpowder, and stale sweat, yet she was able to breathe a bit more easily. The crowds in the street had grown larger as more of the city's population evacuated, clogging the roads and creating impassible conditions.

Jack's breathing returned to normal. He opened his eyes, a glint of dark blue in them, and he kept them steady on hers. "Tell me what you saw."

She could do this two ways: Dispassionately, as an objective observer, or passionately, as a woman and a member of the human race. She rested her forearms on her legs, held her hands out in front of her with palms up, and stared at them, amazed to see, even after a day like today, they weren't shaking.

"Indescribable atrocities. Every man I saw was mired in hunger and despair, and most had bodies ravaged by disease. Wherever I turned, I faced hollowed, sepulchral eyes, and almost inaudible voices. There were dozens of suffering or tortured men, and I couldn't do one thing to help them. Not even offer a cup of clean water."

"Are you sorry you went in there?"

She shook her head. "I'll be forever changed by the experience, but I don't regret going." She paused a moment to take a long breath and let it out slowly. "Braham's had a rough time of it."

"How rough?"

"It could be worse. He could be dead."

"Is he in worse shape than the last time?"

"From what I could see, no. Give him a bath, decent food, patch up his cuts and flayed skin, and his body will recover. Processing and coming to grips with the dehumanizing experience will take longer. Braham can tolerate a broken body better than he can live with a broken spirit. He has stamina and resilience. He drove my car hundreds of miles, an astonishing accomplishment for someone who never had a driving lesson. He's one of the smartest people I've ever met, and will stand up to whatever challenge he's given, but the loss of dignity and pride he clearly endured will not easily be overcome."

"You should have given him a gun instead of pills."

"So he could kill himself?"

"Don't be ridiculous. A gun would have empowered him."

She held up her hands in defense of her actions. "It wasn't in the script you gave me."

"If Warner Brothers played as fast and loose with my scripts as you did, I'd never sell them another one."

He reached for her hand, but she jerked it back. "Don't touch me. I'm crawling with germs. I need a hot bath with strong soap, and then I'll fully debrief you and Elizabeth."

The driver drove toward center city passing columns of refugees strung out along the canal towpath toward Lynchburg, a shifting mass of humanity.

"They have no idea where safety lies, do they?" she asked.

"No," Jack said. "They'll keep running, hoping they can find it. The Union troops won't hurt them, but they'll never believe it. So they'll run in fear, believing Yankees are fiends with horns and hoofs."

"Yankees aren't devils," she said with a grin. "The worst you can say is they have terrible accents and bad manners."

"Ah, spoken like a true Southerner."

57

Richmond, Virginia, April 1, 1865

CHARLOTTE HAD STRIPPED in the kitchen and taken a bath in a wash tub at the back of the room. She asked the servants to burn the uniform. She never wanted to wear the damn thing again. The women had hovered over her, scrubbed her clean, dried, and dressed her. While they took extraordinary care to put her right again, the excruciating pain lodged in her heart couldn't be washed clean. The death and dying at the Battle of Cedar Creek had destroyed most of her romantic illusions about the Civil War. Castle Thunder destroyed the rest.

Jack had encouraged her to rest, to prepare for the long night ahead, but she couldn't. She had learned as an intern, resident, and then as a practicing physician, to work through long, sleepless shifts. She could function well, despite being exhausted.

The parlor door was closed, but she could still hear Jack's crisp, cultivated voice. He must be talking to Elizabeth.

She rapped her knuckles against the paneled wood before sliding the heavy doors open. Candles guttered in the sconces on the wall and flickered from candles placed around the room. Charlotte shied away from shadowy corners and sat closer to the brick hearth, where a warm fire popped and crackled. Knitting her thoughts into coherent sentences had taken some time, but she was now ready to answer their questions about what happened at the prison.

Jack's mouth twitched a little when she entered. His expression assured her he was glad to see her composed, and he wasn't going to make a fuss over her decision to come down instead of resting.

"Whiskey?" he asked.

She settled into the wingback chair. "Make it a double."

He handed Charlotte a whiskey and Elizabeth a sherry. Charlotte passed the crystal under her nose briefly, taking an appreciative whiff of the amber liquid, and then sipped. Hot and delicious warmth started in her throat and spread down into her chest.

"Hmm. That's good."

Jack's long fingers curved lightly around the base of his glass. His expression turned contemplative. He would wait and not push her, although Charlotte knew both Jack and Elizabeth were anxious for her report.

The odd moment of expectant silence ended when Charlotte cleared her throat roughly. "The deprivation was worse than I could have imagined. I counted fifty-two men in sick bay suffering from dysentery, malnutrition, pneumonia and a host of other diseases. Several had infected wounds, but most were dying from secondary contagious diseases. I'd say a half to two-thirds won't survive the night. Leaving a message for Braham with one of those moribund patients was impossible. They were barely coherent. When I realized I had no other option, I insisted on going to the cells used for solitary confinement."

The only outward sign of Jack's displeasure was an infinitesimal twitch in his upper body. If she hadn't been so familiar with the nuances of his temperament, she would have missed it. Elizabeth, however, grabbed a white-knuckled hold of the arms of her chair, leaned forward, and seemed to stop breathing.

"I talked to Hancock, White, and Lohmann. They're weak and undernourished, but not actively bleeding or physically incapacitated."

Elizabeth breathed with relief. "Thank God."

"All three wore leg irons, though. I gave them the *be ready* signal, so they'll be prepared to make a break tonight when we provide the opportunity."

Elizabeth rolled her bottom lip in between her teeth, a thinking pose. "What of Braham?"

"His torture has been more recent and more severe. The lash has shredded his clothes and skin. Open wounds are festering on his forehead and back. He probably has others. I doubt he's eaten in days. He's weak and could barely stand."

"Which will make it harder for him to get away. Did he recognize you?" Jack asked.

"Yes, but I'm not sure he would have if he hadn't heard my whistle first. He even made a move to protect me. I wasn't in danger," she was quick to add. "The guard was being a jerk."

A wry smile teased the corners of Jack's lips. "You probably scared the crap out of him."

"The guard or Braham?"

"You can be formidable, sis, when you puff up like an angry cat. You probably scared them both." He waggled his eyebrows like he often did when he teased her. The levity put a dent in the tension.

Elizabeth refilled her sherry and walked to the window to stare out. The din of cannons still rumbled in the distance. "Richmond will descend into anarchy when the Confederate troops abandon the city. What will the night bring before the Union troops arrive?"

Charlotte suspected the question was rhetorical, and not because Elizabeth believed she and Jack knew the future. Although, considering the information they had shared with her, it might appear they had their fingers on the pulse of history.

Elizabeth dropped the curtain, letting it fall gently back into place. "As the army disengages from its trenches and strikes out to join Lee, we will need to create a diversion to give our associates time to escape."

Charlotte and Jack subtly exchanged glances. He uncrossed his legs and leaned forward. "The situation will create its own diversion. The city council wants all the liquor destroyed, fearing a repetition of what happened in Columbia six weeks ago when the Union troops arrived. Tonight, whiskey barrels will be rolled out into the streets and smashed. The contents will cascade into the gutters and the free-flowing alcohol will cause the collapse of any remaining law and order."

"You paint a dismal picture of the future, Jack," Elizabeth said.

"The rabble will rain hell down upon Richmond tonight," he said.

Elizabeth fiddled with the stem of her sherry glass. "Hell's been here for four years."

Jack nodded. "After tonight the city will be forever changed. There'll be widespread disorder, punctuated by explosions, fires, and pillaging mobs. Your people will have to locate your men, follow close by as they're marched through the city, and wait for the opportunity to break free."

"There are four solitary cells with a prisoner in each one: Hancock, White, Lohmann, and Braham. Those men will probably be grouped together during the evacuation. It will make them easier to find—"

"But harder to rescue," Elizabeth added.

Jack poured another drink. "We need someone trustworthy positioned close to the prison who can notify us as soon as the evacuation begins."

"I can arrange for someone," Elizabeth said.

Charlotte tugged on her ear, fingering the Darwin's Point she'd had since birth. "General Ewell will pull his five thousand soldiers out of Richmond after dark. The streets are already crowded. When the people see the defenders abandon the city, there will be widespread panic."

"Panic is already here. Folks are tracking the advancement of the Union Army from the church spires," Elizabeth said. "Neighbors who have shunned me, even calling me a traitor, have started bringing wheelbarrows of silver and jewelry to the door, begging me to hide their treasures. They should be more afraid of looters than the approaching army."

"General Ewell will systematically burn all the tobacco in the Shockoe warehouse and other buildings to keep it out of enemy hands," Jack said.

Elizabeth patted perspiration from her forehead with a dainty lace handkerchief. "I'm not surprised. What about the bridges?"

"The warehouses and bridges will be torched," Jack added. "Toward morning, the wind will pick up."

Elizabeth searched the face of one Mallory, then the other. "What are you implying?"

Charlotte tried to sound reassuring, but her anxiety over what they faced was clear in her voice. "When fires are deliberately set, they often burn more than the intended structures." Richmond was Charlotte's beloved city, too, and it made her stomach clutch to think so many beautiful buildings would be lost to future generations.

"I don't know where your information comes from or your insight into future events, nor will I ask," Elizabeth said.

A knock on the front door brought Jack and Charlotte to their feet. They followed Elizabeth out into the entryway. When the door opened they heard brass bands and drum corps playing with unusual vigor—dueling patriotic songs from both sides of the trenches.

Gaylord, along with the father and son Charlotte and Jack had previously met, and two others of Elizabeth's friends, entered the house.

A friendly smile spread across Gaylord's blunt features when he saw Jack and Charlotte. "Our people are in place, and ready. We'll get the major out."

Jack nodded and extended a welcoming hand to Gaylord. The dim light threw shadows on Jack's face, emphasizing the strong bones. He looked so much like their father, a man she remembered mostly from family photographs.

Elizabeth gave an intentionally audible sigh. "Good. It won't be much longer now. There's food on the table. Come. While we eat, we can work out the logistics of how we're going to help our men escape."

Charlotte knew what would take place during the night, but there were additional factors influencing the outcome now; Braham's existence was the most glaring one. He should never have been here. He should have died in Chimborazo. And what about the parts she and Jack were playing? They should not be in this century. How would the night change because of them? They all ambled into the dining room where, behind closed doors and curtains, they planned the underground's final mission.

58

Richmond, Virginia, April 1, 1865

EIGHT WEARY PEOPLE sat uneasily around Elizabeth's dining room table, drinking strong coffee and eating chicken soup, bread, and dried apples. With every rifle shot or cannon rumble, Charlotte glanced toward the windows and doors. They were all facing a bleak night, but it would be followed by a sweet victory when the Union Cavalry marched into town.

Elizabeth drew herself up, lifting a glass in a shaky hand. An extraordinary look appeared on her face, something akin to satisfaction, which brightened her eyes. Jack noticed the look, too, and he relaxed his shoulders, and a smiled curled the corners of his mouth. A restless current meandered through the rest of group. Gaylord kept his face steady, but Charlotte could see something going on inside of him—a roiling. He didn't speak, nor did he need to. He was concerned about Braham and the other men, along with everyone else at the table.

Elizabeth tinged a spoon lightly against the crystal and cleared her throat, getting everyone's attention. "For four years we have endured martial law, conscription, underfeeding, and horrendous causalities. It will all end in a matter of hours. Please join me now in a toast."

They all picked up the glasses and stood.

"To the Union," Elizabeth said.

Everyone responded in a lighthearted yet formal manner. "To

the Union."

The toast signaled a temporary lull in the escalating tension, especially among the men. Charlotte well understood the emptiness of heart she'd sensed in these Unionists; the sense of sleepwalking through life and lying opened-eyed at night, finding no rest and knowing only hopelessness. She had seen it in her patients, in their families, and in herself following the death of her mother. To see these men with light in their eyes and hope for their future allowed a semblance of a smile to ease out. The arrival of the Yankees wouldn't solve all their problems, but it would stop the fear and the suffering.

Now, with assignments made and planning completed, the men said their good-byes and left to rescue Hancock, White, and Lohmann. Jack and Gaylord were assigned to rescue Braham.

Jack whispered into Charlotte's ear. "Come with me. I need to talk to you."

She swept into the drawing room behind him like a turbulent weather front. "I'm going with you. Give me a minute to change into pants. You'll need another set of eyes when several hundred haggard looking men march down the street. You can't check them all."

"Maybe not, but Braham knows I'll be there."

"You can't be sure." The words came quickly and without thought.

"Yes, I can. Because it's the underlying message you gave him this afternoon. He'll be looking for me and Gaylord."

"He'll be looking for me, too."

"No, he won't, because he'll be praying you're out of danger."

She sucked in a shuddering breath, steadied herself. "I'll follow you, so you might as well take me."

He collapsed into a chair by the door and dropped his head back, hissing between his teeth. After a moment, he sat forward and rested his elbows on his thighs. "I hate to admit this, but I think Gordon was right. I should have instituted a little more control over your life."

She tried to suppress the dangerous urge blooming in her chest to throw something at him. "*What?*"

The veins in Jack's neck were pumped with blood, his hands opening and closing. "I don't have time for this right now, Charlotte. Don't be an idiot. You don't belong out there tonight. You've read the books. You know what's going to happen. Stay home. Stay safe."

"But—"

"No buts. You put yourself in danger this afternoon. You've used your lucky quota for the day. Stay here. Get your medical supplies ready. You might have more than one patient before the night is over. None of us can do what you can do.

Charlotte sighed, reluctantly convinced. "Take a jacket, hat, and boots for Braham so he can slip into the crowd unnoticed, and take these, too." She gave Jack two pain pills. "The others will have worn off by now."

Jack pointed to a brown paper-wrapped package on the table next to the whiskey. "Jacket and boots. I'll give him my hat to wear."

"I should have known you'd be prepared."

He stood and placed his hands on her shoulders to give her a little squeeze. "Relax and trust me. I'll bring your patient back as soon as I can."

She bit down on the corner of her lip, her eyes fixed on him. "Be careful. Please don't take any unnecessary chances."

As they walked to the front door together, she cocked her head and studied the play of shadows over his face. Although his features were set, he was calm and confident. She had to work at not smiling. The siblings were both very competent people, but their fear of losing each other inevitably got in the way of rational thought, and caused unnecessary stress and anxiety.

Charlotte watched from the open door until he was out of sight. If anything happened to him—

Elizabeth came up beside Charlotte and wrapped her arm around her waist, interrupting her thoughts. "Let's go out onto the terrace. The Confederate infantry is passing through the city."

Charlotte, Elizabeth, and a few of the servants watched from the terrace as the infantry, followed by a mule-drawn supply train, rumbled over the cobbled streets.

"What will happen now?" one of the young servants asked. "Folks say the Yankees will burn Richmond like they burned Columbia."

"Any fires tonight won't be the fault of the Yankees," Charlotte said.

"What time will the prisons be evacuated?" Elizabeth asked.

Charlotte pulled her lower lip through her teeth, thinking. "Now the troops have left, the prisoners will follow."

Elizabeth folded her arms, shivering. "I've seen enough. I'm going back in. It's a warm night, but I'm chilled."

The two women sat in the candlelit parlor. Richmond's mayor had ordered the gas lighting and gas that fed it be turned off, plummeting the entire city into darkness. Candle flames wavered and flickered, filling the room with dancing shadows. A strange paralysis took hold of Charlotte, partly due to the day's trauma, and partly because of the night's promised destruction. Through an open window topped by faded velvet draperies, a warm gust tousled the sheer lace curtains beneath.

The sounds of musket fire and cannon blasts drew nearer, but the shouts right outside the house alarmed her. She hurried over to the window and pulled back a corner of the drapes. Elizabeth joined her. On the lawn, a group of men clustered, shouting. Many of them carried burning torches.

"They've come to burn us out," Elizabeth said, moving quickly to the front door.

Charlotte's sense of unease reached a high pitch. She grabbed Elizabeth's hand. "You can't go out there. Those men are dangerous."

Elizabeth's cold, trembling fingers clasped Charlotte's. "If I don't, they'll burn the house down on top of us."

"Give me a gun. We're not going out there without protection."

Elizabeth exhaled a pent-up breath, "There're a dozen men in the yard. What are you going to do? Shoot them all?"

Charlotte glanced at the door. "I couldn't even shoot one, but they don't know what I'm capable of doing...or not doing. Give me a gun. It doesn't have to be loaded."

"No. You'll get yourself shot. Stay here."

Charlotte put her fist on her hip, huffing, as she tapped her foot on the Oriental rug. "Damn it. I've already been told once tonight to stay put. It's not going to work a second time. If you're going out there, so am I."

Elizabeth swirled her shawl around her shoulders. "Let me do the talking, then. These are my neighbors."

Charlotte snatched her shawl off the coat tree and followed Elizabeth out onto the porch to face a dozen snarled faces with eyes glowing red in the light.

A man reeking of whiskey yelled, "Lincoln lover."

Another yelled, "Traitor."

"We're burning this Union house to the ground."

A man threw his torch, but it landed just shy of the house. Inwardly Charlotte cringed. Although she knew the house would not be burned down, she held onto the knowledge like a mantra, repeating the historical fact over and over in her mind.

"You'll have to kill me first." Elizabeth faced the instigators erect and unbendable, a beacon of bravery. "I know you...and you...and you," she said, pointing.

The mob moved forward, chanting, "Burn it down. Burn it down."

Flames from the torches heated Charlotte's face in the cool night air. For a terrifying moment, she no longer trusted history. Her knees shook, and she was momentarily sure the men would burn down the house. If the house caught fire, she would have to run in and rescue her medical kit. The bag was on the table next to the window in her bedroom. If she got up the stairs, though, would she have enough time to get back down?

Elizabeth stepped to the edge of the porch and, in an unfaltering voice, threatened the mob, saying, "General Grant will be here in the morning. Burn my house and he'll burn yours."

"Burn yours," echoed Charlotte, and the words came out louder than she'd intended. She shifted uneasily as one of the men advanced closer to the house, his threatening torch waving in the air.

The rest of the men muttered among themselves. One man dropped his torch and then another. Charlotte took a tentative breath. There seemed to be a temporary standoff, and for Charlotte hope burned brighter with each extinguished torch. Slowly the grumbling crowd began to disperse and slink off into the night.

Charlotte and Elizabeth remained on the porch, holding hands, shaking.

"Holy shit. Oops, sorry." Charlotte let out the breath she didn't realize she'd been holding.

Elizabeth sighed with relief. "What you said aptly describes the situation."

The women returned to the parlor and headed straight to the sideboard and the whiskey. Each took a big gulp from her tumbler full of the highly aromatic spirit. Elizabeth carried her glass over to the sofa, where she leaned back and closed her eyes.

Charlotte sat next to her. She butted her glass against the crystal in Elizabeth's hand and, with a slight twist of her wrist, the tumblers clinked. "You were amazing. There were a dozen men liquored up and ready to burn you out, and you valiantly faced them down. I wish I was half as courageous."

"Don't ever think you're not, Doctor Mallory."

Charlotte eyed her suspiciously. "I don't think I ever mentioned I was a doctor."

Elizabeth frowned and pinched the bridge of her nose. "Gaylord told me."

Gaylord had always addressed Charlotte as Doctor Mallory, so it seemed logical he would use the title when referring to her. Now really curious, she asked, "What else did he say?"

"To believe you regardless of how outrageous you sounded."

Charlotte lifted her glass to her lips, paused, and said, "Did he say why?"

Elizabeth shrugged, "He didn't have to."

"Why?"

"He reports directly to Grant."

Charlotte's mouth dropped. "Now I know how we got out of Washington so easily."

"The President didn't want to send you into harm's way again, but he knew he couldn't stop you. You were as safe as possible during your trip here."

"Did Lincoln know I was a woman when he sent me to rescue Braham?"

"No. He didn't discover who you were, or claimed to be, until after his meeting with the major."

Now it was Charlotte's turn to sit back and close her eyes, then they popped open and she sat up straight. "Grant orchestrated the last few days. He sent Jack and me to *you*, knowing you would help us rescue Braham. But why?"

"I got the impression the major still has a mission to complete."

Charlotte jumped to her feet. "What mission?"

Elizabeth shrugged. "I don't know."

Charlotte stomped back and forth, thinking while she paced. "What mission could possibly be left? Richmond is being evacuated. The Union Cavalry will be here tomorrow. The city will be under the Union's control. What's left to do?"

She stopped and replayed the last few days. When Gaylord came to Braham's house in Washington, he only told them Braham was working undercover. He didn't mention any assignment. What work could Braham have been doing for Lincoln? Elizabeth kept Grant apprised of what was happening in the city. What else would be of interest?

A light flashed on in Charlotte's brain with the intensity of a two-hundred-watt bulb. "The treasury…the Confederacy's gold. When the government is evacuated, they'll move the gold, and it will be vulnerable to an attack, especially by a person…" She stopped before saying out loud…*who knew in advance when and where it would be moved.* Her thought processes made another giant leap. Capturing the gold would benefit the Union's reconstruction efforts greatly.

Charlotte smacked her fist into her palm. "I've got it. I know what Braham intends to do. He's going after the gold."

"But you said he could barely stand. How can he do anything?"

Charlotte gave a cynical laugh. "You'd be surprised at what Braham McCabe is capable of doing when he sets his mind to a task, and don't forget Jack's with him."

Elizabeth sat rigid on the sofa, staring at her. "Will Jack help him?"

The mystery of what happened to the Confederate treasury had intrigued historians and treasure hunters since its disappearance the night of the evacuation. By all accounts, it was boxed for shipment, delivered to the Richmond & Danville Railroad Depot, and guarded by midshipmen of the Confederate naval academy. Solving the mystery, by preventing it from ever becoming one, would be too big a temptation for Jack to pass up.

"*Absolutely.*" Thinking aloud, Charlotte glanced at the clock on the mantle. "It's almost ten-thirty." Davis's train would leave at eleven. "If Davis is captured, or worse, killed, Lincoln will be blamed and the war could escalate." She grabbed her shawl from the chair where she'd dropped it when they came back inside. "I've got to find them."

Elizabeth followed Charlotte into the hallway. "You can't leave. You promised Jack you'd stay here."

"I promised before I realized they'd be doing something crazy."

"You can't be sure."

"I know them, especially my impulsive brother, and it leads me to only one conclusion." Charlotte flung open the door and dashed out of the house.

Elizabeth ran out on the porch and yelled, "Charlotte, come back."

A steam whistle pierced the night air with its shrill cry. Nothing good could come from Braham's attempt to capture the gold at the depot close to the Mayo's Bridge. He and Jack could get killed or captured themselves, and their lives were worth more than the gold.

Here was another frigging red-light moment. Was she going to sit still and wait, tapping her fingers on the steering wheel while the men she loved put their lives in danger? Going after them might be reckless, but as long as she stayed out of the way of the crazies and avoided areas of the city destined to catch fire later, she'd be safe. Right? She gave a sharp nod, answering her own question.

Her plan was simple. Find them, shake some sense into them, and hurry home before the city became a rioting inferno.

59

Richmond, Virginia, April 1, 1865

BRAHAM DOZED AFTER he swallowed the pills Charlotte had given him. When he woke, the pain had lessened somewhat. With considerable effort, and keeping one shoulder close to the wall for balance and support, he rose to wobbly feet. On Charlotte's one-to-ten-point pain scale, he was down to a six. His stomach, though, screamed ten. He was no stranger to hunger, but actually starving as he was now was a new experience. In the midst of his misery, a chuckle slipped out. Tonight would be a good time for someone to solve world hunger one person at a time, and he'd be standing at the head of the line.

His upper back muscles were still in tight knots. Since the bucking his guards had forced him to endure, no amount of stretching his neck and shoulders had reduced the spasms. Spikes of pain jabbed straight through him, and he groaned.

Shambling, he moved toward the small window until he reached the full length of the chain. Boards were nailed to the opening, blocking out light, but they couldn't diminish the cannons roaring in the background or the shouting mob. The prisoners would be marched through streets packed with half-crazed Richmonders. Spotting Jack would be difficult. He'd have to stay alert and ready for his chance to escape.

He sniffed at the cracks between the boards trying, to get a breath of less rancid air. The faint scents of fish and sulfur and smoke, and something else—whiskey—hit his nostrils. *Whiskey?* Either someone was drinking near his window, or the city was drowning itself in drink. Not a bad idea when an army you couldn't defeat was marching toward your front door.

The squeaky door at the top of the stairs opened. Braham instinctively folded his arms across his chest, opening and closing his hands, breathing through his mouth, and cringing with each loud heel strike. Conversations were too muffled for him to distinguish words.

How should he play this? If he appeared in a weakened condition, the guards wouldn't see him as a threat and might relax their vigilance, giving him an opportunity to escape. If they judged him too weak, would they shoot him, or leave him behind? If the warehouses used for prisons burned down in the city fire, he'd die for sure if he was left behind.

He gritted his teeth against the fear, but it lingered inside of him, making his breathing fast and shallow and his heart hammer. He would appear not too alert, but not weak either. He sat, closed his eyes, and leaned against the rough timber walls of his cell, mentally preparing for what lay ahead.

Sweat poured off him while he waited agonizing minutes for his cell door to open. He counted the crossbars sliding out of the cleats and the doors thrown back. His heart beat faster with each one.

Finally, the guards were at his door, jingling the keys.

Each deep breath he took was a piecing insult to the muscles in his back, cramping and burning like he'd been slammed against the wall.

The crossbar slid back with a heavy, dull noise. *Clunk.* The door swung open, and he steeled his body and mind for the blows he knew were coming.

A guard shuffled into the cell. "*Get up.*"

Braham recognized the voice of the man who had beaten him. He tensed. Any punch would double him over. More than one, and he might not be able to get up at all.

"He can't, Sarge. He's beat up." The voice belonged to the red-headed lad Braham had seen earlier.

"Maybe he needs another beatin'. You want another beatin', *traitor*?" He slurred the word as if it disgusted him to say it.

Braham raised his head. If his mouth and lips hadn't been so dry and cracked, he would have spat on the son of a bitch.

The lad grabbed Braham's arm and pulled him to his feet. "Do it later, Sarge. We don't have time."

Braham hung his head again, moaning softly. The sergeant unlocked the bolt securing the shackle around his ankle. With the heavy weight no longer dragging on his leg, a sensation of weightless filled him with unexpected energy. He bit the insides of his cheeks to conceal his relief. The guard shoved him out into the hall, where the other prisoners waited at the point of a bayonet.

A guard shoved him, knocking him into the wall "*Move.*"

Braham wavered and tried to regain his balance. His fists clenched with fury, and he snapped them tight, like a gunfighter on a draw.

A guard holding a bayonet poked Braham's gut with it, and with a voice rough as rust, he said, "Go ahead. Try hitting me."

Hancock touched Braham's shoulder. "Friend, we don't need a fight. Lean on me."

The guard shoved Braham again, but this time the shoving hand landed smack in the middle of Braham's injured back. He let out a cry of pain.

The guard laughed. "Move out, or you can stay behind permanently, if you get my meaning."

There were three things Highlanders were raised to cherish: their home, a woman, and a good fight. Braham itched to give back what he'd been subjected to, but Hancock wrapped Braham's arm over his shoulder and urged him forward and up the stairs. Out in the enclosed yard the area teemed with hundreds of recalcitrant prisoners flashing belligerent attitudes and bellowing about a forced march late at night.

A sentry handed Braham and Hancock each a hunk of cornbread. "Eat slow. It's got to last three days."

Braham took a bite, spit out a worm, took another bite. He needed nourishment. If he remained in captivity three more days, he'd most likely need a casket.

Sentries with rifles and bayonets herded them into a long formation. Others took positions along the sides to guard the prisoners as they marched out of the prison environs and into the crowded street.

"Stay to the rear," Lohmann said. "We're breaking away soon as there's an opening."

"And go where?" Hancock asked.

"Miss Van Lew's," White said.

Braham had decided to escape at the first opportunity, whether Jack was there or not.

The guards herded uneven columns of weary and tattered prisoners into the city at bayonet point, shouting orders and clearing a path. The prisoners at the front of the lines taunted the crowd, yelling angry slurs. A bystander threw a rock in response and violence flared immediately.

"Now," Lowmann said.

While the guards were distracted, trying to restore order, Braham and his cohorts slipped out of line and mingled with the agitated throng. He nervously scanned the crowd for Jack. "Scatter," he told the men. Then he paused, drawing a long breath which seemed to take forever to fill his battered body. "We'll meet up at Van Lew's. Be careful."

Good things are rare. They're to be cherished, and freedom most of all. Even if someone put a gun to his brain and pulled the trigger right now, he'd had a chance to taste liberty once again, and it tasted sweet on his tongue.

A tap on Braham's shoulder startled him, and he jerked, flinging his fists up quickly. "*Jack.*" Instead of throwing a punch, Braham's squeezed his buddy's shoulder. Then they embraced fiercely. "God, I'm glad to see you."

Jack gave Braham a wry smile, but his eyes remained sober. "You don't look so good."

Braham swept his fingers through his hair in a quick, cursory gesture. "I didn't have time to bathe, sorry."

Jack handed him the jacket and boots. "Put these on so you won't look so bedraggled."

Braham slipped on the jacket, then shoved on a boot while hopping on one foot, then did the same with the other boot. Without socks, the leather rubbed his raw ankle, but nothing could be done about it right now.

"Give me your hat. Most men in the crowd look as scraggily as I do, but they have on hats."

Jack plopped the hat on top of Braham's head. "You want my pants, too? Yours smell pretty ripe."

Braham settled the slouch hat low over his forehead. "Stay upwind."

Jack held out his hand, palm open. "Charlotte said to take these pills."

Braham popped them into his mouth and swallowed. "Got any whiskey?"

"Can't you smell it? The city government ordered all the whiskey destroyed. It was poured out into the street. The mob's getting drunk." Jack pulled a flask from his jacket pocket and handed it over.

Braham took a mouthful, then spit it out. "Damn it's hot." He looked at the flask as if it personally had betrayed him. "I can't believe you put coffee in here."

"You don't need whiskey with pain pills and an empty stomach. You'd pass out on me before I got you back to Van Lew's."

He lifted the flask to his mouth again, but drank cautiously. "I can't go back there yet. There's something I have to do. You go, though. I'll meet you later." Braham pulled his chunk of cornbread out of his shirt and took a bite.

"What the devil are you eating? It's got worms in it."

Braham took another swig to wash down the bread. "You said I needed food in my stomach."

"Elizabeth has food waiting for you. Eat something decent first, then go do whatever you have to do."

"What time is it?"

Jack checked the time on his pocket watch. "Ten-thirty."

Braham took more bites of cornbread, and finished the coffee in the flask before handing it back to Jack. "There's not much time. I've got to go."

Jack grabbed his arm. "Uh, I don't think so. If I don't come back with you, Charlotte will kill me. Either you're going with me, or I'm going with you."

"Come on, then." Braham took off at a fast walk down Cary Street, weaving in and out of the crowd with Jack all but stepping on his heels. In a low, gravelly voice, Braham said, "The train carrying Jeff Davis and the Confederacy's gold leaves in thirty minutes. I intend to stop it. I don't care about Davis, but I have orders to capture the gold."

"*What?* Without weapons and back up? Are you crazy?"

Braham stopped and looked Jack in the eye. "Go home. You're not part of this fight."

The statement brought a little shadow creeping in on the edge of Jack's jaw and the muscle twitched. "Maybe not, but I'm not leaving you alone. Whatever you have planned can't be worse than Charlotte's ire if I go back without you."

Braham chuckled at the image, but it was raw and shaky.

"The major's not alone," a familiar voice said.

Braham jerked his head. "Gaylord. Good to see you." He slapped his friend on the shoulder. "Hope you've kept an eye on things."

He nodded and fell silent as a group of men marched past them, rifles slung over their shoulders. "I followed Davis to the depot. He's sitting in the railroad president's office with Secretary of War Breckinridge."

Braham stared off into the distance, his eyes unfocused. A ripple of tension went through him. "What are they waiting for, then?"

"He's waiting until the very last minute, hoping to hear better news from Lee so he won't have to leave town," Jack said.

"The cabinet members are already on board with what's left of the treasury," Gaylord said.

Braham straightened quickly. His mission had been scattered into the wind like a dandelion, leaving only a bare stem of impossibility, but the wind had changed. He had been spoiling for a fight. Now here it was. "How well is the train guarded?"

"Half of a small regiment, but most of them are busy keeping people who don't have passes from the Secretary of War away from the trains."

Braham raised his eyebrows with a questioning look. "Tell me you've got a couple of those passes in your pocket."

Gaylord held out empty hands. "I tried."

Braham pursed his lips tightly, contemplating his next move. "We need explosives."

"The arsenal will have blasting powder, but we'll run out of time," Gaylord said.

Braham took off in another fast walk. "Then we'll blow the bridge."

"Have you lost your fucking mind?" Jack sputtered. "You couldn't even stand up this afternoon, and now you're running down the street to go blow up a bridge."

A fist came out of nowhere and crashed into Braham's chin. He landed hard on his butt. He stared at Jack, shaking himself hard. "What the hell?"

Jack put his fists on his hips and planted his feet. "Because you're acting crazy. Tell him Gaylord. You can't go blow up a bridge. You don't have time. You don't have the stamina. You're not Superman, and someone had to knock some sense into you."

Braham got to his feet, growling at Jack with steely green eyes. "I'll forgive you this time. But don't ever do it again. I don't claim to be a super man. I have a job to do. Go home."

"Not a super *man*, Super…Oh, damn it. I told you I'm not leaving you."

"If you try to stop me again, Gaylord will tie you to a tree."

Gaylord pulled a length of rope from his pocket, strung it between his hands, wrapped the ends around his palms, and yanked.

Jack waved Gaylord off with an elaborate shoulder shrug. "Put it away."

The wind shifted out of the south. An odor struck Braham's nostrils and made his throat knot. "Fire. We don't have much time. "Let's get out of here."

When they reached the commercial center of town, they found the streets lit by bonfires and torches, and an angry mob carrying off sacks of coffee, sugar and bacon from the commissary.

"What's happening here?" Braham asked a man loaded down with sacks.

"The army took what they could carry off. Told us to get what we needed 'fore the Yankees took it."

"Come on," Braham said. "Let's go."

Glowing bonfires, fed by frantic people discarding papers and incriminating evidence, cast a brassy light over the roaming crowds.

"We can't get through there. The street's blocked," Gaylord said.

Jack checked the time. "It's ten-forty-five. We won't make it."

"We have to," Braham said.

Gaylord led them down a narrow street, through dense smoke. Braham covered his mouth and ran as fast as he could. His heart pounded so fiercely he thought it would burst from his chest. When he reached the end of the street where the air was clearer, he stopped and took deep, heaving breaths.

"I'll go ahead and find a way to enter the armory," Gaylord said.

"Where's all this smoke coming from?" Braham asked.

"They're burning the cotton and tobacco warehouses," Jack said.

Then, like a bomb blast, an explosion rocked the city, sending brick and glass flying in all directions. Doors ripped from houses and chimneys toppled. The impact lifted Braham several feet into the air and sent him sailing into the street. When he hit the ground, his breath left in an audible *ooof.* Pain ripped through him. Debris rained down on him, sparks burned his trousers, and he couldn't move. He couldn't roll over to brush away the fire. Since he was unable to breathe, a momentary panic erupted. He'd had his breath knocked out of him before. If he relaxed, in a minute or two, his breathing would return to normal.

"Braham, where are you?" Jack yelled.

Braham raised his arm, giving a slight wave, and forced out one word, "Here."

Another explosion ripped the night, shaking the ground, and sending more flying debris into the street. Black smoke billowed up in the center of the flames.

Jack reached Braham's side. "The arsenal's blowing up. We've got to get out of here. Can you walk?"

Braham cursed the night. Without explosives, he couldn't blow up the train or the bridge. Through the smoke, he saw Gaylord gimping toward him. Jack helped Braham to his feet and brushed shards of glass off his clothes.

"Give me a damn pistol. I'm going after the gold."

Jack pointed toward the river. "Too late. The train's reached the trestle and is crossing the James."

Braham turned toward the river, kicking at a smoldering piece of wood. "Son of a bitch."

Another explosion, this one on the water, sent shockwaves which shook the earth violently. Braham grabbed a lamppost for support. Flames shot high into the air as one explosion followed another.

"Now what's going on out there?" he yelled.

Jack crawled to the stoop of a burned-out house. "Semmes is scuttling his ironclads in a dramatic finale."

"Move over." Braham dropped his sore, weary body dejectedly onto the stairs next to his buddy, and Gaylord joined them. Braham propped his chin on his hands. "They don't want a damn thing left in Richmond the Yankees can use against them."

The crack and crackling of splintering wood snapped all around them. Fires spit and sputtered, and falling bricks and glass peppered the area. Braham caught Jack's eye and gave him a humorless grin. "Can't anything be saved tonight?"

Jack snatched up the hat Braham had been wearing, slapped it against his thigh to knock off the accumulated dirt and broken glass, and tossed it to Braham. "Just you, I reckon. Let's go back to Elizabeth's. I know a doctor who's standing at the door waiting to get her hands on you."

Gaylord picked up a piece of broken stair railing and used it for a crutch.

"You better come, too, Gaylord. Let Charlotte look at your leg," Jack said.

"It's only my ankle. Nothing a shot of whiskey won't cure."

The pulse was throbbing at Braham's temples. He wanted to get his hands on her, too. He clapped the hat on his head and seized Jack's arm for support. "First things first, buddy—whiskey and a bath. Then I'll be glad to surrender to her healing hands."

60

Richmond, Virginia, April 1, 1865

CHARLOTTE REACHED THE depot, panting from her wild dash through town. She gulped in a smoke-laden breath and started coughing. Tears, from both the coughing and the smoke, tracked down her cheeks. She dropped, exhausted, on top of a crate, ready to rest, if only for a minute.

There were only a few dark and empty trains on the tracks. If one of them was earmarked for Jeff Davis and other government officials, there should be lights and people inside. Did this mean Davis and the treasury had already escaped Richmond?

If Davis had escaped, then where were Jack and Braham? If they had made an attempt on the president's life or tried to steal the gold, there would have been a ruckus. Even now. The only commotion was from the handful of panicked citizens arguing with guards who menaced them with bayonet-tipped rifles.

One of the guards raised his voice, "You'll only be allowed to board if you have a pass signed by the Secretary of War. Those with passes, come forward."

A handful of families presented the necessary documents and ran toward the empty trains. The others, without passes, muttered their objections while snorting audibly as they passed around flasks of whiskey.

There was nothing left for Charlotte to do. As history had recorded, Davis and the gold had escaped. Jack and Braham must have returned to Van Lew's. Walking back up the hill from the depot, Charlotte noticed another blaze. This one was along the water's edge.

They've torched the Richmond-Petersburg Bridge.

The burning bridge reminded her of the story of a trainload of wounded soldiers who had been left at the Richmond-Petersburg Depot. Her memory was fuzzy, but she vaguely recalled the depot catching on fire when the bridge burned, and how a group of doctors organized a rescue party. What had been the outcome? How many were lost? She couldn't remember.

Trudging on up the hill, she hoped to God she'd find Jack and Braham safe at Elizabeth's. She turned the corner on Grace Street, anxiously searching for her men.

But how many wives and mothers and sisters and daughters would never see their men again because they'd died in the Richmond-Petersburg Depot fire?

If those in charge knew the building was going to burn, they could move the wounded out of harm's way.

Charlotte hesitated near the wrought iron fence in front of Elizabeth's house. Could she go inside and forget about the wounded? A nagging voice in her head said *go inside to safety*…but if she went to the Depot, she could do triage in the street if need be. The wounded men probably needed medical attention as well. Jack could take care of Braham for a little while longer.

Gathering her skirts, she dashed toward the crimson glow moving ever closer to the Depot.

People weighed down with sacks of loot filled the streets, making it impossible for her to move quickly. The evening had started out chilly but had turned hot, and now sweat streamed down her face. She unbuttoned her collar. When it didn't bring any relief, she slipped into the shadows, untied her petticoats, and let them drop to the ground. She turned away, leaving them where they lay, but immediately went back. Bandages were always needed. She scooped up the cotton petticoats and walked briskly toward the depot. Without the bulky petticoats, her hem dragged on the ground and swished dangerously close to the many small fires from sparks landing on anything flammable. Fearing her dress would catch fire, she found a ripped seam and tore several inches off of the hem.

Navigating her way around the last few blocks of congested streets was slow going. Widespread disorder combined with fear created a dangerous cocktail, and Richmonders were slugging it down by the gallon. Soldiers rumored to belong to Garey's Cavalry Brigade roamed the streets and smashed store windows with their musket butts. Then those same soldiers climbed through the broken windows and threw the doors open for swarms of looters.

Charlotte stayed in the shadows, away from the chaos and shouts, but she couldn't escape the pungent odors of smoke and fear and sweat.

A Confederate straggler rushed out of a clothing store carrying large bundles on his back and another on top of his head. One of his bundles swiped Charlotte and sent her freefalling onto the street, where she landed facedown on her armload of petticoats in a resounding thud. After a moment or two she stretched and wiggled her fingers. Nothing broken or bleeding. She was very lucky, since shards of glass lay in a glistening layer covering the streets. If she had nosedived into them, her skin would have been cut to shreds.

Carefully she rolled over and sat up, and was repeatedly jostled by the swarm of looters. She had to get out of the way quickly. A break in the milling crowd gave her time to scramble to her feet. Stumbling over debris, she made her way to an unoccupied bench outside a general store with broken windows, a demolished door, and empty shelves.

The coppery taste of blood coated her tongue. She licked her bottom lip and discovered a cut on the inside corner. More sweat slid down the side of her face. When she wiped it away with the edge of a petticoat, it came away bloody. Not wanting to probe the wound with dirty hands, she ripped off a wide strip of the petticoat and bound it around her head, only to discover raising her arm hurt her shoulder. She must have strained it when she broke her fall. The fall had battered her head, scraped her knees, and twisted her shoulder, but she wasn't broken.

She flinched when falling timbers crashed nearby and a chimney collapsed, dropping a pile of bricks only a few feet away. Her heart crawled up her throat and hung there. No serious injuries...yet.

Hurried footsteps ground the pebbles and crunched the broken glass as people streamed past her, like mice scurrying away from a clowder of cats, as her granny would have said.

In the distance a tongue of flames licked over the top of one of the tobacco warehouses. The old South was fading away, and searing regret burned into her heart.

Stiff, blood-matted curls stuck to her forehead, and acrid smoke burned her nostrils. The fires would intensify, and so would the chaos. She had a choice. Turn back or try to save some soldiers.

The decision was made before she even took time to consider it. This was *her* city, regardless of the century. She wouldn't shrug off her responsibilities when Richmond needed her most. She hauled herself up, climbed away from the bench and over the rubble of bricks, and trudged on, weaving through the throng, and avoiding men carrying large bundles.

Finding a clean patch on one sleeve, she wiped her face again, leaving behind dark pink splotches. At least they weren't dark red.

If Jack could see her now, he would not be happy. It was so crowded and smoky, he and Braham could have passed her on the street and not noticed her, especially in her condition.

Taking a circuitous route to avoid the worst of the panicky mob, she reached the depot to find it already backlit by the bright orange glow of flames engulfing the bridge. When the wind changed, as it was destined to do, the fire wouldn't take long to reach the building. She dashed inside to find the doctor in charge.

"My God," she said, coming to a standstill. As far as she could see, men sprawled on the rough wood floor, row upon row of injured and dying Confederate soldiers. How could they all be moved before the building went up in flames? She bit her lip against a surge of fear and cringed at the sharp pain from her forgotten wound.

A surgeon stood by the door watching the conflagration.

She stepped in front of him, getting close so he'd pay attention. "This building is about to catch on fire," she said. "When it does, it will burn quickly. These men have to be moved *now* or they'll be burned alive."

He raised both brows in patent skepticism. "Charles Ellis, president of the railroad, assured us the men would be safe here."

"He's *wrong*. Take a look for yourself. Do you want to wait until the building's burning to find out?"

"I'm not going to move two hundred injured men on the word of a woman who looks like she rolled out of a chimney."

"How about on the word of a surgeon?"

"Go home, *surgeon*."

Charlotte returned his sardonic expression with a bland smile before stomping to within a foot of his face. How many times had she done this lately? "Listen, you son of a bitch…" She slammed her fists to her hips. "I don't give a damn whether you believe I'm a doctor or not." She leaned forward, getting nose-to-nose with him. "But this building *will* catch on fire. It *will* burn to the ground. And if your ego is more important than the possibility I'm right, these men *will* die."

She shot past him and strode rapidly into the cavernous depot, searching for someone who might believe her. Several yards away, a man wearing a dirty white apron was tending to a one of the wounded. "Excuse me, sir." When he turned toward her, she rocked back on her heels, swallowed hard, and, with wide eyes, fell silent.

"Yes, what do you need?" he asked.

The man's clear blue eyes, cool skin tone, and symmetrical face—ears flat against his head, straight nose sitting the perfect distance above his lips, sharp cheekbones, and a gently rounded chin—were dead-on identical to Jack's, and to old paintings in the family portrait gallery. The man had to be Carlton Jackson Mallory, her six-times-great-grandfather.

Awkward? God, yes. She gawked.

"Are you looking for someone? If so, I can't help you." He turned aside, returning to his patient.

"Sir." Her voice cracked. She poked his shoulder with her fingertip, feeling the tight muscles in his neck. "Sir, this building is about to catch on fire, and when it does, it will burn too fast to rescue everyone. We need to start evacuating... *now*."

He was wise enough not to reject her out of hand, but his expression was skeptical. She gauged his mood before pressing on. There was no missing the tension in his body, the stiffness with which he moved, or the anxiety in his red and tired eyes. The enemy was coming, and while the end was imminent, his intensity was well-leashed, an admirable trait for a surgeon.

She touched his arm, pausing for the briefest of moments to figure out her best argument. "From one surgeon to another, I beg you to believe me."

He glanced around the depot, sniffed the air. "Considering the amount of smoke outside, it seems safe enough in here."

"Yes, but it won't be when the fire on the bridge spreads to the roof."

He squatted to check on another patient, pulling the man's shirt aside to look at a shoulder wound. "What makes you believe it'll happen?"

She peered over her grandsire's head. "The wound you're working on looks clean. No redness. An inch in a different direction and it could have shattered the clavicle or hit the subclavian artery. He would've lost his arm, part of his shoulder, or maybe his life. Do you want him to lose it now?"

Carlton Mallory took stock of her with a penetrating expression similar to ones she'd received during her surgical training.

"Look, I know there's no reason for you to trust me. But I'm a student of the Greek philosophers. And logic and firsthand observation of the progress of the fire tell me this depot will catch fire, and these men are in mortal danger."

He surveyed the ceiling, his eyes roving slowly from one corner to the other, his fingers rubbing his chin, as if gauging the time it would take to burn. "Who's your favorite?"

"My favorite what?" she asked, tracking his eyes.

He fixed his eyes on her, as if giving a final test. "Philosopher."

The lives of hundreds of men now depended on her knowledge of philosophy, not on her medical expertise. She blinked. "Plato. Same as you."

Thick lashes lifted, and he examined her more closely. Did he recognize a familiar trait in her face, or notice the hereditary bump on her ear Charlotte had traced back to his wife?

"Do I know you? What's your name?"

Her eyes remained on his, unwavering. Telling him she was also a Mallory would be a mistake, although lying credibly was always a struggle. Behind her back, she interlaced crossed fingers with straight ones and squeezed hard. "Charlotte...McCabe."

"I'm not convinced moving these men is the right decision. Still..." he hesitated for moment, then made up his mind, and nodded. "There's been enough dying, Doctor McCabe. Let's get to work."

Carlton Mallory summoned the other physicians. They trooped outside and reentered a few minutes later, still debating, then nodded their heads in agreement. The evacuation began, slowly at first. Charlotte hurried from patient to patient, identifying the ones who could walk without assistance, instructing them to move quickly away from building. As the encroaching danger became more apparent to everyone, the urgency and speed of evacuation spread with the advancing flames.

A steady stream of soldiers, limping and shuffling, exited the depot, a pitiful stream of disheartened and broken souls. The smoky yard began to fill as dozens of them huddled on safe patches of ground.

Knowing time was against them, she kept one eye on the ceiling, expecting at any moment to see tongues of fire lapping at the eaves. The muscles in her arms, legs, and back cramped from the constant bending and pulling. All her life she had pushed herself to the point of exhaustion, whether it be long, complicated surgeries or running marathons. She had always been able to locate a pocket of reserve energy to make it to the end, but on this night she had already reached the bottom of her last pocket.

All the doctors were running frantically in and out of the depot, hauling patients by their arms and legs, regardless of their injuries. Screaming men still in the building begged to be saved. Others crawled toward the door, leaving trails of blood.

Buckets of sweat rolled down her cheeks, her neck, under her arms. Hair hung in limp, matted shanks about her head. Her dress was ripped and ragged. Her brain, her muscles, her will were all impaired, fatigued by the beating she had taken hauling so many to safety.

"*Get out. Get out,*" Carlton Mallory yelled. He grabbed Charlotte's arm. "The roof's going to cave in. *Get out right now.*"

She jerked free. "I can save one more." The roof was moments from collapsing, the fire chewing at the beams.

A man shrieked to her from the corner. "Help me, ma'am. Please, help me."

Charlotte gauged the distance from where the man lay to the nearest door. When the roof collapsed, he would die horribly. If she hurried, maybe the two of them wouldn't. Every muscle in her body tensed. Her brain flip-flopped from *if I hurry* to *maybe I'll die*. Even in the smoke-filled air, she smelled fear, and knew it wasn't only hers.

He begged while he desperately crawled forward, using his elbows to move him along. "*Help me.*" Empty trouser legs dragged behind him. He had given his limbs for the South. She could not let him die.

"Grab my arms. I'll pull you."

The roof crackled and groaned and sparks rained down on them. With muscles screaming, she hissed through her teeth while she pulled harder. The heat from the flames singed her skin. Her feet slipped on the slimy floor.

Her strength and energy were gone. She humanly could do no more. The roof dropped chunks of flaming wood.

"*Hurry.*" The man's face was distorted with terror and pain, his eyes blazing, reflections of the advancing fire.

Her grip on his arms weakened as the muscles in her back, biceps, forearms, and shoulders simply ceased to function. "No more."

I'm sorry.

And then the fiery timbers supporting the roof plummeted toward them...

61

Richmond, Virginia, April 1, 1865

B RAHAM AND JACK left Gaylord at the boarding house where he
had been staying. Since the rioting mob controlled the main
thoroughfares, they had to weave through side streets, dodging
rioters and avoiding the fires spreading into Richmond's business
center. Frightened women and children ran from their homes as
flames licked at their doors and windows. The mad dash through the
scorching heat back to Van Lew's drained Braham, twisting and
squeezing him like a sponge, until he had nothing left.

He licked peeling lips, gasping for breath. "Need to stop—"

There had to be protection from the roar and crackle of the
flames and shattering glass, but where? Sparks carried by an
intensifying south wind danced on the tops of most of the buildings
and rained down into the street, now hot and littered with fiery
debris. Thank God Jack had the foresight to bring boots for him. He
owed the man his life.

Jack grabbed Braham's arm, tugging hard. "If we stop, we'll
burn. Come on. Only a few more blocks."

Braham staggered up the street, coughing, while exploding shells
soared high into the night's sky, a pyrotechnics display—a dangerous
one—raining burning chunks of wood and melting glass down on
top of homes and businesses. At the rate the fire was burning, there
would be nothing left of the city by morning.

Only the strength of his own will held him together for the last few blocks.

When they reached Church Hill and the Van Lew mansion, the fire was several blocks behind them. Exhausted, they trudged up the stairs at the back of the house and entered, startling three of the women servants who huddled in a corner.

One of the women came forward with a lighted candle held high. "What do you want?"

Braham leaned against the wall, gasping, and began a slow slide to the floor. His legs had turned to mush along with every other muscle. He doubted he could get up again, much less find the energy to wash. There was a dull ache at the backs of his eyes from the smoke, and from days of restless sleep in a cold cell with little food. He lowered his head onto his knees, praying everyone would leave him alone to sleep or die. At this point, he didn't care which.

Jack moved farther into the room. "It's Jack Mallory."

The woman turned to the others. "It's Miss Lizzie's guest." There were a few beats of silence before the woman asked. "Who's the man on the floor?"

Jack hooked his thumb over his shoulder. "Major McCabe. I rescued him from the Castle Thunder evacuation."

"Lordy, Miss Lizzie's been waitin' for news. I'll go tell her you're back."

"No," Braham said in a hoarse voice. "We need baths first."

The women giggled.

"Guess they can smell us," Braham said.

Jack pulled him to his feet. "Us? You're the one who's past ripe. If I ever smell as rotten, throw me in the garbage heap." He dragged Braham into the room where Charlotte had washed after her visit to the prison. "Come on. Get cleaned up, then you can rest."

A servant dumped buckets of steaming water into the tub.

"Keep the hot water coming," Jack said. "And send for the butler."

When the butler arrived, Jack explained the situation and asked him to get clothes for both of them from Jack's wardrobe and to also bring the haversack containing his toiletries. "And don't let the women know we've returned until we're dressed."

The water in the tub quickly turned dark brown as old blood and grime soaked off of Braham. The tub was emptied and filled a second time. The third time, while heat seeped into his wounded body, he gobbled down a hefty bowl of chicken soup.

When the butler returned with clean clothes and the haversack, Braham washed his hair with Jack's special shampoo. Clean and smelling good, he climbed out, feeling remarkably refreshed. He'd been blessed with a hardy constitution, and four years of war had battle-hardened what God had given him. Under the right circumstances—food, rest, and a little tending to his wounds—he could recover to fight again, but this reprieve would not last long.

He intended to use the reprieve to reacquaint himself with the taste and feel of Charlotte's lips.

Jack stripped out of his torn, scorched clothes. "Are you going to shave your ugly beard off?"

Braham scratched at the bristly, four-month-old growth of hair. "You don't like it? I'm getting used to it."

Jack ducked to wet his hair. When he resurfaced he said, "You're asking the wrong Mallory. I don't care, but Charlotte will hate it."

"She likes your three-day-old whiskers look."

Jack chuckled, tilting his head in a yes-and-no gesture. "I'm not sure she likes it. She's merely stopped complaining about it."

Braham combed back his shoulder-length blond hair. "Should I cut it? Most men wear short hair now." He stopped combing and studied his reflection in the small shaving mirror. The cut above his brow gave him a somewhat menacing look. He snarled at it. "Do you think I look fine enough?"

"Jesus, man. What's wrong with you? Remember this. It's all in the nose. Win over a woman's nose and you're halfway into her bed."

Braham set the comb aside, picked up a clean shirt, and slipped it on. He only had a short time remaining with Charlotte and that thought triggered a quiver all the way through him. There wasn't anything he could do about it, though. He couldn't go home with her, and she wouldn't stay with him.

"Hand me a towel, and don't forget the cologne," Jack said.

Braham collected a towel off the shelf and tossed it to Jack.

"I don't know why you're getting dressed. You know she'll want to examine you. And when she sees your back, she'll dope you up and put you to bed."

Braham put on a jacket and straightened his tie. "As long as she's next to me, I won't object."

"Elizabeth won't approve of you sleeping together."

Braham flapped his hand in dismissal. "I don't plan to tell her."

"I suspect she knows everything going on in her house, even what's happening behind closed doors."

Braham slipped his thumbs under his lapels, raising his eyebrows theatrically. "You forget. I'm a master of subterfuge."

Jack tied the towel around his waist, roaring with laughter. "Which is why Johnny Reb caught you twice."

Braham shrugged. "I admit I've had a string of bad luck, but I survived."

"Oh, speaking of surviving. There's a matter Charlotte asked me to talk to you about. Elizabeth spent most of her family's fortune rescuing Union soldiers. She'll die of old age in this house, penniless. I don't have money to contribute, but I thought you might be able to set up a trust fund for her."

"I've got more money than I'll ever spend. I'll take care of it, but wouldn't providing for her change history?"

"If making sure a woman has food and shelter for the rest of her life changes history, then I'm all for it."

Braham reached for the doorknob. "Consider it done."

They found Elizabeth in the drawing room, staring out the window while fingering the cameo brooch at her neck. An uneasy foreboding stole over Braham. A servant in the room had her head down, watching as she poked at something on the carpet with the toe of her shoe. Braham checked. Nothing there. The uneasiness ballooned rapidly.

"I don't believe the fire will reach this far," Braham said.

Elizabeth dropped the curtain and turned to Braham. She seemed...not absentminded, but rather nervous and distracted. Her fingers fluttered about her neck like uncertain moths caught in a lampshade. "It's good to see you, Major. Was there any trouble?"

"No. Did the other men arrive?" Braham asked.

She nodded. "They were taken to safe houses for the night."

"Where's Charlotte? Is she sleeping?" Jack asked.

"She went looking for you."

"*When*—" Braham asked.

"*Where*—" Jack shouted.

"When you didn't return," Elizabeth's fingers fluttered faster, "within a reasonable length of time, and she believed you intended to stop Jefferson Davis from leaving the city with the treasury. Did you?"

Jack collapsed into a chair and buried his head in his hands. "How in God's blue blazes did she leap to such a conclusion?"

"How long has she been gone?" Braham demanded.

"Two hours, maybe more," Elizabeth said.

"Where would she have gone?" Jack asked, moaning, "Oh, God. Where is she?"

Elizabeth's skirts swished as she strode across the room toward Jack. She rested her hand on his shoulder. "I tried to stop her, but she wouldn't listen. She only mentioned the depot."

Braham paced, thinking. If she reached the depot and discovered the train gone, what would she do then? She'd come back . . . unless. "Is there a hospital in the path of the fire? Or an influx of wounded? A place where the injured are gathered for medical care? If she's not out searching for you, Jack—"

"She's knee-deep in somebody's blood. But where? I'm not aware of any hospitals in danger, but there is a trainload of wounded housed in a depot."

Braham paced his way over to the whiskey bottle and poured a drink. "Which isn't remarkable at all."

The statement hung in the air for a moment. Then Jack said. "But it is, I'm afraid. The depot caught fire when the Richmond &

Petersburg Railroad Bridge was torched. As I recall, the army doctors organized a rescue party. But Charlotte wouldn't go there. Not tonight."

"If patients were in danger, wouldn't she move mountains to save them?" Urgency vibrated in Braham's voice.

"The depot's a tinderbox. When it catches fire, it burns…"

Braham had one foot out the door before Jack finished his sentence. *If she survives tonight, she's going straight home, even if I have to carry her through the ages myself.*

Jack followed him down to Main Street, where they found the mob had deteriorated into total anarchy. Braham put his hands on his knees, panting. He had never seen such lawlessness. Every store had been looted, leaving behind destroyed buildings and empty shelves. Fires blazed from Fifteenth Street to Seventh Street.

"*Come on.* We have to hurry," Jack said.

They ran with their jackets over their heads, dodging collapsing buildings. Jack led the way across the short bridge spanning the canal at Seventh Street. Flames shot straight into the sky, and buildings blazed on both sides of the short, narrow street leading to the depot.

When Braham spotted the burning train station, he made a fierce gesture at Heaven, leaped over a pile of smoldering bricks, and ran like he was fire himself, yelling to Jack, "*It's burning.* The depot's burning. *Run.*" His heartbeat hammered in his ears over the roar of the flames.

Rows upon rows of wounded Confederate soldiers languished on the ground some distance from the burning building.

Braham pointed to his left. "Go that way. Ask everyone if they've seen her. I'll try this way." They separated and Braham darted in and out among the wounded men. "Have you seen a woman with yellow hair?"

"She helped me get out, but I ain't seen her since."

Braham heard the same comment dozens of times as he continued to search through the rows of wounded men, all coughing from the smoke.

"Last time I saw her, she was running back inside," a soldier told him.

One side of the building was engulfed in flames and fire was spreading rapidly to the other side. Black smoke poured out of the windows. Braham ran to the only entrance not in flames. "*Charlotte. Charlotte.*" He bellowed, covering his mouth to keep out the blazing hot smoke. Then he yelled again. "*Charlotte. Charlotte.*"

Heat blistered his skin and sweat streamed down his face. The overhead beams splintered and crashed down, cracking with fire. Glass exploded from windows and wicked shards turned into dangerous projectiles embedding in already-injured soldiers' arms and legs.

Braham ran into the building, calling her name, until the roar of the collapsing ceiling jerked him to a standstill. And then his heart stopped. He spotted her dragging a man out of the flames, out of the path of the burning roof, but she wasn't going to make it.

He pumped his legs faster than he'd ever run, but he felt like he was slogging, dreamlike, through a river of molasses. If he reached her, and they couldn't escape the flames, at least she wouldn't die alone. He'd carry her into eternity.

Time stopped. The fire stopped. The burning roof hung suspended. And in that briefest of seconds, he touched her arm and yanked with more strength than he could possibly possess. The momentum pulled her toward him in a perfect pirouette. Her body flattened against him. He folded her up into his arms and ran like hell.

A broken window with shards poking in on all sides of the frame was their only escape. He ducked his head, snugging Charlotte to his chest, and threw himself through it. An anguished, blood-curdling scream came from behind him as the beams hit the floor.

He and Charlotte landed on the ground, tumbled and rolled, but he never let go of her, protecting her head and her back. When they had finished their tumble and roll, he was on top of her, his hands under her, his mouth inches from hers. Her breath gusted on his face. She was alive. His eyes roved over her. Blood trickled down her forehead to her hairline. She was watching him intently, eyes focused and steady. Then she reached up, stroked his cheek, and mouthed thank you before dropping her hand.

"*Braham.*" Jack rushed over and knelt beside him. "Get up. We have to move before the building collapses." Braham rolled over, revealing Charlotte beneath him. Jack gasped. "What are you doing here? I saw Braham plow through the window, but I didn't know he had you in his arms. A man told me you had been sent to a tent set up for the doctors. Are you hurt?"

"Not fatally. Help me up." Once she was sitting up, her mouth twisted abruptly. She cupped her elbows and shuddered, staring at the burning building. The pain glimmering in her eyes was heart-wrenching.

Braham touched her shoulder gently, aware she was, at this moment, as fragile as his Highlander figurine. "I couldn't save you both. I'm sorry." He looked at her almost pleadingly, but her face had shut down completely.

A man wearing an apron black with soot dropped to her side and gathered her hands in his. "Doctor McCabe. Come this way, quickly."

Braham stared at the man. *McCabe?* Then he glanced at Jack who shrugged.

"The entire building is going to collapse," the man said. He supported Charlotte to her feet then sheltered her beneath his arm, brushing away flying sparks falling on her hair and shoulders.

"We've got to get out of here, too. Can you make it?" Jack asked Braham.

Braham's heart was still thumping wildly "I'm bleeding from my head, arms, chest, and hands, and my entire body is screaming with muscle strain and aches, but nothing is cracked or broken. Yes, I can make it."

They had only moved a few yards away from the building when it collapsed in on itself in an explosive *whoosh,* which sent Braham tumbling through the air again. He landed in a soft patch of grass littered with debris and more shards of glass. The heat from the flames alone would roast him if he didn't get out of its path. Using his forearms, he dragged himself through the glass, now bleeding from both old cuts and new ones.

Familiar hands grabbed him under the arms. "Anything broken, now?"

Braham shook his head. "Damned tired of being knocked on my ass. This keeps up, we'll be crawling to Elizabeth's door."

"Let me help you."

Braham shook his head, not wanting to move, stand, or attempt to walk. Jack, however, paid no attention to what Braham wanted, easily lifting him to his feet.

"Where's Charlotte?" he demanded.

Jack looped Braham's arm around his shoulder. "The man wearing an apron took her away, remember?"

Braham's mind was a jumble of puzzle pieces darting here and there, trying to organize themselves into some semblance of order. While he was rooting for their success, he didn't think they'd prevail. If an ax split his head wide open, the pain couldn't be any worse than it was right now. He was almost thankful for the distracting ringing in his ears. "Where's Charlotte?"

"The man…" Jack looked at Braham curiously, one brow lifted. "You're in bad shape. I'll take you to her."

"Aye, ye're a good friend." Braham's words were slurred, but he'd be damned if he could untangle them.

Leaning on Jack, he hobbled toward a tent on the other side of the street, safely away from the line of burning buildings. His progress was painfully slow, as if he had aged years in the past few hours. A corporal put a cup of hot coffee in his hands, and he drank greedily before collapsing into a camp chair, breathing heavily, clarity slowly returning.

Fire crackled upwind all around them. From the noise, Braham couldn't tell if the fire, shells, and explosions were the result of the fires which had been deliberately set to destroy the tobacco and other goods, or from Grant's forces bombarding the city. He refrained from shaking his head in order to give the puzzle pieces time to organize themselves fully, but he needed to clear away the gathering fog of apprehension. Was there a safe way out of the fire's path? They had to find one and get to safety.

Charlotte sat straight as bone on the small cot, clutching a coffee cup with a slightly quivering hand. "How'd you two get here?" she asked.

"Searching for you," Jack said.

She sipped her coffee, then dabbed primly at her mouth with a filthy finger, as calmly as she would have in Elizabeth's drawing room. "How'd you know where to look?"

Jack waggled his eyebrows. "Elementary, my dear Watson."

The man who had brought Charlotte to the tent returned with a blanket. He wrapped it around her shoulders, and then he sat close by, holding his own cup of steaming black coffee.

"Doctor Mallory," Charlotte said. "This is my brother Jack . . . um." She stopped and licked her lips, pointed to Braham. "And my other brother, Braham. We're all McCabes from South Carolina." She then pointed to the man and said, "This is Major Carlton Mallory. He owns a plantation several miles from Richmond, I think he said."

"Did I? I don't remember mentioning it."

Braham detected a flash—just a flash—of possessiveness in Doctor Mallory. Had he, too, become one of her admirers?

Jack's face went pale beneath a sheen of sweat, and he swallowed, his Adam's apple bobbing in his throat. "Thank you for taking care of my...our sister."

Doctor Mallory smiled at Charlotte. "Your sister single-handedly saved a hundred or more men tonight. If she hadn't warned us of the danger, most of the men would have burned alive in the depot. The Confederate Army owes her a great debt."

There it was again; a familiar look of eagerness. If he flashed it again, Braham would introduce Doctor Mallory—who had a remarkable resemblance to the man Charlotte had impersonated—to his bloody fist. It was time to get out of here, even if it meant rushing into Dante's Inferno.

Braham wobbled to his feet. "We need to find a way home. The fire's moving fast. My thanks for the coffee." He dumped the dregs outside the tent and handed the corporal the empty cup. Braham studied Charlotte closely: the exquisite lines of her face, the curve of her nose, the patches of soot below her eyes, the furrow of concentration as she negotiated her goodbyes to Doctor Mallory. Her features, though pale, had lost their ashen quality. The shock had passed. Now she needed to get home and rest.

Charlotte tried to return the blanket, but Doctor Mallory insisted she keep it to wrap around her head, then he wished them good luck, and, as a parting gift, invited them to visit his plantation after the war.

After Braham, Jack, and Charlotte had gone several yards away from the tent, she asked, "Why aren't we staying? Isn't it safe here?"

Braham answered, "These men may be wounded, but I don't care to spend another minute in the midst of two hundred Johnny Rebs. After a week in their prison, I've had enough of them. And besides, we have cuts needing treatment, and Elizabeth is very worried."

She gave him a slight smile. "You're right. Let's go home."

Watching her return to herself triggered a throb of affection in Braham. He took a deep, steadying breath, then another. They had almost died in the fire, and they still might. He had to keep her safe. She was in Richmond because of him, and if anything else happened to her, he would never forgive himself.

"The wind could change again," Jack said. "We've got to get past Main Street. Then we might be safe."

"Go over to Sixth Street," she said.

They plunged back through the narrow street. Firelight as bright as day dazzled their eyes and scorching heat seared their already tender skin.

"Hurry." Braham pulled Charlotte behind him. Unsteady on her feet, she stumbled, so he picked her up again and ran.

"Let me carry her," Jack said. "You can't have much strength left."

Braham had nothing left except his instincts to survive and protect. He refused to let go of her, willing himself forward. "If we can work our way around and get to Capitol Square, we'll be safer. I can make it there." Every part of his body was screaming in agony, but he wouldn't stop now.

"Let me down. I can walk," she said.

Braham snugged her closer to his chest. "I'm not putting you down. Cover your mouth with the blanket."

The crash of falling timbers nipped at his heels, and the roaring crackle of burning wood harried them along. They ran up a side street, then veered onto another. They twisted and turned, trying to outrun the mounting flames and heavy black smoke stealing air from their lungs. Buildings collapsed in their wake as they dashed up hill.

"Run," Jack yelled.

The Capitol finally came into view as Braham wound himself up for one final push, even though the muscles in his arms and legs burned as hot as the blaze chasing his heels. He led the way to the far end of the square, close to Capitol Street. There, he crouched on his knees, cradling Charlotte and grimacing as jolts of pain reminiscent of his bucking torture whipped him with the cutting edge of a lash. He arched his back and gasped for breath, coughing out particles of soot.

"The air is smoky here, too. At least it's not burning our lungs. We can rest for a few minutes." Charlotte rasped.

She didn't make a move to leave the protection of his muscle-twitching arms, but she did shudder. Memories could be painful, and she would remember the young, legless soldier for the rest of her life, while Braham would see the ceiling collapsing toward the exact spot where she was standing. He clutched her tighter until finally his arms gave out. Then he set her down, but kept her close, sheltered by the curve of his body. She held on, too, her arms wrapped around him.

Airborne ash fell in profusion, even where they were sitting. He constantly had to brush it off his clothes and his head and the parts of Charlotte his body couldn't shelter. They sat there for some time while more Richmonders arrived carrying bundles on their shoulders and family and friends on litters. They were all searching for a safe place away from the fires.

"We can't stay. We have to find fresh air." Charlotte eased out of his embrace and stood, using Jack's shoulder for support. Stretching backwards with her hands pressed against her lower back, she groaned, shuddering slightly, as if she were sloughing off her aches and pains. "I can walk now. Just don't ask me to walk fast."

She laid her hand on Braham's shoulder, and he squeezed it, reassuringly. Then he studied her carefully, narrowing his eyes, darting them all over her, to be sure she was unhurt. Thank God she was dressed appropriately. If she had worn scrubs, the sparks and glass which had burned and cut holes in her dress would have shredded the thin surgical fabric from her body. Although in pain and exhausted, the thought of her naked led directly to thoughts of bedding her, which then lifted his spirits with a flood of renewed energy.

They plodded down Broad Street, passing through block after block of stragglers and dense smoke, and tongues of flames still leaping to the sky.

Charlotte's eyes glazed over, and her shoulders slumped, but she kept moving, shuffling one foot forward and then the other. Even in a tattered dress and soot-covered face, she was beautiful. He wasn't sure he'd ever loved a woman other than his mother and Kit, but he had no doubt of the depth of his love for Charlotte.

He took her hand, squeezed it, then put it to his lips and pressed a kiss on her fingers. Life-giving fingers. How could he say goodbye again? Before he did, he wanted one night to superimpose over the memory of the falling ceiling; one night to fill himself with the soft, satiny feel of her beneath him; one night to love her as he would never love another.

62

Richmond, Virginia, April 2, 1865

CHARLOTTE SAT HUNCHED on a stool with her back to the fireplace, brushing out the damp curls of her shampooed hair. The two things she missed most from home were hot showers and hairdryers. This morning, though, a copper tub filled with buckets of tepid water had been a sybaritic blessing. She had soaked and scrubbed until the patches of her uninjured skin glistened.

Her post-trauma body was in surprisingly good condition, considering she had run through Richmond's fiery streets twice, and had spent a couple of hours rescuing wounded soldiers from a burning building. The cut on her head needed only a butterfly bandage. The first-degree burns on her arms would heal without leaving scars. The scrapes on her knees and elbows were minor. The skin on her face had a burn similar to a sunburn after a day at the beach. The skin would peel, but as a child she'd had worse. The fire had singed the hair on top of her head, but her scalp wasn't burned. If she hadn't been so muscled and toned, she wouldn't have made it home under her own power, since neither Jack nor Braham had stamina enough left by the end of the night to carry her.

The memory of the legless soldier's clutched hand yanked from her wrists—and echoes of his dying screams—ricocheted around her mind, leaving her body and soul empty and grieving. The disbelief on the young man's face when Braham tore her away would haunt her to the end of her days. She squeezed her eyes closed and shook her head, trying to dislodge the memory's grip. She didn't want to forget him—the nameless soldier—not tonight, not ever. She would always remember his sacrifice.

She had lost patients before, but the loss of this soldier was different. And it hurt. A lot.

A soft knock on her door forced her to bite her lip and swallow back the lump in her throat. Until the house settled down and she had a bit of solitude, she had to hold her emotions in check. When time allowed, and she could pull her thumb from the hole in the dyke, the flood of tears might drown her.

Jack didn't wait for her permission. "Sis, c'mon, I'm dying of curiosity. Tell me about Mallory. How'd you meet him and when—"

Another knock. "Can I come in, too?" Braham stepped into the room. Neither man had put a razor to the tender flesh of his face. Both had wet hair brushed back, and they were both patched like quilts with bandages on chests and arms and heads.

The faint tremor in her fingers which had begun a couple of hours earlier still lingered. She set her brush aside and clasped her knees to still them. "Why do I bother to close the door? What time is it? Feels like next year."

"Almost five o'clock," Braham said. "Elizabeth has her Federal flag ready to unfold."

"The Union Cavalry should be riding into town about now. We should go welcome the sun and the soldiers," Jack said.

Outside fires still raged and random cannons roared. The parts of the city not engulfed by fire were covered with smoke and soot and ash. "I think we'll hear the bands playing *Yankee Doodle* from here."

"Don't you want to watch?" Jack asked.

There was weakness in her knees and a hitch in her breath as she rose to her feet, grimacing from the stiffness. "Coffee on the portico sounds lovely, as long as there's a comfortable chair."

A restless current stretched among them, leaving a silent thrum in the air. The night's reign of fiery terror had changed them all. It would take a while, at least for her, to come to terms with how close she came to dying. She retreated from the intensity of Braham's eyes by lowering hers. Jack shifted, clearing his throat. "I'll go make arrangements and meet you two downstairs."

The door clicked as he closed it behind him.

"I need to tell you—" Braham said.

"I haven't had a chance to say—" Charlotte said.

She smiled nervously, wondering if she should run into his arms or wait for him to come to her.

"You first," he said.

"No, you go first," she said.

"I'm sorry about the soldier." He stepped closer, his arms moving awkwardly at his side, as if he wanted to touch her but wasn't sure if it was the right move. "When I saw the roof about to collapse on you, I only thought of holding you while we both died. I didn't think we'd survive."

"Thank...you." Her voice quavered, and then she broke down, sobbing. She rushed into his arms and buried her face on his chest, crying gut-wrenching tears. "I was so afraid, but I couldn't leave him behind just to save myself. I didn't think..."

"Let it go, lass." He took a shaky breath and let it out in a loud rush, as if he, too, was letting it all go.

And she did. All of it. The ash and smoke, the screams and the unbearable heat, and the fear. She let it all out until her legs went weak and wobbly, and she slumped against him. He reached down and gathered up her legs, his other arm nestled her close, and, as he held her, his muscles twitched hard against her.

With jerky steps, he carried her to the settee, were he edged down onto the cushions and cradled her against his shaking body, his heart pounding in her ear. Months of pent-up guilt and failure, exacerbated by another close brush with death crashed down on her. Her hands clutched fistfuls of his shirt, squeezing and twisting the fabric.

After several long minutes, or it could have been hours, the rising sun sliced a trail from the open window to the far side of the room. Dust particles floated in the brilliant stream of early morning light. The strange tightness around her heart snapped like a popped rubber band—instantly and permanently.

Her crying trailed off into short gasping noises. Braham pulled a handkerchief from his pocket. "It's clean. Blow your nose."

Her grip on his shirt relaxed and she blew her nose several times, dabbing at her eyes with a clean edge. Gently, his hand nestled her head to his chest. She let it rest there, breathing slowly and deeply, taking in the mingled scents of him and starch and soap and shampoo, and faintly, of smoke.

A hoarse chuckle found its way up from somewhere in her chest, and she looked at him and tried to smile apologetically. "I had fantasies of having wild sex with you. Crying in your arms wasn't anywhere on my list of things to do." She angled her head and studied him, so beautiful, from skin to bone to soul, and was surprised to see glistening streaks on his cheeks. Tenderly, she wiped away the moisture.

She wiped her face, too, or tried to, with the back of her wrist. "I don't think anyone other than Jack has ever seen me cry before."

"You surprise me. I've always seen you as having matters well in hand. I know the lad's death upset you. I'm glad you let it out."

"I only pretend to be made of stone," she said.

He nodded, as if she'd confirmed his suspicions instead of refuting them. "Never thought you were. Your heart longs to feed the world. Most of the time, though, you forget to feed yourself."

She didn't argue, she merely shrugged her tired, achy shoulders and settled back into his embrace.

He kissed the top of head. "I hear "Yankee Doodle." We should go down with the others. Wash your face while I go change my shirt." He set her on her feet and stood, accompanied by popping and cracking in his joints.

"Between your stiff joints and mine, we could create a symphony." On tiptoes, she kissed his lips without lingering. "Thank you. I know I've already said it, but I needed to say it again."

He pulled her close and snugged her into his embrace. "Every nook and cranny of my being is calling your name."

His statement was like a punch to a place low within her. His words made her want to take the leap her heart had always resisted taking. She moved against him until she found perfect alignment, one which sent heat jolting through her. His arousal spoke not only from his heart but from his need. Angling her head to see him clearly, she gazed into his face, lined with character and honor, and tumbled headlong into his huge eyes, her heart saying what words couldn't express.

She took his hand and studied the ropy veins with her fingertips. This hand had grabbed her and saved her life. Lovingly, she pressed it against her breast, close to her fast-beating heart. The universe was contained in this moment, the heat and texture of his skin, his touch, rough and tender and so alive. His nostrils flared, breathing in the scent of her as she did of him. But there was another scent in the air, the musk of desire. She wanted to consume him like the fires they had escaped, to burrow inside of him and know him, every inch of his flesh and blood and heat.

Her name escaped as a moan while his lips rushed over her face. His tongue slipped into her mouth, giving and taking. She cried out, and she pressed herself against him, clawing to be closer to his skin. He devoured her mouth, his short whiskers rasping her chin. Holding the back of her head with one hand, he moved the other slowly, crossed over her breasts, and up her shoulders to her neck, where he held the side of her face with his large, callused hand. His thumb rubbed her cheekbone rhythmically and intoxicatingly, making her giddy with anticipation.

With his breath warm against her face he said, "If we're going to stop, we have to stop now."

"If you stop, I'll scream."

"I'm protecting your reputation. There's a house full of people downstairs waiting for us."

"I don't care."

He looked at her, into her, and she was barely able to pull herself back from the raw and powerful need in his eyes. He wanted to claim her as much as she wanted to be claimed.

"We'll go to Washington tomorrow, to the Georgetown house, and spend a few days together without interruptions." He took her hand and placed it over his arousal. "Never doubt my need for you."

She closed her eyes against the immensity of wanting to make love with him. His warmth was beginning to seep through the layers of clothing between them, but she needed the feel of him against her skin. She rucked up her skirt and placed his hand where he could touch the heat of her desire. His fingers tossed her beneath a giant wave, sweeping her tumbling helplessly in the tide. With her lips against his, she whispered, "Never doubt mine for you."

They nestled quietly against each other in the shadows of dawn, and from outside the window they heard horses rousing and murmured voices. It was almost the end of the war, but not the end of their story. Their end wouldn't come until April 15.

63

Richmond, Virginia, April 2, 1865

Eᴌɪᴢᴀʙᴇᴛʜ, Cʜᴀʀʟᴏᴛᴛᴇ, Jᴀᴄᴋ, and Braham sat in the drawing room lamenting the damage the out-of-control fires had wreaked on Richmond's business center. Twenty square blocks, from 8ᵗʰ Street to 15ᵗʰ Street, and a half-mile from the north side of Main Street to the river, lay in smoky ruin.

Charlotte stirred cream into her china teacup while biting hungrily into a biscuit, the first food she'd had in twenty-four hours. Following the arrival of the Union Cavalry the previous morning, she had collapsed and slept until about an hour ago. She put the spoon on the saucer and picked up the cup, drinking greedily. "Do they know how many buildings were lost?" she asked between gulps.

Elizabeth thumped a finger on the front page of the Richmond *Whig* in her lap. "The paper is reporting from six to eight hundred public buildings and private residences were burned to the ground. The heart of the city is in charred ruins."

Charlotte got up, leaned over the back of Elizabeth's chair, and read the report. At the top of the article was a rudimentary engraving, resembling modern day clip art of burned-out buildings, showing virtually nothing left except chimney stacks and jagged bits of walls. A few pieces of furniture still holding their fragile shapes were tossed out into the street. Gooseflesh prickled down her arms, her chill as much from the picture as from her memories of the roaring flames and shattered glass crunching under her shoes.

Braham pulled a small sheet of paper from his inside breast pocket and unfolded it. "All the banking houses, the Columbian Hotel, the *Enquirer* Building, the American Hotel, the Confederate Post Office, and…" he flicked the paper with his index finger, "…the courthouse have all been lost."

Elizabeth handed the newspaper to Charlotte and picked up her teacup, sighing heavily. "There wouldn't be a building left standing if the Union troops hadn't extinguished the fires. The city should be grateful."

"I'm sure the city government is convinced if the Federal Army hadn't been standing on their doorstep, the warehouses wouldn't have been burned to begin with," Jack said.

"True," Elizabeth said, "but they didn't show up unannounced night before last. They've been bombarding Richmond for months…" Elizabeth paused, interrupted by Braham's jaw-cracking yawn, and then she continued as if nothing had happened. "City officials refused to prepare for evacuation, convinced the day would never come."

Braham patted his fist against his lips as another yawn slipped out. "There've been no complaints. The Mayor said the citizens aren't complaining about the soldiers, and the soldiers aren't complaining about the citizens. There's no fear of rape and pillaging, and the peaceful occupation has eased the city's anxiety."

When Jack had told her Braham had been at the White House of the Confederacy in constant meetings with General Weitzel and his staff, she had been tempted to march over to the general's office and demand he give Braham time off to heal. But she knew even if Weitzel ordered Braham to rest, he wouldn't.

Charlotte returned to her seat on the sofa and studied Braham over the top edge of the newspaper. Even with his shadowed eyes, cuts, bruises, singed hair, and minor burns, she found his presence soothing.

Jack placed his coffee cup on the serving tray, wiped his hands on a napkin, and tossed it alongside the cup. "If you'll excuse me, I have an article to write."

A loud knock on the front door reverberated through the downstairs; the very air in the room seemed to freeze. Braham came to attention, but the corner of his lip curled, hinting at a slight smile, whether in amusement or something else, Charlotte wasn't sure. Jack turned toward the door, eyeing it inquisitively. Elizabeth lost color in her face. And Charlotte, still jittery over visitors who carried torches, cringed and scrunched furtively into the softly cushioned chair.

Elizabeth rose slowly from the sofa, patting the neatly rolled bun at her nape. Before taking a step, she brushed the front of her blue cotton day dress with slightly shaking hands. "I suppose my neighbors are calling, wanting their silver back now they don't feel threatened by their *rescuers*."

Jack crossed the room to the window, pushed aside a corner of the lace curtain, and peered out. The breeze rattled busily among the branches of the trees and shrub. "All I see from here is a warbler sitting in an azalea bush, pouring its heart out. But whoever is at the door has come with a Union Cavalry escort. Maybe General Weitzel is calling on Elizabeth?"

Braham shrugged, his mouth spreading now into a wide grin. "Let's go see."

They followed Elizabeth out into the entryway, where vases belied the devastation outside with fragrant sprays of greenery mixed in with white and purple lilacs. The large bouquets filled the entry with the fresh, sweet scents of innocence and springtime. Charlotte buried her nose in one bouquet and sniffed, cleansing the lingering, stale smell of smoke from her nose.

The butler opened the door, and loud gasps mingled with the delicious spring scents. Braham strode past the others to welcome their guest. "Come in, Mr. President."

Lincoln and his entourage quickly filled the entryway.

Elizabeth hurried forward, extending her hand. "What a glorious surprise. I'm Miss Van Lew. I'm honored you chose to pay a visit, Mr. President. Please, come in for tea."

The President removed his hat, sniffing the air. "The fragrance of your flowers is a pleasant reprieve from the smoky air of center city."

Elizabeth nodded, smiling radiantly. "Let me introduce my guests." She pointed toward Jack.

"There's no need," Lincoln said. "I'm acquainted with the Mallorys, and owe the doctor a debt of thanks yet again. It occurred to me the major might have intentionally gotten himself captured, hoping to set eyes on your lovely countenance once more."

Charlotte stood stock still for a moment, aware of Braham's musky scent among the floral arrangements. A slight flush increased the heat on her cheeks. "I don't know about that, Mr. President. I can't imagine anyone volunteering to spend time in Castle Thunder, no matter what the reason."

"I heard the prisons survived the fire. It's a shame." Elizabeth's voice was heavy with regret.

Lincoln regarded her with a gentle expression and sympathetic eyes. "The crowd earlier this morning was of like mind, madam. But I've ordered they're not to be burned. Instead, the prisons are to be used as a monument to all the loyal soldiers who suffered its horrors." He placed his hand on Braham's shoulder, gripping it, pulling him into a side hug. "I'm sorry for what you endured there."

Braham nodded almost imperceptibly. "It was only a few days, sir."

"Tea is served, Mr. President. Please come have refreshment."

"I regret to decline, Miss Van Lew. I must get on with the tour. General Weitzel was kind enough to point out your residence, saying you were General Grant's correspondent. I've come to thank you on his behalf and mine."

"I did little for a cause so large, but I pray I did all I could."

Lincoln tapped the breast of his coat with a gesture of satisfaction. "You did more than we had a right to ask or expect. You're an honorable and generous woman."

Elizabeth, a true loyalist, humble and unpretentious, bowed her head slightly in recognition of the compliment.

"Major McCabe, I'll be returning to Washington this afternoon on the *Melvern* and would like you to join me. If Mr. Mallory and

Doctor Mallory intend to return to Washington, there is room on the steamer to accommodate them. Now, I must go."

"Thank you, sir," Braham said. "We'll depart for the dock shortly."

The President and his entourage departed as quickly as they had arrived. Elizabeth and Jack went inside, leaving Charlotte and Braham on the portico to watch the caravan, bathed in rays of golden sunlight, travel down the street. Five minutes of the President's time were more valuable than the missing Confederate gold. And no non-military Unionist deserved those minutes more than Elizabeth. It must have taken a creative scheduler to make time for her.

Charlotte glanced at Braham. His hand rested on the hilt of his saber. He wore the smug look men get when they know they've made a lady happy. Guessing his secret, she smiled and rubbed a light hand over his arm. "Asking the President to visit Elizabeth was a lovely gesture."

He laughed, and the sound was rich and sensual. "Ah, lass, I thought it would please you, too. I didn't know you were on such good terms with Mr. Lincoln." He stroked his thumb across her chin and along her jawline. "Are you ready to return to Washington?"

His warm breath fanned her cheek. As if she were under his spell, her eyes were drawn to his lips, parted and full. "As long as you don't let him talk you into another assignment right away."

"I've promised you a few uninterrupted days in Georgetown. I won't let him have those. They're for us." Braham's eyes were dancing now, and she felt suddenly sheepish, and at the same time melting with desire.

64

En Route to Washington City, April, 1865

WHEN THE PRESIDENT decided to remain in City Point, Braham booked the second leg of their return trip to Washington on the only other steamer available, the *Thomas Powell,* a ship loaded with some three hundred wounded soldiers. Charlotte volunteered her assistance, explaining to the surgeon in charge she had worked in a Washington hospital. When he asked her for references, she told him she didn't have any with her. Braham intervened and told the supervising doctor two of Charlotte's references were President Lincoln and General Grant. It proved to be her ticket to surgery, where she spent most of the day. She found some irony in treating wounded who were chiefly from Sheridan's Cavalry. If "Little Phil" made an appearance to check on his men, she wasn't sure what she would say other than thanking him for threatening her. No, she would simply smile and say it was nice to see him, and he'd likely wonder who in the world she was.

By the time the ship arrived in Washington she was exhausted, but glad to be back. Mostly she was looking forward to Braham's promised getaway. He had strolled past her several times during the day, and each time he'd kept his eyes fixed on hers for several beats before moving on. His glances were titillating, and desire for him flooded her every time, turning her disposition from focused to wanton with only a lift of his brow.

Neither of them had mentioned their plans to Jack, and while she didn't think he would care or be surprised, she was still a bit anxious about telling him. Would he scold her and say getting involved with Braham was the same as dating an unavailable and sure-to-break-your-heart married man? If so, he could save his breath, his energy, and later, his *I told you so's.*

Braham hired a barouche to take them to the townhouse. Since the air was balmy, the driver lowered the collapsible hood. She and Braham shared the seat facing the driver, while Jack and Gaylord shared the rear-facing seat. Each twist and turn of the vehicle jostled her and Braham into closer physical contact. Each time her arm brushed his, the touch was erotically charged. Tingling excitement saturated her, burning hot and promising.

Braham whistled and twitched his long, slender fingers against his thigh as if playing the finger buttons on a trumpet to the beat of the tune blowing through his lips. Of course, it made her think of kissing. Wanton. She was becoming a wanton, and she loved the sensation. She couldn't take her eyes off his hand, imaging the pads of his fingers stroking her in sensitive places. She touched her mouth, the cool, smooth skin of her lips, thinking about what an excellent kisser he was. Or, maybe they were excellent kissers together.

The sun suddenly broke out from behind a rain cloud, and she had to shield her eyes against its brilliance. It was then she noticed the bunting and flags draped around the harbor, which brought her lusting to an abrupt halt. "There seems to be a national festival taking place. If the fall of Richmond causes this kind of a celebration, what will happen when Lee surrenders?"

Jack had his notebook and pencil in hand, jotting down observations. "The city will go nuts."

The driver took them past the throngs gathered in the Capitol grounds, all clearly enjoying the bands and festive atmosphere. The men sported ivory-headed canes and women carried gay parasols, which were twirling in the breeze. On crowded Pennsylvania Avenue patriotic mottoes embellished the State Department, flags smothered the War Department, and the Navy had hung up a large model of a full-rigged ship. After the fires and smoke in Richmond, Washington's charged atmosphere made Charlotte imagine Glinda, the Good Witch from Oz, was waving her wand to banish the unsettling power of Charlotte's horrifying memories.

The carriage stopped in front of the War Department building, and Gaylord hopped out, but before the driver snapped the reins, Gaylord passed a note to Braham. Braham unfolded the paper, read it, and handed it back. His face took on a set and absent look, as though he had forgotten where he was.

Gaylord thumped the side of the vehicle, signaling the driver. They pulled away, heading around the corner to the townhouse. The carriage parked, and Braham helped Charlotte down. Her eyes rested on the paneled front door. A warm, cozy feeling of being home settled in the recesses of her heart, similar to what she experienced every time she drove up the plantation's driveway. How odd to realize she had become so attached to this house. But was it really the house, or the man who lived here?

Edward, dressed in his neatly pressed day livery, opened the front door with a flourish. "Welcome home, sir."

Braham handed over his hat. "How's the household, Edward?"

Edward closed the door after accepting Jack's hat. "Fine, sir. And welcome back, Mr. Mallory and Miss Charlotte. Hasn't been the same here since you left."

Charlotte swept off her cape and handed it to the butler. "Thank you, Edward. Have you been out to enjoy the festivities?"

"Yes, ma'am. I was out earlier this morning. Fine day in Washington. Just fine."

Braham shook his head briefly, as if dispelling some thought, and said, "I'd like a bath and a light meal. See to my guests. I'll be in the study."

She met Jack's eyes straight on, and they stood there in puzzled silence, looking at each other. Charlotte's eyes widened. What was going on? Other than raise his brow, Jack didn't answer her unvoiced question. He didn't know either. Braham's brusque behavior must have something to do with Gaylord's note.

Did the Secretary of War intend to send Braham out on another mission? To do what? The war was within days of ending. And where had Gaylord gotten the note? If he'd had it prior to boarding the carriage, why didn't he give it to Braham earlier? If he didn't have it earlier, where in heaven's name had it come from? She frowned when a vague memory came to mind. While locked in traffic on Pennsylvania Avenue, a man bumped into the carriage. Did he pass a note to Gaylord? If so, why the secrecy?

She was too hot, too sticky, and too hungry to waste much energy trying to understand Braham's clandestine activities. Maybe he had decided a romantic interlude with her was a bad idea? If so, she'd go to the hospital and see patients, and that would be the end of it. She flinched at the thought, and her heart hammered in her ears. Feeling rejected wasn't an easy emotion to master.

"I'm going to have a bath and rest. Are you staying in?" she asked Jack.

He shook his head, looking troubled. "Since Braham's using the study, I'll work in my room. I have outlines for several articles I'd like to sell this week. If you need me, send me a—knock on my door, I guess." His mouth curled up in a wry smile over his almost-slip.

She gave him a thumbs-up and marched up the stairs, an indomitable soldier off to do battle.

After a bath, she cleaned and sorted her medical kit and added a few notes to her journal. She didn't write much, but she did jot down descriptions and insights which should trigger her memory when she was ready to recall certain events and people.

Another band had started playing outside the White House. She watched from the window with her hands braced against the frame and peered down into the street. An uneasy feeling settled over her. In a few days, Lincoln—

A knock on her door interrupted her thoughts. "Come in."

Braham entered, closed the door, and came to stand next to her. "What's gotten your attention?"

She lifted up on tiptoes and kissed him lightly on the lips, breathing in the scent of tobacco. He didn't smoke around her now, but she always knew when he had indulged in his favorite bad habit—a cigar.

"What's happened? You shut down after you read the note from Gaylord, and you appear troubled now." With a stroke of her finger, she combed back strands of hair dangling across his brow, concealing the only part of his forehead without scratches or cuts.

He took both of her hands and kissed her palms, not a quick kiss like she had given him, but a lingering one, filled with promise. "There's something I have to do this afternoon, but I've arranged a carriage to take you to Georgetown. I'll join you there for a late dinner, and we'll stay until Friday. I promised you time together. I won't disappoint you. I'll be there tonight."

She caught her lower lip between her teeth, not realizing how much she'd worried he might cancel. Greatly relieved, she sighed. "I was afraid you had changed your mind about going to Georgetown. I understand emergencies. Do what you have to do, and come when you can. What time will the driver pick me up?"

He studied her face, his shoulders relaxing a bit, and his eyes grew less troubled. "Cancelling our plans never occurred to me. The carriage will be here at three o'clock. Can you be ready?"

"I have only a few things to pack."

He glanced at her bed, where she had laid out traveling clothes. "You won't need much."

Heat rushed up her neck toward her face. Rarely, if ever, had she taken the time to plan a tryst with a lover. All she'd had time for was hit and miss sex, squeezed into a complicated life and a full surgery schedule. She did have sexy clothes, although not with her. Well, there was the one thing she had packed at the last minute, a red stretchy chemise trimmed with scalloped lace and a matching thong. "How about a suitcase full of short and sexy things?"

His eyes brightened into brilliant emeralds. "Short and sexy. I saw a picture of a woman on Jack's Facebook page dressed in a…" Braham put his hands on his chest and slid them down to his groin, "…short, black lacy undergarment which stopped at the top of her legs."

She bit back a smile. She didn't have the kind of enhanced body Braham would have seen posing in slinky black lingerie on Jack's Facebook page. If Braham had those expectations, he'd be disappointed. The sexy red thing might not make it into her travel bag after all.

"You're too jaded now. I don't think you'd like my—"

He nudged her chin up, kissed her, and their open mouths fused hungrily. There were no playful nips and licks, but a full-on siege. Then he stopped and took a step back, breathing heavily. "There's isn't anything about you I don't like. You're beautiful. I don't care if you wear a short, sexy thing or nothing at all." He put his hands behind her head and kissed her roughly. "I'll be there late tonight."

She stood there gulping, watching him hurry out the door. The moment she dropped to the stool in front of her dressing table, touching her bottom lip, slightly swollen now from his bruising kiss, Jack gave a cursory rap on her door and sauntered in without an invitation, as usual. When he noticed the clothes on her bed, he gave her a raised eyebrow look. "Going somewhere?"

"Oh." Distractedly, she continued playing with her lower lip, otherwise not moving.

"Charlotte? What's wrong?" He knelt in front of her and put his hands on her arms, squeezing gently. "Talk to me."

The squeeze broke through her temporary trance. "What?"

One corner of his mouth curled wryly as he pointed to her lip. "Do I see a kissing bruise?"

She shook her head, licking the tender spot carefully with her tongue. "I guess we got carried away."

"I'd say so." He got back to his feet, scratching his chin whiskers. "Does your bruise have anything to do with the clothes piled on your bed?"

"Sort of. Braham and I are going to Georgetown for a few days. Alone."

"Really?" Jack took a seat in the wingback chair by the fire, stretching out his long legs. "Are you sure it's a good idea?"

She turned to face him, hands resting on her knees, fingers tapping rhythmically as she had seen Braham do earlier. Now she understood why. The beat matched the rapid pulse of anticipation. "I don't know how good an idea it is, but it's what I want."

He slouched in the chair and crossed his ankles. His feet flopped back and forth like two adversaries getting up into each other's faces, then backing off and going at it again. "It's going to hurt later, you know."

She watched his moving feet, mesmerized. "Stop it."

"Stop what?"

She pointed a finger, waving toward his feet. "Your dueling feet are driving me nuts. Stop it."

He smirked and uncrossed his feet. "My feet aren't the issue. How you're going to put your life back together later is what we're talking about. *Comprende?*"

"As the saying goes, I'd rather have loved and lost than never to have loved at all. And what do you know about broken hearts, other than you've broken more than your share?"

"It goes both ways, Char. I don't enjoy hurting women. It makes me feel bad. They like my image, the parties, publicity, travel, but they aren't interested in the everyday, sweaty part, the grind. They get more demanding on the days I don't shave and forget to eat, or work straight through the night. When the what-about-poor-me drama starts, I kiss them goodbye."

She moved over to the settee and curled up, hugging a pillow. "What's your point? I know you've buried one in there."

"Braham will never be able to give you what you want. So lighten up and enjoy the party. Enjoy the romance. Enjoy the sex. And when you ask him to go home with you again, and the drama starts, be prepared, because he's gonna kiss you goodbye."

"I know." She added a second pillow to her huddle.

Jack's eyes softened. "Then why are you getting involved, knowing you'll get hurt?"

"Because I'm already in love him, and I don't want to spend the rest of my life wondering what it would have been like to be with him."

"Jesus, if it's the experience you're looking for, I know a dozen men built exactly like Braham. You can have sex with one of them. Have a similar experience without the heartache."

She threw one of the pillows at him. He snatched it out of the air and hugged it to his own chest. "You know it's not what I mean," she said, adding another pillow to her collection.

"I hope you're prepared for the heartache, because it'll hurt for damn sure."

"You can't prepare for pain like you can for a test or train for a race. When it happens, you have to live it, feel it. The memories will help me get through the loneliness."

"That's such a crock of—"

She threw another pillow. "Stop. I've made up my mind."

He stuffed the second pillow between his hip and the side of the chair. "I've got plenty of condoms in my shaving kit. Grab a couple dozen."

Her eyes widened. "Couple dozen? Have you forgotten Braham spent a week being tortured in prison, then ran through a city dodging flames and collapsing buildings? He's exhausted."

"Yeah right. You'd better take three dozen. The man's got stamina."

"How many did you bring?" She threw the third and final pillow. "If Braham's honor equals his stamina, he might not show up. He's sending me over there this afternoon because he has something to do. He'll be there in time for a late dinner."

"Does it have anything to do with the note from Gaylord?"

"I think so, but he wouldn't tell me."

"I can think of a couple of things."

"Booth?" She gritted her teeth, and a hot flush settled into her face at the thought of Braham chasing Booth. She seriously considered finding Braham and shaking him until his teeth rattled.

"Before Gaylord dashed off to Richmond with us," Jack said, "he was following Booth. Makes sense he had someone else keep an eye on the actor while he was gone."

She rarely, if ever, drank during the day, and even at night she normally limited herself to a glass or two—except on nights before she operated, when she abstained entirely. The last few months she'd been drinking a lot. She jumped up and reached for the decanter of sherry on a silver tray by the window.

She poured, took a sip, and then another. "What's Braham going to do? Kill him?"

"Braham's tired of killing, but the war's still going on, and he sees Booth as the enemy. In his mind, it justifies whatever he has to do."

"What happened to him being too honorable to murder a man?" she asked.

"His stint in a Richmond prison, maybe. Honestly, I don't know what he'll do, given the choice."

She gave Jack a brief, distracted glance, and tried to smile. "It certainly would put a damper on our getaway."

"Maybe not. Braham wouldn't go to your bed with blood on his hands. So I'd say he's only spying on Booth tonight."

"Great. We both know what kind of spy he is. He'll end up in the Old Capitol Prison, and we'll have to bail him out."

Jack shoved out of the chair and headed toward the door. "I'm going down to the study to work. Be sure to get some condoms, and don't worry. Braham's an honorable man. He'll do what's right."

"About what? Shooting Booth or sleeping with me?"

Jack turned back at the door, and his hand rested on the doorknob; eyebrows raised in thought. "Both."

65

Washington City, April, 1865

A T THREE O'CLOCK, Jack handed Charlotte up into the carriage sent to carry her to Georgetown. "Remember, if Braham's a no-show, I'll come pick you up." He leaned in close and whispered. "And if he does show up, and you run out of condoms, I don't want to hear about it." His smile segued into a chuckle as he waved goodbye and headed back into the house.

"Stay out of trouble. *Please*," she said as he disappeared through the front door.

This was their first separation since arriving in Washington, and leaving him on his own was like leaving a seven-year-old with the car keys. She probably exaggerated slightly when it came to Jack's penchant for trouble. His infractions had been few, but they were typically monumental when they happened. Like the time, he was arrested as part of a biker gang accused of murder. The prosecutor had dismissed charges against Jack after his attorney proved he had only been doing research for a book. But his mug shot and the story were on the front page of the *Richmond Times-Dispatch*—above the fold. She'd lost a handful of patients over that one. They didn't want family and friends to know their surgeon was related to a *murderer*. Yep. Jack was due for a big one. He was a grown man, for God's sake. Surely he could avoid getting shot or locked up for the night.

Suddenly, a strange, almost mystical calm came over her. The first order of business was to put Jack and his impulsiveness out of her mind. She snapped her finger. *Zap.* Not only was she not going to worry about Jack, she wasn't going to worry about Braham, either. She patted her pocket, letting her fingers trace the outline of the sapphire brooch pinned into the fabric. Only two weeks remained in her nineteenth-century adventure, but she wasn't going to think about it tonight.

The celebrations she'd seen earlier in the day continued, fanning out from Pennsylvania Avenue into side streets and on into Georgetown. Compared to her last visit, when wounded soldiers crowded the streets, this trip was delightful.

When she arrived, the butler showed her to a guest room and invited her to explore the house and gardens. She strolled around the grounds, enjoying the sweet fragrance of alyssum along the path, and spikes of yellow forsythia nodding over the tidy white fence lining the sides of the property. Behind a fast-growing privacy screen of willow trees, she found a tranquil garden with a gently trickling brook. Nestled in a rocky alcove sat a long, narrow bench, and a waterfall fell from the top of the rocks into the stream. Anyone sitting on the cushioned bench reading or meditating would remain dry and shielded from prying eyes by the fall of the water. The bench appeared wide enough for a man to recline on for an afternoon nap, or whatever else he had in mind to do. She rubbed a finger gently across her bottom lip, remembering the touch and feel of Braham's tongue when he had licked and nibbled there. Had he kissed other women behind the waterfall? And what if he had? She had no claim to virgin lips or virgin other parts. She'd had a life, and so had he.

As dusk approached, she retired to her room for a light meal and a bath. At nine, she dressed for dinner. At eleven, she undressed and slipped on scrubs instead of her chemise, tense with disappointment. Moonlight streamed through the open windows, dimly illuminating the empty bed. She paced to and fro, trying to suppress the urge to worry about him, but it was impossible. The room was quiet, save for the crackling fire and the gentle creak of the wood floor beneath her feet.

She stopped pacing and stared out the window for some time, watching ropy clouds scud across the face of the full moon and thinking. She had a choice, didn't she? He had promised her time together, and she could either have faith in his promise, faith in him, or she could choose not to. Which one?

She chose faith.

Before climbing into bed she took two condoms from her bag and placed them on the table nearby. She tapped her fingernail against her front teeth. The table was too far away to reach in a hurry, so she tucked the foil packages under her pillow, where they'd be quickly accessible. Then she crawled up onto the high four-poster and snuggled into the soft, feathered mattress. She composed her mind for sleep, clearing it of worries and concerns, breathing in the scent of the burning logs. Soon she surrendered to the sleep lapping at her consciousness like the tide creeping up a rocky shore.

Vivid and erotic dreams of a man nibbling on her ear and murmuring in Gaelic invaded her soothing sleep. Although she didn't understand what he said, she understood the meaning. Finally the nibbling brought her to semi-consciousness. She snuggled against her dream lover, feeling warm and protected. When chest hairs tickled her cheek, she came fully awake.

"I'm sorry I'm late." Braham smoothed her sleep-snarled hair back from her face, one curly strand at a time. "It couldn't be helped." He shifted, easing them into a comfortable position with her head in the curve of his shoulder. His fingers traced the nobs of her spine, one bone at a time, from her neck all the way down to her sacrum, massaging her gently. Her thigh pressed against him, and her smaller leg molded to the hard length of his.

"You're here?" she said in groggy inquiry. It didn't matter if he was an hour late or a day, he was in her arms now, redolent with the fresh, clean scent of soap. He had stoked the fire, and a log cracked, sending a spray of fiery sparks up the chimney. The firelight filled the room with a warm, golden glow limning his tired but smiling face. "Did you get something to eat?"

"Aye, a bite." He kissed her forehead and cheeks, chin and lips.

"This isn't how I wanted to begin our getaway."

Her hand stroked the taut skin and smooth mat of blond hair covering the warm muscle defining the broad expanse of his chest. Beneath her fingers, his heart beat steady and strong. "Since I missed it, tell me what you'd planned to do."

He laughed with a low masculine rumble. "I'll surprise you tomorrow."

"Hmm. So this is merely a warm-up act for the real performance?" Her hand slid down his abdomen, coming into contact with his arousal. She squeezed gently. "If this is a warm-up, I can hardly wait for the real thing."

"I wanted to seduce you with music and wine."

"You seduce me with your eyes every time you gaze at me. I don't need music and wine."

"Good, since I have neither with me now."

His full lips sipped at hers possessively, and their tongues danced in an irresistible and erotic rhythm. His hands slipped under her shirt, and then he flipped her over onto her back. He raised up and stared down at her. "I've wanted to strip these ugly garments off of you since the first time I saw you in them." He gathered the top of her scrub shirt and pulled it over her head. She lifted her arms, but after he had tugged the top off of her, he held her wrists in one of his hands, and stared at her breasts. "My God, you're beautiful."

Her chest turned into a solid sheet of gooseflesh.

He cupped one breast and then the other. "Perfect." And then he eyed her suspiciously. "Are these enhanced?"

She forced her hands out of his and playfully shoved him away. "How could you ask such a thing? How many breasts have you seen? Dozens? How many enhanced breasts have you seen? None? Well, you're still batting zero. Which means—"

"I get the gist," he said, but his puzzled look remained. "I thought women of your century were proud of enhanced breasts. I didn't mean to insult you."

"You didn't. I'm teasing you. I can hear Jack in your questions. He's—"

"Jaded me is what you said before?" Braham dropped down on one forearm and cupped her again.

"Okay. Here's the secret, so you'll never have to ask a woman again. Enhanced breasts don't move the same way when a woman lies on her back. Usually they stay front and center. Real breasts flatten as they fall naturally to the sides."

He squeezed her breasts one at a time, moving them up and around; then he kissed each nipple. "I like yours fine."

His hand moved down her abdomen and untied the drawstring of the scrubs. Her muscles clenched involuntarily at a touch so soft he could have been using feathers. He pushed down the sides of the pants, then reached beneath her. "Lift your hips." She did, and he bunched the scrub pants down her legs far enough for her to kick them aside. His fingers began a slow exploration, lingering over her most sensitive flesh, teasing her in a delicious way. He was playing her, with the care and skill worthy of a finely tuned instrument. But if he played much longer, her strings would snap from overwhelming tension.

"*Please*, don't make me wait." Her hips undulated for emphasis.

He lifted himself over her and paused. "Tell me what you want."

"You." She reached under the pillow for a condom. And paused. Yes, this was what she wanted… and not merely for tonight, but for the rest of her life. She was accustomed to making quick decisions. Living without *him*, but being able to cherish a part of him, would be the consequence of this decision. Her fingers relaxed, and the condom slipped from her hand.

Her body merged with his, into the feel of his skin under her hands and the play of his muscles. His mouth roamed at will, no longer gentle. He devoured her, kissing the smooth curve of her throat and the soft flesh of her earlobe. With his powerful arms, he jerked her close, consuming her with his tongue and lips. He cupped her hip, her breast, and between her legs branding her body with his sensual exploration. Then he lowered himself and placed his mouth where his hand had been. He drew up one of her knees, opening her wider, then slipped a finger inside her. She gasped as her body shivered from the double invasion—almost painfully alive with sensations unlike any she'd ever experienced before.

She raised her hips to evade the exquisite teasing, but moving only enhanced his tender ravishing. His hands gripped her bottom to steady her undulating hips, which had been moving in a rolling, wave-like motion as she drew closer to the edge of sweet release. She dug her fingers into his damp hair, urging him on. But he needed no encouragement, for he knew exactly what to do to please her. Pleasure crashed around her, inside her, and all the way through her as passion took control of her mind and body. She pulled him up on top of her. She wanted him with an incomprehensible ferocity, an instinctual craving.

His thumb slid over the curve of her cheek, the line of her jaw, stopping at her mouth, looking into her with intensity and focus. He made her world spin. A moan slipped past her lips, husky with need.

She welcomed him into the depth of her being. All the wonder, warmth, and strength she identified with him were in his embrace as he entered her. She had never known such tenderness. His lips found hers, molding shape against shape, and then a burst of hunger. His tongue moved farther into her mouth, writing the definition of intimacy and perfect harmony in a flowing script. His lips trembled against hers.

One long, searing thrust sent her reeling with ecstatic sensations. Her body moved fluidly against his as he pulled back and thrust again and again, sinking into her each time with a guttural groan and binding their souls more closely with each stroke. A gasp tore from her throat as she convulsed in helpless ecstasy. He threw back his head, muscles straining in his neck, and gave himself over to her. Bound body and soul, their release washed them over the precipice and tumbled them into a roiling sea of blinding sensation.

66

Georgetown, April, 1865

CHARLOTTE LAY STILL, listening to Braham's soft breathing. Moonlit particles drifted in a beam of light which shone through the partially closed drapes and graced the handsome planes of his face. She'd cupped her hand along his slightly bristled cheek, one leg lay across his muscular thighs, and her head lay nestled in the hollow of his shoulder. Their limbs and arms were entwined like magical, multi-colored threads. She purred with contentment and snuggled, protected from the chill in a sensuous nest of warmth. The scent of sex, so carnal and tantalizing, surrounded them, permeating the sheets and pillows and her imagination.

She shifted slightly, and his hand slipped loosely to her hips. "I hear you thinking," he whispered, his voice drowsy and sleep-deprived. "What's worrying you?"

A prickle of sweat gleamed among the curly hairs of his chest where her arm had rested, and she wiped it away. "Nothing really, except I'm thirsty."

His eyelids fluttered, and he pulled her over on top of him, holding her closer still. "You're probably hungry, too. I'll go see what I can find."

She kissed him and rubbed against his erection. "Hmm...don't go."

He smacked her lightly on the butt. "Keep this up and you'll die of thirst." He flipped her over, trapping her body beneath his and kissed her soundly. "I won't be gone long enough for you to miss me." He slipped out of bed and tucked the covers up to her chin. "Stay warm."

Sighing, she rolled up into the fetal position, already missing his warmth. What they had shared over the last few hours was unique in her experience, and spoke to her on multiple levels. She wasn't a sexual neophyte by any means. But none of her lovers had ever made love to her the way Braham had. He didn't simply have sex with her. He had created an electric atmosphere and conducted an orchestra whose music still filled her mind and heart.

She was smiling, reveling in the ravishing experience, when he returned a few minutes later carrying a silver tray with a bottle of wine and a plate of bread and cheese. Before he opened the bottle, he stoked the fire, which sent out warm heat and the sweet scent of hickory. Every so often the flame popped and sparked when it found a pocket of resin. The fire quickly removed the chill, so she pushed back the covers and sat up, propping pillows behind her back.

Braham dropped his robe on a chair and stood naked by the bed, opening the bottle. She looked at him with heavy-lidded eyes, leisurely studying the solidness of his superbly conditioned body, and the molded contours of chin and hip and thigh. His incision was still pink, but *no one*, other than a surgeon, would ever take time to notice such a minor imperfection. Her muscles tightened in exquisite anticipation and pure, raw desire, which warmed her thoroughly.

He handed her a glass of vibrant ruby wine with touches of orange around the edges. "This is from my vineyards." He lifted the glass to his nose and sniffed. "Gentle, yet striking. Tell me what you think."

She gave the glass an open-air, freestyle swirl, observing the legs of wine as they ran down the sides of the goblet. Her mouth watered. As her nose hovered above the rim, she gave several quick, short sniffs, and then she sipped. "Hmm. Fresh aromas of lime, grapefruit, and earth. Delicious."

His face split into a huge grin, and his eyes, dark and penetrating, fell on her with an appreciative light. He stacked his pillows before climbing back into bed and pulling her into the curve of his arm. Once settled, he picked up the food and placed the plate on his lap.

She nibbled on a slice of cheese while he combed her hair—now wild and curly and tangled—with his fingers. She tilted her head to look into his eyes. "I read a quote once which said something like: 'Lovers don't finally meet somewhere. They're in each other all along.' It's how I feel about you. You've always been a part of me and always will."

He gently traced the curve of her cheek and chin with the look of an artist studying her before creating a masterpiece. He set her glass aside and picked up a small box from the tray he'd carried into the room. "I have something for you."

He removed a ring from the box, took her hand, and slipped it on her right-hand ring finger. "This belonged to my grandmother." Longing suffused his voice.

A brilliant sapphire came alive in a flash of firelight, twinkling and dazzling. Charlotte stared at her hand, speechless, the implications unclear at the moment. "It's beautiful, but I can't accept it. It's a family heirloom."

He set the box aside and refilled his glass. "Of course you can," he said lightly. "It's mine to give."

"But it's not mine to accept," she said, turning to face him with clear irritation in her voice. "This is for your future wife. Unless..." She trembled as a soft, stirring, hopeful desire unrolled from a secret place inside her, then curled upward, spiraling like a candle flame. "Are you asking me to...to *marry you*?"

He raised his eyebrow in a silent question, and his pursed lips curved into what might have been the shadow of a smile.

"Because if you are, I'd marry you this minute, but only if you intend to return to the twenty-first century."

His eyes pinned hers, and he said, "And if I'm not?"

She glanced at the ring and tugged at it. "I can't accept this."

He stilled her hand and held her fingers closed. "Wear it for now."

She slapped his hand away and slipped the ring off over her knuckle, surprised by how perfectly it fit her finger. "No, I won't. And you can't buy me with a sapphire."

He quickly banked a flash of anger. "I'm *not* trying to buy you."

"It looks like it to me. I'm a bottom-line person. Unless you want to go home with me, we have no future. And I refuse to accept a ring which should belong to your wife."

He stared off into the stream of light now peeking through the drapes, his chest heaving. "Then what we shared means nothing to you."

Oh, God. How did this get so twisted?

The turmoil in her stomach turned into a whirlwind, and her head became weightless. Blinking, she tried to see through the forming tears. "Of course it does, and I'm in love with you, but..."

He came to his feet, knocking over the plate of cheese, which crashed to the floor, shards pinging against the wall. "No buts, Charlotte."

Time washed over her as if she was nothing more than a woman made of sand who would dissolve in the ever-changing flow of life, her life. "I can't stay here. This isn't where I belong."

He grabbed his trousers off the back of a chair, shoving his legs into them.

"I've given you my heart, in spite of knowing it will break." She placed the sapphire on the table and closed her burning eyes. Her breath seemed to run out of her forever, like a final sigh.

67

Washington City, April 14, 1865

BRAHAM BALANCED ON the rear legs of a straight-back chair in John Nicolay's White House office, reading newspaper reports of the surrender at Appomattox. If the meeting between Lee and Grant had taken place earlier in the week, he would have attended, but he couldn't risk being out of town tonight.

Lincoln entered the office holding a sheaf of paper, looking bemused. He appeared neatly combed, a marked contrast to his usual rumpled appearance. The legs of Braham's chair dropped to the floor with a loud thump, and he quickly came to his feet, straightening his coat.

"Come with me to the War Department," Lincoln said, seemingly cheerful for the first time in many months.

Braham folded the newspaper and dropped it on the seat of the chair. "Yes, sir."

They walked out into the hall, empty of the day's crowd, where Braham picked up his slouch hat and gauntlets from a table near Nicolay's door. "I thought you promised Marshal Lamon you wouldn't go out at night while he was out of town."

A guard armed with a revolver, one of the four members of the President's security detail, followed close behind. Lincoln adjusted his top hat and shuffled along toward the War Department. "My reply was evasive. I've gone to the War Department every night for the last four years."

"Lamon's concern was not your nightly trips to the War Department. It's going to the theatre that concerns all of us. When you're moving, you're not a sitting target. Although, wearing the stovepipe, you do stick out in a crowd." The corners of Braham's mouth twitched to contain a smile.

He held the door as they emerged into a promise of spring in the air. The temperature had already teased the blooms in the dogwood trees, and young leaves rustled a serenade in the breeze. Occasional fireworks lit up the sky over a populace who had grown accustomed to streaks of canon fire. Braham walked on one side of Lincoln, the guard on the other.

The President put his arm around Braham's shoulders, and while Lincoln's careworn face revealed nothing, he took a deep, shuddering breath before saying, "I had a dream of a corpse the other night. The sound of people sobbing drew me from my bed. I asked who was dead in the White House and a soldier said, 'The President. He was killed by an assassin.' I didn't sleep the rest of the night."

Dread coalesced into a cold snake running down Braham's backbone to coil in his gut. He halted and turned to Lincoln. "Stay home, sir. An attempt will likely be made on your life tonight, tomorrow, or the next day. There are more people out there like Count Adam Gurowski making caustic comments about your policies, and some are actively conspiring to kill you." He stared helplessly into the President's dark eyes. How could he convince Lincoln his life was truly in danger without coming right out and telling him John Wilkes Booth would assassinate him at Ford's Theatre in only a few hours? Braham had to prevent the shooting, but short of locking up the President for the night, how could he? "If you insist on going, I'll stand outside the theatre box and guard the door."

"I have a guard, and I believe the Mallorys are still visiting. Go home to your company. Enjoy the celebrations."

"The Mallorys will not be offended by my absence if they know I'm protecting you."

The skin at the corner of Lincoln's mouth wrinkled with a smile.

"I have seen Doctor Mallory's eyes following you. I would not like to displease her more than I have already."

"She's not displeased."

Lincoln gave no more than a brief snort in reply. Then he took Braham's hand, clasped it, and continued his slow, ambling gait. "This is a critical time, Braham. I don't want the country to know it's necessary to protect the President from assassination. It's unwise to admit a lack of confidence in the people. I have a twenty-four hour guard." Lincoln gestured by nodding his head toward the much shorter plainclothes officer at his side. "Tonight I must go to the theatre. The papers today announced both General Grant and I would see *Our American Cousin*. I cannot disappoint the public."

A sudden rush of fear and helplessness staggered Braham. He couldn't rid his mind of the photographs he had seen while in the twenty-first century of Ford's Theater and William Petersen's house. Lincoln needed to understand the depth of Braham's worry and concern. "If Grant had given you a plain refusal yesterday or early this morning, you would have been able to cancel without as much disappointment. I understand. But, I promise you, the public will be far more upset if you're assassinated at the theatre."

Lincoln smiled at Braham with what looked like an attempt at confident reassurance. "You cannot escape the responsibility of tomorrow by evading it today."

A trickle of sweat ran down the back of Braham's neck, under the queue tied at his nape. "But, sir—"

Lincoln held up his hand to silence further argument, and while there was sympathy in his eyes, there was determination, too. For Lincoln, the matter was closed, but it would not vanish like a vapor, it would manifest into extreme anxiety for Braham. A free fall of perspiration trailed down his back.

They continued in silence until they reached the War Department. "What'd you decide about arresting Jacob Thompson?" Braham asked.

"I told Assistant Secretary Dana, when you've got an elephant by the hind leg, and he's trying to run away, it's best to let him run."

"Guess it means the Confederate marauder is going to escape to England."

The President merely lifted one shoulder in a half-shrug. "Secretary Stanton wasn't pleased with my decision."

The guard reached the entrance to the War Department first and held the door for Lincoln and Braham. The President went immediately to the telegraph desk to check for messages from General Sherman, and afterward remained there with one hand on his hip, his lips pursed, reading the telegrams.

"Sherman is occupying Raleigh. It's only a matter of time before he meets with Johnston and negotiates a surrender."

Braham gave the President's shoulder an affectionate squeeze. "It's almost over."

After Lincoln had read the telegrams, he and Braham returned to the White House, strolling past the gaslights glittering on the surrounding evergreens and the flags. Lincoln remained lost in thought as he shuffled back to his office, where he met with Illinois Governor Richard Oglesby and a group of friends. Braham remained outside the President's door, listening to stories and laughter, but his mind was so fixed on what was about to happen, he couldn't enjoy Lincoln's obvious pleasure.

Braham sat with his head bowed and propped on his hand. His fingers were splayed through his hair, massaging his forehead as he slowly rotated his head back and forth.

"Never seen you so worried, Major," Nicolay said. "Does it have anything to do with the rumors I've heard about you being seen several times this week in the company of a beautiful woman?" Nicolay leaned forward, wearing an expression of amused bewilderment. He lowered his voice. "I've also heard tell she's the doctor the President sent to Richmond to rescue you from Chimborazo."

Braham moved his powerful shoulders in a partial shrug, and he flashed Nicolay a ghost of a grin. "Don't believe everything you hear, John."

Braham leaned his chair back against the wall as he had earlier and closed his eyes. He didn't move when the President's company departed and Lincoln left to join his family for dinner. Knowing the President was safe for the time being, Braham nodded off.

A gentle touch on his shoulder startled him out of a light sleep. He blinked several times as Charlotte's wavy image took form and shape.

"What a surprise." He rose slowly from the chair, still stiff and achy from his Richmond ordeal, and very little rest since returning to Washington. He and Charlotte had made love all night for the last three nights, so he certainly wasn't complaining about his lack of sleep.

A flush appeared on her cheeks. "I'm sorry to wake you."

He stretched, yawning. "The President went to dinner with his family, and I dozed off. I'm glad to see you."

"I didn't mean to disturb you. I know you're tired."

He was certainly glad to see her, but he sensed immediately she wasn't paying a social call. The visit had to be her last plea. Throughout the week they had skirted around and outright avoided any discussion of Lincoln. But, by some unspoken yet mutual consent, the subject had lurked still, dull and gray and ominous.

"Let's go out into the hall. There's a corner where we can have some privacy," he said.

They left the office for a quiet alcove. Their mingled shadows floated together on the wall. Braham pulled her into his arms, pausing to appreciate the fragrance of vanilla from lotion she used on her face. A distinct scent he would forever associate with her. As if under a spell, his eyes were drawn to her lips, parted and full, and the sound of her breathing filled him with desire. He kissed her hard and thoroughly, his tongue teasing hers. The kiss had lasted only a few seconds before she stepped away, ending it abruptly and decisively.

She chewed on the corner of her lip, looking as if she wanted to say something, but she wasn't sure what or if she should. Finally, she said, "Jack and I are leaving in the morning, regardless of what happens tonight. I'll ask you one more time. Please don't interfere."

"How can you ask that of me? You've sat at his knee and hung on his every word. The country needs him desperately. I don't care about the future. I care about right now."

Charlotte's breath hitched. She shook her head, and her unbound gold hair released the faint scent of amber and vanilla. She turned to leave, but he grabbed her arm. The area was quiet, except for the gentle crack of settling timber in the fireplace in the President's nearby office.

He tried to slow his breathing and stop the racing of his heart. He loved her, but she didn't understand that, to him, Abraham Lincoln wasn't a marble statue. "I didn't mean it the way it sounded."

"I don't think there is another meaning. But tell me this, if you stop Booth tonight, what will you do tomorrow, or the next day? The President wants you to chase down the gold. Are you going to stay and guard him for the rest of his term? If you take out Booth, someone else will come along with the same hatred."

Someone behind Braham cleared his throat and said, "Excuse me, Major."

Braham turned on his heels, quick as a panther, to find Nicolay several feet away holding out an envelope with a shaking hand. "Yes, what is it, John?"

"The President would like you to deliver this to Secretary Seward."

Braham backed away from Charlotte and took the envelope, giving it a cursory glance. He made a rough noise in his throat. His jaw muscles bulged, his limbs trembled, but he kept his temper in check. He didn't want to leave the White House unless it was to guard the President, but he couldn't explain why to Nicolay. He paused for a moment, wiping the back of his hand across his mouth, as though to rid himself a lingering rancid taste.

"Why me?" Braham asked.

Nicolay flinched slightly at this; his lips compressed. "You were with him at the War Department this evening and can answer the Secretary's questions, if he has any."

Braham frowned, contriving to look menacing as he once again gathered his hat and gauntlets from the table. "Don't let the President leave for the theatre until I return."

"I'll ask him, but I can't make any guarantees," Nicolay said.

The color had left Charlotte's face, and she stared at Braham with a glint in the dark blue of her eyes, watching intently, brow creasing with new worry. "Lewis Powell will try to murder Seward tonight," she told him quietly. Tiny pinpoints of perspiration glistened on her forehead, reflected by the light of the hall sconces. "Be careful."

Braham's narrow-eyed glance roamed hungrily over her slender form. How could he still desire her with such intensity? He had taken her several times during the night and again early this morning. If they were in his bedroom, he would have her once again. He swallowed, worked his jaw, and finally with effort asked, "How'd you get here?"

"I walked. I'm only across the street. Go on."

"I'll go with you to the corner."

They reached the front door of the White House and a soldier jogged up to meet them, wearing an urgent expression on his flushed face. He took a moment to catch his breath, and then said, "Major, Secretary Stanton wants to see you right now, sir."

"I'm on my way to Secretary Seward's house. I'll stop on the way," Braham said.

The soldier saluted then ran back across the lawn, holding his hat firmly to his head.

Charlotte and Braham walked in silence side by side, barely touching. Her satin skirt swished about her legs, and the breeze blew tendrils of hair around her face. There was a small love bite on her neck where the muscle curved into the shoulder. The memory of morning light on her face, her lips, and nibbling on the silky flesh made him feel a bit wistful and reflective, in spite of his fears for Lincoln.

She glanced at him for a moment, and then her eyes traveled to some indeterminate spot to the side of him and grew distant, as if looking into the future. "If Lincoln dies tonight—"

"He won't."

"If Lincoln dies tonight," she continued, "he'll be remembered as the greatest president the country ever had. If you change history, you change how he'll be remembered through the ages."

A vein in Braham's temple throbbed, and he fell silent, finally accepting he would be unable to persuade her to his position.

"The President's party will fight him over policy, over reconstruction. Possibly, he could be impeached for overstepping executive powers, over passing amendments and laws, or blockading Southern ports. He'll end his term battling criticism, to be remembered as a mediocre man and a mediocre president. You'll rob him of his immortality. Is that what you want?" She let out a long, shuddering breath; her shoulders sagging. The last vestiges of her focused determination seemed to crumble and fall away. "There's nothing more I can say."

While he stood alone, watching her, she went across the street to the townhouse. Each step she took carried her farther away from him. The bond they had created stretched to the point of breaking.

When the front door closed, he swallowed with regret, but there was nothing to swallow. His mouth was dry and scratchy as sand. He bit the inside of his cheek trying to summon a little saliva. Nothing. A sudden instinct engulfed him, as if the blazing roof he had rescued Charlotte from was about to crash down on his head.

68

Washington City, April 14, 1865

WHEN BRAHAM ARRIVED at Secretary Stanton's office in the War Department, the door was closed. A loud, unrecognizable voice could be heard through the walls. He heaved an impatient sigh, blowing air through pursed lips. Should he wait or go on to Seward's house? Stanton was the most powerful man in Washington, aside from the President, and he was also Braham's boss.

He decided to spend a few minutes here, and give his mind time to search the untidy cupboards in his brain for the information he'd read months ago in Jack's books about Lincoln. Large blocks of text simply remained unrecoverable, specifically, the exact sequence and time of the evening's events. This had never happened to him before. He blamed the unusual memory loss on the intensity of his shock when he read the account of the assassination. He had remembered Secretary Seward was attacked around the same time, but he couldn't recall if it happened before Lincoln was shot or afterwards.

The thrum of conversation in Stanton's office showed signs of strain and then went quiet. He would give the secretary five more minutes before he would have to leave for Seward's house. Braham lingered in front of the window, hands braced on each side of the frame, gazing out over the White House. A torchlight procession of employees from the Navy Yard was marching by singing "Rally

Round the Flag." He rocked to and fro on the balls of his feet, as if readying for a quick getaway.

Only a handful of people knew what was supposed to happen during the next few hours. Charlotte and Jack were back in his townhouse, while the others, a handful of conspirators, were moving into their places and preparing to attack. Braham took a deep breath, then gagged at the sour mixture of stale sweat, slightly tainted food, and remnants of an earlier celebration which fouled the air in the room. The odor hung like an unrelenting fog. Desperate for a clean breath of air, he fully raised the window and leaned out, gulping greedily.

He shoved fingers through his hair, and encountered the leather thong securing the queue at his nape. He ripped it out, leaving his hair loose around his shoulders. Before he left town on assignment, he would cut it, but he wouldn't do so while Charlotte still shared his bed. He enjoyed the sensation when she ran her fingers from scalp to ends. If he accomplished tonight what he intended, everything would change between them. When he arrived home, she'd be sequestered in her room, not waiting in his bed. He would never again hear her soft moans of pleasure.

The door to Stanton's office creaked open, and, low-voiced, the Secretary said, "He's rejected my resignation."

Hearing Stanton wanted to resign sent a small jolt through Braham. The Secretary couldn't quit. The President's reconstruction efforts would be hampered, if not stymied, without him. Stanton was a man of steel, unmoved by events or personal feelings. But beneath the hard exterior, he had a powerful and abiding respect for Lincoln. He must stay on as Secretary of War.

Braham picked up his hat and idly threaded the brim through his fingers—an illusion of calm he had perfected. The action was so mundane he appeared unconcerned and relaxed, when what he wanted to do was flare his nostrils and crack every one of his knuckles.

"He knows of your fragile health. Did he tell you why?" the visitor asked.

"He only said I cannot go," Stanton said.

The visitor approached the outside door and grasped the knob, swinging the door open to the creak of old hinges. "The President knows you understand the situation better than most. The country needs you." He reclaimed his walking stick from the cast iron stand and quit the room.

Stanton watched the door close then turned his attention to Braham. "Come in, Major." He picked up a quire of paper from his desk and held it out to him. "Here are two reports describing what happened in Richmond the night of the fires. Both are based on statements made by eyewitnesses. The President has requested a report. I need you to review these, and if you find errors, correct them."

"Will tomorrow—"

"Mr. Lincoln wants it on his desk in the morning. So make yourself comfortable."

The embers in the hearth broke apart with a soft *whuff,* and Braham let his breath out in a long sigh, shoulders slumping in capitulation. He settled into a chair in front of the desk, still warm from the visitor's body. He massaged his forehead, hoping to fend off a headache. Reliving the pain and trauma of the Richmond fires wasn't compatible with recovering the lost timeline and avoiding another headache. His only option was to read quickly, make a few notes, and get out of there. If he didn't save the President, it wouldn't matter what was on his desk in the morning.

Thirty minutes later, Braham had made the final notation on the last page of the second report when a cup of coffee was set on the table in front of him.

"Thought you might need this," Stanton said.

Braham stacked the papers together. "Thanks." He gulped some of the lukewarm coffee. "I've made a few comments in the margins. On the whole, their information is consistent with what I witnessed. Now, I must leave. I have correspondence from the President to deliver to the Secretary Seward."

"Go on then. He was tiring when I visited earlier."

"I haven't seen him since his stagecoach accident, but I heard he'll have a full recovery."

"In time," Stanton said.

The stress of Braham's delay caused a painful tightness in his neck and exacerbated his headache. He rarely had one, but since the beatings in Castle Thunder, he'd had them frequently, along with blurred vision. He took another swallow of coffee, then hurriedly left the building.

Seward lived in a three-story brick house facing Lafayette Park on Madison Place near Pennsylvania, only a short distance from Braham's townhouse. He checked his timepiece—nine-fifteen. It was still early, and there was time enough to get his horse before going to Seward's. He rushed over to his house, but went directly to the stables. Another confrontation with Charlotte would only delay him further.

The time was nine-thirty when he swung into the saddle for the short ride to Seward's residence. There, he dismounted and tied the reins to the hitching post. All was quiet except for the distant din of the Navy Yard employees' procession and the creaks and sighs of tall trees. A small twinge of unease escalated to a high pitch. Nothing was amiss, but the dark air seemed heavy with threat. He removed the cylinder from his .44 caliber Remington revolver, grabbed a new one from his pre-loaded cylinder pouch, and locked it into place.

The moon, two days past full, rose high over Washington. Under its clear, bright light, Braham scouted the perimeter of the house. At the back property line, he stopped and searched for clues to explain his unease. The dense smoke and intermittent bright sparks flying from the chimney in a shower of fireworks caught his attention, but nothing else.

Satisfied the outside of the residence was secure, he cautiously approached the front door, and put his ear to the dark wood, listening. He heard no scuffling or groans to indicate a fight was in progress, nor gunshots, nor screams. If the Secretary had already been attacked, there would be hysteria. And there wasn't any.

He rang the doorbell and waited, his revolver at the ready. The doorman, Mr. Bell, whom Braham had spoken to on previous visits, answered the door.

"Evening, Bell," Braham said, handing over his hat and gloves. "Is the Secretary awake? I have a message from the President."

"He's trying to sleep, Major, but he'd want the message. Miss Fanny and Sergeant Robinson are with him in his bedroom at the top of the stairs. Go on up."

Before ascending the stairs, Braham paused for a moment at the entrance to the drawing room. The gaslights had been turned down for the night, and the fire banked. An unusual stillness prevailed. He'd never been in the room when the Secretary wasn't sitting in his easy chair, surrounded by billowing smoke from his black cigar, swirling a drop of brandy in a glass while regaling his guests with comments about the day's events. Braham blinked and looked away, bringing himself back to his surveillance.

The scent of Magnolia blooms reached him from a vase on the table next to the staircase, but it wasn't the flowers which made his nose twitch. It was the aroma of fried chicken drifting in from the back of the house, reminding him he hadn't eaten since midday. Tomorrow there would be plenty of time to eat.

"Bell, the streets are crowded tonight with citizens celebrating Lee's surrender. They may find their way here to express their gratitude. Guard the door well. Don't let anyone else in."

"Been listening to the music, sir. If anyone comes by, I'll send them on their way," Bell said.

Braham pounded up the stairs, his boots striking the boards with dull thuds. His heart thumped as if he had run for miles. His hand went instinctively to the hilt of the saber clanking at his side. On the landing on the third floor, he met Frederick Seward coming out of one of the bedrooms.

"Evening, Major." Frederick glanced back into the room before closing the door, and said quietly. "Father's almost asleep."

"I have a message from the President, but it can probably wait until morning. No need to disturb him."

Fredrick, seeming ambivalent, raised his brow. He knew as well as Braham his father would want the message from Lincoln, but Frederick preferred his father's rest not be interrupted.

Secretary Seward took the decision out of his gatekeeper's hands, calling from the bedroom, "If it's Major McCabe, send him in, Fredrick."

"He doesn't want to miss any news. You better go in." Frederick shook his head, dark brows drawn together.

Braham hesitated before opening the door, making one last dash through his memory in hopes of deciphering the blurred time sequence, but came up blank. He stepped into the room, his eyes taking a moment to focus as they adjusted to the darkness. Here, too, the gaslights were turned low, and the bright glow from the hearth gave the room spotty, wavering illumination.

Fanny, the secretary's precocious daughter, sat on the far side of the bed reading. She glanced up and gave Braham a welcoming nod. He had had several enlightening conversations with her during dinner parties, and had found her to be both witty and intelligent. He couldn't help comparing her to Charlotte. Both were educated women, conversant in a wide range of subjects. But Charlotte had something Fanny didn't, something intangible and unidentifiable which hovered companionably in the back of his mind, tickling his subconscious and flooding him with a sense of peace. It was more than possible, once Charlotte left, he would never again feel settled in his life.

A sergeant, probably the night nurse, sat near the head of the bed, closest to the door. He stood, acknowledged Braham, and moved to the chair placed at the end of the bed, limping slightly.

"Good evening, Major. Has Secretary Stanton sent another soldier to guard my father?"

Braham tried to smile as he sat in the vacated chair, but his lips felt stiff, unbendable. "No, I bring a message from the President."

The secretary was swathed in bandages. His shoulder was heavily padded, where the head of the humerus had fractured in the carriage accident. His face was badly bruised and his jaw was also broken. "Read me the message," Seward whispered. The extensive metal splint he wore on his head restricted his movements and made speech difficult.

Braham opened the folded piece of paper and squinted in the dark. Fanny, sitting closest to the lamp, turned up the light, and he proceeded to read the news from Sherman.

"Excellent," Seward said. "With Sherman occupying Raleigh, Johnston will see the futility of further resistance. This victory should lead to a meeting between the two generals in the next few days."

Braham was far from relaxed, but forced himself to appear outwardly composed. He didn't want to alarm the secretary or Fanny. "Johnston won't like Sherman's terms of surrender."

"He'll have no choice," Seward said.

Raised voices outside Seward's room alerted Braham to possible danger.

"Frederick must be chasing a rat in the hall," Fanny said.

Braham quickly came to his feet. "I'll see what's going on. Stay here." He drew his revolver, held it flat against his back, and slowly opened the door. A tall, muscular man dressed in fine leather boots, black pants, and a jacket was arguing with Bell and Seward's son. It was Lewis Powell, and he held a small package wrapped with twine.

Braham remained still, but his muscles tightened in readiness. His finger quickly cooled against the steel of the trigger. "Is there a problem here?"

"I must see the Secretary now," the wide-eyed man said in a terse voice.

Braham couldn't come right out and shoot the assassin, but he could guard the door and keep him from entering. "He's asleep. Come back later."

Powell thrust out the package. "I have orders to deliver this medicine to the secretary and instruct him on how to take it."

"Tell me. I'll see the medicine is properly administered," Braham said.

Powell's hot impatience quickly turned into the cold stillness of a predator. "That's unacceptable."

Braham braced himself squarely in front of the bedroom door, the revolver still hidden. If the bastard tried to gain entrance, Braham would shoot him. "You're not getting in to see him. Not tonight."

Powell made a face as if he had heard wrong, and his voice held an even angrier edge when he said, "Step aside."

When Braham didn't move, Powell jerked up a knife and slashed, cutting Braham's forehead. Then, continuing in a downward arc, he stabbed it deeply into the Braham's shoulder. Braham dropped his gun, swaying slightly. Powell then threw a glancing blow to Braham's temple. Braham staggered backwards and fell to his knees with the hot trickle of blood dripping into his eyes. In spite of the screaming pain in his head and shoulder, Braham refused to lose focus.

Frederick threw himself at Powell, who pulled a revolver and placed it against the Secretary's son's head, immediately pulling the trigger. The gun misfired. Powell muttered an oath and smashed the revolver handle against Frederick's skull.

The door opened, and the nurse appeared. Powell stabbed the limping soldier repeatedly in his rush toward the bed.

Fanny screamed. "Don't kill him."

Wobbly and bleeding, Braham clutched the stair railing and hauled to his feet. Blood streamed down his face and shoulder. He swiped his arm across his forehead but couldn't staunch the flow. Bracing his injured right shoulder against the doorjamb, and grasping his revolver in his left hand, he took aim at Powell. Blood partly obscured his vision.

Fanny moved into the line of fire. Both Powell and Fanny appeared as wavy figures in a macabre scene. In the best of times, Braham could hit a target with his left hand, but this was closer to the worst of times. With limited vision and two innocent victims in an unpredictable welter, he wouldn't take the risk.

Gus, the Secretary's other son, rushed past him into the room and grabbed Powell from behind. Powell threw a blow to his rib cage, then slashed wildly, catching him on the head. Gus dropped, clutching his face.

Fanny threw herself across her father's body to protect him, and once again put herself in Braham's line of fire. Powell jumped onto the bed and raised the knife, aiming for the Secretary.

Braham lunged toward the assassin, grabbing Powell's knife-wielding arm. Using the broken revolver he still held in his other hand, Powell clubbed Braham's head. Braham reeled, head spinning, and his world pulsed into black. *If he passed out, the Secretary would die.* He lifted his hand and fired blindly at Powell. The explosion sundered the room. Powell lifted his arm and stabbed the Secretary, then kicked Braham in the chest before fleeing the room.

Woozy, Braham swayed as he climbed to his feet again, bleeding from shoulder and head. He stumbled after Powell, who rushed headlong down the stairs, where he continued the carnage by stabbing Emerick Hansell, a State Department messenger standing guard at the foot of the staircase.

Braham wiped the blood from his eyes, and barely able to see, fired again, hitting the window next to the door, shattering the glass. By the time he made it down the stairs and out the front door, Powell was galloping off. Braham planted his feet, braced his left arm against a lamp post, and pulled the trigger, missing the escaping assassin one last time.

Braham ripped off the bottom of his shirt and tied it around his forehead. Returning to the Secretary's bedroom, he found Seward's body on the floor with Fanny kneeling in a pool of blood next to him.

"Oh, my God. Father's dead, he's dead."

The vicious slash, stopped finally by the metal brace, had opened Seward's cheek, and the skin hung in a flap, exposing his teeth and fractured jawbone. Braham put his hand to Seward's neck and felt a rapid, thready pulse. The secretary still lived.

"I am not dead; send for a doctor, send for the police, close the house," the Secretary mumbled.

Relieved to know Seward yet survived, Braham said, "I'm afraid for the President. I'm going to the theatre."

Both Gus and Frederick climbed to their feet, slipping in the pools of blood.

Braham grabbed a towel off the washstand, rammed it into his coat, and pressed it against the shoulder, then he ripped a long strip from a clean sheet and made a sling for his arm. Satisfied he'd done the best he could for his injuries, he stumbled back down the stairs, leaving another set of bloody footprints.

He had to get to Ford's Theatre to protect the President. His right arm was numb and blood oozed down his coat sleeve and dripped off the tips of his fingers. It took three attempts to mount his horse. The reins were slippery from his blood-coated hand, and his bloody boot kept slipping out of the stirrups. If he could remain in the saddle and reach the theatre, he could warn someone. He galloped away like a crazed man, crossing the unpaved, wheel-gouged, muddy streets. Several times he almost fell off, but managed to keep his seat, grasping the reins and mane as he raced five blocks east and two blocks south to Ford's Theatre.

As Braham galloped down F Street, he could see an unruly, frenzied mob gathering at the corner of 10th Street. He slid off his horse and pushed his way through the crush of humanity, staggering toward the front of Ford's Theater.

"Guards, clear the passage. Guards, clear the passage." Bearers emerged from the vestibule with a small force of guards, shoving gawkers aside. A septet of men supported Lincoln, two at his shoulders, and others supporting his head, torso, pelvis, and legs. They carried him from the lobby, out the doors, and across the stone stairs. The crowd gasped at the sight.

"For God's sake, take him to the White House to die," someone yelled from the crowd.

Braham pushed his way through the half-insane mob and faced Doctor Leale, the army surgeon attending Lincoln. With eyes as steady as he could manage, Braham drew his sword from its scabbard and said: "Surgeon, give me your commands, and I'll see they're obeyed."

Yelling over the din Leale said, "Take him straight across the street and into the nearest house."

Braham fought his way forward, cutting a virtual seam through the mob. Halfway across the street, Leale halted the procession and yanked a blood clot from a hole in Lincoln's head, tossing the gooey mass into the street. Fresh blood and brain matter oozed from the doctor's fingers. Stranded, with nowhere to go, the President of United States was dying in the middle of a street surrounded by thousands of frenzied witnesses.

A man opened the front door of 454 Tenth Street, came out on a high, curved staircase, raised a sole candle, and shouted, "Bring him in here."

The somber bearers carried the President up the stairs and through the doorway, leaving the frantic crowd behind. Braham collapsed on the stairs, holding his saber in a shaking, bloody hand, pointing it at the mob. He had failed to protect his President from an assassin's bullet, but he was determined to protect Lincoln's final moments from the hungry rabble.

Braham closed his eyes and blackness overtook him.

69

Washington City, April 14, 1865

CHARLOTTE STOOD AT the window in Braham's drawing room, listening to the chattering and courting of the mockingbirds under the light of the full moon. The shutters were open, and cool air poured in, both chilly and soft, the way spring nights were meant to be. But this wasn't a normal spring evening. Edward had turned down the gaslights and banked the fires. The darkness didn't bother her, but a strange stillness, broken only by the singing birds perched in the leafing trees, did. The room's cool air stroked her arms, and the hairs rose quietly on her skin.

Jack had managed to procure two tickets to the production of *Our American Cousin* at Ford's Theatre, but she had adamantly refused to go. He, however, couldn't pass up the opportunity to be an eyewitness to one of the biggest events in United States history.

"Braham might succeed tonight," she had told Jack before he had left for the theatre.

"Either way, I'll still be an eyewitness to history."

Charlotte wanted to be as far away from the theater as possible. Jack was a writer; she was a doctor, and they had quite different perspectives on the evening's events. If she had been there and Braham failed to save Lincoln, she would rush to the mortally wounded President's side, and in the process earn a place in history—a woman from the future imprinted indelibly onto the past. In her heart she hoped Braham would succeed. How much her life would change when she returned to the twenty-first century didn't seem to matter right now. She let out the breath she had been holding in a sigh like the April wind. She checked the time on the mantle clock. Lincoln should be at the Petersen's house by now, brain dead.

Unless...

Her throat was sticky as glue. She turned away from the window, willing the tears pricking the backs of her eyes to stay where they were. Needing to loosen the pasty feeling in her throat, she tilted up her glass of whiskey and gulped. Fire trailed down her esophagus, but the alcohol did nothing to soothe the worry and sadness burdening her heart.

The window curtain fell back into place, and she walked over to refill her glass at the sideboard, but the clatter of carriage wheels and the jingle of harnesses pulled her back to the window. Jack, barely visible in the shadow of the gas streetlights, was helping a man out of the carriage. She watched, puzzled. Was the man drunk? When Jack moved out of the shadow, the light glinted off the man's blond hair, and she saw his blood-streaked face.

She ran toward the door, threw it open, and dashed down the front steps. Jack had propped Braham against the side of the carriage. Reaching him, Charlotte immediately checked his breathing, since his head hung limp. His breath warmed her check. She pressed her fingers against his neck to feel his carotid pulse—too fast and maybe a little weak, but palpable. Blood oozed from his forehead, and his jacket had a large, wet crimson stain.

"What happened? Has he been shot again?"

"I don't know." Jack grabbed Braham around his waist and lifted him over his shoulder. "He was unconscious when I found him." Jack rushed up the stairs and in the door, leaving behind a trail of blood.

Charlotte followed closely, suddenly missing her hospital, the efficiency of the ER, and the medical advances which could save Braham's life again. "Put him on the dining room table and get his clothes off. If there's active bleeding, put pressure on the wound. I'll get Edward and my bag." She ran down the hall, calling the butler.

He poked his head out of the kitchen. "Yes, ma'am."

"Braham's hurt. Jack's putting him in the dining room. I'll need clean cloths and boiling water." Charlotte ran up the stairs for her medical bag. On her way back down with her supplies, she patted her pocket, touching the brooch. Regardless of what Braham wanted, she refused to let him die.

Jack and Edward had Braham stripped to the waist. Blood saturated both his discarded shirt and jacket. He had a deep gash in his right shoulder, but there was no spurting vessel. She grabbed her stethoscope and checked his lungs. Sounds were shallow but equal on both sides. The knife probably had not punctured his lung, but she couldn't be sure with him lying down. She would listen again carefully when she could sit him up. His heart rate was fast but regular. His color was good; there was no active bleeding, and his blood pressure was low normal.

Satisfied he wasn't in any immediate danger, she turned her attention to the shoulder wound. A cut rotator cuff could impair the strength and use of his shoulder. For even a preliminary evaluation, he needed to be awake, and if the injury was serious, he'd require an orthopedic surgeon. Even after repair, it could be months before he had full use of his arm again.

The six-inch gash on his forehead was still oozing blood, but it was a bruise on the side of his head which made her recheck her pocket for the brooch. The impact was close to the site of his previous head trauma, which she suspected to be the cause of his frequent headaches. She opened each eyelid and brought a candle close. The pupils reacted. Good.

"How is he?" Jack's voice was jittery with worry and concern.

"He's stable. Heart and lungs seem okay. He's lost a fair amount of blood, but not enough to be life-threatening. I can't tell yet how much damage has been done to his shoulder, and he could well have a concussion."

"What can I do?" Jack asked.

"I need light, then hold him down. I'm going to examine his

shoulder wound for deep bleeders, and then sew up the shoulder and facial lacerations. If he wakes up, he's not going to like the pain I'll be causing him."

While Charlotte organized her surgery table, Edward set an armload of logs onto the brass dolphin andirons and stirred the glowing embers until the fire roared to life, bringing light and heat to the room. He hurriedly lit every candle he could find to supplement the light from the gas lit chandelier.

Charlotte sterilized the instruments and a small tray in a pot of water a house servant set on the fire.

"I need a bottle of whiskey," she said.

Jack grabbed a bottle and handed it to her. "Can't you wait until you fix him before you start drinking?"

"Remind me to laugh later. Now pour some over my hands and the wounds. I don't want to touch the bottle." She checked her instruments, which were cooling on the tray, needle and thread, the position of the lights, and Braham's blood pressure. "Hold the candle close."

Jack moved to the head of the table, holding the light.

Her examination of the shoulder injury revealed a three-centimeter puncture wound. "There're a couple of little vessels I need to tie off. There may be some functional damage, but I can't evaluate it right now. If he's lucky, his shoulder will heal with reasonable function. As soon as I close this, I'll work on his forehead."

Braham woke briefly in an agitated state. Charlotte hit a tender area, and he flung out his free arm, then passed out again. She talked to him to determine his level of cerebral function, but he only responded to pain.

"Do you need anything else, Miss Charlotte? Will the major recover?"

"Grab some pillows and blankets and put on a pot of coffee. And, yes, he'll recover. The major's like a cat, and he still has a few more lives left in him.

Edward left the room and returned shortly with a stack of linens.

Following on his heels, was one of the kitchen servants carrying in a tray of food and a carafe of steaming coffee. She set the tray on the sideboard with cups, plates, and silverware.

"A buffet in the operating room. A luxury I could get used to," Charlotte said.

An hour later, she had cleaned and tied off all the little bleeders she could find, and closed his wounds. The head wound had been more tedious to repair. It was a clean cut, but long and down to the bone. She had closed it in layers. Because the repair would be forever visible, she had taken care with each stitch.

Braham had barely stirred while she worked on his head, and it concerned her. To see if he would respond to pain, but with some reluctance, she pushed on his shoulder wound. He moaned and opened his eyes for a second.

"How'd this happen? Do you know?" she asked.

"No." Jack shook his head, looking sober. "I found him on the steps up to the Petersens' house with his saber in his hand, as if he was guarding the door. He was barely conscious."

"I saw him earlier this evening. He was on his way to the War Department and then to Seward's house. I bet he was knifed trying to protect the Secretary." She cut the last thread and set aside the needle.

"Nice job," Jack said. "You worked the old scar into the new one."

"I guess the assailant skimmed the knife across his forehead, then straight down into his shoulder." She had read the report of what happened at the Secretary's house in the history books. It had been a bloodbath. Had Braham's appearance changed the outcome? He shouldn't have been there, because he should have died at Chimborazo. Maybe the Secretary's injuries weren't as bad as they would have been.

"Let's try to get him to sit up and open his eyes. See if he can swallow a sip of water. If he can, I need you to get the mortar and pestle from my bag and crush two Keflex and two Aleve. We'll have him swallow the drugs mixed with a bit of water."

"Is he going to be okay?" Jack asked.

"He's been on an antibiotic since Richmond, so he shouldn't get an infection. If his brain recovers, yes, he'll be okay."

"Does this mean you plan to stay for a while?"

"Only until I'm sure he's on the mend. I have to get back. I have a medical practice which might disappear if I stay away much longer. Let's see how he is in a couple of days."

With Jack's help, they brought him to a sitting position. Braham grimaced, and his eyelids fluttered. She brought a glass to his mouth and tipped in some water. "Braham, swallow." He did, and the action warmed the chill in the pit of her stomach, but only by a degree or two.

"Get the mortar and pestle and start crushing," she said.

Jack dug the ceramic bowl out of her bag, dropped in the pills, and used the pestle to crush the medicine into powder. "He's been shot, tortured, caught in a fire, and now stabbed. His body can't take much more."

He'd also had several sleepless nights in bed with her. "Occasionally people who suffer concussions lose their memories. This memory might be a good one to lose. Will you check the newspapers tomorrow and see what you can find out?"

Before laying Braham back down, they gave him the medicine mixed with a sip of water. Then, very carefully, they shifted him to pad the table for comfort and elevated his head on goose down pillows to decrease the intracranial pressure. He groaned but didn't open his eyes again.

"I'll sit up with him. Why don't you go rest?" Jack said.

"No. These first few hours are critical. I want to be close by to check his level of consciousness hourly." She shrugged against an almost staggering feeling of helplessness. "There isn't much I can do if he starts to deteriorate."

"If it happens, I won't object to you taking him to the hospital."

"It might be too late."

Jack screwed up his nose as he peered intently into Braham's face. "He doesn't want to go."

She unfolded a quilt and pulled it up over Braham, tugging it to his chin. Had she done everything she could for him? She rubbed a finger between her brows, mentally rewinding the tape of the last hour, then playing it again. Yes, she had. Satisfied, she straightened the creases in the blanket, tucking it neatly under his sides. "Let's see how he does over the next hour."

"Do you want me to move a sofa in here so you can stretch out?" Jack asked.

"It would be more comfortable, thanks." She blew out the extra candles and turned down the gaslights. In the dimness Braham was no more than a dark shape on the table, his breathing slow and hoarse.

Edward and Jack pulled the sofa into the dining room. With cups of coffee in hand, she and Jack eased back against the cushions as quiet descended into the room.

After several minutes, Jack said, "He's a fine man."

"Fine and stubborn."

Jack tilted his head to one side, eyes narrowing. "You're in love in with him, and he's in love with you, but you won't stay, and he won't leave."

"It's hard to imagine never seeing him again."

"After all you've been through," Jack said.

"I'd rather not dwell on it. Let's get him well first."

They sat there listening to Braham's breathing and the crackling fire.

Jack interrupted the silence by clearing his throat. His voice shook slightly when he said, "It was horrible."

Sleep was encroaching on her consciousness, but she heard him speak and jerked upright, shaking herself hard. "What?"

"What happened at the theatre was horrible."

She reached for him, and his arm was tense beneath her hand. He shied away, not wanting to be touched.

"I never imagined it would be…well, like that. I was focused on the play, waiting for the lines Booth believed would produce the most uproarious laughter from the audience and cover the noise of the shot. *'Don't know the manners of good society, eh? Wal, I guess I know enough to turn you inside out, old gal...'*

"When I heard the lines spoken from the stage, something clicked inside me, and I had what I could only describe as an out of body experience. I was there, but I wasn't."

Jack turned away from her, and his eyes fixed somewhere beyond the room, inward probably, where he wouldn't have to share his thoughts or emotions with her. Tonight she wouldn't intrude, would simply give him room to say what he needed to say. She didn't move except to breathe more deeply and hide her knotted fists within the folds of her skirt.

"Lincoln never knew what happened to him. His head dropped forward; his chin hit his chest, and he sagged against the upholstered rocking chair. It didn't sound anything like twenty-first century gunfire. It was more of a *poof* that echoed to the ceiling, and to the stage, and then reverberated through the theatre. No one moved. People weren't sure at first whether it was part of the production, or a celebration, or what.

"Major Rathbone was the first to realize something was wrong. I was sitting close by and had been watching for his reaction. He glanced up, so did I. The smoke from the pistol swirled in front of the gaslights, and gave the crimson upholstery and wallpaper in the box a devilish glow. Booth looked like a demon. His face seemed ghostly against the black of his clothes and hair and moustache. In his right hand he brandished a big knife—bright as a diamond in the stage lights—as he leaped from the box onto the stage.

"I was the only person there who had read the script and knew the storyline. It all happened as history recorded, and everyone played their roles perfectly." Jack's voice fell to an anguished whisper. "Only it wasn't a play. It was real...and the bastard killed one of greatest and finest men who ever lived."

Jack bunched his fists up so tightly they turned white, and the veins throbbed from fingertips to forearm. His eyes closed for a moment to keep her from seeing in too far.

"What happened then?" she asked.

"From the moment of the gunshot to Booth vanishing into the wings, no one in the audience moved. Some gasped; others thought it was part of the play. Major Rathbone shouted, *'Will no one stop that man?'* and then the actress Clara Harris cried out, *'He has shot the President.'*

"Then fifteen hundred people went wild. Some men climbed up on the stage; women fainted, and half-crazed voices shouted to kill the murderer, but by then Booth had left the building."

Jack paused, drinking his coffee.

"What'd you do then? How'd you find Braham?"

Jack looked at her; his eyes searched her face, as if her features held important answers. "Panic erupted, and people shoved each other to get out. I stood there, unable to move. Finally I made my way to the lobby and ended up following behind the bearers who carried Lincoln's body across the street. I kept waiting for the police to rush in and impose order, but they never came. Lincoln almost died in the middle of a dirt street surrounded by a frenzied mob."

Jack didn't move; he merely intensified his stare. "It was real, sis. Not a goddamn reenactment, or a movie, but real."

The anguish on his face made her heart slam against her ribs. She opened her arms, and he fell into them, hugging her tightly. Tears dampened her shoulder as he poured out the fathomless grief of a man who had grown up honoring a marble sculpture until at last he grew to love the man who had inspired it.

Charlotte wasn't the only one who would bear the emotional scars of this trip back in time. These new wounds would be indelibly etched on the whole of Jack's being.

70

Washington City, April 15, 1865

C HARLOTTE RECLINED ON the sofa next to the dining room
table, grateful for the morning sun's warmth and light, while
she reviewed the chart of Braham's vital signs and medication. She
chewed her lower lip as she considered what to do next. During the
night, after Jack had fallen asleep, Braham's agitation had increased,
and she hadn't been able to calm him.

As a last resort, she had climbed up on the table and lain next to
him with her hand on his chest keeping track of the rise and fall of
each breath. She had kissed his lips, cradled his head against her
breasts, smoothed his tousled hair back from his face, and whispered
the words of her heart. Words he would never remember, but they
had calmed him nonetheless. The warmth of his body seeped
through her clothes, dispelling the chill of the night, but not the chill
of their upcoming separation.

He had not been fully awake since Jack brought him home hours
earlier. He had moaned, and sipped water laced with medication, but
he hadn't fully opened his eyes, or followed basic instructions other
than to drink what was offered. She fluffed the pillows and edged
smaller ones beneath his neck and back. She yawned, stretching. The
night had been very long, and she hadn't slept.

Midmorning rays came low through the trees, spilling through
the windows and making shifting leaf patterns on the dining room
walls. The front door opened and footsteps, quick and solid,

thumped the oak floorboards. A minute later, Jack entered the dining room. "How's the patient?"

"His vitals are good; he doesn't have a fever, but he's still not responding as he should. I'm considering—"

"I know what you're thinking, and don't waste your brain cells." Jack plopped down on the sofa and crossed his hands behind his head. "I considered it earlier, and said only if his life was in danger, and it's not now. Right?"

"But he needs to be seen by a neurologist."

"Why? Do you think he has brain damage?" The muscles in Jack's neck knotted. It obviously cost him a lot to ask the question, even more to wait for the answer.

"There's no way to tell until he wakes up."

"Can't you look in his eyes or something?" Jack voice grated past his throat.

"It doesn't work that way." She pressed her hand on his arm in warning and then said in a low voice, "I can't tell if this is exhaustion, a concussion, or neurological deficit. Some people in comas remember conversations. I don't know if Braham is listening to us or not, so let's keep our voices down."

Jack ran his hand through his hair, creating furrows. "Sure, no problem. It's just…"

"I know. I'm tired, too." Moving slowly, she came to her feet, her joints protesting loudly. She pressed her hands on her lower back and stretched. For the last several hours, she'd sat at the table next to Braham, watching him breathe, stroking his face, holding his hand, letting him know he wasn't alone. "What's the news on the street?" she asked.

"I saw Gordon at the War Department. Saw him outside the theatre last night, too. You know the expression, *if looks could kill?* Well, it's how he glared at me. Creepy."

The hairs prickled on her arms, and she shuddered. It was one of those uncontrollable shudders, according to old wives' tales, caused by footsteps walking over her future grave. "You didn't say anything to him, did you?"

"No, I nodded politely and moved on."

"Good, because he scares me. I'm surprised he hasn't challenged you to a duel."

"If he could get away with it, he probably would."

"So, what other news do you have?"

Jack removed his journal from his pocket and opened it to a page about halfway through. "The city's agitated and there's a spirit of revenge. At the New York Avenue Presbyterian Church, the President's pew was draped in black. Stanton has called Grant back to Washington to defend the city. Johnson's been sworn in, but Stanton's in charge. The manhunt for Booth has been going on for hours. Stanton believes there was a conspiracy planned in March, and the Confederacy might be involved. Lincoln took his last breath at seven-twenty-two this morning. Mrs. Lincoln returned to the White House about nine o'clock. I saw them carry the body into the White House in a crude, improvised coffin. It looked like a shipping crate. But you know," Jack paused and tapped the tip of his pencil against his teeth. "Lincoln wouldn't have cared. It was the roughly-hewn coffin of a rail-splitter. There were no bands, no drums, no trumpets, only the cadence of horses' hooves."

"Sounds like you have a story to write."

"Not me. This story will be well documented without my two cents." He glanced up at Charlotte, blinking slightly. "I'm ready to go home."

"It's time you both left," Braham said in a raspy voice.

Mouth agape, she whirled around to face her patient. Jack jumped to his feet and rushed to the table. "You're awake," they said in unison.

He seemed to want to say something more, but couldn't decide what. His mouth opened, but nothing came out for a moment or two. Then, in a hoarse voice he said, "It's over now. Go home."

The coldness in his voice sent shivers from her nape to her tailbone. "We'll talk about it when you're up and moving around."

"I'm getting up," he said. "Where's Edward?"

Edward entered the room so quickly he must have been sitting by the door waiting. "I'm here, sir."

Braham rolled over onto his left side, hissing between his teeth. "Help me up. I want a bath and a shave."

Charlotte got out of Edward's way, swallowing a lump of relief. "You have stitches in your forehead and right shoulder. A bath would do you good, but keep the area around the stitches dry."

She stood at the bottom of the stairs and gritted her teeth as she watched Braham shuffle up, one slow step at a time. When he disappeared onto the landing, she returned to the dining room.

"Do patients always wake up so grumpy?" Jack asked.

"On the crotchety side, but he wasn't so bad. Some patients wake up swinging. I think he woke up remembering what happened and didn't want to talk about it."

"I don't blame him. For months he's been focused on one goal, and he failed. I wouldn't be happy either."

"History survived, and if he thinks we're happy because he didn't prevent the assassination, he's dead wrong. Last night I wanted him to succeed," she said.

Carefully, she wrapped the mortar and pestle in velvet and placed the pieces in her bag next to the pill containers, and then she fastened the clasp, letting her fingers rest on the handle. "If he's going to shut us out, there's no point in staying any longer."

Jack put his arm around her. "We're not going to rush off. You two need to settle things between you."

She leaned into him, sighing. "Why don't you go up and help him? He might be interested in hearing the news."

Jack gave her a squeeze. "I'll do it, but you need sleep. If you're going to make decisions in the next few hours, you need to be rested. You don't want to leave here with regrets."

No, she didn't, but it was impossible not to. Of course, she would have regrets. She pressed her hand on her lower belly. There was one thing which could make leaving him more bearable, but even if it happened, it would never be a substitute for her soldier's love.

71

Washington City, April, 1865

EVERY FEW HOURS Charlotte either knocked or rattled the doorknob or stomped noisily back and forth in front of Braham's locked bedroom, but he refused to talk to her or let her come in. After the second day, Jack gave her a trumpet, very tongue-and-cheekish, and said, "Blow this for six days. On the seventh day, the door should fall flat."

She closed her eyes, exasperated, blew hot air into the mouthpiece, and then shoved the damn instrument against his chest. "You blow it." She had then nodded smartly, turned on her heels, and left…only to return a few hours later and rattle the doorknob again.

At night she sat on the floor with her back propped against his door. She'd roll skeins of yarn she would never use into perfectly shaped spheres while she talked to Braham about random events in her life and travels through Europe and Asia with Jack. The clink of bottle against crystal told her he was awake. Did he hear her? She didn't know, but occasional footfalls near the door made her believe he did. Otherwise, she had no real sense of what he was doing, other than grieving and avoiding company.

Whenever she knocked and pounded, pleading with him to let her in, he yelled at her to leave him alone. Her patience had worn as thin as the line she tried not to cross. He didn't owe her anything. She was a guest in his home, and if he preferred she didn't change his dressings or share his grief, she couldn't very well have him arrested or committed to an asylum, although it was tempting.

Tuesday following the assassination was a warm day, and a spring breeze fluttered the curtains framing the windows in her bedroom. In spite of the warmth, gooseflesh rippled up her arms while she considered what to do next.

If Braham wouldn't talk to her, she might as well go home. Would he even care? Maybe not, but she would. She wanted to see him before she left, partly to check his wounds, but mostly to say goodbye. Short of blasting a hole in the wall, gaining entry was unlikely. Frustrated, she snatched up a pair of boots and pretended they were grenades, lobbing them one by one against their adjoining bedroom walls.

"Great." She didn't blast a hole to climb through, but her bad aim had lodged one of the boots between the wall and the wardrobe. Grunting, she pushed against the oversized piece of furniture, but it wouldn't budge.

"I'm going to the White House. Lincoln is lying in state in the East Room. Do you want to come?"

She glanced around to see her brother loitering in the doorway, his jacket slung over his shoulder and hanging by two fingers. "Yes. When's the funeral?"

"Tomorrow, but it's limited to six hundred people. We can't get in, but I'm sure Braham's on the approved list."

She stopped pushing and leaned against the side of the chest, gasping. "Do you think he'll go?"

"He should, but he'll have to come out of seclusion." The lines of Jack's face cut deep and weariness shadowed his eyes. He took a slow breath and moved his shoulders a bit, as though his necktie was too tight. "By the way, what are you doing?"

She pushed against the wardrobe again, giving it all she had. "What does it look like?"

"Taking your frustration out on a six-foot-high mahogany wardrobe."

She pushed harder on the side of the massive piece of furniture. "Well, I'm not. I'm saving the physical violence for when I get my hands on a particular Union major. Come here and help me. I can't reach my shoe."

He idled in and dropped his jacket onto a chair. "How'd it get back there?"

She fixed him with a direct look. "I threw it against the wall and it bounced."

"I won't ask why."

She stood aside, brushing dust from her hands. "I was pretending it was a grenade." He grabbed the back corner of the chest and pulled, barely straining against the weight. She bent to reach for the shoe. Her fingertips brushed against the heel at the same time she spotted the frame to a door. She blinked, so surprised she couldn't immediately translate the appearance of the door into the significance of its presence. A moment passed, and then she let out a sort of unhinged giggle. "There's a door back here. Push this monstrosity further from the wall."

Jack pulled the piece of furniture out several more feet, leaving a wide gap between the wall and the wardrobe. "I doubt it's a closet. Must be a connecting door to Braham's room."

"If it's unlocked, I can get in to talk to him."

Jack held out of his arm, blocking her way. "Wait a minute. You can't go barging in there uninvited."

She ducked and skirted past him. "Of course I can. I do it every day. If I waited for patients to be ready to see me, I'd waste half my day. I simply enter, and avert my eyes if they're on the commode."

There was a ghost of a smile on Jack's face, although his eyes were dark with concern. "If we go in there, he'll probably have us thrown out."

She gave a brief snort, the verbal equivalent of a shrug. "I don't care. After I change the dressings, he can toss us out, and lock this door, too. We're going home anyway." She took a breath, placed her hand on the doorknob, turned it, and pulled gently. The breath she had held blew out in a rush as she pulled the door open wider. It didn't creak.

A heavy red velvet curtain hung over the doorway, probably to keep heat from escaping either of the rooms by way of the passage. She slipped the back of her hand between the door facing and the edge of the drape, fanned the curtain out of the way, and tucked the bunched fabric into a brass holdback. The dark, tomb-like room reeked of whiskey, sweat, and cigar smoke. She shook her head to clear it and looked up to find Jack's eyes on her, no longer dark, but blue and vivid. He, too, understood at once the complexity and dangers of Braham's use of alcohol to battle depression.

The sunlight gleaming in from her window cast a long beam of golden light into the dimness of Braham's room. The light illuminated several plates filled with half-eaten food, as well as empty whiskey bottles, and discarded clothes. A small, uneasy feeling darted down the back of her neck. She sniffed, but didn't smell rot, or worse.

"Go away. Why are you in here?" Braham's slurred speech was raspy from whiskey and smoking.

She didn't bother answering; it was a rhetorical question anyway.

"Stoke the fire," she said to Jack. "I'll open the drapes and windows and let in some fresh air."

"Leave me alone. I don't want you here." Something hit the floor with a thud. "I need another bottle. *Edward.*"

Jack threw on some kindling and poked the fire. Light sprang up, wavering in swaths of shadow and light over the plaster walls, and the chill quickly dissipated.

Charlotte pulled open the drapes, then went over to the other door and threw back the bolt. "Edward." Within seconds, the butler was standing in the room, holding two bottles of whiskey. "This can't go on. No more alcohol. Draw him a bath, clean up this mess, and bring him his favorite foods. He needs something solid in his stomach."

Within minutes, servants were moving about the room, picking up soiled clothes and empty bottles. Braham slouched in an armchair with his shirt unbuttoned down to the mat of hair on his chest. Unkempt and puffy-eyed, he let his head loll to the side. "Get out, all of you. Leave me alone."

Charlotte bent over him, pressed her hands on the arms of the chair and dug her fingers into the upholstery. "I didn't save you from Chimborazo to see you waste away like this."

"I didn't ask you to save me."

"No, you didn't, but a man who loved you very much asked me to do it."

Braham glared at her and the rhythm of the pulse in his throat closely matched the pounding of her heartbeat. "I failed to do the same for him."

"Your failure, if it's what you want to call it, grants him immortality." From the corner of her eye, she caught the movement of his hand as it inched down into the side of the seat cushion. Thinking he might have hidden a flask of alcohol, she pushed his hand aside and dug her fingers into the crevice. When her hand brushed the smooth-finished grip of a revolver, she jerked upright, gasping with a hot flash of shock, and then she slapped him across his whiskered jaw. His head popped up, and he shot her an affronted glare, clutching the side of his face, red with her handprint from chin to cheekbone.

She snatched up the revolver and held it by thumb and forefinger. "Take this," she said to Jack. "And check the room. See if there are any other weapons. He's not going to blow a hole in his head while I'm here."

"Get out." Braham clenched his teeth and waved a shaking arm. He swallowed hard and visibly. "I don't want you here."

"Right now, I don't give a damn what you want. You're going to have a bath and dinner and when you're sober, we're going to talk. When we've finished, Jack and I will get out of your life."

Braham was not the same man she had witness struggle to get to his feet in the cell at Castle Thunder. That man had the will to live. The man sitting in front of her now, crumbling in grief, had simply given up.

The crackle and roar of the fire interrupted the room's charged silence as one log splintered and exposed another piece of wood to the flame. The aroma of burning hickory quickly displaced the pungent odors in the room.

Braham eyed her narrowly through bloodshot eyes. Most of his hair had escaped the thong and dirty blond tangles fell around his shoulders, reeking of whiskey and smoke. "Where's my whiskey?"

She squinted and rubbed her face, trying to think how best to help him. He didn't need the skills of a surgeon or the passion of a lover. "Coffee. No more alcohol."

Jack squeezed in, gently pushing her aside. "Go on. Let me take care of him."

"But I need to check his—"

"Later—"

Their words collided, and they stared at each other, waiting to see whose glare would win. "Give us some time to talk. It's a guy thing," he said.

She nodded. "Okay."

With a heavy heart, she returned to her room, where she sat in the window seat looking out over the city draped in black. Braham's shouts blasted through the velvet-draped doorway. As the hours wore on, he stopped slurring and his voice softened.

When she hadn't heard voices for some time, she peeked into the room to check on them. The men sat in front of the fire. Plates covered with discarded white napkins sat on a tray nearby, and they held steaming cups of coffee. From where she hovered, she couldn't make out their murmured conversation, but from the chuckling, she knew Jack had accomplished what she couldn't. Quietly retreating from the doorway, she curled up on the settee in her bedroom and closed her eyes.

Later, it might have been minutes or hours, she woke suddenly, listening in the dark. No one had turned the gaslights on, and the fire was cold on the hearth. She stirred, shivering slightly beneath a heavy quilt.

"I've been waiting for you to awaken."

She unearthed herself from the covers and came quickly to her feet. "Why didn't you wake me?"

"I wanted to watch you sleep and listen to you breathe."

Her eyes took a moment to adjust to the duskiness, and then she blinked hard when his dark form, sitting in a wing chair next to the dying embers in the hearth, took shape. "How's your shoulder?"

"Jack said the wounds are healing fine. No red streaks."

She turned up the gaslight and studied him closely, seeing the same emotions on his face she knew were on hers, relief and regret. It was impossible to say which one ranked above the other. "Good."

"I'm leaving soon, and I wanted to apologize for my transgressions."

She pulled up a stool and sat next to his chair, breathing in the scent of him, musk and soap and the polish Edward used to shine the brass buttons on his uniform. "Are you going to lump them all together in one big apology or enumerate them?"

He chuckled, almost soundlessly. "There're several."

"Like stealing my car?"

"That one I'll never forget."

Her lips tightened at the memory of how frightened she'd been when she realized he'd taken her car. Abraham McCabe was a man of many talents.

"I'd best enumerate them so you can remind me if I forget one. Let's see, stealing your car, lying to you, putting your life in danger." He paused and reached for her hand, linking their fingers. His large palm, textured with calluses, and both warm and hard, pressed against hers. Dark bronze skin covered the corded tendons on the backs of his hands, which she traced lightly with her fingertips.

"I never should have taken you to bed when I couldn't offer you a future. But you handed me your heart and body and trusted me not to forsake you. Now I'm doing it anyway. I knew this moment would come, and I feared it more than any battle. You're taking my heart with you, lass."

Then he looked at her, giving her a small smile, but with such pain in his eyes she caught her breath, stricken through to her bones. Drawn to him, she slipped off the stool, knelt between his legs, and placed her hands on his cheeks. His face was warm, and the lushness of his beard stubble was both soft and scratchy. His wide, sweet mouth met hers in a kiss. She closed her eyes against the sting of tears and pressed her lips against the soft, warm flesh of his mouth.

"And you're keeping my heart with you." She lowered her head, and pressed her cheek against his chest, and her tears dampened his jacket.

The door opened, and Jack entered. "It's time to go, sis." He came to stand next to the chair. He laid one hand on Braham's shoulder and placed his other under Charlotte's elbow, lifting her to her feet. "I packed your medical bag."

Charlotte held up her hand to still her brother as she felt Braham slip something into the hand he'd been holding. She opened it to find the perfect sapphire ring he'd given her at Georgetown. And she'd chosen to leave it behind. Shaking her head and swallowing hard, she tried to hand it back.

"I won't take it back," he said. "I want you to wear it so you'll remember me."

Gently she took Braham's hand, placed the ring in his palm, and tucked his beautiful, masculine fingers around it. "I don't need a ring to help me remember you."

The light in the room dimmed almost as if someone had turned down the gaslight, but it wasn't the room which had darkened, nor was it a fire which choked the air with smoke. It was her heart and lungs straining for blood and breath, and her eyes brimming with the tears clouding her vision. She trudged toward the door, believing her heart would crumble into a thousand awkward pieces and crunch beneath her feet.

"*Charlotte.*" Braham came quickly to his feet and pulled her to him, kissing her hard enough to leave a trace of blood in her mouth. Then he whispered so she felt the words as much as heard them. "I'll never forget ye'. Go now, before I canna' let ye' leave."

Jack took her hand and led her through the doorway. She glanced back to see Braham in silhouette, his hair glinting off a beam of moonlight streaming through the window. He turned slightly, and she gasped.

Her shoulders began to quiver with repressed sobs. His long hair would never again trickle across her breasts like the sweetest of lover's touches. Never again would she smooth the long golden strands behind his ear. Now she saw him in profile, she could see what she hadn't noticed before. She had thought he had bound his hair in a tail, but she was wrong. He had cut it.

Jack pressed the brooch and tweezers into her hand. "When you're ready, let's go home."

Part Three

"The best thing about the future is that it comes one day at a time."

—Abraham Lincoln

72

Richmond, Virginia, Present Day

CHARLOTTE SPENT THE next few days in a twilight sleep. Going through the motions necessary to sustain life, but not living it. Numb to everything but her pain. Decisions took effort, so she didn't make any.

In twenty-first century time, she and Jack had been gone only two months, leaving her with four months of sabbatical time still available. When she could think clearly, she'd make a decision about when she wanted to return to work.

Food wasn't easy to swallow. Bitter or sweet, tangy or salty, hot or cold—everything had the bland indigestibility of cardboard. She ate only enough to keep her stomach settled. Even putting on her shoes to go running exhausted her, so she quit lacing them up and left them in a pile on the floor with her other running gear.

Sleeping, however, came as easily as closing her eyes, but only during the day. At night, she cuddled up on the chaise lounge on her screened-in porch and stared into the starlit sky. She withdrew to a place where she could control what was happening to her by refusing to think or feel. Grief, as she'd discovered as a teenager, was not easy to live with.

Whenever Jack called she lied and told him she'd been eating well and exercising, and he'd respond with a snort. He didn't believe her, but he'd probably decided, since she was a health nut and exercise junkie, she'd eventually find her way back from her depression. He wouldn't let her drag it out for long. If she didn't come out of this on her own, he'd intervene, and they'd do something completely random, like a quick trip to London or the Caribbean or Alaska.

A picture on the bulletin board in the kitchen of her and Jack at the family's oceanfront cottage on Hilton Head Island became the impetus to kick-start her recovery. She needed the ocean, the ebb and flow of the tide—sometimes soft and gentle, and sometimes furious. If any place could soothe her and restore her connection to life again, surf and sand had the best chance.

Jack was meeting in L.A. with his agent and two movie producers and wouldn't be home for several days. If glowing sunrises, lazy afternoons, and al fresco suppers at the Inn down the street from the cottage wouldn't snap her out of her funk, she'd need his intervention.

On the sixth day following her return from the past, she loaded her car and drove to the island. Jack had shuttered the cottage for the winter and the house needed a good airing. She threw open the windows and left for the market. When she returned, a cool sea breeze had filled the rooms with the tangy scent of salt and the promise of healing.

She changed into shorts and T-shirt and went out on the back deck with a basket of medical journals, her cell phone, and iPad. It was a gorgeous day for early March: high-sixties and a light breeze, goosebumply cool, but the sun warmed her face.

Her phone rang. She dug it out of the basket, frowning. If Jack was calling instead of texting, something was wrong. "What's happened? Are you in the hospital?"

"No. I'm just tired." The reply was casual, but there was something odd in his voice, off-key. "The producers are requesting changes to the proposal."

"If you make them will they option your story?"

"They might, but I can't find my journal. Did I leave it in your bag? Where are you, anyway?"

Charlotte stretched out on the cushioned lounge chair and wiggled her toes, admiring their trimmed, polished pinkness. "I'm at the island. I stuck the bag in my clothes closet when I got home and never opened it. Go over there and look. Check my mail, too."

"I'm taking a red-eye tonight. I'll go over there tomorrow. I don't remember packing it in your bag, but it's the only place it could be."

"Maybe you left it at…" By unspoken agreement, they hadn't mentioned Braham's name. It didn't mean she hadn't thought about him. She had, constantly. She just couldn't talk about him. "Maybe you left it behind."

"If I did, I've lost six months of irreplaceable research, and if anyone reads it, the stock market could be impacted for the next hundred years. I've got to find it."

"I'm sure it's in my bag. You wouldn't have left it behind." She slipped on her sunglasses and hat and stacked the magazines on the table next to the chair. "I wish you'd come to the island. The weather is decent for early spring."

"How long are you staying?"

"If you won't come down, then I'll come home Friday. It's lonely here by myself."

"Come out to the mansion, and I'll grill steaks. Do you want to invite Ken? You promised him a full report when you got back."

"No, I'm not ready to talk yet."

"I'll see you at the house Friday night about seven-thirty. We'll sit out on the portico, watch the sunset over the river, and drink a bottle of the Australian wine you like. Be sure to text when you leave the island."

"Where's the cat?" she asked.

"Curled up on my bed or catching mice in the barn. Ciao."

By Friday, the tightness in her chest since leaving the nineteenth century finally loosened, and she could breathe without it catching on the lump in her throat. However, more than once she had found herself staring at her finger and visualizing the missing sapphire ring. She would always miss Braham, but she was strong enough to get on with her life. Teary moments would come, but they were simply part of her new reality.

After a cup of strong, black coffee, Charlotte laced up her running shoes and headed to the beach for a five-mile run before she drove home. Somewhere around mile two or three she made the decision to call the hospital on Monday. She needed to work and lose herself in caring for others instead of worrying about herself and a man she would never see again.

She closed up the house and packed the car for the six-hour drive back to Richmond. Before getting on the road, she stopped at Starbucks, ordered a banana smoothie, and while waiting for it, sent Jack a text, but he never responded. Halfway home, she stopped and sent another text. He didn't respond to it either. Shortly before she reached Richmond, she called. The call went straight to voicemail. He could have gone back to L.A., but he would have told her. Regardless of where he was in the world, he might not take her call, but he'd always answer her texts.

Instead of driving directly home, she decided to stop at Jack's condo. The doorman in his building would know if Jack had gone out of town. She parked and took the elevator to the ground level, magnificent with its polished chrome finishes, shiny glass windows, and Italian marble floor. To her, the building was cold and impersonal, but it fit Jack's taste for everything modern from art to fixtures, while she preferred subdued colors and early American antiques.

The doorman wasn't at his desk. He'd probably stepped away to see to the needs of a tenant. She'd wait a few minutes. As she waited, leaning on the counter, she watched the security monitors. There were six: one spied on the exercise room, another the parking garage, one in each of two elevators, the front door, and the playroom. While her eyes were glued to the screens, the doorman returned to his station.

"Hello, Doctor Mallory. Hope you haven't been waiting long."

"Hi Frank. I just arrived. Have you seen Jack? He's not answering his phone."

Frank plopped his right butt cheek on the edge of a high stool behind the counter, raised his eyebrows, and studied the ceiling. "Hmm. Don't think I've seen him since yesterday afternoon. He went out and never came back while I was on duty. But let me check the log." He thumbed through several sheets of paper attached to a clipboard. "There's nothing here."

"Doesn't he always tell the desk when he's going out of town?"

"I've worked here ten years and Jack has always notified the desk even it's a…you know…overnight situation," Frank said, looking at her with one eyebrow raised.

"He said he'd cook dinner tonight."

"We haven't gotten a grocery delivery for him, and he always has an order delivered from the market when he's cooking for company. I'm sorry, Doctor Mallory. Looks like he's MIA."

"Great," she said. "I'm worried and hungry. I'll go upstairs and look around. Maybe he left a note."

She took the elevator to the tenth floor and walked down the long corridor toward his unit. Other than trips to the mountains to write in seclusion, he was always available. He might have caught a plane and flown back to California, but even then he would have called or texted prior to boarding.

She unlocked the door and walked in, sniffing. No mouthwatering, tempting smells wafted from the gourmet kitchen he had personally designed to accommodate his passion for cooking. Thank goodness at least one of them had gotten the gourmet chef gene. She couldn't cook soup in the microwave without it boiling over.

A jade carving of a cat with its legs tucked tightly under its body sat on the table inside the door. She dropped her clutch and keys and picked up the antique. "Well, well, so Jack finally got a pet." She turned it upside down and around. "You're beautiful. And you don't shed. Exactly what he needs." The first question Jack asked every girl who tried to ask him out was do you have a house pet? If she said yes, he said no thank you.

Charlotte placed the cat carefully back on the table and patted its head.

"Jack, are you here?" Calling out wasn't necessary. She'd already sensed his absence in the coolness of the room.

The view of the James River from the wall of windows in the living room brought her to a standstill as it did every time she stepped into Jack's home. In all of Richmond, his unit probably had the best view of the river. The corner office had views of both the river and the city. He had paid a premium price for it, but the view was worth the extra money.

On top of the glass desk sat his MacBook Air and half a cup of day-old coffee, along with a notepad and pen. Something seemed very wrong, but she couldn't identify what caused an odd sensation trickling down her spine other than intuition.

She wandered into his bedroom. An unpacked suitcase rested on a folding luggage rack. The bed was neatly made, and the room would easily pass a white glove test, and so would the bathroom: seat down, sink clean, shower curtain open at both ends to prevent accumulating mold and mildew. She rolled her eyes. He got the neat gene, too, but then he often had overnight guests.

Scratching her head, she returned to the office and placed a call from the landline. He still didn't answer, and the call went to voicemail. Her voice was sharp and shook slightly with concern. "Call me. STAT."

Her brother was fanatical about keeping his Outlook calendar current. He had deadlines and media events he scheduled and then synchronized to his phone. Maybe he'd entered an appointment which would explain his absence.

She booted up his laptop and a document popped open. Curious, she read a few paragraphs about his meeting with one of the conspirators in Lincoln's assassination, Mary Surratt, at her boarding house at 604 H Street NW, shortly before the assassination. Charlotte picked up a pen and sat back in her chair, twirling the Bic ballpoint between her fingers. Jack hadn't told her about the interview. She knew about the one he had with Booth, of course, but not Surratt, and, while she remembered Surratt was one of the conspirators, she wasn't sure what role she had played in the conspiracy. She shrugged, and opened Outlook. Jack had blocked out time for dinner with her on Friday night—nothing else was scheduled.

Sighing with frustration and a heavy dose of worry, she closed the computer and locked up the apartment.

Driving home, she thought about where he might be. Researching was the logical conclusion, but why wasn't he answering his phone? If he was in the mountains out of cell range it would explain no calls or texts, but if he'd gone to the cabin he routinely used, he would have called to cancel dinner. If he didn't call her in the next hour or two, she'd call his agent. Maybe she had heard from him.

When Charlotte arrived at her house, she found her medical bag open on her unmade bed. Obviously Jack had been to her place and looked for his journal. Did he find it? Until he called, she had no way of knowing.

She put the bag back into the closet, unpacked her suitcase, dumped the dirty clothes into a pile, and then slipped into a pair of sweats and a running T-shirt. Dinner was supposed to be at Jack's place. Now she'd have to come up with something to eat. She stood in front of the gourmet refrigerator that had come with the purchase of her house, and cost more than a Honda, and pondered her choices. A bottle of *Cailean*, Meredith Montgomery's chardonnay, a package of cheese, a bottle of water, and a half-gallon of outdated milk were the only items on the shelves.

Go without or carryout.

While she considered Chinese or barbeque, she carried a glass of wine to her office, sat down at the desk, and opened her Mac laptop. She wasn't interested in checking email, so she googled Mary Surratt and discovered she was charged with aiding and abetting her co-defendants. Charotte knew the government had hanged several of the conspirators. Was Surratt one of them? She googled the question and found the military panel had sentenced five defendants to the gallows: Lewis Powell, David Herold, George Atzerodt, Mary Surratt, and Jack Mallory.

For one shocking moment, the steady hand of time stopped dead.

She didn't flinch or look away, but continued to stare wide-eyed at the computer. Then blood seemed to drain from her body, leaving icy cold fear freezing her veins. Jack Mallory? Impossible. She slammed the lid down on the laptop and left the room, wine glass in hand, wandering aimlessly through the house. Her fear faded, mutating into agitation spinning out of control in the pit of her stomach.

On July 7, 1865, the government had hanged a man named Jack Mallory for conspiring to assassinate Abraham Lincoln. Why hadn't she known? Simple. How many people knew the names of the conspirators? How many people could name the Presidents or state capitols? She shrugged as if the answer was obvious. Unless a person was a teacher, a student of history, or author, probably not many knew. She knew Virginia history and Civil War history as it related to the Commonwealth, but that was the extent of her expertise.

But to have the same last name…

The conspirator Jack Mallory had been dead for more than a hundred and fifty years. Her Jack must be secluded in a mountain cabin out of cell range so he could meet his deadline. Time must have gotten away from him, and he forgot she was coming home. He had done it before. It made sense.

She collapsed onto a chair next to the stairs, pushed aside a stack of clean jeans and T-shirts, and glanced up toward her bedroom door. There was a quick way to prove her brother was not the same Jack Mallory hanged for conspiring to kill Lincoln.

Open the puzzle box.

Slowly she climbed the stairs, imaging the terror which must have burned through the condemned as they climbed the stairs to the gallows.

She halted on the top step. This was ludicrous. She was terrifying herself over an improbability. Her bedroom door, several feet ahead, gaped open. With a deep, conscious inhale-exhale and her feet dragging, she crept forward, wading through a pool of shoes and clothes and unread journals.

Clean thongs and bras, running socks without mates, and a couple of empty wine glasses cluttered the top of the dresser. The puzzle box that held her most precious piece of jewelry sat in plain view. Clammy hands reached for it. Now that she knew the solution to the puzzle, opening the box took only seconds. A rivulet of sweat trickled down the side of her face.

Inside was a blue velvet bag with a gold-corded drawstring. Upon her return, she had wrapped the sapphire brooch in the bag and carefully tied a perfect bow.

The bow was now untied.

With nerves curling, she dug her fingers inside the cut velvet, but nothing was there. She drew a trembling breath and swayed a little as waves of darkness washed over her. Everything went faintly out of focus. Her legs turned soft and wobbly, and she fell into a bottomless cavern of despair.

73

Richmond, Virginia, Present Day

CHARLOTTE'S WORLD HAD already been teetering on its axis, but with confirmation of Jack's return to the past and his death, it spun completely off, yet she couldn't cry or scream.

If she could hold her breath and die, she would. Jack had been executed for something he didn't do. How was she supposed to live now, without either of the men she loved? Her heart wasn't merely broken. The executioner had ripped it from her chest while it was still beating.

The house wasn't cold, but her teeth were chattering. She curled into a ball on the floor and burrowed into the pile of crumpled and dirty clothes. Tears soaked the T-shirt where she rested her face. She fiercely gripped a pair of running shorts, squeezing tightly, as if the fabric could wick away her pain.

Nothing mattered now, not even medicine. Sobbing gasps exploded from her innermost core, and she wept until she had no tears left. Finally she drew in a few trembling breaths and fell into numbing sleep.

Hours later she awoke, tense and dry-mouthed. She gulped the last of the wine she had carried upstairs, and needed more, but there wasn't enough wine in the world to ease the pain of her losses. First Braham. Now Jack. She had believed she could struggle through the loss of Braham only because she had Jack. But who would help her through the loss of her brother? The compounded pain was simply too much.

Once again, she stood in front of the refrigerator, staring at the same four items—wine, cheese, bottle water, and sour milk. Forget the cheese. It had green stuff growing on it. She grabbed the wine bottle and a clean glass.

The first time she had tasted Meredith's wine was shortly after her return from MacKlenna Farm. She and Jack never should have chased Braham. But they had, and she'd had unprotected sex, and she might now be pregnant.

She glared at the bottle as if it were solely responsible for her possible predicament. Wine and pregnancy didn't mix, but the odds of her being pregnant were extremely low. She pulled out the cork, but as she tipped the bottle over the edge of the glass, her rational voice told her to stop. Whether she was pregnant or not, the possibility would keep her from using alcohol as an escape. She put the wine back and instead drank a sixteen-ounce bottle of water to rehydrate.

What would Elliott and Meredith think of *this* story? She should call them. There wasn't anyone else she could talk to about Jack. Maybe they could help her figure out what to do next.

She had Ken, but he still had reservations about time travel, and right now she couldn't bear to expose herself to doubters.

Could she go back again and undo what Jack had done? Braham had tried to change history, and he had failed, but Jack had altered what happened at the conspiracy trial and afterwards. Surely she could reverse what he had done. To do it, though, she needed a brooch. Elliott had given the ruby to Braham because he didn't belong in the twenty-first century. Would he let her use the ruby to save her brother's life?

What if Elliott hadn't gotten the brooch back after Braham used it?

She ran into her office to call Meredith. Dashing through the foyer, she banged her shin on the table, knocking over a stack of mail and a pottery candlestick. Flyers and magazines scattered across the oriental runner with its clutter of shoes and socks. The beeswax candle rolled across the floor. She swooped up the mail, kicked aside the shoes, and hurried to the office where she tossed the junk on top of a round oak pedestal table. One of these days, she'd throw out the accumulated crap covering the top and finally have room to eat there.

Now where was her purse? She dug under the mail and found the black clutch and her keys and phone. The phone showed one missed call. Her heart thumped with surprise and then raced with hopeful expectation.

But it wasn't from Jack, and her heart dropped sickeningly. The missed call was from Ken. She sat with her head bent, propped on one hand, and her fingers splayed through her hair. Frustrated, she swept the junk mail across the table with her forearm and most of it fell to the floor.

A first-class letter addressed to her from someone in Maryland teetered on the edge of the table. She didn't know anyone in Maryland. She stared at the letter, wishing it would fall off, too, so she wouldn't have to deal with it.

The sender had written her name in black block lettering—very precise—to get her attention. What kind of person wrote like that? An architect or engineer or even an artist. Written under her name was: *please forward*. She had just discovered her brother was dead, and some stranger wanted her to read his letter. She swiped it off the table.

She scrolled through her list of contacts and found Meredith's number, but before she pushed the call button, she stopped to consider what to say. The best strategy was not to say anything about Jack over the phone. First, she had to find out where Meredith was jet-setting today, the winery in California or the farm in Kentucky. She might even be in Scotland. God forbid. Charlotte didn't have time to fly to Europe. She pushed the send button and said hello to her friend.

"You're back. I can't wait to hear about your adventure." Meredith's voice swelled with excitement.

"We got back several days ago. Sorry I haven't called before now. I'd like to come for a quick visit. Are you free tomorrow or Sunday afternoon? Some things shouldn't be discussed over the phone."

"We're in Kentucky, and we're not doing anything this weekend. Fly up, and while you're here, we'll make plans for Derby. We want you and Jack to be our guests."

"I'll fly out in the morning. As soon as I have an arrival time, I'll send you a text."

"I'll pick you up at the airport. We'll have a girl's lunch in Lexington and shop for Derby hats before going to the farm."

When Charlotte disconnected, she picked the mail up off the floor and drank the rest of her water. There was no way she would be able to bring herself to have a girl's lunch or shop for a Derby hat right now. She'd have to tell Meredith that Jack had disappeared when she picked her up.

A fresh surge of tears trickled down her face, tempting her to curl up on the floor and weep some more. She glanced down at the table, drawing patterns in the dust with a forefinger. The letter from Maryland caught her eye again. The damn thing kept popping up. She ripped open the sealed flap, and removed two sheets of paper.

Dear Dr. Mallory,

For the past several years, I have been doing research at the Surratt House and Museum on the assassination of President Abraham Lincoln and the trial of the conspirators. I came across a letter which appears to be an original written by one of the conspirators, Jack Mallory. I have not found another reference to this letter. It is possible Mr. Mallory's attorney put the correspondence in his case file and never delivered it. Mallory addressed the letter to his sister, Charlotte.

I, along with thousands of other researchers, have done extensive research on the Mallory families living at the time of the war, and have found no reference to Jack. The experts believe Mallory was an alias. Whoever he was and wherever he came from are among those mysteries lost to time.

However, I did discover a few things which might interest you, and which I offer as thanks in advance for any assistance you can give me.

I traced your family tree back to Major Carlton Jackson Mallory, who served valiantly in the Army of Virginia during the Civil War. He had a son Carlton Jackson, Jr., who was only a child at the time. Major Mallory owned a plantation outside Richmond. Vigilantes burned the mansion within weeks of General Johnson's surrender to General Sherman on April 26, 1865. The family eventually sold the acreage to pay back taxes. Today the property is the home of The Lane Winery and Bed & Breakfast.

I have enclosed a copy of the letter I discovered. I have read it dozens of time, and it makes no sense. In addition, there was no reference to a Charlotte Mallory found in the Mallory family tree until you. It's probably why it was never delivered. If you have any information about Jack and Charlotte Mallory in your family archives, I would appreciate hearing from you. I'm sure if there ever was any information it would have circulated long before now, but I would be remiss as a researcher if I failed to follow up on this lead.

Thank you for your time and attention. I look forward to hearing from you.

Her hands dropped to her lap, shaking. "Oh, God, Jack. History has gotten so screwed up." From the very beginning, her goal had been to keep history intact, but now…

She read the letter again. The family history was correct. Nothing new there. Her ancestors had moved to Richmond after the plantation burned, and Major Mallory had practiced medicine until he died. His son taught school, as did the next four Carlton Jackson Mallorys, although the last two were college professors. Jack broke the mold when he went to law school and ended up becoming a writer.

Small waves of pointless panic seized her. There was no way anyone could connect Jack to her ancestors. Even if her name was discovered on Lincoln's second inaugural dinner invitation list or medical records as an attending physician, she couldn't be linked. She was the first and only Charlotte in a long line of Mallorys dating back to the seventeenth century. Thinking back now over the last few months, she realized she had saved the old house from the torch in the fall of 1864, only to ensure it burned in the spring of 1865.

A strange ripple—like when someone tosses a stone into the water—went through her, and the breath hitched in her dry throat, with a faint rasp. Her actions and Jack's actions had a rippling effect on the future. She didn't yet know how far out the ripple extended, but it was there nonetheless.

She gulped, painfully, when she peered at the second page, recognizing Jack's eloquent script. The uneven writing, dark where he had dipped the quill, faded slowly through each line until he dipped the nib again.

Dear Charlotte,

I am sorry for the pain my death will cause you. When the police came to arrest me, there was a fight, and I lost your beautiful sapphire eyes in the place of our last goodbye. After an exhaustive search, no one could locate them, so I was unable to travel again. I pray no one finds them now, for I fear they will never understand their uniqueness, and the consequences could be catastrophic. I hope one day you will claim my body and bury me in the family cemetery at the homeplace close to the river I love.

Tears dropped on the page, puckering the paper in her cold hands.

She didn't know what he was talking about. They had no homeplace. No family cemetery. And what happened to the brooch? Did someone find it? Oh, God, what a mess.

She read his letter again, then again, becoming more confused with each reading. No wonder his attorney never delivered it, and who was his attorney anyway? Surely Braham had represented him. A very uncharitable thought occurred to her. His lawyering skills might be on the same level as his spying skills.

Yes, it was very uncharitable. Braham and Jack loved each other dearly. Braham would have moved heaven and earth, and even hell to clear Jack's name. Which meant someone had planted irrefutable evidence against Jack, but who would have done it...and why? It would all be in the record. She would have to dig through the trial transcript, witness list, and find the evidence used against him. The thought of him languishing in prison, wearing the ghastly hood, and being horribly tortured, made her sick at her stomach. She gagged, leaned over the trashcan, and threw up the little bit of food in her stomach.

No amount of struggling helped her control her emotions. She rolled into a fetal position on the rug and sobbed until her fists were sore from pounding the floor and she had no more tears to shed.

74

Richmond, Virginia, Present Day

W HEN CHARLOTTE WOKE on the floor of her office, it took only seconds for her to plummet from conscious awareness into profound sorrow.

She made a strangled noise and froze, paralyzed by stiffness and pain. She drew her knees tightly up to her chest, sobbing. "I'll get you back. I'll undo this mess. I promise."

She staggered to her feet. What time was it? Her eyes were dry and scratchy, and she couldn't read the small numbers on her phone. She blinked and blinked until finally the numbers one-two-one-three came into focus. Just after midnight. Her stomach complained, reminding her she hadn't eaten in more than twelve hours. First, though, she had to schedule a flight to Kentucky. Then she'd go to the all-night market. She scrolled through her contacts and found the number for the private airline she had used before. Jack wouldn't be around to pay the bill for this trip, but she'd get the money out of savings. It didn't matter what it cost. She was fairly sure they would accommodate her travel plans. Which they did. She had an itinerary confirmed within minutes, with an early departure time of seven a.m. She sent Meredith a text of her arrival time.

After a trip to the market, she chowed down on a late supper of chicken and a spinach salad with sliced almonds, cranberries and chopped eggs. With a full stomach, she set about making plans. She had four months of sabbatical left, and the accountant was still paying her bills. For this trip, she wouldn't need a Confederate uniform, and since she'd left all her dresses at Braham's house, she didn't need to pack any clothes. Assuming the brooch would take her to Kentucky as it had taken Braham, she would have the same two-day trip to Washington. Traveling unaccompanied, she'd be safer dressed as a man, and arriving in the city incognito would give her time to investigate whether or not the government suspected her of participating in the conspiracy, using guilt by association reasoning. She would need to order men's clothing or possibly buy trousers and shirts off the rack in a costume store.

Suddenly, she gasped at an ah-ha moment. Maybe she'd even arrive before Jack's arrest. Which would be perfect. But then she shivered, not only from fear of what she'd find when she arrived in Washington, but from fear of going through the dizzying fog again. Each trip had made her life in the present worse.

Her eyes darted as her mind wrestled desperately to see through the maddening maze which had become her life, and Jack's, too. The irony was they had become characters in the story he was writing.

With a plan for rescuing Jack percolating, she sat at her desk and spent the next several hours reading the transcript of the conspiracy trial. When her eyes began to glaze over, she showered and packed an overnight bag. At six-thirty she drove to the airport. Flying private, she avoided a long check-in line and possible delay at the gate. The plane soared into a dark sky within minutes of boarding, leaving the twinkling lights of Richmond behind, and made a smooth landing in Lexington an hour after sunrise.

Parked outside the TAC Air Terminal at Blue Grass Airport were two limos and a Mercedes, all with tinted windows. The driver's door of the Mercedes opened and Meredith emerged looking as if she had just walked off a photo shoot for the cover of Vogue—dark hair blowing in a gentle breeze, black leather jacket, skinny jeans, Kentucky blue turtleneck, and boots. Her face brightened when she saw Charlotte and her pink mouth turned up in a brilliant smile.

How could anyone look so beautiful this early in the morning?

Charlotte slipped on a pair of sunglasses, not to shield her eyes from the bright morning sun, but to keep Meredith from seeing how puffy and bloodshot they were.

Meredith's strong arms embraced Charlotte with gentle kindness, as if she already understood her pain without knowing the cause. Meredith was not only beautiful, intelligent, and successful, she was also kind-hearted.

And if Charlotte truly was pregnant with Braham's child, the baby would be Meredith's six-times-great-grandmother's first cousin once removed. *Try saying that ten times fast, or better, yet, understanding the convoluted relationship.* Charlotte didn't even have a cousin, much less one so far removed.

She tossed her bag into the back and settled into the front seat, fastening her seat belt. "Thanks for picking me up, and thanks for having me on such short notice."

Meredith smiled, her blue eyes crinkling at the corners. "Wherever we are in the world, our friends are welcome to join us. Elliot and I keep the door open."

"I can't imagine having so much flexibility in my schedule. Having friends show up on the doorstep would send me into a blind panic."

Meredith drove out onto Man O' War Boulevard. "Elliott thrives on having people around. He's a problem solver. He's in his element when he takes charge and bullies his way through a situation. Lord knows he bullied me through chemo. Our life has become so calm, even I'm getting bored. I'm thinking about launching another wine."

"I was feeling sort of antsy when the brooch arrived." Charlotte swallowed, forcing her voice to steady. "Now I'd give anything to just be antsy again."

"Instead of—?"

Fat tears gathered in the corners of Charlotte's eyes. "Scared."

Meredith's eyes were on her now, soft and warm and full of speculation. "This is about Braham, isn't it?"

"Indirectly, but let's talk about it when I can tell it to everyone at once."

Meredith turned her attention back to the road. "Okay. Well, since it's too early to go shopping, why don't we go back to the farm? Mrs. Collins was making homemade biscuits when I left. We can eat first or have a yoga or spin class or go for a run. Whatever you'd like to do. Ted, my trainer, is working my butt off right now. He's available to work with us this morning if you'd like to burn off some of the fear."

"A run around the farm might be—" Charlotte tried to be enthusiastic but failed miserably. Tears streamed down her cheeks. She dug into her clutch for a package of tissues and dabbed at her eyes. "It's bad, Meredith. It's real bad."

Meredith squeezed Charlotte's hand. "No matter what has happened, Elliott and David can fix it. The extent of their creativity and resources boggles my mind."

"This might be beyond even their capabilities."

"One day something might come up which is beyond Elliott's reach, but nothing will ever be beyond David's." A ghost of a smile crossed Meredith's face, although her eyes grew dark with concern.

"I don't think I've ever known anyone who had so much faith in another person," Charlotte said.

"It didn't come easy for me, but Elliott, David, and even Kevin, have never failed me. I wouldn't have made it through breast cancer and childbirth without them. David supported Elliott while he propped me up, and we all three yelled at Kevin."

Meredith chuckled. "Poor Kevin crawled over broken glass for us, and we were so mean to him. We laugh about it now, but we all went through a very trying time for several months. Elliott and I both had moments of doubt, but it all worked out, and we have little Cullen to show for it. As the saying goes, it takes a village. Elliott is the center of an incredible village of loving and caring people. You and Jack are part of our village now."

"For the longest time, it's only been Jack and me. I've never had a circle of friends and family."

"I didn't either," Meredith said. "I married into Elliott's inner circle, and once you're there, you're never alone again."

"You better call Elliott and tell him I'm bringing a problem for him to solve."

"Elliott and David were in a closed-door meeting when I left. Something is going on with them, but Elliott will stop whatever he's doing to help you out. Don't worry."

Charlotte closed her eyes and breathed in the scents of the countryside along Old Frankfort Pike—horses and spring grasses and freshly-turned earth, and she let her breath go with a sigh. For a few minutes she would relinquish fear and worry and enjoy the company of a friend who had been to hell and back herself, and found the love of her life along the way.

75

MacKlenna Farm, Lexington, Kentucky, Present Day

THIRTY MINUTES LATER, Meredith, Elliott, and David sat around the conference table in Elliott's office in MacKlenna Mansion. David had set up a video camera to record Charlotte's statement. As Elliott explained, no one would interrupt her, and she was to start from the beginning and describe everything that had happened to her until the moment Meredith picked her up at the airport.

"Everything?" Charlotte asked.

"Ye' don't have to go into intimate details, just tell us what and when and if any promises were made," David said.

Mrs. Collins came in with a tray of fruit in one hand and a basket of egg and cheese biscuits warm from the oven in the other. "You call me when you run out of food. I'll bring in lunch."

Three hours later, David and Elliott were both rubbing their noses and Meredith was wiping away the tears streaming down her face. Water bottles, empty plates, and half-filled coffee mugs littered the table, along with pages of notes. Reliving the horror of Richmond and the terror she experienced when she discovered Jack was gone had drained Charlotte completely. She slumped in the swivel chair, barely able to hold herself upright.

"I have a question," David said. "Do ye' intend to rescue Jack or prove his innocence?"

Charlotte's head jerked up as if a puppeteer had yanked her

strings. "Rescue him. Get him out of prison as quickly as I can."

Elliott slid across the table the copy of Jack's letter she had brought with her. "David's question stems from this. Do ye' have a family cemetery or a homeplace?"

She straightened in her chair, shaking her head, knowing exactly where Elliott was going with his question. The same one had niggled at her since she first read the letter. "No. After Jack hit the New York Times bestseller list, he bought a condo on the river, and we sold our parents' house in downtown Richmond. When I came back to practice medicine, I bought a place of my own, too."

"That's what I thought," Elliott said.

David took the letter and added it to his notes. "Jack's execution has changed yer family's history."

Charlotte fixed David with a direct look, and clearly enunciating each word for emphasis said, "I don't care."

"Ye' might, if ye' knew what it was."

"Nothing matters but Jack. I need to get him out."

Elliott frowned and rubbed a knuckle slowly down the long, straight bridge of his nose. "Ye'll have to tell him."

"Tell him what? That there's no homeplace or family cemetery. Do you think he'll care? No, he won't. His freedom will be all that matters."

"Ye' might be surprised," Elliott said. "But here's something else to think about. If Jack disappears from prison, how will they explain his escape? The government and the public will blame the warden and guards. There'll be another manhunt. They'll never find Jack. The country will be left with an unsolvable mystery, and the Mallory name will be as sullied as Doctor Mudd's."

"Do you think I care about my name? I don't. I only care about Jack. Nothing else. Not my name, not my medical practice, not my savings or my retirement. Nothing." She licked dry lips and took a gulp of water. "This is my fault. If I had returned home instead of chasing after General Ramseur at the Battle of Cedar Creek, none of this would have happened. I had to see if my twenty-first-century medical knowledge could save him. Because of my ego," she said, thumping her chest, "Braham spent the rest of his life riddled with guilt and Jack was executed."

Elliott pushed away from the table and propped his leg across his opposite knee. Meredith appeared very interested in the lipstick on the edge of her coffee mug, and David stared at his notes, flipping a pen back and forth across the page. Charlotte watched them, wondering what they were thinking…or better yet, what they had not told her.

The charged silence passed when David eventually cleared his throat, and focused on Elliott for a moment. "Jack has to be exonerated. We have to find the culprit who framed him, expose the man, and have the charges against Jack dismissed. The Mallory name might still be stained, but not as badly as it would be if Jack disappeared. I don't advise whisking him away unless it's the last resort."

"I agree," Elliott said. "But what about Charlotte? Jack's execution altered her family history. Once Jack is exonerated, he'll come back with his history intact, no alteration, but it will be different from hers. They'll no longer have a shared history."

Charlotte shook her head vehemently. "What nonsense. No more shared history? Really? I don't buy it."

Meredith tucked her arm in the crook of Charlotte's elbow, and gently bumped shoulders, showing solidarity. "Give us an example, Elliott."

Elliott and David exchanged glances, then David said, "I'll take the question." He opened a folder and leaned forward confidentially. "This is only a hypothetical, because we have no way of knowing what Jack is really talking about. Okay? Are ye' with me?"

Charlotte nodded, but worrisome thoughts were darting in her head like hornets around their nest mobilizing to attack a threat.

"Based on Jack's letter, we know he believes there is a homeplace and a family cemetery." David slid an old photograph across the table. "Look at this."

"What is this?" Meredith asked.

"A picture of Mallory Plantation taken shortly after it was destroyed by fire in 1865. What do ye' see in the background?"

Meredith and Charlotte squinted at the picture. "A cemetery," they said in unison.

"Look at this picture," David said.

"It's The Lane Winery in Richmond," Charlotte said.

"What do you see in the background?" David asked.

She and Meredith squinted again. "An old cemetery."

"What else to do you see?"

"Besides the vineyards, an old willow oak." Charlotte glanced at the Mallory Plantation photograph again. "The tree is smaller, but it seems to be the same tree."

David produced two more pictures. One from the Richmond Historical Society, and the other from a Richmond architectural firm. "Here is a picture of an 1835 painting of Mallory Plantation, and the other is an architectural rendition of what the mansion would look like today if it had survived intact." He spread the four pictures out on the table.

"Now, let's pretend Mallory Plantation survived the Civil War and generations of Mallorys have resided there, including you and Jack. Maybe you or Jack or both still resided there when he went back in time to find his journal. Are you still with me?"

"Sort of," Charlotte said, scrunching her brow while she studied the architectural rendition of the mansion.

"When Jack was executed," David continued, "the mansion lost the protection you earned from General Sherman. Let's say, for argument's sake, after the fire the Mallorys didn't have the funds to rebuild the mansion, so the property was sold. We know it had four different owners before it was purchased by The Lane Winery.

"After the property was sold, we know the Mallorys moved to Richmond, where your six-times-great-grandfather practiced medicine until his death in 1885. His children and his children's children grew up in Richmond like your parents."

"Everything you've said is true," Charlotte said.

"But it's not what Jack is saying in his letter. He wants to be buried at the homeplace. The next time you see Jack, he might be looking forward to returning to the mansion, sitting on the back porch looking out over the river, and drinking a bottle of good California wine."

A sinking, twisting feeling wrapped around Charlotte's heart. "But there's no mansion."

"Under David's hypothetical construct, there will be one until Jack is executed," Elliott said.

"I'm still not sure I buy any of this."

"Look at it this way. There is a memorial to Abraham Lincoln in Washington, D.C. Ye' know it, and I know it. Now, say ye' go back in time and Braham stops the assassination. Lincoln continues his term of office and then retires to Illinois."

"Okay," Charlotte said. "So…"

"When ye' come back to the twenty-first century, the Lincoln Memorial will no longer exist. Ye'll remember it was once there because it was yer memory when ye' went back in time. But if Braham changes history, Lincoln will lose his immortality, and the memorial will never be built. And ye' and Jack will be the only people who will ever know it was once there."

Charlotte slumped in her seat, put her head in her hands for a moment, then slowly straightened. "I see the problem now." She glanced from Elliott to David. "There's no way to fix this, is there?"

"This is only a hypothetical," Elliott said. "It's possible nothing of any significance will happen."

"You're a betting man, though. What does your gut tell you?" she asked.

There was silence, long enough to fill several heartbeats, long enough to fill tomorrow.

Elliott propped his ankle on his opposite knee and jiggled his foot, sighing. "I hate to say this, but I'll bet when ye' and Jack return, ye'll have significantly different memories, life-changing memories."

When Charlotte replied, her voice was soft, and she was careful to keep her eyes on Elliott in order to stay in the moment, to stay connected to a lifeline. "Then I guess we'll simply have to adjust."

Conversation died and they all sat in silence for several long moments.

Charlotte cleared her throat of the knot lodged there. "I grew up in a very loving home. My parents were college professors. I took dance and piano lessons. I had a horse I rode every day. We weren't wealthy, but we had all we needed. I was in high school when they died, and Jack took care of me. If his history is different, then I only hope his was as happy as mine."

Elliott's dark eyes seemed curiously blank for a moment. Then they snapped back to Charlotte. He uncrossed his legs and stood. "This argument is moot if I don't have possession of the ruby brooch."

"Braham said he saw Sean MacKlenna put it back inside the desk," Charlotte said.

Elliott opened the desk's middle drawer, stuck his hand inside, and a secret compartment on top of the desk popped open. "Let's hope it's there now." He withdrew a rosewood box. Meredith, sitting beside Charlotte, grasped her hand in a bone-crunching squeeze. Elliott's expression sharpened for a moment as he opened the box, and then his features relaxed until the corner of his mouth lifted slightly. Charlotte held her breath until Elliott tipped the box for all to see, and then she let out her breath in a long stream of relief.

"There has to be understanding before we go any further with these discussions. Ye' can borrow Kit's brooch, but David is going with ye'," Elliott said.

Charlotte cut a quick glance at David, a hulking six foot two, and two hundred-plus pounds of lean muscle. "Shouldn't it be your decision?" she asked David.

"I had already made it. It's why I videotaped your statement. I'll watch it again and make notes. And I'll have questions for ye' later," David said.

"I've screwed up two people's lives already. There's a good chance you'll be in danger, too."

Meredith leaned in and said low-voiced, "He did several tours in Afghanistan, and he's the Scottish equivalent of a Navy SEAL. He can take care of himself, and you, too."

David put his legal pad of notes into an accordion file with a half dozen labeled folders. "If ye'll excuse me, I've got work to do."

"Wait a minute," Charlotte said. "You said you had already made your decision. How could you possibly have known about Jack?"

"After you called last night," Elliott said, "I asked David to research the end of the war, the assassination, and the trial to see if your name or Jack's showed up. We found what you found and assumed it was your Jack."

"I've been talking with experts and collecting copies of the transcript, witness, and exhibit lists, and the statutes Jack allegedly violated. With this information, his attorney will have an advantage," David said.

"Braham has to be his attorney. You can't give those notes to just anyone," Charlotte said.

"If Braham isn't representing him, then I'll feed his attorney with insider information. He won't turn it down, nor will he question how I got it," David said, and then paused.

"For example," he resumed, "the defendants weren't asked until the first day of trial if they wanted representation. At that point defense counsel had no time for pre-trial preparations or consultations with clients. The notes I have will bring Jack's attorney up to speed immediately. He can, as they say, hit the ground running."

"And the prosecutors will be looking for a staff leak," Elliott said. "Wish I could see it."

"The proverbial fly on the wall," Charlotte said. Then she added, "How long will it take you to collect all the research and be ready to leave?"

"There's more to do than research," Elliott said. "If I send people into a war zone, they go prepared—weapons, funds, identification. It will take a couple of days. Ye' also need to be up to speed, Charlotte, on the proceedings and layout of the courtroom. I've placed a call to Bob Redford. He directed the movie *Conspirator* a few years ago. I want his insights about the trial. I know he did extensive research at the time."

"You didn't tell me that," Meredith huffed. "I tried for years to get him to come to an event at the winery, and he always turned me down. Will he return your call?"

"MacKlenna Farm has been a corporate sponsor of the Sundance Institute for more than twenty years. He'll call."

A trace of humor touched Meredith's face, and she wrapped her fingers around her husband's arm and tugged teasingly on the sleeve of his polo shirt. "You have such an irresistible way about you."

Elliott kissed her. "Aye, my wee lassie, but ye're the only one who thinks so."

"Tell Mr. Redford Jack will make a nice donation. And just so you know, we're picking up the tab for *all* expenses," Charlotte said.

Elliott waved away her comment as if it had no importance. He was no longer grinning, but there was a distinct glint in his eye. "When everyone has safely returned, then we can discuss money."

76

MacKlenna Farm, Lexington, Kentucky, Present Day

CHARLOTTE SPENT THE next three days in David's office participating in videoconferences with experts. She and David had studied Redford's movie several times and talked to the experts he had used in creating the film. Their wealth of information staggered Charlotte, who kept hearing *ker-ching* every time David set up another videoconference.

Her pockets were not as deep as the Frasers', and by her best calculations, she had already spent her savings and would have to dig into her retirement unless she sold the Hilton Head house to a developer. Money didn't matter, though. Jack's freedom did. Both Frasers had told her not to worry about the money, but she did.

Elliott's research assistants discovered a Union officer from Lexington, Kentucky whose identity Charlotte could borrow. The man died at home in the summer of 1865 from wounds he received in the Siege of Petersburg.

What made him of interest to Elliott was Captain Charles Patrick had been a lawyer. Elliott had vetted the captain's historical record and found no connection to any member of the military commission or defense attorneys. If Charlotte wanted to attend the trial, being a member of the defense team guaranteed her admission to the courtroom and contact with Jack. Impersonating a Union Captain wouldn't be difficult, but impersonating a lawyer, even with a script to follow, might be more of a challenge.

"I promise ye', Charley, ye' won't have to say a word." His nickname for her rolled smoothly off his tongue. "Sit there and look menacing," he said, glaring with a tight-lipped, pinched expression.

She surprised herself by laughing out loud, but then stopped suddenly and pressed the tips of her fingers against her mouth to keep another laugh from bursting out. Jack was gone, and she had no right to be happy.

David moved her hand away from her lips and held it in his strong palm, as if it were something precious and fragile. The sudden warmth of the touch rippled the fine hairs of her forearms. Her fingers closed involuntarily on his, and his hand wrapped large and warm around hers. "It's okay to laugh," he said with gentleness in his face. "It doesn't mean ye' don't love yer brother or worry over him."

David's intense, smoldering, dark brown eyes rarely changed, but when he smiled, they took on the coziness of a cup of cocoa, and she melted in the sweet, hot chocolate. There was no tension between them, only general ease in the way he probed and she prodded. They were partners, and if Braham didn't already have her heart, she could easily give it to this man.

The intercom buzzed, and David answered the phone on his desk. "Aye, I'll meet ye' there." He hung up and said to her, "Elliott needs me in the stallion barn. I'll be right back." He pocketed his cell phone and left the room, muscles rippling beneath the fabric of shirt and trousers.

She got to her feet and stretched. From the window behind David's desk, she observed him crossing the yard toward the closest red-roofed barn, admiring the way his body moved with such athletic ease and power.

David was a deadly force to be reckoned with. According to the historical record, the conspirators were incarcerated in the Old Arsenal Penitentiary. If anyone could rescue Jack from there, David could. She said a silent prayer, grateful he was one of the good guys, and on her side.

A description of one of the characters in Jack's last book described David right down to the aviators he tucked into the open collar of his shirt: *He possessed a quickness of mind and body, and protectiveness born of nature and honed by training.* She trusted him implicitly and wanted the trust reciprocated, but if she expected him to believe in her, she had to be completely honest with him. And she was holding back, not ready to share the possibility she might be pregnant.

When she had told her story to Elliott, Meredith, and David, and reached the part about her visit to Braham's house in Georgetown for their getaway, David had quietly left the room. She suspected he had watched it later when he reviewed the video, but by leaving he had preserved her privacy—*protectiveness born of nature and honed by training.*

While she was standing at the window, a reflection of his bookcase in the glass caught her attention. She wandered over to the bookshelf and pulled out a hardback book titled *Knights in Black: The Adventures of the Royal Scots Dragoon Guards.* The red and green tartan cover was one of three with similar book jackets. Jack had recently mentioned reading and enjoying these books by David MacBain. She flipped the book over to see the author's picture and gasped.

"I'll be damned." The breadth of David's experience and knowledge had surprised her at first. Then by the second day she found herself in awe, hanging on his every word. By the third day, she had given up being surprised, but now she was back to being in awe again—or maybe thunderstruck. Was there anything the man couldn't do?

She glanced up to find him standing in the doorway with his hands gripping the top edge of the doorjamb as he leaned into the room. The corner of his mouth curved up, and she had the grace to blush slightly at being caught snooping in his office. "Jack read your books recently and really enjoyed them."

"After yer trip to Afghanistan, ye're probably not interested in reading them. I wouldn't blame ye'."

She shook her head, eyes fixed on him. "I'll definitely read them now. I know the author." She returned the book, placing the spine flush with the edge of the shelf to match the others.

"Come on, then." He motioned with his chin, his smile widening. "Let's get out of here for a while. We need a break."

Her breath hitched at the unexpected invitation, and then she shrugged. "Sure. Why not?"

Five minutes later, they were speeding down Old Frankfort Pike in David's Z-4 with the top down, the wind blowing in her hair. The ends of David's closely cropped hairstyle barely fluttered above his aviator sunglasses.

"Can you fly a plane?" she asked.

"If I have to." The dark lenses hid his eyes, but the way his mouth curled, she knew they were twinkling. He was teasing her—*protectiveness born of nature and honed by training.* Maybe it's what the meeting with Elliott was all about. He and Elliott needed to know if she could emotionally handle another trip back. Honestly, she didn't know for sure, but she thought she could. They probably wanted more reassurance, though.

"I thought we'd stop at Wallace Station and have a sandwich and beer out on the back deck," David said.

"Sounds great, but make mine water."

He shook his head. "Part of this outing is drinking beer. Just one. It won't hurt." He turned into the restaurant's parking lot. "Looks like we missed the lunch crowd." He parked, and they entered the building. After ordering, they made their way out the back door to a picnic table on the deck. They sat in silence for a few minutes, soaking up the sun, until David went back inside to pick up their order. He returned with beers, sandwiches, and a bottle of water.

Charlotte twisted the cap off the water bottle and took a long drink.

"Now, the beer," David said.

"I can't." She spoke softly, her shoulders trembling. "I may be pregnant."

David set down his bottle of Kentucky Ale and peered over his aviators. "Ye're a doctor and don't know for sure?"

"I haven't taken a pregnancy test. I'm several days late, but I've also been through hell and back the last six weeks."

"Six weeks? How about six months." He tipped his bottle and finished off the ale. "Ye' still have a shell-shocked look about ye'."

"Well, thanks."

"We'll stop at the drug store on the way back to the farm. Ye' should know what's going on in yer body. Ye're a brave—"

She shook her head several times, huffing softly. "No, I'm not brave. I even have to talk myself into running a stoplight late at night, even when there's no traffic on the road. And then only when I'm going in to take care of a medical emergency. I lead a safe life, and I don't take risks. The damn brooch has brought nothing but trouble, and after I get Jack back, I don't ever want to see either one of those things again. It may have been a cake-walk for Kit, but the sapphire has only brought me hell and heartache."

There was a small barbed edge to his voice when he said, "Kit spent six months crossing the Oregon Trail in a covered wagon with bad food and burned coffee. She fought a cholera epidemic, killed three men, saw her husband get shot, and barely escaped being raped, and those are the highlights. I wouldn't say she had an easy time of it."

"I'm sorry. It was insensitive of me to assume it." Charlotte shoved a hand through her hair and snagged her fingers in tangled, windblown curls. "Damn. Should have worn a hat."

David snatched off the MacKlenna ball cap he had plopped on his head when he parked the Z-4, hooked it onto her head, and tugged on the bill to set the hat in place. "Now ye've got one. Let's go."

"You know, if I'm pregnant, the baby will be Kit's cousin."

"Not sure how ye'd explain it to a wee laddie."

"Me either, but when he or she grows up, I'll try."

"Either do it, or don't do it, Charley. There is *no* trying—ever."

David tossed their trash and recyclables into the proper containers, moving about the deck naturally. Only the tension in his shoulders suggested he was under any heightened level of emotion.

He paused at the edge of the deck, his chest rising and falling as he breathed in cool air. It was early in the afternoon, and the rays of sun were beginning to shift, slanting down through the trees in the fencerow on the west side of the property. The bright light glowed on his brown hair, highlighting pinpoints of yellow, as if the wind had sprinkled his head with gold dust.

Charlotte joined him next to the stairs leading to the parking lot, tipping her head back to let the rays of sun bathe her cheeks with warmth. She wasn't in a hurry to leave the restaurant and drive to their next stop—a drug store. Being pregnant now wasn't convenient, but she had wanted Braham to be the father of her child. At the moment, though, she wasn't so sure.

"I asked one of the researchers today if she had seen Braham's name mentioned anywhere in the trial transcript. She said no." Charlotte tugged on the bill of the ball cap, trying to put into words the thoughts pressing on her heart. "What could have happened to him? Why didn't..." Her voice broke, and she cleared her throat, trying to regain composure. "Why didn't he help Jack?"

"My internet searches haven't turned up any information, either," David said in a tone indicating mild frustration. "After everything you've said about him, I'm surprised. And I'm rarely surprised about anything."

"I know he was leaving town the day we left Washington, but surely he would have returned." She gripped the railing, turning her knuckles white as she desperately tried to hold the tears at bay, so afraid once they started she wouldn't be able to stop. "I thought he cared about Jack. I thought he cared about me. But I must have been wrong."

"Whatever he did after the war, Braham didn't distinguish himself in any way."

"He had a law practice to return to, and his winery. I wonder if he never made it back to California."

"I've got people looking. They may turn up something, or it's also possible maybe...he didn't survive his last assignment."

"It's the only thing that makes sense, but the war was over. So if he died, it must have been from an accident or disease. Edward, his butler, will know where he is and what happened to him. If he's alive and well, I'm not sure how I'll react to seeing him."

"If ye're pregnant, he's the father, and he deserves to know about the baby."

"Then I hope I'm not pregnant. I don't want a child by a man who would abandon my brother."

"Don't give up on Braham. He might not have represented Jack, but he might have helped in other ways. We'll find out when we get there."

Yes, they would find out, and if she was pregnant, she didn't intend to tell him. Nor would she allow the pregnancy to overshadow Jack's situation. She went down the stairs, clutching her brow. She must have moaned, for David reached her quickly and cupped her elbow, supporting her weight.

"What is it, lass?"

"Besides Braham's betrayal?" The tears flowed freely now. "Everything." She wiped her face with the heel of her hand. David pulled her into his arms and held her, and she cried until she soaked his shirt.

When the tears stopped she said, "I'm sorry, I thought I had cried them all out."

He reached behind him, grabbed a handful of napkins off the table next to the railing, and gave them to her. "Blow yer nose. Ye've been close to tears all morning. It was time to let them out."

She did as he asked, then took several hiccupping breaths. She breathed easier now the tension in her chest had eased. "How'd you get to be so smart?"

He laughed. "Everything I know I not only learned in kindergarten, but I also learned from Elliott, especially about women."

She threw the used napkins in the trashcan, chuckling. "From what I heard about Elliott prior to meeting Meredith, I'm not sure it's knowledge to be proud of."

"Aye, but ye' have to understand. Before he fell in love with the right woman, he fell in love with the wrong one. The first lassie caused him a wee bit of trouble. It took Meredith a while to straighten him out."

"He reminds me of Yoda in *Star Wars,* building his knowledge, experience, and wisdom into others. I can't imagine undertaking this *mission* without his support and," she paused, glancing up at David, "his Jedi knight. I'd never be able to kick evil's butt without you."

"Where would ye' like to start with yer ass-kicking?" he asked, smiling into her eyes.

"Oh, that's easy," she said, letting David divert her focus. "A certain kangaroo court with the power to execute. We'll start there, then I'm going after Johnson and Stanton in the press. The *Tribune, Times, Post, News* and the *World* are five of the newspapers whose editors disagreed with Johnson and Stanton about how the trial should be conducted. I firmly believe those two men bullied Attorney General Speed into writing an opinion supporting their position."

She stopped and slammed her fists to her hips. "An opinion is only an opinion, for God's sake. It doesn't have the force and effect of the law. A criminal court should have tried the conspirators, not a military court. Knowing Jack, he's suffering more from the injustice than the torture."

David rubbed his knuckle across his upper lip as a broad grin spread across his face.

"You're laughing at me."

"Nay. I'd never laugh at a lassie strapping on a gun belt, ready for battle." The lines of his face curved in such an irresistible smile that her own laughter bubbled up in response.

"You're damn right I am, but I have to warn you, I'm a lousy shot."

They meandered toward the car, taking their time, listening to the trees whisper and the chatting and courting of the birds. She had become accustomed to the sounds of nature, to hearing the trills and odd yowls instead of the roar of engines and blasting music.

"I've changed my position since the videoconference this morning," she said.

"To what?" David asked. "Are ye' coming down on the side of the press?"

"I can't believe I'm saying this, because I can't stand the press, but if we can't win the trial in the courtroom, we'll win it in the newspapers."

"And if we can't win it in the press?"

She opened her door and slid into the passenger's seat. "Easy. Do you know where we can get a drone?"

"What do ye' want to do with it? Fly it into the Old Arsenal Penitentiary?"

"Yep. Blast a hole in Jack's cell and rescue him during the confusion."

David's mouth twitched slightly as he cast a sidelong glance at her. "I can see it all now." He spread his hands as if clearing the way of visual obstructions. "On the left, we have the steady hands of a surgeon operating a drone's controls. And on the right, we have a writer inciting the public to reject the Attorney General's opinion as both unlawful and a gross blunder in policy."

In spite of her distress, Charlotte laughed. "You have a future in either politics or the theatre."

Chuckling, David put on his seat belt and started the engine. "The ancient Greeks and Shakespeare had it figured out. They combined the two and created political theatre."

"Great. If we had a script ready, we could press our case on the stage, too."

"Thank goodness we don't. I have a feeling we're going to have our hands full as it is." He tapped her on the head. "Hold on to your hat and tell me why you dislike the press."

"It's a long story."

"It's a nice drive back to farm." He pulled out onto Old Frankfort Pike for a scenic drive back to the farm. "Tell me yer story, and I'll tell ye' mine."

"During my residency, one of my first gunshot victims almost died on the table. We worked on him for several hours. It was touch and go. By the time we finished, I was exhausted. Several reporters were waiting for an interview. They reached me first and caught me off-guard. I said, 'He coded on the table…' Before I could complete the sentence to add…the patient was resuscitated by the anesthesiologist, the reporters were spreading the rumor he was dead, upsetting the family members sitting nearby. I caught hell from the hospital administrator and the Chief of Surgery. And it's the last time I've ever talked to the press."

"And now ye' want to use them?"

"Better to use them than be abused by them. So what's your story?"

"A reporter in Afghanistan asked me what it felt like to be a hero. Another reporter shouted over the question, asking me what I was going to tell the widow of one of the men I'd rescued. I hadn't known he had died."

Charlotte squeezed his arm. "I'm so sorry."

"I was, too, but my sorry didn't warm her bed at night."

77

MacKlenna Farm, Lexington, Kentucky, Present Day

C HARLOTTE PROPPED HER foot on the bottom rail of the white plank fence surrounding the paddock adjacent to the MacKlenna mansion. A gorgeous chestnut stallion with three white stocking feet trotted past her before stopping and lifting his head, his nostrils quivering as he sniffed the air.

"What do you smell, gorgeous?"

The stallion trotted toward her corner of the fence.

Charlotte sniffed the air, too—freshly turned earth, manure, magnolias—scents unchanging from one century to the next. The whiteness of the clouds was still as fierce against the dark blue of the sky as it had been in Washington. The blue was not as dark as Braham's uniform, however. She sniffed again, this time to stop her runny nose. The pregnancy test was negative, and she had only herself to blame for dashed hopes. At thirty-eight the odds of getting pregnant without the use of fertility drugs were very low. Even with drugs, her chances were iffy.

"That's Stormy. He's a time-traveling stallion."

She jumped when Elliott spoke from behind her. "Guess that means Kit either took him with her or brought him back."

Elliott joined her at the fence and rested his forearms on the top plank. "Kit knew she'd need a horse to ride. Took a million dollar stallion on a thousand-mile trip through the wilderness. Ye' should have seen Stormy when he came home. Ribs were showing. Kit wasn't in much better shape." Elliott rubbed the horse's forehead and Stormy flicked his ears in response.

"Why didn't she take him back the second time?"

"She intended to, but at the last minute it came down to breeding. She didn't want to introduce a twenty-first-century stallion's bloodlines into the nineteenth-century."

"Is that an indirect way of asking me if *I'm* breeding?"

Elliott lifted only one shoulder in a shrug, and then he pursed his lips a little, as thoughts flashed half-formed across his face. After a moment, he said, "When Meredith and I were dating, she told me she never wanted to see me again. I wasn't a very nice person, and I deserved the verbal blow to the jaw. A few weeks after she kicked my ass to the curb, she got clobbered with a double whammy."

"Meredith told me she was diagnosed with breast cancer at the same time she found out she was pregnant." Charlotte patted Stormy's neck. Basking in the attention of two people, the stallion's muscles relaxed and his eyelids began to droop. "If you were being a jerk, I'm surprised Meredith told you. She must have been very scared."

"Aye, she was. Her doctor encouraged her to tell me in case she became too sick to care for the child. She showed up here one night and told me I was going to be a father. I was thrilled, of course. In the next breath she told me she had breast cancer. I had recently lost Kit and my father, and I wasn't going to lose Meredith, too. We had a difference of opinion about how to handle both situations. I wanted her to fight for her life. She wanted to fight for the baby's."

"Now she's healthy, and you have little Cullen."

"Aye, it's true. But the point I'm trying to make is we don't understand why we have the trials we do. If we give up, we'll never receive the blessings to come afterwards." Elliott gave the horse a final pat and linked his fingers, rubbing one thumb with the other in a distracted sort of way. "In the last few years, I've known two women who were pregnant in difficult circumstances. Both found a way to be joyful in spite of hardship. Whether ye're pregnant or not, find your place of joy and rest there. It's where ye'll truly be blessed."

Charlotte stopped petting the horse, swallowed hard, and then asked, "Do you think I can find it?"

Elliott turned his head to look at her, and his eyes held a depth of understanding she had never seen before. He gathered her into his arms, hugged her tightly, and the muscles in her back yielded slowly as tension subsided.

"I know ye' will, lass. Now come inside. We have last-minute preparations. It's almost time to go."

She backed away from him, barely breathing, watching his eyes. The tension which had barely subsided ramped back up. "We're going today?"

"We're waiting for the FedEx truck. As soon as we receive the last delivery, all will be ready. Your clothes arrived from the tailor. We've gathered every piece of relevant research, and David's testing the drone."

She stared at Elliott, baffled, and then simply blinked, making no sense whatever of this. It had only been two hours since she had mentioned a drone, jokingly. "He got one?"

Elliott nodded, eyes intent on hers. "It was either the first or second item he added to his want list."

A warm ripple of shock thinned the air in her lungs. *Why hadn't he told her?*

Evidently her thoughts showed, for Elliott said, "He ordered the drone to use for reconnaissance, but he's leery of introducing a UFO and possibly PE-4 into the nineteenth century. He likely won't use it, but he won't leave anything to chance, either"

"A drone and plastic explosives?"

"Kit took an assault rifle and saved a wagon train from a stampede. Nothing much came of it except a few journal entries about a mysterious gun."

"Changing history wasn't such a big concern when she was saving lives, I guess."

A slight smile turned into a wry glance as Elliott's mouth tucked in at one corner. "I told Kit she couldn't go back in time and change history, since it might obliterate her life. When Jack returned to find his journal, he got caught up in something that changed yer family history." Elliott took her arm. "Come on, let's walk." They turned toward the mansion, following a brick path around the paddock. "This will get tricky for ye', lass. When ye' exonerate Jack, he'll be coming home to a plantation which for ye', doesn't exist. Ye' and David will be the only people in the world who will have any memory of the plantation being destroyed and never rebuilt."

"But you'll know, won't you? I mean, we're having a discussion about the plantation right now."

"When you go back for Jack, ye're taking with ye' everything ye' know today. Ye're a doctor, ye' grew up in Richmond, and yer parents were teachers. Those memories are not going to change. When ye' see Jack, his memory will not be the same as yours. He'll be ready to return to the homeplace—"

"Which doesn't exist for me."

"When he's exonerated and saves the plantation, it will then exist in the future. It's what ye'll return to—to the world of Jack's memories, not yours."

78

MacKlenna Farm, Lexington, Kentucky, Present Day

CHARLOTTE TIED THE narrow black cravat into a small, flat bow and primped in front of the mirror. Satisfied with the look of trousers, shirt and vest, she slipped on a matching jacket and smoothed the front. The tailor had done a remarkable job in a very short time.

The shoulder-length wig she wore belonged to Meredith. When Meredith's hair fell out during chemo, Elliott had it made to match perfectly the color and texture of her hair. Meredith had hated wearing it, claiming it was too hot. She rarely wore it then. Since her hair had grown back, she gladly contributed it to Charlotte's costuming.

Charlotte pulled the hair into a queue and tied it at her nape with a leather thong. Transformed now into Charley Duffy, she paused in front of the mirror again, studying her appearance. There was something odd about the costume. She shrugged uncomfortably from the breasts binding and adjusted the cravat. The suit was too fitted, too perfect, and too brown. If she were going to dress like a man, she preferred to be a soldier, not a dandy.

She fluffed her beard with a few swipes of her fingers to give it a more rugged look, and then turned away from the mirror.

Her mind drifted from her clothing to her conversation with Elliott. What he'd said played like a short, looping video. It was possible she and Jack would no longer have shared memories, and the thought gave her a sense of leg-weakening helplessness, sharpened by grief. If she gave in to despair now, she'd be unable to focus on ensuring they'd at least have a future, with or without shared memories.

The Frasers' Maine Coon cat, Tabor, ran into the bedroom and leaped onto the bed, where she immediately burrowed all ten of her pounds into the middle of the pillows.

"You goofy cat. Don't you know you're not a person?" Charlotte sat on the edge of the bed and cuddled Tabor, who purred for her. "If you stow away in my bag, I'm sending you back. One trip to the past should be enough for a cat like you."

How in the world Kit managed to take care of a menagerie while traipsing across the country in 1852 boggled Charlotte's mind. The logistics of getting from Kentucky to Washington were complicated enough, and she only had to worry about herself.

"Is that really you?" Meredith's voice came softly from the Charlotte's doorway, startling her. She jerked her head around to see her friend's wide-eyed stare.

"Yes and no. Usually I have a sense of the person I'm portraying, but I have no clue who this man is." Charlotte glanced toward the mirror, squinting, as if refocusing would bring clarity. It didn't.

"Elliott thought he might have upset you earlier. Are you okay?"

"I think so." Charlotte gave up hoping for character insight and hugged Tabor goodbye.

"Good. He was worried."

Charlotte picked up the carpetbag with her medical supplies and clothing and joined Meredith, scratching at a bug bite on her hip. "He told me when the two of you met, he wasn't a very nice person. It's hard to imagine."

"He had good days, and those were fantastic," Meredith paused, and seemed to drift off, then returned as if she'd suddenly remembered what she was saying. "When the pain in his leg worsened, he depended on drugs and alcohol to get him through and then he became verbally abusive."

"I've seen similar things happen too many times. I'm sorry he went through it, but he looks healthy now."

"He is, thank God. It's been more than two years since he's had a drink. He'd be okay now with a glass of whiskey or wine, but he won't…" She paused again, curled her bottom lip over her top one. Something was definitely on her mind.

"Are *you* okay?" Charlotte asked. "You seem distracted."

"Do I? Well, hmm." Meredith dismissed Charlotte's observation with a shrug and seemed to remember the point of her visit. "Come downstairs. Elliott and David are waiting."

Charlotte had never seen Meredith so befuddled. Was she sick again? Had her cancer spread? Had she received a bad report? No, if it was true, she'd have all of Elliott's attention, but at the moment he was single-mindedly focused on Jack's rescue. Either she hadn't told Elliott, or her distraction had nothing to do with her health and everything to do with something else she'd discovered.

Charlotte shouldered her bag and followed Meredith down the stairs. "This is my third trip and I'm more scared this time than I was the other two combined."

"I often think about what Kit endured and wonder if I would have had half the courage she had. But I know for sure I don't have the courage you do," Meredith said.

"Don't discredit what you did. You delivered a healthy baby after an attempted murder, breast cancer surgery, and chemo. It's remarkable. No, it's amazing."

"I can't wait to meet the woman who has the emerald brooch," Meredith said.

Charlotte stopped on the stairs, almost tripping, and looked at Meredith. "It might be a man. But whoever has it, I hope to God, their journey isn't as traumatic."

Elliott jaunted out of the office and watched them descend the stairs. "I hope so, too."

She leaned against the newel post before stepping off the last riser, thinking. "Knowing someone else will go through a similar experience is not very comforting right now."

David joined them with a golden retriever close on his heels. He slipped the strap of her bag off her shoulder. "It's not about comfort. It's about finding true love, and there isn't a damn thing easy about it."

"What do the brooches have to do with finding true love?" she asked.

"It's complicated, and we shouldn't let it distract us." David beckoned her to follow with a cock of his head. "We'll tell ye' everything we know when ye' return."

Charlotte crossed her arms. "No. I'm not moving until you tell me what the stones have to do with true love."

Elliott sighed, scratching the back of his head. "Sean the first told Kit a story she later recorded in her journal in 1852. She left the journal for me to find in the future. According to the story, over four hundred years ago, a laird's wife was kidnapped. Three brothers went to rescue her. When they returned her to her husband, the brothers were each rewarded with a brooch. One was a ruby, the other a sapphire, and the third brother received an emerald." Elliott cleared his throat. "The stones bring true lovers together."

"*What?*" Charlotte put her hands on her hips and stomped to within a foot of Elliott. "*Are you serious?* This has all been about finding true love? What. A. Bunch. Of. Crap."

Elliott threw up his arms. "I'm merely telling ye' what I learned. Ye'll meet Sean shortly. Ask him."

"*I will.*" She marched into the office, then stopped, and turned back toward Elliott, who was standing in the doorway, looking rather perplexed. "The stone gods got it wrong this time. You know that, don't you?"

He sort of smiled and shrugged. "I don't have any control over the stones, Charlotte. I don't get to decide who gets them or where the stones take them. My job is to prepare people for their journey. This isn't about what's before ye', or even what's behind ye. It's about what's within ye'. When it's all said and done, if ye' can say ye're a happier and better person and have a fuller life than you did before, then the brooch will have given ye' all it was meant to give."

"I want my brother back, but even when I get him back, we

won't know anything about each other because we'll have different memories. I can tell you right now, when this is all said and done, I will *not* be a happier and better person." She grabbed a tissue from the box on the desk and wiped her eyes. "I'm sorry. I don't mean to take this out on you. You're right. You didn't pick me. You've given me everything I need to succeed. It's up to us now to bring Jack home." She went over to him and held out her arms for a hug. "Thank you so much."

Elliott pulled her into his arms and squeezed. "Ye'll be fine, lass. Trust yer intuition and ye'll turn 'round right."

She wasn't sure what he meant, but when she returned home she'd have plenty of time to reflect on his Elliott-isms.

David set her bag next to his on the conference table. Then he pulled out his cell phone and handed it to Elliott. "Don't run up my bill while I'm gone."

Elliott hugged him. "Ye' got everything? Money—"

David held up his hand. "No litany, please. We've gone through this a dozen times. If I've forgotten anything, we'll make do." He turned toward Charlotte. "Are ye' ready, Charley?"

"As ready as I'll ever be."

Elliott handed the brooch to her, and she quickly turned it over to David. "You steer this trip."

He gave it back. "I can't. This trip is yer destiny. Not mine." David looped the straps of his bags around his shoulders.

"Are you armed?" she asked.

He flipped open his jacket, revealing a revolver tucked in its shoulder holster.

"Good. If we land in the midst of a battle—"

He gave her a thumbs-up signal. "I got yer back." David's dark brows drew together, as though the late afternoon sunlight bothered him now that he was without his aviators. He caught her eye, and gave her a wry grin.

She tried to give the Frasers a smile, but her lips felt stiff. Days of preparation had led to this moment. Her heart hammered suddenly in her ears. God, she couldn't believe she was doing this again. It was definitely going to be the last trip. A trickle of sweat ran down between her bound breasts as the brooch heated in her hand.

David tapped her on the head. "Hold on to yer hat."

The tension broke, her anxiety faded, and she smiled. "I'll hold on to my hat. You hold on to me." She opened the stone, took a breath, and then stammered through the Gaelic spell once more. As the fog swirled around her feet, she added a silent prayer.

79

MacKlenna Farm, Lexington, Kentucky, 1865

WHEN THE FOG lifted, Charlotte found herself on a tree-lined drive leading to the MacKlennas' front porch. Instead of asphalt, the driveway was a dirt road full of muddy potholes. The fragrant smell of burning wood hung in the air. When she and David had left the future, the buds of the trees had been bursting open in the spring-like breezes. Now brilliant sunshine streamed through the dense stand of elm trees. Dark green, fully leafed branches formed a canopy on both sides of the road. The season had jumped ahead from late March to May or early June. It wasn't hot enough to be summer.

She glanced at David. His face was unreadable, but not his eyes, which were scanning the landscape. He was perfectly still, a warrior assessing danger and weighing risks. Then he seemed to relax and adjusted the weight of his two large carpetbags. "The wee farm looks the same but different. If ye' had put me in the paddock out of sight of the house, I would have still known where I was."

"It's beautiful, regardless of the century. Do you think the architect intended the Doric columns to resemble sentries guarding the house?"

"Thomas MacKlenna designed the house to resemble Monticello. In 1790, they probably needed protection."

Charlotte hopped over another mud puddle and around the next one. "Do you know what you're going to say?"

David drew a long breath, and his shoulders squared beneath his well-fitting jacket. "Thought I'd leave it up to ye'."

"Well, thanks. I guess." She hadn't given much thought to meeting Sean MacKlenna. To her, he was a necessary stop on the way to Washington. Although she was interested in meeting him, she didn't want to delay their departure. A cup of tea, a friendly chat, then they'd ask for transportation to the train station. "I'll tell Mr. MacKlenna I'm a friend of Braham's."

David stepped aside to let Charlotte climb the portico stairs ahead of him. "Braham might have told him about ye'."

"Probably. Or maybe he just mentioned a doctor. He had to explain how he came from the future somehow."

Reaching the front door, David clanged the big brass doorknocker. "Shall we see who's at home, then?"

Charlotte fingered a bullet hole. "These look recent."

"Aye, they do. Looks like they repaired some of the holes but left others. Wonder why?"

A butler dressed in fine livery, opened the door, and Charlotte forgot all about the holes. "May I help you?"

"Aye, is Mr. MacKlenna at home?" David asked. We're out-of-town acquaintances and have business to discuss."

The butler opened the door wider and invited them inside. "Sur. You'n wait in 'a parlor."

Other than stains on the hardwood floors which seemed lighter, and the paint on the walls more vivid, the residence hadn't changed. The same or similar eighteenth-century antiques filled the rooms.

David studied the painting hanging over the fireplace. "I wonder what happened to this painting. As many years as I've been visiting the mansion, I've never seen it."

A man shorter than David with lanky brown hair and intelligent eyes entered the room and noticed David admiring the painting. "Eilean Donan castle close to—"

"Dornie," David said.

"From yer accent, I'd wager it's not far from yer home."

"Not far," David agreed.

"I'm Sean MacKlenna."

"I ken yer name. I'm David MacBain. As I lad I spent time at the MacKlenna estate…" he paused, then continued, "with yer niece Kit."

Sean glanced from David to Charlotte, then back to David. "Ye' came through the time portal, then?"

Charlotte extended her hand. "I'm Charlotte Mallory."

A line furrowed between Sean's brows as he searched her face.

She gave her beard a little tug. "You'll have to excuse the disguise. We thought it would be safer for me to travel as a man."

A devilish spark rallied in his eyes. "Ye're the surgeon who saved Abraham's life."

Her cheeks flushed, and she nodded. "Yes, sir. I didn't give him a choice in the matter, and then he wasn't pleased when I wouldn't take him back."

"He also said he wasn't in love with ye', but ye' could see the denial on his face as easily as the scratch on his nose. He kens the stone's power, but he's fighting against it."

She looked at Sean wide-eyed and interested. "It's true, then, what Elliott said about the stone and finding love?"

"Aye, lass, 'tis true. The stone will lead ye' to the one of yer heart."

She pursed her lips with disappointment. The sapphire brooch might have led her to Braham, but it had no power to hold them together. She eased her shoulders with a little sigh and placed thoughts of hearts and stones on the back burner to simmer indefinitely.

"We're in a hurry to get to Washington," she said. "I hope it's still 1865."

"The date is May 5, 1865," Sean said.

She glanced at David. "It's soon enough, right? Nothing's happened in the trial yet."

David nodded. "Nothing yet."

"Thank goodness. Oh, here," she said, dropping the brooch into Sean's hand. "You can put this back inside the desk."

"Elliott is going to wear it out. I just popped it into its wee box, and here it is again." Sean placed the brooch in his jacket pocket. "I'll return it shortly. Elliott might decide to pay a visit too."

"When his son is older," David said, "Elliott will make the jump. He misses Kit. I do, too. Have ye' heard from her lately?"

"Aye, a telegram last week, but Cullen arrived this morning from Chicago. He's on his way to Washington."

A warbling whistle came from down the hall, beautiful music from a talented whistler. The tune might have been Bobby McFerrin's *Don't Worry, Be Happy*. Charlotte cut a quick glance toward David. The corner of his lip tilted up. The whistling preceded a man's appearance in the doorway. "Did I hear my name, Uncle?"

Charlotte blinked at the tall, dark-headed, John Kennedy-esque man who entered the room, smiling. His powerful presence wasn't just because of the Kennedy look. It was charisma. She couldn't explain it or define it, but it oozed from his pores. She wasn't easily impressed by looks, fame, fortune, or celebrity status, but Cullen certainly got her attention.

"I was telling our visitors ye' arrived this morning."

Cullen approached her, extending his hand, studying her with eyes which held her enthralled. "I'm Cullen Montgomery."

"I'm Charlotte Mallory," she finally managed. *So this is the ghost of MacKlenna Farm.* David had told her all about Cullen's hauntings. At first she found it hard to believe, but why not? The farm was enchanting. It might as well have a ghost, too.

Staring at her, oddly, Cullen's outrageously long dark lashes fluttered as he blinked several times. Obviously, he didn't trust what his eyes were telling him.

She tugged on her beard. "I don't look like a Charlotte, do I?"

His laugh was almost musical—full and vibrant and contagious. "Aye, my wife wears trousers, too, but she has no facial hair."

Charlotte grinned. "You know what they say. You can take a girl out of the twenty-first century but you can't take the twenty-first-century out of the girl."

Sean and Cullen exchanged glances then both threw back their heads and laughed.

"I'm sorry Kit isn't here to meet you." Cullen wiped tears from his eyes. "You came through with the brooch, aye?"

Charlotte removed the wig, shook out her hair, and then slowly peeled off the beard. "David and I have come back to save my brother."

"What happened to him?" Cullen asked.

She shifted uneasily and threw a glance at David. He shifted, too, moving closer to her. If they were going to be thrown out of the house for being connected to one of the conspirators, he'd be there to protect her. She cleared her throat and steeled herself. "He was arrested for conspiring to kill the President."

Cullen's eyes widened, but otherwise he hid his emotions. "Jack Mallory?"

She tensed and nodded with only a slight lift and dip of her chin.

Cullen pressed his fingertips together, bouncing them slowly off of each other, moving to the silent tick of a metronome. Finally, he stopped tapping his fingers and put his hands on his hips. "Braham sent me a telegram to come to Washington."

She gasped, clutching her chest. "*He did? When?*"

"A week ago. He asked me to come to Washington to help him defend one of the conspirators. Why?" Cullen asked.

She broke into a relieved smile. "It's a long story, but thank God, he's all right. We've been worried."

Sean gestured down the hall. "Let's retire to my office. We'll have more privacy there, and ye' can tell us yer story."

"We have a tradition," Cullen said. "The person telling the story brings the whiskey."

David dug into one of his carpetbags and pulled out a bottle. "Woodford Reserve. From a local distillery, or will be."

Cullen took the bottle and read the label. Then he clapped David on the back. "Unless your story is longer than an hour, we won't die of thirst."

The group entered the room with the familiar vast mahogany desk, full bookshelves, and floor-to-ceiling windows with glorious views of the pastures beyond the house. Charlotte came to a standstill right inside the doorway, taking in the scents of tobacco and leather. While the room appeared the same, the absence of Elliott made it seem somehow smaller.

"Do ye' want a drink, Charley?" David asked.

"Yes, please." She was drawn to the open window behind the desk and inhaled a lungful of afternoon air, cloyingly warm for early spring, but fresh and sweet from the roses beneath the window. There weren't roses outside Elliott's window.

"Here's yer drink, lass," David said, handing her a half-filled crystal glass. "Come, sit down. Today is the last time ye'll need to tell yer story."

Sean rearranged the chairs so they could sit in a circle. Charlotte began her story, and when she reached the part about Braham's disappearance, David picked up the tale. From there, Sean added to the story, telling them about Braham's appearance and the fight with the Reb deserters.

Charlotte shook her head, groaning. "I was afraid it might happen before he fully recovered. Are you sure he wasn't hurt?"

"Aye, a wee scratch from broken glass. I told him I'd send him back to ye' if he got shot."

"I'm surprised he didn't surrender right then," she groused.

Sean laughed, but she hadn't meant it to be funny.

Sean finished his story and Charlotte continued with the next part of hers, ending with her return to MacKlenna Farm. Three hours later, with everyone up to speed, David poured a final round of whiskey, emptying the bottle.

Not long after Charlotte had begun the story, Cullen had stopped her to fetch a journal and pencil, and had taken notes. Now he flipped through the pages. "Why do you think Braham didn't go home with you after the assassination? His boss was dead. The war was over, and, knowing him as well as I do, I'm sure he was in love with you."

She stared at her hands and considered Braham's state of mind the last time she saw him. "I'm not sure I can explain it." She looked up into Cullen's eyes, seeing warmth and understanding, and she knew she could trust him.

She straightened, saying, "I think several things combined to keep him here. After almost dying at Chimborazo, his degrading treatment and abuse in Castle Thunder, and his failure to save Lincoln, he was compelled to reclaim his honor. Although he'd never lost it, he believed he had. He was looking for a way to restore what he lost. Will he find it? I don't know."

"His honor pulled him into the war when I tried to keep him out of it. But he had made a pledge to General Sheridan in 1852. A pledge he shouldn't have made, but I'm thankful he did."

"Stubborn man." Charlotte pulled a tissue from her pocket and wiped her nose.

Cullen chuckled. "He's a McCabe and a Highlander. You can't expect anything less." Then he eyed her speculatively. "And what about you? Do you love him enough to give up the life you have and stay here with him?" Cullen asked in a low, even voice, but it resonated throughout the quiet room. She could tell from his tone he wasn't judging her. But beyond the simple question was an undercurrent of more than curiosity. She pressed her lips together to avoid giving him a hasty answer. He deserved more than a quick yes or no.

David opened one of the carpetbags at his feet and withdrew a stack of papers. "We have a copy of the complete record of the conspiracy trial." The interruption was transparent to everyone, and Cullen turned his attention to David, politely leaving his question hanging in the air unanswered.

"The evidence against Jack is circumstantial, but Stanton doesn't care. There's no due process, no presumption of innocence, no jury of their peers, and no appeal. The trial is only a formality before guilty verdicts are handed down."

"The *New York Herald* predicted the trial will start next week," Cullen said.

"On the tenth, the commission will ask the defendants if they'd like to seek counsel. We have to be there then and prepared to represent him," Charlotte said.

Cullen made a notation in his journal. "The earliest train leaves in the morning. Until then, I'd like to study your documents."

David handed over a six-inch stack of papers. "These are the pertinent pages relative to Jack. There are more than forty-six hundred pages of testimony. We have the entire record with us."

Cullen stared at the bags on the floor next to David's chair. "Forty-six hundred pages won't fit in the bags your carrying."

"I have the rest in another format and it's easily accessible," David said.

"When you read through the transcript, you'll notice Braham's name is never mentioned. We don't know why. We thought he might have been killed before the trial, but since he sent you a telegram, we know he's alive. But we don't know what part, if any, he played in the trial."

"Is my name there?" Cullen asked.

"No," she said, shaking her head.

Cullen thumbed through some of the pages. "Who represented him?"

David flipped through a few pages then pointed. "A Mr. Patterson. We don't know anything about him, and he did a lousy job."

Charlotte frowned. "Quite an understatement."

"I'll start reading immediately. Anything else I should know before I begin?" Cullen asked.

Charlotte put her hands on her knees and leaned forward. "We don't know if I've been implicated, too. It's why I intend to arrive wearing a disguise."

Cullen picked up the papers and fanned them. "Are you mentioned in any of these pages?"

She shook her head. "I'm worried I might…"

"…be considered guilty by association," Cullen said.

"That could be what happened to Mary Surratt. Her son, John, had well-known ties to Booth, but the police were unable to find John. So Stanton went after Mary, hoping John would surface to protect his mother. He didn't."

Sean reached into his pocket and pulled out the brooch. "Since ye' don't have the sapphire, ye' best keep this. Ye' may need to make a quick escape." He returned the stone to Charlotte. "When ye' find the sapphire, give the ruby to Cullen. He can bring it back when he makes his return to trip to California."

Charlotte pinned the brooch to the inside of her jacket's lapel. "Let's pray we find it, or we might have bigger troubles than changing the outcome of the trial."

"Don't worry, lass. Ye'll find the stone, or the stone will find ye'. It's not finished with ye' yet," Sean said.

Cullen nodded as if he agreed completely. "You can be sure of it."

80

Washington City, 1865

T HREE DAYS LATER Charlotte, Cullen, and David arrived in Washington, dirty and tired. Delays in Cincinnati, Parkersburg, and Baltimore had tacked an additional day onto their two-day journey. While Cullen and David had remained calm throughout, Charlotte had been pissy with conductors, snappy with fellow travelers, and downright rude to anyone who mentioned the conspirators. The food on the train was barely edible, the accommodations were atrocious, and the overcrowded cars had made it impossible for them to discuss Jack's situation. Thank goodness Sean had insisted they bring a basket of food with them, or she would have starved.

When they disembarked in Washington, she was so thrilled to be off the train with its never-ending clacking, she almost knelt down and kissed the ground. She didn't, but she did squint against the glaring overcast sky. Ragged clouds streamed in from the south, and the scent of ozone heralded stormy weather ahead. Nothing new.

She wondered why she was irritable and caustic. David even asked what happened to the woman he'd met at MacKlenna Farm. He'd been joking, of course, but there was underlying seriousness in his tone. She was extremely worried, which kept her from sleeping, which made her more crotchety. Fatigue she could handle. Fatigue combined with worry and stress she couldn't, at least not for long.

How was Jack handling the daily rations of soft bread and salt meat? He had a healthy appetite, but he also worked out daily. He'd lose weight for sure, and without exercise he'd have no outlet for his frustration and fear. She'd seen creepy pictures of the torture hoods the prisoners were forced to wear and imagined Jack suffering from wearing the heavy canvas tied tightly around his head with cotton pads placed over eyes and ears. He could withstand some sensory deprivation, but not seven weeks of it. He could lose touch with reality and start hallucinating.

Was Stanton a sadist, devising such an instrument of cruelty? Was it his purpose? To induce mental and physical suffering? Or was it to keep the conspirators incommunicado? What in God's name could they say to each other which would make any difference in the outcome of the trial? The men were outcasts, beyond the pale of human sympathy, but one of them *was* innocent.

No wonder she couldn't sleep.

While Cullen went to hire a carriage to take them to Braham's townhouse, she and David sat on a bench and looked out over the city.

"I've been all around the world. Seen the worst parts of it, but this," he gestured with his arm to emphasize his point, "is not an undeveloped country. It's not contaminated by twenty-first-century noise and pollution." He shrugged. "I don't know what it resembles. A movie set, maybe."

Charlotte gripped the edge of the bench and fell into a slow, comforting rock. "I thought so, too, until I saw the suffering. When men are bleeding all around you, it quickly becomes very real."

"Ye' jumped into a situation most people would run away from."

She stopped rocking, and her knuckles turned white from gripping the bench, but she couldn't loosen her grip. "I've been critical of Civil War surgeons for years. Now I know firsthand they did the best they could with limited resources. In modern warfare you normally don't have hundreds of injuries to deal with at the same time. In this war, the surgeons saved the ones they could and later wept over the ones they couldn't."

David placed his warm, strong hand over hers and lightly

squeezed. He didn't speak. He didn't have to. He'd lost buddies in Afghanistan, and from what she'd read on the back jacket of his book, he'd almost lost his life saving the wounded while under heavy fire.

"There's Cullen." David patted her hand, stood, and hefted the bags onto his shoulders. "Come on, Charley. The clock's ticking."

She spotted Cullen about twenty yards away, chatting with the driver of a barouche. "I don't think the carriage has a meter like our taxis."

She glanced up and met David's eyes. He didn't need aviators to hide what he was thinking or seeing. His beautiful, hooded brown eyes did it naturally. Impossibly full lips tipped up into a smile, and he flipped the brim of her top hat, exposing her face to the sun.

"Glad to see ye' retained a bit of yer humor. I think it's the beard ye're wearing making ye' short-tempered."

"Let's hope I can take it off when we get to Braham's."

The city was once again in high spirits. National colors bedecked the buildings, replacing emblems of mourning. Passengers on the train had mentioned the muster out of a million men had begun at the end of April, and thousands of soldiers were pouring into the city. Camps were miles long and wide on every slope and ridge. Charlotte sat tense in her seat, observing the restless and impatient people bumping each other as they traversed the sidewalks.

"Are ye' okay?" David asked.

"This is my third trip here. The first time I was scared to death. The second time, I was excited, anticipating a romantic getaway with Braham. This time I'm scared again, but not for myself."

"We'll get him out. I promise."

Charlotte gave his arm a pat and a squeeze. "Promises are easy to make. They're impossible to keep."

"Not all of them are, Charley."

Cullen stopped whistling a Bach tune she recognized, but didn't know the name of the piece. "David's right. I've got some ideas, but I have to talk with Braham first. Keep your eyes on the prize, lass."

"Paul and Silas, bound in jail. Had no money for to go their bail. Keep

your eyes on the prize, hold on," Charlotte said. "It's an American civil rights song. I guess Kit taught it to you."

A distant stare turned Cullen's face into an expression of pensive admiration. "Music stopped for her one day, and she swore she'd never again play the guitar or sing. It wasn't easy, but she found her way through the darkness, and music is alive in her heart today. The days ahead will get darker, but you'll hear the music again, too."

The carriage stopped in front of Braham's townhouse and Cullen alighted first.

"Let's not tell Braham's butler who I am until we find out if I'm under suspicion. We don't know what happened when the police arrested Jack. Edward might have given him up. And we have to find the sapphire brooch. If we don't, Braham will have to take Jack to the future and then come back for David and me."

"We'll work out logistics later, but I agree we should keep your identity secret until we know your status. Although I don't believe Edward would betray his employer's friend," Cullen said.

Charlotte threw the strap of her carpetbag over her shoulder and stepped down to the sidewalk. "He might if the police threatened him, as they did most of the witnesses."

David glanced up and down the street, then turned slowly, looking at the park and the White House in the distance. "Great location. Let's go inside. We're not going to learn anything standing out here."

Above the rumble of heavy wagons on the hard-packed dirt came the sounds of spring, barks and yelps of dogs from a neighbor's yard, and birds singing in full voice from the elm tree in front of the townhouse. The second-floor windows facing the street were located in the two rooms she and Jack had used. His was close to the tree. Hers looked out over the front door.

Cullen led the way to the front door, but stopped before knocking and said to Charlotte and David, "Since I'm expected, I'll introduce you as business associates from Kentucky."

Edward opened the door quickly after Cullen's knock. A sour expression turned to one of pleasure when he recognized Cullen. "Welcome, Mr. Montgomery. Come in. Colonel McCabe will be glad to see you."

"Afternoon Edward." Cullen turned toward Charlotte and David. "These are my associates Charley Duffy and David MacBain. Braham doesn't know I invited them, but he'll be glad for the help, I'm sure."

"Did you say *colonel?*" she asked.

"The major was promoted to colonel for his assistance during the attack against Secretary Seward," Edward said.

A strange ripple, like pebbles thrown into a pond, went through Charlotte, and her heart seemed to sigh. She hoped being rewarded for his service would go a long way toward restoring Braham's perceived loss of honor.

"They should have made him a general," Cullen said. "Where is he, by the way?"

Edward lowered his head, shaking it. "At the Old Arsenal Penitentiary, trying to visit Mr. Jack. He wasn't involved in Mr. Lincoln's death. I know it for sure." Edward sighed, woefully. "I wish Miss Charlotte was here, but the colonel, he said he didn't expect her to come back, and we had to take care of Mr. Jack. Lordy, if only she was here…"

She dug her fingers into her wig, ready to rip it off and reveal herself. "Edward—"

David placed his hand firmly on her back, a warning gesture, and she shut her mouth.

"We'd like to work in Braham's office while he's gone." David's hand remained pressed against her. "Could ye' lead us there?"

"Yes, sir. Leave your bags here. I'll take them upstairs and see to your rooms."

Once inside Braham's office with the door closed, David turned toward her, arms crossed over his chest, eyes hot and glaring. "We had a discussion on the street about keeping yer identity secret. Thirty seconds later, yer ready to come clean. Ye' can't, Charley. Ye'll compromise the mission." He pressed his hand hard on her shoulder, forcing her into a chair. "Sit and remember this is about Jack, *not ye'.*"

Cullen slipped off his jacket and hung it on the back of the desk chair. "If the police come looking for you, they'll pilfer through our research, which would be devastating for Jack."

"Okay, you got my attention." So did a wave of nausea. She put her feet up on the desk and rested her head against the wall.

"Ye' look like the blood drained from yer face. Are ye' sick?" David asked.

She nodded. "I think I caught something on the train."

"Ye' sure ye're not pregnant," David said.

"I told you I failed the test."

"Ye' get false positives and negatives with those, don't ye'?" David said.

"Rarely. But I don't have any pregnancy symptoms."

"Nausea is a symptom. Kit's had it with every bairn."

Charlotte glared, jaw clenching. "So is travel, bad food, and no sleep. *I'm not pregnant* and don't either of you mention the possibility again."

The men busied themselves rearranging Braham's desk to make room to work. David unbuttoned his jacket and hung it on a coat hook on the back of the door. He rolled his neck, settling the leather of the shoulder holster more comfortably. There was something odd about his pistols.

"Are you carrying Glocks?" she asked.

"Aye."

Cullen cocked his head. "Kit had a fancy automatic rifle. You should have seen her setting her sights on several hundred buffalo. I'd never been so scared. Our lives depended on a weapon I knew nothing about, and she acted like she was at target practice."

David laughed. "Even as a kid, she had more guts than sense. Nearly got me killed a time or two."

"We got a wee lassie Kit calls her mini-me. From what you're saying about Kit's childhood, mini-me is an apt description."

David slapped Cullen on the back, laughing. "Hope ye' survive to see the lass married."

"It's Kit who'll likely not survive. Tell Elliott, will you? He'll be glad to hear she's getting back the trouble she gave her father and godfather."

Charlotte watched the exchange between Cullen and David, awed by the depth of love they had for Kit. Now she understood the glassy-eyed look in Elliott's eyes every time someone mentioned her name. How blessed, to be so loved by so many people. She only had Jack, and their relationship was threatened. Her throat became painfully tight, and she swallowed back a gallon of tears, which, if allowed out, would swamp the room. Time to get back to business. She cleared her throat.

"You've had several days to study the court record. What do you think?"

Cullen eased into the desk chair, retrieved a stack of documents from his leather-bound briefcase, and spread them out on the desk. "I have a list of questions. I've also identified the weaknesses in the case against Jack."

"What does your gut tell you?"

"Exactly what ye' told me. Seward wants the defendants convicted. A military trial will be an injustice. However, with the current sentiment in Washington and around the country, odds are almost certain even a jury of their peers would convict them all."

"But at least they'd have a jury and their day in court instead of Seward's generals with verdicts already in hand. What about the testimony? Did you find anything you can use to help him?" Charlotte asked.

"Several pieces of key testimony against the defendants, and Jack in particular, were obviously manufactured, exploited, or coerced. After reading through the documents ye've given me, it's obvious the defense had no time to prepare. We have time now. We also have the witness list. We'll be ready."

Cullen thumbed through several sheets until he found one in particular. "Do ye' know anything about this?" he addressed Charlotte. "A witness, identifying himself as a cabbie, testified he dropped off a man and woman at Major McCabe's house, picked up Jack and Booth, and delivered them to the National Hotel. Do you know the identity of the couple?"

Charlotte dropped her feet with a loud thud, mouth agape. She shot to her feet, fists slamming to her hips. "*What a damnable lie. Yes, I know the couple.*" She breathed heavily, battling outrage for a bit of emotional control. "Colonel Gordon Henly and Charlotte Mallory." She rolled back her eyes, shaking her head. "What a lie. It was the last date I had with the asshole colonel. We had been to the theater, then had dinner at the Willard, where I saw Braham for the first time since he had disappeared and driven to Kentucky. Gordon and I had a disagreement. It was more of an argument, really. When we arrived back at Braham's townhouse in *Gordon's carriage,*" she said with emphasis, "driven by *his driver*, we met Booth, who had just finished an interview with Jack. And, by the way, I was furious with Jack for inviting that man to Braham's house."

"Why was Booth here?" Cullen asked.

"Jack said it was too noisy at the National Hotel, and he wanted to tape the conversation secretly."

Cullen gave her a puzzled expression.

"With a recording device," David said. "It's like a stenographer reading the words aloud. Ye' don't have to read them. Ye' listen."

"Like an iPod?" Cullen asked. "I listen to music on Kit's iPod."

David arched his brow. "After all these years it still works?"

"Kit says the sun charges it." Cullen waved his hand. "We digress. Continue with your story."

"When Gordon saw Booth, he fawned all over the man. Then, after Booth left, Gordon and Jack went back to the Willard—in *Gordon's* carriage again—to find Braham. If the cabbie testifies to delivering Jack and Booth to the National Hotel, he's lying."

"What was Gordon's relationship with Jack?" Cullen asked.

"Gordon hated him. He thought Jack was to blame for my lack of interest in him, and Jack...Well, Jack has a certain effect on women. Gordon didn't like it at all. He fancies himself a ladies' man, but he couldn't compete with Jack."

"Do ye' think he would go so far as to implicate Jack in the assassination?"

"Gordon is a drug addict," she said, her voice shaking a little. "He loathes Jack, and he's obsessed with me, or was."

"*Why* didn't ye' mention this in yer video statement?" David asked, eyes blazing.

She shrugged with a tight movement, almost a flinch. "It didn't seem important."

Cullen made a choked noise. "*Important?* It's the key that unlocks our defense."

Excited voices from the hall alerted them only seconds before the door swung open, and Braham stomped into the room, noticing Cullen immediately.

She fixed Braham with a direct look but he hadn't noticed her yet.

The lines of his face curved in sudden joy. Braham went quickly to the desk and embraced his friend, clapping Cullen several times on the back. "Damn, it's good to see you." Then he noticed David and his eyebrows shot up. "What are *you* doing here?" He glanced from Cullen to David, and then back at Cullen.

As if remembering there was another person in the room, he jerked his head in Charlotte's direction. The red of his scar was clearly visible above his eye. He pressed his lips so tightly together they were barely evident in the depths of his neatly clipped beard. He took a step toward her, and she moved backwards, her heels scraping against the wall. The air seemed sucked from the room. She bit her lower lip, trying to think of what to say, but nothing came to mind as he advanced closer, then closer still, until he stopped within inches of her.

The memory of their last moments together seemed to cross his face, and the hint of a smile, wry yet painful, showed in his glistening eyes. He traced the curve of her lips, and then a pinched look of shock replaced the smile, giving way to slump-shouldered sadness. He pulled her into his arms, and in a voice as soft as his breath on her cheek, he said, "Ah, Charlotte, I'm so sorry."

His tears fell silently upon her cheeks.

81

Washington City, 1865

CHARLOTTE LEFT THE men and retired to her bedroom to compose herself, change out of her miserable Ace bandages and facial hair and clean up a bit. When she returned, only a little refreshed, but more comfortable without the beard and wig, she heard voices behind the closed doors leading into the parlor. She put her ear to the door but couldn't distinguish voices or words. She doubted anyone other than Braham, Cullen, and David were in the room, so she knocked and opened the door at the same time. The men made a move to stand, but she made a stopping motion with her hand.

"Don't get up on my account," she said.

Braham stood anyway and came up to her. "I hope, since you're my guest, you'll at least allow me to fix you a drink."

She fingered the hair above his scar and pushed strands out of the way so she could see the injury. "It's healing well. How's your shoulder?"

"I had a surgeon at the hospital where you worked remove the stitches. He asked me if you'd sewed me up. Said he recognized your handiwork."

"Really?" She smiled, pleased by the compliment.

Braham poured a glass of whiskey and handed it to her. "They thought well of you."

She took a restorative gulp, sighing blissfully as the amber-colored liquid trickled down the back of her throat, extending tendrils of warmth and comfort into her chest. "What have I missed?"

Braham waited until she settled into a corner of the sofa before taking a seat across from her. "We've been talking about Cullen's lad, Thomas. We knew you'd want to be part of the discussion concerning Jack, so we've been waiting for you."

Braham wasn't being truthful. There was no look of subterfuge, no averting of his eyes, but she could feel a heaviness in the air. They'd been discussing her. Maybe she was overly sensitive right now, but she didn't think she was completely off her game.

"I've asked Stanton what evidence the commission has against Jack, but he's refused to tell me. I believe whatever he has is circumstantial. If Jack had sold at least one article to the newspaper, it would support his claim of being a writer. But he didn't. Do you know why?"

"He never told me," she said, "but it probably has something to do with his writing style. His undergraduate degree is in journalism, but he writes differently than reporters do now."

The muscles tightened around Braham's eyes as if he were confused. "He told me he studied pre-law, not journalism. I asked specifically why he studied pre-law before going to law school."

"No," she said, shaking her head. "You're mistaken. It was journalism. In fact, he had a part-time job working for the Richmond-Times Dispatch."

Braham leaned forward in his seat, both hands gripping his glass. "He said his mother arranged a position with a Richmond law firm. He worked in the file room and ran errands while in college."

A sinking, twisting knot wrapped around her throat. "My mother didn't have any friends who were lawyers." She said it slowly, enunciating each one, as if he was a child who couldn't hear or comprehend.

"Charlotte," David said in a warning tone, and her head shot up. "This is what Elliott was talking about when he said ye'd have different memories."

Braham glanced at her and repeated David's statement as a question. "Why would you have different memories?"

"Elliott believes it's because of Jack's execution—" David said.

Braham came up out of his chair. "*His what?*"

Cullen shoved a piece of paper into Braham's hand. "Read this. It's a copy of his death warrant."

Braham read out loud, his face crumpling like the paper in his shaking hand: "*Finding.* Of the specification, Guilty. *Sentence.* And the commission does therefore sentence the said Jack Mallory to be hung by the neck until he be dead, at such time and place as the President of the United States shall direct, two-thirds of the members of the commission concurring therein." Braham grabbed the edge of his chair, swaying slightly, his face ashen. "How in *God's* name is this possible?"

Faintly startled by his tone of voice, she said, "It won't happen now, but it did happen. Let me ask you this. We found a letter Jack wrote to me, asking me to claim his body and bury him in the cemetery near the homeplace by the river he loved. Do you know what he's talking about?"

Braham stared, fixing her with his brilliant green eyes, full of turbulent thoughts she couldn't read. "You don't?"

She shook her head.

He turned slowly red and seemed to swell. He opened his mouth in a futile search for words. After a long moment he asked, "You don't have any memory of growing up at the plantation?"

"Why would I? I didn't grow up there. We lived in Richmond a few blocks from Virginia Commonwealth University, where our parents taught history and philosophy."

"Ah, lass, you did grow up there." His voice was scarcely louder than the beating of her own heart. "Your parents weren't teachers. They were United States Senators. So were your grandsires, back six generations. The Mallory name is the most prestigious name in the Commonwealth, and you're an heiress."

She flapped her hand, dismissing him. "Impossible. Where did you hear this wild story?"

"I've been to your mansion. Stayed there while I recovered after Chimborazo. I've seen the family portraits. I've read the history of the plantation from the mid-sixteen-hundreds to the deaths of your parents."

Silence filled the room until his words, short and brutal and impossible, echoed off the walls. Her brother was in prison for conspiring to kill the President, and the life she had known didn't exist, according to Braham. As soon as they exonerated Jack, they would return to a life she knew nothing about, but if they lost the case and lost Jack, she'd return to the life she knew without him. Could anything be more screwed up? Although Elliott had warned her that could happen, she hadn't truly understood the significance.

David came over to her with the whiskey decanter and refilled her glass. "Drink, Charley. Ye' said it didn't matter if yer histories might be different. What mattered was freeing Jack. We'll save the plantation, too, if we can."

"I'll send my man to Richmond to warn Doctor Mallory. If he knows there's a plot to burn the house, he can be prepared. When does it happen? Do you know?" Braham asked.

"Soon, I think," she said. Then she realized what he intended to do. "But don't you need Gaylord to help with the investigation here?"

Braham cocked his head in David's direction. "I think that's what David intends to do."

Charlotte put down her glass and sat forward in her seat. With her fingers linked, her thumb rubbed nervously at the first joint of her index finger. "But Gaylord has contacts who might prove helpful."

"It will only take him a few days to get there, warn Mallory, and return." Braham nodded as though verifying something to himself. "David's a very resourceful lad. I've seen it for myself. He'll make contacts of his own. By the time Gaylord returns, David will know what needs to be done."

Charlotte quit worrying the joint of her finger, picked up a small pillow on the sofa, and hugged it to her chest. "Elliott worked up an identity for me so I could appear in court as counsel, too. But I'll need something to do."

"I don't know what Elliott had in mind, but you *will not* go to court. Can you imagine the trouble we'd have if you were recognized? I beg of you, for Jack's sake, please don't do anything rash. We'll give you assignments every day so you won't feel helpless, but I can't defend your brother if I have to worry about where you are and what you're doing."

She glanced up and caught Cullen's eyes. He gave her a faint, tired smile. "I'll need yer' help in handwriting the motions we're going to file. I intend to read all forty-six hundred pages of testimony, and I'll need ye' to summarize the documents."

"You brought all those documents with you? How?" Braham asked.

"David has a…" Cullen used his hands to form a longish square. "A magic box. You read the index, click on the document you want, and magic takes you there."

"An iPad?" Braham said.

"A MacBook," David said.

"I'll read every page, too," Braham said. Then he raised an eyebrow. "But don't you need a charging device?"

"We'll use solar power," David said.

"We know the identity of the one hundred ninety-eight witnesses the prosecution intends to call. We'll interview the ones they haven't sequestered," Cullen said. "And file a petition for a writ of habeas corpus with Judge Wylie of the Supreme Court of the District of Columbia."

"How do you intend to get around the Habeas Corpus Act of 1863?" Braham asked.

"The act specifically states the President can suspend the privilege of the writ of habeas corpus under certain conditions *during the present rebellion.* Our position is the present rebellion should be considered over when the last battle is—was, by the time we file— fought on May 13, which lifts the suspension."

"Let me see it," Braham said. Cullen handed him a copy of the act and he quickly reviewed the short document.

"We have a three-pronged approach. One, Habeas Corpus Act of 1863 is no longer in full force and effect because the *present rebellion* is over; two, military tribunals do not have jurisdiction over civilians in states where civilian courts are operating; and three, torture is forbidden under the Eighth Amendment. We'll be breaking legal ground with the cruel and unusual punishment argument."

"The petitioner in *Ex parte Milligan* prevails with the question of jurisdiction. Here's a copy of the case," Cullen said, handing the document to Braham. "In writing the opinion for the majority, Justice Davis said, *The Constitution of the United States is the law for rulers and people, equally in war and peace, and covers with the shield of its protection all classes of men, at all times, and under all circumstances.*"

"What's the date of the case?" Braham asked, flipping pages.

"The decision's dated April 3, 1866," Cullen said. "Elliott's research team drafted a brief based on the *Milligan* case, but with facts relevant to ours."

"If Stanton can exert power over the United States Supreme Court, then he'll be single-handedly undermining the United States Constitution. The press should enjoy debating it," Cullen said.

"Do you think we could interest the petitioner's attorneys in the *Milligan* case to join us?" Cullen looked through the copy in his hand. "The attorneys are James Garfield and Jeremiah Black. Black's a former United States Attorney General and Secretary of State. He might be interested."

"Garfield is a future President," Charlotte said. "He'll be assassinated, too."

"I don't remember anyone mentioning the lawyers' names in our preparations," David said.

"I took an undergraduate class in law and medicine," she said. "We studied the case. The President was shot twice in the back. One bullet barely missed his spinal cord. There was testimony at the trial saying Garfield died because of medical malpractice."

"Two Presidents assassinated within…" Cullen said.

"Sixteen years," Charlotte said with a nod. "Then, twenty-one years later, President McKinley is shot, and President Kennedy sixty years later. I only mention it because those assassins, or the ones who survived, had jury trials."

"Were those Presidents shot during times of war?" Cullen asked.

"No," Charlotte said, "and arguably neither was Lincoln. Lee surrendered the week before the assassination. If you'd asked anyone on the street, they would have said the war was over. The official position, however, was even though Richmond had fallen, the Confederate government was on the move and still functioning."

David flipped through pages of a yellow legal pad. "Elliott's research team said not to file anything until after Jeff Davis is captured on May 10 and the last battle is fought on May 13."

"I'm curious about Elliott's research team," Braham said. "What'd they think they were doing?"

"Helping Jack write a screenplay," Charlotte said. "I told them two movie producers were waiting on script revisions before they agreed to invest millions of dollars. We were in a rush, and they worked overtime." She swallowed a large gulp of whiskey. She'd have to take out a second mortgage to pay the bill, but it didn't matter. Nothing mattered but getting Jack back.

"I *don't* condone the actions of the conspirators," she continued as soon as the whiskey had burned all the way down her throat, "but I believe in the Constitution and the Bill of Rights. We're a country of laws. And Stanton and Johnson are throwing them out the window to get quick convictions. I know their friend was murdered, but they're not going to kill my brother in their thirst for revenge."

Her breathing was loud and ragged in her ears. She glanced at Braham. His pain was evident in his sad eyes and the tightness around his mouth. "You were tried by a military court *in absentia* and convicted. The court had jurisdiction over you because you were a soldier. This military court does not have jurisdiction over civilians."

"The argument didn't get Mary Surratt anywhere," Cullen said. "But if we file a writ earlier, and the judge decides the commission does have the authority to detain Jack, we'll have an appealable decision."

"What's to stop Johnson from signing an order stating the writ is suspended in cases such as this, as he'll do for Surratt?"

"If he does, we'll take two actions," Cullen said, "First, we'll encourage Congress to impeach Johnson, arguing he acted outside the bounds of his constitutional authority. Second, we'll file a lawsuit against the President claiming his authority to suspend the writ of habeas corpus expired at the end of war."

"What's our goal, other than to free Jack?" Braham asked.

"In the present climate, we won't prevail with our legal challenges, but we'll cause a serious debate in the legal community from here to New York, and we'll try the case in the press, too," Cullen said.

Charlotte gave Cullen a level look from beneath her brows. "Do you think we have any chance of winning?"

Cullen's eyes never left hers as he shook his head. "No. It's possible we'll cause enough public debate the commission will reconsider its rush to judgment. Which will give us more time to move our case through the courts."

She set down her glass and buried her face in her hands for a moment. Then she looked up, hot tears forming in her eyes "I get so frustrated thinking about what they're doing to Jack. It makes me sick." She sniffed and pressed the back of her wrist at the base of her nose. "The first person to see Jack has to take him back to the twenty-first century. I don't care about history. I don't care about the plantation. I don't care about the trial. I want my bro...bro...ther back."

David rose quickly and knelt down in front of her, his knees cracking like a pop of a pistol. He took her hand in his. "We've gone through all of these arguments. We have to see the trial through and get Jack acquitted."

She cast her eyes down and fixed them on their tightly clasped hands.

"Look, Charley, I've read every interview Jack's given. I talked to his friends, his agent, those who know him best, and there wasn't one of them who didn't think he could withstand deprivation and torture for a limited time. Trust in him and have faith in his legal team. We'll get him out."

She put her arms around David's neck and bathed his hard, muscular shoulder with her grief. There wasn't anything soft about him but his heart. Although he was balanced on his haunches, his arms tightened around her. He didn't try to calm her. He didn't pat her. He simply held her. When she stopped crying, Braham handed her his handkerchief. She wiped her eyes and blew her nose. Calmed now, she smiled at David, brushing at his wet shirt. "Thanks for the shoulder."

Standing, he squeezed her hand. "Keep yer eye—"

She gave him a thumbs up. "On the prize."

Braham plucked at his moustache distractedly. "I'll make discreet inquiries about the attorneys who will represent the petitioner in the *Milligan* case. Whether they want to join us or not, we need to have motions ready to file in the District of Columbia Court as soon as we're appointed Jack's attorneys."

"When you make an appearance, you'll get crosswise with Stanton. Remember, he's your boss," Cullen said.

Braham sighed, making a brief gesture of frustration. "Former boss. I'll not stand idly by while he abuses the constitution. I'll resign prior to becoming attorney of record."

Charlotte cleared her throat delicately. "How should we handle Gordon?"

Braham wheeled on her with a ferocious glare. "*How the hell* is Henly involved in this?"

She cringed as Cullen handed Braham a page from the record. "A man we believe is Henly's personal driver is on the witness list. Here's a copy of his testimony. Charlotte says it's fabricated."

Braham's hand shook as he read the statement. "Booth was here? *In my house?*" His glare intensified. "Why didn't you tell me?"

A hot flush burned up her neck to her cheeks. She shot him a quick glance, not sure whether to apologize or duck and run. "Jack and I decided…not to. It was a mistake, I admit. But at the time you were bent on killing him."

"It does explain why Jack and Henly showed up together at the bar at the Willard not long after Henly took you home," Braham said.

"It might be in Jack's best interest if you're not the attorney of record. We might need you to testify," Cullen said.

Braham scratched his chin. "We have two days to consider the ramifications. First we need to draft the writ."

"Already written," Cullen said.

"When'd you find time?" Braham asked.

"I didn't. Elliott's research team drafted complaints, motions, and briefs based on mid-nineteenth-century law. When we start filing documents, the commission will feel blindsided, and Stanton will believe there's a security leak."

Charlotte's empty stomach reminded her she hadn't eaten. "Let's go to the Willard for dinner and show Washington Jack has a formidable force behind him."

"*No,*" Braham, Cullen, and David said loudly, and in unison.

Charlotte jerked back away from the blast of testosterone. "I thought—"

"We've got to be inconspicuous," Cullen said. "We don't want to show our hand, especially to Henly. If he knows you're in town, he might conveniently manufacture an incriminating statement to get you locked up in the Old Arsenal, too."

"Do you mean I can't leave the house without this disguise?"

"It's exactly what we mean," Braham said. "But wear whatever you want inside. Your identity is safe with the staff. David, however, can come and go as he pleases. The city is so crowded no one will be suspicious of a newcomer hanging around the hotels and clubs," Braham said.

"Do you think we should decamp to Georgetown where we'll have guaranteed privacy to prepare for trial?" Cullen asked.

"Once you take on Jack's representation," Charlotte said, "you'll be ostracized. It's what happens to Captain Frederick Aiken, Mary Surratt's attorney. I don't think people will throw bricks through your windows, but you never know. Today you're a hero. No one will understand how you could agree to represent one of the conspirators."

"I'll be yer ears on the ground," David said. "I'll follow up with the witnesses as well. And since Henly is a drug addict, I'll push him a bit. Make him nervous."

"Whatever you do, please be careful," she said.

"Ye' know I will, Charley, and while I'm gone, ye' need to rest. Ye' haven't slept much the last three days. Ye' won't help Jack if ye're too tired to think clearly." David emptied his whiskey glass and set it on the table. "If ye'll excuse me, I'd like a bath. Then I'll start at the Willard. I want to find Henly tonight and start surveillance, but I'll need a description."

Braham returned the carriage driver's statement to Cullen. "I'll be at the hotel later. I'll give you a signal when I spot him or anyone else of interest."

Cullen gathered his papers and his half-emptied glass. "I'll be in the office."

Charlotte yawned as she crossed the room and set her empty glass on a silver tray next to the decanter. "I'm going to take a nap. If anything develops, wake me up." She spoke quickly to Edward about bringing a tray to her room. As tired as she was, though, she didn't think she'd be able to stay awake long enough to eat. But when he brought up a tray a little while later, the plate of chicken salad and piece of pound cake revived her.

She was standing at the window, gazing out toward the White House when someone knocked on her door. "Come in." Charlotte turned, half expecting Jack to walk into the room. She smiled at Braham.

"We'll get him out. I don't know how. But we will, and we'll get your life back the way it should be."

"It's too late. This situation has already changed my life irrevocably. No one can undo what's happened to me, but I don't matter. Jack does."

"You matter to me, lass. To Jack, too."

"Whatever you tell him, please don't tell him my future changed.

We'll get it sorted out later."

"I promise."

David walked past her door, then quickly returned. Leaning against the doorjamb he said to Braham, "I'll meet you in the billiard room at the Willard in a couple of hours."

"David, wait." Charlotte rushed to the door and grasped his arm. "About Gordon—"

"I've met plenty of men like Henly. I can handle him."

"He's an abusive man and can be vicious. Don't turn your back on him. Be careful."

David tugged on her earlobe. "Get some rest, Charley. Ye're barely able to stay on yer feet. *Do not* wait up for me. I'll give ye' a report at breakfast."

She smiled and waved. "Okay." When she turned and caught the wounded expression on Braham's face, her breath hitched. "What's the matter?"

"Nothing. I've got to go. Get some rest." He brushed past her, but she caught his arm, tugged on it, and pulled him back into her room.

"You can't just leave without explaining. What's the matter?"

"I noticed the way you look at him. That's all."

"And how do I look at him?" she asked.

"Like I want you to look at me."

She wrapped her arms around his neck and held his eyes. "I love you, Braham McCabe, and if Jack hadn't gone missing, I'd still be at home crying over you."

Tension melted and his shoulders relaxed. He put his hands around her waist and pulled her to him. "Is he your rebound guy?"

"What? Where did you get such a notion? Never mind. Dumb question." She yawned. "David's too young for me and lives in Scotland most of the year. Of course, it's not as bad as loving a man who lives in the nineteenth century. At least we're in the same universe."

"Too young for you?"

"Well…I have heard younger men have more sexual stamina."

Braham pulled her close, pressing her against him. "I'm not ready for a rocking chair yet, lass." He ran his fingers up into her hair, cradled her head in his hands, and kissed her.

Somehow their loss and pain and longing was transformed by this one kiss, so warm and tender. It was everything she had missed and hungered for. The scent of him, leather and soap, and the taste of sweet whiskey on his tongue. She dug her fingers into his short, luxurious hair, missing his long locks, but he could be bald and she'd love him all the same.

His arms were around her now; his fingers exploring the length of her back, lightly reading the knobs of bone like Braille. He gathered the hem of her shirt and pulled it up and over her head. She drifted into the arousing feel of his touch. Bending his head, he nibbled down her neck and licked along the line of her collarbone, sending tantalizing shivers over her arms and chest and belly.

He kicked the door closed and threw the bolt. Then, smiling faintly, he bent and blew softly over her breasts before he suckled. Never had a sensation felt so sweet, so intense. She arched her back, pushing herself deeper into his mouth, craving his touch, and pushing aside thoughts of the heartache once she lost him again. He untied the drawstring to her pants and let them fall to the floor. She untied his cravat as he unbuttoned his shirt, popping the last ones, sending them pinging and rolling across the floor.

He was kissing her now, and his moustache tickled her face. The kisses were hot and leisurely, as though they had the whole night before them. No kiss had ever made her feel so hot and shaky. There was only one thing she wanted, and she couldn't get to it fast enough. Braham backed her closer to the bed, kissing her while removing his clothes. When the backs of her knees hit the mattress, she toppled over onto the coverlet, laughing. He kicked aside his pants and joined her.

She kissed the scar on his shoulder, pleased at how well it had healed, but when his lips found hers again, she forgot about his wounds. Her body opened to him like her heart. He reached between her thighs, and when he touched her, she shuddered.

Slowly, she began rotating her hips against his hand. Then he slid the hand beneath her and lifted her hips, drawing her to this mouth. She gave a gasp of delighted shock and then keened a sigh of pleasure. She wrapped her hands around the bedpost, breathing heavily, and gave herself over to the consummate skill of his tongue. His beard tickled pleasantly against her inner thighs, and she became lost in the sensations, surrendering to the primal urges throbbing rhythmically through her. She edged toward release, moaning deliriously, and he tickled her with the softest of kisses.

"Let go, my sweet," he said.

And she did, clipping the last restraint of consciousness, before soaring and spinning endlessly toward completion.

Moments passed, and in a dreamy state, she floated back into her body now damp and pink. Her heart pounded, and every beat echoed throughout the room. She sprawled against him, and he smoothed his warm hands over her back, teasing, until his fingers settled on her hips.

Between their bodies, his erection throbbed against her, and he uttered a guttural noise when she stroked him. She raised her head and inched up to kiss his lips, reveling in the musky taste and scent of them both. Groaning, he flipped her onto her back. A flame kindled his eyes with desire so hot, so sensuous, so demanding she couldn't help but yield to him, wrapping her legs around his hips. As he drove into her, all rational thought evaporated.

82

Washington City, 1865

T HE NEXT MORNING, Charlotte awoke in a darkened room, momentarily confused. She'd slept in so many different beds lately, she had no idea where she was. A feather mattress and covers wrapped her in a cocoon of warm comfort, and she wasn't inclined to move. As a whiff of Braham's musky scent penetrated her sleepy brain, she smiled lazily, remembering their hours together locked in each other's arms.

Vaguely, she remembered him leaving the bed. He had kissed her goodbye, told her to sleep well, and left through the door to his adjoining room. She had expected him to come back to her bed, but he must have arrived home late.

Like a train jumping tracks, her mind skipped from her temporary happiness to the image of Jack's head strapped in the ghastly hood. She jumped out of bed in a panicky rush, running toward the door with a scream lodged in her throat. She slapped the closed door with both palms, breathing heavily.

"Dear God, give him strength to endure."

She gripped her arms across her chest and took several slow, calming breaths as she paced the room naked. A crack of daylight filtered through the split between the closed velvet drapes. She wrapped a shawl around her shoulders before flinging open the curtains, letting sunshine warm the room. Her panic slowly subsided.

What would it be like to wake in suffocating darkness and silence and have no drapes to open? If she let her mind dwell on the agony Jack was enduring, she wouldn't be able to function. In order to help him, she needed her mental faculties to be operating at their highest level.

After a quick bath, she dressed in one of the day gowns still hanging in the armoire, and then she ventured down the stairs. Cullen's whistling drew her to the study.

"I recognize the tune," she said. "*Take Me Home, Country Roads.*"

He got to his feet, smiling. "One of Kit's favorites. She likes country music. I think if anything could pull her back to your time, it would be the music."

Charlotte poured a cup of coffee from the sterling service tea set on the sideboard and sipped the strong, hot brew. "I'd love to meet her. I've seen pictures of her. She's a beautiful and gutsy woman. You were lucky to have found her."

"We didn't have any choice in the matter."

"Oh, why? Because you couldn't fight the stone's magic?"

With a faint look of uneasiness, he nodded. "Once you get caught in the stone's fog, you're in for the duration."

"It's different with Braham and me."

"I wouldn't be so sure," Cullen said, returning his attention to the stack of papers in front of him. "But we can talk later. Right now we have a lot of work to do."

Her lips were trembling ever so slightly and she hoped Cullen hadn't noticed. She set her cup down on the side of the desk where she had arranged a workspace. "Is there food in the dining room? I'm starving."

"There was earlier, but I don't know if it's still there. Ask Edward. He'll see a meal is prepared for you."

She escaped to the dining room, where she found eggs and bacon warming in a chafing dish, plus bread and butter, and fruit. She fixed a plate and returned to the office, now more composed. "Where are David and Braham?"

Cullen continued writing without glancing up. "David went to spy on Henly, and Braham's nosing around the War Department."

"They must have found him last night. Good. Did either of them say what happened?"

The sleeves of Cullen's shirt were rolled to his elbows, revealing ropy, veined forearms with a dusting of fine black hair. He pushed the sleeves up higher to keep the fabric from dragging across the paper and smearing the ink. "They played cards."

"I bet David lost."

Cullen glanced up, drawing his brows together in thought. "Why do you think that?"

"It's usually what happens. The bad guy thinks he's playing an easy mark, so he bets heavily. The good guy loses, and later sets up another game to 'win his money back.'"

Cullen set his pen aside, laced his fingers, and put his joined hands behind his head, chuckling. "You're right. It's exactly what happened. Makes me wonder which one of you is the writer in the family."

Charlotte jabbed the eggs with her fork. "I dabble. Jack reads what I write, laughs, and then very sweetly tells me to go back to the operating room. I don't have much of an imagination."

"You're a critical thinker with a creative mind. Even without a legal background, you've grasped complicated issues, and you're able to ask intelligent questions. Braham told me once I'd never met a woman who challenged me intellectually until I met Kit. I believe he's found the same thing in you."

"The majority of our conversations have revolved around his injuries. In the last few months, he's been shot, knifed, whipped, beaten up, and almost burned alive. As for the rest of our interactions, well," she blushed, "we haven't done much talking."

Cullen dropped his hands, coughing discreetly.

Quickly changing the subject she asked, "How much did they lose last night"

"A thousand dollars."

She choked on her coffee. "*Ker-ching*. My bill keeps going up. I'm paying all expenses, and unless David wins the money back, his gambling losses go on my bill, too."

One corner of Cullen's mouth lifted in a confident smile. "Braham staked him. From what I heard, Henly's reckless, and with David's skill at cards, he'll easily win back what he lost."

She picked up the coffee pot and offered to fill Cullen's cup before refilling hers. "You and Braham have been friends for a long time."

"Since we were lads. The war's changed him. Hardened him. When he gets back to California and puts the war behind him, the old Braham will reemerge."

"You hope," she said.

Cullen's concern was belied by a glimmer in his eyes, and a wry smile teased the corner of his lips. "Kit will kick Braham back into shape in no time."

"If anyone can, she can, but tell me this…" Charlotte picked at the last of the food on her plate, wondering if she wanted an answer to the question she was poised to ask. "What advice, if any, did Braham give you when you discovered Kit was from the future?"

"Marry her, and if I didn't, he would. He didn't know they were first cousins at the time, though."

She asked without thinking, "Was he in love with her?" And then regretted the question. If he was in love with Kit, Charlotte didn't want to know it.

"No, he was needling me. And it worked."

The front door opened, and Cullen and Charlotte quieted. Their hands hovered above the documents, ready to quickly snatch them up and hide them in the safe. Seconds dragged by, and perspiration broke out on her forehead. Then Braham's resonant, full-throated laugh echoed in the hall. Her skin pulsed with heat and waves of soothing warmth flowed over her. She glanced at Cullen and found him observing her, a smile softening his face.

Braham entered the room grinning. When he saw Charlotte, he bent down and kissed her lightly on the lips.

"Have you had a productive morning?" she asked.

He untied his cravat and unbuttoned the top buttons of his shirt. "I met with Stanton and told him I intended to represent Jack. He told me it would ruin my career. I almost slugged him."

Only then did Charlotte realize he was putting his reputation on the line for Jack.

Braham poured a cup of coffee and pulled a chair up to the desk, squeezing Charlotte's knee. She placed her palm on top of his hand and drew small figure eights on the back of his hand with her fingertip. The touch was a tinderbox. Braham shifted in his chair and so did she. She reclaimed her hand, choosing to defer the spark which she knew could quickly roar into a conflagration.

"There's something I've been wondering about," she said. "Jack came back to find his journal. Did the police confiscate it?"

Braham shook his head. "Edward found the notebook and locked it in the safe. The police found Jack upstairs, dragged him outside, and tossed him into a heavily guarded wagon."

She cringed. The vision of Jack dragged out by the police and then forced to wear a canvas hood would hammer relentlessly at the edges of her consciousness.

"In the letter Jack wrote, he said he lost the sapphire and was unable to travel again. Do you know anything about it? Did Edward find the brooch?" she asked.

"Jack might have hidden it. Edward said officers tore the house apart while doing a thorough search. When I see Jack, I'll ask him," Braham said. "If he believes one of the officers stole it, then I'll have David and Gaylord get the names of the arresting officers. Once we know who they are, we'll find the stone."

"What happens if someone opens it?" Cullen asked.

"The latch is broken. It's tough to open," she said. "Most people wouldn't notice the fine line around the circumference of the stone, and would miss the broken latch. A jeweler, though, would notice both."

"If a police officer stole the jewelry from an assassin's room and was caught, he might be implicated. I think he'd hide it until the trial is over."

Cullen got up and stretched, twisting one way, and then the other. Charlotte compared the two men, their similarities and differences. Cullen moved and spoke with an ease Braham didn't have. Although she hadn't known him before the war, she suspected four years of fighting had stolen his spontaneity. Would he ever get it back?

Cullen picked up a paper and handed it to Braham "Do you know where David is today? I'd like him to talk to the people on this list. It includes several newspaper editors."

"He'll be back after dark. He doesn't want to be seen coming and going from here." Braham pursued the list. "Do you have the motions ready for tomorrow?"

Cullen handed over a stack of documents. "This motion requests General Hartranft remove the hoods because they violate the cruel and unusual punishment clause of the Eighth Amendment. The next document is the writ of habeas corpus to be filed on May 13."

"And if President Johnson signs an order cancelling the writ?" Braham asked.

"The third document is a petition claiming the President of the United States acted outside the bounds of his constitutional authority by suspending the writ of habeas corpus, and thus violated our client's Sixth Amendment right to a trial by a jury of his peers." Cullen frowned. "Do you have any idea what's going to happen when we file this?"

Braham seemed to consider the question, and then nodded brusquely. "There'll be an uproar. Can't be helped."

"We have to get the hoods removed," Charlotte said. "It's...it's barbaric."

"The country is angry right now, and there's no sympathy for the conspirators," Cullen said.

"I know," she said, "but General Hartranft is using hoods and heavy iron balls indiscriminately. Some conspirators are hooded, some aren't. It's the same with the iron ball. From what we've been able to learn, Jack has both. Forcing prisoners to wear hoods is cruel and unusual punishment, and in violation of the Eighth Amendment." She paused, feeling suddenly helpless, and her throat was tight and scratchy with fear. Her plea emerged as a whisper. "You have to make them understand."

"We will," Braham said. "We don't need all of them, though. We only need five. To convict Jack, they'll need a majority, and a two-thirds vote brings an automatic sentence of death. We'll get five to vote for acquittal."

Braham turned to Cullen "What day will the verdicts be sealed?"

"June 30," Cullen said. "The prisoners sentenced to death will be told on July 6 and executed on July 7. We have less than eight weeks."

Charlotte thumbed through the stack of papers, looking for the file with the commissioners' bios. She had studied them on the train. "I've read all the members' bios, and I think you should speak directly to General Wallace. He has a brilliant legal mind. But what's more interesting about him is his reputation is tarnished because of what happened at the Battle of Shiloh."

"I know Wallace. He's a good soldier. What happened at Shiloh was a misunderstanding."

"Which is my point," she said. "He'll be able to identify with it when you argue Jack's been wrongfully accused. But you have to get his attention. Our research indicates he was distracted during the trial, drawing sketches and writing letters. He's a writer and, in fact, will write a famous book titled *Ben Hur*. If we can find one of Jack's articles, maybe we can get him to read it."

"Have you seen Jack's journal in the safe, Cul?"

"I didn't pay any attention to what was in there. I'll look." Cullen ducked under the desk, shuffled papers for a couple of minutes, and then popped up again with a leather-bound journal in his hand. "Is this it?"

Charlotte nodded. "I bought it for him to use when we made the trip last December. Here, give it to me. I'll read through it to see if there is anything we can use for an article."

Cullen handed it to her, and she quickly fanned the pages covered with Jack's legible handwriting, so different from hers, with rounded letters and wide, looping *l*s. Her throat felt tight, and she slammed the journal closed. "I'll look at it later."

Braham squeezed her shoulder and must have sensed she didn't want to talk about something so intensely private as her brother's journal, so he changed the subject, saying, "We have to keep in mind this commission is not legally bound to follow the common law rules of procedure. They'll rely on the laws of war instead. They could deny every motion we make. In fact, we should expect it."

"Then we'll feed the press," Charlotte said. "Perhaps the only way Jack will escape this nightmare is by vanishing into thin air."

"Let's give the process a chance first," Braham said.

"Do you see a morality issue here, Braham? Are we cheating?" Cullen asked.

"We have an innocent client, and unless you find a law we're breaking, I intend to use every document we have. Nothing we do will impact the four who will hang or the four who will be sentenced to prison terms. In answer to your question, Cul..." Braham sighed heavily. "I don't know."

"Well, if you find evidence leading you to believe we are, don't tell me."

83

Washington City, 1865

T HE NEXT MORNING Charlotte rose early and dressed in the Union captain's uniform she'd brought with her. She expected a full-blown battle with Braham the moment he saw her, and she was prepared to fight dirty if necessary. How dirty? Would she go so far as to lock the door between their rooms? No, but she'd threaten.

She tiptoed down the stairs, avoiding the creaky boards, and stood at attention next to the front door. Braham and Cullen were arguing a point of law. It took a moment for her to figure out why their voices were raised and then she realized they were debating. Braham was arguing his case and Cullen was rebutting, pointing out flawed and irrelevant arguments.

Finally, Cullen said. "You're ready."

"Thanks for your help. There's no other lawyer I'd try this case with."

Two handsomely dressed men, one in uniform and the other in civilian clothes, strode out of the room, both carrying leather briefcases. Their somber demeanor was one of confidence. There was no doubt in her mind Braham and Cullen would win Jack's case in the press. Convincing the commissioners of his innocence would take more than a tailored suit and a well-prepared case. The generals would require indisputable evidence, and Jack's attorneys didn't have it, yet.

"Good morning, Captain. I didn't know you were waiting. How

can I help you? I'm in a bit of a hurry," Braham said.

Charlotte smiled inwardly. Braham had left her bed only a couple of hours earlier, and he didn't recognize her. Confident she could pull this off, she stood a little bit taller. "I came to escort you to the Old Arsenal Penitentiary, sir. Secretary Steward thought you'd need an escort today."

Braham crossed his arms, cocked his head, and glared. "Even if you changed your eye color, lass, I'd recognize you. You're not going."

Her eyebrows shot up, and she took a step forward. "You must have me confused with someone else, sir. We're providing escorts for all known counsel as a courtesy today."

Braham snatched his slouch hat from the coat tree, frowning. "The third member of Mr. Mallory's defense team will be down shortly. You can escort him. Good day, Captain."

Charlotte backed up to the door and spread her hands, guarding the entrance. "Okay, I surrender. But please, let me go today for the arraignment. Jack will ask me later to describe the first day. You *have* to let me. I promise I won't ask again."

Braham glanced at Cullen, who had his fist pressed over his mouth, but failed to hide the smile peeking out on either side of his fist. Braham paused for a moment, and his frown deepened. "I'm not trying to be mean, lass, but—"

Cullen walked to Charlotte's side in front of the door as if to join her in her plea. "It won't be a full day of court, Braham. Let her go see her brother."

"Never expected you to abandon me, Cul." Then Braham's expression lightened a little. "Seeing Jack so disheveled might make you worry more."

She wrapped her hand around the porcelain doorknob, smelling victory. "But it might make me worry less."

"Here're the terms then. You cannot signal Jack with a cough, sneeze, whistle, or whatever childhood signals you have in your repertoire. There's too much at stake. I won't introduce you. You'll sit in a corner and remain silent. Do you agree with these conditions? And will you give me your word?" He narrowed his eyes obviously watching for any tells signaling she was lying.

If she gave him her word, she'd have to honor it. Could she? Jack could recognize her sneeze in a group of five hundred people. Could she keep from sneezing or sighing or clearing her throat? If she couldn't, she'd better stay home, which was unacceptable. Without trust, she and Braham had nothing but great sex. "Yes," she said, taking a resolute breath, and then she experienced a shudder of annoyance over having to submit to his conditions in order to go to court.

He shoved his briefcase into her hands and stomped out the door. "Be useful, then. Don't make me regret my decision."

The carriage pulled up as they exited the house. As a senior officer, he climbed in first. She sat on the bench opposite him, studying his mood. His feathery brows were knitted in concentration. Over the last several months she had seen him dying, angry, depressed, forlorn, defeated, abused, aroused, tensed, and playful, but never this singularly focused. He was brilliant and formidable, and the most passionate man she had ever met. Without a doubt, he and Cullen would possess the best legal minds in the courtroom. Having the trial transcript gave them an advantage, but it was their ability to comprehend complex legal issues and apply them to the present situation that revealed their true genius. Her faith in both men was absolute.

They rode in silence down Pennsylvania Avenue, circled the Capitol to Delaware Street, and turned down the hard-packed, dirt road toward the penitentiary. The closer they came to the prison, the more fear knotted every limb and squeezed her chest, making it hurt to breathe. She was no stranger to fear. She'd been in a battle, faced Grant, gone into Castle Thunder, and run through the burning streets of Richmond. Any one of those experiences she'd prefer to face rather than the danger she now faced with mouth dry and heart pounding. There was so much at stake. If she were caught, all three of them might end up incarcerated. Then it would be up to David to blast his way inside to rescue Jack. She wiped her palms on her wool trousers, second-guessing her decision.

Braham took her hand, squeezing it lightly. "Don't forget to breathe, lass. Focus on why you're here. If you feel faint, bite your tongue or pinch your arm. We'll only be there a short time. I've got to represent Jack. If I'm worrying about you, I can't give him my full attention. If you don't think you can handle it, the driver will take you home."

She squeezed his hand in return. "You always know when I need a word of encouragement. I don't know how you know, but you do."

"I see it in yer eyes."

"I didn't know my anxiety showed."

"Only to me," he said.

Braham sat back in his seat and stared out the window, tugging on his chin thoughtfully. The corner of Cullen's mouth tucked in, a small, secret expression indicating he knew more than he was willing to say. She had seen a similar look dozens of times over the last several days. Once Jack was out of prison, she would demand an explanation. Pressing Cullen now for one was pointless. During the hours they'd worked together, she'd learned he was as stubborn as Braham.

Their driver halted behind a long line of carriages near the gate. They alit and followed the crowd toward the entrance. Water surrounded the prison on three sides, making it one of the most secure and heavily guarded places in Washington. You could walk up the White House stairs and knock on the President's office door, but you couldn't get near this courtroom without a pass. Braham showed his pass, and they were allowed inside. They made their way across the entrance courtyard toward the cell block, the largest of three buildings inside the walled prison.

She had the floor plan memorized. She knew the layout and position of the newly constructed courtroom in the northeast corner of the third floor, and where on the raised platform Jack would be sitting.

David had a three-dimensional map of Jack's cell on the second floor, and another one of the path from his cell to the courtroom. He knew how long it would take to scale the outer wall of the prison under cover of darkness, cross the yard to the cell block, climb the wall of Jack's building, infiltrate the cell, and disappear with him. Just thinking about it made her shudder.

When she saw the crowds and squads of armed soldiers, the hair on her neck prickled at the palpable, almost physical expectation of vengeance swirling sickeningly in the air.

Cullen whispered, "Keep yer eyes…"

"On the prize," she answered under her breath.

They entered the building to find General Grant arguing with a young private, who was looking cornered but bravely telling him, "Sir, new gas lines were installed in the courtroom. You can't take your stogie upstairs."

Grant was a bit taken aback and gave the young soldier a hard look, then said, "You're following orders, and I commend you for it." Grant turned toward the stairs, still holding his burning cigar, and came face to face with Braham. "Congratulations on your promotion, Colonel. Well deserved. I suppose you're here to testify about what happened to Secretary Seward."

"I've been called to testify, sir, but I'm here to represent Jack Mallory."

The general shook his head. His expression was kind but serious, and there was no lack of conviction in his tone. "You're making a mistake, Colonel. Your career in the military will be tarnished."

"So I was told by Secretary Stanton, but my client is innocent, and I intend to prove it."

Grant took one last puff on his cigar before extinguishing it in a silver-hinged ashtray sitting on a table next to the stairs. "Is your *lofty* goal worth your reputation?"

"It's worth my life, sir." Braham's voice didn't sharpen, but it resonated with strong commitment.

"I've never known you to be wrong about anything, Colonel. I pray this one mistake doesn't haunt you for the rest of your life." Grant nodded and preceded them up the stairs.

A hot numbness swept over her when she gazed into Braham's eyes. What she saw there almost broke her heart, and she had to look away, fidgeting with the clasp on the leather briefcase. Cullen nudged Braham in the arm, and whistled a haunting melody from Bach or Mozart or Beethoven or one of the other classical composers she couldn't keep straight. Braham shook his head wordlessly.

Boot heels and spurs thumped and chimed on the crowded stairs and sabers clanged as everyone climbed to the third floor. Braham led the way into the whitewashed courtroom, which was already packed with spectators lining the west side of the room. He rounded up three chairs and squeezed them in at the defense table, where several other lawyers had already claimed seats. Nodding his head, he acknowledged them but didn't make introductions. Charlotte sat between Braham and Cullen, holding tightly to the briefcase in her lap. It was creepy being here. There were a few lawyers on one side and the whole United States on the other.

She glanced around the room, taking in the details. Later, Jack would want to know her first impressions.

The defense table was in front of a raised platform edged by a wood railing. The platform was constructed to accommodate eight prisoners and seven guards. Mary Surratt and her attorney sat at a separate table next to the defense lawyers. Additionally, there were two long tables. One for the press. The other, a green-baized-covered table, was on the east side of the room with a clear view of the witness stand and the raised platform. In the center of the table was a stack of law books. Charlotte wondered if they would ever be opened.

The commissioners entered the courtroom, talking among themselves. Judge Advocate Holt, lead prosecutor, took his place at the head of the commissioner's table, closest to the witness stand. Charlotte eyed him with suspicion, knowing he would write rules as the trial progressed and share them with no one, at least no one on the defense teams.

Once the commissioners settled into their seats, Presiding Judge General David Hunter ordered the prisoners brought into the room.

With the exception of Mary Surratt and Dr. Mudd, the prisoners were heavily shackled and hooded.

Jack sat in the middle of the platform, only a few feet from Charlotte, close enough to touch, and she was so tempted to do just that, she unintentionally cleared her throat. Braham shot her a *don't do it again* look.

She visually examined her brother with a surgeon's eye for detail. The wrinkled, sweat-stained linen of his shirt clung to his chest and shoulders. Although he was filthy, there were no bloodstains, and his clothes weren't torn. He sat straight in his chair. His head didn't wobble, and he appeared alert. He wasn't trembling. His shackled hands were of normal color and rested easily on his knees from relaxed arms, although there was some redness around his wrists from the constant rubbing of metal against skin.

She'd been holding her breath without realizing it, and now she let it out with silent sigh of relief. If she could only see his eyes, she could get a better read on his emotional health. For now, though, his body language conveyed a strength which made her hopeful. At least he was visited daily by the Arsenal's army physician. Would the doctor understand Braham's memorandum on sensory deprivation and encourage General Hartranft to dispense with the hoods sooner than he did historically? She would pray he did.

General Hunter read the charges against the prisoners and each was asked if he or she objected to any member of the commission. Charlotte held her breath again. Following the establishment of Guantanamo Bay Detention Camp in 2002, Jack had written several articles about the similarities between the trial of the conspirators and the treatment of the detainees. And he'd read the biographies of all the members of the military commission, and studied their war successes and failures.

When Hunter asked Jack if he objected to any member, he said with a voice which carried throughout the room, "I object to the presence of General Hunter and General Howe. They have both just returned from a two-week tour of mourning with the President's remains. I further object to General Hunter…"

Braham exhaled a seething breath though gritted teeth.

"…who fought against Mosby's Rangers in the valley, sitting in judgment of Mr. Powell. I further object to General Hunter on the grounds he might be seeking atonement for the embarrassment caused by General Early in 1864. Lastly, I object to General Wallace, who might be seeking redemption for his military blunder at Shiloh."

The courtroom erupted. Several reporters jumped out of their chairs and raced from the room. General Hunter banged his hammer repeatedly, demanding silence, but the clamor continued. Both Cullen and Braham remained expressionless. Charlotte did not dare look at the commissioners.

Jack had sealed his death warrant.

"Your objections are noted and *denied*." General Hunter's voice rose several notches in volume.

When the room began to calm, Cullen leaned over and whispered. "Draw an accurate layout of the room. Identify who you can, and where they're sitting, and make a note if you recognize any of the spectators."

While the arraignments proceeded, Charlotte drew a floor plan, stretching her neck to see on the other side of the three columns dividing the room. Very little air came through the four barred windows, and it was already sweltering. By July, she knew the temperature in the room would reach a hundred degrees.

Many of the people in the room she recognized from photographs. A few of the female spectators looked familiar, but she couldn't put names and faces together. Rattling chains drew her attention back to the platform. The prisoners were standing.

Cullen leaned over and whispered to her once again. "Don't watch them leave. Show me your notes. *Now*."

A wrenching pain lodged in her chest, but she obeyed Cullen. She picked up her notes, and they huddled together in low-voiced discussion.

After the prisoners had been removed, General Holt and the commission determined the rules of procedure. Not being a real court, the commission had a great deal of latitude. Holt advised the commission several witnesses, fearing retaliation, would testify in secret.

"Which must be why there's no record of Jack's accusers," she said.

After the rules were established, court adjourned for the day. Braham stood, indicating it was time for them to leave. He gathered his papers and slipped them into his briefcase.

"Let's go," he said.

On their way out of the courtroom, General Holt stopped Braham and said, "This will ruin your reputation. You're a hell of a soldier. Step aside before it's too late. Your client…well, it's better to get out now."

Holt's attitude unnerved and infuriated Charlotte. The prosecutor had no idea what being in the courtroom cost Braham. He had spent months planning to save the President's life and had failed. A man he loved as a brother was charged with a crime Braham had tried to prevent and failed. He wasn't about to let his failure end Jack's life. Braham shifted his feet, pretending Holt's comments didn't matter, but not quite pulling it off.

"I loved President Lincoln," Braham said, "and I'll grieve for him the rest of my life. I pray for the day those responsible pay the ultimate price for what they've done. But I know beyond a shadow of a doubt Jack Mallory is innocent. He did *not* support the rebel cause. He did *not* participate in a conspiracy, and I intend to prove it. Good day, General."

Waves of weariness seemed to drag on Braham as they walked back to their carriage. Charlotte jogged to keep up with the two long-legged men. As soon as they were safely inside the carriage and out of earshot of soldiers and spectators, Braham groaned.

"*What* possessed Jack to alienate the commissioners before the trial even started? I could wring his neck. If they could have voted right then they would have put him in front of a firing squad. *Good, God.*" Braham scrubbed his face with his hands. "I'll never be able to redeem him in the eyes of the commissioners." He sat, utterly motionless while a silent pall settled over the interior of the carriage.

Charlotte didn't say anything. Then after several minutes, she asked, "Did you see Gordon?"

Braham wore a cold, contemplative look as he studied her. "No, where was he?"

"Standing several feet behind you while you were talking to Holt, hissing like an angry serpent. I'm surprised you weren't scorched by the steam."

"So *that* was Gordon," Cullen said.

Charlotte raised her voice excitedly. "You saw him?"

Cullen nodded as he teased the corner of his lip with his index finger, giving her a wry smile. "I did, and I agree with yer assessment."

She shivered briefly in spite of the heat. "I didn't want to look at him too closely. He gives me the creeps. What'd you think of his eyes? I didn't get a good look at them."

"They were glassy," Cullen said.

"Good. The more pressure he's under, the more laudanum he'll use," she said.

Cullen bounced his fingers now instead of his usual steepling. "David believes Henly framed Jack, but it seems excessive for a jealousy motive."

"Jealous lovers kill people all the time," she said.

"Yes, but for unrequited love or unfaithfulness. Not an elaborate plan to frame someone for a crime," Cullen said.

"Add in revenge and you've got a very credible motive," she said.

A question lifted Cullen's brows. "Why would he want revenge?"

Braham leaned forward, elbows resting on his knees. Intense interest showed on his face. "He wanted the position working for Lincoln. He outranked me, but I got the appointment. He's had no use for me since."

Cullen and Charlotte both stared intensely at Braham.

"Jesus. If Henly's done all this to get even with me, I'll stick a knife in his bloody, black heart."

84

Washington City, 1865

T WO DAYS LATER, Charlotte handed Braham his briefcase and kissed him goodbye at the door. He carried a signed writ of habeas corpus, a motion to compel General Hartranft to discontinue the use of hoods and excessive restraints, a motion to allow Jack to testify on his own behalf, and a motion compelling the general to make available for interview certain witnesses held in detention. When the motions were filed, the courtroom would explode, and she hated missing the excitement.

When the daily newspapers arrived, she spread them out on the dining room table to read the press reactions. There were filled with praise for Braham and Cullen's legal prowess. Several members of the Washington bar weighed in on the constitutional challenges presented at the military trial and in federal court. Braham and Cullen were touted as brilliant, though a couple of editorials claimed Braham's legal maneuvers were insane. One newspaper went so far as to say the courtroom shenanigans provided the best entertainment Washington had seen in over four years, and Colonel McCabe was the only actor on stage who'd been given the script. Charlotte pictured smoke pouring from General Holt's ears over this particular comment.

President Johnson had suspended the writ as Braham anticipated, and Cullen had immediately filed suit in federal court claiming the President had acted beyond the scope of his legal authority. The legal community found the arguments fodder for endless debate, and the demand for courtroom passes far surpassed availability. Lawyers and journalists pressed for details about the motions Colonel McCabe intended to file on his client's behalf. The topic of Jack's guilt or innocence was ignored. The reports, interviews, and editorials all focused on Braham and Cullen's legal arguments.

The publicity was taking its toll on Braham, and although he hadn't mentioned it to her, she knew he believed he had crossed the line he'd drawn the day Cullen asked him if he thought they were cheating. General Holt was making up the rules as he went along, and to Charlotte, *that* was the real cheating. His railroading meant Braham and Cullen had to use everything at their disposal to save Jack.

Sorting through all the motions and briefs gave her a giant headache. Cullen left her a list of tasks every morning, and it took the majority of the day to mark off only the first few items. It was tedious work, and her hand cramped from writing hour after hour.

In the evening, after she'd eaten alone, she decided to take her work to her bedroom. She straightened the office, locked up the research, and took only her handwritten notes. Propped up in bed to read, she quickly fell asleep. Male voices coming from the parlor woke her some time later. She ran a brush through her curls then hurried downstairs to join the men.

Braham, Cullen, and David were relaxing with their feet up, jackets and cravats discarded, cigars and pipes and whiskey glasses in their hands. The story David was telling had them all laughing. When she entered the room, they all got politely to their feet.

"Please sit. You've had a long day." She waved her hand in front of her face to clear a window in the pungent smoke. "I'll even ignore the cigars." After pouring herself a drink, she joined Braham on the sofa.

He took her hand and kissed it. Then he tilted his head to one side, narrowing his eyes. "You've been asleep. We woke you."

She pushed away his concern. "I dozed off waiting for you. I read the early papers. Did you? I'm sure you cringed over the 'script' line."

He frowned behind a cloud of cigar smoke. "I did."

"The best research in the world won't help a man who doesn't have the innate intelligence to understand it and use it effectively. The commissioners are going to resist because they don't understand how you can do what you do. The only way they can fight you is to shut you up. But the press won't let them get away with it. Thank God for the press. I wish I could be there, but I know my presence is a burden."

"I live in fear of the day someone rips the beard off your face and exposes you." Cullen said, pointing his cigar at her.

"I'll kick 'em in the balls before I let it happen." A quiet cough punctuated her comment. The smoke in the room was overpowering, but these men were on a path fraught with danger, and if they wanted to smoke, she wasn't about to deprive them of their simple pleasure. "Did I hear David talking about Gordon as I came downstairs? What's the latest with him?"

David drew on a pipe and blew rings into the air. The new ring struck the remnants of the old ring, and they both disintegrated in a haze. "We've played a few games. His losses now tally over five thousand dollars, and tonight I won the family business."

"Excellent. What kind of business?" Braham asked.

David removed the pipe between his teeth and said, "Lumber. Near Cincinnati."

Cullen pointed with his cigar held loosely between two fingers. "It should be a very profitable business now the war has ended."

"How long are you going to keep playing him? He can't have much left to wager."

David's pipe threatened to go out, and he drew on it heavily until the bowl glowed red. "When he left the table tonight, he said he'd be back tomorrow. I believe someone is staking him. Gaylord is following up."

Charlotte put the edge of her glass to her lips, wondering. "Why would someone stake him? Does Braham have more enemies than we were aware of?"

The men laughed, and Cullen said, "Several new ones, lass."

Braham bit down on the end of the cigar. "Start with Johnson and work yer way down to the court reporters borrowed from the Senate."

Charlotte fanned her way through the smoke, heading to the cabinet to refill her drink. "Braham, do you think Gordon knows there's a connection between you and David?"

"It's possible."

She refilled her glass, replaced the stopper on the decanter, and sipped her drink. "If he loses everything, including his backer, he'll blame you for his gambling losses, too."

"At this point, lass, he'll blame me if it rains."

She moved over to the window and gulped in a few lungfuls of smokeless air. "You need a bodyguard."

"Cullen and I now have two apiece. David has a dozen."

Braham patted the cushion next to him, inviting her to come back. She shrugged. As long as she stayed in the room, she wasn't going to escape the smoke. She sat, tucked her feet beneath her on the sofa, and leaned against him. Being with these three men made her heart ache for Jack. He would have loved this moment—drinking whiskey and smoking cigars with the guys. The least she could do was enjoy it for him.

"I wish you had told me about the bodyguards earlier. I've been so worried."

"Cullen and I didn't know about them until we left for court this morning. Nice lads. Former sergeants. Gaylord arranged it, interviewed a hundred men, and selected sixteen burly ex-soldiers. David trained them. Starting tomorrow, you'll also have a guard, twenty-four hours a day."

"Seriously?"

David turned the pipe over and knocked the dottle out into the ashtray. "Gaylord told them he was starting an agency. Their future employment would depend on how well they performed this assignment. They have no families to return to, and were glad for the work."

She chuckled under her breath. "So we have our own police force now."

Braham placed his warm hand over hers. "Something like that. This is a dangerous game we're playing, but a necessary one. When I subpoena Henly next week, he may become aggressive. We have to protect ourselves."

"He'll be a hostile witness, won't he?"

"Aye, and if he lies," Braham said, frowning. "I'll have to call you to the stand."

She glanced up at him. His penetrating look of concern cut straight through her. He didn't want her on the witness stand, and she didn't want to testify, but for Jack, she would do anything. "Maybe if Gordon knows I'm in town and prepared to testify, he'll think twice about lying."

Cullen puffed on his cigar, blowing rings of his own which seemed to entertain him. "We can't risk exposing ye' until the last possible moment."

She fiddled with the small cameo brooch pinned at her collar. It had belonged to her great-grandmother and Charlotte had accidently left it behind on her previous trip. It reminded her of the lost sapphire. "Did you ask Jack what happened to the brooch?"

Braham blew perfect rings into the air and calmly said, "He tossed it and assumed it went out the window."

Charlotte sat bolt upright. "He did *what?*"

Braham put his arm around her shoulder. "The police would have taken it, and he knew Edward went over the grounds twice a day, pulling weeds and picking up trash. He assumed he would find it."

"What'd Edward say?"

"He hasn't seen it. He even raked the entire yard. If it was there, it's gone now. He questioned all the members of my staff. No one has seen it."

A trickle of sweat ran down the back of her neck. "Damn. Then we have to assume it's gone for good, which means you'll have to take the ruby and escort Jack home, and then come back for David and me."

"Once we prove Jack's innocence, we'll solve the logistics problem."

"I wish we'd never had access to the ruby. You wouldn't have been able to come back on your own, and I wouldn't have come chasing after you."

Cullen cleared his throat. "Let's leave the ruby brooch out of this. Without it, I never would have met Kit."

"Then she could have married me," David said.

Cullen glared at David, jaw muscles rippling as he ground his teeth.

David ducked and crossed his arms in front of his face in mock terror. "Just kidding. She's like my little sister."

Braham turned his head so his cheek rested against Charlotte's hair. The faint rasp of his whiskers made scratching noises near her ear. His unusual public display of affection surprised her, tickling her insides.

Cullen puffed his cigar. "You're not planning a trip to California, I hope."

David clamped down on the lip of the empty pipe, clicking his teeth. Then he stretched out his long arms and cracked his knuckles one at a time. "Hmm. Do ye' think we'll have time for a quick trip, Charley?"

She gave David a teasing smile. "Don't drag me into this."

David made for the cabinet and the whiskey decanter. He gave Cullen a light punch on the shoulder. "Ye're a lucky man. Ye' and Kit are creating a fine legacy for yer heirs. I'd love to see the lass, but ye've nothing to fear from me." David refilled his glass, and he and Cullen clinked their drinks. "*Slainte.*"

Braham kissed her cheek, and she turned toward him, searching his expression, but she could read nothing other than tiredness in his eyes.

"It's getting late," Cullen said, "and I still have work to do."

Yes, it was late, and she wanted time alone with Braham, to nestle in his arms and hear his heartbeat, and know he belonged to her. For now. She had no illusions about what they shared. It wouldn't—couldn't—last beyond the next few weeks. But while they were together, she would store up a lifetime of memories.

She loved him, and as many times as she had recited the manta, *I won't stay and he won't go*, she prayed every day he would change his mind, because she knew she couldn't change hers. She couldn't give up twenty-first century medicine. The soldiers she hadn't been able to save, the ones she could have saved in her time, had been heartrending. And she missed the freedom women had to vote, to work outside the home, to participate in government, and to even run down the street in athletic shorts. Her predecessors had made sacrifices so she could do what she did every day, and while she often took her rights and privileges for granted, she could never give them up permanently. Did it make her selfish and shallow? Maybe. But she knew herself well enough to know she couldn't give up her life, not at forty, and not even for love.

Yes, the life she returned to wouldn't be the same, but the hospital would still be there, and Jack would be there, and Ken would continue to pressure her to date his friends. Life would go on. She would feel pain. Her body would crave the rumble of Braham's laughter, the warmth of his hands, and the gleam in his eyes, expressing the words of his heart. She would miss his jokes, his teasing, and his protection. Good things were rare, and they were to be cherished. But most of all, she would miss his love.

She attempted a smile but wasn't sure she managed. "What's on the calendar for tomorrow?"

"Cullen will be in federal court arguing motions. I'll be with Jack."

"Then we need to get some sleep," she said.

Cullen stretched and headed out of the room with his whiskey and cigar. "I'll be up for a while working, and will leave a new list for you to attack tomorrow."

Charlotte cleared her throat nosily, expressing her complaint. "I haven't finished today's list yet. But you know what? Now I have a bodyguard, I can go to the park."

On her way to the stairs, Braham cupped her elbow and pulled her to him possessively. "Wear your disguise and obey your bodyguard."

"Unless Stanton wants to arrest me for participating in the conspiracy, too, don't you think I'm safe?"

His nostrils flared slightly. "I don't, and you should never take your safety for granted."

85

Washington City, 1865

C HARLOTTE'S DAILY HABIT was to begin by devouring the newspapers. Another reporter had mentioned Braham seemed to be the only player who had read the script, and she cringed to see the line now printed and reprinted in all three papers. She had visions of the military invading the house in search of stolen War Department files.

Stanton had to be livid. Good for him. Let him loose sleep wondering if he had an informant in his office. No need for informants when you had strategically-placed listening devices. She had learned about them only this morning, when Cullen handed her pages of transcripts to be locked in the safe. David had planted bugs in both Stanton and General Holt's offices. When Braham had suggested to Cullen perhaps they were cheating, surprisingly, Cullen had laughed, claiming he knew about tape recordings, and he wasn't going to debate the ethics of using them in Jack's case.

Braham had subpoenaed Gordon to testify, and, according to a conversation which took place in Stanton's office, Gordon had complained bitterly to the secretary about having been promised anonymity. Stanton had warned him if he failed to testify in public the prosecution's case against Mallory would fall apart. He was the only person who could testify about seeing Jack and Booth together talking about an *event happening in April*. A blatant lie, which, if he maintained it on the stand, would force Braham to call her as a rebuttal witness.

It would take the talent of an actress like Meryl Streep to pull it off, and she was no Meryl Streep. All the prosecutor had to do was ask her if she knew of the plot to assassinate Lincoln. She was a horrible liar, and he would be able to see the truth on her face.

Tickets to the trial had become the hottest commodity in Washington. She pleaded every day to go, but Braham was adamant and so was Jack. If she had to testify, her identity had to remain a secret until they called her to the witness stand.

The public debated the Habeas Corpus Act of 1863 and Braham's claim of the end of the war having suspended the act's authorization. Stanton had halted the draft and removed all travel restrictions in and out of Washington, and had been quoted as saying, "Since Lee's surrender, the threat to national safety had passed away." Cullen used those facts while arguing his case against President Johnson, which was proceeding through the federal court system. Would it do Jack any good? Probably not, but it was keeping the press enthralled and their case in the public eye.

The military court denied the other motions Cullen had drafted, except for allowing the hoods to be removed during court. But they were shoved back over the defendants' heads before leaving the courtroom at the end of each day.

Her emotions soared and plummeted while she read the news. She didn't care about the plantation. She didn't care if the Mallory name was held in disdain in perpetuity, like Mudd or Booth. She only wanted to rescue her brother, go home, and reclaim her life. Whatever it turned out to be.

Sergeant Jonathan Clem, her bodyguard, entered the dining room. "Excuse me, ma'am. Edward said you'd like to visit the park this afternoon."

Charlotte folded the newspapers and added them to her collection in a basket on the floor. "Give me five minutes to put on my wig and beard, and I'll be ready to go."

The clouds had disappeared, and the crowds hadn't yet arrived. They'd picked a good time. The sugar maples had fully leafed and the winding paths were lined with purple irises.

"Are you going to stay in Washington?" Charlotte asked Jonathan.

"If a permanent position opens up with Mr. Gaylord, I'll stay," he said. "There's not much for me back in Illinois. My folks passed on while I was away at war, and I lost my two brothers at Gettysburg. No reason not to stay here, if there's a job."

She pulled her hat down to shade her eyes from the glaring sun. "I'm sorry about your brothers. Were you at Gettysburg, too?"

There was a sudden flutter of motion behind her as a man leapt from the bushes, gun in hand, and clobbered Jonathan over the head. She took a breath to scream, but the heavyset man, who reeked of sweat, slapped a hand over her mouth. The hand smelled of garlic and onions, but she tried to bite him anyway. He pressed his hand harder, squeezing her cheeks painfully into her teeth. She bit the soft tissue inside her mouth instead of his hand when she tried again, and a metallic taste coated her tongue.

She elbowed him in the chest. But before she could go for his eyes or throat, he planted his arm across her middle and pulled her back against him. This maneuver pinched both of her arms against her body and tightly squeezed her ribcage. As strong as he was, she couldn't break free. Her adrenalin went haywire.

He muffled her screams as he carried her toward a waiting carriage, while she kicked furiously at his shins. Her muscles strained to break loose, but with her back pressed against his solid chest and her arms and hands locked down tight, she was helpless...*except for her head.*

She head-butted him, but he didn't loosen his grip. He bit down on her earlobe, and his hot, garlicky breath and spittle sprayed across her skin. "Try it again, bitch, and you won't like what I do to you." He was breathing nearly as hard as she was. The pressure from his squeezing hand on her face made her eyes water. The violence in him reeked as nauseatingly as he did.

Her survival instinct erased the initial shock and panic. She tensed, readying herself to fight to the end. If he got her into a carriage, her chances of living through a rape or beating would diminish considerably. She couldn't see further than the moment, a single heartbeat between life and death. She kicked backwards at his shins and knees, but the man was built like a linebacker, and his increasing fury tightened his grip. She continued to fight, to squirm in his viselike arms.

She panted in short gasps, her heart beating frantically. They neared a carriage. She had only a handful of moments left. Once inside, she'd be defenseless. She raised her legs and pressed them against the door, pushing back against him, and at the same time gouging at his rock-hard legs with her short nails. She attempted another head-butt, and he bit down hard on her ear. A warm trickle dripped into the canal.

There was a shadow of a man inside the carriage. "Back up. I'll open the door so you can get her inside," he said in a recognizable voice.

Incoherent terror engulfed her. She couldn't escape, and she knew they would hurt her, but she refused to stop fighting. Her life was at stake. Her attacker backed up, her legs fell, and she dangled several inches off the ground. She kicked him squarely in the kneecap, and his leg buckled, but he didn't release his grip. When the door opened, he tossed her onto the floor as easily as a sack of flour, and then piled in behind her. The driver slapped the reins on the backs of the horses, and the carriage drove off at a gallop. She glanced up to see Gordon smirking, and she swallowed back tears of panic.

"Well, well. What do we have here?" Gordon ripped off her beard, taking a layer of skin. She screamed, and he slammed his fist into her jaw. A wave of dizziness hit her. He dropped to the floor, straddled her, and twisted her wrists so hard she thought they had snapped.

"Doctor Charlotte Mallory. Did you think I wouldn't recognize you? It's your eyes, my dear." He let go of her hands, now numb and useless. He slapped her hard. His family crest ring hit her cheekbone and made her eyes water. Black pain bloomed from the center of her face, and the violence of the slap took her breath away.

His wolfish grin broadened, revealing yellow canine teeth, and his eyes blazed with fury. He was crazed with the need to assert his dominance over her. If he hit her again with the anger seething though him, she would lose consciousness and her life. He punched her in the ribs, forcing the breath from her lungs. "You're nothing but a whore." He punched her again. "Tonight you won't be warming McCabe's bed. You'll be begging me to fuck you."

Barely able to speak, she hissed, "You can't get it up."

He cocked his head, eyebrows lifted, as if he had heard wrong. Then he snatched his gun up off the seat, holding it above his head by the barrel. Her eyes widened, then squeezed shut in reflex as he clobbered her on the head with the butt of his revolver.

86

Washington City, 1865

ONSCIOUSNESS RETURNED SOME time later, but Charlotte wished it hadn't.

Had she wrecked her car? She had no memory of an accident. Why was it so dark and cold? She shivered and tried to shake off the chill, but it only made her head throb worse. Did she hit the steering wheel? Must have. Her face hurt, too. She touched her cheek. It was swollen, but not cut. There was pain in her mouth. At least one cut on the inside. She ran her tongue over her teeth. A couple molars wiggled slightly, but none were missing. Her airway was open, but taking deep breaths hurt. Maybe bruised or cracked ribs. She ran her hands down her arms and legs. Everything moved. There was no external bleeding. No belly pain.

She tried to open her eyes and realized they were already open. Total darkness surrounded her. No cracks of light. No red exit signs. Where the hell was she? On the ground. She must have been thrown from the car. There was a dank, sour, musty smell in the cold air. She wasn't outside in the dark. She was inside. Then she hadn't been thrown from a car?

The trauma came back in a terrifying rush. There had been no car accident. Gordon had kidnapped and beaten her, and must have dumped her here. How long ago? And where was she?

Oh, God, her head hurt. How long had she been unconscious? She had no memory of riding in the carriage or being dumped wherever she was now. There were no voices. No footfalls above her, below her, or around her. She managed a feeble yell. "Help." Nothing. She was completely alone in the terrifying darkness.

Why did Gordon take her? Braham would be going crazy by now, wondering where she was, and so would David. Neither of them would stop looking until they found her.

But if Braham was looking for her, he wouldn't be in court defending Jack. Was that what Gordon had planned? The bastard. She bristled at realizing she was pawn in a game she couldn't win.

She prayed Braham would continue to concentrate on helping Jack and let David find her. Meredith had said David could do the impossible.

Would Gordon kill her? Not right away. He'd make her suffer first. Hah. Like she wasn't already. How long could she live without food or water? She could last weeks without food, but she'd be dead in a few days without water. And what about the cold darkness? Her coat wasn't very warm, but it was May, not January, so she didn't have to worry about hypothermia. There were a few cracks of light in the ceiling, but when the sun set...Oh, God, it would be like wearing a hood. How long could she handle sensory deprivation? Not long at all.

She cupped her elbows and shuddered, remembering Gordon's twisted face as he was posed to smash the revolver butt down on her head. She took as deep a breath as she could, stilled the scurrying thoughts in her throbbing head, and rolled her shoulders, trying to stretch raw nerves to calm them.

The stench in her prison intensified. It seemed to clutch her face like the man with the onion hand. Something close by was dead. The scratch of rodents triggered an immediate wave of panic. *Not, rats. Anything but rats.* She curled up into a ball to make herself a smaller target.

Gordon had clobbered her hard. Meredith's wig probably saved her life. What if she had a concussion? She had lost consciousness, and now had severe head pain and queasiness. For the next few hours, she'd have to stay awake. But what if she got confused? No one was there to help her.

Her stomach roiled, and she turned her head to the side and vomited what little she had in her stomach. She wiped her mouth with the sleeve of her jacket. Pain lanced through her face and jaw, and she groaned as she rolled back on her side.

The scratching of rodents inched closer. She used the moldy straw on the ground to wipe up the vomit and threw it in direction of the scratching. *Take my lunch and leave me alone.* Sitting here helpless wouldn't keep the rats away. She had to move.

When she put her hand out, her fingers touched a dirt-packed wall. Maybe she could dig her way out. With what? Her nails? She always protected her hands and kept her nails neatly trimmed and buffed. So, no digging. In the darkness, locked in fear, she squeezed her eyes shut. Pinpoints of light flashed behind her eyeballs. Stars. Millions of bright, twinkling stars pointed toward home.

She dozed, dreaming of the messy bedroom she left behind, and when she woke, rats were scampering lightly across her shins, frequently changing directions. How many? One on her right leg shifted its weight and skittered higher, toward her thigh. Its nails pricked her skin through her wool trousers. Another one crawled over her left ankle and chewed on her leather shoestring. A third one gnawed on her shirt in the center of her chest.

"Get away from me." Kicking and batting at the rats only made her head throb harder, and the damn creatures didn't scurry far. She couldn't stop them from coming back. It hurt too much to try. She rolled to her side and raised herself to a sitting position, pulled her knees to her chest, and struggled to remain alert. If she had to lecture today, what would she teach the students?

In the middle of the lecture, she fell asleep again, and woke with a jerk and a scream. A rat had burrowed beneath the cuff of her trousers and clawed its way up her leg. She held her head between her hands to keep it steady and kicked frantically. She couldn't get the rat out. It was next to her knee, inside her pants. She pounded on it through the material. Its teeth sank into her skin at the side of her calf.

"Oh, God, it's *eating me.*" She hit it again and again until warm liquid flowed down her leg, and its teeth relaxed. She shook her leg and it fell away.

Her mouth was cotton dry, and her voice was barely a whisper.

She dozed again, head lolling against the wall. She woke to a rat nibbling on crusted blood on her neck. She lifted her hand and swatted it away, then leaned back against the wall, and very slowly, as to not jostle her head, she pulled the wig the rest of the way off and used it to cover her face. It smelled of blood and sweat.

She closed her eyes, needing to see the stars again, her light in the darkness.

If she removed the binding around her breasts, she could wrap her hands and face and neck. She needed to do it now. If she waited, she might not have the strength in an hour, but if she took off the binding, her ribs might hurt even more. No, leave the binding in place. She wasn't sure whether it was onion-hand's squeezing or Gordon's punches which had damaged her ribs. It didn't matter now. The pain of breathing was getting worse, probably because she was panicking. Slowing her breath, she fell back asleep.

A rat woke her, gnawing on her bitten, bloody ear. "Get off me," she slurred. She grabbed it, yanking and tearing the soft flesh of her ear before its teeth released. She threw it as hard as her exhausted arm could manage.

God, she was thirsty. All she wanted was a little sip. And a cracker would settle her stomach. Water. A little bit of water would be enough. Something was wrong with her. She was tired, so tired. And her brain couldn't think. Were her eyes even open? In the pitch black, she couldn't tell, but she could see the stars.

A bee stung her butt or a damn rat bit her. "Ouch." She dug her hand down inside her trousers and found a hot, hard spot high on her hip. It was the same spot where she had noticed a bug bite while at MacKlenna Farm. But now the spot was tingling. She was so tired. She slid down the wall to the ground again, curled up tightly, and went back to sleep.

A flash of light from above woke her. A rat's sharp toenails clung in her hair. A shadow, black against black, glided stealthily toward her, much bigger than a rat. She cowered in the corner, shivering. "Where are you, David? Help me."

87

Washington City, 1865

B RAHAM AND CULLEN returned home tired but exhilarated after a long day in court. The prosecution had produced four witnesses in their case against Jack. Each one testified to seeing him with Booth within weeks of the assassination. Braham had been unable to shake the witnesses' testimony until he asked the question, "Was the defendant writing in a journal or on a piece of paper during the conversation?" Each witness answered yes, which bolstered Jack's defense of being in the process of interviewing Booth for an article.

On redirect, General Holt asked the witnesses if Jack was talking in a low or normal voice, and if he seemed concerned others might overhear the conversation. Each witness testified he wasn't whispering.

On recross, Braham asked the witnesses if they overheard any of the conversations. Each testified they heard Jack and Booth talking about their favorite playwrights, and which theaters in Philadelphia and New York had the best performance spaces. The witnesses claimed the conversations were boring.

General Holt asked on re-redirect why they hadn't mentioned the conversations during their initial interviews. Two witnesses claimed they hadn't been asked. The spectators snickered, and General Hunter slammed his gavel, demanding order in the courtroom.

If anyone was keeping a tally, the defense was ahead, but the prosecution's most damning witnesses, the carriage driver and Henly, were scheduled to testify the next day. Braham and Cullen had a long night of preparation ahead.

Although Braham wanted to go straight home to see Charlotte, Cullen insisted they stop at the Willard for drinks. They didn't need the alcohol, but they did need to be seen in public. Jack was innocent, and swaying public opinion was part of their strategy. Being at the Willard made them accessible to other lawyers, businessmen, members of society with influence, and, most importantly, President Johnson's political supporters.

They arrived home around nine to find Jonathan Clem alone in the parlor, dozing in a straight-back chair. Braham tossed his briefcase on top of a table hard enough to rattle its legs. The porcelain knick-knacks clinked, and he cringed. Kit had bought them during a visit to Washington, claiming the room needed a feminine touch. He turned back quickly, holding out his hands in case any toppled off the table.

Cullen laughed. "Kit wouldn't be happy if you broke one of her treasures."

Startled, Clem jumped to his feet, clearing his throat, his hat gripped in his hands.

Braham straightened the figurines. "A soldier doesn't need breakables in his damn parlor." He glanced at the startled sergeant. "Evening, Clem. Where's Doctor Mallory?"

In the glow of the gaslight, the soldier's face appeared unusually haggard and lined. "Sir, she was...kidnapped this afternoon from the park."

Braham dropped the angel figurine he'd been holding. "*She what?*" He stomped over to the contrite sergeant and grabbed his shoulders, bunching the fabric of the shirt in his hands. "*Why aren't you out looking for her?*" Fear mixed with rage froze the breath in Braham's lungs. A quiver of panic leached all reason from his mind. He shook Clem until Cullen pulled Braham back, hard, and his grip on the sergeant's shoulders loosened.

The color had drained from Clem's face. "Mr. Gaylord told me to stay put and wait for you."

Braham's heart raced. He swept his fingers through his hair in a quick gesture, trying to harness his raging fear. "*Where's MacBain?*"

"He was riding over to Maryland today to interview witnesses. Mr. Gaylord sent a man after him. It's all I know."

"Where's Gaylord now?"

Clem shrugged. "I can track him down. He leaves messages around town so he can be found."

Now, rock-hard anger the size of a fist lodged in Braham's throat. "Then go find him, *now.*"

Clem ran out of the room, slamming the front door on his way out of the house.

Edward entered the room with a broom to sweep up the broken china.

"You didn't ask the sergeant what time she was taken," Cullen said.

"Three o'clock," Edward said. "Or thereabouts."

Both men faced the butler. "Did ye' see what happened?" Braham asked.

Edward shook his head. "No. I was at the door when Miss Charlotte went out. Within an hour, the sergeant returned, blood dripping down his head. Said, he'd been hit over the head and when he came to, Miss Charlotte was gone."

"Did he see the men? Were they hired thugs? Young, old?" Cullen asked.

"They were wearing soldier's trousers," Edward said. "I sent one of the maids out to leave word at the shop up the street for Gaylord to come quickly. He came, talked to the sergeant, and then left, saying he'd get his men out to search the city."

Braham's jaw worked in barely controlled rage. "Why didn't you send word to me?"

Edward dropped his head. "I knew you and Mr. Montgomery were working on Mr. Jack's case. I'm sorry if I did wrong, sir." He glanced up at Braham, a sheen of tears in his eyes. "I didn't think

Miss Charlotte would want you to abandon Jack for her. She's told me every day, 'Jack comes first, Edward.' Whatever else happened around her, Jack had to come first."

Braham collapsed in a chair and buried his head in his hands. "You did the right thing, Edward."

Cullen poured drinks and handed Braham a glass. "Do ye' think Henly took her?"

Braham studied the glass for a moment before taking a quick gulp. "Yes. I don't think he'll kill her, but he'll hurt her." He set the glass aside and got up again to pace the room, thinking.

"Do you think he'll rape her?" Cullen asked.

Braham punched his fist into his palm, smacking it again and again. "He's had her for six hours. He implicated Jack in a conspiracy, he's capable of ruining her life, too."

"But would he—?"

"*I don't know.*" Icy fear grew in Braham's chest. "His drug addiction might have made him impotent. At least Charlotte thinks it has."

"Which could make him more violent," Cullen said.

Braham's hand shook as he picked up the glass again and held it at his lips. "As soon as Gaylord gets here, I'm going out to look for her. You stay and prepare for tomorrow. You'll have to handle the cross-examination."

"If you find Henly, for God's sake, don't play into his hands. We need him on the witness stand tomorrow."

Braham swirled the contents in the glass, staring at the golden liquid as if it held answers. "If he's hurt her, I can't make any promises."

The door opened, and David rushed in. "I got an urgent message. Has something happened to Jack?"

"Charlotte's been kidnapped." Cullen said.

David's face held his usual immutable calm, but his hands clamped into tight fists. "How long ago?"

Braham took a short, calming breath. "Six hours. She could be anywhere in the city. Gaylord's men are out searching. We just sent for him. He should be here shortly to give us a report."

"I'll find her." The ruthlessness in David's voice was chilling. He rolled up his sleeve and pushed buttons on the special watch he wore, much like the one Braham had seen on Jack's wrist. David wore his device high on his forearm and out of sight. "Elliott anticipated this. If we were at home, I could locate her within seconds. This equipment will take longer."

"How much longer? Days?" Anticipation tightened the back of Braham's throat.

"If it works, minutes." David's broad shoulders tightened, and his muscles were starkly defined beneath the tight fit of his linen shirt. The room grew quiet, motionless except for the occasional flutter of a curtain hanging in front of the open window. David kept his eyes on his watch. "Braham, do ye' remember how Charlotte and Jack found you in Kentucky?"

Braham walked up behind David and looked over his shoulder, glancing at the watch. "Elliott called it a tracking device."

"Charlotte has a tracking device similar to those used to locate Alzheimer's patients who wander away from nursing homes. I just activated it. If it's going to work, we should get a signal very soon." Within seconds, the watch beeped. "Bingo. She's about two miles in a northeasterly direction. At home, I could give ye' a street address. Here all I get is a general location."

"How do you know you've found Charlotte? The kidnapper could have taken the device," Braham said.

"Or, it could be lost like the sapphire brooch," Cullen said.

David gave Cullen a dark, sideways look. "It's implanted in her hip. She doesn't even know she has it."

A vision of Charlotte *au naturel* with David's hands on her left Braham aghast. "You put the device inside of her without her knowledge?" Anger bubbled to the surface, and he raised his fist to slam it into David's face, but Cullen caught his arm.

"Why didn't you tell her?" Cullen asked, holding tight to Braham.

David shrugged. The movement was tight, impatient. "It's a

device. I didn't know if it would work here or not. Besides, knowing she had the implant could have given her a false sense of security, and we didna need her going off half-cocked."

Outwardly, MacBain appeared unruffled, but a small tic in his jaw as he ground his teeth told Braham the lad was truly worried about Charlotte. Braham's eyes stung, and he turned away, noticing for the first time one of her shoes peeking out from under the sofa. Fear settled on his shoulders like a confining cloak he couldn't shake off. "If you know where she is, then let's go."

David shook his head. "I need backup. We'll wait for Gaylord." He left the room and leaped up the stairs, taking them three at a time.

"Do you think the signal will lead us to her?" Cullen's voice held doubt.

"I drove a car five hundred miles from Mallory Plantation to MacKlenna Farm, and Jack and Charlotte found me using a similar device. It fit in the palm of my hand. I hope the one Charlotte has implanted is a wee bit smaller."

"Do you think Henly took her?"

"I know he did. If I'm spending my time looking for Charlotte, I can't be in court fighting for Jack."

"He's forcing ye' to choose one Mallory or the other." Cullen's voice was low and gravelly.

"Whichever one I don't fight for, he'll kill, or, in Jack's case, perjure himself and let the commission send Jack to the gallows. When I get my hands on Henly…"

Cullen squeezed Braham's shoulder. "We'll rescue her, and you'll destroy Henly on the witness stand and exonerate Jack."

"Let's get the lass back first."

David reentered the room dressed in black pants and shirt, plus a black cap, and he'd covered his face with black paint. He hoisted a bag over his shoulder. "Braham, if ye're coming, ye' have to stay out of my way. I have no doubt ye' could rescue Charlotte if I weren't here. But Jack needs you more than she or I do right now. I can extract Charlotte and set up reconnaissance to catch the kidnapper.

But I can't do it if ye're in my way."

"If you're expecting me to stay here, you're wrong."

"Ye' can go. But when I tell ye' to stay put, ye' stay. If ye' get shot, Jack's chances of beating these charges diminish. Gaylord's out back. Let's go."

David hustled out of the room. Braham turned to Cullen. "If anything happens to us, get Jack out and take him home. He'll see you get back to MacKlenna Farm."

Cullen nodded. "I've no heart for traveling to the twenty-first-century, but I'll see to it."

They hugged each other, slapping backs. Braham left the house by way of the rear door, and found Gaylord in the barn with David.

"Where're we going?" Gaylord asked.

David led his horse out of the stall and tossed on its saddle blanket. "Two miles in a northeasterly direction. What's over there?"

"It must be near the docks. One of my investigators discovered Henly has an interest in a vacant apartment building, unless he's lost it at the gaming tables, too."

"If that section of town closes down at night, it will be to our advantage." David lifted the saddle, placed it gently on the horse's back, and tightened the cinch. "Where are the rest of your men?"

"Canvassing the city. As soon as we know Miss Charlotte's location, I'll pass the word."

As soon as Braham saddled his horse, the men mounted up and David led the way. The moon appeared only as a sliver, thin as a nail paring. The pattern of stars which formed the Big Dipper were clearly visible in the night sky. They rode through the city in silence, and fear tightened in a band around Braham's chest.

A wire stretched from David's ear to his watch. He stopped at intersections to study a map, using a small light which snapped on and off with a click of his finger.

They traveled down a street lined with residences, businesses, and a few warehouses, sticking to the shadows cast by gaslight. The traffic was light, with only a rare carriage or a man on horseback. David stopped on the side of the street, dismounted, and signaled for Braham and Gaylord to wait for him. He took his bag and disappeared into the darkness.

Braham dismounted, his heart squeezing in his chest. He was responsible for this. He should have been honest with Charlotte from the beginning and explained she couldn't stop him from returning to his time, and assured her whatever happened was not her responsibility. But he hadn't done it. Instead, he'd endangered the lives of both Charlotte and Jack.

David returned after several minutes. "Found her. She's in a root cellar beneath a three-story building. She's alive."

A small shudder of relief skimmed through Braham, gradually releasing the tightness in his neck and shoulders.

"There's a guard sitting in a chair next to the outside cellar door. The first floor is unoccupied. I'm going to break into the building, cut a hole through the first floor, and bring Charlotte out through the hole. Gaylord, you keep an eye the guard. If he attempts to enter the cellar, take him down. Once we get her out, we'll plan twenty-four hour surveillance of the building until we catch the men responsible."

"Is she hurt?" Braham asked.

"I can't tell. She lying on the ground and not moving, but she could be asleep."

"Did you see her through a window? I'll stay out of your way, but I have to see her for myself," Braham said.

"Come on," David said. They went around to the opposite corner of the building from where the guard was positioned. David gave Braham an odd-looking pair of binoculars. "Ye' can see her lying curled on the ground."

Braham saw a reddish-yellow human figure, curled in fetal position. "How do you know it's her?"

"The signal puts us in the right location."

"How do you know she's alive?"

"If she weren't, we wouldn't be able to see her. The object has to emit heat in order to be seen. I'm going to open a hole in the floor above her." David pointed to a window up above. "I'll go through first. When I know it's safe, ye' can come in. Now, give me a leg up."

Braham laced his fingers and hoisted David, who raised the window and silently dove into the room and out of sight.

88

Washington City, 1865

B RAHAM SAT ON his haunches, waiting impatiently for David to come back for him. A part of him hated MacBain. He was a good lad, intelligent, and resourceful. Elliott trusted him implicitly, and from what Cullen said, Kit adored him. From the rare facial expressions David allowed to show, he obviously was in love with Charlotte. Braham was sure he'd never admit it, though, and maybe only another man in love with the same woman would notice the occasional discreet glances. Nothing inappropriate, but they were there—a smile, a flash in the eye, a brush of the hand, small gestures.

What would happen when they returned to their time? Charlotte had said David was too young for her, and he spent most of his time in Scotland, but Braham was certain the lad would spend most, if not all, of his time in Richmond if he believed he had a chance to win Charlotte's heart. Unless Braham intended to go live in her time, he mustn't stand in the way of their happiness. And no matter how much he loved her, he couldn't go with her. If the trial went the way he and Cullen expected over the next two days, the Judge Advocate would have to drop all charges against Jack, and the time-travelers would be free to return home.

A light flashed in the window. It was David's signal. Braham sprinted the short distance from his secluded spot between buildings and reached the window within seconds.

"Give me your hands," David said.

Braham grasped David's arms, scaled the wall, and then rolled through the open window, landing softly on the floor. "How is she?" he asked, climbing quickly to his feet.

"I cut a hole through the floor and heard her moaning. I'm going in now. I'll need ye' to help us out."

"Can you see her?" Braham asked.

"She's only a few feet away, curled up in the corner now. It's good. She's moving, and she's conscious." David sat on the edge of the hole, dangling his legs. It was about an eight foot drop. He put his arms through the straps attached to his bag, snugging it to his back. "Keep an eye on the window till I call for help." David then dropped through the opening and Braham reluctantly returned to the window.

"Where are you, David? Help me."

Charlotte's plaintive call for him cut through Braham's heart in sharp, jagged slices. The lad was the man she wanted in her moment of darkness, not him. A strange, tight sensation gathered around his eyes, and he wiped them with his forearm.

"I'm here, Charley." The unutterable tenderness in David's voice took Braham by surprise and the vise around his chest tightened.

"I knew you'd come," she said hoarsely.

The looming, dense clouds had lifted now, shredded away by a light breeze, allowing dark streaks of a starlit sky to show through the breaks, much as David's appearance had broken through Charlotte's darkness, bringing light and safety.

"I'm going to check ye' over before I move ye. Where do ye' hurt?"

Braham listened closely, holding his breath, praying Henly had not...

"My head, mostly, and my ribs."

"How 'bout yer neck?"

"It's okay. I think."

"Did he rape you?"

"No..."

Braham had been holding his breath, and now he let it stream out of his lungs.

"But I have a hot spot on my butt, and rats have been trying to eat me."

David chuckled. "It's not a bite, lass, but ye' might slap me after ye' hear what I did to ye'."

"I doubt it. Let's get out of here."

"I've checked ye' over. There doesn't appear to be anything broken, and ye're not bleeding. I'm going to carry ye' a bit, then lift ye' up to Braham—"

"He's here? He should be in court, not looking for me."

"Court's over for the day. If I hurt ye,' tell me to stop."

She made a noise like someone absorbing a body blow.

"I'm sorry. What hurts?"

"My ribs."

"I'll be easy. But we have to get ye' out of here."

Braham moved over to the hole and prepared to grab her. They were right below him now. His heart jumped into his throat. He almost had her in his arms.

"Try to keep her head steady," David said. "I'm going to pass ye' up to Braham now, lass. It will hurt a bit, but try not to cry out."

Braham grabbed her beneath the arms, and she cried out.

"Grip her around the waist," David said. "She might have a broken rib or two. Her breasts are bound, so I can't tell."

Braham pulled her through the hole. "I've got her." He wanted to hug her to him, but he didn't dare squeeze her. He very gently kissed her forehead. "Thank God you're all right."

"I didn't want you to come for me. Jack needed you more. Are you sure you're not missing court?"

"I'm not." He chuckled, relaxing into a warm pool of relief. He picked straw out of her hair and clothes.

"How long have I been down there?"

"Six or seven hours."

"I thought I might be there for days. How'd you find me?"

"It's a story for David to tell you."

"Thanks," David said. "I got the tracks covered. Help me up."

Braham set Charlotte aside, grabbed David's arms, and hauled him up.

"As soon as I seal the hole, we'll get out of here. Take Charley over by the window and keep watch."

Braham held her shivering body in his arms as he squatted next to the window, watching. A few minutes later, David tapped him on the shoulder. "I'll go out first. Then ye' can hand her over before ye' climb out and close the window."

Braham nodded, and David slid out of the building. After a quick check of the premises, he returned for Charlotte. Braham passed her through the window and followed them out.

"Take her home," David said, handing her back to Braham. "I'm going to work out surveillance with Gaylord. I'll see ye' at the house later. If she goes to sleep, wake her every hour. Make sure she knows where she is and can follow commands, like squeezing your fingers."

"If I have a concussion, it's mild," she said. "Other than the headache and the initial nausea, I'm okay."

"We'll observe ye' anyway. Now go."

Braham held out his hand, and David clasped it. "Thank you," Braham said.

"Let's get the other Mallory home safely, too, and then my job will be done," David said.

Braham glanced at Charlotte, then at David. "No, I don't think it will be."

The trip home was uneventful, and Braham kept the horse to a slow walk to keep from jostling Charlotte. "Can you tell me what happened?"

"One of Gordon's goons grabbed me and threw me into a carriage. Gordon hit me several times. Next thing I knew, I woke up in the cellar. I hate rats."

"I don't like them either. David got to you within thirty minutes of finding out you were missing. He's a fine man."

"Meredith said he could do anything. I knew he'd find me." Charlotte closed her eyes and drifted off to sleep.

He gazed down at her dirt-streaked face. Even smudged and

bruised she was the most beautiful woman he'd ever seen. Her time living in the past had scarred her, and when this was all over she and Jack would need time to heal. Maybe they would consider coming to his vineyards to rest for a while. Later, he would ask, but for now he only wanted to hold her close. And as he did, his silent tears fell gently into her hair.

89

Washington City, 1865

C ULLEN'S CRITICAL EYE roved over Braham, who had worn his best uniform for this critical courtroom appearance. Epaulets with silver embroidered eagles graced both shoulders. Around Braham's waist Edward had tied a yellow sash. The jacket buttoned up to the throat, forcing a slight lift to Braham's chin. Polished spurs with large rowels were buckled with fine leather straps to top-boots made with ornamental stitching of red silk. As Edward hooked a long sword with a jewel-studded hilt to his side, Braham stood quite still, his face devoid of emotion.

"If your intent is to intimidate, you've accomplished it well," Cullen said.

"I'll be in a room full of generals, Cul. Intimidation is not my intent. I only wish to remind them Lincoln and Stanton had faith in my judgment, and there's no call to doubt it now."

Charlotte entered the room through the adjoining door, carrying a cup of coffee. Cullen gasped inaudibly at the sight of the bruises on her face, now a deeper purple, extending from the left side of her eye down to her chin.

She stopped and smiled slightly. "You look dashing. The female spectators won't be able to take their eyes off of you."

Braham kissed her on the lips, and Cullen smiled inwardly, longing for his wife. They started every day with long kisses, and he missed them terribly, especially today, when he felt a strong need for

Kit's tender touch and understanding.

Braham pushed aside Charlotte's hair, revealing a bandaged ear. "How do you feel this morning?"

"Sore, but very grateful. My head still throbs, but it's on the mend. I probably had a concussion last night, but I'm thinking more clearly this morning. I have scratches, but only two bad bites. I cleaned them both and smeared antibiotic ointment over them. All in all, I'm pretty good."

She turned to Cullen and gave him a quick hug. Her vanilla-scented hair reminded him of Kit, and he missed his wife even more.

"Thank you for everything you've done," she said.

"I would never have forgiven myself if I hadn't come, and likely Kit wouldn't have forgiven me either."

Braham tucked Charlotte into his arms. "We'll send you news as soon as we can." She lifted her face and they gazed into each other's eyes. Cullen was so touched by the love he saw there he glanced away, not wanting to intrude.

"Half of Gaylord's men are stationed here, both outside the house and inside. You'll not be alone. You're not a prisoner, but for your own safety, you're not allowed to leave, even if you beg for a walk in the park. If any of the guards surrenders to your wiles, they'll be drawn and quartered. So spare the men and behave."

She gave him a demure look.

Cullen turned toward the window to hide another smile and inhaled the morning air, heavily scented with honeysuckle from the garden below. He knew Braham would surrender to Charlotte's charm within seconds. Charlotte was a beautiful and intriguing woman, and from Cullen's experience with strong-willed women, she'd damn well go outside, threats notwithstanding, if she needed a bit of air and exercise.

"How do you feel about today?" Her brow creased, and her voice was soft, with a curious emphasis in her tone.

Braham softly touched the crease in her forehead. "We've planned for every contingency. There'll be no surprises."

Cullen smiled again, shaking his head, his index finger gently tapping his chin. Charlotte had completely ignored Braham's admonishment, and he allowed it. As Kit would say, Charlotte had Braham wrapped around her little finger. And it would tickle Kit to see it.

Edward gave a final brushing to Braham's jacket and trousers, flicking off small wisps of lint. "You're ready now to face the enemy, Colonel."

Cullen, Braham, and Charlotte followed Edward in an orderly procession down the stairs. Saber and spurs clinked with Braham's easy stride. At the door he collected his revolver, hat, and gauntlets.

She gave Braham one last goodbye kiss. "Good luck, soldier."

Braham cleared his throat and stood ramrod straight. "I'll bring your brother home, or die trying."

Cullen tucked his briefcase under his arm, took Charlotte's hand, and kissed it. "I know you'll worry, regardless of what I say. So I'll leave with one of Kit's favorite ditties, a Shaker hymn I believe."

Tis the gift to be simple, 'tis the gift to be free,
Tis the gift to come down where we ought to be,
And when we find ourselves in the place just right,
Twill be in the valley of love and delight
When true simplicity is gain'd,
To bow and to bend we shan't be asham'd,
To turn, turn will be our delight,
Till by turning, turning we come round right.

"What a beautiful song. There's a message there, but I'm missing it today," Charlotte said.

"Turn, Charlotte, and you'll find yourself in a *place just right.* Kit did, and I know you will, too."

90

Washington City, 1865

THE COURTROOM ALREADY buzzed with speculation about the identities of the prosecution's star witnesses against Jack. There were opinions bandied about, but no one knew for sure, including the defense, or so the prosecutor believed.

Heads turned as eyes followed Braham to his chair. There was no mistaking the spectators' looks of admiration. Several newspaper articles had appeared yesterday describing Braham's exploits as a master spy. Somehow the public now knew about his near-death experiences in Richmond.

Folks were curious about the hero lawyer representing a conspirator, wondering why he would risk his reputation for such a distasteful assignment. Cullen and Braham were betting if the citizenry's consciousness was aroused, they might take another look at the evidence against their client. It had been part of the defense's strategy from the beginning, including leaking certain information. After today, the defense team hoped to have the press firmly on its side, and with the press came public opinion.

Braham and Cullen took their seats at the defense table, put their briefcases aside, and then sat quietly, with hands clasped on top of the table. When General Holt entered, he scanned the table, noting the absence of law books and papers usually stacked in front of Braham. He glared, giving Braham a questioning lift of his brow.

Once the commissioners were seated, the defendants were

brought into the courtroom and their hoods were removed. Jack blinked at the sudden bombardment of light in his eyes. Braham nodded with only a slight dip of his chin while raising his thumb. Jack blinked again, gave Braham a quick nod, and settled into his seat.

Cullen had never seen his client outside of the courtroom, but Jack's demeanor when compared with the other defendants clearly set him apart. The press commented on his intelligence and compassion, and his proper courtroom demeanor. Press reports attributed it to his pose, which drew attention to his best attributes: penetrating blue eyes, sculpted features, muscular frame, and large, relaxed hands. To Cullen, the lines around Jack's eyes and mouth made him look tired. Otherwise, he appeared to be holding up well enough, although his clothes and hair were more and more disheveled. Braham and Cullen had always before insisted their clients dress in their best Sunday clothes for court appearances. It wasn't possible for Jack.

General Hunter pounded his gavel and Cullen turned in his chair. Today his assignment was to observe the commissioners, members of the press, and spectators, and to note their body language and facial expressions.

If the defense would ever completely win over the commissioners and the press, it would happen today. Later, the arguments which triggered favorable reactions would be the ones Braham stressed during closing arguments.

"General Holt, call your first witness in the case against Jack Mallory," General Hunter said.

Holt pointed to the guard standing next to the witness room. "Send in the witness."

A man worn down by life and age shuffled into the room swiping at shanks of thinning, dirty gray hair. His pursed lips and shuttered eyes gave him a sinister appearance. Holt directed him to the witness stand where he stood, holding tightly to the rail, whether for balance or fear, Cullen couldn't tell. A combination of both, most likely. After being sworn in, Holt asked him to state his name and occupation.

"Name's Troy Stroker. I'm a hackney driver."

"Who is your employer?" Holt asked.

Stroker licked his lips. "John Howard. It's his livery stables where I rent my carriage."

"Do you recognize any of the defendants in this case?"

Stroker turned, wobbled a bit, then pointed at Jack.

"Let the record show the witness identified Jack Mallory. Now, Mr. Stroker, did you have an occasion to pick up Mr. Mallory and deliver him to his requested destination?"

The witness wiped his mouth on his sleeve. "Yes, sir. It was in March. I picked him and Mr. Booth up at a residence next to the Lafayette Park. I remember because the Booth fella called the defendant there…" Stroker pointed over his shoulder toward Jack. "Called him Mr. Jack Mallory. I thought it was odd."

"Where did they ask you to take them?" General Holt asked.

"To the National Hotel."

"Did you hear any of their conversation?"

Stroker shrugged. "Just a word or two. Theys was goin' to celebrate their April plan."

"Their April plan?" Holt raised his brow, glancing at the commissioners for effect. "You remember those words specifically?"

"I do, sir. I do. Thought it were odd. But I remember. Came to tell you right away after the shooting and all."

"Did anyone ask you to make the report?"

"Oh, no. No. No. No one asked me. I did it on my own."

"Thank you for being such a good citizen, Mr. Stroker. No more questions for this witness."

"Colonel McCabe, your witness," General Hunter said.

Braham stood. He tapped his fingertips on top of the table, looking straight ahead. Several members of the commission leaned forward slightly, waiting. The press also waited with pencils poised. Finally Braham said, "Who's your employer, did you say?"

"John Howard."

"And how long have you worked for him?"

"A few weeks."

"Who did you work for previously?"

"Ah," Stroker licked his lips, swallowed.

Braham rubbed a finger down his nose, thinking. "You did have an employer, didn't you? A former employer?"

"James Pumphrey," Stroker said under his breath.

"I'm sorry. I didn't hear the name." Braham kept his face impassive.

Stroker was rather flushed, and he said, loudly, "James Pumphrey."

"Do you know if Mr. Pumphrey has any connection to this case?"

Stroker gripped the railing, released his fingers, then gripped again and again. "He rented Booth the horse he rode the night of the shootin'. *But I wasn't working for him then.*" Stroker's excuses spilled out so quickly his statement sounded like one long word.

"I believe you testified your employer before Howard was Pumphrey. If you weren't working for either of those men the night in question, then who were you working for?"

"I was driving for several people."

"Isn't it true, Mr. Stroker that you were driving for only one customer?"

Stroker went pale and his eyebrows shot up. "No."

"Maybe you have your dates confused, and you were driving for Mr. Howard. Is that correct?"

The spectators were leaning forward in their seats now.

"No, he done fired me."

"Then who?" Braham hissed, low voiced but emphatic. "Mr. Stroker, who were you working for?"

Stroker gnawed on his lower lip. His eyes flitted between Braham and General Holt. "I was drivin' fer Colonel Henly."

"Colonel Gordon Henly?" Braham asked.

"Yes sir."

Gasps erupted from the spectators. The buzz turned into a loud rumbling which quieted with Braham's next question. "How long had you been driving for the Colonel?"

"Since last year."

"So in the last year, you didn't work for either Mr. Pumphrey or Mr. Howard. Is this your testimony?"

"No. I mean—" Stroker broke off in the middle of the sentence and shot Braham a startled look. "Yes. It's what I mean to say."

"You testified earlier you drove Mr. Mallory and Mr. Booth to the National Hotel. Did you have other fares that evening?"

"Yes," Stroker said, his eyes cast down.

"And who did you pick up?"

"I drove the colonel to the theatre."

"Was he alone?"

Stroker's lips trembled. He compressed them briefly before saying, "He was with a lady."

"After the theater, where did you take them?"

"To dinner at the Willard Hotel."

"After dinner, where did they ask to be taken?"

"To a residence—" Stroker stopped, appearing to consider his next statement. Apparently, he found no alternative but to tell the truth. "A residence across from Lafayette Park."

Braham's eyebrows rose for effect. "Is it the same location where you testified earlier you picked up the defendant and Mr. Booth?"

Stroker nodded.

"Speak up, Mr. Stroker. The court reporter can't hear nods," Braham said with a hint of wry humor.

Cullen kept his eyes on the commissioners. No one needed to cup their ears to hear. Braham's booming voice carried clearly throughout the courtroom.

"Yes, the same location."

Many of the spectators whispered to each other now.

"Is there anything about your previous testimony you would like to change at this time?"

Stroker, blinking, glanced between Braham and General Holt. "I might have been mistaken about my passengers."

General Holt's arm rested on the table at his side. His fist opened and closed repeatedly.

"So," Braham said, "would like to tell the court who you actually picked up that night and where you delivered them?"

Stroker ran a hand over his hair, looking around the room like a ferret searching for an escape route. "After the colonel dropped the lady off, I took the colonel and Mr. Mallory to the Willard."

Without a twitch or a blink, Braham said, "Thank you, Mr. Stroker. No further questions."

"General Holt, do you have further questions of the witness?" General Hunter said.

"Yes, I do. Mr. Stroker, why did you testify you picked up Mr. Booth?"

"Well, sir," Stroker said, his Adam's apple bobbing. "The Booth fella, he came out of the house where the colonel and the lady had gone, and he asked for a ride."

"And did you give him one?"

"No, sir. I told him I was waiting for the colonel. He said thank you and walked on down the street. Real nice like."

"No further questions." Dejection was as clear in Holt's voice as it was on his face.

"Do you have further questions, Colonel McCabe?" General Hunter said.

Braham remained silent a moment, steepling his fingers. "Mr. Stroker, did you hear either Colonel Henly or Mr. Mallory say anything during the ride to the Willard?"

"Yes, sir. The colonel said he'd been a fan of Mr. Booth's for many years but had never met him."

"And what did Mr. Mallory say?" Braham asked.

"He had no use for the man and didn't intend to write a flattering article about him."

"Thank you. No further questions," Braham said.

Holt stood. "One final question. You perjured yourself earlier in your testimony, how do we know you're telling the truth now?"

"I guess you don't, sir, but I got no reason to say nice things about Mr. Mallory if he's done what you say he's done. And the colonel told me if I was confused about what happened that night, then he'd remind me. Thing is...my memory is pretty good, but the colonel wanted me to remember what happened jes' the way I told you first."

Holt sat, shaking his head.

"Colonel McCabe, do you have further questions of the witness?" General Hunter's voice held an exasperated tone.

"Mr. Stroker, is there anything else the colonel asked you not to mention? Like what the two of you were doing yesterday afternoon in Lafayette Park about three o'clock?"

"Objection. Beyond the scope of re-recross-examination," Holt said.

The witness's mouth dropped open. "Ah, ah..."

"No further questions," Braham said, and strode back to their table.

91

Washington City, 1865

GENERAL HOLT HAD a brilliant legal mind, and had been Lincoln's chief arbiter and enforcer of military law. He knew not to ask a question if he didn't already know the answer. Cullen and Braham had bet Holt wouldn't ask Stroker what he and Henly had been doing at three o'clock on the previous afternoon. If he had asked, Braham and Cullen would have had to adjust their strategy, but as long as Henly was sequestered, they would still have the benefit of surprise during Henly's cross-examination.

Since Gaylord had not sent a message, Cullen and Braham knew Henly wasn't aware Charlotte had escaped. He was probably waiting until after his testimony to dispose of her. Just thinking about it had Cullen wishing he'd been given the assignment to cross-examine the colonel, but Braham had assured Cullen his emotions were under control.

Now it was show time.

"Call your next witness," General Hunter said.

General Holt pointed to the guard standing outside the witness room. "Colonel Gordon Henly."

Henly limped into the room, grimacing, dressed in a clean, pressed uniform complete with saber and revolver. However, his boots were scuffed and muddy. When he had shaved, he had missed the whiskers close to his ears. His eyes were bloodshot, his face was pinched, and he was breathing heavily. He did not look well.

"Please state your name and current position," General Holt said.

Unkempt wavy brown hair flowed loose over his collar. "Colonel Gordon Henly, on special assignment to the War Department. I'm currently supervising the discharge of our troops."

"How long have you been on special assignment?"

"Since I recovered from the wounds I sustained at Cedar Creek and my regiment was given to Colonel Taylor."

"Are you familiar with the defendant, Jack Mallory?"

His upper lip twitched in disgust. "Yes, sir, I am."

"Would you tell the court how you met the defendant?"

"I was on my way back to the War Department one afternoon in late December when I saw the defendant's sister on the corner outside the Willard Hotel. She was sitting on her trunk, left in the cold by the degenerate Mr. Jack Mallory."

"Objection," Braham said. "The statement is inflammatory."

"Sustained. The witness will refrain from characterizing the defendant," General Hunter said.

"Doctor Charlotte Mallory was sitting unaccompanied in the cold while her brother attempted to secure transportation. I ordered my sergeant to stand guard over her luggage while I escorted her into the hotel, where I subsequently met her brother."

"And what happened during the meeting at the Willard?"

"Doctor Mallory told me they were staying with her cousin, Major McCabe, and I offered to escort them to the major—excuse me, the colonel's residence."

"Did she indicate which one of the colonel's residences she intended to visit?" General Holt asked.

The spectators' questioning eyes glanced at Braham. His affluence hadn't been mentioned in the press before. A number of women smiled shyly. A handsome and wealthy bachelor was always of interest.

"Doctor Mallory and her brother intended to travel to the colonel's residence in Georgetown. I asked why they weren't staying in Washington. They were unaware of his townhouse across the street from Lafayette Park, so I escorted them there."

"And did you have an occasion to recommend Mr. Mallory as a possible contributor to an editor at the *Times*?"

"Mr. Mallory gave me a copy of an article, an unpublished article he had written following the Battle of Cedar Creek. He asked me to show the article to editors I knew who might consider buying one of his stories."

"And did you have an opportunity to show this article to anyone?"

"I did, and the editor at the *Times* agreed to read it. He said he would consider purchasing articles from Mr. Mallory."

"And did Mr. Mallory ever sell any articles which you are aware of?"

Beads of sweat dotted Henly's face, and he wiped his forehead with the back of his hand. "He has never sold *one*."

"Objection. Calls for speculation. Unless the witness has read every newspaper around the world, he has no way of knowing how many articles Mr. Mallory has sold," Braham said.

"Objection sustained. You testimony is limited to your personal knowledge, Colonel," General Hunter said. "Continue."

General Holt picked up a sheet of paper and glanced at it briefly. "Tell us about the events of the evening in early February, when you attended the theatre with Doctor Mallory."

"Doctor Mallory agreed to accompany me to see the comedian J. S. Clarks. After the theater, we had dinner at the Willard, and then I took her back to Colonel McCabe's residence."

"And what happened when you arrived at the colonel's residence?"

"Doctor Mallory and I were standing in the foyer when Mr. Mallory and Mr. Booth came out of one of the rooms, laughing and talking about an event in April. The men were in high spirits until they saw me. They immediately sobered and made quick introductions. Mr. Mallory and Mr. Booth then left. Shortly afterwards, I said goodnight to Doctor Mallory and left."

"Did you have an opportunity to see the Mallorys on other occasions?"

Henly's eyes brightened. "I did. They attended the inaugural party. They approached me." He glanced down at his nails and picked at them, as if the topic of discussion was painfully distasteful. "I felt uncomfortable and escaped their company as quickly as possible."

General Holt set the sheet of paper aside and accepted another sheet from General Hunter. He pursued it quickly. "Did you notice anything particular about their demeanor during the inaugural evening?"

"They spent an inordinate amount of time staring at President Lincoln and talking behind Dr. Mallory's open fan."

"Thank you, Colonel. No further questions."

"Your witness, Colonel McCabe," General Hunter said.

Braham sat still as calm water for a long moment. Then he pushed his chair back, scraping the legs across the hardwood floor. He stood, smoothed down his jacket, and approached the witness stand at a leisurely pace. "Colonel, what did you and Doctor Mallory discuss over dinner at the Willard the night in February?"

"We talked about the show, I believe."

"Were you fond of Doctor Mallory?"

Henly flipped his hand in dismissal and rolled his eyes in disgust. "Not as fond as she was of me."

"Why not? She's a beautiful, intelligent woman."

"Much too strong-willed for me. She lacks discipline."

Braham folded his arms and his mouth twitched in what might have been a faint smile. "She's a surgeon, and she lacks discipline? Would you be more specific?"

Despite Henly's obvious efforts at self-control, his frame was quivering with indignation. "She told me medicine was the most important thing in her life and she never intended to marry."

Cullen was as enthralled with the testimony as was the rest of courtroom, which usually buzzed with side conversations. Now every eye and ear was focused on the exchange between Henly and Braham. Newspaper reporters were madly scribbling.

Braham shrugged. "Why did you care whether she intended to marry or not?"

"Because I considered…" Henly paused before starting again. "*I didn't care.* Considering how strong-willed she is, it's best she doesn't impose her will on any suitable gentleman."

"Like yourself?" Braham asked.

"I will *not* tolerate such behavior."

"Who do you blame for not squelching her strong will?"

"*Her brother,* of course."

Braham paused a moment to let the comment sink in. It did. The female spectators were chatting behind open fans covering the lower portions of their faces. Several commission members took deep breaths and eyed General Holt.

"Did you speak to Mr. Mallory about his sister's behavior?" Braham asked.

"I did. The same night as a matter of fact." Henly's voice was unnaturally loud and angry. "I told him he should exercise more control over her."

"When did this conversation take place?"

"In the carriage." Henly wiped perspiration from his forehead. "I misspoke. It was later when I ran into him at the Willard."

Braham steepled his fingers and tapped them together. "So you returned to the Willard after you left Doctor Mallory? If you didn't ride in the carriage with him back to the Willard, where did you find him? In what room?"

Perspiration popped up on every inch of skin on Henly's face. "In the billiard room."

"Going back to earlier in the evening, was there any time during your dinner with Doctor Mallory when you left the table?"

He barked a laugh. "I don't recall."

"Isn't it true you had to restrain Doctor Mallory from going into the billiard room?"

Henly slammed his fist on the railing. "I *told* her brother she was out of line and should be punished."

Braham turned toward the commissioners with a hint of a smile.

"What did you expect Mr. Mallory to do? Turn her over his knee and give her a whooping?"

"Of course not."

The women in the courtroom giggled.

"Isn't it true, Colonel Henly, you said to Mr. Mallory, and I quote, 'A slap never hurt any woman, it keeps her in line.'?"

"No, I did not."

The commissioners had all turned in their seats to face the witness stand, riveted to the testimony, even those members whose attention usually wandered. Braham raised his eyebrows, but said nothing. It was a planned maneuver to keep Henly in an anxious state.

"Why did Doctor Mallory want to go into the billiard room?"

Henly roared, full of indignation. "*To see you.*"

"Why did you object to Doctor Mallory seeing her cousin?"

"*Ha.* You're not cousins. You're…*lovers.*"

Cullen's heart was thudding at a breakneck pace. The testimony was proceeding exactly as they planned. The next few questions and answers were critical.

"Why would you think we're lovers? Have you spied on Doctor Mallory's bedroom?"

"Certainly not." He punctuated his comment with a wild gesture.

Braham walked over to the defense table and Cullen handed him a small bag. "If you have no interest in Doctor Mallory, why do you care who she takes as a lover?"

There was an audible intake of breath around the room. Braham was besmirching Charlotte's reputation, but it couldn't be helped. Cullen prayed she'd forgive them.

"I *don't* care." Henly's voice was tight with suppressed rage.

"Between your command position and when you began your assignment to the War Department, were you offered other opportunities?"

Henly's nostrils flared. "No."

"Was there a position working for President Lincoln which you applied for and were passed over in favor of another candidate whom you outranked?"

"I wasn't interested in the position."

"I'm sorry." Braham turned toward the commissioners. "Did you say you weren't interested in a special assignment working directly for the President of the United States? Did you tell him you weren't interested?"

Henly snarled. "Of course not."

Braham twisted to look at the witness. "What did you tell Mr. Lincoln?"

"That I'd be honored to accept the position if offered."

Braham turned back to the commissioners. "So you lied to the President of the United States. Is this what you're saying?"

"*No, it's not what I'm saying?*"

"The court would be interested in your explanation, Colonel. And after you explain why you lied to the President," Braham then turned back to the witness, "maybe you'll explain why you've lied to this court."

"I haven't lied."

"Then tell the court when you last saw the person wearing this." Braham opened the small bag, pulled out Charlotte's wig, and tossed it to Henly.

He fumbled, gasped, and then let it fall to the ground. "*How dare you?*"

Braham picked up the wig and nonchalantly straightened the hairs. "How dare I what?"

Henly's rage was back now, rising, smoldering behind his eyes. "*Insult me.*"

"How much laudanum do you take a day for the pain in your back? I believe you said you were wounded at Cedar Creek. Is that correct?"

"Yes."

"Is that why you needed a henchman to grab Doctor Mallory from Lafayette Park yesterday? Because you're too impotent to do it yourself?"

"I don't know what the hell you're talking about."

Braham approached the witness stand, still holding the wig. "Isn't it true, Colonel, you hated Jack Mallory for having no control over his sister, because you had intended to propose to her on the night in question?" Braham paused, allowing his question to thoroughly penetrate the observers' consciousness.

"Isn't it also true, Colonel, you hated me for getting the job you wanted, working for the President of the United States?

"Isn't it true, Colonel, you kidnapped Doctor Mallory yesterday afternoon and dumped her badly beaten body in a rat-infested cellar so I would have to choose between looking for her," Braham paused and pointed toward Jack, "or representing her innocent brother?

"Isn't it true, Colonel, you framed Jack Mallory?"

The spectators in the courtroom erupted, and General Hunter banged his gavel. "Order. Order in the courtroom."

Henly snatched his revolver from its holster, pointed it at Braham, and pulled the trigger.

92

Washington City, 1865

C HARLOTTE WAITED QUIETLY on the sofa in the parlor, reading an article in an old issue of Annals of Surgery. She'd read it five times and, while she didn't remember much about the article, she did remember the first few words of the objective: "To evaluate the effect of implementing a multidisciplinary…" Well, okay, she didn't remember it, either.

She closed the magazine with a snap and stuffed it into her knitting basket, which contained balls of yarn, needles, and whatnots. She had dropped her grandmother's cameo brooch into the basket several days ago, after she had worn it, so she wouldn't forget it again.

Idly, she rose and ambled over to the window to lean out, looking up and down the sidewalk. Two men in the park across the street came to attention, watching her closely. Another guard standing near the front door glanced up, grimacing. The window might as well have bars.

A scratching sound startled her. She jerked, gasping, but it was nothing more than a breeze coming through the window and skimming across the tabletop stacked with clipped newspapers. Her breathing eased, and she rubbed her arms against a slight chill. Rats. The memories of them crawling and nibbling all over her wouldn't leave her alone.

Stir crazy, she paced the length of the foyer—back and forth and back and forth, annoying Edward, who glanced up from his perch near the door every time her heels clacked off the edges of the hallway's Oriental runner.

It was after five o'clock. The men had not returned, and there had been no word from the prison. No newspapers. Nothing. If she didn't hear from Braham or David or Gaylord within the next thirty minutes, she was going to scream "fire" and dash out of the house.

On her next trip down the hall, she went into the office for the umpteenth time to see if Cullen might have left a list of assignments hidden under a law book or stuffed inside one. She opened a book titled, *A Treatise of Legal Philosophy and General Jurisprudence* and thumbed through the pages. Nothing.

The front door opened. She dropped the book and ran out, coming to a sudden stop, her heart in her throat. When she found her voice, she shrieked, "*You're free.* They did it." She ran to Jack and threw herself into his arms, hugging him. She groaned as his squeezing arms tightened.

"I'm sorry, sis." He loosed his grip. "Braham warned me Henly punched you." He touched her face, lightly. "I'm so sorry."

"Forget about me. Where've you been? You look fantastic."

He smirked.

"No, I mean you're…" She brushed his lapels. "…all clean and dapper." The fragrances of a barber's talcum powder and new clothes filled the air in pleasing waves. She stood back and scrutinized him. "Lost a few pounds. Ten, maybe. Food wasn't so good, huh?"

He stared at her, eyes fixed wide, blue and unblinking above a small twitch of a smile. "Yeah, it was pretty bad. The hoods were worse. Thank God I spent so much time with the monks. Without mediation and the ability to go into deep trances, I'd have lost my mind. I spent hours in my head sitting by the river, reading."

"Knowing you could do that kept me sane. So, Braham and Cullen accomplished everything they planned to do today."

"You should have seen Braham. He was brilliant. I'd pay a million bucks for a video and pictures of the expressions on Hunter and

Holt's faces. True brilliance. When this movie is produced, it'll win a dozen Oscars."

Cullen and Braham opened the door and entered the house, laughing. Braham ambled toward her with a smile playing around his mouth, and he pulled her gently into his arms. "I told you I'd bring him home or die trying."

David and Gaylord entered behind Cullen. She waved her hand at the whiskey fumes being exhaled by all five men. "If I lit a match, the house might explode. Y'all stopped to celebrate while I paced, dying for news."

"We had to wait for Jack. He didn't want to see you until he'd had a bath and shaved. While he did, we…" Braham pointed, carefully but tipsily, to Cullen, David, and Gaylord. "…shopped for new clothes for him."

"We couldn't bring him home naked," David hiccupped.

They deserved to get drunk, smoke cigars, and tell tall tales until the wee hours of the morning, but when they started singing Scottish ballads off-key, which they were bound to do, she was going to bed.

"Why are we standing out here? I hear a bottle of whiskey calling my name," Jack said, leading the way into the parlor.

"Hold on a second. Before y'all get too drunk, you need to tell me everything. Please. I'm dying to know what happened," she said.

Braham poured a round of drinks, and they all found a seat. She scooted in between Jack and Braham on the sofa.

"There were a couple of tense moments," Braham said.

"For me, not for him," Cullen said. "Braham pulled Excalibur from the stone. He was in the…What's the expression Kit uses?"

"Zone?" Braham said.

Cullen snapped his fingers. "Yes. That's it. We'd rehearsed the questions and anticipated Henly's responses, but reducing his laudanum to keep him on edge—" Cullen paused and gave a small head bow to David, "—was brilliant."

David nodded. "Thank you, but the credit goes to Gaylord. "He'd already been inside Henly's house. He knew where the medication was kept and the location of every weapon Henly owned. Once we diluted the laudanum and put blanks in all the guns, it was just a matter of babysitting until he reached the prison."

"Wait, wait. Time out," Charlotte said, making a T with her hands. "I'm missing something. *Who* did you think Gordon was going to shoot?"

Cullen, David, and Gaylord turned their heads slowly in Braham's direction.

She gasped, glaring up at Braham, open-mouthed. "You set yourself up to get shot in order to prove Henly's guilt? You're *insane. All of you.* What if he'd used another weapon?"

Braham's mouth quirked wryly as he met her eyes. Then he pounded on his chest with his fists. "Bulletproof vest."

She ran her fingers through Braham's hair, gripped a few strands, and shook his head. "It doesn't protect your head. Did David forget to mention such an important detail?" A muscle twitched by Braham's mouth, and she shot him a sharp glance tinged with amusement.

Cullen chuckled. "Stubbornness would protect his head."

Gaylord cleared his throat and smiled. "David promised he'd give me the vest to keep. So hand it over." There had never been a hint of a smile from Gaylord. His grin now widened, revealing straight white teeth.

Ignorance was truly bliss. A host of illegal activities had taken place over the last couple of weeks. The illegality had never bothered her. It was the danger the men had risked which would feed her nightmares.

"Have you talked to Stanton?" she asked.

"Before they would release Jack, I had a sit-down with Generals Holt and Hunter and Secretary Stanton. They wanted to know the name of the informant who passed me confidential information. I told them there was no security leak. When they pressed me for specifics, I told them once you and Jack were safely away from Washington, I would divulge my source."

"What will you tell them?"

Cullen rolled his eyes toward her dramatically. "He's throwing Gaylord under the cart."

"*What?* You're not. Not after all he's done for us." She ran her hand gently over her face, trying to adjust to this information.

Gaylord was the first of the men to howl with laughter. "Don't worry, Miss Charlotte. I worked for the colonel in California, and came to Washington with him. When General Grant found my skills useful I adopted the code name Gaylord. Tomorrow I'll head back to California and reclaim my identity. The colonel can throw me under the cart. Stanton will never find me unless I want to be found. Like you, ma'am, I have several disguises."

"Will you tell me your real name?" she asked.

"Henry Bayford."

She gave him a worried frown. "What about the men who were promised jobs?"

Gaylord lifted one shoulder in a slight shrug. "There were no guarantees. They'll get a bonus."

"So it's all over?" she asked.

Jack stooped forward as if he bore a terrific weight. The indirect lighting in the room exaggerated the hollows of his drawn face, and there was a haunting behind his eyes. He nodded, squeezing her hand. "This part of it is. We'll talk about the changes in our lives later." His voice thickened, and he fell silent.

Time stopped for a heartbeat, and she looked at him through tears flooding her eyes. "So Braham told you about our memories?"

Jack took a shuddering, sighing breath. "He explained it on the way home. I'm so sorry, sis."

She hugged him and held him as tightly as she could. "We'll adjust to whatever we find when we get home. We have each other and nothing else matters."

Memories of their ordeals would linger, but they would have each other, whether Jack lived in the two-hundred-year-old mansion from his memories or the chrome and glass condo from hers.

An expression came over Braham's features she had never seen before—a look of sorrow, regret, and weariness mingled with relief.

The war, his suffering, and the trial had worn him down and changed him irrevocably. It was time for him to go home, too. Time to rest, nurture his vines, and recover. With his war record and courtroom victory, his future was guaranteed. Although he was raised in Scotland, he was born in America. He could run for President of the United States.

She swallowed painfully. The two men she loved most in the world were hurting, and she was powerless to help them. All she could do was love them.

She opened the brass-mounted mahogany humidor on the table in front of the sofa. "Breakout the cheroots, boys, and pour me another drink. We've got some celebrating to do."

93

Washington City, 1865

CHARLOTTE AND BRAHAM lay snuggled in each other's arms. His heart was beating fast, and she could feel it as though it pulsed in her hand, and she took comfort in the warm familiarity of his body. They had made love in a slow, erotic, and passionate tango.

Later, he had teased her playfully, and she had expressed her pleasure in moans loud enough for the entire household to hear. She didn't care. This was their last night, and they were the only two people in her world. Their bond, forged in trust, was an incredible aphrodisiac. He had awakened her at least twice more, pulling her to him with urgency, his hunger for her insatiable.

The room was dark, although a slice of the moon showed thought the split in the curtain. She scooted closer to him, and he spooned against her back, his arm around her. The gentle rise and fall of his breath blew softly across her shoulder until at last they slept.

Now the bedcovers were askew, and she shivered slightly in the early morning chill. Braham must have sensed her need for warmth. He snugged her closer to his side, and she drifted back to sleep. She woke again as the sun crept through the partially open drapes. Braham was gone, and his side of the bed no longer held the heat from his body.

She would not stay abed without him. Quickly, she bathed,

mourning the loss of his musky scent on her skin. After dressing in a traveling gown, she packed her medical kit. She needed nothing else. The rest of the beautiful dresses would stay and could be given to the staff or sold. She wouldn't need them. Her reenacting days were over. But she did want her grandmother's cameo she had previously left behind.

The open knitting basket sat on the table by the window. She dug through the contents looking for the brooch, and gasped when she found the piece of jewelry. The pin on the back of the cameo linked itself with the pin on the back of…the sapphire brooch. *How on earth?*

She collapsed in the chair, holding the jewelry in her hands. It could have stayed lost for all she cared. If she didn't want it, what was she going to do with it, besides keep it away from Jack? If she confessed now that she found it, then she, Jack, and David, could return to the present from Washington instead of traveling back to Kentucky.

Jack knocked and opened her door. "Hey, Char, you ready?"

She slipped the brooch into her pocket. "Almost. Give me a couple more minutes. I'll see you downstairs."

Braham came to the door and said to Jack, "We'll be down in a wee bit." He entered the room, closed the door behind him, and leaned against it. "Have you ever been to Napa during the harvest?"

She leaned forward in the chair, studying his face. His brow was furrowed, and he looked tight-lipped and pale. Was his heart breaking as much as hers? "I've been to Napa, but never in the fall."

He came further into the room and stopped when he reached the table with her medical bag. He fiddled with the handle. "During the harvest, thousands of grapes are picked. The grapevines covering acres of undulating landscape begin to go dormant and the leaves turn bright red and gold." He turned to look at her, his eyes glistening. "The land smells fresh with the aroma of fermenting wine. You wake up before sunrise when the air is cool and crisp, and the scent of wine hits your face. It's the most beautiful and exciting place I've ever been."

He ran his hand over the smooth leather of the case. "I want to take you there, Charlotte. I want to wake up with you and hold you and smell the grapes. I want to make love to you under the vines in the moonlight. Come with me. Let's put the war and the trial..." His voice broke, and he breathed haltingly through his nose. After a moment, he began again. "Let's put all this behind us. Come with me. If we leave now, we could be at my winery before the harvest begins."

She jumped up and ran to him, and they held each other. "I can't go with you. Jack and David are ready to go, and I have to return to my medical practice. Come with us."

His body quivered against hers. "I can't leave. Not now. I need...I need the land, Charlotte. I need to put my hands in the soil and prepare the earth for new growth in the spring. I need to find myself again. If I go with you, I'll be running away. This war has taken my soul. I've spent the last few years lying and cheating. We even broke the law to win Jack's freedom. I'm not sure what's right and wrong anymore. I have to find my way back to the person I was."

"I'll wait for you." The words didn't catch in her throat. She was saying she would wait for the rest of life.

"No, you mustn't do it. You have to make a life for yourself. Find a man who will love you and give you children."

His words were like a cold wind blowing through holes in her heart. "I don't want another man. I want you."

"You can't spend the rest of your life waiting for me. Promise me you won't."

"I can't promise."

"You have to. You have to let me go."

She gazed into his eyes, and what she saw there broke her heart. She had to tell him what he wanted to hear, even if her own heart knew it was lie. "I'll let you go, but only if I find someone I love more."

"I want you to be happy."

"How can I be happy without you?"

"I'm broken, Charlotte. My bones ache with every move I make. You deserve a man who can give all of himself. I can't do that. Not right now."

"I'll help you find your way back. There are doctors—"

He covered her mouth with his, murmuring, "I have to love you once more." He carried her to the bed, lifted her skirts and petticoats, and took her. It wasn't lovemaking. It was possession. And then when it was over, he kissed her softly, brushing his lips across her face as if memorizing with his lips the contours of cheekbone and brow, of lips and chin, seeking to know her mind and spirit and the heart beating beneath his hand.

She looked away and breathed in and out slowly to keep her composure, because looking into his eyes was like looking into the night sky and watching the stars burn out one by one, until only infinite darkness remained. "I have to go."

He held her close one last time, his heart pounding against her cheek. Finally, his arms relaxed. She disentangled herself and straightened her clothes, his seed warm inside of her.

"Goodbye, Braham. I'll always love you."

She hurried from the room with her knitting basket and traveling bag and went downstairs where David, Cullen, and Jack were waiting in the parlor. When David saw her, he picked up his bags and hoisted one over each shoulder.

"I don't look forward to the train ride back to Kentucky. It's long, hot, and crowded," he said.

"We don't have to worry about going back to Kentucky, because look what I found." She held up the sapphire brooch."

Jack gasped, clearly shocked. "*Where'd* you find it?"

She held up the basket, shrugging as if the answer was obvious. "When you tossed it toward the window, I guess it bounced in here."

David's face split into a huge grin. "*Great.*" He handed the ruby brooch to Cullen, placing it in his palm with a slight smack. "Will ye' return this to Sean with our thanks?"

Cullen squeezed his shoulder. "I'll be glad to. I'll also tell Kit about your books. I know she'll be happy about your publishing success."

Charlotte gave Cullen a hug. "I'm so glad I met you. Meredith will be envious. Kit's a very lucky woman."

Unable to see through the tears, Charlotte fumbled with the tweezers until David took them from her hand and opened the brooch's clasp. She didn't glance back up the stairs. Instead, she steadied herself, laced arms with Jack and David, and spoke the Gaelic incantation for the last time.

Part Four

"Every man's happiness is his own responsibility."

—Abraham Lincoln

94

Mallory Plantation, Richmond, Virginia, Months Later

CHARLOTTE SAT IN her rocking chair in a room on the second floor of Mallory Plantation, which had been recently painted in soothing, muted colors. The sunlit room had been used as a nursery for more than two hundred years. Jack told her both of them had slept here as babies. She had no memory of it, though. Instead of grieving the loss of shared memories, they had decided to focus on making new ones. And in a matter of hours, a brand-spanking new one would arrive.

When she reached her eighth month of pregnancy, she had decided to move into the mansion. She wanted Jack to be a part of her baby's life, and with his busy schedule, living with him was the only way to be sure that would happen.

Contractions had begun in her back several hours earlier. She hadn't told him until daybreak, but she called Meredith to let her know the baby was coming a few days earlier than expected. She and Elliott should arrive by late morning. Knowing Meredith would be with her during labor and delivery had help reduce Charlotte's anxiety.

"Charley," David called from the hall. "Where are ye'?"

"In the nursery," she said, rubbing her tummy while she rocked.

He entered the room carrying what looked like a banana smoothie, came to a hurried stop, and studied her face. "From your expression, the contractions must be stronger."

"A little bit, but they're not bad yet." She held out her hand. "Did you make me a smoothie? Thank you."

He put his hand on her belly and pressed gently. Around week thirty, he had belly-mapped the baby and drawn a beautiful picture on her stomach of the baby, cord, and placenta, all floating in blue-rippled water. He knew the exact location of head and butt, and palpated her belly regularly to be sure it didn't move out of the birth position. The picture had washed off, but its image had settled nicely in her brain.

David prepared for the birth the same way he prepared for everything else in his life. He read every childbirth book written within the last five years. He interviewed doctors and midwives. He studied childbirth videos. He planned for contingencies. He drove her nuts.

And she was grateful for every moment he'd spent with her.

"I put a little peanut butter in the drink, too. Thought it would give ye' an energy burst. It's going to be hard work to push the laddie out."

She gave him a teasing smile. "Both you and Jack insist it's a boy. I hope y'all aren't disappointed when it comes out a girl."

"I insist because I know," David said.

"No, you don't. Not unless you bribed the doctor." She took the milkshake-like drink and stirred it with the straw. "You're so sweet. Where'd the bananas come from? I thought I ate the last one."

"Jack went to the store."

"You've got to be kidding. He stopped working on his manuscript for five whole minutes just to go out and get a banana?"

David nodded, looking somewhat bemused. "He said he could run errands, but it was about all he could do for ye' right now."

"He can't deal with me in pain. If he can't fix me, he's useless." She took a sip of the cool, refreshing drink. "Yum. You'll have to give me your secret recipe."

Jack entered the room carrying a cup of coffee and the newspaper. "I'm useless at what?"

"A few things, but I was talking about how you can't handle seeing me in pain," she said.

He settled on the settee next to the baby's crib, one brow lifted in a question. "I did okay in Richmond the night of the fire, didn't I?"

"I wasn't hurt then. I was in shock and exhausted, but I wasn't bleeding."

"I beg to differ. I wish I had a picture of you. You were bleeding in several places on your head and arms. But you're right. If you'd been seriously injured, I probably would have fallen apart at the seams."

David kissed the top of her head. "I've got a telephone conference in five minutes. It'll probably take a half hour, but I can cut it short if we need to hurry to the hospital. I'll be downstairs. Call if ye' need anything."

"Thanks, sweetie," she patted her belly. "I think the two of us will be okay."

Jack stretched out his legs and sipped his coffee. "So, how long do you think it'll take before he or she decides to…you know…pop out?"

She rolled her eyes dramatically. "A baby doesn't simply pop out. It's going to take a while. Probably the rest of the day."

Jack looked older these days. His incarceration and the trial had aged him a bit—matured him, maybe. "I'm glad David's here," he said, "You're right, when the time comes, I won't be much help."

"It's okay. You went to get the bananas." She lifted her glass in a thank-you salute. "You know…one of my first memories is of you freaking out when I fell off my bike. I was probably about five years old. You took one look at the blood running down my legs and the tears and snot streaming down my face, and you ran like the Devil was chasing you."

A smile flickered briefly across his face. "My memory is the police showing up to tell Mom that Dad's campaign plane had crashed. She collapsed on the floor, and you started screaming louder than you were already. I was ten, you were five. I couldn't help either one of you. My dad was dead and my life was shattered."

"I am sorry, Jack. It had to have been a horrible day. I know you idolized him. So did I."

"There wasn't anything he couldn't do. He taught me to hunt, ride a horse, and even how to read a Senate bill. And then he was gone. I didn't handle it well."

"He taught you to love history, too. You went to his college classes while you were still in high school and you couldn't stop talking about what a great teacher he was."

"I'm sorry it's not one of my memories. Sounds like a good one."

"But you saw him introduce bills in the Senate. It's a good one *I* don't have."

"From what you've said about Dad, I'd prefer your version of my past rather than my own. Not only did you have him longer, but he was home every night. In my memories, Mom and Dad were rarely home. They were always campaigning."

"I don't know if it's worse for a boy to lose his dad at ten or twenty. At either age, it's life-altering."

Jack glanced around the nursery he had helped her decorate, insisting it be filled with boy sorts of things, too, particularly University of Kentucky basketball and New York Yankee paraphernalia. She had enjoyed shopping with him, and the expeditions to the mall and specialty shops had helped them both heal.

"I really screwed things up, didn't I?"

She shrugged with a bare lift and fall of her shoulders. "It is what it is. We'll deal with it. At least we'll never bore each other retelling old stories."

"You wouldn't have been so kind before. You would have cussed me out, and I would have deserved it. Have you noticed how different you are now?"

She patted her belly. "I'm definitely different. I'm carrying around what looks like a bowling ball."

"Not just that. You're as relaxed as you used to be only after a long run. There's sadness about you, but it's not hopelessness. It's more like a wound that's almost healed, but it's still red around the edges. Having David here has been good for you."

She picked a small book up off the table. Jack had found it in a book store in Los Angeles. It was titled *The Abyss of War*, and had been written by one Michael Abraham McCabe. "Thanks for this. I can't believe you found it."

"It was on a shelf behind the table and chair set up for me to sign books. I stretched and my hand knocked it off the shelf. My hair practically stood on end when I realized who wrote it."

"I understand now what Braham was trying to tell me about being broken." She thumbed through several pages. "*The experience left on a generation horrible scars which would remain long after the war. I hear in the silence even now the cries for help. Men begging for a drop of water. Calls to God for pity.*" She shivered. "Later he quotes Lincoln saying, *If there is a worse place than hell, I am in it.*

"Then Braham continues, saying he can't find his way out, he can't stop the cries, the pleas for help he hears in the night." She thumbed to another page marker. "*I can't rid my mouth of the taste of gunmetal or rid my mind of the painful memories of the years I failed to live up to my ideals.*" She thumbed to a page toward the end of the book. "*The war changed me profoundly. It touched everything and left nothing unchanged, and left me a different person in every respect. There is now a great divide between who I was, who I am, and who I will become.*"

She closed the book and held it to her breast. "I will treasure this always. It's a precious gift." She patted her belly. "Perhaps our impending progeny might read it one day."

She swept her hair, longer now than it had ever been, to one side and let it drape over her shoulder. When she noticed Jack running his eyes over the fall of hair, she said, "The day we got back from Washington, David undid my hair, and kept doing it until I stopped wearing it pulled back. He knew what happened in the past would haunt me for the rest of my life if I didn't let my hair down, relax, and stop worrying. You know I still have occasional flashbacks, and I'm working through them, but I'll never forget what happened. I pray Braham found peace in the person he became."

A popping sensation startled her and fluid gushed down the insides of her legs. "Oh my God." She glanced down at a spreading wet stain on her maternity leggings. "Looks like my water broke."

He frowned at her dubiously. "Are you sure you'd didn't just pee in your pants?"

"I think I can be trusted to know the difference," she informed him sarcastically. *Her baby was coming.*

"Seriously?" he said.

"Yep."

Jack jumped up, spilling coffee down the front of his shirt. "*David.*"

David pounded up the stairs and appeared at the door with his phone pressed to his ear. He pointed to let them know he was on a call.

"*Hang up the goddamn phone. Her water just broke.*"

David's face lit up with a big grin, and he nodded. "I have an emergency. I'll call ye' later." He disconnected the call and hurried to Charlotte's side to help her stand. "Jack, go get her bag and meet us at the door."

Jack pointed to the diaper bag on top of the dressing table. "Do you want me to take the baby's bag, too?"

"No, leave it. We'll get it tomorrow," David said.

"You know you'll need it. Why not take it now?"

"*Leave it*, Jack," David said, giving him a look which brooked no further comment.

Charlotte was well aware she was a high-risk patient and something could happen to her or to the baby. She'd never discussed it with Jack and didn't intend to now.

"I need to change my clothes."

"Only a quick change. I won't let ye' delay any longer. Ye' should ha' gone to the hospital hours ago."

A few minutes later, with David at her side, she waddled down the stairs. Jack waited by the front door wearing a clean shirt and holding her overnight suitcase, laptop bag, and purse, chewing on a corner of his lower lip.

"Leave the laptop here. If I decide to check email, I'll use my phone."

He put the computer bag on the table. "God, you *have* changed. Do you want your purse?"

"I'll take it," she said, tucking the clutch bag under her arm. "Give the car keys to David. I'd rather he drive. He's calmer than either one of us."

Jack, sighed with obvious relief, and chucked the keys to David, who barely managed to catch Jack's bad throw. "Maybe I'll stay here. Call me when it's over."

She quivered with the effort not to laugh at her brother, whose anxiety level was probably ten points higher than her own.

David glared at him, and, with a slight edge in his voice, said, "Get yer ass in the car. Ye're going with us. I won't have Charlotte worrying about ye' while she's trying to birth a bairn. Ye' can pace in the waiting room with Elliott."

The cat rubbed up against Jack's leg, and he scratched her head. "I'll be back later, Cat, and we'll talk about giving you a name. I guess you're here to stay."

95

Virginia Commonwealth University Medical Center, Richmond, Virginia

"**W**HY AREN'T YE' here already? If ye' don't get on the plane now, ye' won't make it, and Charlotte wants ye' attending the birth." David disconnected the phone and refilled Charlotte's empty cup with ice chips. "They're on their way to the plane, and they'll be here in less than two hours."

Charlotte adjusted her bulky frame, searching for a comfortable position. "What took them so long? I thought they were leaving two hours ago."

David put his arm around her back and helped her straighten in the bed. "A mare."

Charlotte groaned. "Elliott's not vetting anymore. Why'd he have to be there?"

"He has high hopes for the foal. It's one of Stormy's."

She crunched on the ice. "Where's Jack?"

"Pacing in the waiting room, on the phone with his agent."

"I forgot the New York Times bestseller list comes out today. I bet he made it again."

David placed his hand on Charlotte's bulging tummy. "He didn't say."

Even before David had belly-mapped the baby, whenever he was with her, he had caressed her stomach. She had asked him why, and he had shrugged, saying he owed Braham for saving Jack's life, and he wanted Braham's child, as he grew, to feel the warmth of a man's love, and hear the burr of his Scottish accent.

She placed her hand over David's, appreciating his warmth and strength. His hand reminded her so much of Braham's, with its long, slim fingers and powerful grip.

"Are you sure you want to stay in here during the birth?" she asked.

He kissed her forehead. "After going through those classes, I wouldn't miss it."

"Did you clear your schedule when you talked to your agent earlier? I'd love for you to stay a few more days."

"I told her I wanted time with my godchild before I left town. She gave me two weeks, but then I have to leave. She's scheduled a book tour starting the first of next month."

"Geez. Between your tour and Jack's, the baby and I will have to find a bookstore to get five minutes with either one of you."

Jack popped his head in the door, but didn't venture into the room. "I talked to Ken. As soon as he finishes rounds, he'll be on his way. He said to wait for him."

Charlotte laughed. "We're not waiting for anybody." Unless it was for Braham. If she knew he was on his way, she—they—would delay as long as possible. "Come in here and sit with us."

"No, thanks. I'll wait out here. Where are Elliott and Meredith? I thought they were supposed to be here by now."

"There're only now leaving the farm."

"Well, if you need anything, I'll be in the waiting room." The door *whooshed* shut behind him.

She heaved a sigh. "Do you suppose if I told Jack I wasn't in pain and I simply wanted him to hold my hand, he'd stay?"

David shrugged. "Ye' know him better than I do. What do ye' think?"

"I don't know him as well as I used to."

David poured more ice in her cup. "Has he changed so much?"

Something about the way David was looking at her, as if he could see inside her mind, made her heart knock lightly against her ribs. "No, but I have. Jack's noticed, too."

She rolled onto her side and closed her eyes for a few minutes. "Sometimes when I close my eyes, I see rats. I never saw them in the darkness, but I felt them. At night, when the baby moves and wakes me, I wake up thinking I feel them crawling on me again."

David didn't move, but something changed in him. He straightened, and then he quickly settled into his skin again. "Why are ye' thinking about it now?"

She licked her lips, and popped another ice chip into her mouth. "Moms and babies die, even in hospitals."

He set the ice pitcher on the table with a smack. "I killed them, Charley. There were four. They'll never crawl on ye' again. They'll never bite ye' or scare ye'."

She fingered the scar on her ear. "You never told me."

"No point in mentioning it, if ye' didn't. If I had only stayed in Washington and sent someone else to Maryland, ye' wouldn't have spent more than fifteen minutes in Henly's hell hole." As he spoke, the tiny lines around his eyes tightened with strain.

"Everyone was doing what they could to free Jack. Gordon gets all the blame. Come here," she said. He leaned in, and she kissed him very lightly on the lips. "You saved my life." She gasped and pressed her hand against her back. "Even with the epidural, I feel a different kind of pressure with this contraction." She pressed the call button.

"Can I help you?"

"I think something is changing. Will you send my nurse?"

The nurse arrived within thirty seconds. David rested his hand on Charlotte's shoulder and she squeezed it.

Finishing her exam, the nurse pulled off her gloves and covered Charlotte's legs with the sheet. "You're getting close. You're about eight centimeters dilated."

Once the epidural was in and she had no longer needed to breathe through contractions, Charlotte had given the okay for a few visitors. Word had spread, and most of the OB nurses had run in for a quick hello. It wasn't just because they knew her. Not only had

Charlotte hung a life-sized, drool-worthy poster of Braham on the wall of the delivery room to use as a focal point, but David was there, and had dressed casually today. His shirt clung to his muscled shoulders without a single wrinkle, and the seams of his jeans strained against bulging thighs. A drool-worthy poster and a drool-worthy man had elicited more than a few appreciative glances from Charlotte's well-wishers.

The Fraser clan arrived about noon. Four-year-old Cullen climbed into a chair and kissed Charlotte's tummy. "When's my cousin coming out? I brung a present. Mommy, can I show Cousin Charlotte my present?"

Meredith pulled a stuffed horse out of her bag, and Cullen clapped his hands. "I'm going to name him Thunder."

"Cullen," Meredith said, "it's the baby's toy, not yours. The baby gets to pick a name."

"Okay. I'll tell my cousin to name the horse Thunder." He jumped down and took David's hand. "Uncle David will you take me to get a hot dog? I saw the restaurant. Come with me."

David glanced at Charlotte, shrugging. He adored the child, but she knew he didn't want to leave her side.

"It's fine," she said. "We have plenty of time."

"Okay, buddy. Let's get Jack and have us some hotdogs."

Cullen ran from the room, yelling, "Cousin Jack. Cousin Jack."

Meredith closed the door, rolling her eyes. "If I had half of his energy…" She gave Charlotte a hug. "How're you feeling?"

"Good so far."

Elliott glanced around the room. "Nice artwork."

"For nine months, I've thought Braham would change his mind and join me. A full-sized poster is the best I can do, though. I want the baby to know him."

Meredith patted Charlotte's hand. "This baby will have friends and family who will love him and spoil him. Even our dear friend Louise called about an hour ago. She and her partner Evelyn are ecstatic. If you don't get to Scotland soon, they'll come here."

"I might have a renter for yer house," Elliott said. "Unless ye' want to sell it."

"I probably will, but not right now. A renter would be great. Is there anything you and David can't do?"

"Ask me in three years," Elliott said. "If we do a good job training the foal born this morning, he'll have a shot at the Triple Crown."

"What did David have to do with it?"

Elliott smiled. "He picked the mare."

Charlotte squirmed for a moment and decided to push the call button "Would you tell my nurse I'm getting a lot of pressure down low?" The doctor came in while Charlotte was still speaking. "I think I'm ready."

"Let's take a look."

"I'll get David," Elliott said as he gave Charlotte a quick hug and left the room.

The exam was quick. "You're fully dilated. With the next contraction, let's see what you can do."

The next two hours were grueling. Meredith hovered on one side of the bed, David on the other. They held her legs, propped up her back, and breathed with her.

At one point, Charlotte said, "That damn Braham McCabe, if he walked in here right now, I'd throw something at him. I'll never do this again."

Meredith and David chuckled.

"Don't you dare laugh," Charlotte said. "This isn't fun."

"One more contraction, and your baby will be out," the doctor said.

Charlotte took a deep breath and pushed her child out. Her head dropped back on the pillow. When the baby cried, so did she.

"It's a boy," the doctor said.

David's face flushed with his excitement. "Congratulations, Mom. I told ye' he'd be a boy."

She glanced at the poster, barely able to see through her tears. "We have a son, Braham."

"He's perfect, Charley."

Meredith swiped at her own tears. "And beautiful." She gave Charlotte a hug. "I'm going to go tell Elliott and Cullen. I'll be right back. Do you want me to send Jack in?"

"No, not unless he wants to. You can tell him, too," Charlotte said.

The doctor clamped the cord, handed David a pair of scissors to cut it, and laid the baby on Charlotte's belly. David beamed like any new father.

For nine months he'd come for extended visits and had taken on all the responsibilities of an expectant father. He held her head when she threw up. He brought her ice cream and pickles when she had cravings. He took her to the beach when she was bitchy. He told her she was beautiful, and he stayed up late with her when she couldn't sleep.

And never once had he complained or asked for more than she was able to give. This was his moment, and she was so happy he was there to share it. He was more than the baby's godfather, and she wished her heart was free to love him as he deserved to be loved.

Meredith returned with Elliott, Kevin, Jack, Cullen, and Ken for a quick peek.

"He has a penis, Daddy. That means I have a boy cousin. Yippee. I want to play with him. Can he ride my pony?"

"He's only a baby. He can't play yet," Meredith cautioned."

"When's he going to stand up like Stormy's baby did today?" Cullen asked.

"Not for a while."

"Congratulations, Charlotte," Elliott said, smiling. "I'm going to take Cullen to the playroom. Text me, Mer, if you need anything."

Jack walked over to the bed, wearing a relieved smile. The corners of his mouth trembled slightly. He kissed Charlotte on the cheek. "Congrats, sis. He's beautiful. It wasn't as bad as I thought it would be. Maybe next time I'll stay with you."

"There won't be a next time, Jack. You missed your shot."

"He's a big one," one of the delivery nurses said.

"You don't have to tell me," Charlotte said. "How much does he weigh?"

"Nine pounds, five ounces, and he's twenty-one inches long."

After the nurse cleaned, diapered, and wrapped the baby up tightly, she returned the newborn to Charlotte to nurse. "Do you have a name picked out?"

A stew of emotions welled up in her as she gazed at her precious child. "Lincoln Michael McCabe Mallory."

96

Sacramento, California, 1869

S ENATOR MCCABE ARRIVED at the Leland Stanford Mansion
promptly at nine o'clock. Melissa Mills, his companion for the
past year, elegantly graced his arm. The evening fundraiser for the
Republican Party had been on his calendar for several weeks. Leland
Stanford, along with his partners in the Central Pacific Railroad,
Charles Crocker, Mark Hopkins and Collis Huntington, were hinting
at the possibility of backing Braham as the next gubernatorial
candidate. If he decided to run, he would need not only their
financial support, but their influence.

"Good evening, Senator." Stanford shook hands with Braham
and kissed Melissa on the cheek. "My dear, Melissa. I'm sorry to hear
your father is indisposed this evening."

"It's Papa's gout. He'll be fine in a few days."

"I'm pleased to hear it. I believe your godmother has visitors
from New York she'd like you to meet. Ah, here's Jane now."
Stanford kissed his wife, "If you ladies will excuse us, I have
business to discuss with the Senator."

Glancing at Braham, Melissa batted her eyelashes flirtatiously
over the ivory lacework of her fan. "Don't be long, darling." She
then linked her arm with her godmother's and the two women
sauntered away with their heads together, chatting in soft under-
tones.

Braham cocked his head, watching the lithe, coquettish brunette glide across the room. He had yet to bed her, preferring the company of his mistress, and often wondered if Melissa would even enjoy the marriage bed, or tolerate it only to produce an heir. Regardless, he would likely marry her within the next year.

"Come to the library, Abraham. I have a new bottle of blended Scottish whisky you'll enjoy."

Braham followed the railroad tycoon, dismissing thoughts of the woman he regularly bedded and the woman he wasn't inclined to bed at all.

After pouring two glasses, Stanford handed one to Braham. "Have a seat, Senator. Cigars are on the table."

Braham extracted a cigar from the humidor, lit it, and relaxed in one of the two leather wing chairs in front of a roaring fire, crossing one leg over the other.

Stanford remained standing in front of the fireplace with one arm resting on the mantel, cigar propped between his fingers. "Your term as Senator is up next year, and the party wants you as our candidate for governor. Within six years, with Melissa at your side, you'll reside in the White House. California needs you there, Abraham."

Braham pulled a short draw, then removed the cigar from his mouth and studied it, blowing out puffs of smoke. "This is somewhat of a surprise, although you have hinted at it."

"Come now, Senator. Don't be coy. You've been on the path to the governor's office since you stepped onto the floor of the Senate. The White House is the obvious next step. My partners and I can make it happen."

What Leland was offering were not only financial support and influence, but also a promise of victory. Braham puffed again, and the smoke wreathed up around his head. "I'm flattered. However, I couldn't possibly give you an answer without discussing the ramifications with my law partner. Being governor would preclude my practicing law. I'd hope my clients would stay with the firm, but clients are fickle when it comes to lawyers."

"Mr. and Mrs. Montgomery are on this evening's guest list. Dinner will provide the perfect opportunity to bring him around to our point of view. He'll quickly see the benefits for all Californians to have one of our own in the White House. Of course, my business associates require legal representation on a variety of matters. I'm sure Mr. Montgomery could handle a multitude of issues brilliantly."

A knock on the door interrupted their conversation. With an edge of impatience, Stanford called out, "Come in."

The butler stepped into the room. "Sir, the governor's carriage arrived. Mrs. Stanford asked that you join her at the door."

Stanford waved away the servant. "Yes, yes. Tell her I'll be along." He puffed on his cigar. "As soon as I have your answer, you'll be free to call on Melissa's father. He should be recovered from his gout attack and will be pleased to entertain your offer for his daughter's hand."

Braham cleared his throat discreetly.

"Timing is everything, Senator. Announcing your upcoming nuptials and your bid for governor at the same press conference will guarantee the announcement appears simultaneously on the front page of every newspaper in California and in the society columns. Now, we don't want to keep the ladies waiting. Shall we go?"

Braham stubbed out his cigar and emptied his whiskey glass. His plan was falling into place like expertly arranged dominos.

Thirty minutes later, Cullen and Kit arrived. After kissing his cousin, and remarking on how beautiful she looked in a green silk gown matching her eyes, he and Cullen went out onto the balcony for a private conversation. Kit and Melissa remained inside, chatting amiably.

"What are you going to tell him?" Cullen asked.

Braham leaned against the railing, folding his arms. "I don't want to live in Washington ever again."

"It's not the same city you left four years ago, and you still own two houses there."

Braham steeled himself against the riptide of memory. "I need to sell them."

A silence followed. Cullen fixed him with a frown. "Charlotte is not coming back. Sell the properties."

"But—"

Cullen gave him a friendly slap between the shoulder blades. "It's time you proposed to Melissa and started a family. You're forty-six years old. Run for governor. After two years, if you still don't want to run for president, tell the party you want another term as governor."

Braham took a long, silent breath and opened his hand, revealing a sapphire ring.

Cullen eyes held a glint matching his half-smile. "You've got the ring. You've got the girl. Propose this evening. What in God's name is holding you back?"

Braham felt an uneasy rumble in his stomach and put the ring away. "Do you think Charlotte married David? He was in love with her."

Cullen pointed with his index finger. "If you're expecting me to tell you to go to Charlotte, I'm not going to do it." Then he tapped Braham's chest with the tip of the finger. "You have a beautiful, intelligent woman who loves you. A political career which leads to the White House, and, as a heavy investor in the continental railroad, you're one of the five or six wealthiest men in the country. *This* is where you belong."

Braham turned away from Cullen. He put both hands on the railing, leaned forward, and rocked slightly on the balls of his feet. "It's not the advice I gave you almost two decades ago."

Cullen ran his hand through his hair. "Goddamn it. The situations are completely different."

"I still love her."

"Then you should have gone four years ago. It's *too late* now."

The French doors opened, and Melissa and Kit joined them on the porch. "There you are, darling." Melissa kissed Braham on the cheek, then looked from one man to the other, and flitted her hand about her head. "I feel the remnants of a serious conversation in the air. Would this be about you running for governor, or something else of great import?"

Kit gave Cullen a probing stare, and raised an eyebrow, giving her husband a signal Braham had seen her use before.

Cullen switched his focus to Melissa. "You're too astute my, dear. Shall we go inside? I need a drink." He took Melissa's elbow and smoothly guided her through the doorway, leaving Braham and Kit on the balcony.

"I get the feeling you're trying to solve the problem of world hunger again. I might be able to help."

Braham opened his arms and Kit melted into his bear hug. He rested his chin on top of her head. "You've always been able to read me."

"It's because we're so much alike." She pulled away from him and looked up into his eyes. "Whatever's going on with you has nothing to do with Melissa or running for governor. So what is it?" Instead of waiting an answer she said, "It has to be Charlotte."

He fell silent, astounded as always by Kit's insightfulness. There was no point in denying it. She'd badger him until he confessed. "What gets me—what surprises me, is the way thoughts of her catch me so unaware." He bowed his head and stroked his furrowed forehead with the tips of his fingers. "Once she's in my head, she'll stay there for hours, and I'll relive every moment we had together. He dropped his hands and looked again at his cousin. "As the years go by it happens more often, not less."

Kit took his hand in hers. "When you came home from the war, you were a broken man. Cullen and I both worried about you. The first harvest was heartbreaking to watch. You looked over your shoulder constantly. I don't know if you were expecting the enemy or Charlotte to surprise you, but you were on guard. It wasn't until you had faith the grapes would grow again on empty vines that your soul was able to heal, but it didn't heal your heart. And that's why Charlotte's on your mind. She's still holding pieces of it."

He chuckled. "Not pieces. Chunks. And I want my heart to be whole again, too."

"If you're feeling the tug to go to her now, don't let Cullen or anyone else stand in your way. Not only should you go. You must go."

97

San Francisco, California 1869

A WEEK LATER, Braham entered Cullen's office at the law firm on Montgomery Street and dropped a signed Last Will and Testament on top of the open book on his desk. "I made you executor of my estate. If anything happens to me, liquidate all my assets, convert the cash into gold, and bury it."

Cullen leaned back in a swivel desk chair, fingering the steel and gold dip pen in his hand. "Should I draw a treasure map so you can find it in the afterlife?" A fleeting smile crossed his features.

Braham sat in the chair on the opposite side of the desk from his childhood friend. This was going to be a hard sell, but Cullen couldn't stop him from doing what he truly wanted—no, needed—to do. Although he hoped for Cullen's blessing, Braham was prepared to leave without it. "If you follow my instructions, I won't need a map."

Cullen picked up the document and perused it quickly. "According to this, Kit is your sole beneficiary."

Braham crossed one leg over the other, and when he did, the crease stayed straight. "I want her to sell everything I own, except the vineyards and the horses. Those she's to keep. Liquidate the rest, then turn the cash into gold."

Cullen harrumphed. "And bury the gold?"

Braham nodded. "In my casket."

After a few seconds of silence had elapsed, Cullen remarked in a sarcastic tone, "I take it your remains won't be in your casket."

"No, they won't."

Cullen tossed the document onto his desk, and stood, pounding the top with his fist. "*Don't do this.*"

Braham uncrossed his legs, put his hands on his knees, and got to his feet, pressing his fists at his hips to keep from slugging Cullen. "Nothing you can say or do will change my mind."

"We're too old for fisticuffs." He strode to the sideboard and poured two whiskeys. "Kit hasn't spoken to me in a week. She told me if we didn't work this out, she'd take the kids and go with you." He handed a glass to Braham.

Braham took a restorative gulp and followed it with another. "Since she hasn't left your sorry ass by now, she's not going anywhere."

There was an awkward silence. Then one corner of Cullen's mouth curved up in wry acknowledgement. He sat on the edge of the desk, sipping his drink. "Except for the years you were gone during the war, we've been together every day since we learned to walk. I can't imagine growing old without you." His voice was soft now, wistful. "Why are you giving up everything, including possibly the White House, for Charlotte, when she wouldn't give up anything for you?"

"Charlotte saved my life, and in doing so, she almost lost hers and Jack's."

"You can be grateful without leaving home."

Braham set his glass on the end of the desk and scrubbed his face with his hands. "You don't understand, do you? She did it out of love. Not love for love me, but love for her country, for Virginia, family, and tradition. She put everything at risk, and she almost lost it all. It's why we fought a war. But I didn't want to fight. I didn't go to Washington for lofty ideals. I went because I'd given Sherman my word."

"You made the promise to Sherman because of me." Cullen reached out and squeezed Braham's shoulder.

"Charlotte is the most honorable, fearless, and loving woman

I've ever met. And I don't want to spend another day without her. She's calling me, Cul. You want to know why I can walk away from my law practice, the governor's office, and possibly the White House? The answer is simple. Because I want Charlotte more."

Cullen returned to his desk chair, picked up Braham's Last Will and Testament, and leafed through the pages. "What will you do in Charlotte's time? You can't practice law."

"Since the Mallorys still own the plantation, I assume they will continue to own it in Charlotte's lifetime. I'll have money to build her a house on the property, and I'd like to start a winery and breed horses."

Cullen folded the will and tucked it into his top drawer. "What if she's married?"

Braham's brows shot up, and he looked at Cullen, shrugging slightly. "Then I'll be a part of her life in any role she'll allow me to play."

"How are you going to pull this off?"

"I'm going to MacKlenna Farm, and I'll die either by accident or disease. When you have all the gold, bury it in my casket."

"What are you going to tell Stanford and the other members of the party?"

Braham rubbed a hand across his mouth, wiping away a drop of liquor. "I have business in the East to settle, and when I return, we'll make an announcement."

"And Melissa? What about her?"

"I'll tell her the same thing. I wish I could make it easier on her, but I can't, Cul."

"You're giving up everything for a long shot."

"I'm giving up this life, for the one I truly want, and I'm willing to bet Charlotte still loves me. And hasn't married."

Cullen opened his calendar and thumbed through the pages until he reached the present month. "When are you going to Kentucky?"

"Next week."

"Now that the railroad is completed, it won't take months to get there." Cullen dipped his pen into the ink then scratched a note on the calendar. "Kit and I are going with you."

"You don't need to do that."

"Yes we do. If you're going to die, we'll want to attend your funeral."

98

MacKlenna Farm, Lexington, Kentucky, 1869

TWO WEEKS LATER, the train carrying Braham, Cullen and Kit from Cincinnati approached the Lexington depot. Kit hadn't visited her uncle since the summer of 1853, and she had never met her aunt. For the last hour, Kit had primped and paced up and down the aisle of the train, moving about in an unfocused sort of way, quite unlike her usual decisive strides. The swishing of her skirt and bumbling movements had disturbed other passengers. Finally, Cullen grabbed her around the waist and plopped her into her seat.

She shot him an angry glance. "Why'd you do that?"

Cullen merely smiled, not bothered by her tone. "The man across the aisle was about to do the same. Be thankful it was your husband who manhandled you and not a stranger."

She pursed her lips in speculation, looking from Cullen to the man across the aisle. Then she shrugged and fiddled with her clothes, ironing the front of her dress with the flat of her hand.

When they reached the depot, Braham immediately spotted Sean and Lyle Anne waiting on the crowded platform. Kit's aunt, a woman in her mid-forties, appeared as anxious as Kit, patting at the hair at her nape. What was it about women which made them afraid having one hair out of place or a wrinkle in their clothes would somehow make them unacceptable?

They disembarked and Kit almost tripped as she hurried to her uncle.

"Kitherina." Sean grabbed her in a bear hug and swung her around, swishing her skirts. "I'm so glad to see ye', lass. How're those bairns of yers?" He set her down, beaming with excitement. "Oh, excuse me. Kit, this is your aunt, Lyle Anne."

Lyle Anne's wide eyes stared at Kit, obviously baffled by her unorthodox behavior. Then finally her face brightened, and her small, pink mouth reversed her lips' downward droop and she beamed.

Braham pressed the crook of his finger against his lips to contain his smile, but his shoulders trembled with suppressed laughter.

"I haven't seen Kit this spirited since I met her at Fort Laramie in '52," Braham said, low-voiced, to Cullen.

Something moved in the backs of Cullen's eyes. Surprise? Acknowledgement? "I've had glimpses, but mostly I see spirit play out in our wee lassies."

"For your sake, I hope they don't race Thoroughbreds or jump into swollen rivers."

Cullen slapped Braham on the shoulder. "I can only hope."

When they reached the farm, the ladies went to visit the nursery, and the men found their way to Sean's office for whiskey and cigars.

"Your telegram said you're on your way to Washington, but didn't say why. Is this in preparation for a presidential campaign?" A broad grin creased Sean's face.

Braham puffed on his cigar. "No. The trip is only to provide a reason for my absence. We let it slip to the press we were going to Washington for business and on to New York on a shopping expedition."

"What are ye' really planning?" Sean watched Braham closely.

Braham made a quick glance behind him to be sure no one was coming in. "I've come to MacKlenna Farm to die."

Sean's head jerked back, brow furrowed and he became tight-lipped and pale. "Are ye' ill, then?"

Braham rolled the tip of the cigar along the edge of the ashtray and tapped it gently to let the ash fall. The plan he easily concocted suddenly seemed impractical to implement. "It seemed the best place to disappear. I can die here in peace, and that will be the end—" He blinked hard for control. "The end of Braham McCabe."

Sean puffed smoke out through his lips in genial disbelief. "Ye're intending to go to Charlotte's time, then?" He pointedly fixed Braham with a look Braham returned undaunted. If Cullen had been unable to convince Braham to stay, Sean didn't have a prayer.

Cullen ambled over to the bar, refilled his glass, and then took a long gulp. "After I settle Braham's estate, I'll convert all the cash into gold. The gold will then be shipped here to be buried in Braham's casket."

"So, I'm to dig up the coffin months later and bury the gold."

"I know it's a lot to ask," Braham said.

Sean waved him off, laughing. "I'll be able to say, 'Braham McCabe died and took his gold with him.' Based on your reputation, no one would doubt it. Of course, we'll have to bury the gold in secrecy, or I'll have treasure hunters digging up the entire cemetery."

"If the timing doesn't matter to you, I thought we'd go for a ride tomorrow. My plan is to be thrown from a horse and break my neck. Since there's no family to inform, there's no reason to delay the funeral. It might seem heartless, but Cullen could explain he's following my wishes to dispense with a wake and bury me immediately."

"Ye're sure this is what ye' want? There'll be no coming back."

Braham smiled at him in an attempt at confident reassurance. "I don't intend to come back."

"If ye're set on this course, we'll bury ye' tomorrow, but tonight, I think we should drink and sing a few ballads. We'll give ye' a proper Scottish wake tonight before ye' break yer neck."

The next morning the men saddled their horses and left on Braham's "fatal" ride. And that afternoon, on a cool, crisp fall day with the fiery yellows of beech trees and the vibrant reds of maples providing a glorious backdrop, Kit, Cullen, Sean, and Lyle Anne laid to rest Colonel Michael Abraham McCabe, war hero, lawyer extraordinaire, California Senator, and philanthropist, who would be missed by those who loved him.

After the minister departed, Kit and Cullen joined Braham beneath the sycamore tree, its brown-yellow leaves forming a canopy over the small cemetery.

Braham hugged Cullen tightly, seeing their lives flash behind his closed eyes. "I'll miss you, Cul."

Cullen wiped away tears but more came. "Saying goodbye to you is ripping out my heart. The only consolation is I know you're not dead and will have many happy years to come."

"I'm sorry I left you on the trail all those years ago."

Cullen grabbed him around the neck, pulling him close. "You've more than made up for it."

Kit wrapped her arms around Braham. "I can't imagine life without you. There will always be an empty chair at our table."

He kicked at the pile of red and gold leaves at his feet. "I think it's my cue to go."

In spite of Kit's distress, she laughed. "When I thought I'd lost Cullen, and had to go home to save my baby, it nearly broke my heart to leave the Barretts and Henry. A saying of my grandmother's saw me through the heartbreak: 'The day will come when you believe everything is lost, but in fact, it will be a new beginning.'" She took a deep breath and nodded to him.

"Live a full life, Braham, love Charlotte with all the love you have to give, and never look back. You're going where you're meant to go. Now go with God."

Kit took Cullen's hand. Together they walked away. Braham followed their fading silhouettes until they disappeared over a small knoll.

The time had come. He opened the ruby brooch and whispered the Gaelic words he had first heard one night years ago in Chimborazo, *"Chan ann le tìm no àite a bhios sinn a' tomhais an gaol ach's ann le neart anama."*

99

MacKlenna Farm, Lexington, Kentucky, Present Day

WHEN THE FOG evaporated, Braham found himself standing in the middle of MacKlenna Farm's driveway. Several vehicles lined the curve in front of the portico, with signs on the doors identifying the drivers as electricians, florists, party planners, security providers, and caterers. The front door of the mansion stood wide open, and dozens of people marched in and out like a well-organized army. Braham half expected to see General Grant on the porch, cigar in hand, ordering the troops about.

Braham cautiously entered a foyer redolent of flowers, dodging men carrying boxes and crates. Of the dozens of people rushing past, not one offered assistance.

Until the event concluded, maybe he should make himself scarce and wander the rolling green hills seamed with plank fences and enjoy the horses.

Or, he could hike over to the cemetery and visit his gravesite.

He squeezed around a large metal box on wheels caught on the threshold and escaped to the portico, out of the way of the troops. Hanging baskets filled with velvety blooms of rich purple draped the porch, seeming to turn even darker under the warm sun. The all-powerful Elliott Fraser must have specially ordered the cloudless blue sky. Braham leaned against the corner of the house, crossed his feet at the ankles, scraped his whiskers with his fingers, and watched men set poles for a large, white tent.

A man jumped up on the porch and plowed right into him.

"Oh, jeez, excuse me," the man said, grabbing Braham's arms to keep them both from falling. When they straightened and looked at each other, Jack Mallory's face split into a wide grin. "I've never been *so glad* to see anyone in my entire life." He hugged Braham, slapping his back with exuberance. "You couldn't have picked a better day to arrive. You're the mint in the julep, buddy. *God*, I can't believe you're here. Have you seen Charlotte yet?"

Braham swiped at the tears in his eyes. His heart was now lodged in his throat. "She's here? Where?"

Jack pointed toward the side of the house. "Over by the barn." He then gave Braham a scrutinizing look. "You need to clean up first. Come up to my room and take a shower. I'll find you something more appropriate to wear."

Braham jerked his thumb in the direction of the vehicles. "What's going on here?"

"It's Derby weekend. Elliott and David's horse is an early five-two favorite for the Kentucky Derby tomorrow. There hasn't been this much hype surrounding a horse in over a quarter of a century. The three-year-old stallion is a favorite to win the Triple Crown, and right now he looks unbeatable."

Braham hustled up the stairs, following Jack to the second floor landing. "Is the race here on the farm?"

Jack led him down the hallway and into his guest room. "It's at Churchill Downs in Louisville. The farm is hosting a breakfast in the morning for a few hundred of Elliott and Meredith's friends. Afterwards we'll take limos to Louisville for a day of racing. The Derby's not until late tomorrow afternoon." Jack opened the closet door and shoved back hangers, searching through neatly arranged jackets, shirts, and trousers.

"How long have you been here?"

"A week. Charlotte and I decided we didn't want to miss any of the festivities this year. So we came up early."

Braham tossed his bag on the bed. "I packed my kilt. I only need a shirt and jacket." He looked around. "Where's the bathroom?"

Jack pointed to the door on the opposite wall. "Through there."

Braham headed into the adjoining bathroom, looked at the controls on the wall in the stall and scratched his head. He didn't want cold water, and he didn't want scalding water. Finding the perfect temperature, he had discovered, took practice. Today, he didn't have time to experiment. He turned the handle to the left then put his hand into the stream of water. He got it right first try, he stepped into the warm spray, grinning.

"Shampoo, shaving cream, razor—everything's in the shower." Jack carried a light blue shirt and navy jacket into the bathroom and hung the clothes on a hook.

Braham rubbed shampoo into his shoulder length hair. "Do you think she'll be glad to see me?"

"Are you kidding?" Jack folded his arms across his chest and leaned against the sink, laughing. "She has a life-sized poster of you she kisses every night. What do *you* think?"

"I was afraid she might have found someone else." Braham turned off the water, grabbed a towel, and stepped out of the shower.

A man with a recognizable Scottish burr called from the bedroom. "Jack, where are ye'?"

Still chuckling, Jack said, "In here."

David entered the bathroom carrying two beers and came to an immediate stop, squeaking rubber-soled boots on the marble floor. "Well, I'll be damned." He shoved both cans at Jack, pushed up his sleeves, and slugged Braham in the gut.

Braham dropped to his knees, sucking wind like a man with asthma. "What the hell was that for?"

David scowled, fisting both hands. "Because you waited more than three fucking years to show up."

Braham pulled to his feet. "It's been over four for me."

David threw a right-left jab to Braham's gut, although not as hard as the first punch, and Braham doubled over. "I thought ye' were smarter than that," David said.

Braham grabbed hold of the counter, weaving slightly. "If you're going to hit me again, go on and take your shot. Let's get this over with."

David relaxed his rigid stance and said, in a lighter tone, "I'm done. Get dressed and I'll give ye' a welcome hug. I don't hug naked men."

"What naked man aren't ye' going to hug?" Elliott entered the bathroom and grabbed the doorjamb when he saw Braham. "Well, I'll be damned. When did ye' get here?" Elliott extended his hand and shook Braham's with a forceful grip.

"He just arrived. But I wasn't about to let him hug my sister until he cleaned up. David thought he needed more than a bath."

Elliott crossed his arms and glanced from David rubbing his hand to Braham rubbing his belly. Elliott made a noise deep in his throat which didn't need interpretation. "Well, get dressed, then. The van's ready to take Stormy's Sun to the track and Meredith wants a group picture. Ye' best be in it." He smiled at Braham. "Ye're part of the circle now."

"Charlotte doesn't know he's here, Elliott. Don't ruin the surprise," Jack said.

"She's yer sister." Elliott walked out of the room, shrugging. "Ye' know her best. I'll at least warn Meredith. David, I'll see ye' at the barn."

A few minutes later, standing in front of the mirror dressed in kilt, blue shirt and blazer, Braham brushed the tangles out of his hair. His jaw quivered, and he cleared his throat roughly. "Are you sure she'll be glad to see me?"

Jack popped open one of the cans and took a long pull on the beer. "She'll be thrilled."

Braham pushed his hair behind his ears. "How do I look?"

"Like a damn Scot in a kilt. How do you think you look? Come on, let's go."

Suddenly, panic grabbed a foothold in a pocket of fear, and Braham hesitated. "I don't want to see disappointment on her face. Maybe you should tell her I'm here. Give her time to adjust to the idea before she sees me."

Jack tugged on the jacket's lapels. "Once she sees those legs, she'll be smiling. Trust me. I wouldn't lie to you."

Braham dug his hands into the pockets of the jacket, and his heart lurched. Throughout his life, when he needed courage most, it came from unexpected places. His fingers clasped the length of a thin, cotton cord—the cord, which had tied the hood around Jack's head—the cord Jack had asked his guard if he could keep. Jack had tied it into multiple knots on the way home from the prison. Admiration and satisfaction clashed with Braham's unease and wholeheartedly won the day.

With a much lighter step, he sauntered down the stairs and followed Jack through the loud, hectic kitchen. The scents of ham and fresh-baked rolls filled the air. He breathed in the delicious smells, his mouth watering.

"Stay here. I'll go see what's happening," Jack said, leaving the house through the back door.

Braham grabbed a ham biscuit off a tray on the counter while he waited, and ate it in two bites, then wolfed down a second and a third to the disapproving glare of the caterer.

"My God. I don't believe it."

Braham turned his head in the direction of the voice coming from the hall leading into the kitchen. There was something familiar about it, but the man, weaving his way around the cooks, and coming in Braham's direction, wasn't anyone he recognized. He only knew a handful of people anyway. The brown-haired man, sporting a two-day beard, was tall and lean, but several inches shorter than himself. The man must have mistaken Braham for someone else.

He extended his hand, but the welcoming gesture was at odds with his twisted smile. "I'm Ken Thomas. It is you, isn't it? McCabe, right?"

Braham nodded with dawning recognition of the name, if not the face.

"You're a sight for sore eyes." Ken's gaze traveled down to Braham's midsection, then back to his face. "Last time I saw you, you were recovering from a bullet in your belly. When'd you...*arrive?*"

Braham shrugged. "Thirty minutes ago."

Doctor Thomas crossed his arms and glared. "It takes a lot of nerve to keep a woman waiting for more than three years."

Braham grimaced, scratching his chin. "I told her not to, but I'm grateful she did."

"You don't deserve her."

"I won't argue with you."

"She never stopped believing in you."

"She never should have started."

"I should punch you."

Braham spread his arms at his side, opening his body for another punch from one of Charlotte's protectors. "Go ahead. I deserve it. David already has—twice."

The doctor rubbed his knuckles. "Lucky for you, I'm a healer, not a fighter."

The door swung open and Jack entered the kitchen. "Oh, hi, Ken. When did you get here?"

"Just walked in and saw Braham. How's Charlotte taking the news?"

"She doesn't know yet. The photographer is placing everyone for a group shot with Stormy's Sun. We need to get in place before Braham comes out. The photographer knows he's coming, so he'll be taking pictures."

"Okay." Ken slapped Braham on the shoulder. "She'll be glad to see you." Ken left the house whistling.

"There're two dozen of Elliott's friends out there," Jack said. "They've all heard about you and will want to meet you. You can do it later. Charlotte's waited a long time. Take her upstairs. No one will bother you there. Give me thirty seconds to get in place." Jack blew out a breath. "I can't believe you're finally here." He gave Braham a hug. "Love ya, man."

Braham calmed himself and kept his breathing slow and deep. His eyes stayed fixed on the open door as he counted. When he reached sixty, he strode out toward the paddock. The heavy wool of his kilt swished about his legs with each easy stride.

A beautiful chestnut with white stocking feet stood in the center of a group of people. Braham scanned the crowd, searching for Charlotte.

Then a child's voice piped, "*My daddy.*"

There was some murmuring, and people looked around.

"It is *too* my daddy. Look. Let me down. I gotta hug him right now."

Braham glanced in the direction of the child's voice and spotted a small, blond-haired lad, wearing a blue shirt, tan pants, and a navy jacket, running toward him with open arms. The odd moment caused Braham's heart to kick up with an extra-hard thud. He blinked, looking at a miniature of himself. The lad ran straight to him with his little arms raised.

"Pick me up. I want to kiss you, Daddy."

Braham hoisted up the lad, who immediately gripped his little arms around Braham's neck and kissed his lips with a warm, wet smack. "Love you, Daddy."

The words rang in Braham's heart, and tears welled at the sight of his son—a child conceived in a moment of deepest desire.

Braham's heart beat wildly as he searched the crowd for Charlotte. The sun glared down on a stunningly beautiful woman chasing after the lad with long, shapely legs. Her curls blew wildly about her face, and a short dress, matching the blue of her eyes, molded to the luscious curves of her body.

Charlotte came to a sudden, breathless stop. Her head cocked, staring at him in utter disbelief through tear-filled eyes. Then the most radiant smile he'd ever seen brightened her rosy-cheeked face.

Braham knelt on one knee, his kilt swirling around him, his son in his arm. He held out the sapphire ring and said, "I love you, Charlotte. Will you marry me?"

She dropped to her knees, tears streaming down her face.

"Will you accept this ring now with my promise to love you and our children? To protect you and our children, and live *here* and *now* with you for the rest of my life?" His heart stopped beating while he waited for her answer.

"I…will marry you."

She held out her hand and, with his heart crashing happily around in his chest, he slipped the cherished ring on her finger.

"I marry you too, Daddy."

Braham pulled Charlotte into the curve of his arm and kissed her. The kiss moved like a warm, blossoming light from the center of his heart to the center of forever.

Lincoln patted Braham and Charlotte's cheeks. "I want to kiss Daddy, too."

Charlotte smiled into Braham's eyes. "Kiss your daddy, Lincoln. He's finally come home."

100

MacKlenna Farm, Lexington, Kentucky, Present Day

L ATE ON DERBY night, after everyone had gone to sleep, Elliott sat up in bed studying a family tree. Meredith had received a one-inch stack of documents from her research team a couple of days earlier, but with all the pre-Derby activities, he hadn't had time to read even one page. Now, reveling in Stormy's Sun's Derby victory, Elliott was too hyped up to sleep. He removed his reading glasses and tapped a corner of the frame against the papers.

"If I read this correctly, Michael Mallory from Ulster married Lorna MacKlenna, who was James Thomas MacKlenna's two-times great aunt."

Meredith pulled back the sheets on her side of the bed and climbed under the covers. "Yes, and Charlotte and Jack are direct descendants of Michael Mallory, who immigrated to America in 1613 and founded Mallory Plantation."

"How am I related to Michael Mallory?"

Meredith rolled over on her side and propped up on her elbow. "I haven't counted the generations, but Lorna is probably your twelve- or fifteen-times great aunt."

Elliott gave a small grunt of amusement. "That's pretty far removed."

"Almost to Adam and Eve."

Elliott put his glasses back on and thumped through the pages again. "Didn't I see a letter from a law firm in Edinburgh?"

"Keep looking. It's in there."

He tossed the pages on the floor next to the bed. "I'll look later. Give me a synopsis."

"Their client hired them to deliver the brooch, a family heirloom, to Charlotte. They won't reveal the client's identity. Sorry." She rolled over, turned off her bedside light, and then fluffed her pillow. "It makes me wonder though if the person knew of the stone's magic and wanted to get rid of it just as much as Charlotte did."

"That would make sense."

Meredith yawned. "The research budget is in the stack, too. The team in Scotland is plugging into a database the names of all MacKlenna family members and the families MacKlennas married into all the way back to the fourteen-hundreds. It's going to cost you."

"I'll sell more Apple stock."

"I know for a fact you've never sold one share of your Apple stock."

Elliott rolled over and sat on the edge of the bed. "This time I might have to." He patted Meredith's hip affectionately. "I'm going to check on the boys."

"They're fine. They were so tired when they went to bed, they shouldn't wake up until late tomorrow morning. It was a big day for everybody."

Elliott made a small sound of pleasure. "Especially Stormy's Sun. The pressure will be on him now to win the Preakness and Belmont."

"If he's half the horse his sire is, there's no doubt in my mind he'll win it all."

Elliott climbed out of bed and slipped on a pair of gym shorts. "Don't fall asleep, I'll be right back. I haven't finished celebrating."

Meredith yawned again. "I'll be waiting. Oh, I forgot to ask. Did you talk to David? Is he okay with Braham's sudden appearance?"

"David's not the type to live with unrequited love. After Lincoln was born, he gave up hope."

"I know he said it, but—"

"There're few things in this world ye' can believe without a doubt. One of them is the word of David MacBain. He's fine, Mer. Ye' don't have to worry."

Elliott walked down the hall, smiling when he passed Charlotte's bedroom, hearing soft moans and the rhythmic squeak of the bed. She and Braham might not come up for air before the Preakness in two weeks. Braham had done well at the track earlier in the day. He knew horses. He had won a $2 Superfecta and the $1 Supper High Five, but Jack had to collect the winnings of more than a hundred sixty-five thousand dollars, since Braham had no identification. First thing Monday Elliott intended to create an identity for the lad, complete with college diplomas and a passport. Before they went to Baltimore for the Preakness, Braham would have all the documentation he needed to collect his winnings. And then there was a small matter of millions of dollars in buried gold needing to be converted into cash.

Elliott opened the door to the boys' room and tiptoed in, side-stepping a Legos racetrack, but his bare foot landed squarely on one of a hundred Hot Wheels forming a long line around the track. Elliott cursed under his breath as he hobbled across the room.

Seven-year-old Cullen and three-year-old Lincoln were sprawled on the bed crosswise, smelling of soap and freshly washed hair. Their pajama shirts were rucked up over their tummies. Elliott laughed silently. Careful not to wake them, he straightened the boys in the bed and pulled up the covers.

Cullen shifted slightly and mumbled something, but then quickly lapsed into the deep breathing of sleep again. Elliott stood still for a moment, listening to the sounds of the night. Satisfied the boys were safe, he kissed their heads.

Stopping at the door on the way out, he glanced back into the room, remembering all the nights he had come up to check on Kit when she was small. He wouldn't be kissing either of the boys if she hadn't gone back in time. But her absence would always leave a hole in his heart.

"Wherever you are, Kit," Elliott whispered, "may God hold ye' and these precious boys in the palm of His hand."

The End

"The better part of one's life consists of his friendships."

—Abraham Lincoln

*   *   *

Thank you for reading

THE SAPPHIRE BROOCH.

I hope you enjoyed reading this story as much as I enjoyed writing it.
Reviews help other readers find books.
I appreciate all reviews, whether positive or negative.

About the Author

Katherine graduated from Rowan University in New Jersey where she earned a BA in Psychology with a minor in Criminal Justice. Following college she attended the Philadelphia Institute for Paralegal Training, before returning to Central Kentucky where she worked as a real estate and tax paralegal for over twenty years.

Katherine is a marathoner and lives in Lexington, Kentucky. When she's not running or writing romance she's enjoying her five grandchildren: Charlotte, Lincoln, Cullen, Henry Patrick, and Meredith.

Please stop by and visit Katherine on her social media sites or drop her an email. She loves to hear from readers.

website: www.katherinellogan.com
blog: www.katherinelowrylogan.com
Facebook: www.facebook.com/katherine.l.logan
Twitter: @KathyLLogan
LinkedIn: www.linkedin.com/in/katherinellogan
Pinterest: pinterest.com/kllogan50
Shelfari: www.shelfari.com/o1518085100
Goodreads: goodreads.com/author/show/5806657.Katherine_Lowry_Logan
Google+: plus.google.com/+KatherineLowryLogan/posts
Email: KatherineLLogan@gmail.com

If you're interested in Kit and Cullen's love story you can find THE RUBY BROOCH (the Celtic Brooch Trilogy Book 1)

* * *

If you're interested in Meredith and Elliott's love story you can find THE LAST MACKLENNA. This story is NOT a time travel romance

* * *

If you would like to receive notification of future releases

Sign up today at KatherineLowryLogan.com or

Send an email to KatherineLLogan@gmail.com and put "Sequel" in the subject line

Look for THE EMERALD BROOCH in late 2015

Author's Notes

This book could not have been written without the input, support, and encouragement from Carol Parrot and Ken Muse. Thank you very much!

Notes about events in the story:

- A Confederate surgeon did tend to General Ramseur's wounds at Belle Grove Plantation, and General Custer sat at his bedside off and on during the night. No one told the general, though, that he had a daughter named Mary. Most of the wounded were buried at Belle Grove temporarily until they were removed and interred in their final resting places.

- The sequence and times of events in Richmond were altered slightly to accommodate the story, as were the conditions at Castle Thunder. It was a brutal place but my muse took it a step further in creating the dungeon scenes.

- General Benjamin F. Butler, commander of the Union Army of the James, referred to Elizabeth Van Lew as his "correspondent in Richmond, and General Ulysses S. Grant considered her valuable enough to order personal protection for her when he entered Richmond. However, there is no indication that she ever met President Lincoln. After Grant was elected president, he nominated Elizabeth for the position of postmaster of Richmond, which Congress approved. The government paid her $5,000 for her service and several of the prisoners she had helped sent her money. Elizabeth died in 1900. The city condemned the mansion in 1911 and it was torn down the following year.

- The assassination attempt on Secretary Seward was a bloodbath. Lewis Powell's wild rampage left five people seriously injured, but he didn't kill anyone. Braham's role in the events of April 14, 1865, is entirely fictional. Although I was tempted to let him overpower Powell, I didn't want to further alter the real story.

- According to Carl Sandburg in *Abraham Lincoln: The Prairie Years and the War Years,* Seward's house did have a doorbell.

- Braham and Cullen's legal maneuverings are products of my imagination, although the Habeas Corpus Act of 1863 was an actual act of Congress. For those of you with legal backgrounds, or like me, love legal thrillers, I decided not to include objections to Braham's witness badgering. He wouldn't have gotten away with it in today's courtroom, but in a trial where defendants had almost no legal rights, I gave him some leeway.

- The tracking device David implanted in Charlotte's hip is also a product of my imagination. Technology isn't available for implanting a chip of that sort in a person.

- Everybody needs an Aunt Mimi! I don't have one, but I have a sister Mimi, and she has created genealogy notebooks for all of her siblings. The complicated MacKlenna Family tree will be available in the near future!

- As for time travel, altered memories, and the locations of the brooches at any given moment, I decided to let my muse take the story in a fun direction without worrying about time passing and snowballing effects.

- Will David ever get his HEA? Yes, stayed tuned!

Special Thanks to my fantastic early readers: Joan Childs, Shirl Deems, Virginia Simpson Geffros, Jessica Hartwigsen, Tamara Logan, Ken Muse, Nancy Qualls, Theresa Snyder, and John Wickre, Ph.D., and an extra special thanks to my editor Faith Freewoman, Demon for Details Manuscript Editing, who did an amazing job with a very long manuscript.

Bibliography

Agonito, Rosemary, *Miss Lizzie's War, The Double Life of Southern Belle Spy Elizabeth Van Lew,* GPP, Guilford, Connecticut 2012

Cartmell, Donald, *The Civil War Book of Lists,* New Page Books 2001

Carr, Richard Wallace and Carr, Marie Pinak, *The Willard Hotel, An Illustrated History,* Dicmar Publishing 1986, 2005

Casstevens, Frances H., *George W. Alexander and Castle Thunder, A Confederate Prison and Its Commandant,* McFarland & Company, Inc., Publishers 2004

Cunningham, H.H., *Doctors in Gray, The Confederate Medical Service,* Louisiana State University Press 1958, 1986

Furgurson, Ernest B., *Ashes of Glory, Richmond at War,* Vintage Books 1996

Green, Carol C., *Chimborazo, The Confederacy's Largest Hospital,* The University of Tennessee Press 2004

Hesseltine, William B., *Civil War Prisons,* Kent State University Press 1962

Hoehling, A.A. & Hoehling, Mary, *The Last Days of the Confederacy, An Eyewitness Account of the Fall of Richmond, Capital City of the Confederate States,* The Fairfax Press 1981

Kauffman, Michael W., *American Brutus, John Wilkes Booth and the Lincoln Conspiracies,* Random House Trade Paperbacks, New York 2004

Lankford, Nelson, *Richmond Burning, The Last Days of the Confederate Capital,* Penguin Books 2002

Leech, Margaret, *Reveille in Washington 1860-1865,* Simon Publishing 2001

O'Toole, G.J.A, *The Cosgrove Report,* Grove Press New York 1979

Sandburg, Carl, *Abraham Lincoln, The Prairie Years, Volumes One & Two,* New York, Harcourt, Brace & World, Inc.

Sandburg, Carl, *Abraham Lincoln, The War Years, Volume One, Two, Three, & Four,* New York, Harcourt, Brace & World, Inc.

Steele, Volney, M.D., *Bleed, Blister, and Purge,* Mountain Press Publishing Company 2005

Swanson, James, *Manhunt, the 12-Day Chase for Lincoln's Killer,* Harper Collins Publishing 2006

Varhola, Nichael J., *Everyday Life During The Civil War, A Guide for Writers, Students and Historians,* Writer's Digest Books 1999

Varon, Elizabeth R., *Southern Lady, Yankee Spy, The True Story of Elizabeth Van Lew, A Union Agent in the Heart of the Confederacy,* Oxford University Press 2003

Wyman, Donald Paul, *The Chosen Path, Based on the Life of Elizabeth Van Lew,* iUniverse, Inc., 2007

Made in the USA
San Bernardino, CA
24 July 2015